PRAISE
MASTER (

Sexy, decadent, powerful and fun — exactly what you want in a date and in a book!

Margaret Cho
Author, *The One I Want*

For me, reading *Master of O* evoked old feelings and also stirred new ones. The story has the quality of lived experience, elegantly yet explicitly capturing the way a certain elite likes to play. Modern erotica seems to have recently piqued the interest of the mainstream, but *Master of O* keeps its promises!

Dita Von Teese
Author, *Your Beauty Mark*

This is *The Story of O* for the new millennium. Brash, crass, terribly hip and framed in decadence and a fierce, in-your-face passion for fetish. An epic saga of desire so powerful it consumes the hearts and minds so elegantly hidden beneath designer names, fantastic settings and couture kink.

Laura Antoniou
Author, *The Marketplace*

In *Master of O*, Ernest Greene expertly manages a deft balancing act of sacred and profane. If you are looking for a wickedly debauched romp, you will not be disappointed. But look out — it is the truly thoughtful and profound narrative of transformation that will sneak up from behind and hold you captive!

Jillian Lauren
***New York Times* Bestselling Author,**
Some Girls: My Life in a Harem

Ernest Greene's long, loving riff on the most significant sexy book of all time is the real deal — gripping and pervy, knowing and witty, sexy and moving. If *The Story of O* played out today, here's what the other side of that classic tale would look like: brainy and literate, scarily observant of the details of the kinky LA good life, where exotic furs are faux, whips are Jay Marston, flight attendants wear translucent blue latex, and the power-trappings of masculine dress finally get the fetish stylist they deserve. Read it for the dead smart vocabulary and cryptic Jethro Tull reference, or read it for the hot, hot characters and the searing sex — but read it!

Carol Queen, PHD
Author, *The Leather Daddy & The Femme*
and co-founder of The Center for Sex & Culture

Ernest Greene's *Master of O* masters the reality of life in a dominant/submissive relationship. Written from the inside of the BDSM culture, *Master of O* is infused with hot sex, laced with pleasure and desire, sadism and masochism and sprinkled liberally with some fictional mystery dust. The delicious result takes the reader into the minds of both dominants and submissives in a way only someone with intimate knowledge of the real world of BDSM can accomplish. Other books are fiction with a dose of fictional BDSM. This is the real thing with a small smattering of fiction. I highly recommend this book to anyone who isn't satisfied with fifty shades of anything and wants to get the full 100%!

Ricci Joy Levy
Exec. Dir., Woodhull Sexual Freedom Alliance

Ernest Greene was put on earth to write *Master of O*. Reading this erotic noir is like rediscovering Mickey Spillane and the entire oeuvre of Grove Press in one sitting. Greene insightfully captures the psychic mysteries of S&M longing in this super-hip and trenchant thriller. His characters are superbly drawn and achingly sexual. *Master of O* is an astonishing novel. Why haven't we heard of Greene before this? He is a master storyteller.

Mel Gordon
Author, *Voluptuous Panic:*
The Erotic World of Weimar Berlin

MASTER of O

a novel by ERNEST GREENE

Daedalus
Publishing
Company

Daedalus Publishing
2807 W. Sunset Boulevard
Los Angeles, CA

www.daedaluspublishing.com

ISBN 978-1-938884-04-7

DEDICATION

This book is dedicated to my loving, forbearing wife Marie without whose constant support and encouragement this book could never have been written.

ACKNOWLEDGMENTS

Though it may have been my hands on the keyboard I did not do this project alone. I had encouragement, advice and research assistance from some lovely people and I want to thank them for making *Master of O* possible.

First and foremost, my undying gratitude goes to Mel Gordon, who inspired me to attempt this venture and continues to set a wonderful example as a writer, a teacher and a scholar. I was fortunate also to have the editorial services of Gram Ponante, a fine author himself whose light deft touch improved the rough draft enormously while leaving the animating ideas undisturbed.

Thanks also to Ricci Levy, who read the manuscript while it was still under construction and became a tireless advocate for it. I owe much to my mysterious friend Wicklow for his superb scholarship in providing background on the source material. Rick and Tina, leather title holders and inspiration to us all, much obliged for your support all through the process.

Further thanks are due to Joel Tucker, who went out on the financial limb to publish this work, having never done anything like it before. He committed his resources to make it work, without which it wouldn't have. Likewise Shawn

i

Gentry, who managed the project for Daedalus Publishing, is to be thanked for his passionate and protective approach to the original material, as well as for his elegant cover design. Shawn, you got this thing done. Also at Daedalus, my thanks to Chris Hall, for his saintly editorial patience in buffing the manuscript to its current luster.

To Al Gelbard and Sarah Early, my close friends who believed from the start and kept me moving forward during the inevitable periods of low morale that accompany a long creative venture, much gratitude.

Though I'm ever so sorry he never lived to read this book, I owe my friend Emerson Semple for copious inspiration.

Robert Nevans, thankfully still very much with us, provided technical guidance in the brave new world of electronic publishing without which I would have been exposed for the lazy Luddite I can be all too easily.

And a special note of appreciation to Dita von Teese. You were a muse in absentia throughout. I hope you're happy with what you read.

Ira Levine, aka Ernest Greene
February 2014

FOREWORD

I read *Story of O* for the first time when I was still in my teens. I didn't know much then but one thing I already knew was that my sexuality wasn't emerging in the same way as that of those around me. I don't believe I ever had a sexual fantasy that wasn't fundamentally sadistic and in which I had power over my partner. I also don't remember one in which these factors were influenced by my feelings toward the object of my desires. There was no anger or hostility behind them, just a natural instinct toward cruelty and possession. That those I might cruelly possess would welcome such a thing was more or less a given.

To say that the book was a revelation is to understate its impact. For the first time I saw on paper vivid descriptions of my own fever dreams of conquest and surrender. Whatever critical things I might have to say about Pauline Réage, who I've come to know under two additional names as a result of informal scholarship, I give her unwavering credit for her grasp of visual detail and her ability to create believable characters in exotic circumstances. It was a very hot, very compelling read.

And yet, when I was done with it, I threw my Grove Press paperback against the wall in frustration. I'm not going to spoil the ending for those who still haven't read the original (which they should do right now before bothering with the rest of my ramblings here) but I think it fair to say that after a tremendously dramatic first two acts, it sort of comes apart. I was exasperated by the lack of any resolution that made sense in light of what had come before. I don't mean a happy ending, an unhappy ending or any ending of a particular sort. I'm just talking about an ending of some kind after having had such powerful emotions stirred by the experience of reading O's story. Where was the catharsis? Even Sade got Justine off-stage by having her struck by lightning, a fairly clumsy *deus ex machina* but incontestably consistent with the anti-moralistic dystopia in which his narrative was set.

Later I would come to understand the circumstances under which *Histoire d'O* was written and the author's reticence about seeing it in print at all, much less investing the effort necessary to conclude it in some way that would satisfy teenage boys living in Denver, Colorado twenty years later.

She'd written it as a somewhat sardonic gift for a lover with whom she didn't share the experiences or the interests packed into the book's few but powerful pages and never imagined it would see the light of day, much less become a significant influence on late twentieth-century fiction and remain in print continuously for six decades. We have every reason to believe from her late-life interviews as Ann Desclos that she felt as charitably toward O as Sir Arthur Conan Doyle felt toward Sherlock Holmes – not very. Like Conan Doyle, she wanted her best-known invention to go away and quit distracting readers from her more important work.

But O wouldn't lie down for that. There were things almost beyond imagining that she would do to please those to whom she'd surrendered herself but there were things she would not do for them, for those who fell wildly in love with her in their dreams or even for the mortal woman who created her, and quietly unveiling all her mysteries before fading into obscurity was not one of them.

I felt at the time that there was another story that had been left untold, a further suspicion validated by the writer's own later reflections. She had glimpsed a whole world but didn't care to enter it and tantalized us with her extrapolations from what she'd casually observed. I never understood why O, who was unstintingly depicted as a voracious, conscienceless sexual predator prior to her first encounter with René, gave it all up for a young man who seemed little more than a cipher – shallow, capricious and altogether unworthy of such devotion.

O's submission to Sir Stephan was somehow a bit more comprehensible, even though she felt none of the affection for him she ostensibly maintained for René. This makes sense only if you discard Jean Paulhan's completely risible contention that the physical and psychological pleasures of masochistic sexual slavery had nothing whatever to do with O's limitless obedience to two entirely different men.

Subsequent experience of my own suggests that Paulhan was lying in the service of having his lover's book taken seriously as literature rather than dismissed as pornography. This was disingenuous on his part and dishonest on hers. Whatever she didn't know about real BDSM people, Réage-Aury-Desclos understood the plain logic that no one ever took a second whipping out of love. For someone who seeks only to suffer and serve, O is suspiciously orgasmic under circumstances inconsistent with romantic martyrdom.

Even back then, a virgin myself, I got it that someone was telling a real whopper here. If I hadn't read Paulhan's whining yet defiant apologia first and then seen the story arc run over by a bus that could have been driven by Michael O'Donahue at the end I might not have reacted with such exasperation. But as the whole thing was presented, I found it an infuriating tease, as if the writer knew a whole lot more but didn't care to expose it or herself to the accusations that it would surely bring.

In this she set the precedent for mainstream writers who take on the subject of BDSM to this day with a disclaimer to the effect that none of their understanding is derived from their personal histories. If that were true, why would we find any of what they have to say credible in the slightest? They aren't recounting voyages to distant planets no one else has ever visited. They're telling us about people they know a bit but whose company they don't care to be seen as keeping.

Well that's just bullshit, and Desclos finally owned it, at least a little, toward the end by admitting that the characters were people she'd observed in passing and that secret sexual cabals were not all that uncommon among the band of mystical intellectuals with whom she traveled, particularly in her earlier life.

She was, in fact, bisexual and had a long and passionate affair with the English socialist Edith Thomas. Prior to WWII she had been part of a circle of rightist intellectuals with an inchoate nostalgia for feudalism. After the war, in which she had fought for The Resistance, she kept faster company among models and actresses as well as her fellow members of The French Academy. Her publisher, Jacques Pauvert, was a friend of Paulhan and also a bit of a showman who had ginned up a *succès de scandale* by publishing Sade, something Sade had attempted himself with much less salubrious results. O, we discover, was short for Ondine, an acquaintance known for her heavy drinking and affinity for violent men. While the novel is no *roman à clef*, my hunch that it was grounded in some measure of reality and that we were only being spoon-fed parts of that reality appears to have some foundation in fact.

My job, my calling in life, was to explore those foundations in fact in the most personal way possible, to "fix" the story by living it openly and giving myself to it completely, hoping to return with more complete and reliable information. I could not be O any more than Desclos could have been. I'm neither female nor submissive. The former was obvious to everyone and the latter was obvious to me. But I could be O's master. I could hardly do a worse job of it than the ones she'd been given to and there was no other life possible for me in any case. I had about as much chance of being vanilla as Liberace had of being straight. It just wasn't happening.

Fortunately, as I would learn, kinky people have radar for each other somewhat similar to "gaydar." A girl a year ahead of me in school – a cheerleader with seemingly no reason whatsoever to take an interest in a singularly unpopular brainiac – initiated me into the life I would live from then on by suggesting that I tie her up with scarves and spank her with a belt before we had conventional intercourse the first time. How much more do you need to know about me than that I found this not the least bit peculiar and threw myself into all aspects of it, including the fucking, without hesitation? That proved to be the schematic on which virtually all my subsequent relationships right up to the present have been constructed.

While I don't think that's the case for everyone who engages in this kind of sex from time to time, I think it's orientational in the way that being gay is orientational to those of us for whom the alternative would be celibacy rather than convention. I've been the dominant partner in BDSM relationships virtually exclusively for over forty years and I suppose there's little point in wishing I could be something else at this late date. It's a good thing I'm not.

There are some very fucked up things about my life, but my sexuality isn't one of them. I believe kink, like gay, is at least partially heritable and there are other members of my family in at least four generations who seem to carry a sort of "marker" for this kind of sexuality. I can see it clearly in some and not the least in others. And they can see it in me. If you get around to reading the rest of this book, you'll find that family dynamic very much at work, as I'm pretty sure it was at work in René and Stephan.

Alas, the novel's author didn't like those guys much and wasn't very interested in them. It could be argued she didn't like O either, but at least found her artistically engaging.

What got to me when I read the book, what gets to me whenever I see heterosexual dominant men portrayed in books and on film, is how simplistically they're designed and how utterly inexplicable their appeal to the fabulous women they invariably attract. There must be something about them – about us – that some very powerful women find so compelling they're eager to be bound, lashed, ass-fucked, passed around among friends, branded and pierced in order to fulfill their wishes. Reading about them or seeing them on the screen we wouldn't have a clue where that appeal might lie. How in the world do Mickey Rourke and James Spader hook up with Kim Basinger and Maggie Gyllenhaal? Yes, they're successful men with all the outward trappings, but these things alone hardly explain their attractiveness, especially when they're otherwise so difficult to like.

Once again, the problem lies with the observer. The writers who invent these characters are nothing like them and can't see them as anything more than damaged products of catastrophic childhoods, the kind of shallow psychiatric motivation against which aspiring writers are wisely cautioned in Creative Writing classes. Because straight men rarely speak honestly with one another about the specifics of their sexual habits, those who are not kinky could well be having drinks with a beautiful and fascinating woman's master and have no clue about it. That cluelessness is a dead zone in which only toxic stereotypes can flourish.

I've spent a fair amount of time among other sexually dominant men and the most I can tell you about them with any degree of assurance is that they were in no way like their fictional counterparts and, more importantly, in no way like one another outside of their sexual proclivities. One of the hard lessons I've learned in my decades of being out and living among those with whom I could be is that we are not all brothers and do not all see who we are and what we do in the same way, much less in the way that outsiders see us.

We have no special claim to authority over those who submit to us and are guilty of no specific sin in accepting their submission. They're all different and so are we. Some of us are caring and sensitive as are some of the women with whom we're compatible. Some of us are selfish and conscienceless, as are some of them. We're pretty much human in all the usual ways and human in one particular way peculiar to our kind. That's my story and I'm sticking to it. Indeed, I've stuck to it throughout my entire career in writing and in filming and I'm not likely to let go of it now.

I first came to Los Angeles under the thin cover of pursuing a career in mainstream screenwriting. I had a bit of early success and plenty of false encouragement but that didn't really matter because it was only a façade to begin with. I really came out here to find others with whom I shared that specific human peculiarity and devoted myself to it with an enthusiasm that, applied to writing screenplays, might have made me a lot of money, the one thing I regret about the course I ultimately chose.

I made one attempt to write a comedy about Bettie Page set at the height of her career, with which I'd become familiar while working on a piece about her for *Rolling Stone*. While everyone who read it had nice things to say about it, I was told in no uncertain terms that it would not get made (which it might have been a few years later, as someone else's version did end up in production with disastrous results). I took that as an invitation to pursue other kinds of employment if this was the material that interested me.

Thankfully, being a pervert is much less of a disadvantage to a pornographer. Let me say right now that it's not entirely helpful even in that endeavor. Porn producers aren't as different from mainstream producers as either would like to believe. Both are surprisingly conventional when it comes to sex overall and are content to let the sausage making be carried on by others far from the golf courses the producers frequent.

I've never pretended to be normal and thus have never been a welcome presence in the executive suites (such as they are) of porn barons. They prefer to keep me on the set making what I make which they can sell at a considerable profit without having to spend much time in my company. God forbid that someone who got into porn because he wanted to express certain ideas about sex should ever be in charge of anything when it's understood the occupation is a cynical dodge to turn a few bucks off the shameful needs of the hooples. A sincere pornographer is a reproachful reminder of the underlying energies that propel the whole enterprise. It's best to keep them at barge-pole distance.

Nevertheless, in pornography my mission was not to be thwarted. If this were the only medium in which I would be permitted to express myself on the subject of sexual sadomasochism I would accept it for that purpose no matter who ended up taking the profits.

If I found *Story of O*'s portrayal of BDSM overall and dominant men in particular disappointing, the porn equivalent would prove enraging by comparison. My first kink-porn gig was as a bondage rigger, a position not yet officially recognized on the end credits of XXX vids, for Marilyn Chambers' last feature before her first retirement in 1984. And what a gig it was. Marilyn proved charming and cooperative, relaxing while I crawled all over her petite, next-to-naked chassis as I tied her to a bed. I got paid a hundred bucks for this and, looking back, think it may have been my best hire as a crew hog.

Subsequently signing on with what was then the biggest producer of "specialty bondage videos" in the same capacity, I soon discovered that porn's ideas about any kind of unconventional sexuality were no less ugly and inaccurate than those of the mainstream entertainment business of the time.

"Bondage videos," for those lucky enough never to have seen one from the era, existed in an alternate universe where there were no men, no directly sexual activity and a whole lot of pissed off women who tied each other up and beat on each other for no apparent reason. Neither dominant nor submissive players were coached to show any pleasure in what they did. The dominant women barked and scolded. The submissive women begged and whimpered. Eventually some contrived plot twist reversed their positions so that the barkers now begged and the beggars now barked.

It was an ugly, brainless and completely inaccurate conception of the real world in which I spent my off hours learning and loving and living among the fascinatingly diverse crowd that made up the non-commercial BDSM scene back in the day. We were few in number at the time, Madonna having not yet made corsets and spanking trendy, and most of us would not have been considered conventionally attractive in the way the younger kinksters I meet now tend to be. But we brought great enthusiasm to what we did, practiced it with meticulous care for the safety and pleasure of our partners and, unlike the preposterous melodramas shot in the cheesy studios where I worked, understood that the purpose of it all was sexual satisfaction in equal measure for everyone involved.

It took me seven years of tendonitis-inducing rope work on concrete floors before I finally got behind a camera. When I did, I sighted it on gunning down every rotten cliché I'd helped the no-talent hacks who I'd worked for foist on the public. The formula for my videos was simple: Hire appealing women with some affinity for bondage, get them naked, tie them down with their legs spread and have other appealing naked women get them off by whatever means. It may not have been a particularly sophisticated approach, but people liked it and I sold a lot of Mylar.

Eventually I found employment with bigger production companies capable of supplying bigger budgets and open to new approaches. By then BDSM was an expanding blip on the cultural radar screen and the long-held belief (founded on nothing in any state or federal law) that showing penetrative sex with bondage would result in certain prosecution had faded away. Not surprisingly, Larry Flynt helped me debunk that myth by making me editor of his new kink-sex magazine, *Taboo*, and giving me latitude to publish explicit images of BDSM sex in a form recognizable to those actually engaged in it personally.

All of this led up to the day when I finally got my shot at "fixing" *The Trouble with O*. I was funded to make an ambitious X-rated feature based on the original novel. Unlike the drearily literal 1975 soft-core version, my picture would be set in a modern-day Los Angeles where, by then, a vibrant leather community had kicked its way out of the closet and partied openly in a wide variety of venues frequented by an oddly charming mix of off-beat characters. Within that community people made no secret of the physical satisfaction they derived from sexual power play and neither did the casts in my "O" pictures, including the three different female performers who played the title role in the different segments of the trilogy I shot.

I also made a point of scripting the dominant male players to be appealing and sympathetic, two things that could not fairly be said of the men in the novel, or in much of any other depiction of BDSM I'd read or seen anywhere.

There are certainly lots of undesirable dominant men out in the world. I'd met quite a few over the years and I continue to encounter them, try though I might to avoid it. Fortunately, there were and are charming, funny, skillful and self-aware men who enjoyed being on top. There were and are women who derive great erotic satisfaction from submission and sensation play and by no means are they all mental cases practicing DIY psychotherapy to work through traumatic and abusive childhoods.

In fact, I had learned over time that kinky people were neither more nor less fucked up than vanilla people. They were sexually oriented in an unconventional way but were often otherwise quite conventional with quite conventional vices and virtues, joys and sorrows, strengths and deficits.

And while more and more women emerged from the shadows to speak and write the truths of their lives as enthusiastic submissives, the men who provided the particular kind of intimacy they enjoyed remained largely silent and invisible. Submissive women, it turned out, were much better able to make the case for the legitimacy of their sexual orientations than dominant men. Women were more assertive about claiming their desires and defending them from ignorant criticism, I suspect, because feminism had opened a larger dialog about female sexuality for which there was no analog among men.

Thus, while O got her say, and a chance to defend herself from strident critics who saw her as a destructive projection of the worst kind of misogyny, Stephan and René remained voiceless clichés, presumed to be motivated by that very misogyny to which submissive women were accused of catering.

While I've met my share and then some of gender essentialist imbeciles (genders notwithstanding) and I'm not about to deny that abusive and exploitative relationships are neither more nor less common among kinky people than among vanilla people, I reject the whole notion that their failings result from their kinks, or vice versa. It's easy to overstretch the comparisons between being sadomasochistic and being gay, but spend enough time amid either crowd and you'll hear it said that the one thing about their lives that isn't fucked up is their sexuality.

I get why dominant straight guys have bad reputations. All complaints to the contrary dismissed as deserved, most of them are victims of the worst kind of character assassination, the kind originating within. I'm made very uncomfortable by the politics of some dom guys. One great thing lost from back when our numbers were few and diversity was the only thing that made it possible to get together a quorum for a good party was the social irrelevance of gender, which carried absolutely no behavioral expectations whatsoever. That's no longer the case, which is one reason why gay and straight leather people no longer party together as they once did. It's not the fact that there are more straight people around than there used to be but rather the cultural baggage they bring with them.

No, women are not all naturally submissive. No, masculinity is not essentially dominant. No, there has been no cultural deviation from the immutable laws of nature that has emasculated men and forced women into shouldering responsibilities for which they aren't constructed. And there's no such planet as Gor. That's all just preposterous and I don't blame anyone for finding it offensive. I might if they don't. I don't believe that "real" masters won't recognize there's such a thing as domestic abuse and sexual predation in their midst. Such foolishness mostly originates online among self-styled experts who know even less about the realities of BDSM than Anne Desclos did.

The Internet invited a huge number of people to this party all at once and a certain percentage of them simply don't belong here. I'm sure I'll be accused of the dreaded "One Twue Way-ism" for writing that and I'll know immediately why I don't care what comes after that accusation. There is no one true way but there are many false ways and they're not hard to spot.

One thing I did not set out to write was a polemic in support of dominant men. I just wanted to rescue a couple of particularly misunderstood ones who happen to be the most familiar pair of their kind in all of Western literature from their enchantment as malevolent specters. I wanted to do something for René and Stephan and for all the women who ever wanted what was good in them and were left grieving over their lack of any other substance.

One thing little noted but quite acute about Anne Desclos' original writing was her observation of a certain class of bourgeois perveratti that emerged in the post-war Paris where she lived and worked. Once a center of high culture devastated by the humiliations of a war that's still a very touchy subject among French people, the Paris of 1956, like modern Los Angeles, found a new identity for itself as a purveyor of popular culture – particularly fashion and film – instead. This made it, like L.A., a natural venue for self-reinvention.

It's no accident that O is a fashion photographer who seduces models and that the men in her life are shady entrepreneurs whose exact occupations are never revealed. As we know, the author wasn't unfamiliar with this type of person. O viewed them all somewhat snobbishly (if you doubt me I suggest re-reading the description of Jacqueline's family in the novel) and would undoubtedly have felt the same for their latter-day counterparts here.

A similar class has long existed in this city, where money and power buy all sorts of sybaritic pleasures and shame is in short supply. We read in the tabs quite frequently about the mishaps befalling them and their hapless partners. There's some *schadenfreude* about that in a place where most people work very hard and don't get much, but overall we tolerate this class because they employ us and in some way we hope, without justification, to join them. Then others can look scornfully upon our excesses while we indulge ourselves without remorse. We should be so lucky.

Nevertheless, BDSM is no more immune to the attentions of that class than any other source of enjoyment and though they may not show up at big fetish events (well, actually some of them do but everybody's dressed in a way that makes them invisible to celeb spotters), they do have a parallel if more exclusive BDSM circle of their own. When it came time for my re-thinking of the source material, it was in that milieu where it fit most naturally. If we're dealing in wish fulfillment here, why limit those wishes to the exclusively sexual? Why not address the way in which certain objects become fetishized the way that some lives become fetishistic?

O's inventor certainly didn't back away from that question. Another hint to the dark comedy of manners underlying the poison-pen love letter *Story of O* is generally thought to be is its casually subversive mentions of objects and locations that absolutely identify the players' place in the social matrix of Paris circa 1954. An Hermés scarf, mentioned by name, has the same meaning now that it had then. It's totemic and iconic and wouldn't it be nice if we could afford one?

Unlike Ms. Desclos, however, I'm a crass pornographer and I'm no subtler in my rendering of economics than in my depiction of sex. I deal with class discord quite bluntly in these pages and I'm sure that will be the source of plenty of annoyance among those who don't get invited to CMNF parties in Pasadena mansions. Everyone else can enjoy the cocktail of *noir* and glam I've mixed up here guiltlessly. Someday I'll write a gritty book about what it was really like to be a leather person in the Reagan era but this isn't it.

Nor is this book programmatic in any way. One of the sadder things about *Story of O* is the extent to which it's become an ideal of sorts, a blueprint even, for a certain kind of master/slave relationship to which real people in the real world aspire. Again, a close reading of the text, which is honest enough to show us the beauty of such a life, reveals an unsparing vision of its cold-bloodedness. Is that really a thing any of us would want? We might like to visit Roissy for a few days, but live there? I suppose some would but most of us rather like the vibrant, zany mash-up of marginal sub-cultures we've got now and would find the lives of O, René and Stephan pretty drab by comparison.

I also expect to take some heat over the un-PC lack of discussion concerning consent, negotiation and other critical ethical matters where BDSM IRL is concerned. I don't in the slightest mean to dismiss the importance of these things. I've just created a slightly altered universe in which they're already understood by all in order to spare us some exposition that would have to come at the expense of a fun story. There are other, better tutorial works out there for those in search of such details. I've given many workshops and written many serious instructive pieces about the moral mechanics of BDSM and I will do that too again one day, just not this day. In the meantime, don't try this at home, folks.

All I'm offering here is a luxury vacation with some fellow travelers a bit more congenial than the characters who inspired them. These are the polished, pampered companions with whom we will get down and dirty for a few hundred pages of a modern fairy tale. If it's a good one, it will expose us to some truths about human nature the way the best fairy tales do. But it won't be our story and it won't give us any instructions or demand of us any new way of doing what we already do.

What I've written is a modern, noir-inflected L.A. story about a couple of jolly, sadistic lads who get much luckier than they deserve with an extraordinarily beautiful and accomplished woman who needs a certain thing that they're uniquely adept a providing. She sees them as they are as clearly as she sees through the lens of her camera and can enjoy them at a certain focal length. I'd suggest readers of this fat brick of a book do the same. It means to be honest about certain matters usually cloaked in deceptive rhetoric by discussing them in surroundings that remind us constantly of how deceptive appearances can be.

I have no greater purpose than to speak frankly about the kind of sex I know best, as I have been doing for three decades now. This time I'm doing it in words instead of pictures but ...

well … you'll know what I mean. Give these people a chance. You might find things about them to appreciate. I know I did.

CHAPTER ONE

Everything in the enormous hotel bar was bright and blonde: the gleaming veneers of the square, modern furnishings, the pin-spots studding the ceiling, the leather upholstery on the stool where Steven Diamond was parked with his shoulders squared – even the bartender, golden hair spilling down the back of her snug, black uniform jacket. The bar crowned a glass and steel tower so high stray wisps of marine layer drifted by the vast expanse of surrounding windows. The sun had almost dropped into the sub-coastal murk and the streetlights of downtown Los Angeles had begun blinking on far, far below.

Alone at the end of a pale, varnished expanse of wood as long as a bowling lane, Steven surveyed his city in the quiet before the corner office crowd would rush in to drink away the day's frustrations.

Steven had none. The deposition had gone well. As usual, he'd scheduled it for the end of the day when both the prosecutor and the material witness were eager to get home. It might have cost Steven a billable hour, but he was not one to roll the meter. With the retainers he commanded, there was no need.

But then there had been the call from Ray. Ray, Ray, Ray. While his work was as free of frustrations as only that of an extremely competent mercenary can be, his personal life had some stubborn complications. At one time hehad resented his younger half-brother fiercely, not only for the easier road he'd traveled, but also for the delight he'd brought their mother through what seemed to Steven fairly modest accomplishments. But though he didn't share Ray's last name — Vincenzo — Ray was all that remained of Steven's bloodline.

Like most confidence men, confidence was the one thing Ray lacked, having never been tested in the world without Steven to pluck him out of its tiger pits and dry wells. He couldn't help trying to convince others, hoping to convince himself.

Earlier today, he'd been typically insistent on the phone. He had something wonderful for Steven. He couldn't describe it. Steven had to see for himself. In the first three minutes Steven added up three good reasons to be suspicious. Ray's wonderful discoveries had often turned out to be expensive in unexpected ways. Some were worth it.

Curiosity alone, inspired by the excitement in Ray's voice, would have gotten him to the end of that bar. If Ray ended up bringing Steven a problem, he'd just solve it like all the others.

From the paneled offices of Bunker Hill to the marble corridors of City Hall to the sweaty, institutional-green antechambers of the Stanley Mosk Courthouse to Men's Central off Santa Fe, Steven knew every back room where a fix could be put in. If ever a city could appreciate a resourceful criminal attorney, this was it. No one worked the system's levers more smoothly. For those who could afford him, he was the best legal mechanic in town. And for those who couldn't, he was occasionally inclined to do a bit of fixing anyway. Sometimes an owed favor was as bankable as a fat cashier's check.

Morgan, the tall, lean, part-time actress who brought him his club soda with a twist was one of those for whom he had put in a *pro bono* fix. It was just a simple DUI with no priors and a good bartender in a place frequented by Steven's clients and competitors was useful.

Like so many, Morgan had come out here for the movies and made a few, her athletic frame strategically draped with scraps of animal skins. On camera, she'd usually died heroically, but even the stunt players agreed she probably could have eviscerated most them without spilling a drink. A trim and tanned forty, she still did some theater now and then but had stopped going to open calls.

"You think Sheriff Delgado will resign?" she asked, setting Steven's drink dead center on the black napkin. Steven swirled the ice cubes and took a swig.

"I think they'll describe it as wanting to spend more time with his family."

Steven's voice was the smooth baritone of a radio announcer selling something expensive. He'd polished it over many hours persuading judges and juries to believe the patently ridiculous. On the West Side, they gossiped about film stars. Down here the inside talk was politics.

"Even if the grand jury doesn't indict the S.O.B.?" Morgan had hung onto her tough-girl delivery as well as her taut physique. Steven liked that about her. She was a pretty good saber fencer too, a legacy of her reign as sword-and-sandal queen. The two of them occasionally clanged steel.

"He's been dead meat since they term-limited the Supes. The new board may not like the way he runs the department, but they'll miss him when he's gone. Delgado may be crooked as an ant-eater's nose, but he takes care of those who take care of him."

Morgan glanced toward the door where Julian, the thin, elegant host, greeted a young couple.

"I think your party has arrived," she said.

"I hope it turns into a party. Anything involving my brother is suspect."

"Let me know how it turns out."

Morgan turned to the barback just as Julian led the couple to Steven. Steven stood to greet them, exchanging a back-thumping embrace with the younger man in the blue leather jacket. Steven wasn't just taller than Ray. The vast span of his back and his tree trunk legs made him seem of an altogether more massive species.

Ray had always been a rather delicate boy, but with his hipster goatee and his expensive, skinny, blue-tinted shades he remained conveniently ageless. He may not have been a rock star, but he knew how to play one on TV.

Julian started to pull a stack of menus from under his arm.

"Would you like to be seated now, or have a drink first, Mr. Diamond?"

"We'll take the drink, but just one."

Julian flashed his professional smile as he pulled out the two adjacent barstools.

"I'll hold you to that Mr. Diamond. We're slammed from 8:30 on."

"I have a feeling this will be an early dinner."

Turning from Ray, Steven looked at his younger brother's companion for the first time. In a city full of beautiful women, most in some kind of trouble, Steven had met many but never lost his appreciation for the truly exceptional few. He'd seen a picture or two of this one in *Forbidden*, Ray's magazine, but there was much that pictures did not convey: her surprisingly small stature and formal bearing, the dark luster of her shoulder-length bobbed hair; the yielding warmth of her brown eyes emphasized by luxuriant, expertly-applied theatrical lashes; the extravagant fullness of her slightly-parted lips (lacquered a subtly wicked red). A black jet choker accentuated the slender grace of her neck. She stayed out of the sun: her complexion fair, almost porcelain. She couldn't have been much over thirty.

A short silk-satin jacket, closed at the neck with lingerie hooks, fell straight from breasts all the more ample on her petite frame. The top of a full, corset-waisted circle-skirt rose barely to the hem of the jacket. Where her skirt ended just below her knees, Steven noted the black, seamed stockings; the patent pumps with very high, slender heels and the red soles that every woman in L.A. coveted. Elbow-length leather gloves with buttoned wrists and turned back cuffs were rather retro and a bit wicked also. She carried a small deco clutch beaded in silver and black.

If this was Ray's surprise, it was one of his best. If Dodger Stadium were filled with young women in big hats, sunglasses, and black trench coats, Steven could stand on the pitcher's mound and know with absolute certainty which would come down and kneel in front of him. The straightness of O's spine and her quiet, deferential manner, among other subtle cues, suggested she'd be the one.

Ray took her by the gloved hand and brought her forward. "Steven, this is O. O, my brother Steven."

Ray placed O's hand in Steven's. Her squeeze was firm, but fleeting. Steven's look was long, leisurely and appraising.

"Your brother's told me a lot about you," O said, glancing just once into his eyes. Her voice was soft, a bit deeper than expected, but her enunciation quite clear.

"He's told me absolutely nothing about you," Steven replied. "What is O short for?"

Ray laughed. "Even I don't know."

"How refreshing. Someone who can keep a secret. If more people did that, I'd be out of business. A pleasure to meet you, O."

Steven held onto O's long, slender, gloved hand as he helped her onto the adjoining barstool. How effortlessly she swept the skirt aside with her free hand so it fell around her when she sat down, revealing nothing in the smooth movement. She did take in a short, sharp breath when her backside made contact with the leather seat. Not much under that skirt, Steven surmised. And under the draped blouse, perhaps a hint of hardware, though he couldn't be sure.

Steven waved Morgan over. She actually blinked and looked twice at O, a major display of interest for one accustomed to seeing some of the world's most tempting arm-candy.

"What can I bring you fine-looking folks?" she asked cheerfully, cocking an eyebrow at Steven.

Steven tilted his head toward his brother. "He'll have a G and T, Bombay Sapphire." He turned his attention to O. "For you?"

O seemed tentative, almost hesitant. She glanced over at Ray. "May I get a Campari and soda?"

Ray pondered a beat, as if pronouncing on something important. Steven knew gestures of authority were far more common than authority itself.

"Why not?"

Morgan's other eyebrow went up. "And you, Mr. Diamond?"

"What do I usually have here, and do I like it?"

"Right then. Campari and soda, Bombay Sapphire gin and tonic and a Stella with a glass." She turned back toward the bottles.

"They know you pretty well at this place," Ray said with a laugh.

"I prefer taking my mysterious encounters on friendly turf. If you can't afford one, I can buy you a tie."

Steven reached across O to tug on the open collar of Ray's dark blue shirt. Ray's face exploded into the bright, boyish smile no one ever tired of seeing.

"Unlike lawyers, magazine publishers are not required to cinch their necks with remnants of ancient heraldry." Ray turned to O. "Steven became a lawyer so he'd have an excuse to dress up every day."

O took a photographer's inventory of significant details. Steven's flamboyant style provided plenty of those, anchored by a bespoke double-breasted black wool-crepe suit with important roped shoulders. It was accented with a black-silk rose stick-pinned through the left lapel, a rather daring red shirt, a black tie embroidered in red with the "Death or Glory" skull-and-bones motto of the British 17th/21st Lancers, a black pocket square with rolled red edges and mirror-polished, wing-tip paddock boots O was sure had come off the benches at John Lobb. He was, without a doubt the most elegant man she'd seen on this coast. And he wasn't even gay. No gay man had ever looked at her the way Steven did.

Though she knew Steven and Ray were only half siblings, she had expected at least a superficial resemblance. There was no hint at all of Ray's even features in Steven's hard mug. His was a fighter's face, all weathered angles and small scars. His close-cropped hair had gone almost entirely white, his merry blue eyes hooded by up-angled brows. He had a dreadnought of a chin and a grin so dazzlingly white and even, she half-wondered if he concealed a second row of teeth behind it. He looked to be somewhere north of fifty, but his lightness of movement belonged to a much younger man.

"Actually," she said, "He looks like a friendly devil."

"And so I am," Steven said, raising the glass Morgan had just filled for him.

"To friendly devils and beautiful women in black," he said. The three of them clinked crystal. Steven's hands were strong, immaculately manicured, a silver signet ring with a plain, black onyx shield instead of a cipher on the third finger of his right. On his left wrist he wore a big moon-phase watch with so many complications O wondered how anyone could actually tell time with it.

O was a bit too careful in her movements. Steven suspected he frightened her at least a bit. It was a common reaction among certain women and not necessarily unpleasant for either party. He imagined she felt it right where she liked to and had to restrain herself from rubbing her bare thighs together under the skirt. Steven mercifully suggested they take a table.

It was right next to one of the giant panes through which the tower's looming height was more apparent. It looked down on the machinery-cluttered roofs of other very tall structures nearby in which lights had also begun to come on. Dusk was a swift affair in the L.A. basin and darkness closed in fast.

That O sat up very straight, heels planted firmly on the floor, knees slightly parted so the full skirt fell between her thighs, did not escape Steven's notice as Julian drifted a black napkin over her lap. O's lips remained slightly parted as well. Someone whether herself or another, had gone to a lot of trouble training this woman to broadcast the right signals.

Steven waved off the wine list, pulled a slender leather envelope from an inside pocket and put on a pair of large, perfectly round, black-rimmed spectacles. With O seated between them, menu unopened, Steven and Ray caught up on each other's respective enterprises while surveying the narrow strips of cream-colored paper between the leather covers.

O remained silent. Her mouth had gone parched and she was afraid to call attention to her dilated pupils. She took a sip through the red straw of her aperitif.

"What's good here?" Ray asked.

"The lack of music," Steven replied. "But I'll probably have the salmon tartar and the lobster ravioli."

Ray laughed.

"What, no *Wagyu* filet?"

Steven was a dedicated carnivore who drank beer, smoked cigars, kept late hours and still had a BP of one hundred over sixty-five and a resting pulse of fifty-eight.

"Next time. You have it and I'll take a bite. What does O like?"

Talking about her in the third person raised the curtain for the act to follow. Any session – and this situation had all the hallmarks of one in the making – begins at first meeting. How it goes after depends greatly on the opening moves.

Glancing over at O, her elegant, gloved hands folded on the white tablecloth, Steven already looked toward dessert. It wasn't just O's beauty that stirred interest somewhere further south than his stomach. Her muted theatricality seemed full of promise. All Steven knew about O was that she was the star photographer for Ray's magazine; or rather, the magazine with Ray's name on the masthead and Steven's signature on the articles of incorporation.

"My guess would be the *frisée* salad and the Dungeness crab cakes," Ray suggested.

Steven smiled at O, flashing those predator's teeth. "Was he right?"

She shrugged, causing a mild disturbance under the black satin jacket. "Ray always orders for me. It's a luxury, not having to decide something once in a while."

"Every time she looks through the viewfinder she has to make a choice," Ray explained. "Fortunately, she makes most of them right."

The waiter, a tall, young man with an affable manner no doubt cultivated for auditions, was next to the table as soon as the men's menus touched the linen.

"Good to have you back, Mr. Diamond," he said, certainly sounding sincere.

"Nice to be back."

"Until the craziness starts," the waiter said in a stage whisper.

"You'll get us out in time I'm sure," Steven replied, proceeding to rattle off their selections, which the waiter repeated, withdrawing after a quick bow.

Ray told O that Steven knew everyone in town.

"Only the important people," Steven said. "Parking valets, waiters, executive assistants, sales associates, you know, the ones with the real power."

They all laughed. O's laugh was light and musical and, Steven suspected, not often heard. He could do with more of it.

Latin kitchen messengers wearing black aprons brought over small cups of mushroom consommé and big, flaky popovers to keep them busy until the first course. Ray juggled one of the hot popovers onto O's bread plate.

"You've got to try these. They're evil."

He tore one apart, buttered a section and offered it to her. O unbuttoned her gloves and slid them off, neither hurrying nor making a burlesque act of it, and draped them over the arm of her chair. She took Ray's offering whole, with no affected delicacy. For the first time, Steven saw the silver shackle ring on O's hand. He'd seen many versions of the standard door-knocker design, but this was the most elegant – clean and simple, big enough to catch the watchful eye but not out of proportion to O's slender fingers. O's nails were short and perfectly buffed a medium pink as carefully chosen as everything she wore.

The ring was definitive. O was someone's slave. Ray undoubtedly thought she was his, but Steven had doubts.

"Definitely evil," she pronounced, neatly dismantling the pastry, allotting half a pat of butter to each side.

"She can eat anything and never gain an ounce, just like you," Ray told Steven.

"Shooting burns a lot of calories." O swallowed a second bite.

"I've seen your work," Steven said. "You go for the strenuous angles."

"She's got a lot more stamina than I do," Ray interjected. "And she's not afraid of getting messy."

"I just look like I would be," O said. There was that laugh again.

Steven fixed his cool, blue sharpshooter's gaze directly on O's face. "More importantly, you understand the content. It shows in every frame."

O shifted uncomfortably in her seat. This conversation was no longer about photography.

The rest of dinner was occupied with the current state of the magazine business, which was hurting, and criminal practice, which wasn't. No one seemed to be hurrying through the meal, but the air was heavy with expectation. All agreed, or rather the men decided, to take a nightcap at Steven's place, which was nearby. Steven called for the check. Ray made a feint toward his inside jacket pocket. Steven stopped him cold with an upraised hand.

"Your money's no good here," Steven said, taking out a long, silver-edged wallet and an ornate black-resin fountain pen as big as a cigar and encircled with silver Art Nouveau scrollwork. Steven barely glanced at the check before tossing a black charge card into the folder. The slip came back in about ten seconds and he signed off on it with a flamboyant flourish. Lawyers signed their names to lots of things. Steven wanted his clients to feel they got their money's worth of his trademark purple ink.

Collecting O's vintage fur shoulder wrap and exchanging farewell handshakes with Julian, Steven, O and Ray shouldered through the grumbling throng waiting to be seated, O safely between them. They rode the heart-stopping glass elevator down forty floors to the garage. Steven presented his claim check and a crisp twenty, exchanging a few jolly words in fluent Spanish with the valet captain. Steven had meant what he said regarding whom it really counted to know well – those left alone with either one's food or one's car.

O stood at the curb, Steven and Ray a few steps behind, studying her carefully. Even the roomy circle skirt couldn't entirely obscure O's high, hard handful of an ass.

Ray elbowed Steven, grinning.

"Just your kind of view," he said quietly.

"Quite scenic."

Steven's mind wandered back to a weekend in a double suite at Principe di Savoia in Milan with a couple of splendid French whores they'd picked up at a café in The Galleria after a surprisingly unexceptional performance at La Scala. Choosing partners for the first round, Ray had made both girls bend over in front of Steven to spur a quick decision. They had all been laughing back then. Tonight's engagement, Steven suspected, would be no laughing matter.

Steven's car was parked right up front and when the runner kicked it over, the high-pitched whine of the turbocharger whistled through the tiled cavern. The sedan was the only one of its kind, a two-tone black-over-silver Jaguar of an older body style with a strong retro feeling. But there was nothing retro under the sheet metal. It was one of a handful of street-modified S-Type-R racing models that had been imported to the U.S. and it was terrifyingly fast. Ray's anthracite-gray BMW came right up behind it. O started toward its passenger door, but Ray blocked her way.

"I want you to ride with Steven."

It wasn't a suggestion. O did not hesitate, going straight to the passenger side of the Jaguar and waited for Steven to assist her by her gloved hand into the low, body-contoured leather seat. She got her skirt under her with just a flash of a stockinged leg that would have raised the dead.

Steven slid in behind the wheel and popped the shift lever into gear. The dashboard lit up red around clusters of old-fashioned white-faced gauges. The burl wood and stitched leather cockpit still smelled like it had just rolled off the showroom floor. O sat still and straight, knees and lips never touching.

Steven slid back the cover of the glass moon roof as they eased out into the street.

"Look up," he said. "It's almost like being in Manhattan."
O gazed upward at the glistening office towers forming a canyon around them, baring her tender throat in the process.

"It's a lovely view," she agreed. "But it's not Manhattan."

Steven sighed. No it wasn't. Were it not for Ray, he might
be practicing there instead. Though both Steven and Ray had
grown up entirely in California, Steven had lived all over the
world. He'd moved back to Los Angeles after their mother
died, only to be reminded daily why he left in the first place.

The car was tight and silent except for the high note of
the turbo. It didn't ride like a luxury car; the tightly sprung
suspension translated the bumps and dips of L.A.'s neglected
streets up through the frame. O looked over at Steven's chis-
eled features.

How must it feel to be so comfortable in one's body?
Again, O experienced that strange hot-and-cold feeling deep
down. Ray had hurt her, and seen her hurt, many times, but
she wasn't scared of him. In some way, he was a boy, and boys
had never frightened O. Boys were easy. This elegant monster
was most definitely not a boy. Beyond that, she wasn't sure
what he was.

"Ray's very happy since you've been together," Steven
said. O hesitated to talk about Ray, even with his brother. Especially with his brother.

"He's told you that?"

"He doesn't have to. He's an expert at looking like he's
having a good time, but I used to watch him stare out the window on rainy days, back when we still had them here, and
wonder what was bothering him."

"Did you ever find out?"

She clearly expected a more complete answer than he was
prepared to give.

"Yes. But I haven't seen him like that since you came
along."

Crossing Figueroa, skyscrapers gave way to low, grimy commercial buildings with signs in Spanish, bright lights pouring from open doorways. Knots of dark-skinned people clustered under the street-lamps and around the big boxes and tents on the dirty sidewalks here and there.

"Welcome to the nicer part of Skid Row," Steven said, aware of O staring out the window. "They've cleaned it up a lot. Most of the dealers have moved over to Sixth Street."

"You know this area rather well, Mr. Diamond," O said, a bit archly.

"It's convenient to the places I visit my clients. I can be at The Federal Detention Center in seven minutes."

"Quick service."

"Not if you're sitting in the Federal Detention Center."

The dingy gray landscape of *taquerías* and murder motels gave way to the patchy greenery of MacArthur Park. The dirty lake in the park's panhandle reflected the lights from a tall square building, buttressed in concrete X-frames, at the far end. It still looked like the Late International-Style office tower it had once been. When Steven pulled up to the massive steel gate of the parking structure they caught the headlights of Ray's car behind them in the mirror. Ray had his stereo turned up so loud they could both hear it.

Ray was in high spirits. Since The Plan first came into his mind, he'd thought of little else, working through the fine points, making all the arrangements, carefully rehearsing his lines in the mirror at home during O's stay in Pasadena. Now it would all play out just as he intended. Ray never stopped expecting his endless procession of schemes to do so, no matter how rarely that happened.

The steel-mesh gate rattled open and the cars descended the spiral ramp into a cavernous automotive museum. The floor was covered in spotless black-and-white flagging. Rows of overhead fluorescent lights popped on as they passed a sensor to reveal the most lavish garage O had ever seen, complete

and the leather box shut with a firm click. Removing the red and black pocket square, Steven shook it out, folded it neatly and slid it into a narrow drawer with many like it and many others more ornate. There was another drawer for glasses an optometrist might have envied. The wallet joined a dozen more in a locked cabinet and the fountain pen slid into a vertical rack inside a glass case crowded with fine writing instruments. His big moon-phase watch joined a dozen others in a motorized Tourbillion auto-winder with a skeleton movement.

He caught a quick glimpse of himself in the three-way fitting mirror. Steven's looks didn't inspire vanity, but his style did. Style, his mother had taught him, was a weapon in the arsenal, and Steven enjoyed shedding his armor less than he enjoyed putting it on. He'd gotten the dimple in that tie just right today. Shame to wreck it. Steven had often stayed dressed for the girls who fetishized the power-suit guy, but on this occasion, everything must go.

Steven unknotted the tie as carefully as he had earlier pulled it into the perfect four-in-hand. No yanking on the woven silk. The tie department was a controlled riot of color where today's choice, snugly rolled, went back to its cubicle in the red-and-black section.

He tossed his brightly-lined suit jacket lightly onto the leather bench, revealing his devil's red braces. Back in the day, a gentleman never showed his braces to anyone with whom he was not intimate, and in their way, these were racier than the more pornographic embroidered ones he wore expressly to be seen.

In the now open-collared red shirt, one of a dozen he had Turnbull make up for him, and the suit trousers with their razor-edge waist-to-cuff pleats, Steven briefly considered going back out to O just as he was. Remembering that this was not a seduction, he settled the braces on their hook, hung the suit in the DB department (laying the broad lapels flat to avoid folding over the peaks) and treed the boots before sliding them into the half-dozen shelves of footwear. The shirt went to the dry-cleaning compartment; underwear and socks went to the concealed hamper.

For one moment, Steven looked at himself naked.

He was already feeling the first hot flush of the drug hitting his system and he didn't yet know the precise interval for O at which anticipation turned to boredom.

From the long bar of robes and dressing gowns, he continued today's theme with a heavy, black-silk Turnbull&Asser, its wide, quilted shawl lapels and matching cuffs piped in red. How many pairs of skull-embroidered velvet slippers could one man wear in a lifetime? Steven's own extravagances made him cringe occasionally, but now was not the moment for introspection. O was expecting him to be his bad self, what most women wanted from him. He lowered the lights and headed out to tonight's arena.

As expected, he found O in the living room, displayed as precisely as all the artifacts he kept under glass. Stripped to her red-soled pumps, stay-ups, the long gloves she'd impulsively slipped back on, and the collar around her neck, O knelt on her high heels in the middle of the dragon rug. Her knees were wide apart, her hands still laced behind her head like the condemned awaiting execution, shoulders squared, breasts out, chin straight, eyes lowered.

When Steven stopped and stared, a slight tremor washed over her, though of course she didn't turn her head to look at him. She was the one there to be looked at.

Steven was perfectly rude about taking in the view, making her stand at attention, walking around her, looking high and low. Yes, there were surprises. O could have rouged her nipples a shade darker so the rings stood out more, but they were far from inconspicuous. Though only an inch and a half in diameter, they were wicked thick, agonizingly stretched from an initial ten gauge to their current six. Plain stainless with black hematite captive-bead closings, they clearly wanted to be grabbed, weighted, tied, and made to hurt.

Steven took in the slender shoulders and spectacular, natural teardrop breasts of the type for which women in this town paid vast sums and still didn't get. O's belly, flat and cut from fanatical exercise, her perfectly-sculpted pink lower lips; the high, tight buttocks and long straight legs with slender ankles; all comprised a fine inventory and both of them knew it.

Steven could see O's pulse thumping in her carotids. A droplet of sweat trickled in each armpit. He was quite certain she was dripping elsewhere too. The tightening, throbbing bulge rising under his silk robe was just as apparent to the two of them.

Steven let her stay at attention as he plucked the half joint from the ashtray and fired it up with the giant lighter, inhaling a big hit. He approached O at leisure, his head wreathed in smoke. He seemed so accustomed to having whatever he wanted, absolutely devoid of shame or doubt, and she was alone with him at last. Nothing stood between him and whatever he wanted of her. He stopped in front of O's face, tracing her cheek with a fingertip.

"I love this moment," he said quietly. "So full of promise."

In the heavy silence of the vast room, its lights dimmed, the illuminated city at their feet, they shared an interval of limitless possibility. Steven held the joint up in front of her. O leaned forward and took a hit without using her hands. Steven got the closer look he wanted, impressed by the lean muscularity beneath her flawless skin.

"You're a fit bitch, aren't you?"

"I try to maintain myself in good working condition, Sir."

"You stink like sweat and sex," he said. "And no perfume. I like that."

"Sir has a keen sense of smell."

"Not always a blessing in this world, but right now, I'm quite grateful for it."

Flicking the roach into the porcelain ashtray with the logo for Cohiba Cigars on a glass end table, he pulled O into him and kissed her, his hands reading her body like Braille. He was good at these things, neither tentative nor rough. His lips pressed hard on hers, but his tongue explored her mouth with surprising delicacy.

Skilled fingers rolled the steel rings back and forth beneath the tinted, stippled flesh. Steven loved the sensation of hard metal moving under tender skin. O's already-half-erect nipples crinkled up around the jewelry. Her blue web of milk veins stood out against the paler skin of her breasts.

Steven's other hand came up between her legs and took hold firmly at their juncture, his warm palm pressing against her wetness. O managed to hold position, but there was no resisting the urge to rub against his open hand. O's clit was almost embarrassingly large even when soft, which it most certainly wasn't now, and it had its own agenda that would not be denied.

Wrapping his hand in her hair, he pulled her face back from his.

"You're also a fast starter," Steven said. He didn't overdo it, but a little humiliation spiced the mix. For people like themselves, without the knowledge of shame there could be no pleasure.

O's voice came out huskier than she would have preferred. She wanted to be cool to this man, but it seemed impossible. She was uncomfortably aware of her visibly rapid breathing.

"I have no resistance to pleasure or pain, Sir," she said as matter-of-factly as possible.

"And I can see why Ray has no resistance to you. I imagine most men react that way."

"Some women as well, Sir."

Steven laughed, face splitting into a wide grin. He was nothing if not jolly, but how deep did that go and what lay underneath? Her hair still wound into his grip, there was no avoiding his gaze.

"I'm sure. That must be helpful in the studio."

"Sometimes. Models can be very competitive."

"Why does that not surprise me?"

When he kissed her this time, it was much deeper and rougher, his strong hands plastering her up against the heavy silk of his robe. The kiss lingered, but when it was over, he pushed her away a carefully calculated distance and slapped her across the left cheek with perfect precision, exactly in the middle of the fleshy part, just hard enough to sting and leave a light hand print. O didn't flinch. In fact, she looked up at him with a surprised smile.

"You really know how to hurt a girl, Sir," she said brightly.

"Lots of practice," he said.

Taking her by her collared throat, he smacked her across the right breast with a loud splat. The ring at the tip flashed in the light.

"Ouch," O said, still smiling at him as the stinging spread out from the point of impact. Yes, he was an evil bastard and he wanted her to know it.

Spinning her like a top, he gathered her in against him back to front. Something thick and hard poked through the smooth fabric of the robe to rub against the groove between O's buttocks. O wondered if that where he would go first. Ray said he liked doing girls up the butt. If so, he wasn't in any hurry, stroking the front of her body firmly up and down with one hand while the other still gripped her solidly between the legs. A shivering moan rose from deep in her chest. She was so small in his arms, gloved hands at last disentwining to reach back around his bullish neck.

"You're made for this, aren't you?" he whispered in her ear, which was decorated with a simple diamond stud edged in jet to match her stowed necklace.

"Made to be used, Sir?" she asked with mocking inno-cence.

"Made to play the slave."

O stiffened, suddenly offended. She broke the embrace and turned to face him.

"You think this is just play for me?"

"It's certainly a convenient way of getting what you need. After all, you're only following orders. It's not your fault."

Her tilted eyes narrowed at his taunting. Her clenched teeth were straight and white.

"I never pretend to be virtuous. If I didn't like myself as I am I'd be some other way. Sir."

"Well," Steven said pleasantly, "another thing we have in common. I won't judge you for your nature if you won't judge me for mine."

O felt her flash of anger fade. It wouldn't be easy, staying mad at this guy. She cocked a perfectly plucked eyebrow at him.

"And what nature is that, Sir?"

"Cruel but generous. And pathologically cheerful."

He came forward suddenly and scooped her off the rug like a rag-doll. His shoulders seemed even bigger with her gloved arms wrapped around them. He gave off a faint cit-rus scent, something subtle and expensive. O couldn't refrain from smiling when he swung her around, carrying her toward the vast, steel-topped table. It had been a long time since a man had made her feel so weightless. She extended a leg for his visual pleasure.

Effortlessly, Steven conveyed her to the longer side of the table, moving a chair out of the way with a velvet slipper be-fore perching her on the edge so her feet dangled just off the floor. Finding her balance, she put her hands back behind her head and opened her knees as far apart as possible. The neat, straight line between her thighs popped open in full, dewy bloom.

"My, she's a naughty little thing, isn't she?

O's shoulders rose and fell, taking her breasts along.

"She has a mind of her own, Sir."

"With which you seldom disagree. Very smooth, too. Shave or wax?"

"Laser, everywhere from the neck down – arms, legs, everywhere. I've always hated hair on my body. I started shaving at fifteen but I could never get it all off. Now I'm like this permanently."

"I admire your dedication. Take off your gloves. I want to see what you do when you're alone."

The table was chilly under O's backside, but she got herself as comfortable as possible on it, unbuttoning and tugging off each glove, folding them onto the table next to her left leg. One hand went to her right breast, twisting and tugging hard on the fat ring. The other dropped straight to her lower lips, squeezing them together and rolling them back and forth. Steven smiled to see that her pink nail polish was a dead match for the color of her most intimate flesh. He would have wagered the building he stood in that her pedicure was identical.

O could certainly have made a performance of masturbating for him, displaying herself far more bawdily, but he hadn't asked for that. He wanted to know what she did when she was alone, and this was how she started, gradually, working into a slow, circular massage that made her inner juiciness quite audible.

Steven appreciated the precision of her obedience. Sliding comfortably in against her nylon-sheathed thigh, he unhitched the tasseled belt of his robe to join in.

It was often difficult for O to keep her eyes down, but not when there was something worth looking at. They went straight to the rigid flesh that popped out to greet her. Both at work and at leisure, O had many occasions to appreciate male anatomy when it justified her interest, but that was far too seldom. Steven had just what she liked: not much longer than usual, but appealingly girthy, with a narrow, cleanly circumcised head expanding rapidly to broad bulge, then tapering back in with a slight upward curve. It was rock-hard and clearly very happy to be so close to her.

Steven rubbed it against the stocking, holding her by the neck.

"Sir has a nice one, if I might take the liberty of saying so."

"I'm quite attached to it myself.""Permission to touch?"

"By all means."

O's touch didn't disappoint. Still masturbating with one hand, the other was warm and her grip was firm and assured, her stroke slow and knowing, with a slight twist at the end. Steven felt the swelling increase, the throbbing grow more urgent.

"You're quite accomplished at that, aren't you?"

"I'm glad you approve."

"Of the fact that you're a slut who's an expert on cocks?"

"Yes, Sir. I'm dreadfully promiscuous."

"I'm shocked. Hands back now."

O was approaching the edge, but she stopped short and complied. Steven took O's nipple rings and a healthy chunk of the meat in which they were anchored between his thumbs and index fingers

"Tell me when it stops feeling good."

He began to pinch, the pressure rising gradually until O's head swam and she moaned.

"You enjoy being hurt this way," he observed.

"Yes, Sir. You can go harder if you like."

O's pain tolerance followed a familiar bell curve, rising as she approached orgasm. No doubt, it would descend rapidly after climax.

"Shall I give you a safeword?"

"I've had them before but never used one ... Sir."

"Fine, then. Just tell me if something's wrong and I'll take that into consideration."

When he pulled her up by the rings almost off the edge of the table, she let out an unexpected yelp. He kept her up there a long minute, her shoulders lifted and back straightened to relieve the pressure, her laced fingers tightening behind her collar.

"Is that something you don't like?"

"No, Sir," O said between gritted teeth. "I can take a lot there before it hurts in a bad way."

"Very good. One thing you will be forbidden is modesty in any form. If you're to belong to me, nothing must be concealed, physically or otherwise."

"Understood, Sir."

"Down you go, my dirty girl."

Placing his open hand against her breastbone, he gave O a surprisingly hard shove, landing her flat on her back on the table. It felt freezing under her, shaking loose a cry of surprise. Her freshly abused nipples suddenly popped up even harder as a wave of goose bumps rolled down the length of her body.

"It's meant to be cold. Put your legs on my shoulders and lie still."

O rested her ankles lightly on either side of his face, expecting the abrupt penetration for which they both certainly appeared ready, but Steven was not one to be hurried, ever. Instead, he bent down and slapped her face back and forth. He kissed her repeatedly, starting at her yielding mouth. Working his way down her collared throat, he paused at the engorged tip of each breast to tug the rings between his teeth for a moment. Then he continued down the furrow of her belly, his lips warm and dry on O's skin. She tried to stay still and open, but she really didn't want what was coming next.

It wasn't that O disliked oral stimulation, but most men were so god-awful at it she'd rather they didn't try. All that frantic flicking, usually concentrated in the most obvious spot. Please, let this one not be that way.

Much to her surprise, Steven ate pussy like a dyke. Fastening his mouth around her splayed parts, he sucked her wholly into his mouth, applying his tongue in lazy circles across the entire landscape of her membranes.Involuntarily, O felt her legs wrap tight around his neck, hearing what sounded like a muffled laugh from far below. She wasn't the first woman he'd surprised in this way.

Picking up speed, licking and sucking harder, neither shy nor aggressive, he went at it systematically, carefully noting every twitch and gasp, adjusting his motions accordingly. As Steven once advised Ray, "Show me a master who doesn't give killer head and I'll show you one who's soon to be replaced."

O grabbed the edge of the table, clutching with all her might. He'd let her do most of the work herself and now had only to apply the necessary attention directly to her clit. Steven applied himself to it with careful determination, one hand wrapped around a rocking thigh, the other snaking up to close over her throat above the collar. His grip tightening, he felt her whole body stiffen and arch.

"Please, Sir," she gasped. "Permission to come."

Sliding a hand over O's wet parts to keep her warm, he looked up at her with an evil grin.

"Does girl deserve it?"

"Please, Sir. Girl needs it."

"Then girl will pay the price after."

"Gladly, Sir."

Steven dropped his head back into her lap and O's heels pressed into his shoulders as the bright flush that always gave her away spread over her chest. She went rigid, slapped her palms down on the surface, threw back her head and let out a shockingly indecorous howl. Her entire body clenched into a crunch, lifting half off the cold steel. Her hands flew to the back of his head as he felt her pelvic bones grind against his face. He exhaled sharply through his nostrils, burrowing in deep, but halting his movements until O's spasms faded. He knew better than to suck past the money.

Slowly detaching himself, he leaned into her flushed, damp face. O's hair fell to one side and her eyes were closed so tight the mascaraed lids wrinkled.

"That seems to work," Steven said.

"Yes, Sir. Thank you, Sir," O panted.

"I like the way you taste," he said. "Get up."

"I'm a little dizzy, Sir."

"I should hope."

He stood straight, took her by the hands and pulled her onto her perilous heels. O swayed slightly, seeking her balance.

"Here, I'll make it easy for you."

Swinging O around, Steven placed her hands flat on the table, yanking her hips back until her rump grazed the front of his robe. He casually kicked her ankles wide apart, exposing a long, shiny, liquid streak down the inside of her right thigh. O made no attempt to brush it away. She was certainly more stable in this position, but even as the whirling subsided in her brain, she felt a chill of anxiety. He said he was cruel and generous. She guessed the cruel part was next.

"Lovely. Stay just like that."

Steven left her there, strolling over to the silver-handled crop dangling from its hook. He was in no hurry about it. To her disappointment over the years, O had found many men couldn't concentrate on more than one thing at a time. Somehow, she suspected, that wouldn't be a problem here.

Steven lifted the crop by its pommel-ring and cheerily tossed it in the air. It did a single loop just under the lights and dropped, handle-first, into his grip. Since she wasn't meant to look, the flourish was not for O's benefit, just a spontaneous expression of exuberance. This property was now his, for however long, to enjoy as he pleased. At the moment, it pleased him to hurt her. There was no anger in his lust, just cruelty as he had promised. He strolled over, pacing slowly back and forth behind her.

O's composure had limits. Her eyes began following him under the fringe of her hair. It was all she could do to keep her head still.

She'd expected strong legs from all that fencing, but not the dancer's sinews or the loose-limbed gait. Steven's gut, visible through the widening split of his robe, was even harder than hers, a slab of flagstone mounted on his sharply defined waist.

Already knowing the strength of Steven's arms, it dawned on O that if she cared to resist him in anything, it wouldn't matter at all. And from the safest perspective, down between her open legs, she saw that up-tilted ram rise even further. The anticipation of hurting her got him harder. This delicious realization made O dizzy again.

Finally, he stopped behind her. Tucking the whip under an arm, he dropped a hand between her shoulders, pressing her tits to the steel surface, still only slightly warmed by her body heat, and pushing down on her back to extend her hindquarters to him. O reached for the opposite edge of the table, figuring she'd need to hold on tight. Satisfied, Steven stroked the side of her face softly with the business end of the crop. He felt a wave of tenderness for her, as he always did toward those who endured to satisfy him.

The leather was smooth against O's cheek and smelled of regular dressing.

"It's my favorite," Steven explained, "ideally balanced and easily controlled. I assume you're still light-headed."

"A bit, Sir. It was a very powerful orgasm."

"Girls are always more pliable after the first one. And particularly sensitive. They're far more readily broken by pleasure than pain, which is why I never deny them, though I still expect the courtesy of a request before coming."

"I'll try to remember, Sir."

He moved in close, rubbing his cock along her flank, his hand finding its way underneath her to the right spot. Even a gentle contact made her jump, heels clicking back on the floor as quickly as possible. Such tiny lapses always amused him.

"Here's the deal," he said. "If it's too hard, raise your right foot. If you want more, wiggle your ass."

"That wouldn't be impertinent, Sir?"

"It's never impertinent for a slave to show off her ass."

Stepping back, Steven went to *en garde*, crop extended. Every girl took the crop differently. Steven never ceased to marvel at the variety of their responses.

The first stroke was light and crisp, delivered to the lower curve of O's butt-cheek with a slight upward cut at the point of impact. It hardly stung, but conveyed the general idea. Steven always gave fair warning. He was good about that.

Moving behind her in an unhurried stride, he took his time, positioning himself for each blow.

In his head, as always, Steven made choices. Whip. Touch. Fuck. It was an intoxicating combination of sensations, but his choices, once made, were never haphazardly mixed. He worked the crop in precise half-circles over the tops of O's rear curves, each impact a bit harder, painting a deeper-hued stripe, proceeding from light pink to crimson as the instrument traveled back and forth like a metronome.

Steven watched and listened with complete attention – the speed at which the color rose on O's flesh, the increasingly rapid contractions of her diaphragm, the accelerating sway of her hips. Steven liked making girls ask for it, beg for it. Their pleasure was his power.

Every ten strokes precisely, he paused, draping his arm around O's waist, balancing the whip on her tail bone and sliding his fingers under her, around her wet zone, sometimes inside, probing expertly for any spot that produced a particularly intense response.

If O typically found men's tongues disappointing, she positively dreaded their big fingers mauling her insides. But this man did not maul. He pushed buttons with the expertise of a skilled pilot.

Uppercuts to the lower surfaces now, swift and sure to the point where the line between pain and pleasure was more brightly drawn, though O was equally happy on either side of it. She was only distantly aware of her swaying rump, inviting him to strike harder.

Steven never declined such an invitation. He loved the meaty thump of leather on muscle, the rippling of skin outward from the point of impact, the knowledge that not only was he inflicting pain on someone he desired, but inducing her to like it.

The crop's broad head distributed the energy as widely as possible, but it lacked nothing for bite. Now the focus moved inward, making O jump with the sudden, hard shots to the inner thigh. Liking the effect, Steven lingered, laying a row of triangular prints laddered from knee to crotch on both sides.

Curiosity overcoming both etiquette and common sense, O lifted her head and looked straight back over her shoulder at him. He was masturbating unabashedly with his unoccupied hand, smiling broadly, gleaming eyes focused to coordinate his aim. His movements were as smooth as she presumed his saber advance to be. That hard, weathered face bore none of the usual affected sternness or stagy detachment that had become so wearying during the final days before Ray had reclaimed her from The Mansion.

Steven was in the moment, fully relaxed and loving it. O wasn't the kind of selfish pain-addict who simply lived to have her itch scratched until it bled, submitting only for the purpose of seducing a partner into helping her get her freak on. She liked to see a man enjoy her so thoroughly. Pleasing made her confident and the indisputable evidence of Steven's pleasure stood up between his legs like a tree-branch.

He had always been the kind of kid who tied up other kids, and when he reached puberty, he tied up girls. His first, a year ahead of him in school and improbably a cheerleader, had asked him to spank her with a belt before the first time they fucked.

Steven was convinced that there was a kind of transponder in those genetically oriented toward sexual cruelty that sent out a signal to others like themselves. He'd been turned down on his terms of engagement very few times in his life, and he had never hesitated to state them clearly. Whatever guilt or shame so many men seemed to have over such impulses had been left out of him at the factory, along with certain other usual components, including jealousy and the urge to reproduce.

"Put your head back down, silly girl," he said, "and we'll see if I can keep your mind from wandering."

The sharp snap up between the legs commanded O's attention wonderfully. She let out a yelp when the leather connected with a wet splat, but the tingling that followed, building atop the growing heat of the surrounding regions, was delicious.

"May I have another please, Sir?"

"Oh, absolutely. Have a couple."

He delivered them smartly, with hardly a respite in between. O gasped and moaned.

"Thank you, Sir. That's wonderful. Would Sir like me to count?"

Steven cringed.

"Oh god no. I hate formality for its own sake. I'll whip you until I'm ready to do something else."

He continued a long time, halting unpredictably to massage O's hot spot as he'd seen her do it, pinched between her neat, hairless labia. Back to whipping, he never stayed in one place too long, distributing the strokes evenly, left and right, high and low, until O's ass glowed red all over, highlighted by darker crimson streaks.

Rubbing his fingers lightly across it, he could feel the rising welts. They weren't deep and wouldn't bruise. Most of the color would be gone by the next day, but for a first time, they served their purpose, providing him with an alluring view. He set the crop on the table where she could look at it and moved in behind her.

Pausing one last moment to look at all those splotches of scarlet, he took her by the hips and made a hands-free, unhurried entrance, the head of his cock pushing into O's tenderized opening very slowly with a single, drawn-out thrust.

Normally, he would have greased her up with some silicone lube first, but his earlier probing had satisfied him that she was wet enough already. She moaned and he felt her whole body go limp on the table. Snug and warm within, she was a perfect fit in every way, her small stature making it easy for him to slide in from the rear despite her tall heels.

Never one to hurry his indulgences, Steven took her in long, slow strokes, feeling her strong internal muscles grasping for him at every withdrawal. Swinging his hips in slow circles, he held her down flat with a hand in the middle of her back. It was a gesture she understood the way a well-trained horse understood a light tug on the reins and she stayed completely still from the waist up, only lifting her heels slightly and swiveling her pelvis each time he filled her again. The heat of her fresh welts tingled against Steven's hard abs. He couldn't resist raising the temperature with occasional random blows from an open hand, each of which spurred O into grinding back harder.

Steven relished the control his chemically boosted arousal gave him, allowing him to speed up or back off without losing one PSI of internal pressure. He could stir O's insides with lazy orbits; deliver a hard volley of pounding strokes, then back down again long before anything unexpected could occur.

Steven couldn't remember a single unscheduled orgasm in his entire life and doubted he'd ever have one. O, however, let out a pitiful whimper and began hammering at him so hard she rocked the heavy table. Her back heaved and her voice was high and thin when she pleaded for permission. Though it was a courtesy he demanded, Steven never said no to such a request, knowing that the more orgasms a woman had the more she was likely to, and that always worked in his favor.

After a few particularly deep, rough jolts, he slammed his hips against O's sweaty backside and held her tight around the middle. O wailed, shaking her head from side to side, babbling out her gratitude along with assorted invocations of various deities and a few curses. This time, the telltale red flush rose along O's spine. He stroked her affectionately while her breathing slowed to normal.

"That must have been a good one," he observed calmly, his hard rod still now, but pulsing inside her from the blood pumping through his dilated vessels.

"Yes, Sir. Thank you, Sir. Penetration works best for me, but you can also get me off with a vibrator if you like."

Steven laughed. "You really don't hold anything back, do you?"

O was still breathing hard. "It's a slave's duty to keep her master informed, Sir."

"I appreciate your honesty." Steven could read his partners with the expertise of vast experience, but preferred not to have to.

"I'm going to enjoy you from the front now," he said, sliding his arms under her shoulders and raising her onto her feet. O staggered a bit turning around and her face was as flushed and sweaty as the rest of her, stray wisps of hair clinging to her cheeks.

"Want to see first?

"May I?"

He guided her over to the mirror so O could admire the neat rows of stripes. She brushed them with her fingertips. Their burning and itching went straight to her center.

"They're beautiful, Sir. Thank you."

"I'm sure you could take it harder, but you get the general idea."

Steven wondered what was required to wring genuine pleas for mercy from those full lips. Perhaps he'd find out sometime, but it wasn't his usual objective. He was only vicious enough to satisfy his needs and didn't seek limits as ends in themselves. It hadn't always been thus.

He swung her around into his arms and kissed her hard. She gave it back to him, letting a small squeal escape her nostrils when he reached down and squeezed her ass.

"You're mean, Sir," she panted when their mouths separated.

"You noticed that."

"But you could be meaner if it pleases you."

There were places in Steven he rarely visited anymore, though as a younger man he'd spent a lot of time there. He sensed that was precisely the geography O wished to explore, but it would have to be his choice and he wasn't ready to make it yet.

He took O by the wrist and led her back to the table, once again seating her on the edge. This time, the cold steel felt good under her seared backside. She deliberately shifted her weight on it, ostensibly settling herself in, splayed open with her hands out of the way.

O was nice and sweaty now. Clever girl: the blush on her lips and tits might be colorfast, but her mascara was clearly meant to run and small, black rivulets trickled from the corners of her eyes. Steven knew it had been a gamble, or possibly a presentiment. Not all men liked criers. As it happened, he did.

"You do mess up nicely," he said, putting his hand to her wet face. O suddenly broke form, grabbed his wrist and held it tight, squeezing out a few more black droplets between her shuttered lids. But she smiled at the same time. Steven stroked her face gently for a moment and then ordered her back into position.

Undoing the tasseled belt of his robe, he shrugged it off, catching it neatly over one arm as it fell and laying it next to O's things on the couch. Turning back, he allowed her the privilege of a good, long look.

In addition to his most obvious landmark, Steven had other striking terrain features – a spectacular red *irezumi* dragon, surrounded by red and yellow flames and bright blue waves, covered his entire left shoulder, winding down his arm just to the stopping point of a short-sleeve shirt. He noticed her studying it.

"Gift from a Japanese client for whom I did a favor."

"Beautiful," O said. She didn't have a thing for ink, had come to think of it as a fashion cliché that couldn't be donated to The Salvation Army. But Steven's seemed to fit him perfectly like everything he wore. Not far from it, on his other shoulder, was something she really didn't expect to see: a deep, perfectly round scar she was pretty sure she recognized. Daringly, she reached out and touched it with a fingertip.

"Not so beautiful."

"It was a 9mm, through-and-through. Gift from a less satisfied client." He dipped his shoulder to show her the exit wound in back.

"And here I'd assumed it was from an ex-wife."

"She and I parted on better terms. Anyway, it didn't break any bones or hit anything vital."

"That was lucky."

"If I was lucky I wouldn't have gotten shot. Now sit up straight."

She did it gravely, setting her shoulders and properly lowering her gaze to Steven's velvet slippers, taking just a beat to see him through the viewfinder. For all the evident mileage, Steven had the battered perfection of an artifact from a distant era, all muscle and sinew, solid as marble. The idea was a little absurd but the *frisson* was real.

O was on a blind date in ancient Crete without a ball of string to find her way back out of the labyrinth where Ray had offered her as tribute. What if she couldn't? What if this was the date that lasted forever? O didn't believe in forever, and reality intruded with a sharp rap to the side of her left breast.

Just as he had from behind, Steven applied the crop with unerring aim, planting bright red blooms around O's aureoles before giving her hard, downward slaps across their heavily ornamented tips. Whipping over piercings was tricky, but Steven had much practice at smacking the upper surfaces without catching the rings.

O couldn't stay silent under his precision hammering of these tender regions. She tried not to squirm. Throwing his aim off would make things worse. She did gasp, whine, whimper and cry out. Now Steven was breathing hard and the pulsing further below was unmistakable. The more he hurt her, the more he enjoyed himself.

Moving to each side, Steven laddered a row of vermilion splotches down her torso, stretched long as she arched back to absorb each impact fully. The leather bit deeper each time. Few men seemed to understand the erogenous potential of a woman's belly. O loved being whipped there, or caned, or flogged, or lashed. She loved the rippling vibration through her ovaries that seemed to sink down straight through her liquid interior. Struck abruptly across the cheek with the crop, she let her head swing with the momentum, slowly coming around to look him in the eyes. She wanted him to see how wet she was there as well as elsewhere. Nothing opened the taps quite like a stinging smack in the face.

Steven wasn't surprised. O's signals were polished but not subtle, much like his moves. Finely tuned alarms began to wail softly in the back of his mind. He wasn't in a listening mood.

Coming forward, he pushed her over, ordering her to lift her legs wide. O did it, knowing where he'd concentrate next, starting with her smooth thighs and working up to the place where the whip would sting best. Quick and just hard enough, the slapping of the crop's flap made O's legs quiver. Some penetration would be lovely now. Even a passing spike of guilt for Ray, a perfectly satisfying demon lover in his own way, couldn't distract her from the hunger this hard man inspired.

Tears flowed freely now, running in rivulets off her cheeks, pooling on the table. He grinned down at her affectionately.

"I'll bet you're eager to show me your appreciation, aren't you?"

"Any way you like, Sir."

"Good, then," he said.

Slipping his hands beneath O's perspiring back, Steven easily slid her to the far side of the table so her head fell off the edge, affording her a brief, inverted look at the night skyline through the windows before his bulk blocked her vision. That big, hard shaft hovered over her face, which she lifted to run the point of her tongue along the underside. Nice and smooth. She could have licked it like ice cream all night, but that wasn't the plan.

"Open," Steven ordered brusquely.

O's parted lips fell completely wide as he stretched her arms out by the wrists and held them down on the table. Slowly, Steven slid his cock into her wet mouth. This was a challenging test and he knew it. If he felt her teeth, he'd let her know, but he didn't. Instead, he saw the slight swelling under her delicate collar, heard her wheezing breath through her nostrils, watched her belly heave when she finally started to cough and choke. But she let it happen, keeping her head still while struggling for air. O even kept her legs open to afford him the best view.

Steven withdrew just as slowly, spilling thick spit down O's face. After all, she had said she didn't mind getting messy. He let her demonstrate her well-schooled lips by not pulling out completely. He had yet to meet a submissive woman who didn't take pride in what she could do with her mouth. O definitely had bragging rights in that department, but he would indulge her vanity only so far. For Steven, mastery was the subtle balancing of what was desired and what was required.

Again, he went to the choke point. Again, O's breasts rose and fell as she did her best to breathe around him, but ultimately the coughing and gasping racked her small body once more. Steven sped up, giving her just enough time to suck in some air before packing her face each time. His hands found her thick nipple rings and tugged upward, but O stayed flat on her back. This one had her pride. Was it about impressing Steven or not disappointing Ray? She knew he would hear all about this.

It was neither. O would have preferred to be on her knees, demonstrating the talents she'd cultivated with such extensive practice, but Steven chose to use her this way instead and that was all that mattered.

In most men to whom she had submitted there was always an anxiety she could feel. They were afraid of hurting her, afraid of breaking her. They didn't realize that, despite her appearance, she despised being treated as a china doll.

Watching the huge muscles tense in Steven's legs when he rocked in and out of her mouth, O realized that by treating her with such brutal selfishness he was showing her the respect she had been missing. Suddenly aware her hands were free while he mauled her breasts, she daringly reached behind him and took hold, forcing him in even deeper, deliberately gagging on his invading hardness. This was so wrong and she was so down for it.

O needn't have worried about Steven. He'd long understood that women were not fragile. Nor were their tastes particularly refined. While the appearance of fragility might attract men, too often it brought out instincts opposite those that appearance was meant to inspire. Why affect vulnerability if not to encourage violation?

The grip of her small hands and the rocking of her head even as she struggled for every breath might conclude the proceedings more abruptly than planned.

The first person a master must master is himself. Summoning all his willpower, he slid free of her hungry lips and squatted down to face her.

"You're entirely too good at that," he said. "It could be dangerously habit-forming." He took her by the hair and kissed her, oblivious to the rivers of saliva contributing to the further ruin of her makeup. She kissed him back ravenously, and then shook loose, wet hair flying.

"Please, Sir," O panted. "Please, girl needs fucking so badly."

"I think you've earned it."

Steven stood up straight, his wet lance gleaming in the lamplight from above, and went back to the other side of the table. He pulled O to him by the ankles quite roughly, sat her up, encircling her small shoulders with his big arm, and stepped in, carefully guiding the thick head fisted up in his hand to where O's naughty opening waited eagerly.

Steven took possession in his usual, unhurried way, letting her feel every inch go in, one by one, holding her upright and impaled as if she were weightless. He felt the heat pouring off her, the need clasping at him in her depths. Usually, even in these moments, some part of Steven always looked on from a distance – thinking, remembering, comparing, and engineering the next move. At the moment O could have eaten his head like a female mantis and he might not have noticed.

Fully settled in, he flattened his free hand to the small of her back and moved inside her in lazy circles, sliding in and out with agonizing slowness, savoring the physical connection each time. Having extracted O's tears, now he wanted something else.

She gave it with her languid mouth, her nuzzling of his neck, her hands sliding up and down his broad back. As much as he could be hard, she could be soft, pressing her stinging breasts against his iron ribcage, swinging her hips to match his movements, raising and lowering ever so slightly, seeking the sensation of being shafted deep with each in-stroke.

O's breathing grew hard and husky and her legs wrapped around his middle, respectfully urging him to do what she so needed, but he held her up a long time, moving in and out in those maddeningly extended rotations. She tried to stake herself against him harder, but the edge of the table didn't give her much leverage. She could only fuck him back with aching core muscles.

Not utterly indifferent to O's plight, Steven tucked himself under, slamming into her from below, tilting her forward all the way onto him repeatedly. It was without doubt the deepest O had ever been fucked. The friction of Steven's pubic bone against her recently mistreated clit compelled her back toward the precipice.

"Okay, dirty girl, back down you go."

This time he lowered her to the table more gently, never slipping out of her for an instant. Settling her hips just so, he lifted her legs and placed them over his tattooed shoulder, crossing her black-clad ankles and resting them on his collarbone. He looked over at the red-soled shoes and grinned.

"Isn't that pretty?"

He kissed her ankles, rubbed his face against them, as he swayed into her depths.

Held down to the table with one hand gripping her neck and the other working deviously at the critical junction between her captive thighs, O had little resistance to Steven's now-relentless pounding.

Babbling out a desperate plea for release she sat up suddenly, throwing her arms around him and sobbing into his nearly hairless torso. Steven stroked her head, bending down to kiss the top of her skull as he held her close.

"Good girl," he whispered in her ear. "My turn now."

With that, he laid her back down carefully. O shook like a wet kitten. She was covered in sweat, suddenly aware that she must reek from the exertion. One eyelash was starting to come off and black streaks trailed down toward her chin. Neither of them cared about any of it.

Steven rolled her onto one side, tucking her legs under her so her heels hung off the table. It wasn't a comfortable position, but she didn't care about that.

Grabbing the far edge, O impaled herself on him with all her considerable strength. Holding her by hip and ankle, he worked her back and forth, enjoying the graceful S-curve of her body as she lay on her side. Hardly moving himself, he pistoned her against him harder and faster, his strong hands tightening around her hip bone and leg, adjusting her until the angle, the friction, were just right.

Instead of the killing thrust O expected, he drew almost all the way out at the last minute and slowly slid back in, roaring like a beast, taking his release by the inch. O could feel the hot spurts and convulsive shudders all through her from the inside out. It went on a long, long time and when it was over Steven made no move to disengage. Flipping O onto her back, he leaned down and let the weight of his upper body lie over her.

The room was so quiet now, just the sounds of breathing gradually growing softer and more even. Eventually, Steven stood up, placing a hand over O to keep her insides warm while he slowly extracted himself, wet and dripping.

"You're very good at that," he said with jovial affection. It didn't take Steven long to regain his composure, ever.

"You did most of the work ... Sir."

"I'm immune to flattery."

Steven deftly slipped off O's pumps, standing them neatly on the table, offered her his hands to help her up. Normally preferring the highest heels possible, at this moment she was quite glad to be flat-footed. Steven led her over to the couch and fell back into it, pulling O onto his lap.

"I'm forced to admit it. For once in his life, Ray was right about something," O said.

"What's this?" Steven asked, glancing over at the ashtray. How convenient.He took what was left of the joint and fired it with the giant lighter. Taking a puff, he handed it to O, who steadied her breathing and inhaled a deep drag.

"Thirsty?" he asked.

"Dying, actually."

"Can't have that."

Steven slid out from under her, settled her into the couch and went to the massive steel refrigerator in the open kitchen on the other side of the immense room.

"What'll it be?"

"Water's fine. Thank you, Sir."

"Water it is."

Taking a tall glass decorated with a German beer logo from the cabinet, he poured O some bottled water. For himself, he took a long pull from straight from the neck.

Handing her the glass, he wrapped her in against him.

"Do you prefer Sir or Master?" O asked after a gulp or two.

"Anything but master. Sir is fine."

"So Sir, did I pass the entrance exam?"

"I certainly enjoyed entering you, if that's what you mean."

O turned to look him in the eye, amused and exasperated.

"No, that's not what I mean."

"Now that you've been alone with me, are you still game for Ray's bargain?

O had to think about that a minute. It had all kinds of risks. Ray was her principal employer, the publisher who had liberated her to make the images she had always wanted to. And he was her lover. Until tonight, she would have considered him as much her owner as any man or woman could be. She already knew that Steven's definition of ownership would be more complete.

And what of his feelings for her? Could he have any? She looked at him, smiling and smoking. It didn't seem likely. That, at least, made the whole thing feel a bit safer.

Steven had come around from his initial skepticism. He was not one to want a thing and not have it and O definitely fell into that vanishingly small category of things wanted and not already possessed. Nothing came from Ray free of entanglements. Pervy girls could be troublesome, especially if they knew they were luscious. But Steven was nothing if not a problem solver. If this adventure ended badly he would put in whatever fix was required as always.

O caught sight of herself in the round mirror. Never had she seen herself so completely, deliciously wrecked, but it wouldn't do for Steven to remember her that way.

"God, I'm frightening," she said, covering her eyes. "May I take a quick shower, Sir?"

Steven found the monkey's fist with the keys on it, carefully slipped the collar from O's neck, and stood it up on the table in the shape of her name.

"Bathroom is to the left down the small hallway behind the pool table. There's a clean robe hanging on the back of the door."

"Must I wear it?"

"As a general rule I'd discourage that."

O put down her glass, slipped to her knees, touched her forehead to Steven's hands. Then she stood up, turned her back and strolled out to the bathroom, consciously straight-ening her posture. He admired the departing view. O certainly knew how to roll her hips. That little open space at the tops of her legs was indeed inviting, not to mention her firm, still-blazing backside.

Looking up at the smoke curling into the light, Steven felt a vague unease. He preferred having Ray owe him instead of the other way around. Ray's judgment was, to be charitable, uneven at best. Steven had accepted the hard, adult truth that things seemingly too good to be true generally were.

Listening to the water blasting away at O's body from the multiple heads in the vast marble and glass shower from the open door of the guest bathroom, Steven felt unusually comfortable with her presence there. Sex was the easy part. Conversation could be taxing. But he really didn't want her to go.

Stubbing out what was left of the joint, Steven slipped the silk robe on loosely, letting it hang open with the belt dropping to his sides. He ambled toward the black-surfaced pool table, snagging a pair of wireless headphones off a wall-mount next to the bank of giant flat-screens. Scooping up a compact remote en route, he punched in a code, dropped the remote in his robe pocket and put on the headphones.

At the table, he racked the classic-style balls with circled numbers using a silver Tiffany Atlas triangle, spotting the lead ball and aligning the rack exactly square. From a narrow cabinet on the wall he took out an alligator-skin cue case, popped it open and assembled an ebony stick inlaid in bone around the butt with the Jolly Rogers he so favored.

The well-used cue ball, another token from a client, was incised with a corseted woman raising her bum to the perfect point of contact where the cue would strike. It always made Steven smile to sight in on that tiny derrière.

As he spotted the white ball behind the scratch line, Chris Isaak poured out of the headphones, singing "Wicked Game" in his wounded voice. Steven sang along, not caring that without the instrumental accompaniment his voice would be *a capella* and certainly off-key. If she were lucky, O wouldn't hear him over the running water. Actually, Steven was a better singer than he gave himself credit for, but was fortunate not to have to make his living that way. He considered himself blessed to have as little contact with the entertainment industry as possible.

Putting down the Fifteen on the break, he began his relentless progression around the table. Steven took as long as he needed for each shot, tapping the balls with as little energy as necessary to drop them, one by one. At this, he could have made a living. He loved the simple geometry of the table, as his suave and corrupt Uncle Sol had taught it to him. The angle of incidence equals the angle of reflection. If only things worked out so predictably anyplace else. Stopping after each ball fell into the leather webbing, he chalked up with a battered silver chalk holder, a legacy from the long-departed Uncle Sol, engraved with Steven's initials.

Through Chris Isaak's keening, Steven heard the clapping of strong but delicate hands. He looked up to find O watching him. Except for a towel turbaned around her head she was as naked as ever. The hot water had really brought out the marks he left on her. Face scrubbed clean, she was almost more exotic completely unadorned.

Steven lifted off the headphones and lowered them to his shoulders.

"Enjoy your shower?"

"Particularly the lower nozzles, Sir. Very thoughtfully situated. And the bidet is a nice touch. Quite considerate of your female guests."

"Not entirely. I like watching them use it."

"So nasty-minded, Sir. I like that in a man."

Placing her hands on the edge of the pool table, O leaned forward just enough.

"Are you trying to distract me?" he asked, not at all annoyed.

"Wondering if it's possible."

He tapped the cue ball and the Six fell like a shot duck. Moving around behind O, deliberately brushing against her damp back on the way, he proceeded to play the last three shots without even looking up at her, dismantled the cue and returned it to its case.

"I didn't think it would be easy," O said.

O tugged playfully at the loose robe cord as he draped his arms around her.

"This could be useful for tying someone's wrists," she said helpfully crossing hers in front of her, dipping her eyelids with affected shyness.

"We're past the point of appropriating household objects. You're welcome to stay the night."

"Is that an order?"

"You'll know when it is."

"Then I'd better not. I'm shooting tomorrow afternoon."

"I certainly don't want Ray bitching at me over you missing work. He'd be right, too. If my wants get in the way of your pictures, you have to tell me."

"Sir has seen my pictures, I take it."

"Without them, I'd have made Ray sell the magazine a year ago. Print is a lousy investment unless it offers something consumers want to own. Your pictures make *Forbidden* collectible."

"And you know what's collectible, don't you? I could serve you again before I go. You still haven't had my ass."

"Disappointed?"

"From what Ray said, I expected ..."

Steven silenced her with a finger to the lips.

"Were you disappointed that I didn't fuck your ass?"

"I wasn't disappointed in anything, Sir. But I can take more."

"Don't worry, you'll get plenty of that and everything else."

O looked up at him seriously. No more teasing now.

"Then you and Ray intend to go through with your bargain."

"More to the point, do you?"

O looked disconsolate.

"Why do you force me to make choices instead of just forcing me to do what you want?"

She turned her back to him, leaning against his chest, putting her hands over his. His voice turned firm and business-like.

"I'm sure it would be easier for you, but things can never happen that way. The day you refuse is the day it all stops. I won't let you forget that, even if you try."

"I think I should go now. I can take a cab."

"I'll call Ray and have him pick you up. I'll see you here again on Friday at four in the afternoon, unless you refuse."

"I'll be here, Sir. Please email me with any special instructions for delivering myself."

O sounded sad. Steven turned her around to face him.

"Look up at me. There's no escape from choices, O," Steven said firmly. "Not to decide is still a choice."

"I've made mine then, Sir. May we leave it at that?"

He told her to go get dressed.

O's mood seemed to brighten a bit just at being given a simple and direct command.

"Yes, Sir. Right away."

O padded off to collect her clothes while Steven called Ray from the phone in the kitchen. Steven's tone was affable and reassuring. Everything was fine. O would tell him all about it. At that, she looked back from doing up her skirt, mouth open as if to say something, but Steven cut her off, leaving the receiver uncovered so Ray could hear.

"That's right, O. Tell him everything in detail. You have no privacy from him — either of us."

"I understand I'm common property, Sir."

Her tone had reassumed its natural formality.

"Property maybe, but certainly not common."

Steven went back to talking with Ray. O went back to dressing. She'd had more than a good time with Steven. Something had changed with the sealing of the bargain and she knew there was no undoing that. What she did not know, but feared, was what lay ahead.

There was danger where these men wanted to take her. They might not know it yet, but O did. The deal had been struck and she'd hold them all to it, whatever the final cost.

CHAPTER THREE

F*orbidden*'s creative operations were headquartered in a storied Hollywood landmark from the city's High Kitsch era. Built to resemble an ocean liner of sorts, it had a wide, round, glassed-in front like an old-fashioned tugboat bridge. A stumpy mast with a revolving globe on top jutted up from the low façade and porthole windows ran back along either side. Ray had been offered more than the whole magazine was worth in exchange for the lease, but he needed the cachet worse than the additional cash.

Surrounded by oft-refurbished machine-age furnishings that had been there since the original owner, Ray occupied the expansive front office facing Sunset Boulevard. In a city full of tragically hip addresses, Ray's was among the most coveted. Like most things, he didn't take it too seriously. One of the rare things he did take seriously was displayed on the big Mac studio monitor atop his desk return.

"I still like Number One," Ray said, shaking his head. He studied the three prospective covers for the next issue of *Forbidden* from his out-of-period Aeron chair, leaning all the way back to simulate the perspective from the sidewalk in front of a newsstand. Jasper, the art director, sat on the edge of Ray's cluttered desk and looked over his shoulder, a dubious expression on his long, gaunt face.

"Number Two shows more skin," he said.

Tall and slender, immaculate in his buttoned-up, slim-cut jacket, stovepipe trousers and green brogues, Jasper's high-pitched voice and languid manner fooled some into thinking him gay. Jasper was, in fact, straight, vanilla and happily married a dozen years with a couple of kids. He had no kink.

"Did you email JPEGs of these to Albert?" Ray asked, referring to *Forbidden's* notoriously reclusive editor.

"He liked Number One too," Jasper said with a discouraged eye-roll.

At any magazine, the cover was a recurring nightmare from which there was no awakening. The easy choices were rarely right and the right choices were rarely easy. But it was the cover that sold the book and Ray knew he'd pay the price of a bad call in the sixty-day numbers. It didn't help that he and Jasper saw completely different things when they looked at the three options from the photo layouts inside the issue. Jasper was a consummate technician. He understood everything about photography and product design and could make the complex graphics programs recreate The Sistine Chapel ceiling. But he was essentially a hired gun with no personal feelings toward a particular target. He had assembled everything from flagstone-size coffee table books about yachting to classified pages for *The Recycler*. To him, everything was an element, the key art essentially no different from the logo font. Ray didn't need intuition from him.

It was Ray's instinct that guided the magazine toward its readers' darker impulses, for which his own served as the template. The best piece of advice he'd ever gotten was from a cranky, wheezy old video director with whom he'd shared a five a.m. breakfast at The Grande Luxe in The Venetian during the big annual porn convention in Vegas.

"I don't care what kind of bullshit these guys make up about how they set a shot," the director had growled. "All I know is that behind every successful image there's one guy's hard-on."

For this magazine, Ray was that guy, and looking among the three contenders on the monitor, he wasn't as sure as he wanted to be which made his divining rod twitch most inside his Italian jeans. Albert's was the only other libido he trusted as his own, but Albert made no pretenses when it came to the book's visual content, or anything else for that matter. He had an informed opinion but that was as much as he could or would give.

"Number Two is definitely hot," Ray agreed. There was no denying it. A tall, naked blonde shackled to a rust stained concrete wall with her hands over her head and the tails of a flogger frozen in motion across her sleek haunches, she looked back over her shoulder with a credible expression of distress on her high-cheek-boned face. She was certainly perfect in that predictable way. Her blue eyes looked ready to tear at the next stroke and her glossed lips seemed to tremble over her even, white teeth as if pleading for mercy. Posed half-turned, her expertly augmented breast was truly alluring. She was a vision of suffering beauty.

And yet the feeling wasn't there. Ray would have loved to fuck this girl and fuckability was definitely an important criterion for a cover model. But the whole shot seemed too staged. Something was missing.

Number Three, a tiny redhead strapped to a column, was also appealing. She had a giant ball-gag stuffed between her bright red lips and the straps were well placed – around her neck, above and below her breasts and around her middle. The dressage marks on her chest and belly were believable. Ray, however, was finicky about ink and this girl had a couple of scratchy tattoos he found distracting. It always made him a bit sad to think about how some of these models would feel in a few years when the pigment started to break up.

The cover to which Ray's eyes kept returning was a risky choice. Also blonde, and spectacularly voluptuous, she was much more dressed than the others, wearing a simple white blouse and a short, tight leather skirt. She was tied to a wooden chair with her arms behind her and her legs very neatly secured with loops and hitches of rope. The blouse was ripped open to show her fantastic cleavage and the skirt was hiked up to the legal limit.

It was a pose that could have come from an old crime magazine cover. It would have been rack-legal even then. But the facial expression was what Ray found fascinating. The implication was clearly one of abduction and captivity, but her face was simultaneously defiant and seductive, as if daring whoever had taken her to do his worst.

If Number Two made him want to fuck her, Number One made him want to slap her, hard and repeatedly. Getting a scared look out of her would not be easy.

"Show me Number One with some Greeking and the logo," Ray said, motioning toward the screen.

Jasper leaned past Ray and tapped out a couple of commands on the split keyboard. Instantly cover lines of random characters popped up on either side of her and the logo fell across her face.

"Have to cut into that," Jasper said. Ray rolled back in his chair so Jasper could get in closer. Using the mouse on the desk, Jasper pulled down the outlining tool from the style menu and deftly positioned the model's head over the second and third letters across the top of the page.

"Let's see a fifth color and a white drop shadow," Ray suggested.

A few more keystrokes and the model's blue eyes popped out over the hot-pink type. Jasper stood back and looked at the screen through his stylish narrow spectacles.

"It certainly works," he admitted. He never pretended to understand more of the desired effect than he actually did, which was one of the reasons Ray trusted him.

"That's what I want," Ray pronounced after a long pause. "Go with it."

"No problem," Jasper replied, turning to head back to his own office. "It will be on your desktop in an hour."

"Careful on that UPC block."

"You mean this magazine has a UPC?"

Jasper pulled a half smile, stretching his lanky frame on the way out. He slipped easily through the arched doorway even as Ray's pneumatically sculpted managing editor, Lena, slithered in.

Ink-black hair piled high, short-sleeved, red angora sweater tight enough to get attention and pencil skirt narrow enough to keep it, she clacked across the tile floor in her strappy thrift-store sandals, a thick stack of clipped papers clutched to her ample bosom.

"Proofs are here," she announced in a voice too chirpy for her age, leaning down to set the clipped pages in front of Ray. Lena had an impressive full-sleeve tattoo of flowers and vines. Her nails were painted black. Lena had a lot of nice going on there, but she was so not Ray's type. For all his bohemian affectations – his blue shades, his leather vest appliquéd with Maltese crosses all over the back, his chunky silver bracelets and embroidered black silk shirt – Ray took his glamour dry of irony.

He looked up at her in his friendly way.

"Are they any good?"

"No, they suck. Of course they're good. The Fernando strip rocks, the Lilith interview is nice and dirty, but O's set blows everything else away as usual."

Lena glanced at the monitor where the cover prospects were still on parade.

"Go with Number Two. More skin."

Ray slapped his forehead.

"Goddamn it, I figured you of all people would see why I took Number One."

"Too Retro."

Lena shrugged.

"Anyway, an O image is always safe, and the set really delivers so it's not just a tease."

She clacked back out, leaving Ray to sort through the yet-unassembled issue. He took a Sharpie from his desk drawer to initial each sheet. This was the last chance to catch any mistakes, but after the book had gotten through Art, Editorial, and Copy, he really didn't expect to find any. That was good, because four-color fixes at this stage cost eight hundred bucks each.

Signing off, Ray's attention wandered back to O's return from her evening with Steven. She'd been even quieter than usual in the car. Her face was scrubbed and her hair tied back – not how she usually returned from these missions. Most the time, O simply patched her makeup and ran a brush through her hair so that Ray could appreciate her well-used condition. She must have had something better to show him.

O's perfect little jewel box of a house was set back behind high walls and automated gates in a pricey neighborhood across from Griffith Park. Among the oldest in the area, it had belonged to one of Griffith's editors back in the day, but now she'd made it very much hers.

Built like a very large bungalow, its scale was just right for her. The living room was blindingly white from its tufted silk walls to its overstuffed furniture to its draped, vaulted ceiling. It was simple, spare luxury at its most polished, right down to the Daumier originals on the walls. Ray never felt entirely comfortable there, which was how O preferred it. No one was to be entirely comfortable there but her.

That's why the bed in the robin's-egg blue bedroom was only a small queen, though buried in pillows fluffed with the down of an entire flock of geese. O had led Ray directly there, flipped on the lamps on either side of the bed and stripped with her back turned to him. Unlacing the corset skirt, she had let it slip to the floor for him to fully appreciate the patchwork of welts and streaks Steven had left.

Ray smiled, remembering rocking back on the bed, laughing.

"Man, he must really have liked you."

O had turned to face him, teary-eyed. Her body was even more spectacularly decorated in the front, from an already yellowing thumbprint on her neck just above the collar to the crimson streaks all over her breasts and belly to her swollen, still-shining lady parts.

"Your brother is very mean, Master," O had declared, turning in the light to show Ray the evidence from every angle. Even the stockings were gone now. Naked in her high heels, O looked every bit the martyred slave. "See how he hurt my poor, little pussy?" She'd spread it open to show him that she was marked even there.

In truth, she had been tired and confused. But it was always easy with Ray, both his greatest virtue and most disappointing failing. In his recollection, O had been eager to share her intimate suffering with him, when her real intention had been to address his anticipated lusts with the greatest possible dispatch.

Pirouetting once under in the light, she had sunk to her knees and crawled over to him.

"Shall I tell you all about it, Master?" she'd asked. She knew Ray coveted the title as much as Steven found it preposterous.

She'd already started unzipping him, recounting every lurid detail she could remember in a low, throaty voice. He had come out of the gate already hard, her small hands grasping and stroking him as she spoke. From this angle, swallowing Ray whole was easy, without gagging or retching. He remembered her looking up at him pitifully, then diving on him as if ravenous. O had still been wet and tingling, but that was more of a nuisance than anything else. She had given Ray service, pure and simple; to be enjoyed for the quality of it she delivered.

It hadn't taken long. Ray recollected the undulations of O's neck muscles as she had gulped down every drop. Afterward, she'd been asleep in his arms five minutes later, respectfully declining his offer of anything in return. The big, purple wand vibe had stayed in the drawer of the damask shrouded nightstand.

O, who usually slept like the dead, found herself restless and unable to get comfortable. Slipping quietly out of bed, she'd gone to the quartz-white kitchen and made herself a cup of chamomile with the electric kettle. Pouring the steaming liquid into a giant yellow cup emblazoned with a French brand name, O had drifted back to the bedroom doorway. Ray, who tended to run hot, had been halfway on top of the covers, clutching the long down pillow to his smooth chest. O had looked at him a long time as she sipped her tea. She couldn't imagine ever ceasing to find him beautiful, with his wavy black hair and his aristocratic bones.

Buff and healthy as he was, something about him seemed fragile, especially compared to his brother. O considered herself to have absolutely no maternal instincts whatsoever. Her biological clock, as she liked to put it, came without batteries. And yet she felt protective of Ray, responsible for him. He depended on her for so much – the covers and sets for his magazine, the dazzling entrances they always made together at fetish events, the envy Ray's possession of her inspired among his friends, the easy routines of erotic circus magic that were all he required of her in public venues. Until tonight, she'd felt secure in the life they shared. Staring down at him, she wasn't so sure.

Fortunately, Ray had slept through O's moment of doubt and remembered only the good stuff. He was like that.

Picking up the proofs from Ray's desk, Lena bustled out with all her formidable bustling capabilities evident in the tight pencil skirt. Ray hired attractive women, but he kept his distance from them. Well aware of his unsteady judgment, he was a model of decorum with his employees.

Maybe Steven was free for a drink. He doubted he'd get much out of him, but he was eager for anything Steven might let drop about last night. He was just about to call Steven's cell phone when the big, black Range Rover pulled up to the curb. It was a loading zone, but the bumper bore a bright yellow commercial vehicle permit.

The door popped open and Marie climbed down into the late-afternoon glare, looking around from behind the graceful curves of her huge, concealing Tom Ford shades before shutting the door.

Ray went to greet her at Reception. She was chatting up Alden, the fey, black preppy Ray kept around mainly because his humorless demeanor discouraged free-lancers from loitering. Marie's celebrated derrière, displayed in tight black lambskin leather jods today, looked most spank-worthy, but he could easily imagine how quickly his kneecap would meet one of her tall riding boots.

"Hey Marie," he said, sliding up to rest his elbows on the marble next to hers. "Want to preview next month's cover?"

Marie enfolded him in her tight, black, ruffled blouse. Athletically built to begin with, Marie maintained every curve with the assistance of a personal trainer and the best cosmetic surgeon in Beverly Hills. Well into her forties, she was firm everywhere. Ray squeezed her back with genuine affection.

Though Marie was Ray's former sister-in-law, she had a maternal intelligence that O lacked and which he had never stopped craving since the loss of his own mother well over a decade ago. Usually if he wanted to see her, he had to seek an audience either at The Mansion or in the smaller house she kept for herself on Franklin Avenue. She tugged playfully at his big, silver belt buckle. His jeans came away effortlessly from his flat belly a couple of inches.

"Boy, I'm going to take you down to Go-Burger and feed you a couple of chocolate malteds."

"Never could keep the weight on," he said with a touch of smugness.

"We should all have such problems. I dropped by to show you something that might interest you."

Back at Ray's computer Marie took a USB key engraved with a Cartier panther off a chain around her neck and jacked into the one remaining slot of a hub bristling with cables.

While they waited for the file to load, she asked how it had gone with Steven and O.

Ray thought it must have been a success because O had jumped him when she got home. Marie wasn't convinced. Up at The Mansion, O had proved herself an expert at using protocol to work the guests. She never spoke unless spoken to or lifted her eyes except on command, concealing her pleasure at all the beating and buggery so as not to spoil the illusion of broken acquiescence. She also held the record for servicing the most men and women in the shortest time, yet all they did was praise her. Marie respected O's artistry for what it was.

A new Preview window opened on the screen, revealing the most mesmerizing head shot Ray had ever seen. The girl's light auburn hair fell in wisps around her heart-shaped face. Her exotically ovoid eyes were an unnaturally brilliant green, but the jewel-tone contacts couldn't completely filter out the mischievous sparkle. She had a small, button nose that made her pink lips – the lower slightly pouty, the upper a perfect Cupid's bow – all the more lush and inviting. Her neck seemed impossibly long and slender. Her half-smile revealed a single incisor slightly out of alignment, the kind of flaw French casting directors always insisted a girl must have.

She wore no makeup, no jewelry, and, given the bareness of her milky shoulders, quite possibly nothing at all. Ray looked a long time, stroking his beard. Other than that rebellious tooth and ears large enough to poke through her brushed out hair she seemed almost inhumanly perfect.

"You've got my attention. How old is she?"

"Getting your attention has never been much of a trick. She's twenty-four. Her name's Jacqui. Just wait. She gets better."

Marie leaned in to toggle through the JPEGs. The first few were all face shots, and though there was no mistaking this face, all were different. Jacqui grinned like a kid on her way to Disneyland. She looked as if she was about to burst into tears because Disneyland was closed. She squeezed out a single, perfect tear, seemingly out of place with a playful smile. The green eyes narrowed. The lips projected as if she were about to come out of the screen and dive for his lap. She was anguished and pitiful without inspiring sympathy.

"An actress?" Ray asked.

"Too lazy. She'd rather lie around getting high, listening to her iPad and having her muffin munched. She's super-smart when she's interested; completely redesigned our web page in half a day. Wait, it gets better."

Marie clicked through the JPEGs. As the camera moved back, Jacqui's slender, unadorned body came into view. The rest of her was as creamy as her shoulders. In the waist-up shot, the tips of her perfect teacup tits were so pale as to be nearly invisible, making her even more doll-like. Her waist was long, her belly deeply grooved to a long, lozenge-shaped navel. Her abdomen was absolutely flat and her shaved vulva was a split, ripe peach, less the fuzz. Her legs went on and on forever.

The back view were particularly gamine, those legs leading up to a rump that seemed to belong to a younger girl. Her sinuous back had a slight sway to the right. At least five-foot-seven, she might have been a marble caryatid.

"She can't be that lazy. She must put a lot of work into looking this way."

"Nope. She just smokes a lot and does a few extra laps in the pool before eating a breakfast that would floor a lumber-jack. You forget what it's like to be her age. She comes home after drinking all night looking like that and wakes up the next day looking like that."

Marie dropped into one of the barrel chairs fronting Ray's desk.

"What do you think?"

"Is she up at The Mansion?"

"I'm keeping her at my place for now. She mainly prefers girls anyway."

"Why am I looking at her?"

"I want her shot for the magazine."

"Why? You'll only inspire more competition."

"I have no competition, darling."

"Forgot that part. What will she do?"

"Whatever I tell her."

"Boy-girl?"

"She has plenty of experience with boys."

Ray stood up, started pacing.

"What's in it for you?"

"She wants me to make her do it and I oblige. The secret of being a successful domme is giving the right orders. Order people to do what they want and they usually obey. She'll make great advertising. I'll put on an up-charge for her at The Mansion when I finally put her up there. Even I wanted her for myself so I brought her to Franklin Street. Now I have to keep her motivated."

Ray sighed.

"As good a reason as any. Has she done hardcore stills?

"Oh my, yes. She's a shameless exhibitionist and a natural talent."

Ray stopped behind Marie, massaging her shoulders. Marie relaxed into it, eyes closing. Like his brother, Ray had good hands.

"She's definitely cover quality. Whom should I put her with?"

"Somebody who really gets it. She's also a dedicated masochist."

"Maybe I should do her myself then."

Marie lightly lifted Ray's hands off her shoulders and turned to face him.

"I want O to shoot her."

"You think O would prevent me from fucking her?"

"She'd probably stick it in for you under other circumstances. But in the studio I trust her to pick the best partner and get the best set."Ray stood up straight, giving Marie a jaunty salute.

"Aye, Aye, Ma'am."

He went behind the desk to download the images.

Marie came over and kissed Ray on top of the head.

"That's a good boy. I can always count on you."

He looked up at her with mock innocence.

"To do what?"

"Whatever you think is in your own interest. That's one thing you share with Steven, besides some random DNA."

Marie perched on the edge of Ray's desk.

"This thing you're doing with O and Steven, why?"

"I already told you. It's payback."

"You're much too selfish to go to so much trouble, even for your brother."

For once, Ray dropped his implacable geniality.

"Last night I woke up and O was just sitting there, staring at me. I think she's restless. Once she has something, she needs something else."

"So you figure that by putting her through training at The Mansion and then offering her up to Steven, you'll keep her from wandering off."

Marie casually took Ray by the edges of his vest.

"Are you sure she's the one who's restless?"

"O gives me everything I want. Why would I be restless?"

"Maybe what you really want is what you don't have. You and O may share that trait."

He reached up and tapped her forehead with his index finger.

"You're over-thinking it. Steven and I have played this game before. Some women have short attention spans. When they get antsy I send him in at halftime as a relief quarterback. By the gun they'll both be ready to have her back in the locker room."

Marie ran a weary hand across her eyes.

"God, I hate sports metaphors, especially applied to sex. Trash that drive for me, please."

Marie pulled the USB key, dropping the chain back over her neck. She leaned down into Ray's face.

"Careful, coach. If you lose control of the ball, you may have more trouble recovering it than you think."

"I thought you hated sports metaphors."

"I hate a lot of things men like. Never stops me from joining in. Call me when you have a shoot date for my girl."

"You won't have long to wait."

"I never do."

Ray stood for a hug before Marie strolled out, celebrated rear carriage swinging casually.

Ray looked at Jacqui's pictures on the monitor again. He envied the guy who would do her in the studio. Unlike his brother, Ray was still young enough to desire the unattainable. Marie was right about that. But he had O, owned her thoroughly enough to share her, just as she had said at dinner. What prize could be less attainable than that? Still, his eyes strayed back to Jacqui's images as they collapsed into the folder on the desktop.

Ray's commute wasn't quite as short as Steven's, which amounted to going out one door in his rooftop lair and in another. But it was a dream by L.A. standards, just a mile or so up at the end of Outpost Drive. Despite the time of day, it only took a few minutes in the BMW, most of them spent at or near a dead stop, listening to Tom Waits. It was getting toward fall and the descending sun blasted through the windshield on the westbound leg. Eyes shielded by out-of-production side-lens Persols that resembled welding goggles more than sunglasses, he still had to pull down the visor.

Pulling up in front of his mid-century glass-box house cantilevered out from the hillside, Ray was surprised to see Steven's black Bentley coupe parked out in front. Was this Family Week and someone forgot to tell him?

Not a nest builder like Steven, Ray's place was spare and bare, furnished with a few Shagadelic pieces perfectly period-matched to the house, though all were modern reproductions. Steven's worsted suit jacket and trousers hung over the back of an Eames chair near the glass doors leading to the westward facing rear deck. His double-breasted vest, complete with watch fob, dark gray shirt and silver silk-satin tie were all neatly folded on the seat. The outline of Steven's head and naked shoulders were just visible, looming out of the Jacuzzi. Ray snagged a bath sheet from the stack next to the sliding doors and went to greet his brother.

Arms out of water, head back so his disturbingly round, dead-black shades reflected the fading light from the murky sky, Steven clenched a conical *figurado* between his teeth, a slender, aromatic plume of smoke rising from the glowing end. His customary mineral water with a twist sat near at hand on the teak slats surrounding the tub. On a folded towel, Steven had placed a Royal Hawaiian Hotel ashtray and his favorite pocket lighter, a big DuPont inlaid with silver and mother-of-pearl.

Ray sat down next to him, knees to chest, wrapped in his own embrace.

"Admit it. I have the better view," he said.

Ray's vista extended from The Strip directly below straight out Mulholland Drive toward the ocean, though the air quality wasn't good enough to see much past the wooded hillsides where richer folks lived.

"I suppose, if you like suburbia."

"Hollywood is not suburbia."

"You asked for my opinion."

Ray gave a disdainful snort as he stripped down, tossing his clothes haphazardly over a wooden deck chair from a scrapped ocean liner.

"I take it things went well in the courtroom today or you wouldn't be soaking triumphantly like an eagle in my birdbath."

Ray slipped naked into the water across from Steven, hardly rippling the surface. The water and the air were almost the same temperature.

"Things never go well in any courtroom. That's why I keep my clients as far away from those places as possible. The judge takes one look at Julio and wants to send him over for life and a half. I got another postponement. If we're lucky all the witnesses will die of old age before we ever go to trial."

"Old age or other causes."

"They'll be none of that stuff. I tell all my clients to say daily Novenas for the prosecution's witnesses because if any misadventure befalls them I walk away from the whole case, no refund on the retainer. I remind them that when they are violating the law they do not break the law."

"No wonder you got shot. You'll never guess who dropped by the office today."

Steven puffed a great cumulus of expensive smoke out into the general pollution. "Marie."

Ray's brows knitted in vexation. "How the hell ..."

"She called me earlier. I think you've got her worried."

"Marie doesn't care fuck-all about me."

"Worried about me, that is."

"I guess somebody has to be. She's a got a new girl she's pimping for a photo set. Very hot. Everything I like. But I think she was just trying to get my attention."

"I'm sure she succeeded."

"O's shooting Marie's girl this week, although neither of them knows it yet."

"And this has what to do with me?"

"I'm getting to that part. As soon as Marie had her deal closed, she started poking around about our new arrangements."

"Of which she doesn't approve."

Ray shrugged. "Like anyone could tell. She seemed puzzled by the whole thing."

"You don't really expect anyone to understand, not even Marie." There was a touch of scorn in Steven's voice that Ray ignored.

"Nope. She thinks I'm trying to unload O on you because I'm ready to move on."

"I thought of that. Too obvious. And besides, why?"

"You haven't told me much about what went on between you and O."

"I figured you'd get the details out of her."

"It wasn't very difficult. I'm still her master too, you know."

"Hold onto that thought. I consider her strictly on loan."

"But you do want to see her again ... soon. She said you told her to come back Friday."

"I haven't shown her the playroom yet."

"That kind of surprised me."

"I don't do these things by the numbers. We were having a good time where we were so we stayed there. Why the fuck is this so fucking important to you?"

"So you're here for the same reason Marie showed up in front of my desk."

"Not so much. She's curious about your ends. I'm more interested in your means."

"I still want O in my life, but I know her too well to think I can keep her all to myself."

Steven took another puff. "You really ought to try one of these. They're sensational. *C.A.* gives them a ninety-two."

"I'd rather live, thanks."

Ray was silent and pensive for a moment. "O sets a very high standard. Sometimes it's hard to meet."

Steven pointed at Ray accusingly with the cigar. "For you it is. You have the concentration of a hamster."

Ray laughed. "And again my brother busts my balls."

"Nana loved you and I loved Nana. You're about all she left me."

Now Ray shifted uncomfortably. This was a tender topic Steven brought up more often than Ray would have preferred, which would have been never. "It's not my fault she left your dad. It's not my fault I was the last thing in her life she still cared about."

"And it wasn't your fault that you were in school and I was the one who walked in and found her hanging from the staircase."

Ray's face hardened. "I guess this conversation is about over." He started to get up out of the small pool.

"Sit down. I have something else to say that you might want to hear."

Ray settled back into the water. "That would be a nice change."

"O made a very favorable first impression to put it mildly. I admit I've thought about having her all to myself."

Ray's expression turned grim. "Why would I want to hear that? I didn't say I intended to give her up. I said I wanted to share her."

"What if O doesn't agree?"

"You think it was that good for her too?"

"I think there's eventually going to be a decision and it won't be ours. So if she wanted just one master and he turned out to be me instead of you, would you consider all accounts square?"

Ray thought about that a long moment. Yes, there was a growing distance between O and Ray. During his visits with her up at The Mansion, she'd been like a stranger to him, adhering to protocol so strictly he might as well have been another anonymous patron. He'd expected her to be like a kid in her first week at camp: clinging to him, not wanting him to leave her.

But as Marie said, she'd made herself right at home up there. Ray figured Steven would satisfy her need for epic cruelty he couldn't quite fulfill, and with that hunger safely sated, maybe she'd be more amenable to her domestic arrangements with Ray, if that was what he really desired. The seeds of doubt Marie had planted were quick to germinate.

O was valuable to him in so many ways. Who could possibly replace her? Though he thought of himself as loving her, maybe he just needed her and feared he couldn't think of a better way to hold on to whatever it was they had. It was a risky gambit. Steven could take anything he wanted from anyone. That, too, had always been the case. Was Ray actually inviting him to prove it once again?

If O were Steven's and not his, she would still be in his life, still working for him but no longer requiring him to live up to her exhausting standards.

"That would certainly be a sacrifice," Ray said at last. "But I think you're just testing me. I don't believe you want anyone all to yourself, except you."

Steven switched on his most dazzling smile.

"O's a remarkable girl, but I'm happy on my own. I always say that whoever forces the decision loses. If O does that, she'll either choose you or neither of us, because I'm not available. And that huge load of guilt you carry around about me – you need to set that down. You took a much harder hit from mom's death than I did. And you're not nearly as high-maintenance as she was. I came up here to thank you for a truly exceptional gift and to tell you to quit trying so hard. O's exceptional in every way and if I were looking, I'd be looking for her. But I'm not looking. I'm content to keep things as they are. I wanted you to know that because I figured you'd be having second thoughts."

Maybe, but an unspoken "for now" seemed to hang in the steamy air between them.

Steven climbed out and wrapped a towel around his middle.

"Morgan and I have a match at eight."

Ray got out as well. They hugged, but their bodies didn't touch below the shoulders.

While Steven dressed, Ray made himself a Bloody Mary in the kitchen, pouring himself an extra half shot of Absolut.

"Sure you don't want one of these?"

He held up the glass for Steven to see, rattled the ice.

"That would only make it easier for Morgan to kill me. And she likes killing me."

"I'll make sure O shows up on time and ready Friday."

"No worries. She'll see to that."

After Steven left, Ray picked up his shoulder bag and carried it into the small home office he'd made from one bedroom. Sitting bare-ass at the desk, he plugged the portable drive into the back of his computer and pulled up the file of Jacqui's pictures.

CHAPTER FOUR

The Downtown Athletic Club was an elegant relic from the Prohibition era, its red stone façade squeezed by glass and steel on either side. The slightly faded floral carpets, tufted library furniture and vaulted dining room were as much of a different time and place as the wooden courts, blue-tiled indoor pool and three-corner billiard room. The gyms had been redone with mirrors and modern machinery, but the top floor fencing salon, still accessible by an elevator with a manual operating handle (supplemented with a standard row of buttons since the last human operator had retired ten years ago) was unchanged. Four narrow lanes illuminated by long skylights during the day, and pendant lamps with green glass domes at night. There was a bank of cracking leather theater seats along one wall, but not many came to watch fencing anymore.

When Steven emerged from the green painted locker room in his distinctly non-regulation, custom-made black tunic and mask, saber over his shoulder, Morgan was already practicing lunges on the varnished killing floor. Wearing the traditional whites, she hadn't masked as yet and her blonde hair was tied back tight. She really was quite the magnificent

Amazon in any armor, even simple canvas. Without looking over, she shouted to him without interrupting her warm-up.

"I got here early so I thought I'd start without you."

"It won't do you any good. You're already dead."

Morgan lowered her saber, Steven raised his mask and they met mid-lane for a friendly hug. He didn't know how long she had been practicing, but her breathing was steady and she hadn't started sweating yet. With Morgan, as with Steven, it was hard to tell when she was exerting herself.

"At least I won't die of old age halfway through the first match. I'm always afraid you'll have a heart attack."

"I'd need a heart for that."

"I know. You're such a mean old bastard. How did whatever it was go the other night?"

Morgan went to her gym bag for a swallow of bottled water.

"I managed to get through it without needing a defibrillator."

"The girl was quite a looker. We don't see her type at the restaurant very often."

"What type is that?"

"The atypical type. Definite style of her own. No bling. No flash. Kind of retro but not as a statement."

"Did you come to fence or to talk?" Steven asked, flexing his blade. It was a Leon Paul, made up at their shop in London for his precise height and weight. The guard was heavily engraved with rings of crossed bones. Morgan used a lighter, shorter weapon, but it was well-matched – a present from a stuntwoman with whom she'd had a brief romance on one of her low-budget features.

"Didn't know you were in such a hurry to lose. Positions?"

"My pleasure."

Steven lowered his mask and they retired to opposite ends of the strip. Each did a few quick squats and stretches before coming to *en garde*. Though saber fencers generally eschewed courtesies, Steven and Morgan had fallen into the habit of raising their blades in a friendly salute. What happened next was neither friendly nor courteous.

"*Commence!*" Morgan shouted, launching off the floor and flying toward the center of the strip, blade extended. Steven came at her low and fast. Unlike foil fencing, which allowed scoring touches only on the torso, saber fencing descended from cavalry combat, in which unhorsing an opponent was as good as fatal, so scoring on the head and arms was also permitted.

Assuming that Morgan would try to decapitate him, Steven thrust his head forward, deliberately presenting a preferred target. Morgan went for it with a slash so close Steven heard the steel whiz by his ear as he tilted his neck just far enough to prevent a touch. Morgan was quick to recover, executing an acrobatic turn to come back at him from the other side, but it was too late. He lunged up from underneath and planted the point squarely between her breasts. She lifted her mask and looked down at his flexed blade.

"Pure luck. Go again?"

"That's why we're here."

When Steven signaled the engagement, Morgan came at him more cautiously. She even managed a parry when he took a slash at her upper-right quadrant, shoving him back with her guard. Breaking free for a split instant, she backhanded him across the chest with the blade's upper edge, a legal score in saber fencing.

Steven fell to his knees, flipping up his mask with his sword hand and clutching his chest with the other.

"You got me!" he announced with a laugh and fell onto his side. Morgan kicked him lightly in the ribs with a white boot.

"Get up, old man. I'm not done killing you yet."

"Old man? Now I am wounded," Steven replied, still laughing.

Back to *en garde*, Morgan peered at him through narrowed eyes before dropping the mesh over her face.

"This time you're really going down," she warned him.

Steven bowed and saluted respectfully, but his attack was furious. He'd stopped fooling around without any noticeable change in demeanor and his opponent realized it too late. Before she could advance to meet him at the center point, he flew right past her, smacking her hard across the upper arm with his saber's triangular lower edge. She let out a yelp, dropped her weapon and grabbed the spot where he'd struck.

"Ouch! You fuck!" she yelled.

Steven's mask hinged up to reveal a broad grin.

"Want me to kiss it and make it better?"

She shot him a glance as lethal as any thrust.

"Okay, that was pretty good for a senior citizen. But if you do it again I'll kick you in the nuts."

"I don't think that's a valid touch," Steven said as he crossed back over the green centerline to assume his stance once more.

This time, it was a longer, more even engagement, steel clashing so lightning fast their gauntlets would have been a blur to anyone watching. Letting out a rebel yell, Morgan spun sideways when Steven made a pass at her abdomen. He actually stumbled going past her and she couldn't resist sending him sprawling, face down, with a swift kick to the hindquarters. He rolled over to find her point in the middle of his chest this time. Both were breathing hard now. When Steven pulled off his mask, his face was covered in sweat.

"If you get any better at this," he said, "I'm switching to a shotgun."

Half an hour later, they were showered and dressed (Morgan in tight jeans and a loose, low-cut top, Steven in a hounds-tooth hacking jacket and slacks), downing beer and munching burgers in the club's snack bar, the only one of its three restaurants still open at that hour. With its faintly nautical décor grown a bit shabby, it was scheduled for the next phase of the renovation, undoubtedly meaning yet another levy for Steven and the rest of the membership.

"You need to work on that temper, Morgan," Steven said with no condescension at all. "When you take a touch you get mad and lose your shit. You're actually a better fencer than I am but your anger keeps you from beating me."

"That's not the only place it gets in my way. I can't seem to keep either a boyfriend or a girlfriend, or even a job."

Steven felt a sudden wave of apprehension.

"You didn't get fired, did you?"

"Nope. Quit."

"That sucks. Where will I take people when I want to feel important?"

Morgan laughed so hard she almost sprayed beer out her nose.

"Like you have to work to impress a bunch of thugs who already think you're Jesus. I'm moving to Vegas. Going to work that pirate ship gig at Treasure Island."

Steven shook his head.

"You're going to hate it out there."

"My agent can't even get me *Celebrity Apprentice*. I'm finished here. I'm tired of mixing drinks. I'm an entertainer and I want to entertain people, even obese tourists in Bermuda shorts. Won't be the first time I've dressed up in something skimpy and to do something lame."

"As your lawyer, I have to advise you against buying real estate in Las Vegas. Rent someplace and wait until the prices stabilize."

"As your bartender, I'd advise you to get yourself a real girlfriend."

Steven was genuinely surprised, a rare occurrence.

"Where did that come from?"

"You meet a lot of lonely people working behind a bar. I think you're one of them."

Steven threw back a gulp of beer and laughed.

"I have the perfect life. Why would I want to fuck it up? I love you, really, but there are things you don't know about me."

"I know you're a big perv, if that's what you're talking about. Nature doesn't do one-offs. Somebody's out there looking for you right now."

"A month later she'll be looking for somebody else. For a certain woman at a certain time in her life, the most important thing is exploring the experience I have to offer. After that, the most important thing is to take whatever she's learned from me and put it to work with a guy she can actually have. That guy would not be me."

Morgan held up her hands in a gesture of surrender.

"Okay. I'm done. Two things any good bartender knows are when to cut off a customer's drinks and when to stop giving advice."

Steven put down his hamburger, wiped his hand on his napkin and reached over to put it on Morgan's strong arm.

"I'm really going to miss killing you."

"I'll miss killing you too."

The lights in the snack bar started to come up.

"I think they're trying to tell us something," Steven said, finishing his last bite and draining his glass.

"Come out and visit me sometime. I'll get you comps at TI."

"I might just do that. Don't forget to take your saber with you."

"Aargh, matey. I be tradin' her in fer a cutlass."

They both laughed as Steven signaled for the check. This time Steven pulled out a solid sterling pen about the size and shape of a zeppelin and signed the check before the elderly waiter finished putting it down.

Parting with Morgan after an embrace long enough to hint at sex that might have been, Steven took the ancient elevator down to the lobby, where he presented the claim check for his car and headed outside to wait at the curb.

This was the great equalizing moment in L.A. life. Steven had stood at curbs waiting for cars with movie stars and moguls, judges and celebrity chefs, overdressed garmentos, high-end dentists, symphony musicians and the usual assortment of wannabes and also-rans. All held colored tickets clutched in hand and the exasperated, "What, did he park it in Barstow?" looks on their faces.

The Jag, still his favorite of all the rolling stock he owned, pulled up smartly. He stood for a moment by the passenger door, remembering O's compact curves settling into the seat, her heels swinging in from the side, the way she buckled in so deftly with those gloved hands. For the first time in more years than he cared to count, he wondered what another person might be doing at that moment, and what she might be thinking in regards to him. The sensation was troubling and he pushed it from his mind as quickly as possible, sliding in behind the wheel and cranking up the stereo.

CHAPTER FIVE

The strobe power packs beeped and popped when O test-fired the big Leica. For an instant, a brilliant flare from the tripod-mounted umbrella lights illuminated the center of the darkened studio. O, dressed in a plain, black bra top, black tights and red, knee-high Doc Martens, stood next to the small, torso-shaped iron cage dangling from the ceiling and studied the light meter in her hand. She frowned, hung the meter from a cross bar on the cage by its lanyard and went back to the wheeled cart where her cameras, memory cards, batteries and filters were all laid out on an immaculate blue furniture blanket.

"Still a little hot," she pronounced. "Try raising them about six inches."

Roger, O's assistant, leaned over from the stepladder next to one of the stands and slid the shaft up, lifting the shiny aluminum umbrella. A wiry, balding gaffer who had once lit glamour shots on giant sound stages, Roger took it slow, tightening the stand and dismounting the ladder, wheeling it over to pop up the second umbrella. O watched carefully, judging how much spill she'd get from each.

She sighted through the viewfinder, lining up the empty cage dead center, and pushed the shutter button, triggering another brief explosion of brilliance. Putting the camera down, she went back to the meter, which was set to read when the packs fired. O pondered, head cocked to one side.

"I want some hair light from the back. Let's pump up that slave pack a little."

"On it," Roger said, trudging toward the back of the set to tweak the power unit on the small strobe mounted to a rail below the ceiling. It was always tricky, shooting in a black space so the foreground details were clear without losing the feeling of cavernous gloom. It didn't help that the studio Ray had rented for O was so enormous.

The ceiling, vaulted and braced with huge struts like a barn, was at least thirty feet high. The distressed flats, dulled to look like old concrete, were twenty feet back, arranged to intersect like the corner of a room. The vast floor layered over with black painted slats textured and riveted to look like steel plate contributed to the impression of a bleak and empty chamber. The atmosphere was as sinister as O could have wanted, but the place soaked up light like a black hole.

O strolled over to the makeup chair to see how Jacqui's face was coming along. Jacqui lounged naked with a robe over her lap so any elastic marks would fade. She had ear buds stuck in her head and a copy of *Wired* spread across the robe. Her thick, naturally auburn hair was tied in a big knot on top of her head. Renata, the compact, butch-cropped makeup artist fluttered around Jacqui in her sleeveless shirt and cut-offs, dusting blush on the model's cheeks.

"Light on that, please," O instructed.

"You sure you don't want any foundation?" Renata asked.

"Like she needs it with that complexion. And she was probably out partying all night."

O reached up and plucked one earbud out of Jacqui's skull. The spacy electronic tunes of Carbon Based Life Forms leaked from the tiny speaker.

"Weren't you?"

Jacqui, who had the high, trilling voice of a teenager, didn't even look up.

"Only until two-thirty. Well, maybe three…"

She pretended to look guilty.

O laughed. "In about ten years you're going to have to start working at looking like that."

"In ten years I'm going to be living on a ranch in Wyoming not giving a fuck," Jacqui replied, leaning forward to kiss O on the forehead. "It's so cool that you're shooting me. That was one of the things I wanted to have happen this year and we're already doing it. Your work rocks hard, man."

"I'm glad you appreciate it. Models aren't easy to impress."

"A lot of the people doing this material aren't that impressive. You bring some serious mojo to it."

The next question was sure to be personal. It was time to change the subject. "Like the cozy set we built for you?" O asked.

Jacqui looked around with an exaggerated shudder. "Nice and creepy. Bad things could happen to a poor girl in a place like this."

"Natalie Wood drowned off a yacht," O said. "Bad things can happen to a girl anywhere."

Jacqui rubbed her long hands together gleefully. "So what's happening to me today?"

"Just the usual. Rigid shackles, torture, fucking. Like I told you on the phone, you can pass on anything you don't want to do. It's not an endurance contest."

"Maybe not for you, but I like to push myself. Terror is one of my better emotions."

She gave O a huge, frightened face that made them both laugh out loud. "My pitiful isn't too shabby either." Jacqui stuck out a fat, trembling lower lip and widened her eyes to saucer-size.

"Remember that one," O said. "I'm going to want it."

This bright, fearless, slightly geeky beauty had a lot of good images in her. O's annoyance at Ray for slating a shoot without consulting her faded at the prospects.

When it came to work, O and Ray had a separation of powers agreement. The office was his. The studio was hers. O hated having models pushed on her. There was usually some agenda that involved getting some guy laid and the model usually took advantage. At least Ray wasn't a modelizer. This was strictly about good pictures and good pictures made up for everything.

"Now, about the fucking part ..." Jacqui began.

"God," O thought. "Here comes the bad news." She'd already inspected Jacqui's lab report so she knew what the bad news wouldn't be.

"Could you please ask him not to whisper dumb jokes in my ear when I'm trying to fake an orgasm? I don't want him in my butt all night."

"I'll see what I can do, but you've worked with him before. He's an obnoxious, little prick who ..."

"...shows up on time," a cheerful male voice broke in. Both of them turned.

Calvin, an unremarkably handsome, dark-haired, dark-eyed man just shy of thirty, strolled across the studio in his distressed motorcycle jacket and ripped jeans. He was very much Master Right, or at least Master Right Now, among the small group of players who specialized in on-camera domming. Neither he nor O knew just why.

He came over and kissed O on the cheek, blowing Jacqui an air kiss so as not to mess up Renata's work.

"Hey, you," he said to Jacqui, "how come you didn't call me when you were up north?"

"They'd already booked me with someone else."

"You could have requested me, you little shit."

"I don't want people thinking we're married."

Calvin made a gagging noise. Jacqui tossed the magazine aside and stood up, looming over him a good three inches.

"You better be good and mean to me today or I'll kick your ass."

"Not before I ream yours."

O looked back and forth between them.

"Excellent. A grudge fuck. I can work with that energy."

She turned to Renata.

"I want a lot of eyes, and some lips. A little redder than they should be. Don't make her too innocent."

"Right. Just a hint of her inner slut," Renata said.

"Exactly. How long?"

Renata waggled her head from side to side, looking at Jacqui.

"Half an hour, maybe."

"Make it twenty."

O needed to confer with Fiona, her rigger, who was at the equipment table, zapping herself on the bare forearm with a Neon Wand. The gas-filled tube at the end of the generator lit up a nice, hot red-orange, but the spark seemed a little weak.

"The strobes will wash that out," O said.

"Thought they might."

Fiona used few words, uttered in a tight monotone though she had been known to burst out laughing at odd things. Small-breasted with killer legs and butt, it was Fiona's face that both men and women found hypnotic. She had the high cheekbones from her exotic Eastern European blood, but her eyes were light grey flecked with yellow. Her hair was a deep and lustrous black. She was impressive in black jeans and a cropped T-shirt that showed off her muscles. Focused and disciplined, Fiona had been hurt enough during her performing days to respect the close tolerances at which a bondage rigger worked. That, and her creative mean streak, made her the best. O wouldn't shoot without her.

Fiona cranked up the knob at the butt-end of the Neon Wand, stepped on the foot switch and gave herself another jolt. This time there was a loud crackle and pronounced whiff of ozone in the air, but Fiona didn't flinch.

"That should read," O said.

"Think it's too much for internal?"

O stuck out her own arm so Fiona could shoot a loud spark at it. O didn't flinch either.

"We'll get a few good jolts on the tits and then crank it down a little for the hardcore. Jacqui likes to be pushed."

A slight smile distorted the purposeful straightness of Fiona's lips.

"This should be a fun day," she said, putting down the wand and moving on to shake out the rest of her gear.

"We'll be setting up for covers first. I'll need her in the cage."

"Let me know when."

"Now would be good."

As the cage descended, O did another lighting check, catching Fiona in the shot. Doing a digital instant replay on the Leica's wide finder screen, she studied the results intently.

Fiona had the front panels of the cage, now suspended waist high, hinged open as Renata shuffled Jacqui, dressed only in green flip-flops to keep her feet clean, under the modeling lamp. O grabbed the Leica.

"Okay gorgeous, stand right there," O said.

Shaking out her cascading auburn waves, Jacqui stood still in the halo from above while O took her first test-shot. The packs popped and beeped again. O looked at the preview panel.

"I already don't like that. Roger, hook me up with a ring-flash, please."

It was amazing how quickly Roger could move when the photographer had camera in hand. These were dangerous moments, employment-wise. He took the heavy unit from O, quickly wiring it with a circular reflector mounted at the end of the lens hood. He did a couple of trial pops himself before giving it back. For one long moment, O looked at Jacqui just standing there. One inch taller and this girl could have been on the catwalk. O wondered if Jacqui knew how lucky she was. She could even have a tiny, sexy belly under her navel without some agency ordering her to get lipo or seek new representation. O had come up through the rag trade and despised it as only an intimate could.

"Okay Fiona, let's get her in there."

Fiona eased Jacqui toward the cage by her biceps.

"You just sort of sit back into it," Fiona explained.

Jacqui slipped into the narrow nest of bars effortlessly. She'd been bound so many different ways by so many different riggers she could have made a living as an escape artist. The contact of iron on skin raised a body-length shiver and a tsunami of goose bumps.

"Holy shit!" Jacqui cried out. "This thing is fucking fur-reezzing!"

"You'll heat it up," O reassured her while Fiona locked the bars into place around her body. She helped Jacqui thread her long legs through the openings at the bottom so they dangled vulnerably in mid-air. Jacqui kicked her flip-flops neatly off the set.

"It's tight too," she said, shifting around as much as she could to see what movement she really had. The cage was designed to fit bodies even smaller than hers as closely as a suit of armor. The leg segments opened her wide, and there was a strategic gap in the ironwork running from the top of her pelvic arch under and around to the base of her tail bone. She looked down at it with raised eyebrows.

"And really, really nasty. Can I borrow it on Saturday?"

"Not unless you take Fiona along," O said. Fiona said she'd be happy to help out but she had another booking.

When the stage was clear, O told Fiona to crank up the cage. Jacqui made a noise like a kid on a swing as it rose. O stopped the hoisting with a palms-down grip gesture.

"Yeah, that's very nice," she said, eye welded to the viewfinder. This moment of promise approached the feeling she'd had when Steven circled her while she stood naked at attention in his living room.

"I'm going to take a couple of bracketing shots. Give me some deer-in-the-headlights."

Jacqui's face was suddenly transformed into a mask of frozen dread.

"Too much," O said, shaking her head. "Dial it down about twenty percent."

Jacqui grinned. It was so much easier working for someone she knew had been in the same position more than once.

"Perfect!" O exclaimed at the slightly less dramatic version. "Stay just like that, but lean forward as much as you can and squash your tits against the bars. Need the nips blocked for the cover."

"Well, they're certainly nice and hard," Jacqui said calmly, pressing her flesh into the cold metal. She really did look fairly pathetic.

It was as important to her as to O that the results came out right, or she was suffering through this for no good reason other than a highly combustible paycheck.

O fired away, squatting low, standing on a stepladder and lying on the floor. She had Fiona rotate the cage thirty degrees for some side shots.

"I wonder if I could spin around in this thing," Jacqui mused.

"Why not? Just try not to giggle."

O nodded at Fiona, who grabbed the cage and twirled it like a *piñata*. O wasn't happy.

"Doesn't work with the ring light," she pronounced, ordering Fiona to steady things up.

Once the cage was still, O moved in closer, centering Jacqui from the waist up in the finder. This was it.

"Okay," O said in a near whisper, "you've been hanging here for hours. You're in some Eastern European hellhole and you've pissed off some cops who thought you were hot and you know they're going to have their fun with you for a few days before they let you go. You want to play along, but you're scared shitless you'll fuck up and they'll really hurt you. Now, give me that."

Jacqui's pathetic face would have made angels weep. O gritted her teeth, held her breath and fired off a dozen shots, perfectly cropped to fill a cover with Jacqui's delicious anguish of anticipation.

O flipped back through the digital frames, amazed as always when something came out just like she'd imagined it. O held the camera up so Jacqui could look at herself on the screen. Jacqui's face lit up.

"Bitchin'!"

"That's our cover. Now for the easy part."

It was true. The rest of the shoot lay ahead; it would be strenuous for all, but to O, that cover shot was the reason for all of it.

Fiona rolled in a long, steel table full of sinister implements and Calvin clunked over behind her in heavy boots and a rubber apron, completely exposed from the rear.

"Come on, O," he whined, "do I really have to wear this thing? I mean, it's so gay."

"They didn't tell you about the part where she gets out and pegs you with a strap-on?" O asked with a smirk. She promised she wouldn't shoot him from the rear.

"It's not like anyone wants to see your naked, hairy man-ass," she reminded him.

"I'll have you know I shave my ass twice a week. What do you want me to do with her, boss?"

O told him to start with some fingers. Calvin crossed to the cage, looked up at Jacqui and carefully started playing with her.

"Could we get a little lube, please?" O asked of no one in particular. Fiona ran in with a black bottle, poured some viscous liquid on Calvin's fingers, and gently applied a generous dose to Jacqui through the opening in the bottom of the cage. Jacqui smiled down at her.

"I'll make you stop doing that in about a week," she warned.

"Nice wax job," Fiona said.

"Hurt worse than anything that happens here."

Fiona cleared the set and Calvin moved back to First Position, his fingers once more in play. O caught Jacqui in an authentic moan. Calvin really did know his way around a woman's body – one reason he was on every girl's "yes" list. Satisfied that she was ready, he slipped a couple of fingers inside.

"That's great. Stay just like that. Jacqui, look down at him like you'd do anything to please him. More fucking equals less torture."

Jacqui could easily do seductive and desperate at the same time. O captured that from a half dozen angles, having Jacqui move around as much as the steel embrace would allow so she could show off everything they'd had to conceal for the cover shot.

"Calvin, no more Mr. Nice guy. Get the long cattle prod from the table."

Calvin picked up the yard-long rod with a big battery box at one end and double electrodes at the other. He looked it over and whistled.

"Now that is a wicked unit. I assume there are no batteries in this thing."

"Sorry to disappoint you, but no, there aren't," O assured him.

"Damn. I've always wondered what one of those felt like," Jacqui said.

O rolled her eyes and looked at Fiona.

"It sucks," Fiona said succinctly.

"I do better faces when I don't have to fake it. Let's give it a try and if I can't deal I'll crash out on it."

O shrugged. "Okay Fiona, go ahead and sting it."

Fiona shook her head but loaded up the battery box and handed the hot prod to Calvin. It had already been rewired to reduce the voltage by half but Fiona saw no reason to report that.

"Now what's my motivation again?"

O reminded him that he was a sadistic little fuck who liked torturing helpless girls.

"I can do that."

She told him to start with Jacqui's right foot. He pulled her leg out straight, applied the contact points to her arch, and pushed the button just for a second. Jacqui yelped and rattled her cage.

"Ow! Fuck!" Jacqui yelled.

"I think we can take the batteries out now," O said calmly. Fiona started over but Jacqui stopped her.

"Let's just do it and get it over with," she insisted.

"Fine, but no screaming," O cautioned. "It gives me a headache."

For the next half hour, Calvin worked Jacqui through the bars of the cage, carefully placing the prod with the contacts on either side of each nipple, then to her labia and finally across her anus, which O shot lying on her back from underneath, zoomed out wide for maximum depth of field to capture Jacqui's suffering.

They broke for lunch, the models sitting around in hotel bathrobes swapping gossip while gobbling down sandwiches from the upscale deli nearby. O never ceased to be amazed at how performers could pack it away, but then most of them didn't need to do a four-inch reduction with a corset unassisted.

They set up for the hardcore as Roger cleared away all the bags and napkins. Jacqui was stretched on a Y-frame, wrists overhead in steel manacles, ankles far apart, body-straps liberally applied in between.

O asked if she could move at all. Jacqui tried a few muscle groups to no avail.

"Not going anywhere."

"Let's get some singles on this," O said. "Roger, I think we'll need the kinos down toward the bottom of the frame to get a good arc."

Roger unfolded a pair of long fluorescent tubes in corrugated cardboard housings and laid them out to cast their light upwards. They gave off a nice, soft glow.

Satisfied with the placement, O shoved the wheeled ladder toward Jacqui's face, sending Roger up with the camera. Roger popped the packs and O, squatting next to Jacqui with the meter, took a reading. Looking at the image on the camera display, she smiled, turned it over and held it above Jacqui's face so she could look.

"I think that works," O said. "See? We've got the strobe on your face and upper body and we let your legs fall away from the light a little so when he zaps you we'll catch the lightning in the bottle."

"Nice," Jacqui said. "Could I get a couple for my blog? I want to write about this."

"No problem. I'll res them down when I get home and email you a few."

"Thanks. You're nice to work with."

"Only because you are."

Free at last of the hated apron, Calvin stood by, stroking himself and looking Jacqui over. Whatever he was thinking made him visibly happy. O called for the wand.

"Flying in," Fiona said, dragging the cord behind her. It was a harmless gizmo in comparison to the prod, making lots of sparks but causing only a mild static tingling where it touched flesh. Calvin had used it many times and didn't need to be told to start at the breasts, working down. Jacqui made screaming faces but heeded O's warning about doing it for real. Besides, this was cake, although when he actually put the glass tube at the end of the wand inside her and tapped the button, it felt like a swarm of small, angry wasps. It had to stay on a bit for O to get the sparks at just the right aperture.

The final set-up was simplicity itself: a waist-high bondage pallet with rings around the edges. Jacqui and Calvin sat on a couch making out while the rest of the crew humped gear and lights. She was already on her knees sucking him when Renata came to patch her makeup.

"You can join her if you like," Calvin said to Renata.

"Only if you want me taking a side of knackwurst with my lunch," she replied. She didn't have much patience for boys, especially this one; she'd had to put up with him on every set she'd worked for one whole week this month already. Fortunately, no male performer stayed at the top for long.

O had Fiona position Jacqui ass-up on the pallet, wrists clamped between her ankles with a straight steel bar. Calvin gave into the impulse to tickle Jacqui's left foot with the tip of a cane from the equipment table.

"Do that again, genius boy, and they'll be two for knackwurst," Jacqui warned.

"I just need a few strokes on each foot," O said, already thinking toward the coming wrap and her drive home. She was sweating, and the heavy camera had begun to make her arms ache. Though the ring flash was long gone, the thing itself weighed a ton. Pro Leicas were still made with steel bodies, and there was no substitute for Zeiss glass.

Jacqui took half a dozen sound strokes on each foot, now deliberately taunting Calvin.

"Lovely, Sir. May I have another?" she said after each.

O made him count to three before every stroke so she could catch the cane in the air and then the impacts on Jacqui's ass and feet. Once she'd gotten five frames on all targets, she couldn't help asking, as she unsnarled her sync cord if Jacqui preferred sting to thud.

"I'll take sting any day," she said. "Floggers remind me of a car wash. It's too bad he can't mark me because I've got a vanilla girl-girl tomorrow."

"Another time. Let's get some sexy here. Calvin, find an angle where you can put it in her mouth. I want to see some good cheek stuffing."

"Copy that."

He leaned down, somewhat awkwardly to pack Jacqui's mouth. How the boys stayed hard during all this remained an enduring mystery to O. Even a chemical boost wouldn't give most men whatever it took to shake their spears at a room full of people without losing some concentration. But however uncomfortable the position, Calvin kept his edge, finding Jacqui's mouth and putting it to work. As O had hoped, the pose made for some messy work. Spit was always a good prelude to other bodily fluids.

Climbing up behind Jacqui at O's instruction, Calvin eased into her pussy first, doing long, slow strokes for the camera.

"This is such a tease," Jacqui griped through gritted teeth.

"We'll loan you a vibrator afterward."

"It's cool. I'll get off during the anal if you let him go for a few minutes."

"First I need an initial penetration shot. Then you two can have at it."

O took the careful entry of Jacqui's narrower channel low and slow, making the obvious even more obvious. For an instant, she was distracted by the thought of Steven. Why hadn't he done this to her when he had the chance? When would he? All that was his decision. Her decisions counted in only one place anymore, and this was it.

Given the go-ahead, Jacqui and Calvin worked through the agenda, somehow able to stay in character. Jacqui looked back at him with utter hate. Calvin grinned sardonically, waiting for Jacqui to arch up in a wave of real spasms. Just for a moment, her face scrunched down in a way that wasn't consciously appealing. Thankfully, O caught it in time. She loved documenting women's orgasms, which she saw far too rarely shooting stills. Nothing ever went on long enough for most girls to come from it. Jacqui was not most girls, in a variety of ways. O realized they had things in common.

"I can go any time you want," Calvin offered helpfully. It was a two-minute warning no experienced porn photographer would ignore.

"Okay, Jacqui," O asked. "Where do you want it?"

"Gotta be a facial, don't you think?"

With a face like hers? O didn't usually like what she considered a tired convention of vanilla porn, but given Jacqui's situation and how good she still looked in it, O decided not to duck the cliché. She had plenty of other unpredictable stuff already. While Calvin sprinted off to the bathroom for a quick rinse, O sat down next to Jacqui, still in her rigid bondage, and showed her some RAWs on the camera back. Renata shared the viewing experience while blotting Jacqui's upper lip with a makeup sponge.

"You're really good at this," Jacqui said with genuine awe.

"You make my job easy," O replied.

"Maybe. I can build a website from scratch in a day, but if I had to take my own pictures for it, I'd never get it online."

"I knew you were a closet geek. You should get together with Fiona— she's the queen of Photoshop, not that you need it."

Jacqui gave O a very frank look.

"I wouldn't mind getting together with you some time."

Mercifully, Calvin strolled back from the bathroom, whistling.

"Good to go," he announced.

O spotted him next to Jacqui's face and moved in, sitting on the floor to see how much air she could get on the pop. She asked Calvin to please try and miss her.

Jacqui opened her mouth wide while he masturbated over her for a remarkably short time. One bad feature of stills was all the starting and stopping that made the final flat-out dash to the finish an ordeal for some of the guys. Not for this boy. However annoying, he was certainly reliable. Jacqui caught almost all of it on her tongue, rolling her head just enough to let it stream out the corners of her mouth and all over everything. Everyone in the room applauded, even Fiona, who rushed in to take Jacqui out of the hard restraint.

"I'd call this a good day," O said. "Thank you both. I'd like to shoot you again."

It was only half a lie. She'd be delighted to shoot Jacqui any time. Calvin she'd rather shoot with an elephant gun, but she'd probably end up using him regardless. Male performers who could do their bit with bound female performers were a pretty small club.

Free at last, Jacqui stood up and gave a mighty stretch.

"That's what I love about good bondage," she said, giving Fiona a hug after Renata had cleaned up her wrecked face with a baby wipe. "It feels so fine going on and even better coming off. Somebody toss me my flip flops, please."

O found them and handed them directly to Jacqui, who was covered in sweat and smelled strongly of sex. O could feel Jacqui's body heat and it stirred her own uncomfortably, especially when Jacqui spontaneously used O's shoulder for balance while standing up. She asked O if she could look at a few more pictures from the shoot. O obliged, flipping through them on the laptop onto which Roger had already started downloading them. They flew by in a fantastic blur of erotic violence.

"I'd love to have some of these shots for my site," she said wistfully, knowing how hard it was to get use rights on work for hire.

"I think I can talk the boss into that if you give the magazine a credit."

"No big."

"And tweet about it. And write it up for your blog."

"Done deal."

They shook hands on it and Jacqui went off to a second bathroom to shower separately from Calvin. Somewhat to her own surprise, O found herself following along.

In the white, clinical bathroom, Jacqui sang to herself, off-key, while O watched her through the translucent curtain.

"Want me to wash your back?"

Jacqui pushed the curtain aside and turned around. O found a big sponge and some liquid soap. She worked away at some of the grime left over from the steel cage.

"You have no idea how good that feels," Jacqui sighed.

"You'd be surprised."

"I can tell you're one of us. You know too much to be just another human tripod."

"Well, your hints aren't exactly subtle."

Jacqui turned her wet face to O and kissed her on the lips.

It went on a few seconds longer than expected, threatening to turn into something else. Jacqui finally broke it off.

"Your hints aren't all that subtle either, Madame Photographer."

"I like flirting with girls if they're wired like I am," O said with a casual shrug. "They're better at it than boys."

Jacqui reached out and took O's hand, looking at the big shackle ring.

"Whoever he is, he's a lucky guy."

"He's the owner of the magazine, but he's not all that lucky. He gets in his own way."

"I can't imagine much gets in your way," Jacqui said over the noise of the streaming water.

"I take a detour here and there, but I stay on course when it comes to work."

"Riiight. That's why you're in here with me."

"I'd like to continue this conversation. I'm doing some stills for a latex catalog next week. All singles. Doesn't pay a ton, but you can keep the outfits."

"Fuck, yeah! What day?"

"Tuesday."

"I'll put it on my phone calendar when I get out."

Mission accomplished, O excused herself. She rarely did this kind of thing anymore, though she'd once been the terror of her boarding school locker room. She'd gone after girls relentlessly because that's all there were. After meeting dick, however, O had pretty much given up her Sapphic enthusiasms. There were rare exceptions. Jacqui might be one of them.

O handed Jacqui a towel as she stepped, dripping, out of the shower.

"I'll get back with you right away about Tuesday," she promised.

Jacqui gave her a quick hug, all hot and pink and damp from the spray.

"I'd like that," she said on her way out of the bathroom.

O wondered what was happening inside herself, a place where she didn't spend much time as a rule. Tired and achy as she was after a typically strenuous studio day, she couldn't deny her impatience for the coming Friday.

CHAPTER SIX

F riday morning before dawn, Steven's recurring dream played its twice-yearly date in his head. There had been no script changes in the twenty years he'd been having it. It was always a bright summer day in Venice. Steven, still in his thirties, stood on the fantail of a vaporetto as it pulled up at the dock of The Hotel Cipriani. Seated under an umbrella at a table on the dockside deck were his father, his mother and her brother, his wicked Uncle Sol. All wore white – his father a miraculously unwrinkled linen suit, his mother an Escada dress with nautical gold trim, his Uncle Sol a crisp polo shirt and pleated white ducks. His father held a glass of wine, his mother a vodka tonic and his Uncle Sol the characteristic double Cutty with one rock. As the launch nudged against the dock's fenders, they all smiled at Steven and raised their glasses, inviting him to come ashore and join them.

But he never did. Somehow, even in his dream, he knew if he got off that boat he'd never get back on. It wasn't a frightening dream. Everyone, himself included, seemed calm and content. All three of his closest ancestors had passed through this life in what seemed like a long weekend. Steven took it as both reassuring and cautionary. There was still time, but never enough. Sooner or later, mostly sooner, everyone said goodbye. Attachment to this world or anyone in it would ultimately end at this destination.

Steven's eyes popped open and he stared up at the concrete ceiling over his bed in the yellow luminescence from the short-wave radio time display on the nightstand. The shades were down over the glass wall, and no light came from beneath. Somewhere deep in the empty park across the boulevard someone was playing the violin, quite expertly. Once again, Steven laughed at the town where The Department of Incidental Surrealism was the only agency that worked overtime. The music sounded like Brahms, but definitely no lullaby. Steven wondered if there was a law against aesthetic bullying. There sure as fuck should have been.

It occurred to Steven that if he were sleeping with someone, he might wake her up and tell her about that dream. The few women who had ever enjoyed sleepover privileges understood those privileges did not include entry to his inner life, to the extent he admitted to having one.

Only Marie knew about the dream, along with all the other things only she knew. Keeping secrets wasn't just her business. She was good at her business because doing so came naturally to her. Marie had something shocking on almost every rich and powerful man in town. They never worried over anything they'd confided to her.

Steven doubted there was such a thing as an easy life, but if there were, he hadn't been cursed with it. The genteel bohemian poverty of his father's struggling years had been considerably less genteel in private, particularly when an abundance of alcohol and a shortage of money had combined to form nitroglycerin. But the old man had been as stubborn as his mother was demanding. He had stood on his artistic ambitions and his political convictions like a bronze statue, until eventually the plaque of recognition and success had been laid at his feet. Like most monuments, his was essentially posthumous. He was gone from an aortic aneurism a year after accepting a chair at Stanford. The Blacklist, or more aptly his reaction to it, had killed him long before he had bled out on the way to the E.R.

Steven dealt with people whose lives had been smashed by scandal every day. Some put the pieces back together better than others. He gave his father middling grades. But more importantly, he viewed his old man's bitter life as a cautionary tale. Those who couldn't work the system would be worked by it. Very early in life Steven had decided he would not be one of them.

Not surprisingly, his father had left them with more name than money, and his mother had found ways of using one to secure the other. Her erotomania, as much as her unearthly beauty, had made her most appealing to a certain kind of man, and Steven had met many of them growing up. He had learned much from observing them but none had made a difference in his life, including Ray's old man, who Steven had never cared to know well.

Oddly, it had been his friend Martin, easily able to afford the tuition where Steven had been working his way through college on a partial scholarship, who had first suggested the Navy as a cruise to a law degree on the taxpayer's tab. Martin had come from an old, influential East Coast Jewish family and had political ambitions some time in uniform might facilitate.

Like so many of Martin's ideas, it had proved sound but more complex in execution than expected. It hadn't been until after they'd signed up that the whole business about Navy JAG lawyers prosecuting marines for shooting their officers had come to light. Safe to say, the people had gotten their money's worth out of both men by the time their six-year hitches were up.

At that point, they'd made it all the way to cushy billets at NATO headquarters in Brussels. Martin had been half-inclined to re-up, but Steven had wanted to see something more of life than could be viewed from a deputy attaché's office. Martin had recognized a possible résumé item for a future DA or mayor or governor in Steven's crazy idea. Steven had more personal reasons for returning to Los Angeles to become a PD.

To be sure, the office view of a deputy public defender in The County of Los Angeles had looked out on more open terrain, if not necessarily so well groomed. As it had turned out, Steven's call had been a quick way to notoriety and the big retainers that came with it. One thing he'd noticed growing up as that rare species, the native Angelino, was that the lawyers handled all the money, whichever direction it might be headed.

The two of them had quickly earned a rep for infuriating the DAs by dusting them off on seemingly impossible cases. They had worked way into the night and way past their pay grades. But after Martin had appeared next to a newly busted society madam on Channel Nine News, their reputations were made.

The madam, whose name was Marie, had walked on a dismissal with prejudice. The private practice of Beren–Diamond Associates had hung out its shingle in a faintly seedy suite of offices near the Capitol Records Tower in Hollywood. Again, Steven had instinctively made the correct choice. Their early client list had been drawn from shadowy figures that scraped together livings on the outskirts of Tinsel Town by providing for the peculiar indulgences of its louche aristocracy.

At first, the practice had been the juridical equivalent of Lourdes, where processions of the bent, the broke and the busted, the coke dealers, pimps and hired muscle to the stars, had lined up for as much justice as they could afford. Martin, with his Sephardic good looks and reassuring manner, had been the public face of the firm, while Steven had been the closer who sat down with prosecutors in chambers and hammered out face-saving agreements.

Between them they had unlocked the jailhouse door for so many shady characters, they'd become known by the nickname of The Devil's Own, after the lawyers' regiment recruited from The Inns of Court at London's Old Bailey. Being military buffs like many retired officers, they had even looked up the regimental insignia – a scaly demon with wings, horns and a pointed tail – to imprint on their business cards and stationary.

That logo had been replaced by the somber "Death or Glory" skull-and-bones of the 17th/21st Lancers on Martin's demise.

After having put in enough cheap fixes to demonstrate their aptitude for beating the system, they had begun to draw the big-money cases – the movie-star murders, the seven-digit embezzlements from production funds, the big-name vehicular homicides, the Social Register domestic violence beefs – that had moved them downtown.

Even as their retainers had soared, Steven, who had known enough financial insecurity to last a lifetime, had lived modestly, restraining the tendency toward extravagance he'd inherited along with his prodigious libido from his mother. He had invested in real estate when the market was just taking off. Selling most of it (except for the building in which he had taken up residence and a few other choice properties) just in time, he'd awakened one fine morning to the realization that he'd gotten rich. Barring a kind of imprudence to which he was not given, he would stay that way for rest of his life.

It was only then that he had entered the luxury living phase of museum-grade watches and Saville Row suits. Literally making money in his sleep from all the dividends and interest on his accumulated revenues, he had reached that tipping point beyond which it was almost impossible to outspend his ongoing income.

Good thing too, because he had known, standing next to a sobbing Ray at the gravesite of their mother in Forest Lawn, that he had acquired a costly dependent. In the middle of all that, Steven's marriage to Marie had come and gone with remarkably little fuss, bother or expense, but from Ray there would be no divorce. Whatever Steven's judgment of their mother, she had loved Ray, sheltered and coddled him, leaving him essentially defenseless in the world. Ray was as much family as Steven had left and Steven wasn't about to let go of him.

Ray had entered that ominous event horizon in his twenties when a few wrong moves could send a life spinning down a black hole. Since his handsome wastrel of a step-father had traded in their mother on a younger model, beginning the final downward spiral into the binge drinking that had concluded at the end of a length of maroon sash cord, Steven had done his best to look after Ray by long distance, advising and subsidizing where he could even from the distant shores of Japan, The Philippines and Europe during Steven's hitch in the Navy. The habit had stuck.

And there had been one other thing, discovered during a surprise visit to Tokyo Ray had managed during a term off after his second year at Cal Arts. In a specialized "love hotel" where they had ended up spending most of Ray's ten-day stay, they had come to recognize something else they had in common with their mother, something they could share only with the women they both attracted, or with the pricey *hentai* whores they hired in *Shinjuku*.

What Steven had seen of Ray during that visit to Tokyo was no phase they happened to be going through at the same time. Both men bore an indelible marker that probably went very far back in their lineage. Steven's father had been convinced Genghis Kahn had raped some ancestor of their mother's. Not everyone in the line had inherited that wild-ass DNA, but those who did got heavy doses. In the women, including two of their cousins, it had emerged as destructive promiscuity. In the men, it had found a different expression.

If, as Steven had learned in college Psych class, all the characters in a dream were players in the dreamer's internal drama, Steven was his own ego, his mother and uncle his id and his father his super-ego, all assembled for the dockside meeting at The Cipriani. Not until he finally sat down and ordered a drink of his own there would Steven ever be free of any of them.

Steven's fortune was already made when Ray had first come to him with the mad idea of financing a magazine just as the Internet had turned into a vast paper-shredder for publications. Steven hadn't rejected the proposal out of hand as he would have from anyone else. Steven had learned in his own hard climb that only the authentic self could succeed, and whether Ray knew it or not, his inspiration came from the most authentic part of his character.

Steven had ordered the incorporation papers, with himself as CEO, drawn up immediately and written a six-digit check to start *Forbidden*. Like most of Steven's bets, it hadn't really been a gamble. *Forbidden* had paid out well to both of them in a variety of currencies.

The violinist in the park finally stopped playing, presumably silenced by the LAPD. In the deep, delicious silence before the early rush, Steven realized that O would be visiting him in a few hours. A slow smile crept across his sardonic face and a distinct stiffness began to rise under the red sheets. He would need all his strength soon enough. Turning over, he fluffed the huge down pillow before lowering his head into it. In seconds, he was asleep again, untroubled by further visitations from the dead.

It was near ten when Steven finally rolled over again. One thing he never liked about the law was how much of it was practiced early in the morning, a misery for a confirmed night owl and a factor in his determined efforts to avoid trial proceedings. The gavel usually came down at eight-thirty, not a civilized hour for dishing out just desserts.

Sliding into a more casual, brushed cotton version of the robe he'd worn with O, he toggled the wall switch that raised the shades with a quiet whirring of electric motors, letting the sun blast through yards of glass. It would be hot out there today.

On Friday mornings an alliance of charitable groups distributed food packages donated from the leftovers of local restaurants to anyone who lined up in the park across the street. The white vans were curbed and unloading. The mendicants – street dwellers, old folks, young immigrant families, crazies and an increasing number of dazed exiles from the middle class – were already waiting. Every week, the lines got longer and the piles of white-plastic-wrapped donor packages got smaller.

Steven understood to his red roots that the income polarization he saw, living where he did, more vividly than most, was unsustainable. He'd already off-shored much of his wealth, but this city was his home and the thought of fleeing it as it went up in flames did not appeal. Shaking his head, he turned from the window and sauntered off to the marbl- floored luxury of his bathroom. So far away from the street heat and yet so close. That awareness was his retirement package from the Public Defender's Office. That and Marie.

Now fully awake, he confronted himself in the oval mirror amidst all the black marble. With his stubble grown out, he really did look part werewolf. Opening the mirror and revealing a medicine cabinet to rival a chain pharmacy, he plucked a small tube of testosterone gel from its box, used the back of the screw-cap to punch the seal, dropped one arm of his robe and squeezed the clear goop into his opposite hand. He smacked his upper arm with the gelatinous dollop and rubbed it in thoroughly. As with the blue diamonds, Steven didn't depend on synthetic enhancement, but with low PSA levels, why not enjoy the extra jolt of badass with which it kicked him into gear?

Next came some whitening grit and a mechanized toothbrush to get those predatory gnashers gleaming, followed by a generous application of Trumper's violet shave cream, applied with a Lucite-handled badger brush big enough to paint a barn.

Rather than lathering in swirls, which could break the bristles, he slapped it on in back and forth strokes, as if he were, in fact, painting a barn. Satisfied with the thickness of the lightly scented lavender layer, he went at his pale but surprisingly abrasive whiskers with a terrifying pearl-handled Damascus steel straight razor. It was stropped so sharp it seemed like it would make eyes bleed just to look at it, but Steven had absolute confidence with the lethal instrument, whisking off great swaths of lavender foam and shavings with nary a nick.

It had been a bloody business acquiring the technique, but nothing left his face quite so smooth. A quick rinse, a stinging application of Kiehl's blue astringent and Steven felt ready for the arena once more.

A motion sensor brought up all three of the big flat screens, each tuned to a different news channel, as Steven strolled by on his way to the front door. The morning papers, including *The New York Times* and *Los Angeles Times*, plus a few specialized trades, waited outside.

Gathering them up and dumping them on the table, Steven went to the steel prep counter in the kitchen where the timer on an industrial cappuccino maker the size of a slot machine had already kicked on the built-in grinder. It made a high-pitched whine shredding the Jamaican Blue Mountain beans while Steven headed to the fridge for some milk to steam.

A few minutes later, Steven sat at the table, swigging the frothy brew from an enormous cup imprinted in French with the menu of The Bistro of All Hours. He sorted through the papers quickly, knowing he wouldn't have time to read all of them, or even any of them fully, before work. Steven always went straight to the local news first to see if there was any trade to be found in the previous day's misdeeds.

There were a couple of possibilities. The comptroller of an industrial town in the unincorporated part of the county had been indicted for cooking the property tax books. It would be boring but the numbers were large enough to inspire at least a bit of mild curiosity. Further inside, there was something more luridly entertaining, a major cable producer with a notorious temper had managed to get himself arrested after a pugilistic encounter at The Palm with a director he'd recently fired. They were probably all lawyered up by the studio already, but show biz egomaniacs tended to go through counsel pretty fast. He'd consider catching them on the rebound after they'd fired the first team on the field.

Now here was something juicy enough to make Steven fold back the paper and fish his round specs out of the top pocket of the robe. It was a homicide case right in his neighborhood, and grisly in the L.A. tradition. A young Hassidic diamond dealer had been arrested at The Bonaventure with a box of rocks and the severed head of a business associate in a suitcase as he attempted to check out.

This could be challenging. There was big money in the diamond business and if, as Steven suspected, the beef was over conflict diamonds of unknown origin, someone would pay him well to make the whole thing go away. The Case of the Headless Hassid. It had a nice ring to it. Something else for the book he'd never write.

By now, Steven had no justification to continue working at all, aside from his love for the cut and thrust of criminal practice. He certainly didn't need the money. But he had never lost his fascination with the human drama behind a high-stakes felony beef. Rich defendants not only paid well, they had interesting motives, and Steven was a diligent student of motives.

Steven circled the story with a big, yellow swipe from the Mont Blanc highlighter he kept at hand during his morning police blotter survey. Sooner or later, after all the familial hand-wringing, someone would mention his name. He'd expect the call to come from the defendant's rabbi.

Steven had only one work-related meeting scheduled for that day, having found Fridays pretty useless after the early phases of most trial proceedings, but he was rather looking forward to it.

First, however, there would be forty-five minutes in the small, mirrored gym off the side of his bedroom opposite the dressing area, where he would work his way through all the shiny cross-training machinery before finishing up on the treadmill.

Steven's was, as Ray observed, the world's shortest commute. Dressed in a black double-breasted blazer with sterling buttons, black-and-cream herringbone trousers made from the hair of celebrity goats, one of his black T&A shirts with triple-button cuffs, a gray silk-satin tie and buffed brogues, he popped out his steel front door, strolled past the double elevator banks and right through the glass entrance in the opposite wall. The sign on it still read "Beren and Diamond, Attorneys at Law."

Martin had been gone a decade, but if he ever decided to drop back in from the afterlife that Steven, a casual atheist, did not believe existed, he'd find his position secure. Steven had kept the extra office space for visiting associate counsel essentially undisturbed from the way Martin had left it when it was his own.

Steven's English secretary Constance looked up from her desk when he entered. She was quite a stunner, with her ginger hair tied back and her fitted, navy-blue suit buttoned up to her neck to cover her Himalayan geography, but Steven simply regarded her looks as added distraction value in dealing with clients. She did the brusque efficiency act superbly, forgot nothing, anticipated his needs and shared a sardonic appreciation for the slippery intricacies of the law.

Constance was already a paralegal. Steven subsidized her continued studies toward eventually passing the bar, thinking one day she might occupy Martin's former post. The job was always easier with another hand on deck, but only one trained to Steven's own methods would be up to the cases that would come through the glass portals.

"Good morning, Mr. Diamond," she said cheerfully. "Was it a good walk then?"

"Most invigorating, Miss Barton. When you get a minute, please bring me Mr. Adelstein's file."

She handed him a blue folder already sitting on her desk.

"Would this be the one, by any chance?

"I seriously doubt chance had much to do with it."

He took the folder and headed toward his sanctum with it under his arm.

"When Adelstein gets here, make him wait fifteen minutes."

Elizabeth looked puzzled.

"Any particular reason?"

"So he'll be asking himself that same question."

"Silly me," Constance replied, lightly slapping the side of her head.

Once inside his deco-style chambers with their huge Lalique screens, Steven settled in behind his giant round desk in front of the windows looking toward downtown. He snapped on the green-glass-shaded Bestlite and opened the folder, flipping through his notes one last time, shaking his head. This was going to be a very short meeting. He charged a full hour for any portion thereof, so this could done as swiftly as possible, which still wouldn't be quick enough for his liking.

At twelve-fifteen sharp there was a double knock at the door. Constance showed in Harold Adelstein; slight, natty and balding in his Canali suit. He'd brought along some young sandy-haired fellow Steven didn't recognize. Steven unfolded himself from his chair for the customary handshakes.

"Hello, Steven," Adelstein said. "I'd like you to meet our staff counsel, Tom Dillard. He'll be working with you on the case."

Steven shook Dillard's hand.

"Pleased to meet you. Would you mind waiting outside for a moment?" Steven asked in a pleasant tone. Dillard looked confused and annoyed. Adelstein's expression was more wary. He was a politician with a politician's instincts.

"I really think I should be in the loop, since this involves the whole organization," Dillard said, trying to sound resolute, though he knew inside he was a minnow between two sharks.

"It's okay," Adelstein reassured him. "I'm sure we'll need you back in shortly."

Dillard shuffled out, shooting a resentful look at Steven before closing the door behind him.

"What was that all about?" Adelstein asked, his hard little face trying to manage a convincing glower that never got past a sneer.

"You don't want him to hear what I'm about to say. Have a seat, Mr. Adelstein."

Steven motioned toward the round, green leather couch that formed a perfect half-circle in front of the desk. Adelstein sat. Steven flipped open the file.

"I had a drink with the U.S. attorney," he said. "A couple of drinks, actually. We did a little informal discovery."

"What did you find out?"

Adelstein shifted nervously, crossing his legs to show off his clocked socks.

"You have two problems. They've been all through the foundation's bank records for the past ten years already and basically they believe you did what the indictment says you did."

Adelstein's irritation was evident in his voice.

"That's supposed to be news? Why would they have indicted me if they didn't think I was guilty?"

"That's a broad philosophical question we can address another time. The important point is that they believe they can take you in front of a jury and get a conviction. You remember when you were a kid and you told your parents not to make a federal case out of something you did wrong? You're going to find out where that expression comes from."

"They're bluffing. We're the biggest HIV/AIDS serving organization in the world. I've got a wall of plaques from the UN. Every NGO in the world knows we're indispensible."

"That's where the second part of your problem comes in. I believe you did what the indictment says you did."

Face flushing, Adelstein leaned toward Steven's desk.

"What the fuck are you saying?" he demanded.

Steven put on his glasses and pulled a single sheet of columns and numbers out of the folder "According to this 501c3 filing here, your foundation claims fifteen million dollars in non-receipted expenses that it nonetheless insists are legitimate deductions from last year."

"We run programs all over the world," Adelstein said, voice rising. "How are we supposed to get receipts for buying off some local warlord so we can distribute ARVs on his turf?"

"I'm sure that would play well enough to an IRS auditor, but a jury might want to know about this."

Steven pulled out another piece of paper from the file. This one was a computer printout, clearly a bank statement of some kind. He tossed it across the desk at Adelstein, who glanced at it as if it were a poisonous snake and sank back into the couch.

"They don't have warlords in The Republic of Andorra, Mr. Adelstein," Steven said in an affable tone. "I've been there. It's a picturesque tax haven up in the Pyrenees. Just about all they've got are sheep, banks and Ferrari dealerships. I imagine the infection rate is pretty low among Basque sheepherders. That's your bank account, isn't it, Mr. Adelstein? And the non-receipted fifteen million is in it."

Adelstein leapt to his feet, slammed his hands down on Steven's desk. Steven didn't flinch.

"You're supposed to be on my side."

"As an officer of the court, if I'm convinced you committed the charged offense, I can only advise you to plead guilty. They take a dim view of lawyers suborning perjury."

"Is this about money?" Adelstein fumed, leaning in even closer toward Steven. "How much more do you need to do induce you to do your job?"

Steven looked up at him, face composed.

"Sit down, Mr. Adelstein."

Seeing the look in Steven's eyes, Adelstein sat down on the edge of the couch, but still looked ready to spring.

"I don't see why you can't represent me if we avoid a trial. There must be some kind of deal you can cut."

"Quite possibly, but I don't do child molesters, charity frauds or faith healers. If I thought they were out to get you undeservedly, I'd defend you for free. But I don't think that. I think you're an AIDS profiteer and I don't want your business."

Adelstein slumped. This wasn't how things were supposed to go.

"You'll defend murderers and drug dealers but not someone who helps sick people for a living?"

"Murderers and drug dealers are down-home crooks. You are a jive-ass crook. I'm sure you help sick people, but from one look at that piece of paper, I can see that you help yourself first. I don't know who didn't get their meds as a result, but I'm sure they'd agree that murderers and drug dealers have a stronger claim on their sympathies, as they do on mine. With all that money you can retain excellent representation, but not from me. I'd very much like you out of my office now. Go work on your tan at Lompoc for a couple of years."

Steven tossed the two pages back in the folder, closed it with an air of finality and shoved it across the desk at Adelstein, who stared at it a moment, shot Steven a hateful look, then picked it up and stormed out, trying unsuccessfully to slam the door behind him. Steven had long since had it mounted on a hydraulic hinge from similar exits.

Putting his hands behind his head, he tilted back his big chair. A smile spread across his face. He might have just sent a million dollars in fees out of the room, and that wasn't ideal, but he'd worked hard for the privilege to send business away.

Constance entered a minute later, iPad in hand.

"Well that was certainly brief," she said.

"Not brief enough. Anything else on today's calendar?"

"Alana Wallace from The Southern District of Missouri called. She wants to set up a phoner for four o'clock."

"On a Friday afternoon? I thought civil servants were supposed to be lazy. Push her off until Monday and tell her I'll buy the drinks when I see her in Kansas City."

"Right. On my way to the law library."

Constance turned brusquely toward the door.

"Why don't you get some friends together and go have a few drinks? Nobody ever died wishing they'd spent more time in the law library."

She glanced back at him.

"I'll take the motion under advisement. Enjoy your weekend, Mr. Diamond."

"I have every intention of it."

Constance raised an eyebrow at him prior to departure.

Steven glanced at his watch, today a Franck Mueller with a black, rectangular face and serif numerals in bright colors. O was due at four p.m. and Steven had preparations to complete. The instructions he'd emailed her had been quite precise and specific. He was certain she would follow them to the letter, especially the part about being punctual.

CHAPTER SEVEN

Steven needed to fortify himself for the coming exertions; nothing too heavy, but substantial and rich in protein. Calling down to the desk from the kitchen phone, he dispatched one of the security guards to Langer's, after seventy years still the best deli in the blueberry bagel wasteland of Southern California, and ordered an avocado and bacon sandwich on toasted sourdough, dry, with mayo on the side.

Steven barely had time to set one place at the table with a black linen mat and napkin and pour himself a big glass of apple juice before the security guard knocked.

Not only had he brought lunch, he'd picked up Steven's mail from the desk. As always, there was a ton of it: piles of glossy catalogs for expensive stuff he either already had or didn't want, solicitations for good causes to which he'd already contributed the maximum deductible amounts, court documents with the seals of various jurisdictions on them and plenty of windowed bill envelopes. He tossed the lot on a glass-topped hall stand next to the door, fished a twenty out of his robe pocket and sent the security guard on his way.

Normally, Steven would have flipped through the day's dispatches while demolishing his lunch from one of the black and silver Jolly Roger plates stacked in the island's drawers, but he was preoccupied with more attractive diversions.

Dishes rinsed and in the sterilizer, paper debris swallowed by the immaculate white cylinder of the Vipp can, it was time to put the elegant esquire back in his closet and bring on his roommate, Mr. Hyde. Suppressing an unusual urge to hurry, Steven put away the parts of his civilized persona methodically as usual, threw the red and black robe over his shoulders and headed for the back room.

Fully a third of the building's top floor, it could have accommodated a bowling alley with room left for a snack bar. Icongruously bright and cheerful, it bore no resemblance to anything that might be called a dungeon, making it all the more sinister – a scary playground for grown-ups.

The walls were painted a dark shade of plumb, the floor a rink of glistening black diamond-plate rubber. The big windows came all the way back to the west wall of the building and with the shades up it seemed airy and safe.

But then there were the appointments: the black-rubber upholstered queen-size bondage bed trimmed all around with ring-bolts and short chains; the tall standing cage; the straight-backed steel interrogation chair fitted with attachment points, including a frightening angle-iron at the top for securing head-gear; the industrial-strength manual hoist bolted deeply into the cement ceiling; and the black steel suspension bar hanging from a beefy shackle-bolt at the end of its thick, black rope.

There was also the padded spanking horse with inward-tilted leg-rails, straps across the back and shackle points fore and aft; the thickly padded section of wall with sturdy steel circles at each corner; and the rope anchors that hinged up from flush-mounted plates in the floor, which slanted gently toward a center drain. In one corner, there was a gynecological suite, complete with an electrically articulating exam table and knee crutches, overhead lamp, and spotless Mayo stands, their metal trays arrayed with gleaming instruments that made most women want to cross their legs.

One wall was hung with racks of whips and floggers of every size and description. Two shiny steel cylinders in front of it were densely forested with crops and canes and dressage sticks. The whip collection shared space with big diamond-plate steel cabinets filled with implements of pleasure and torment. A large glass-front case displayed an awe-inspiring phalanx of dildos, all different sizes, shapes and colors. A big, blue tool box adequate to a racing garage stood in front of a red-steel peg-board festooned with leather cuffs in assorted sizes and colors, pre-cut lengths of chain, bins full of padlocks, chromed spreader bars, hoods, leather bondage sleeves and polished steel shackles.

The opposite wall, closest to the bed, was half-covered in floor-to-ceiling mirror, its back corner a cozy padded alcove where visitors could sit and rest, render intimate services or just admire the brutally sexual, exquisitely executed art on the walls, picturing beautiful women in extremis too dire for the living room gallery. Even in the cozy space, there were floor bolts and rings around the bases of the comfortable roll-tufted banquettes for locking chains.

A glass-doored closet was stuffed with brightly-hued latex costumes in all styles and sizes, along with rows of corsets draped over hangers and shelves of the cruelest shoes imaginable, including steel high-heeled sandals with big, round studs lining the insoles and locking steel ankle bands.

A long drain board with a steel sink and overhead cabinets matching those on the wall took up what was left of the back of the room, save for a doorway into another bathroom, equipped with an open, black-tiled shower, hoses and nozzles dangling from its ceiling amid a forest of nautical steel chains. There were also a black bidet and matching toilet back there, these too surrounded by hardware for securing the user in place. A glass cabinet next to the double sink contained every kind of medical plumbing attachment invented since the discovery of rubber. A glass-front case next to the sink had been stocked with enough lubes and potions to grease down a medium size tractor factory.

All through the place, light boxes set into the walls and ceilings and controlled by wireless switches could change the ambience from stygian to clinical with the touch of a pad.

Steven, robe-flaps fluttering in his wake, laid out his gear for the day, starting by wheeling two steel carts from the bathroom wall to one side of the bondage bed. The tallest held unopened bottles from the bathroom lube stash, boxes of baby wipes, plenty of disposable black nitrile gloves on the top shelf and an intimidating assortment of stainless steel insertable phalli on the second. The bottom shelf was for a tall water bottle and a pile of washcloths.

The largest cart was reserved for electrical gear. A small but powerful suction pump with coils of clear-plastic tubing and electrical power cable draped over the pressure gauge sat on top next to a rack of clear plastic cylinders ranging in size from barely bigger than a pencil to the diameter of a clarinet. On the next shelf down was a generator box equipped with lights, dials, meters and sockets. Steel baskets of coiled wires stood at the ready next to it, along with a padded plastic case of attachments that might fit in almost any aperture of the human body.

From a drawer under the top shelf of the electrical cart, Steven took out a power strip, dropped it on the floor, plugged it into one of many diamond-plate trimmed sockets along the baseboards. He switched it on and connected the suction pump and the signal generator. From that same drawer, he pulled out three big, heavy-duty vibrators, jacking one into the power strip and laying it on the tall cart nearest the bed, mating a second with a curly overhead cable so it hung like the trouble light in a repair garage and connecting the third to a socket next to the padded section on the west wall.

The operating room kick-bucket for used toys and discarded wipes sailed across the floor at Steven's swift shove with a foot, stopping when it hit the bed squarely between the two carts. He wheeled a full-length mirror on a stand to just in front of the bed, checked to make sure it framed the faces of anyone pointed toward the window.

As an afterthought, Steven hung the tall cart with mean clover-clamps on short chains and a ball-gag he estimated would strap into O's mouth appealingly, if not exactly comfortably.

Getting every detail in place took longer than it should have, as usual. Fortunately, he had only a few more things to collect. From the pegboard he selected a set of exquisitely made patent-leather wrist and ankle cuffs with locking hasps, surcingle straps and pad-eye-mounted one-inch stainless rings.

The single most important item came next. From a plain, white cardboard box in the bin of the tool chest, he took out a matching collar, stiff and high enough to remind the wearer of its presence without restricting her head movements unnecessarily.

This was no ordinary collar. It was decorated with a wide, heavy silver plate riveted to the leather just right of the centermost of three rings, roughly the size of those O wore through her nipple flesh. At the suggestion that a few of Steven's watches were nearly due for their yearly tune-ups, his jeweler had shortened the turnaround time on the plate from a month to two days. O's single initial was cut out of the silver plate, revealing the shiny leather beneath. Steven had chosen a German Blackletter font for its severity. He'd riveted on the plate himself.

This collar, while still distinctly feminine and certainly elegant, had none of the fragility of the silver one Ray put on O. It suggested, correctly, that both the collar and its wearer were intended for heavy use.

Steven scooped up a handful of common-keyed padlocks from the wall, grabbed a one-foot length of chrome chain, snagged a bottle of water-based glide and brought down a pair of size six patent fetish pumps with round toes and viciously steep stiletto heels from the closet shelf.

After tossing these items into a steel mesh basket, he tapped out a couple of codes on the hand-held control pad, lowering the shades and bringing up the room lights to create a crepuscular, uniform glow that might have equally suggested dawn or dusk.

On the way out, he took one item off the cart, a steel cylinder with a chunky ring and wide disk on one end and a fat, hard, tapered bulb at the other. He weighed it in his hands. This would be the first and most important test.

Back out in the living room, he went over the steel top of the dining table with a few squirts of glass cleaner and a dishtowel. It wouldn't do to have O's fine rump seated on a less than pristine perch. Steven meticulously arranged the collar, cuffs, locks, chain, lube, wipes, shoes standing at attention and finally the steel appliance at the end of the table opposite the kitchen. From the nearest bathroom, he borrowed a plain hand mirror, and set it next to the collar. Rearranging some pillows against the arm of the silver couch, he borrowed a big, black towel from the bathroom and laid it over them, creating a comfy nest.

O was due in twenty minutes and Steven still had to dress. Something not too intimidating for a first solo date would be good. Slipping into a pair of butter-soft lambskin drawstring pants with wide legs that would slip over the immaculately buffed riding boots he pulled on with red-handled hooks, he completed the ensemble with a woven silk pop-over shirt closed at the neck with Chinese frogs.

As a rule, he never took the pills until his dates actually arrived. Many seemed to suffer mysterious delays and unexpected scheduling conflicts. He'd have bet his whole bankroll

O would appear as promised. She took promises seriously. Their arrangement with Ray had all the earmarks of a very, very bad idea, but that never stopped much of anyone from doing much of anything.

Tossing down the blue diamonds while passing through his bathroom, he went out to roll a nice, thick joint. He barely had it done when the slightly tenuous taps came from the other side of the steel door.

Steven sauntered over to open it, deliberately taking his time. Anxiety was part of the sweetness and he intended to extend O's as long as possible.

Glancing up at the military time clock above the refrigerator in the kitchen, he noted that she had knocked just as the second hand crossed the double zero. It made him smile wondering how long she'd been out in the hallway waiting for the exact moment.

O entered with such perfect form her heels didn't even click on the concrete. She fell lightly into Steven's arms, gripping him with surprising strength during their long, ravenous kiss. Finally coming up for air, Steven pushed her back just far enough.

"Let me see," he said, closing the door behind them.

O wore less makeup this time, just smear-proof red lip stain and a bit of water-fast color around the eyes. It didn't seem an occasion for black tears. O's hair was tied back in a practical ponytail, leaving her face completely undefended. She had assembled the ensemble he sent over for her with predictable attention to detail. Her tight, white blouse was buttoned up modestly to the neck over her regular, silver collar, but the sheer material showed off the plain black-satin demibra underneath, her steel rings protruding rudely above the cups. The wide black-patent belt was done up tight, proving O didn't need a corset to easily reduce her waist an inch or two. The black skirt, a salaciously shorter version of the one she had worn to dinner, swung loosely about her hips, so brief if she bent over her the bottoms of her ass-cheeks would show. She was barelegged in tall ankle-strap heels that matched her belt. Her only contribution had been a medium-size patent-leather thrift-store handbag in mint condition with a bamboo handle, which she dipped at the knees to set down next to the entrance, should rapid flight become necessary. It paid a daring girl to be prudent.

Recognizing an implied command, O lifted the front of her skirt with freshly manicured fingertips, nails the same match for her membranes as before. She was predictably bare underneath.

"You're a good girl, O," Steven said, kissing her again. O continued to hold up the skirt so Steven could grab her rudely between the legs and pull her up to deepen his exploration of her mouth. "And a wet girl."

"A scared girl, actually, Sir," she replied breathily. "I kept wondering the whole way how I'd explain being dressed like this if I got pulled over. Now that I'm here, I'm even more scared."

Steven smiled.

"It doesn't seem to interfere with your enjoyment."

O looked down with an embarrassed smile. "It enhances it, Sir. I hope I never stop being scared of you, at least a little bit."

"I'll try to prevent that." Leading her into the living room, he offered a drink.

"Just water, Sir. But I'll smoke with you if you have something available."

Steven the joint from the rolling box and tucked it behind his ear. Bringing down a glass from over the sink, he shot a stream of cold, filtered water into it from the narrow spigot next to the big sprayer dangling over the basin.

O joined him in the kitchen, receiving the glass from his hand in both of hers.

"It's like a blast-furnace out there today," she said, taking a couple of gulps.

"I can tell."

Big, round stains had formed under O's armpits, making the material of the blouse even more transparent.

"Sir's instructions specified no antiperspirant, O said, visibly embarrassed. "I hope I don't stink."

"Not yet, but I expect you will later."

This time O smiled directly into his face.

"I'm sure you will see to it, Sir. Should I just kiss your boots now or wait to be told?"

"Two things a slave can always do to make a good impression are kiss her Masters boots or show him her ass."

O gracefully descended to hands and knees, lowering her face to Steven's boots while flipping up the lewd little skirt onto her back. Steven felt the heat from O's lips right through the leather of the riding boots. He leaned back on the counter and casually rested the boot she wasn't polishing with her tongue between her shoulders, lightly pushing her face lower. O compensated by lifting her tail higher. He never hurried through things or stopped before they were completed, switching boots so O could demonstrate her devotion to the other one.

"You'll be happy to know these boots have never been outdoors since I had them made. They're only waxed, never polished. I don't think bootblack is flattering on a woman's face.

O lifted her lips to speak without looking up. "That's very considerate, Sir. I'd do it anyway, of course."

"Of course. We'll come back to this," Steven said matter-of-factly. "There are a few things I like done a certain way consistently. Get up and I'll show you."

O rose, smoothing down her skirt, folding her arms behind her and straightening her spine. Steven could see the slight change in her nipple rouge through the blouse. He gave her rings a friendly tug that brought her close.

"Better shade this time. Not quite so whorish," he observed as she winced.

"Thank you, Sir. Though I am your whore."

"You'll have the opportunity to demonstrate that. Come with me."

Taking O by the back of the neck, he steered her from the kitchen to the end of the table, where she took in everything arrayed for her with a quick glance, a fleeting smile crossing her lacquered lips. Steven knew what he wanted down to the smallest detail. She liked that ... a lot.

"You'll start on your knees, of course."

"Naturally, Sir."

O dropped more quickly this time, lifting her hair so Steven could unlock the collar she wore for Ray, which he parked on a chair, and close the patent collar around her neck, kissing her nape in a familiar gesture that made O stiffen a bit. Well, they were brothers after all. A few similar mannerisms were to be expected. She felt the click of a small padlock at the back of the collar. Her hands went to it reflexively. This was very different from what she was used to wearing. Her fingertips brushed the silver plate. Steven smiled.

"Have a look."

He brought the hand mirror down in front of O's face, which registered total amazement and pure delight. The tagged collar was a grand gesture, and grandly presumptuous. The significance of such a thing was hard to overstate in their world. It meant, in terms anyone of that world could not mistake, just who she was and that she was taken. The collar itself was so different, too: heavier, higher and stiffer, with rings on the side as well as the front, practical as much as decorative. It was the collar of a working slave, if a much-treasured one.

O felt the full weight of Steven's ownership as she continued touching it, even though doing so without permission was probably forbidden. Her neck seemed all the more fragile encircled in the wide, unyielding collar.

"What do you think?" Steven asked.

"It's beautiful, Sir.

"It suits you. You're a strong little bitch who merits a collar to match her hardware."

"I could take it a notch tighter if you like," she volunteered.

"Later perhaps. Up, please."

Unlike Ray, Steven never affected a commanding tone. His unfaltering politeness was a bit chilling, making O's underarms even wetter, the cool breeze on them from the air conditioning tightening the stippled flesh around her big nipple rings again. She could hardly think of Steven without that happening. The effect had caused her some moments of embarrassment in public, but there was only so much she was willing to cover up in the name of public decency when the hot Santa Ana's blew.

Steven took hold of the front collar ring, pulling her around to face him and holding it up high to tip O's head back for a long, probing kiss. She kept her hands behind her back, but pressed her body against his at every possible point of contact. She could feel that knowledgeable touch under her skirt, the subtle pinching and rolling that made her whimper into his mouth and lift one foot off the floor so she could rub a knee lightly up between his legs.

"You certainly don't miss an opportunity, do you?" Steven asked drily.

"A slave's first duty is to get some when she can," O said.

"I expect you'll have no problem with that one," he said, going back to kissing and touching, feeling her everywhere, over and under her "uniform." It was a little like being back in boarding school, only this time O was on the receiving end of what she usually did to other girls.

Backing off a short distance at last, Steven started O's orientation. "I'd like the shoes, skirt and bra off, please."

O slipped out of her street shoes, unhooked the skirt, and folded it on the table. She did the amazing girl trick of unbuttoning her blouse, undoing the front-opening bra clasp between her breasts, releasing the shoulder straps and pulling the whisper of satin out of one sleeve. When Ray sorted her wardrobe after her return from Pasadena, he had made her get rid of a fortune's worth of AP and La Perla bras that hooked in back.

She immediately buttoned the blouse back up, placing the discarded bra atop her skirt. Something about the light, translucent blouse that really concealed nothing made O's lower half seem all the more exposed. To enhance the effect, O tucked the tails of the blouse up into the wide belt, so the line of demarcation between dressed and naked was even more obvious. She automatically went up on her toes with her hands behind her head when the kissing and touching started again. The swelling under the soft leather of Steven's trousers left no doubt he liked what he saw.

Holding O by the throat rather tightly, he easily slipped a couple of fingers into her. "Seems like you started without me."

"I couldn't help myself, Sir. I've been like this all day."

"I assume you prepared yourself accordingly."

"Yes, Sir. I skipped dinner last night. Then I gave myself a deep purge with a full quart of water. I made it a little hotter than usual and held it a full twenty minutes. It was quite uncomfortable."

"Poor darling."

"I wasn't forbidden to masturbate during, which helped a bit. I did a quick bulb flush before coming over, just to be safe."

"I appreciate your thoroughness."

O laughed that quick, musical scale. "Anything worth doing is worth doing to excess, Sir."

"That's so good," Steven said. "I may have to borrow it."

She reminded him that he had the right to use anything she called her own.

"I'm not sure that applies to copyrighted material. Cuffs next. You know how to put them on?"

"I believe so."

"Start at the ankles."

"Naturally, Sir."

O took the cuffs and applied them as if she'd done it a hundred times, neatly wrapping each ankle so the flap faced backward on the outside, clicking shut the locks and threading the retaining straps under them. The cuffs were made of black garment leather on the outside. The inside was lined with soft glove leather colored a dark, bloodlike red. She made a very precise business of getting the shiny stainless steel rings even, creating as much of a spectacle of the whole process as possible.

"I can see you're familiar with this type of restraint."

"They're from The Stockroom, Sir. I use them in the studio all the time."

"Doesn't surprise me," Steven said. "They are the Gucci of bondage gear."

O stood up straight, leaning back on the edge of the table with her legs planted wide apart, still on tiptoe. She seemed perfectly at ease, shaking her small-boned wrists to make sure there was just enough room in the leather circlets for her to rotate her hands if needed. Her decorum didn't waver despite Steven's deliberate distractions between her open thighs. He knees trembled a bit when he found a particularly worthwhile bulge behind her pubic bone, but O never looked up from her tasks until she was completely cuffed, the short chain locked between her wrists.

Steven didn't just enjoy having his way with women's asses for the physical sensation of it, though that was certainly a consideration. He tended to start back there by way of establishing his authority over that which was least easily surrendered.

Holding up the bulbous steel plug by its ring in front of O's face with one hand and gripping her collared throat with the other, he explained.

"I've found that once you have a girl by her ass and neck, you pretty much have her altogether."

"I agree, Sir. It certainly works that way with me."

He handed O the plug, which weighed as much as blackjack. She knew just what to do with it. Setting it down for a moment, she slipped on the black rubber gloves as if going out to the opera, making sure they were wrinkle-free all over. She held up the lube bottle.

"I.D., My favorite brand, Sir. How did you know?"

"It's a bit thicker than the silicone stuff," he said. "Most find it better for anal use."

Steven's face had taken on a stern seriousness. Much as O's cheerful mood amused him, it bordered on levity, which was not acceptable. She sensed that immediately, assumed an equally solemn demeanor and went back to work. Bracing her hands on the edge of the table, she lifted herself off the floor and settled onto the surface. It was as cold as she remembered, but it felt good after the blistering heat of the streets, intensified by her own rising internal temperature.

She was grateful to be unshod for a change so she could scoot back and plant her feet on the tabletop for balance. Half-sitting, she squeezed a big droplet of clear liquid from the bottle onto her gloved right index finger and lay back, breathing deeply as she rubbed it into the tight, pink orifice she'd been expecting to have violated in some way from their first meeting. If he wanted her to do it to herself first, she'd make the most of it.

He was such an appreciative audience she enjoyed showing off for him, a most unusual sensation. Unlike the girls she shot, O wasn't particularly exhibitionistic by nature, though she accepted that being exhibited came with the territory.

Steven watched closely as O massaged her sphincters open, first with one finger, then adding a second. She didn't rush it, displaying a tiny gape for his viewing pleasure while he casually stroked her inner thigh. He could have done something more intrusive, but he wanted this labor to be entirely her own. O treated it as such, making not a sound beyond her increasingly heavy breathing while she opened the passage for what was to come.

Grabbing the steel plug with her clean glove, O frosted the fat head of the monster with a swirl of grease and put it directly to what seemed, still, an impossibly tiny entrance. She took in a deep breath, bit her lower lip and started working it through the rings of muscle in slow circles, her wrist chains rattling, angling it this way and that until the ring at the base tilted slightly upward. One patient, unrelenting shove and the large sphere slipped in, sphincters closing behind it to clutch at the shaft. O made a guttural growl deep in her throat.

"It's rather large," Sir," she observed, regaining her breath.

"You don't expect me to be sympathetic, I hope."

"No, Sir. I want you to enjoy my discomfort as much as I do."

Steven patted her on the cheek affectionately.

"Very thoughtful," he said, smiling down at her. O finished settling the plug in place, the wide, thick steel base that kept it from going deeper up against the her so only the ring stuck out. Satisfied that she'd inserted it fully, O rolled onto a hip so Steven could watch, plucked a baby wipe from the box and dabbed away any excess lube from the edges of the steel plate with exaggerated daintiness. Then O crisply snapped off her gloves, one over the other, with the used wipe bundled within. Pushing the debris aside, she laid back down, open for business.

Steven slipped a couple of digits in O's unobstructed pussy to examine the way the bulge at the end of the plug rearranged her internal anatomy.

"Nicely packed in there, isn't it?"

"Rather delightful, actually."

Steven picked up the last remaining item, the pair of patent fetish pumps. They were as high as could practically be stood in, completely unornamented so as not to distract from their classic simplicity. Steven's fetishes were simple and elegant. He might like a rococo fountain pen, but his animalistic appetites responded only to that which improved the savor of bare flesh.

"They're your size," Steven warned, handing O the shoes. "But they're brand new and the pitch is very steep, so they might be a bit difficult to walk in at first."

"I can appreciate difficult, Sir," O said, carefully perching on the edge of the table so as not to put her weight on the plug ring. Bending over smoothly, she slipped one shoe on each foot and stood into them. Her legs were perfectly straight and her balance completely steady.

"I could probably dance in these," she said, smiling happily. "Thank you for finding such comfortable ones, Sir."

Steven cocked an eyebrow. "If I didn't know better, I'd think you were showing off."

"Certainly not, Sir," O said with wounded dignity. She shoved away from the table and did a quick circuit around it. Every motion was perfect, head high, chest out, torso straight, legs firm, steps in a smooth line so the heels hardly clicked on the bare concrete surrounding the big, red rug under the table. O's hips rolled and her ass swayed like those of a Vegas chorus girl, the shiny plug ring rocking lasciviously back and forth with each stride. She returned to stand at attention directly in front of him.

"Now that's showing off, Sir."

"I see you've done this before," Steven said.

"Not with half a pound of steel up my ass," she replied, "But I like the way holding it in exercises me back there."

"We'll see how gracefully you can walk after we have our smoke."

He sat down on the couch next to the spot where he'd laid out the towel for O, plucked the joint from the behind his ear and fired it with the huge lighter. O strolled over smoothly and stood in front of him with her hands behind her head and her legs wide apart until he motioned her to sit down. She did it carefully, very much aware of the steel ring under her. As usual, he feet were flat on the floor, separated by a few inches, and her lips were parted.

O looked straight ahead at the now inert flat screens. For all her external poise, Steven knew she was already at the boiling point inside. The rapid rise and fall of her breasts through the scrim of fabric, the dilated eyes, the visible pulse above and below the collar, the ever-spreading stains in her armpits were clear signals. Steven understood that something in O wanted to run away, but something stronger wanted to be back on her knees in front of him. That she did not run inspired a wave of lecherous tenderness.

"You know what we're going to do now?"

"Whatever you want, Sir."

"We're going to make out right here."

"Sweet."

She turned to face him and he took her in his arms, kissing her fervently while at the same time slipping a hand underneath her as she leaned into his embrace. He slipped a finger through the plug ring, working it in and out gently. O moaned, her arms wrapping his shoulders once again, the chain between her wrists dropping around the back of his neck. She tried to keep her feet down, but there was no way. Her ankles rose under her knees so she could squirm into his lap, making the most of her nakedness from the waist down. His leather pants felt deliciously smooth against her skin. Her chest rubbing against his, she buried her face in his shoulder. He held the joint in front of her face so she could smoke with him.

"Permission to touch, Sir?"

"Absolutely."

O's chained hands dropped between her open thighs as she rubbed against him, feeling the hardness under the soft leather. He let O demonstrate her dexterity, continuing to offer her puffs from the joint, for as long as he could manage, concentrating on continually adjusting the ring from below with his other hand, making her twist and pant, gripping him harder.

"That seems to work," Steven said with a smile.

"So does this," she answered, unbuttoning his trousers. There was nothing under them but him and she got her hands on the part she wanted, holding it in place so she could slip down to wrap her lips respectfully around the head.

He let her greet him properly while he took a few more hits, inhaling deeply. This was just part of the tease and he didn't let her get serious about it, bringing her up for another kiss and a shotgun hit before putting out the roach and ordering her to lie back against the arm of the couch. He told her to stretch out. The distance was perfect. Her fully extended legs were just long enough for her to stroke his inner thigh with the toe of her shoe. Letting her legs fall open, she showed him everything – her obvious wetness, the movement of the ring as she clenched around the plug inside. She stroked his rigid meat with the inside of a well-muscled calf. Steven ordered her to undue the top three buttons of her blouse. She pulled it wide open for him.

"I do think I found a better color for my nipples, Sir," she said, looking down at them.

"Your jewelry stands out against it nicely."

O couldn't help laughing.

"It stands out against everything, Sir. I have to be very careful what I wear. And sometimes I'm not."

O looked Steven daringly in the eye, her chain rattling musically when she shifted her hands from his parts to hers, careful to ask first, unlikely as it was that he'd refuse.

"I'm a very dirty girl, Sir."

"I'm shocked," he said, casually mauling O's exposed breasts.

O fluttered her eyebrows. Her tone couldn't have been more innocent, or insistent.

"But it's true, Sir. I love getting fucked. I've lost count of how many men and women have done it to me. Most of it was meaningless, but I enjoyed everything I could. I started when I was far too young, first with other girls. I even lived in secret with one of the women teachers for a whole semester. She was the first one to whip me. She was in love with me and I lied and cheated on her."

Steven played with the cuff on O's right ankle, lifting her leg by it.

"Is that why she whipped you?"

"No, no. That was just for fun. She never found out. But I certainly deserved it. I've lied and cheated on everyone who ever loved me until your brother. I deserve the worst things you could do to me, Sir."

"That is pure recklessness," he said, warning her genially with a wagging finger. "I need no provocation to do things to you. Mean things. Sick things. The better I like you, the more cruelly I'll treat you."

"You can't blame a girl for trying ... Sir."

"Actually, I think you'll be very well-behaved where I'm concerned, not that it will spare you anything. There's no point in lying to me. People do it all the time and it never works. And there's no way you can cheat on me because I'll insist you have sex with others regardless. It's just not possible to get me to do anything I don't want. I don't doubt your capabilities as a femme fatale, merely immune to them."

O looked at Steven with genuine surprise. She wasn't used to such candor and if it was intended to be reassuring, it worked. Many times she'd seen the anxiety behind Ray's attempts to charm her. If this man even had anxieties, they were unconnected to women overall and her in particular. That was a relief.

"The truth," he said with a shrug, "is that I have no inner life. You shouldn't fret about it. I certainly won't." Digging the monkey's fist key ring from his trouser pocket, he unlocked O's wrist chain with a brass key she'd never seen before. The padlocks stayed on with the cuffs. Putting away the key, he kicked back again.

"Take off the rest of your clothes. We're going for a short walk."

O finished unbuttoning her blouse, pulling the tails out of her belt and letting it slide off her shoulders. The belt went over the back of the couch. Steven stood up and signaled O to do likewise.

"Turn your back to me."

She did it. This time he pulled a small steel loop out of his pocket, brought her hands behind her back and snapped the cuffs onto the loop. His motions were quick and sure. Steven really did like working with this hands. Sliding one arm under both of hers, he squeezed them together, surprised at how easily O's elbows met in the back. Again, those slender shoulders. Snagging the ring rudely protruding from her bottom, he began walking her toward the windows as if she were a convict in some particularly perverse prison.

"Are you sure no one can see in here, Sir?"

"Yes I am. Would you care if they could?"

"I'd probably like it."

"I like bringing out the worst in you."

Despite the punishing heels, the awkward position and Steven's merciless manipulation of the bulbous steel shaft buried inside her, O walked in step with him confidently, even managing to get some through his open fly during the journey past Steven's bedroom and a long gallery wall of progressively more obscene artwork leading to the back room.

She couldn't help pausing at one she particularly liked. It was a Roman scene of a deliciously naked blonde girl spread-eagled on a horizontal frame at about waist height. Before her stood a swarthy, equally naked man with a huge erection which the frightened girl stared at helplessly. O knew what would happen next from image of a creamy, buxom redhead on the frame behind her receiving a brutal pounding from a soldier wearing only his gaudy, plumed helmet. It couldn't have felt all that bad, because the redhead's face was transported with ecstasy and she arched as high as her bonds would allow for deeper penetration.

A spectacularly statuesque domina, resplendent in a cutaway gown revealing her noble knockers, supervised the process with a long snake whip the diameter of a garden hose. The blonde probably feared that more than the other instrument with which she would soon become intimately familiar.

"Like that one?" Steven asked, swinging O around so she could inspect it. She examined it carefully, still milking and stroking with her fettered hands.

"They'll probably keep her there all day," O mused.

"They certainly would you, by popular demand."

She gave him an extra squeeze. "Sir knows what a slave loves to hear."

"If you manage to make it through today ungagged I'll be very surprised."

For her slight impertinence, he pulled up on the ring and tightened his arm around her elbows, swinging her face-front again to pass through the open steel door of the back room.

Once inside, Steven stopped so O could take a good look around. Her expression of delighted wonder reminded him of his first visit to F.A.O. Schwartz during a short trip to New York, where his father gave a lecture at the 92nd Street Y.

Back then, Steven wanted everything and could afford nothing. Now he owned everything he wanted, including the warm little package rubbing his cock against her bare backside.

"Please tell me I don't ever have to leave this room again," O said, overwhelmed by all the possibilities.

"I think that myself sometimes. When I'm done with you today you're welcome to look around and ask all the questions you want."

"Thank you, Sir. How would you like me to demonstrate my gratitude first?"

"By turning around."

Steven let go of O's arms, though not the ring, seizing her ponytail as she pirouetted to face him. Another yank tilted her face back for another long kiss. O moaned. She loved being kissed while handcuffed. If she ever felt a stirring of romantic feeling, it was during that moment.

The silk and leather were pleasant against O's nakedness, but he knew she wanted what was underneath. Pulling up on the ponytail and the plug ring, he maneuvered her in front of the mirrored wall.

"I think I'm overdressed," Steven remarked, leaving her standing at attention while he skimmed off the knit shirt and sat down on the edge of the bed to rid himself of the leather trousers. Steven turned to look at O and let her look at him in nothing but his boots.

He deliberately struck a Tom-of-Finland pose with his hands on his hips, aware of just how non-hetronormative his style might appear. On him, the boots-only look was something quite different. With his weathered face and battle-scarred physique, he was like a gladiator, or something that lived in the darkest chamber of The Tower of London. O's knees buckled and she sank to the floor, rubbing her face against his leather-sheathed calves, looking up at him imploringly.

"Please let me kiss the soles, Sir," she begged. He lifted them one at a time and let her apply her lips to the smooth leather surfaces, which were as immaculate as objects of worship should be. O's fetish for boots duly noted, Steven had every intention of letting her worship them at length. First, however, he had some magic to perform.

Taking a red vinyl cushion shaped to conform to a petite pair of buttocks from a low shelf at the head of the bondage bed, he placed it squarely in the middle of the bed's black rubberized surface. Lifting another key from the railing around the tall cart along with the water bottle, he returned to where O knelt stock-still, watching him.

"Thirsty?'

"Sir knows my mouth gets dry when I smoke pot and other parts of me get wet."

"Try again."

"Please Sir, may I have some water?"

"Much better."

Steven took a large gulp from the bottle and leaned down over O's face. She opened her mouth so he could spit the water down her throat. She only lost a few drops out the corners of her lips when she swallowed it.

"One more please, Sir?"

He did it again, knowing she tasted his saliva along with the cold water.

"Thank you, Sir," O said, coughing a little from the sudden flood. Slipping behind her, he freed her wrists, tossing the steel ring aside and nodding toward the bed.

"Go lie down over there. Settle your tail just off the edge of the cushion."

Still very aware of the invasive ringed plug, O started by sitting carefully on the cushion, one bottom cheek in each hollow, then lowered her shoulders and stretched out her arms and legs. He had positioned her just high enough so she could turn her hands over and grab the edge if she had to. O was acutely aware of what parts of her were most visible in this position. Moving around her, Steven locked both of O's wrist cuffs and one of her ankle cuffs to the short chains at the head and foot of the massive altar. Looking over at the mirrored wall, O could see just how sacrificial she appeared.

"I look good on black," O observed.

Steven agreed. He sat on the bed between her legs, lifting her unrestrained ankle and teasing her with the plug ring. "Wonder why I left this one loose?" Steven asked.

"For my more convenient use," O answered, lifting it out of his hand and touching his chest with a potentially lethal heel. Steven smiled, raising O's loose leg and pushing it back toward her chest.

"And it provides excellent visibility this way," he explained, directing her attention back to the mirror. She was certainly as splayed as she'd ever been.

"I think you're going to like this. I know I will," he said, flipping on the small vacuum pump atop the larger cart. It whirred to life, chugging like a model railroad engine. From the rack of clear cylinders, Steven chose a large one, about four inches in diameter, snapping it onto the end of the long, clear plastic tube draped over the vacuum gauge. Taking the cylinder in one hand and a remote control with a single button and a long cord in the other, he stretched out alongside O and put the remote in her right hand.

Hold that," he instructed her, casually stroking her stretched body with a confident hand, pausing to tweak her big rings.

"We'll need you a bit wetter to start," he said.

"I'm not sure that's possible," O replied, sincerely wondering. That was before he went down on her. Her head lolled to one side and she bit her lip. Just like before, she was amazed at how a big, barrel-chested man so accustomed to satisfying his own wants could lavish such bliss on parts of her that until now only lesbians seemed able to find. He took his time with it too, leaving her to wonder when the pump would come into play. As a final touch, he took a dab of silicone lube from the black bottle on the tall cart and swirled it around O's by now very hard clit.

"You're quite pretty down here," Steven noted, as if looking at a fresh-cut flower.

"Thank you, Sir. I think it's one of my better angles."

He reached up and swatted her across the tits hard enough to sting.

"That gag is definitely on the schedule. Now here's how this works."

Very carefully, Steven placed the open end of the cylinder over O's wet membranes. She felt a slight suction immediately as her tissues rose inside the clear plastic. It was a subtle sensation, enhanced by the pump's vibrations.

"Now, tap the red button."

It was somewhat odd, controlling this device with chained hands. But when O pushed as ordered, she nearly lifted off the table, letting out a yelp of surprise. It didn't hurt, but the pump was more powerful than it looked.

"I told you to tap it, not smash it down. Try depressing it slowly. The harder you push, the more powerful the suction."

O was more careful this time, slowly pressing more firmly as the sensation went from mildly stimulating to intensely erotic to downright painful. She held it at exactly the point of maximum endurance.

Steven smiled down on her.

"I knew you'd hurt yourself with this thing. I want you to, but not so it can't stay on for at least ten minutes. If you move your finger on and off the button, you'll find the pump sucks at you more politely."

He was right about that. The intermittent vacuum was like getting cunnilingus from a giant mouth.

Steven cocked her free leg back and told O to check out the mirror.

It was a shocking sight. O's gleaming pink surfaces rose almost three inches up the cylinder, obscenely expanded against its clear walls as if turning her inside out.

"That's amazing," she said breathlessly. Steven hacked time on a nautical clock mounted to the far wall.

"Ten minutes, starting now. I want you to torture yourself with it. Just don't damage anything I'll want later."

With that, Steven made himself comfortable next to O while she worked the red button, pushing it down further and holding it longer each time. He caressed her heaving chest, toyed with her big nipple rings, and stroked her hair. She felt his hard shaft rubbing casually against her leg. Through the haze of sensation, O realized that he was treating her very tenderly.

"Am I doing this right, Sir?" O asked a bit tentatively.

"You suffer quite adorably."

Gently pinching her nostrils shut so she could only take in air from him, Steven kissed her for a long time, noticing that O now had the button fully depressed, the cylinder filled with shiny, dark-crimson girl meat.

When he let go of her nose, her eyelids rolled back and she stared into his face, seeing nothing but affection.

"That's right," he said in answer to her unspoken question, "the more you hurt, the more lovable I'll find you."

O felt herself inching toward climax, but that word "lovable" was a bit alarming. She told herself he meant it in the casual sense, as opposed to something she didn't care to imagine.

"It does hurt, Sir," She said, her eyelids half-closed, "but not in a bad way."

"I think you'll appreciate the after-effects," he said, sliding off the bed to retrieve a hand mirror from the pegboard. O never ceased to be amazed at his perpendicularity even when attending to some minor task. She suspected he did something to keep himself that way, but she didn't care. Every hard cock was a validation to her and she needed only the evidence, not the motive.

On the way back, he consulted the clock, surprised as always at how quickly the ten minutes went by, and told her to let go of the button. The cylinder came off with a wet pop and when O saw her most private anatomy in Steven's hand mirror, she gasped. Everything down there was swollen to twice its natural size. Red and shiny like a just washed apple, she lay open as if freshly sliced.

"If you think it looks tender, wait until you feel it."

Again he lowered his face between her thighs, sucking in all that newly distended flesh between his lips. O twisted in her chains, neither willing nor able to escape his focused attentions. His occasional tugs on the ring protruding from O's bottom added new sensations to the intoxicating mix. Something was going to happen soon, one way or another.

Steven had done this often enough to know when that point was reached. O's tightening sinews and waves of shudders gave her away. She was easy indeed. Steven preferred the susceptible ones.

Certain of the moment, he hoisted himself over O's small body, easily sliding into her with no hands as he lowered his weight carefully on top of her. He took his time getting in until she was completely full, packed front and rear, unable to influence his slow, revolving, pistoning penetrations even if she'd wanted to. She almost certainly did not. "Like being fucked in both holes at once, isn't it?" he asked, grinning down at her.

Not unfamiliar with that sensation, O agreed it was similar, but this was really better. The pump had sensitized her to the friction of every stroke and each full insertion depressed the steel bulge back into her ass in the rudest way. When Steven started to speed up, she knew she wouldn't be able to hold out long and so did he.

"Sir, please Sir. Begging permission to come," O gasped.

"There'll be a price for it."

O whimpered. She had assumed that but it didn't matter now.

"Please, Sir. Whatever you want to do to me after."

"Fair enough."

Steven slammed into her harder and faster. Wrapping one hand around her throat, he supported himself on the other so he could look down into her scarlet face. O wheezed and sputtered at the light choking, but went completely rigid from head to toe, grinding her pelvis, one of the few still mobile components of her frame, against him. She tossed her head back and forth, screaming louder than might be expected for such a small woman. Steven had long ago learned that when it came to volume, physical size didn't count. He didn't mind. There were no neighbors to complain.

At the summit, Steven stopped still, letting O clutch at him from the inside. She was strong in there. If he weren't so hard, she might have pushed him out, but buried deep with his entire body weight behind him, he had her pinned like a butterfly. He could feel the oily sweat ooze from O's smooth surfaces as the spasms finally quieted.

"I'll bet I could get another one out of you right away."

"Probably, Sir," O panted.

"Now about that gag..."

When Steven approached her face with the red ball and strap, O automatically lifted her head so he could buckle it behind her collar and positioned the rubber sphere in back of her teeth. It shaped her lips in a perfect circle. The red was a good match for their color. Back on top, Steven kissed her affectionately over and around the gag. She couldn't kiss him back and he couldn't get his tongue past the barrier, but that made it sweeter somehow.

He did as promised, entering her more abruptly this time in a single, solid stroke. Pounding harder and faster than before, he took her right to the peak and pushed her over. This time she lay completely limp under him, her sopping ball-gag against his cheek, her breath coming in short gusts from flaring nostrils.

"You'll be more sensitive to pain now," he observed calmly. "Women can take a lot when highly aroused, but they're more vulnerable during their refractory periods. Lift your head. I want to hear you scream."

The gag came out with a wet pop, spraying a mist of spit. It was a good thing O didn't mind getting messy, because Steven was the type to get her that way. He stroked the faint impressions the gag straps left on her cheeks.

"I get the feeling you've done this before, Sir."

No reason not to tease him a bit. O was going to be hurt anyway. Better to hang for a wolf than a sheep.

Steven depressed a lever, lowering the suspension bar. Most electric hoists made nasty grinding noises, but this one was nearly silent as the bar dropped to what Steven guessed would be an appropriate height. Padded straps already waved from either end.

Steven unchained O from the bed, sat her up slowly, holding and kissing her until he was confident the dizziness had faded.

"Ready to stand up now?"

"Do I have to keep my shoes on, Sir?"

Steven thought about it a moment.

"Actually, I think I want them off."

O reached down and slipped the pumps from her feet, standing then neatly side-by-side. Steven helped her up gently but she was still a bit woozy.

"Get moving, indolent whore," he said in a friendly way. Like his brother, Steven didn't curse or hurl insults. O had had more than her share of barking doms. There was no hint of anger in anything he did, just pure sadistic enjoyment and gratitude for the woman who provided it.

Steven never stopped smiling, still keeping those predator's teeth on display. He was fully in the moment, enjoying everything: from the rising smell of sweat and sex on O's body, to the way she came up on her pedicured toes, however unsteadily, as soon as he got her vertical. She walked with surprising grace to stand under the suspension bar. He held her close, lifting her arms so her still-cuffed hands could slide into the padded straps, which he buckled just tight enough so she'd feel secure.

"Grab hold," he instructed. Her grip closed on the leather. It was soft but strong, made of many layers. How much had Steven invested in all these things? How long had it taken him to create this luxury torture chamber? Had he built all this himself? She was prepared to believe it.

Satisfied that she wouldn't slip free, Steven went to the controls on the wall-mounted hoist and slowly took her up until she was stretched taut, taking just enough weight on the balls of her feet to keep her arms from hurting. O's high arches would eventually cramp from the position, but that was part of it. If everything felt good, there would be no contrast and she needed that contrast. Seeing him select a whip from the wall, she knew the contrast was coming.

Steven slung the short, thick single-tail, beautifully woven in red and black with a feathered end, over his shoulder. In her hyper-extended pose, O could only respond with her mouth when he kissed her. He held her tight for a moment. Then he took hold of her nipple rings and pulled up, making her dance in a circle like a marionette. O squealed at this, but the squeal sank to a sigh when he massaged her nipples and rubbed his hardness against her lower belly, now dripping with perspiration and lube. There was that mysterious tender feeling again. It made her a little uncomfortable, but she thought she could get used to it.

Steven didn't worry about anything when he was in the midst of a session. He trusted his instincts not to let him go too far in any one direction. It was instinct that inspired him to go from kissing O to slapping her face and body. She could do nothing to shield herself or pull away and the slaps were firm. O, however, was tough and she wanted Steven to know it.

"I don't mind being punched, Sir."

"Is that a suggestion?"

"I wouldn't presume. But I do seem well disposed for it."

True enough. Steven took a step back and gave her two quick, light blows with his closed fist on her tight belly, leaving pink knuckle prints. O sucked air, but couldn't move a muscle. It was rather tempting. He gave her two more, one on each breast, and then two more, reaching around to strike her butt-cheeks. O whimpered and whined, but when he grabbed her between the legs, she was dripping.

"Isn't violence lovely?" he asked.

She smiled warmly at him and said he was a beautiful monster.

Steven bowed with an elaborate flourish at the compliment. Dragging the whip from his shoulder, he casually flipped it up in the air to straighten it.

"Will it cut me?" O asked. Scars were one of her few hard limits.

"No. The split ends dull it. But you will feel it."

Steven circled her like a matador, picking his targets. O's hard, little butt seemed the right place to start. The leather swished through the air, the feathered end connecting with a sharp report. O twitched, but that was all she could do. Steven concentrated his attention back there for a bit, alternating sides as always, laying on neat, straight stripes. Just for fun, he gently wrapped her a couple of times, bringing the tails up on her belly. Gradually, he worked his way north toward her shoulders. He was never sure why, but many women found the space between their scapulae erogenous. Sure enough, O moaned and did her best to round her shoulders and present a better target. She was bright red there before Steven moved to the front.

"I like that whip," she said, after he kissed her. "It feels just right."

"It's one of my favorites," Steven agreed. He went to work on the front of O's body. It was a trickier business, especially with the need to avoid snagging her nipple rings. To get the whip high enough to strike O's breasts without hitting her face required careful placement, but all that saber fencing paid off in this room. Soon O's tits were also striped, along with her belly. She tried to remain still so as not to mess up his aim, but when he snapped the tips up between her legs, she couldn't help twisting and lifting a knee. Very quickly, she recovered, turned back around and thrust out her hips, daring him.

Steven never resisted such dares. Coiling the single-tail, he smacked at her still-engorged pinkness, making her dance involuntarily. Each time she went out of position, she quickly turned back to present again. Steven smiled.

"I think we need something more specialized for this."

From one of the baskets, he took a short, black crop with a twisted wood handle and a loose flap. He held it up in front of O's face for a good look.

"Hermés?"

"How did you know?"

"The twisted shaft."

"Of course."

He smacked her lightly on the cheek with it. She made a purring sound.

"That feels nice."

"It will feel even nicer here."

He swung it up to catch her crotch with the flap. O gave a little jerk of surprise, but she smiled.

"You're right. Thank you, Sir."

He slapped her most fragile spots with it, and not lightly either. O gasped with each blow but held very still. Steven could easily read her mind. Yes, she would feel all that attention when he fucked her next, which would be soon.

Returning the whip to its place, he came back to take O in his arms.

"Do your feet hurt?

"They're starting to."

He slipped the toes of his boots under her aching arches so she could put her weight down on them. She sighed, falling in against his solid mass of body weight as much as the restraints allowed.

"You know I'm going to cane them next."

"I thought you might, Sir."

"Then I'm going to cane your ass and fuck it."

"Please, yes, Sir. I've been waiting for that. But if you're going to fuck me there, it would be very generous of you to let me pee first so I don't lose control when I come."

Steven looked down into her face with wicked glee.

"Do you really need to pee?

"Yes, Sir. I really do."

"I'm not convinced."

O knew this game well. She looked desperately into his eyes, made her most pleading face.

"Oh please, Sir. Please let me pee. I need to go so bad."

She even crossed her legs as if trying to hold it in.

"Bravo. A splendid performance. Would melt the heart of a statue."

He reached up and freed her from the suspension straps, but rather than letting her sink into his arms, he took her under the collar and made her stay on tiptoe as he led her over to the floor drain.

"You can squat down right here," he told her, "legs open please."

O couldn't contain a scornful look.

"I do know how to piss like a proper slave, Sir."

Lowering herself over the drain, she stayed up on her aching arches and spread her knees wide. O had done this and worse in front of so many men and women it had lost all shame for her and become rather amusing. She looked up at his cock, hovering just inches over her lips.

"May I suck you while I do it?"

"Of course. I expect it when I'm so generous with you."

"I'll remember that, Sir."

Taking the head in her mouth, O easily let go a surging stream from between her legs with no inhibitions at all, tinkling musically on the steel strainer over the hole in the floor. Deftly holding her balance, she lifted her head just enough to take him in her mouth, concentrating on the head and corona while emptying her bladder as noisily as possible. Steven could certainly have enjoyed her labors for longer, but his ability to stick to the plan despite pleasant distractions was essential to how he operated. He withdrew and squatted down to kiss her while she squeezed out the remaining drops into the drain. She looked him right in the eye, completely unabashed.

"Might I have a wipe, Sir?"

He brought one over from the cart and held O by the throat while she blotted, then led her over so she could drop the wipe in the kick bucket.

"You really are such a naughty thing," he said cheerfully.

"Very naughty, Sir. Even you might be surprised."

"I look forward to that."

Steven walked O back to the bed, once again controlling her by the rings on her collar and the base of the steel shaft continually invading her from behind.

He positioned her on all fours, parallel to the mirror, pressed her shoulders down until her breasts and face rested on the surface.

"Look in the mirror."

O glanced over, studied her position a moment or two.

"Always like this?" she asked.

"Yes. Always like this."

From the other basket he brought out a thin, rattan cane, the thing O dreaded and treasured the most. He stroked her back with it, tracing the tip down to her tail bone.

The impacts on O's backside came precisely spaced at ten-second intervals. He didn't spare the rod. It bit deep each time, laying rows of double welts over the now pink curvature of O's ass, top to bottom. She held perfectly still, though these strokes were like lightning bolts compared to the comforting splat of the crop. This was quality pain. She'd had little enough of it to know how rare it was.

After ten stripes to each buttock, he saved five more for each of her feet, which he ordered her to raise. It was very trying, keeping them elevated as the cane seared her aching arches, but that was the point. Something good was coming soon. By contrast, it would be even better.

O kept her head down, but she heard the mean stick drop back in its basket, felt Steven's weight on the bed next to her.

"It's time to show your appreciation."

O looked over and smiled at him in the mirror.

"Ah yes, something at which I excel."

O slid off the bed onto the floor and crawled over to where Steven sat on the edge. Starting at his boots, she worked her way up, stroking and kissing, until she could get her mouth over the top of his upright stalk.

She was all business about it, taking him right to the back of her throat, holding him there until she choked, then easing off to suck at the head, swirling her small skull under his hand. She felt him rest his boot across her back. Clearly, this was not to be hurried by either of them.

O was very quiet in her labors. This wasn't about her and that's why she liked doing it so much. From the moment he went in, his cock never left her wet, hot mouth. She could swallow it whole and slide back out to the very tip without letting it drop for an instant. Buried to its full depth in her gullet, she could still swirl her tongue out from underneath to lick some sweat. O loved the taste of male excitement. When she rolled her eyes up at him, mouth stuffed, he could see the blazing heat behind them. As promised, she excelled.

Steven knew she would happily have had him finish there, but when he felt there was a danger of that happening he pulled her off by her ponytail.

"That's delightful," he said. "However, there is one more item on the menu.

O knew what that would be. He ordered her to climb back up and kneel next to him. She did it with her knees curled under. He handed her gloves and a baby wipe from the cart.

"Take the plug out now, please. I have other uses for that hole."

"Of course, Sir," O said. "No girl is really a slave until she's given her ass to her Master."

"Well put."

While O gloved up, Steven wrapped himself around her, wanting to fully share in this moment of dirty intimacy. O understood completely, nuzzling into his chest while slowly withdrawing the steel bulb from her depths. It emerged with a wet pop, accompanied by a small squeal. That thing really was big. She dropped it into the kick bucket next to the bed with a loud clang, throwing her gloves in after.

"How does Sir want me?"

"In the traditional manner."

O composed herself on the bed, facing the mirror in front of the window and neatly aligned with the one on the wall so she could be viewed from every angle. Crossing her hands on the bed, she lowered her face to them and lifted her other end as high as possible. Every movement was beautiful and graceful. Every day in the studio O was reminded of the importance of presentation.

Stroking O's back, Steven watched her relax around her newly unblocked orifice, which gaped slightly from lengthy packing. The heavy steel had worked well to open the channel.

Taking a blue-lidded plastic bottle of water-based gel from the table, Steven squeezed some out onto his fingertips, rubbing it into the outer rings of O's flexing muscles. They yielded to his touch easily. She was no stranger to this use.

Still, he wanted her to want it as he did, to crave it. With his clean hand, he gave her the vibrator from the cart.

"You have permission to use this at any time," he told her.

"Thank you, Sir. I may need it for the second one."

With that, Steven put another squirt of lube on himself and took careful aim at the tiny target, slipping in a millimeter at a time, feeling O's tightest passage give way to him. She sighed, her whole body seeming to go soft and floppy around the rigid object invading it.

Steven had done this with many, many women over many, many years. Though most enjoyed it thoroughly, he'd never found one so completely accommodating before. O truly loved it. She loved it because it was wrong and dirty and sometimes hurt. She loved it because she was more sensitive there than anyplace on her body. She loved it because it was so inherently violative.

Her list of reasons wasn't much different from Steven's.

He slid in and out of her slowly, rotating in lazy circles, holding her fast against him with an iron grasp around her hips. Soon, instead of moving in and out, he started sliding her back and forth while remaining stationary, impaling her repeatedly. She'd been silent up to that point, but her breathing grew steadily heavier and she gave a low, guttural growl, more animal than human.

The first climax swept over O without warning. She froze, back rising, every muscle tensed inside and out, and howled for permission, which Steven was pleased to grant. At that point, it wouldn't have mattered one way or the other. Once again, her entire body seemed to contract around the point of entry. He'd never felt anything quite like it and he wanted to feel it as often as possible.

This time, as soon as O's spasms ceased he started pounding into her. O groped around for the vibrator, got it up under her and flipped it on, first to the low speed, then rocking the switch back to crank it up. Steven could feel how hard she ground it against her pubic bone.

Looking down at her, back, ass and legs shining with sweat and lube, covered in stripes and splotches, he hammered her mercilessly. O cried out, jamming the vibrator against her as hard as she could. Steven felt the internal rippling again, slid out almost to the point of exiting, then slowly pushed all the way into O, coming in waves, a contraction at each stopping point. O knew she would never tire of the way Steven did that. O shut off the vibrator and dropped it as Steven's hot spurts poured out of him and into her.

O made a purring sound deep in her throat. She knew he would make his demands without hesitation. That was how she liked to be treated and, at last, she'd found a man who was fine with it. When Ray had her like this he always seemed worried about hurting her, which he frequently did, and sometimes had trouble getting off. Whatever his faults – O suspected they were as big as the rest of his personality – Steven didn't have those problems.

Returning to earth, Steven found a wipe to hold under O and slipped out of carefully, making sure nothing dripped where it shouldn't. Knowing how clean she was inside, she would gladly have sucked out a few last drops. She'd make sure he knew that before next time. Limbs quivering, she sank to the bed flat on her belly. Steven lay down next to her and turned her on her side, enfolding her in a long embrace.

"You're awfully good at that," he said.

"You did all the heavy lifting, Sir."

He kissed her for a long time before finally rolling over and pulling her half on top of him.

"I don't know about you, but I'm hungry."

O laughed. "Shall I check out your fabulous kitchen and see if I can find you something for dinner, Sir?

"I've already made plans, but I like the thought of you working in the kitchen. Shower before eating?"

"With your permission."

"I can get you messy again later if I want."

Steven gently helped O up off the bed, sticky and sweaty and shaky as they both were.

"I'll teach you how to clean everything up later," Steven said, noting O's knitted brows as she surveyed the shambles they'd made of the room.

"There's something I want to do right away if Sir will allow."

"I wonder what that might be."

"I'll be right back."

O scampered out of the room on tiptoe, her movements light as a dancer's. She was back in a moment, a smaller point-and-shoot version of the Leica in her hands.

Steven watched O make her way around, shooting photos of all the evidence: the discarded whips, the loose chains, her shoes still standing at attention, Steven's abandoned clothes, the contents of the kick bucket, the machinery on the carts with its tubes and wires snaking down, a close-up of the smeared plastic dome used to make her swell up.

Steven was fascinated by the methodical way she went about it. He'd seen police photographers cover crime scenes far less diligently. O explained that she intended to make a book of such images one day.

"I used to shoot the debris whenever Ray and I played but I sort of got out of the habit."

"Glad to have inspired you again."

O went to the mirror last, shooting her striped and stained body from the front first, then turning around and handing the camera to Steven. She was still covered in lines and splashes of red like a living Jackson Pollack.

Steven framed her head to foot before moving in for a few close-ups of her crimson tail feathers, where he considered his work the neatest.

"Bend over."

O grabbed her ankles so he could document her swollen, still slightly ajar entrances.

"Thank you, Sir," she said, taking the camera back. "I think we may be starting a new phase in my project."

"Those cane strokes are really going to sting under hot water."

"I'll be sure to turn up the pressure."

O picked up her shoes and sat carefully down on the edge of the bed to slip into them.

"I like a girl who puts her shoes on first."

"I do it that way even when nobody's watching."

Steven unlocked and removed her collar. O took her camera and strode off down the hall, Steven watching her sway gracefully in her impossible heels. Steven weighed the smudged collar in his hand. Ray had brought him something wonderful.

CHAPTER EIGHT

Half an hour later, following a quick scrub in the black marble vault of his own shower, Steven stood at the phone in the kitchen, speaking rapidly in Japanese as O emerged from the guest bathroom, her hair turbaned once more. She was back in her pumps. Steven wondered if O was insecure about her height. O's collar, wiped clean inside and out, sat on the counter next to him. She knelt on the hard sealed-concrete floor for it while he held the phone crooked in his shoulder to finish the order. He hung up and clicked the lock shut.

"*Arigato*," O said with a slight bow when she stood to face him.

"*Do-itashi mashite*." Steven returned her bow.

"When did you learn to speak Japanese?" O asked.

"I was stationed in Tokyo for a year during my Navy hitch. I met a future client who advised me to keep working on it so we could stay in touch. You?"

"I just know a few words. I worked with Nobuyashi Araki on some magazine stuff there."

"That must have been fun."

"He's friends with everybody. Got to meet all kinds of interesting people."

"Dinner should be here in a few minutes. Need a robe?"

"Not unless you want me to cover up. You always keep it so nice and warm in here."

"Much as I enjoy dressing up to go out, at home I prefer nudity-inducing warmth."

O circled Steven's forehead with an index finger.

"The wheels never stop turning in there, do they?"

"I try to raise the probability of a desired outcome. Be a good slave and set the table for us."

"*Hai, Sensei!*"

O headed for the cabinets over the sink.

"The sushi stuff is in the third one on the left."

It was all there, covered bowls for miso soup, authentic rectangular plates with sushi menus printed on them, a roll of sterling silver chopsticks and a pile of straw place mats. O gathered it all up, putting two place settings at the end of the table nearest the kitchen. Steven watched her movements with continuing fascination. Unlike most modern women, O was constantly aware of her visibility.

"Sir, if I may ask," she said, straightening out the chopsticks on the black linen napkins, "why don't you have a cook?"

"For the same reason I don't have a butler, a driver or a junior partner. People are the most expensive luxuries and sooner or later they all fuck up. I have a discreet cleaning service that comes in three days a week, a bunch of restaurants that will put anything I want in a cab, and a first-rate surveillance system backed by armed guards to provide perimeter security."

"Not very trusting, are you?"

"If you did what I do for a living, you wouldn't be either."

"What makes you think I am?"

Steven pondered that one for a moment, but the ringing of the phone interrupted him. It was the guard from downstairs. Dinner had arrived.

"That was quick," O said, amazed.

"Go find me a robe."

O proved she just how quickly she could move in high heels as she darted toward Steven's dressing room. She stopped short with a gasp. She'd seen luxury, and even excess, many times, but nothing quite measured up to the splendor of Steven's closet. It was the Taj Mahal of closets. The Versailles of closets. O could have spent a week just looking through it in fascination, but she had an urgent mission to complete. Steven needed a robe. It didn't take long to find the right section of hanging bars, but which robe? There were at least a dozen of them. The choice was obvious: a long, black-and-white silk kimono decorated with twin richly embroidered dragons. She fetched it back to him just in time for the knock on the door.

Steven slipped on the robe and told O to stay just where she was, clearly visible from the elevator hall. This would be interesting. Steven opened the door to a stylish young Japanese woman in a black shirt and black jeans. Steven greeted her in Japanese and she replied likewise, handing him two large, white bags in return for a pile of cash Steven took from a red alligator wallet sitting out on the counter.

The woman looked at O with frank curiosity, doubtless noticing O's marks, bowed but didn't speak to her. She smiled at them both when Steven made his farewells, backing toward the elevator with an even deeper bow.

"Am I mistaken, Sir, or did you just exhibit me to a non-consenting stranger?" O asked, taking the bags into the kitchen to unload.

"Ayako?" Steven laughed. "She used to hostess at a club in Osaka for my friend Nakagawa-san. He owns the restaurant where she works here. I'm sure she's laughing in the elevator now."

"I enjoyed it. It's very humbling to be treated as a decorative object."

As always, Steven watched O's movements with fascination as she set everything out on the table. The long row of sushi bites was neatly arrayed on a narrow ceramic tray. The hot appetizers got round platters and the steaming bowls of miso soup were set on the straw mats.

Steven fetched a towel from the bathroom, tossing it over O's chair so she wouldn't have to sit her bare bottom, which was still quite red, on the cold, hard aluminum chair.

"Bare metal is fine for me if you want to see me sit up very straight," O offered. "Or I can be on the floor at your feet if you prefer. You can feed me as you see fit."

"We'll never make it through dinner that way," he replied. "Beer or sake?"

"What can I get you, Sir?"

"Beer is my usual."

"Duly noted."

O took two small, chilled glasses from the freezer, where there were several sizes and shapes from which to choose, then broke out a tall Kirin from the lower compartment.

Steven sat down with his back to the window so O could enjoy the lit-up cityscape he saw every night. He casually stroked her between the legs when she bent at the waist to pour his drink. She didn't spill a drop.

"Such a pretty *manko*," Steven said, deliberately using the vulgar word for O's intimate anatomy. She thanked, him in Japanese, using the more lady-like *manka*, slyly asking if Master was referring to just the part of her he was touching or to all of her. He assured her he meant both. They laughed and O sat down on the covered chair.

They tore into the split soft-shell crab and gyoza while they waited for the clam miso soup to cool.

"These are fantastic," O exclaimed, chomping into half a crab with that same absence of affected manners Steven had noticed in the restaurant. There was a proper protocol for everything. For dining naked with her Master, it was lusty and shameless. She even kicked off a shoe and casually slipped her small, soft, warm foot under his robe to keep him entertained while he enjoyed his appetizer. She had to slouch down a bit to do it, making the effect even more lewd.

"You let me get away with a lot, Sir."

"It's fun to see you like this."

"Looking like I do in the world of erotic photography I have to be pretty schoolmarmish most of the time. I don't need to be that person with you."

"How about with Ray?"

O thought it over.

"I can be playful with him too, but it's different. He's kind of like that with everyone."

"I'm envious of Ray's cool-dudeness."

"I liked it at first, but now it annoys me sometimes. I don't really like being the grown-up wherever we go."

"It can be draining," Steven said with a sigh, yanking a clam from its shell deftly with the silver chopsticks.

"I make his world into such a child-safe day nursery he never really had to grow up."

"Why do you do it?"

"Maybe I give him too little credit."

O shrugged.

"Sometimes I think I give him too much. But I'd never have had the confidence to shoot what I do now if he hadn't encouraged me."

"Can't fault his judgment there," Steven conceded. "He was right about what you could do for the magazine."

"So why won't you let him try an online version?"

"How did we get around to talking business here?" Steven adroitly snatched a slice of dark red tuna off the long platter. O looked at it disapprovingly, causing Steven to pause with the morsel balanced precariously in mid-air.

"What?"

"Is that Bluefin?" she demanded.

Steven looked at it.

"I hope so. They charge enough for it."

O leaned forward, fixing him with a steely glare.

"You know they'll all be gone within a few years."

He shrugged.

"This one's gone already."

He popped it in his mouth, eyes rolling with gustatory delight.

"God, that's delicious. Want one?"

O continued glaring.

"Doesn't it bother you that your money is helping destroy the oceans?"

"I give ten thousand bucks to Greenpeace every year. I think that entitles me to a couple of pieces of endangered fish that were already on ice before I got to them. If the Bluefin fishermen had to depend on me, they'd all be dry-docked by now. Here, have my other bite."

He extended it to O on the end of his chopsticks. After a brief hesitation, she took it. Instantly, her scowl was replaced by a swoony expression.

"See?" Steven said. "We eat what tastes good. I'm not prepared to live in a yurt subsisting on goat's milk in the name of virtue. What do you think cameras are made from? Plastics, toxic metals hand-mined by ten-year-olds in Nigeria, the labor of sweatshops in China, that's what. So how about it, O, shall we share a yurt together?"

"I'd probably enjoy it. You'd beat me daily like a good barbarian."

"Personally, I'd rather vacation in a suite at The Ritz."

Steven tried to top off his glass but O snatched the big, brown bottle from his hand with lightning speed, pouring for him.

"*Sensei* isn't supposed to fill his own glass," she said.

"*Gomen nasai.*"

Finished, O pushed her plate aside, came around to sit on the table next to Steven. She held out her hand for his chopsticks, which he surrendered without protest, and began feeding him the remaining bites of sushi, one at a time, patiently waiting for him to swallow in between.

"You never answered my question, Sir," she said a bit sternly.

"About an online edition of *Forbidden*? Ray plant that in your pretty head?"

O looked fleetingly offended.

"No Sir. I planted it in his. Print publishing is a dead end. Our long-term market is on the Internet. I've used all my persuasive tactics to get him interested in the idea and it seems to have worked."

"Why does that not surprise me? I'm just not sure you've harnessed your powers for the cause of good. We're getting fifteen bucks a copy for *Forbidden* now. And because we restrict supplies so they don't quite meet demand, we charge half of cover to retailers. Every single issue sells out because it's a beautiful, rare thing pervs want to own. You think we can clear six bucks on a download version any thieving weasel can find for free on Google once the torrent sites get hold of it?"

"Albert knows this really smart kid, Sir. He thinks he can build a platform for it that would actually attract subscribers. It couldn't hurt to talk with him at least ... Sir."

Steven seized O by the right nipple ring and pulled her down to kiss him.

"When you go back," he said evenly, "tell Ray he's not to use you for pitching purposes. If he has any ideas he thinks I'd consider, he can call me himself during office hours."

He gave O's ring a mean twist. She yelped.

"Yes, Sir!"

When he let her go, she rubbed the offended nipple tenderly.

"Ray didn't ask me to bring it up with you, Sir."

"I trust your curiosity is satisfied. Clear the table. Rinse the dishes. Put everything in the sink."

Finished cleaning up, O knelt beside Steven's chair, her head down.

"Slave offers herself for punishment if she pissed Sir off by talking business when she shouldn't have."

Steven turned to take her face in his hands.

"I don't mind talking business with you. Unlike my brother, you might have a head for it."

He lifted O under the arms, shoved his chair back and planted her in his lap.

"Don't ever worry about displeasing me," he told her. "I won't let you."

O's face brightened. "I like that idea very much, Sir. It makes me feel safe." O nuzzled Steven's face, smiling her naughty girl smile. "Would Sir like to see a preview of my next set for the magazine? I brought it along just in case."

"I'd love to!" he said, giving her a squeeze around the ribcage. "I'm you're biggest fan."

Squirming lasciviously in his lap, she felt the expected response almost immediately.

"You're my hardest fan," O sad, reaching under herself to give him a squeeze.

"Pictures."

She let go, jumped off Steven's lap and hustled over to her handbag where she fished out a thumb drive from her handbag. It was entirely paved in red Swarovksi crystal rhinestones. Steven admired it in his hand.

"Only you would have something like this."

"That's just what I thought when I bought it."

He took her by the wrist and started for the front door.

"Where are we going, Sir?"

"The office. There's no one up here and it will give the guys at the security monitors a thrill."

O didn't have time to express her concerns before they were out by the elevators and headed toward the glass doors opposite. Steven tapped the keypad. The small waiting room lit up as they entered.

"I've never been naked in a lawyer's office before," O said, still a little nervous.

"That speaks well of your prior counsel. You know the one thing slaves are absolutely forbidden is modesty. I'd assumed they'd taught you that at the Mansion."

O bristled.

"I was never accused of it ... Sir."

Steven led her to his private chambers and dialed up the dimmer switch. The view through the east windows of downtown glittering so nearby was truly magical, the more so for the round-sided chairs and other relics of Old Hollywood Elegance.

"Permission to look around, Sir?" O asked, already doing it while Steven pressed some buttons that opened the top of his desk so his Mac could rise from within.

O had been in the offices of many rich and powerful men. That was where they really lived and there was much revealed in them to the practiced eye. A giant world map, dry marked with major drug trafficking routes, covered one wall. The Trophy Wall was opposite.

They all had them, these mini-monuments to minor achievements, but some of Steven's weren't so minor. The certificates told quite a story. There was one certifying him to practice before The Supreme Court, and something similar from The International Criminal Court at The Hague. There were three citations from the Navy for his JAG service, letters of thanks from Amnesty International and The Southern Poverty Law Center and an award from *The Harvard Law Review*. There were multiple diplomas, including a JD from Loyola Marymount and an honorary doctorate from The University of the Americas in Mexico City. There was also his round, glass case of fencing trophies, of course. He'd made certain his clients knew they were paying for a seasoned mercenary.

The framed photographs told a slightly different story. Always smiling, Steven's big arm draped the shoulders of grafting politicians, movie-star murderers, rocker dudes wearing shades indoors and druggie chick singers in Chrome Hearts jackets. A motorcycle gang carried a grinning Steven through some hamlet up north. Steven sang along with a major *narcocorrido* balladeer while the musician's pneumatic *telenovela*-star wife gave planted a big lipstick print on Steven's cheek. These were the people O figured a criminal attorney would know. More surprising was the number of shots with respectable citizens from academia, big-ticket charities, the arts and legit politics. Steven moved among all their worlds as welcome guest, effective supporter and, when necessary, fearsome protector.

Only a few relics of personal history made the cut. From Steven's Navy days there was an aging image of Steven and Martin whose polished good looks were a nice counterpoint to Steven's angular features. They were gotten up in full mess dress at some embassy ball.

O didn't know much about Martin yet. She didn't know that Martin, unlike Steven, came from money. Martin had bought Steven the bespoke uniform from Gieves and Hawkes, inspiring Steven's enduring taste for Row tailoring. In the struggling early days of the practice, it was Martin's trust fund that had kept the lights on. In another shot they smoked cigars with their feet up on a battered desk, an *L.A. Times* front page featuring the acquittal of a society murderess spread out between them.

The picture O liked best of all was of Steven and Martin from twenty years ago, dressed for court in blue chalk stripes and gray flannel respectively. A striking young blonde woman, destined to wed them one after the other eventually, stood between them in a stylish polka-dot-silk summer dress. Each had an arm around the woman's middle. There were palm trees in the background and just enough of the tail end of a

Cadillac to date the image circa mid-1990s. Steven seemed authentically carefree.

"Okay, I think this thing is in a mood to work," she heard Steven say over her shoulder. She looked around to find him watching her survey the wall.

"Quite the rogue's gallery," Steven laughed. "Especially if you include the ex-presidents and the former governor."

O pointed at the woman in the polka-dot dress.

"Is that Marie?"

"Yes," Steven sighed. "My one attempt at matrimony."

"And that must be Martin."

"Good looking, wasn't he? No wonder I lost out."

"Marie ended up married to your partner. That must have left a mark."

"They should have been together from the start. I'm sorry they didn't have more time. What else has Ray spilled about my intimate past?"

"That's about it, Sir. You don't confide in him much."

"I save the good stuff for the few people who keep it to themselves."

"Like Marie?"

"We're here to look at your pictures, not mine."

O stood behind him at the round desk.

"It's an interesting coincidence," O said. "The girl I shot is living with Marie at the moment."

"There are always girls living with Marie. She makes sure Ray gets the pick of the litter."

At the touch of a hidden button, the keyboard drawer slid out over his lap. O gave him the glitzy drive so he could plug into his keyboard port, their faces lit by the glow of the big studio monitor. When the outboard drive icon popped up, O reached over him to drag the JPEGs to Preview, lingering just long enough for him to cop a really good feel.

The window opened to the first image of Jacqui hanging disconsolately in her cage. "Cover?" Steven asked of the hanging cage image.

"I hope so."

"It should be."

O knelt next to him, working the computer mouse from the floor with one hand while working him under the arm of his chair with the other.

Steven congratulated O on her unorthodox approach to market research.

"This is the only index that always points the right direction, Sir."

O had not intended to be a pornographer, but like many other things she had not intended to be, she could only be the best at it.

Steven made occasional comments as O clicked through her pre-edit, but she paid closer attention to his physical response. He got steadily harder as the sequence grew more brutal. He even had her to go back to the shots of the long cattle prod probing Jacqui through the bottom of the cage. He observed that the redhead gave really good face.

"Her name is Jacqui, Sir. We were actually shocking her. She insisted on it."

In O's hand, Steven was as hard as the overhead pipes. Jacqui penetrated on the Y-frame with the Neon Wand worked even better. The worse Jacqui suffered, the steelier Steven felt.

They took some time getting to the finale. Steven had swiveled his chair so O could suck him while clicking through the frames. Not only was she not bothered that Steven's attention was as focused on Jacqui's violation as on her labors, she was flattered by his response to both. Lots of girls can give good blow jobs. Taking pictures that inspired men to need them immediately was a more complex achievement.

Then there was the added benefit of feeling used in a completely selfish manner. Casually winding his fingers in O's hair, Steven rocked her head up and down as if he were masturbating, which he was, in effect, only with O's mouth instead of his own hand.

By the time Jacqui took it in the face onscreen, O was swallowing in deep, noisy gulps, Steven's hands gripping the back of her head as he unloaded down her throat. She didn't choke, gag or sputter. She even managed to stay on her knees with her back straight, though her shoes had slipped off her heels and her face was definitely rosier than when she started. She held perfectly still until he let out a long, low sigh of satisfaction.

Steven eventually let go of her hair, stroked it smooth and smiled down at her.

"Thank you for the compliment, Sir. Now I know that's a good set."

They both laughed, and he motioned O to sit on the desk. She did so, swinging her dangling, uncrossed legs.

"I don't think I've ever shot a better model," O said, remembering others back to the beginning of her career behind the lens. Only a few stood out from the blur of mouths and breasts and legs and hair colors.

"I take it she's a genuine enthusiast," Steven said, still looking at the final images on the screen.

"Beyond a doubt, Sir."

"That clarifies a few things, but it doesn't explain why Marie would act as her agent."

An hour later, after thoroughly cleansing and putting away everything they'd used earlier in the day, O lay on her side on his hard mattress. Her small form fit like a puzzle piece against his solid bulk, her ass in his lap, his arm draped around her shoulders, one breast firmly cradled in his large hand.

O still wore her collar and he'd locked one cuff around her right ankle, running a light chain from it to an anchor point on the bed frame. The chain was long enough for her to reach the old-fashioned chamber pot, complete with an unblinking blue eye painted on the bottom of the interior in the French manner, in case she needed it during the night. Tired and sore inside and out, O knew she would sleep soundly.

Something about Steven made her feel oddly safe. He'd switched on the air-conditioning, making them perfectly comfortable under the down quilt he'd pulled up to their necks. Listening to his breathing settle into a steady rhythm, O drifted off, rubbing her unfettered foot against the cool smoothness of the ankle chain.

CHAPTER NINE

The interior of the Mercedes coupe, after the gull-wing doors hinged down, was a space capsule: compact, equipped with every electronic device that could be mounted on a car and tightly sealed from the outside world. Steven preferred to be fully insulated when crossing La Cienaga to the west. The coupe was also his optimal delivery vehicle for weaving through the midday traffic on Sixth Street from the tower on the park to the pink-and-green opulence of The Polo Lounge.

The appeal of the place, which seemed little changed through several renovations, was utterly lost on Steven. It was too bright and too loud and the crowd it drew – ancient, bejeweled Hollywood royalty, agency suits, producers half his age in blue jeans and un-tucked dress shirts, forgotten record biz execs squiring heavily blinged Hip-Hop babes – included too many ex-clients. The gaudy pink and green flower arrangements matching the pattern the carpet didn't help.

Nevertheless, it had taken him three days to book lunch with Marie and this was where she wanted to have it, so there Steven sat, giant green menu in hand, round spectacles parked near the end of his nose, waiting for her entrance.

As usual, she made people look up. Marie's close-fitting, classic navy-blue suit and snug, white French blouse dramatized her athletic stride through the dining room. Her hair was up in a tight *chignon* and the shiny leather shafts of her Laboutin boots disappeared somewhere under the skirt.

Eyes and whispers followed her while people tried to figure out if she was Somebody. At least one other diner, a balding studio exec, must have recognized her, judging by the speed with which he buried his face in *Variety Online* on his iPad as she passed his table.

Sliding next to Steven in the pink booth, she kissed him on the cheek and studied the menu over his shoulder.

"The *frissée au Lardon* looks good," she said. Giving Steven her usual once over, she remarked on the cleverness of his disguise. In his hounds-tooth hacking jacket with pleated back and game pockets, his draped slacks, his black fine-wale corduroy shirt and pearl gray ascot, he could have been any of the comfortably retired moguls living in the surrounding canyons. The last thing Steven wanted was to be mistaken for an executive vice-president in charge of anything.

"And you look good too, for a hard-working crook defender impersonating Clark Gable."

"That's what you get for dragging me over here in daylight," Steven said dourly.

Putting down the menu, he turned and hugged her hard enough to make her push him away.

"Are you sure you don't want to get married again?" he asked, almost seriously.

"To you? I think once was enough for this lifetime. You're certainly in a jolly mood today."

"When am I not?"

"When you don't get your way. I'm sure that's not a problem with O."

"You haven't even met her."

"I've read all her feedbacks from The Mansion. She made quite an impression up there."

"She's good at that. I'm still surprised you enabled Ray's scheming."

"Why? I don't remember signing anything exclusive where your scheming is concerned. He showed me some video that convinced me O would be a good draw. Besides, he's clearly playing over his head and starting to tire. I thought the idea of sharing O with you was one of his better ones."

The waitress came by to take their order. Steven requested an off-the-menu club sandwich in counterpoint to Marie's chic salad, making matters worse by ordering a Diet Coke to go with it. After the waitress moved on he continued his history lesson.

"You never have much confidence in your brother," Marie said, sipping the iced cappuccino that appeared unbidden in front of her.

"More than he has in himself, but his elaborate plans seem unusually vulnerable to the law of unintended consequences."

Marie looked at Steven knowingly.

"You have no intention of splitting O's custody with Ray, do you?"

"For once, my intentions aren't relevant. I'd be happy to keep O blissed-out in sub-space for him if I thought it would work. But the more she gets, the more she wants. I'll bet that's just what the reports from The Mansion said."

"She followed every single rule to the letter. Her service was exemplary."

"Because it was demanded of her. Ray's too casual for O. He's not stupid and he knows she's drifting away. He figures between the two of us we'll keep her around."

"You're pessimistic about this."

The food arrived almost instantly. One thing Steven did like about the place was quick service that allowed either a swift return to the office or a quiet retreat to the bungalows out back.

"It's too late. He's already lost her. When she and I were alone it was like she'd found water in the desert."

"Ah, yes. The monster no woman can resist."

"You find me pretty resistible. It's impossible to wreck a sound relationship from the outside. Theirs is a house of cards waiting for a stray breeze."

"You don't really intend to keep O all to yourself?" she asked incredulously.

Steven looked appalled.

"I don't want anyone all to myself. I just want her whenever I want her. But I still need her to keep shooting for the magazine. I'm determined that Ray make a success of something in his life and if she wanders off, *Forbidden*'s prognosis is guarded at best."

"Then this is really about protecting your investment."

"Fuck that. The money I'd lose if it went out of print tomorrow wouldn't even make a dent. I just don't want to carry Ray on my back like an overgrown papoose for the rest of my life. You know how discouraged he gets."

"Like his mama," Marie said sadly.

"Exactly. Luckily for everybody, I'm a little better at fixing things than Ray. In fact, I think you already have just what I need to correct the situation. Excuse me for this."

Steven looked around to make sure no one was watching before violating one of his cardinal rules. Slipping his smart phone from an inside pocket, he brought up the small screen and slid it across the pink tablecloth to Marie, whose eyebrows rose at the image displayed. It was Jacqui hanging in the cage.

"Well, the shoot seems to have come out right. I'm sure the rest of the pictures are equally good."

"And I'm sure Jacqui will be eager to show her appreciation. You must really like this one."

For once, Marie seemed caught off guard.

"I do fancy her. She's very ... sophisticated for someone her age."

"Which is about half yours. The long-term prospects would be pretty dim based on that alone."

"I suppose you'd know," Marie said, growing even gloomier.

"Yes, and I'm fine with it. You're doing career favors to keep Jacqui on the leash the same way Ray is outsourcing O to you and me to keep her from getting restless with him. Just remember that kind of thing has a shelf date. We need to consider what comes next."

Marie took a last look at Jacqui's image and slid the phone back to Steven, who made it vanish as quickly as possible.

"What do I have to do?" Marie asked.

"Very little. O will handle the heavy lifting. When we're a little further along, I'd like to send her to you for a bit of polishing. While she's there, I want her to get to know Jacqui better. Much better."

"So she can deliver Jacqui to Ray. You know that's insane. If he can't hold onto O ..."

"I didn't say I thought it would last. But it will spare O the necessity of breaking his heart and fleeing, which I suspect is her pattern. If she thinks she's made good by Ray, she can go on working for him and serving me without feeling like she shot Bambi's mother."

"I didn't realize O was so conscience-stricken," Marie said.

"You'd be surprised who suffers from that malady."

Marie looked Steven in the eye, as if seeing him for the first time. "For all your *kvetching*, I think you like being everybody's daddy."

Marie shrugged.

"Let me know when you're ready. I'll make sure O and Jacqui get some face time together. But O will have to take it from there."

"I expect her to take it all the way to the door of The Mansion."

"Steven, really. You're not serious."

"As a rule, no. About this, definitely. I want Jacqui delivered to Ray up there, as his slave."

"I can't guarantee that."

"You won't have to."

Steven signaled for the check. Marie put her hand to the side of Steven's face. "I miss you," she said.

"We'll be seeing more of each other in the near future."

It didn't sound as reassuring as he meant it to.

CHAPTER TEN

Ray had probably seen his mother happy more often than anyone on earth. Even though her operatic ambitions had washed away in the riptides of his father's political turmoil and her own tidal drinking bouts, she had still played the white baby grand piano in the living room for him every day after he got home from school. He'd sit next to her on the white bench in the sunny front room of their Santa Monica bungalow while she tripped through the keys, her repertoire stretching comfortably from Bizet to Gershwin. One day it would be Carmen's sultry *Seguidilla*, the next, appropriately, "I Got Plenty of Nothin,'" from *Porgy and Bess*.

Though Nana's mezzo-soprano had been badly corroded by vodka, cigarettes and the desert climate and her piano playing had never been more than serviceable, Ray had treasured those impromptu musicales. In whatever once-elegant, now-tatty dress she managed to get on, when she sang the transformation of her melancholy features was the show's principal draw. An uneven student, in and out of trouble with the school authorities, Ray possessed one gift denied everyone else, the ability to make Nana happy, at least for brief intervals.

Having pegged Ray as "the creative one," and thus more her progeny than the steely, pragmatic Steven. She who had pushed him in the art classes that eventually got him to The Rhode Island School of Design.

Ray had done much better than expected there. Between playing in art bands, some of which went on to chart-topping stardom after he left them, and polishing his charm on girls who wore black lipstick, Ray blitzed his graphics courses. There were still some at RISD who disdained electronic composition, but Ray sat down at the computer with the same confidence his mother showed at the piano. But unlike his mother's, Ray's keyboard work wasn't just competent. Though intended as something of knock when his mid-term assignment was described as having "the commercial touch," Ray didn't take it that way.

In fact, he already had an agenda to which a commercial touch would be essential. Unlike so many arts grads that emerge with their diplomas and no marketable skills or specific plans, Ray had inherited a touch of Uncle Sol's hustle. By the end of his junior year, his course was charted.

Ever the chick magnet, Ray tended to attract the ones who shared the interests he'd discovered during his stay with Steven in Tokyo. Latex was becoming fashionable then and a tall, Teutonic merchandizing student at FIDM liked posing in it for him while he burned through a few rolls of old-fashioned emulsion film for his photography classes.

Looking at the prints from a particularly good session in the darkroom one night, it came to him that the fetishistic ad spots showing up in mainstream fashion magazines, the increasingly ubiquitous images of Bettie Page in places where girls in black lingerie didn't usually appear and the emergence of an underground club scene (of the kind Providence had long incubated) full of kids sporting ink and steel were trend indicators lying in wait for an early adopter. Europe already had whole magazines that straddled the line between kinky porn and fashion. Was America ready for one of its own?

Ray's senior project, essential to getting that sheepskin for the wall of the cool, post-modern office in which he envisioned himself, was a boldly constructed slick mock-up of just such a magazine, and it barely got by with a C-plus.

More importantly, when he did squeak through graduation, it landed him a job working for *Seams*, a foot-and-leg pin-up book back in L.A. It had been a small operation, which was useful in broadening Ray's portfolio to include everything from laying out pages in InDesign to working potential advertisers on the phone.

At *Seams* Ray met the kind of friend who would do for him what Martin had done for Steven. Albert Beebe was the kind of snide, erudite pervert Ray needed to deal with the one part of publishing that eluded his understanding – that journalism thing. Albert wasn't just a J-school grad. Ink was in his blood. His old man had started as a research assistant at *The New Yorker* under Harold Ross. Heavy-set and rumpled, with his thinning, slicked-back hair and square specs, Albert had exuded an air of ironic detachment that permeated even the free-lance fluff on which he'd subsisted since getting bounced from Condé Nast in one of the Shakespearean office intrigues for which the firm was justly infamous.

Fortunately, Albert was also an avid porn hound, the more bizarre the better. He had a collection of pre-legalization stuff to rival Ray's own. He assiduously cultivated contacts on that side of the fence, writing for *Hustler* under a pseudonym (a privilege rarely granted free-lancers) and getting himself on the VIP list for all the "controversial" openings at galleries like Luz de Jesus, Tamara Bane, Todd Feldman and Merry Karnowski. Albert and Ray had put together the pitch package that Ray had, with much trepidation, presented to Steven.

Ray and Steven hadn't spent much time together since Nana's death, though that event had much to do with Steven's decision to settle back in Los Angeles. There were rifts left over from their cracked childhoods. They'd essentially been brought up in two very different families. Steven had just started making real money springing crooks and though he'd always been generous with Ray, he'd never shown much interest in Ray's ambitions and seemed unlikely to invest in them. Ray was simply all the family Steven had left, the only living witness to what they'd been through. Taking care of Ray was also taking care of himself.

There was something more. Ray's visit to Tokyo had cemented a bond between them far stronger than Ray realized. Steven, who had a pretty clear idea by then of how the family dynamic worked, saw in the seemingly mad plan Ray and Albert presented to him a way to convert that common dynamic from a liability into an asset, one that might carry some interesting perks.

"Make it dirtier," Steven had advised on seeing the high-style pilot issue of *Forbidden*. "Much dirtier."

Albert had expressed some legal concerns about pushing this particular envelope, but Steven had already added a few prominent porn producers to his client list and was pretty sure he knew where the edge lay. He would have to vet all issues before they went to press, of course, but printed material was notoriously hard to prosecute, freedom of the press being specifically enumerated under The First Amendment. He seriously doubted the feds would come after an arty magazine when video shooters were busily stuffing baseball bats up girls' tailpipes out in The Valley.

With a quarter million dollars of Steven's money, *Forbidden* began its gradual ascent to arbiter of all things fashionably perverse. What Steven had assumed would end up a K-1 loss expanded from a modest revenue stream – a trickle really – to one of his better holdings, at least in terms of ROI.

As other sex magazines had died off like mayflies, *Forbidden*'s relentless testing of boundaries and sleek, modern look had kept it vital. From bondage with visible penetration to models pissing; to models pissing on and in each other; to the increasingly brutal sets O had taken to shooting lately, *Forbidden* had always gone a bit further than anyone else in print, on video or online and done it in style.

Still, the market had finally begun to change and Albert had seen it happening first. The arrival of hardcore Internet kink smut had made staying ahead of the curve, especially while fighting the uphill battle against rising costs of paper and printing, increasingly difficult. Its niche content and consistent quality had given it an edge against the grungy, blurry, shot-in-a-garage look of the early BDSM sites. But when someone sharp finally came along to spend a whole lot of money building out a tremendous facility equipped for every kind of deviant reenactment, spun off a dozen specifically targeted URLs and began a campaign of scorched earth promotion, *Forbidden*'s numbers started to soften even though its devoted reader base didn't.

Ray and Albert rarely saw each other face to face once they hooked up a remote server at Albert's Craftsman bungalow in Mount Washington. Albert's copy, which was as sharp and combative as ever, now came in by wire and Albert, who had always tended to be reclusive, stopped hitting the party circuit with Ray not long after O took Ray off the single guy market.

Albert preferred the company of other writers, if anybody, to that of the models and photographers among whom Ray and O had become something of an *uber*-couple. Though perhaps one of the vanishingly small number of successful, heterosexual L.A. bachelors in the creative trades, he preferred women as friends rather than lovers. He'd discovered just in time that he was prone to quick-setting obsessions, and that, combined with his taste for the already taken or the militantly single, had presented him with a difficult choice. He could have gone on having passionate, short-lived entanglements ending in dramatic meltdowns. Instead, he had become much the sort of part-time recluse as other men in his line upon crashing against the wall of middle age.

But when Albert wanted to make his presence felt, he certainly knew how to do it. Ray's BMW parked on a narrow, hilly street in Mount Washington at midday, just as Steven and Marie finished up their lunch amid the swells of Beverly Hills, was material proof. Ray got lots of advice from lots of people, but Albert was one of three to whom he paid attention.

Sitting on the flagstone terrace looking toward downtown, Ray and Albert huddled over a stack of printed out invoices from advertisers and distributors. Neither was a businessman, and they certainly didn't look the part either – Ray in his usual leather jacket and jeans, Albert in his gray sweats – but the one business they were in together, they understood well and valued beyond its material worth. *Forbidden* had achieved what few magazines do. It had put its stamp on the aesthetic of a rapidly expanding sub-culture. Now it was in danger of becoming irrelevant to that very subculture. The numbers were still good, especially in a weak economy, but Albert and Ray had seen them better in the past. This wasn't the kind of trend line either editors or publishers liked looking at.

"Check this one out," Albert said in a deep, sonorous radio-announcer's voice (made gravelly by regular exposure to cigarette smoke and hard liquor) as he handed Ray a purchase order across the redwood table.

"Curtis still takes twenty thousand of a number," Ray said, surveying the order.

Albert shook his head mournfully. "My friend, that's down almost thirty percent from five years ago. And we've lost nearly twenty percent of our advertisers."

Ray shrugged. "It's structural. A lot of small newsstands and specialty retailers have gone under in the past few years. We're still strong over the counter where they've still got counters."

"What about the subscriptions?"

"They're off a little, but that's not a big part of the mix. Most people don't really want this magazine showing up in their mailboxes, even with the Mylar wrap."

"These are bad indicators, Ray. If we don't raise our Q-Factor, they're going to get worse."

"Which brings us back to Eric. Steven's dead-set against a website regardless of who designs it. We're talking about a whole new start-up, and we'd be coming in late. Even established sites are struggling to monetize their content. Steven's not sure *Forbidden* translates to a competitive web product."

"It doesn't have to be competitive. It gives us a presence on the web so that demographic knows we exist. We don't need to monetize it. It's just a vehicle to sell into the new media market. The content cost would be minimal. Hosting, processing and bandwidth are very competitive right now."

Ray shook his head, impressed as always by Albert's firm grip on the tail of the *zeitgeist*. He was several years older than Ray, but when it came to the hippest new music venue or the hottest designer in town, Albert always dusted Ray off.

"We have to bill users something so we can run credit card charges as proof of age and with no live streaming, or even video feeds, all we've got to attract people is still images, which don't work in the Internet."

"I'm thinking retail here, Raymond. Eric's design work is great. He'll do a lot of splash effects, give the thing an elegant shine like an upscale shopping site."

"With only one product to sell? How is that supposed to work?"

Albert finished off a glass of papaya juice. "Maybe you can cut a deal with the guys up north to give subscribers to their sites a break rate if they order through ours. We can trade them some ad pages."

"They believe in print ads about as much as I believe in subscription sites."

Albert took off his square specs and rubbed his eyes wearily. "I'm telling you, bro, if we don't start hooking some younger readers we're going to be an archaeological artifact in a couple of years. The only way to get to them these days is through those tablets. This is not going away, but if we keep trying to pretend it isn't there, we will."

"Would it make you feel better to know that O's already broached the subject with Steven?"

"O? What influence does she have over Steven?"

Ray grinned at his friend. "It will be way TMI if I tell you."

Albert actually loved gossip, but not about people he knew personally. "I don't care how, but we've got to get Steven to hear Eric's proposals. Otherwise, the writing is on the wall, not on the page."

"Okay. I've read it. Now, how about something to read for the next issue?"

"Already on it, Chief. Girl copy goes up on the server tomorrow."

"Coolio. Let's give O a chance to do her magic. She sold me on the idea. Maybe she can sell my brother on it the same way."

Albert rolled his eyes. "Do you have any idea what it's like to manage a family business when you're not family?"

"One of these days, I'd like to find out." Ray stood, gave Albert a kiss on his balding head and promised to call when he had something to report.

By the time Ray got back to O's place, the light was already starting to fade, but the heat hung on. Coming inside, he wasn't surprised to find O naked, laying out clothes for both of them in the upstairs bedroom. Ray stopped in the doorway, taking in the road map of pain Steven had charted all over O's body. The welts had started to turn color by now. The deeper stripes left by the cane and dressage whip stood out in distinct double lines.

"Wow, he really worked you over, didn't he?" Ray asked, kissing O from behind. She turned so he could see the thin streaks across the tops of her breasts as well.

"He's very thorough, Master. And I'm sure next time will be worse. I hope you don't find the marks off-putting."

Ray smiled, pulling her in against him. "Just because I don't do that to you doesn't mean I don't enjoy it when someone else does."

Ray was the first and only man she'd met who didn't need to go the whole distance with her to cheer her on. He wasn't like her, or his brother, but he was fine with both of them as is.

"So," Ray said, flopping backward onto the bed and pulling O on top of him. "How shall I make use of your poor, tortured body?"

"No mercy for either of us tonight. We're due at Art West for Sam Brennan's opening."

"Shit!" Ray yelled, jumping up and smacking himself on the forehead. "How could I forget that?"

"Other things on your mind, Master?"

"Just a few. What am I wearing?"

O surveyed the black, floral-embroidered shirt, velvet blazer and black jeans she'd laid out for him and the black satin corset-laced sheath dress she chose for herself. She asked Ray's opinion.

"I think if my skin looked like yours, I'd go for something looser."

"I kind of like the idea of feeling my wounds all night."

Ray smacked O's Technicolor bottom. "I'm sure I'll benefit from it later."

Ray did a quick change into his dressier look, laced O into her clinging dress and slipped the silver collar around her neck before they headed back toward Hollywood.

The gallery was a deep, narrow space on La Brea Avenue in a newly trendy stretch of retail shops for those in search of the latest two-hundred-dollar distressed t-shirt. As usual,

Sam had drawn a good crowd, both in size and composition, of what Albert had dubbed The Perveratti. There were tall models in rubber dresses and platform heels clustered around photographers in sharp, narrow-lapelled jackets and brightly hued brogues. There were a few gray heads mixed in who might actually buy Sam's large prints. Many of the girls pictured in them were among the rubber brigade in attendance, but considerably more revealed. The work was all black-and-white, nothing too explicit, and filled with affection for inked bohemian babes.

Sam himself, a modest, good-looking guy with one leather jacket to his name had a big grin on his face and a plastic cup of white wine in his hand. He chatted with one of *Forbidden*'s regular contributors, Josh Blaine. The slender Blaine resembled a young Jimmy Stewart and was every bit as affable as Brennan, but their work couldn't have been less similar. Blaine's stuff was spectacularly raunchy, filled with tight ropes, rubber tubing, and spewing bodily fluids. Both had the same models lined up to shoot with them. Brennan's work they could show their mothers. Blaine's, probably not.

O collected lots of hugs and kisses and Ray lots of firm handshakes on the way back to greet the honoree. Why not? Ray was a member of the check-writing class and O was getting some of his bigger checks. This didn't mean the loud greetings were insincere. It was actually possible to make real friends in Los Angeles but the more helpful they could be, the more real they tended to become.

The magazine's photographers got man-hugs, of course, and Brennan, notoriously shy in public, got a butt-squeeze from O.

"Red dots yet?" she asked him.

"A few. Alan Cantor and Eve Forzieri are here. I think they might take home a big one of Jacqui. Eve's painted her a few times."

"I'm going to be hanging in her show next month," Jacqui announced brightly, swaying between the photographers with a full cup of wine in hand. She wore a sapphire blue latex cheongsam trimmed in red, red pumps and just-fucked hair. She'd never been more beautiful, or less for that matter. She was also a little tipsy.

"You're just hanging all over town, aren't you?" Sam said, giving Jacqui a friendly squeeze around the waist.

"Hey, I dig hanging," she replied. "Will you shoot me again if I sell? I love having your stuff in my portfolio."

"I'll shoot you," Blaine said, very 'aw shucks" about it.

Jacqui pointed an accusing finger at him. "You will not, you nasty, dirty boy. I don't want pictures of me with spooge running out of my nose all over the web."

O brought Ray forward.

"Jacqui, this is Ray Vincenzo. He owns the magazine we did the pictures for the other day. Ray, this is Jacqui."

They shook hands, Ray's face lighting up when Jacqui smiled at him.

"Thanks for the hire. It was a fun gig," Jacqui said. "Have you seen the pictures yet?"

"They're terrific. We're putting one of the cage shots on the December cover."

"Okay, no lying now. Do my thighs look fat coming out of the bars?"

If Jacqui had any fat anywhere it would have shown in the blue dress she wore and it didn't.

"Nothing a little Photoshop won't fix," Ray said innocently.

Jacqui took a friendly swat at him with her satin clutch.

"Is he always this charming?"

"It's O's fault for taking me out in public," Ray explained.

"It's always my fault. That's part of my job description. Speaking of being out, how come you're not up at Marie's?"

"Do I look like Rapunzel to you?" Jacqui said. "I've got my own keys and I come and go when I want. Marie was going to be here but she had to go up to The Mansion for something."

She took O by the hand.

"Mind if I borrow her for a minute?"

"Promise to bring her back?"

"No."

As she pulled O away through the crowd, three sets of male eyes followed the two of them closely.

"Nice meeting you, Jacqui," Ray called out after their departing backs. Jacqui looked over her shoulder and yelled above the crowd noise.

"You too, Ray."

"So that's him," Jacqui said, as if summarizing everything that would ever be known about Ray.

O confirmed that it was indeed Ray.

"He's cute," Jacqui said after some reflection.

"And knows it," O added. "Where are we going?"

"There's someone who wants to talk to you."

Before O could ask further questions, they came face to face with Alan and Eve. Jacqui lunged forward and gave each a big hug.

Alan was tall and gaunt, bald in the front with long, wavy gray hair trailing down over his shoulders. Eve was small and round with Southern Italian features and a kindly, maternal air. She called Jacqui "Sweetie." Both were casually dressed, but Eve had a spectacular Bauhaus necklace draped down her front. O had to stretch up to give Alan an air kiss before Eve took her by the hands.

"Okay, you. Enough excuses," Eve said, looking O in the eye. "When are you going to come pose for Alan so I can paint you?"

O looked a little uncomfortable.

"Are you sure you really want me for that?"

"Yes," Alan insisted. "She's quite sure."

"Here," O said. "Look at this." She snuggled under Jacqui's arm and pointed at the tall redhead. "Five-seven." She pointed at herself. "Five-three. You're going to need a short canvas."

"That's the great thing about painting as opposed to photography," Eve said. "I can make Toulouse-Lautrec six feet tall if I want."

"Seriously," Alan said. "Come on out to the house. I'll shoot a bunch of pictures and you and Eve can decide which one she should work from. Then we'll go to Nobu or someplace."

"It's really fun," Jacqui reassured her. "I'll come out with you. You can bring ... um ..."

"Ray," O said.

"Right. Bring Ray and we'll all hang out by the ocean. It's beautiful there."

"I can see I'm surrounded," O conceded. She was flattered but she hated modeling. She had no problem composing her body, much less showing it off. It was her face that never felt quite right.

"I'll talk to Ray and we'll see what's on the calendar. After more hugs, O went looking for Ray. She found him standing in front of Jacqui's portrait. Shot with Sam's characteristic natural lighting, Jacqui stretched out in ballet boots and nothing else on a fainting couch. She looked rather like a Modigliani gone to the devil. Her smile was sly and knowing.

"She does terror well too," O reminded Ray.

"I know. You showed me in your pre-edit. Marie was right about her. She's right about most things."

O said she'd like to meet Marie. Ray promised she would.

Josh stopped them on the way out to introduce a new model that had appeared in a set O and Ray edited a few days earlier. She was a pretty, skinny thing, her face a bit rougher without the benefit of pro makeup but still quite the hot little Goth Lolita in her cheap, black-lace body suit worn under a leather corset she was too thin to need. Her hair was dyed blue-black to match her nails and she had big, stretched ear-piercings from which dangled a tinsmith's assortment of mismatched hardware.

Ray hugged her as if he knew her. He did find her faintly familiar, but assumed it was from looking at her in Josh's photos. She couldn't have been much older than twenty, but she carried herself with a spurious air of world-weariness. Before O, who had recognized the girl instantly, could stop him, Ray introduced himself. The model, whose name was Roxie, burst out laughing.

"You don't remember pissing on me, do you?"

For once, Ray had no comeback. He looked so genuinely embarrassed, O felt sorry for him.

"Wait a minute. You're the girl we met at the party in Vegas after the awards this year," Ray said, doing his best to recover. "Your hair was blonde then."

"It was shorter too," Roxie said. "But I still had this."

She turned to display a row of corset-laces tattooed down her back, disappearing into the top of her catsuit.

Roxi was, indisputably, the midnight snack Ray and O had taken back to their suite at The Venetian, where O had bound her to a railing and tongued her over the edge while Ray whipped her with a flogger he tossed into his suitcase before the drive out. After that he'd buggered her while O held her cheeks open, gotten her face good and messy and put in her in the shower of the pink marble bathroom where he hosed her down from head to foot with the beers he'd drunk at dinner.

"Well, I'm a jerk," Ray said with a hopeless shrug. "But you did look great in Josh's set."

"It's cool. I had a great time with you guys. Josh has my number. Give me a call. We'll have a few drinks."

"I've got your number in my phone," O said, hastily pushing Ray toward the exit. "I'll text you."

O and Ray laughed all the way to the car.

"I feel like such a schmuck," Ray wailed at the moon.

"You can't be expected to remember every girl you piss on, Master," O said with mock sympathy.

"You're not helping," he replied, nearly stumbling off the curb.

"Don't worry. When she sobers up she'll probably forget running into you."

After a light, late dinner in the noisy bar of a new boutique hotel on Hollywood Boulevard, they went home, hardly speaking in the car, which Ray drove just a bit faster than usual.

Once in her front door, O immediately sank to her knees and kissed Ray's boots, lingering so he could enjoy the faint stripes still visible above the top of the corset dress. Reaching up, she found him hard, as usual. Rising to tug down his zipper with her teeth, O pulled out Ray's cock, rigid as ivory with that lovely curve in it, so she could suck on it for a bit. Ray moaned and fell back against the door, his fingers finding their way into her hair. Keeping her arms folded behind her back, she did that thing at which she excelled for as long as Ray could stand it before he had to pull her off in a spray of spit.

Shedding clothes as they went, it didn't take long to reach O's bed, where Ray scooped her up and settled her on her back. He dived in next to her, kissing his way down from her yielding lips. Lacing her fingers behind her head, O spread her legs, bent her knees and pointed her feet so they just touched mattress as she'd been trained at The Mansion. Ray had never insisted on this protocol but O liked the idea of practicing for Steven next time. He was conscious of details others missed. O worked hard to get those details right.

Ray lingered over every bruised, streaked, splotched inch of her, sucking her ringed nipples, which were still tender enough for him to easily elicit a slight gasp when his lips sealed around each in turn. There were lovely sash cords already knotted around the legs of the bed and O wouldn't have minded being tied down, but Ray didn't want her that way this time.

He came up satisfied that she was wet and swollen where she needed to be, settled his weight on his elbows and slid into her. She stayed in position for the first few strokes, just to feel like the good slave she was, before wrapping her arms and legs around Ray's back. Ray could have fallen on her, fucking her hard if he'd wanted. It would have hurt in a few places but O wouldn't have minded. In the beginning, Ray had hurt her often and she always had marks. Things hadn't been that way for some months before her stay at The Mansion and he hadn't whipped her once since she'd returned.

Nevertheless, it didn't take long before O felt her insides clamping around him. O did love the way Ray rode her. No one had ever gotten her to come so quickly and easily just from penetration, but it worked with Ray every time. She slammed her hips up against him for a few final, violent strokes, let out a short, sharp cry and went stiff beneath him. He wasn't far behind her. At the critical moment he grabbed her breasts hard enough to bring back the memory of her recent whipping, pushing himself off so he could look down at her. He pumped her so full she could feel the hot fluid leaking down her thighs.

A minute later, he was asleep with his back to her. O lay staring at the ceiling for a long time, working up the nerve to slip quietly out of bed and call Steven at home. After several rings, she was about to give up when Steven answered. He sounded wide-awake and pleased to hear from her. Heading for the shower to rinse Ray off and out of her, she started to apologize for calling so late. He cut her off, and promised to call security downstairs with instructions to send her right up. She hardly bothered with make up and wore nothing under her simple blouse and skirt as she slipped quietly out of the house.

Less than an hour later, she found herself stripping completely bare in Steven's back room, losing even her shoes and stockings. She presented herself standing on her toes, hands behind her head and legs as wide as she could keep them while retaining her balance. No part of her body would be protected from whatever he had in mind. Sprawled on the bondage bed in nothing but his riding boots, he watched her, reading the urgency of her need in every movement.

Steven's plans, made in haste but nonetheless thoroughly, and the instruments to inflict them, had already been laid out. He kept O standing for some time, walking around her, touching, grabbing, and slapping as he pleased while she struggled to hold position. Lifting her even taller by her heavy nipple rings, he looked down into her dilated eyes and asked if she was scared of him.

"Of course, Sir. You always know how to frighten me."

"I can smell it," he said. "And taste it." He took a long lick at O's glistening right armpit. She hated that "no antiperspirant" rule because it gave her away so reliably. "Definitely wet here," Steven said before slipping a couple of fingers into her. He nearly tipped her backward before bringing them out, slick and shiny. "Down here as well. Fear really does become you O."

Steven chained her to the bondage bed so tightly the slight lift of the shaped cushion underneath her buttocks pulled her limbs taut. She felt genuinely helpless, despite knowing he'd let her go if she indicated the slightest hesitation. It was her lack of hesitation that made her helpless. She needed to ride the roller coaster and she needed to ride it now. That was how O thought of it. The rides were frequently scary and not always pleasant, but they ran on tracks with no real danger. The same sensation on a freeway off-ramp would have been an entirely different matter.

From the large cart Steven took a couple of intimidating devices. There was some kind of figure-eight-shaped hard rubber plate with a long screw handle sticking up from the center. Chains with evil clover clips dangled from a cross piece near the top. He'd also selected a very large black Lexan plug with metallic stripes up the side and trailing wires to the electrical box with all the meters and dials on the cart's second shelf.

As always, he started with kisses and caresses, warming O up for what was to come, though some part of her actually wished he'd get on with it, disregarding her responses altogether. O pictured herself a real slave or captive at the mercy of an able and charming torturer. Would that have been a good thing in real life, or would it have proved less confusing to be tormented by someone for whom she felt no attraction at all?

Steven was a merry monster. He never pretended to conceal his sadistic indulgences behind the alibi of punishment, and never affected a stern demeanor when the physical evidence of his delight was undeniable.

The black rubber surgical gloves were a nice, creepy touch, applying the liquid silicone to her front parts in Steven's usual practiced manner. For her smaller hole, he squeezed some blue gel from a big tube onto the black plug, coating it thoroughly.

"It's a saltwater suspension," he explained, surveying the greasy, obsidian bullet, "which makes the connection stronger."

Leaving O to think about what that might portend, he parted her lower cheeks with two fingers on which he'd also slathered the gel, slowly packing her tight rear socket with the wired plug. It wasn't bigger than her usual steel one, but it had felt particularly invasive. O knew it did tricks.

Before turning on the box, Steven devoted his attention to O's chest, placing the Lexan plate directly on her sternum and whirling the cross bar down until the chains and snaps hung directly over her rings. It wasn't difficult to figure out how this gizmo worked. Steven attached the clips to her nipple rings and twirled the ball at the top of the handle until the bar rose high enough to pull her breasts into pointed minarets, her pigmented flesh under the rings feeling particularly exposed to whatever. Nothing hurt yet, but O had no doubt that would change soon.

Steven stretched out comfortably next to her, one booted leg thrown across her chained one, one hand now cranking the stretching frame ever so slightly tighter, a millimeter at a time, until O finally winced from the traction on the points of her breasts.

"When I turn on the control box," Steven explained, "you'll feel a slight warmth inside. As I raise the current, the sensation will rise to a thumping, rhythmic pulse. I can vary the speed, intensity or frequency by manipulating the dials. I'll ask you how each setting feels since I'm sure I'll want to do this from time to time in the future."

By then O was sweating all over and felt embarrassingly aware of the need to relieve her bladder, but didn't thought it a good time to ask.

At the push of a button, the control box on the cart had lit up, but O had felt nothing other than the intrusive presence of the plug itself. It wasn't until Steven reached over her and began slowly twisting the dials that the sensations grew more complex.

The warmth came first, as promised, followed shortly by an insistent, deep surging that made her muscles clench involuntarily. The sensation wasn't unpleasant at first, but when Steven slowed down the frequency so that the current came in discrete shocks, O felt herself involuntarily jerking against the chains. And when he ramped up the current a little, O knew she would have betrayed all her friends in the underground in a heartbeat.

Meanwhile, Steven cranked the stretcher a bit tighter, creating a different kind of throbbing in her nipples. Steven turned her face toward him with a strong hand.

"Suffering yet?"

"Yes, Sir. A little."

"That's nice," he had said in a very pleasant tone before upping the current enough to make O squeeze her eyes shut.

"You're very beautiful like this," he said gently, casually masturbating at the spectacle of O's twitching helplessness. She thanked him for the compliment and he kissed her as tenderly as she could ever recall, smiling down into her face, by then knitted with the concentration of endurance.

The tenderness was real. Beautiful women in agony had inspired cathedrals full of art. Cruelty was Steven's way of expressing his affection for them and the more he cared for one, the more he would hurt her. Looking up at his face, happier than O had ever seen him, the ride seemed more than worth the price of admission.

Rewarding O's docility under duress, Steven adjusted the box to deliver the current at a higher frequency. Suddenly what had been excruciating became delicious. O's breathing grew labored while Steven pinched the stretched tissue under her rings.

"I could take a little more, Sir," she gasped.

"Of what?"

"Of everything, Sir."

Steven twisted the screw a few turns, then brought up the voltage coming through the wires. O cried out, her limbs rigid, but no plea for mercy had escaped her lips. Satisfied that it wouldn't, he kissed her repeatedly, feeling the pulsations through her whole body. He stroked her hair, smoothed the tensed muscles of her concave belly and caressed her face, which he turned to his so he could fully admire her distress.

"Would Sir like to turn it up to maximum?" she asked with all the courage she could muster, voice high and thin.

"It's at seventy-five percent now."

"I just want to know what it feels like."

Steven obliged. O moaned deeply, her body undulating as much as the chains would allow. She shook her head rapidly from side to side, but refused his offer to turn it back down.

"You're a very good girl," he whispered, "and good girls should be should be properly encouraged."

He brought the big vibrator down from the head of the bed, flicked it on and applied it carefully where it would do the most good.

O's orgasms went on and on, the interior pulsations triggering another wave as each passed. It wasn't until she froze and let out an animal yowl that Steven finally switched off both the box and the vibrator. O lay trembling for several moments while he drank in the spectacle, slowly releasing the tension on her rings with one hand until he could unsnap the stretching device from her rings. He tossed it casually onto the carpeted strip between the bed and the mirror where O usually knelt, crawled and generally showed off for him.

Releasing the chains, he turned her over to remove the electrified plug. When he settled in comfortably over her small back, she knew just what was coming, keeping her legs open and arching her rump for ease of entry. The fading tingle of the electricity made his gentle passage into her depths all the more exquisite. All through what followed, he'd played with her hair and whispered praise in her ear, even as his pounding grew more relentless until she felt the inevitable surge of liquid heat deep inside.

CHAPTER ELEVEN

Unexpected things became normal. The shades were up in front of Steven's open-walled bedroom. It was the first gray Sunday afternoon of the fall. Steven and O spent it in bed reading *The New York Times*. Steven had tuned the bedside radio to The BBC World Service. He sat up against the headboard, his black silk jacquard robe mostly open. His glasses were on and his polished aluminum Tolomeo lamp lit up *The Week in Business*. O, collared, wearing locked and laced ballet ankle boots with seven-inch heels like those Jacqui had on in the gallery pictures but otherwise naked, lay on her back perpendicular to Steven, reading *The Sunday Magazine* with her head propped against his leg. O's ankle chain trailed down the mattress. Her old marks had faded quickly, so they'd made a few new ones the night before.

"Ever been to Dubai?" O asked.

"Haven't had the pleasure. I was in Bahrain a couple of times in the Navy. I guess it's the same basic deal."

"Some incredibly rich guy flew me over there to shoot naughty pictures of his girlfriend once."

"Sounds dangerous."

"Everyone was very nice. It was kind of funny actually. The girl was an American. Very attractive. She had it all planned out. She wanted to act and she figured she'd take home enough cash to finish school and live in Manhattan for a couple of years."

"What brings this to mind?"

"She's back in New York." O held up a center-spread interview in the magazine. "She's opening next week in a new Richard Foreman play."

Steven thought her plan had worked pretty well. O wasn't so sure. "I wonder what happened to the pictures. I warned her about that. They live forever and show up where you least want them too."

"I suppose she didn't care."

"Evidently not. Says here she's writing a book about her life as a harem girl."

O turned over, resting her chin on Steven's thigh. "What's happening in the world of finance?"

"You own any Spanish bonds?"

"Nope."

"Then I wouldn't worry. All this shit is written in boring boardroom code to discourage ordinary people from reading it, but it will all be news next week. It's always the same these days. A few people sweat about what they're going to do with all the money that keeps piling up while the rest look for inspiration in puff pieces on successful mid-life career change."

"You could have been one of those guys, couldn't you?" O asked. "You know, the guys who go to Davos and have Putin's cell phone number."

"Davos is better without satellite trucks and if Putin needs a criminal lawyer I'm sure he'll call."

Steven tossed the paper off the bed. "Tell me honestly, O. Have you ever met a really rich guy who was interesting?"

She thought it over carefully. "Rich-rich or showbiz-rich?"

"Rich-rich."

"Nope."

"The only good reason for having money is to facilitate getting laid. Those jokers' idea of kink is sitting around degrading currencies in a heavy arbitrage session."

O lolled onto her back, waving her legs in the air. "God, these shoes make me lazy. I can't do anything but fuck in them."

Steven rolled on top of her. "A little laziness is a virtue in a great whore."

"How so, Sir?"

"She needs to be comfortable with spending a lot of time horizontal."

O laughed when Steven brought her boots up next to his face, rubbing against them as he slid in. This was the only time O was permitted to cross her ankles and she took advantage, using them to lever herself down onto him. He was hard as usual. O realized she rarely saw him any other way. She knew about the blue pills but when she inspired him with a casual gesture he never seemed to need them.

It started to rain outside. O loved the way the big drops sounded on the huge windows. The spattering on the deck made a nice counterpoint to Steven slapping her face and breasts as he pounded into her. They worked up quite an appetite for dinner and while Steven showered O did closet duty.

O, who attracted fetishists the way honey attracted bears, had been dressed in many ways by many different men. She'd been a school girl, a nurse, a tavern wench, a *fin de siècle* courtesan, an Allen Jones mannequin table, a prison inmate in a numbered T-shirt dress too short to conceal anything, a dirty peasant girl in rags and a spoiled society brat in nothing but a long mink coat and multiple strands of pearls. O enjoyed costuming her models in much the same way. She joked about playing dolls with them.

But until Steven, she had never recognized the full fetish potential of men's clothing. They wore so much of it, and, at

least in Steven's case, there were so many tiny details to inspire obsessive attention. To O's evident delight, Steven had
impulsively shared with her something no other woman had
ever been granted – full access to his mighty closet. He had
taken her on a complete tour, opening every cabinet and
drawer, showing her which hanging bars held which types of
jackets, shirts and trousers, even allowing her into the locked
compartments where he stored his watches and jewelry. It was
all pretty overwhelming and O frantically went back through
every item with a notepad, carefully inventorying everything
from braces to ascots to gloves after he left for court that day.

In the most charming service he'd ever been rendered
by a slave, O applied her own encyclopedic knowledge of costume and natural photographer's knack for styling to assem-
bling his look. He had only to tell her where they were going
and give her a general idea of the level of dress required. She
would set to work with fierce attention, laying out a suit he
would have chosen, a shirt he would be certain to approve,
a tie that couldn't have been better matched, cuff links as elegant or whimsical as required, socks, boots, scarves, belts,
stickpins, hats, pocket squares, wallets, card cases, pill boxes,
pocket knives, even watches and pens.

Her ability to predict his choices was almost preternat-
ural. Dressed only in her collar, a pair of high-arched mules
she had tracked down to resemble those she'd worn at The
Mansion and stay-up stockings, she meticulously fastened every button and raised every zipper. O pretended to be undis-
tracted by any liberties he took with her body while allowing
herself none with his, though there were times when she had
to will herself to button his trousers without slipping a hand
in first.

She always brought along a couple of wardrobe choices
for herself, offered Steven his pick, then dressed herself quickly but impeccably, making no fuss over it. The same pride of
craft Steven displayed in the back room, O brought to the mir-

ror. While Steven ran down the list of possible restaurants for tonight, O's mind wandered into troubling territory.

She could no longer deny how she rarely felt such excitement at the prospect of returning to either her own house or Ray's, who she now regarded as his brother's protégé and little more. Once he'd been the sovereign of her most secret longings; now she experienced those longings more intensely with each visit to Steven's. There she could immerse herself entirely in all the challenging ways she was required to please him.

Ray was only demanding at work. In the office, he exuded some of Steven's relaxed awareness, fielding phone calls from disgruntled advertisers, evaluating portfolios submitted by aspiring shooters, blue-penciling an occasional word from Albert's cover lines and, most critically of all, doing the final photo-set edits with O.

Unlike Steven, with whom she rarely saw others, Ray liked to get out in the world with her at his side. At clubs and showcases and films and plays they pointed out hot girls to each other and shared edged speculations about the real lives and occupations of the various types they spotted. The man in Prada was probably an oral surgeon while the stubbly guy in the faded sweatshirt was this month's hot director. The D&G woman with the nice boob job was certainly a trophy wife, but the angelic young thing who looked like somebody's niece home from Barnard on vacation was probably a partner at some ferocious new agency.

Then there were The Scene events. Steven avoided them religiously. Ray had to see and be seen at all of them. In grubby studios meant to look like medieval dungeons but more closely resembling charity-sponsored Halloween dioramas; in cavernous warehouses broken up into exam rooms, jail cells and interrogation chambers; in dark discos packed with sweaty steampunk kinksters, O and Ray traded jibes above the relentless din of techno thrash.

O wore earplugs to preserve her hearing, but Ray never seemed to mind the racket. Sweaty and grinning, he hugged and kissed and hand-shook his way through every room. He knew everyone and everyone knew him, at least by sight. Together they watched all the showy dommes in pirate outfits doing their Florentines and cracking their snake whips, all the *shibari maniaku* weaving their suspension harnesses and all the pro-dommes getting their boots blacked by naked men with weights dangling from their scrotums.

Shouting above the din, Ray promised phone calls and emails to a motley assortment of aspiring producers, shooters and posers while O entered contact information in her phone from the prettiest girls in the room. Some might be good on camera. Others might be good off camera. All were good to have on her contact list.

Coming home from these events, they were usually both drained and done in. O's feet hurt from her heels and she was covered in sweat and shine under whatever rubber confection she peeled off the minute they got in the door. Ray was usually asleep by the time she came out of the shower.

They were still living the dream, but it was different now that it included Steven.

While Ray's uses for O had grown comfortably predictable over time, O never knew what to expect when summoned to Steven's quarters. The important thing was that Steven always knew exactly what he wanted. It both thrilled and frightened her to realize that, at least for now, she was what he wanted most.

CHAPTER TWELVE

The first time Steven called unexpectedly during the day, O was just back from scouting a location and, by a fortunate coincidence, wearing a blouse and skirt. Like all her clothing since Ray's post-Mansion purge of her wardrobe, they opened in the front for practical purposes. Steven told her to come straight up to the office.

Through the drudgery of law school, Steven held onto some illusions about the drama of his profession. As a Navy prosecutor, presenting actual cases to actual courts-martial where he made his arguments before sober-sided fellow officers, he had clung to the idea that law practice need not be mostly paperwork. Steven enjoyed arguing cases. He liked dazzling courtrooms with his forensic skills.

The grim reality of lawyering as a profession became undeniable during his tenure with the PD's office. The place was pretty much a conviction mill. Big crimes were ground down to small crimes by convincing defendants to plead out rather than shooting craps before juries of retired postal workers. Guilt or innocence was less important than past records and a particular DA's inclination to go for a long sentence. Steven learned to do as much of his job by phone as quickly as possible. It wasn't his preference, but it was in his clients' best interests most of the time.

When he and Martin had moved up to the majors, defending some of the most notorious characters in a town where there was open competition for that status, Steven found more use for his love of the theatrical. Some cases required Oscar-worthy performances persuading juries to believe Steven over their own lying eyes.

Many came with famous names attached. Some cases put him on the evening news for a week or two at a time. Every so often, Steven ended up playing pundit on national television when marquee names or big issues were involved, though Steven's bemused candor made him something of a loose cannon in front of the camera. Sometimes he even litigated for worthy causes in which he took a personal interest. As advertising for the firm, at least, his street-smart cockiness played well.

But when the cameras were absent, which was most of the time, Steven's on-the-clock hours weren't that different, aside from the pay grade, from those spent filing briefs at One-Ten Hill Street courthouse back in the day. It was still all about haggling for justice. The more you could afford, the more you got and the more easily it came.

He wasn't kidding when he said his job was keeping clients away from courtrooms. He'd become a virtuoso at that. The definition of a job, after all, was something you wouldn't do if not paid for it. The better you did it, at least theoretically, the better you got paid, meaning the less of it you had to do. While he still had enough fun at the gig to keep him from retiring on his investments, he'd learned to retain his edge by carefully mixing work and play. When there was a choice, he tilted reliably toward play. That's why he called O.

Constance showed O into Steven's chambers and left quickly. Steven got up from his desk to pull O into his tight embrace, kissed her hard and long, his hand gliding down her spine to grip her backside. With no small talk first, he ordered her to strip. Today he had a different test for her.

O folded each removed article of clothing, stacking them on the couch while Steven watched. O never vamped the process, though she was quite aware of what she showed Steven each time she bent, straight-legged, from the waist to add another item to the pile.

When she was down to her shoes, she knelt on the carpet next to Steven's chair. To her surprise, Steven ordered her to stand and perch on the edge of the desk with her legs open and her hands in the correct position behind her head.

O planted her heels firmly to pose for him as vertically as possible, only the under curve of her bottom resting on the cool, polished wooden surface of the desktop. Leaning forward in his chair, Steven sucked her girly bits into his mouth and reached up to pinch her nipples, holding her that way long enough to induce a bad case of the shivers. Acutely aware of Constance in the outer office, O struggled to stay quiet to the very edge of orgasm, at which point the phone mercifully interrupted with a loud buzz.

Steven patted where she was wet while parking a Bluetooth headset resembling a flying saucer in his right ear. He went right on playing, stroking her stiff clit and working his fingers in and out of her sopping depths, as he talked. His greeting was cordial and relaxed, even as he grinned at O's struggle to stay in position, his words coming to her through the fog of her arousal.

"So," he said. "How did you like the proffer I sent over?"

There was a brief pause for a reply that made Steven smile even wider, though it didn't distract his casual attentions to O's intimate anatomy. "I knew you'd hate it, but it's the best I can give you. My guy walks with no time or your guy walks with no time. Which guy do you want to see go away worse?"

There was another long pause, during which O seriously wondered if her knees might buckle. The incoming voice was loud enough to be audible right through the headset, though O was too far along to understand a word.

"Come on, Ben, let's just skip calling each other illegitimate sons of illegitimate sons of camel driver's whores. I'm trying to do you a favor. Without my client's testimony you'll be dick-in-hand in front of the grand jury. If you have to immunize him to get it, he'll be out on the street anyway. If you let him testify voluntarily, he'll go right back into business and you'll be able to build a case against him in a few months."

Steven laughed out loud at the response, even as O was near tears from frustration.

"No, I will not promise not to represent the son of a bitch. You can either send the crook you've already indicted over for a dime right now and possibly cut a plea bargain on my guy for a nickel at some later date or you can go home with your pockets inside out. Sign off on the letter and you'll get my client's singing lesson in your office tomorrow afternoon."

The pause was shorter this time and O could no longer hear the other lawyer's voice. Steven nodded, a victorious grin on his mug.

"See? Now was that so hard?" he asked into the microphone. "Let's make it five o'clock. Afterward I'll take you and Ashley out for a couple of drinks and we'll have dinner at The Water Grill, my treat."

After what sounded like a friendly farewell, Steven clicked off the earpiece and put it in his pocket, turning his attention to O. He stood up and brought her near enough to feel her body heat through the tropical worsted of his blue double-breasted suit.

"Don't you ever represent any innocent people, Sir," O said through clenched teeth.

"Innocent people can't afford me. Besides, it's less of a challenge."

"You enjoy getting bad guys off?"

"Not as much as I enjoy getting good girls off. Be a good girl and bend over the desk."

O did it joyfully, reaching across to grab the opposite edge. Steven unbuttoned his fly, springing out like a jack-in-the-box and fucked O roughly, taking his victory lap inside her as she lay across the cool, varnished surface. She came so intensely she had to bite her bare arm to keep from crying out. After he'd had his fill of her, he sent her off to clean up in the small but luxuriously appointed bathroom, complete with yet another bidet before helping her dress. He kissed every inch of her exposed flesh before making it disappear behind each button. There was a question on her mind that took some courage to ask.

"The way you spring those criminals, Sir, it is payback for what The Blacklist did to your father?"

Steven gave that some serious thought and conceded that it was a logical theory. "But for all his bitching about how it destroyed his career, I'm not sure he would have had one without it. He might have ended up teaching at a junior college forever if he hadn't been such an excellent martyr for the cause." Watching O straighten her clothing, he thought about it a moment longer, shrugged. "Have to admit, though, I do like busting the system's gear teeth. I could have gone to work for the ACLU or the SPLC, but the government expects to lose civil rights cases and it doesn't bother them the way it does when I make them cut loose crooks they really want to prosecute."

"Even if it means setting dangerous criminals free, Sir?"

"Locking them up doesn't make them any less dangerous. They go right on running their games from the slammer while the taxpayers pick up their meals for them. We've got more people behind bars than any other country on earth. Do you feel any safer?"

O conceded that she didn't.

"The real crooks who wreck the lives of millions from their Wall Street offices will never see a day behind bars anyway. My crooks tend to be the wrong color or speak the wrong language so they're the ones who get caught. I see no noble purpose in pumping up some wannabe appellate judge's résumé with a lot of slam-dunk convictions of guys who are going to end up dead or in jail someplace anyway."

Thinking of her family, O felt a sudden hot rush of resentment for her own class. They were exactly the kinds of people no law could touch and she understood Steven's resentment for their immunity.

Changing the subject, Steven praised O for her obedience and sent her on her way, Constance not even looking up as O headed out to the elevators.

A few days later O shot a photoset at the studio with a naked female model and a suited male partner in an office setting. Adding her own touches, she had the man use a cane on the female model, a petite brunette with a fabulous back view, after bending her over the desk. Then she had the girl suck him while he kicked it in his chair, pretending to talk into an old-fashioned phone. They'd finished with the girl's stockinged legs and high heels up in the air as he splattered her tits while she lay on her back on the desk.

Looking through it later, O and Ray had a good laugh together.

"I should have let my brother have you sooner," Ray said, flipping through the images on his display. "Think of all the great layouts that would be piled up on the shelf by now."

O told him not to fret over it. "You'll get your sets."

CHAPTER THIRTEEN

The next time he called, Steven instructed O to put on full makeup "as slutty as possible," and present herself at his place at nine-thirty p.m. When O arrived, she found the large table covered in green felt and set up for blackjack, with decks of gilt-edged playing cards and stacks of clay chips. The sight made O's stomach flutter. As usual, Steven (dressed tonight in a hunter green velvet smoking jacket with frogs across the front) was quite affectionate, only allowing her to kiss his matching green velvet slippers before dragging her to her feet for some serious making out. She was beginning to understand Steven's twisted thinking too well and could broadly anticipate what was coming. However, her new devil was all about the details and they changed constantly.

Steven prepared her in the back room, starting with a new pair of Wolford stay-up stockings, straight from the package. O wondered whether he shopped for such things himself or simply called and had what he wanted sent over. He collared her with the customary kiss on the nape, then made her do the cuffs herself. He fitted them with small brass bells that clipped onto the rings, adding loose chains in between that would only slightly hobble her movements. This pair of ankle cuffs had snug stirrup straps that would have prevented her from kicking off her punishing patent heels, even if she'd had a mind to, though the very idea was too undignified to contemplate.

For once, he added a bit of costume, a tiny, black latex apron edged with a white latex ruffle, far too short to conceal anything a viewer might want to see or touch. Steven knotted the rubber straps in back with a huge bow.

From a drawer in the back room's tool chest, Steven brought out a leather-covered tray, its red surface trimmed in black patent to match her restraints and a curved cut-out to hold it against her body. A buckled strap ran around the back to keep it in place. Lighter straps swung from the front corners. O knew enough about bondage to instantly comprehend how this was all meant to work.

Steven parked the tray up against O's belly and instructed her to hold it there so he could buckle the belt snuggly around her middle. The narrow straps were equipped with snap-hooks that attached neatly to her collar rings, holding the tray level at right angles to her ribcage. Steven walked her over to the big mirror and had her do a turn so she could appreciate the effect. It was quite lewd, presenting O's breasts on the tray along with whatever libations she expected to serve. The makeup was heavy enough to make her look like the fuck-doll she knew she would soon be.

But for whom? Steven offered no explanations as he showed her to the bar station at the kitchen island and quizzed her on how to properly mix various cocktails. O wasn't much of a drinker, but she had once dated a bartender during her swing-dancing period and was quite adept with a shaker. The way the motion made her breasts bounce would undoubtedly contribute to her popularity.

O was relieved that there were only three extra places at the table, knowing she was in for a long evening.

In the kitchen Steven was using an ice cube and stainless steel tongs he'd taken from the bucket she'd just filled to run up and down her from behind, where she was completely exposed, when the slim, black B&O phone mounted on the wall rang. Steven gave permission for his guests to be sent up.

O was left in to finish setting out a tray of canapés from the huge refrigerator while Steven greeted his opponents – two men and a woman. All were lawyers, very high-ticket judging from the expensively casual way in which they dressed. They were also younger than Steven, and far from unattractive, though O would have served them at Steven's command if they'd been a scouting party of Vikings.

The woman – slender with short blonde hair and some nice architecture well presented by the black-satin open-necked tuxedo shirt and side-striped trousers she wore – was the only one to acknowledge O's presence, going to the kitchen to check her out. She started to ask O's name, but Steven cut her off, explaining that O was under orders not to speak. It was the first O had heard of this order, but she was grateful for it. She had a hard enough time talking to strangers with her clothes on.

Steven relayed all the drink orders and O set to work pouring and stirring while they stood around the island and talked shop. One of the men, tall and sandy-haired, had just taken a staff position with the mayor's office. Another, a buff black man in a tweed jacket and Oliver Peoples specs with slim black frames who exuded a carefully cultivated air of nonchalance, had just finished up an eighteen-million-dollar construction contract for a new wing at LACMA. The woman was taking a case on appeal to the State Supreme Court.

None of them seemed uncomfortable, or even surprised, at O's all-but-naked presence, though they did turn their attention to her at Steven's suggestion when she shook up a vodka martini for the woman. Her hungry gaze made O uncomfortable, but she suppressed a smile at the thought of how the distraction she provided would work to Steven's advantage in the upcoming match. He'd undoubtedly planned it that way.

Once they all sat down, O made a circuit around the table, dipping at the knee with her hands behind her head to serve each drink. She wasn't surprised at all, much less offended, when each in turn felt her up, the woman lingering longest to tug on O's thick nipple rings. She asked Steven if he'd had them put on her. He explained that she came from the factory that way.

Steven took the dealer's position and the play got serious, both on and around the table. When not fetching refreshments or trimming cigars, O found herself constantly and rudely toyed with by everyone in the room. Each time she leaned over to clear an empty glass, someone groped her tits. For a time, the woman had her stand to one side and massaged O's crotch with a practiced hand while deliberating whether to raise or fold. O could see everyone's cards, of course, but betrayed nothing by her deliberately doll-like demeanor. If O was to play this part, she would play it as correctly as she could figure out how.

The tinkling of the bells on her cuffs could be heard over the low conversation with each trip to the kitchen. Steven had suggested they all make their requests of her through him to spare her the necessity of a verbal response. He knew that when the tray was fully loaded with black crystal double-old-fashioned glasses, it was heavy enough to be a strain on her back and having to work around the short chains was not easy. But as always, she immersed herself in the situation without complaint. By midnight, most of the girls he'd known would have been begging for a break from the evil fetish pumps, but O never gave any master the satisfaction of hearing her beg until at the limit of her endurance.

It was a weeknight, thankfully, and not intended for a prolonged match. O suspected the cards might be just a pretext, though clearly a profitable one for Steven, who had pretty much cleaned out all his friends by the fourth game. There was some predictable whining and griping, but it stopped quickly when Steven offered them all O as a consolation prize.

It was just what O had expected, ending up on her knees at each chair for a few minutes, getting everyone in the mood while Steven put away the game set, excusing himself to deposit everyone's money in the wall safe in his closet. He took off O's tray, much to the relief of her aching spine and neck, and unlocked the chains between her wrists and ankles.

Steven returned to find O splayed on her back on the table with one cock in her pussy, one in each hand and the woman sitting on her face. No one was to leave without getting off and O did whatever necessary to achieve that result. The black man came in her the conventional way, as Steven had the first time: supine with her heels in the air. O was glad for it, as he was long and the position kept him from going too deep. The sandy-haired guy sat in a chair while she performed on her knees. As anticipated, the woman was the most demanding. Folding O over the table, she retrieved a short, sharp single-tail whip from her handbag and used it all too competently. It was a real stinger, even for O, who involuntarily lifted one foot at a couple of particularly cutting strokes. O was relieved to be back on her knees with a mouthful of the woman's lightly scented anatomy demanding her full attention.

O's ass, of course, was saved for Steven, who took it on the dragon carpet after the others left. O answered honestly that she'd come with every one of them, but had the most fun with the female lawyer. O could never form a real romantic attachment with a woman, but generally preferred them for casual encounters. A quickie shoved up against the wall by a strong man was fun, but she was enamored of every part of women's bodies. With men she rarely noticed anything much about them above the waist.

Sticky and sweaty with her own fluids and those of others, she was pleased to shower with Steven and spend the night in his arms. He told her she'd made him very proud, which she already knew, but it was still nice to hear.

Returning home in the morning, she found Ray waiting for her, watching CNN. She'd barely gotten in the door before he set upon her, not even bothering to strip her fully, merely unbuttoning her blouse and skirt and nailing her to the floor.

O noted with some concern that Ray, whose sexual appetites were unpredictable, invariably made use of her every time she returned from Steven's. He was always especially rough when she had fresh marks.

CHAPTER FOURTEEN

Steven impulsively chose the seldom-driven black Rolls with its polished stainless steel bonnet for the long ride out to Malibu. He certainly enjoyed his riches to the fullest but never identified, or wanted to be identified with, the entitled class. He despised them not from any inherited ideological sympathies, but rather because he'd come to know them too well personally. Helping millionaires get away with murder hadn't exactly endeared them to him. He knew what he thought when he saw a Rolls glide by on Wilshire Boulevard – that the person in it had probably done something evil, or some ancestor of his had done something even worse, in order to pay for it.

Steven considered all his possessions loot he'd liberated from the spoiled and/or corrupt clients he'd gotten out of the trouble they'd gotten themselves into. Still, if his old man ever saw him driving that car, Steven would have had a lot of explaining to do. And with his father, explanations had rarely proved effective.

Long ago, unlike his father, Steven had embraced the idea that a fair person could succeed in an unfair world. Absent that belief, he'd still be working the PD's office and wouldn't have the resources for what *pro bono* First Amendment cases he took or his filings on behalf of political prisoners held in countries he would never visit. If he gave away everything he had to the poor and deserving, all he'd succeed in doing is adding one more member to their ranks.

Such were the rationalizations of a man in a perforated leather lambskin jacket and cap from Hermés driving his Rolls out to Malibu on a sunny fall afternoon with his brother and two beautiful women. Reclining in the massive, red-piped black leather front passenger seat, Ray took a hit off a joint, exhaling the plume of smoke from his nostrils.

"Gotta hand it to you Steven," he said, "you really know how to live. This is the only way to travel."

"There are many ways to travel. This happens to be one of the more comfortable."

Glancing at the GPS display in the dash, Steven saw they still had ten miles to do down Kanan Road before hitting the PCH. It was Wednesday and traffic was light. The sere hills surrounding them weren't very scenic, but they'd be out of them soon.

Ray turned and offered the joint to the girls in the back seat. Jacqui, who wasn't being photographed today, wore no makeup, her hair in a messy ponytail, narrow shades, a big, baggy cashmere sweater and tight leggings tucked into laced-up knee boots with medium heels.

O, who was being photographed, still worked on her face in the mirror behind the back seat's burl wood fold-down picnic table. Her gray, wool-knit dress was unornamented, cut tight to the waist but falling in pleats from there down to the tops of the leather bows atop her grey suede peep-toe pumps. Like all her remaining clothes, the dress buttoned up the front and its snug tailoring clung to her braless breasts, their big rings quite obvious through the fine fabric.

O wore nothing under it per her standing orders, but as a photographer herself she knew Alan would appreciate having an unlined body for his camera. O hated the way elastic creased skin. Even though these shots would be seen only by Alan and Eve, who took her paintings from his pictures, O expected no less of herself than of her own models.

After spending so much time at the viewfinder correcting floppy feet and drooping shoulders, O felt awkward and self-conscious in front of the lens. Steven and Ray both wanted her to be a subject for Eve's spectacular pin-up paintings and the photographs were a necessary intermediate step, as Eve was too slow and meticulous to work with live models.

Steven called out to the girls as he took the joint from Ray, who had actually put on a suede sport coat for the visit, though the gray chambray shirt and matching tie dressed it down in an artsy way.

"Anybody want some music?"

"What have you got?"

"New Katy Perry?"

"Sweet!" Jacqui cried out with a thumbs-up gesture. Steven tapped a couple of buttons on the dash and the Rolls' mighty sound system turned the leather-scented interior into The Royal Albert Hall.

Coming down through the last switchbacks before the coastline, the car's leveling system kept it from leaning into the turns. The cold, dirty Pacific loomed in front of them, endlessly blue, flecked with white from a light southerly wind. Steven swung right onto the highway and headed north.

O was nearly finished applying just the few touches of mascara and liner she'd need to accentuate her fine features. She was grateful for the smoothness of the ride, though she could have done her own makeup on camelback if necessary.

O glanced over at Jacqui. Even with her long legs stretched out straight, they didn't reach the front seat. O suspected Jacqui had felt gawky and out-of-place most of her life, never realizing how pretty and smart she was until all of a sudden this dazzling butterfly had burst its cocoon. Since the day of the shoot, O had felt a longing for Jacqui she hadn't experienced toward another woman since she'd been with Ray. O had enjoyed herself with many girls over the past two years, mostly for Ray's entertainment. At The Mansion, where those girls who had not been bisexual when they arrived quickly became so just to break up the monotony of endless miles of dick, O had certainly not held back. But Jacqui belonged to the mysterious Marie, Steven's one real intimate and not a person to be antagonized.

And there was something about the way Ray looked at Jacqui in the rear-view mirror that disturbed O. There was no room for jealousy in their world and O wasn't given to it anyway, but she was protective of those few for whom she cared. She felt a *frisson* of danger in Ray's evident attraction to this girl. She hardly seemed to notice Ray's presence and O never caught her giving him that appraising look reserved for a potential lover under consideration.

Winding along the shoreline, Ray cranked up the charm to see if he could tease anything useful out of Jacqui. He didn't get much. She acknowledged that she was staying at Marie's, but offered no details regarding her circumstances there. She was from Wyoming, of all places, but certainly didn't want to talk about that. She had been working as a dancer at a notoriously raunchy club in New York when she met Marie, which left much unexplained.

Though Ray had an easy congeniality with women that most found disarming he hadn't shown Jacqui anything to make her drop her guard thus far. Steven would count on O to disarm her.

Alan and Eve lived on one of the bluffs above Zuma beach in a house they'd designed – a sort of Moroccan villa with industrial details. The treacherous terrain underneath was reinforced with a mountain of concrete and the driveway was narrow, steep and winding.

Steven threaded the Rolls smoothly up to the tiled courtyard where Alan and Eve waited to greet them. This was technically a workday and Alan had dressed for it in black jeans and a denim shirt with carpenter pockets. Eve had thrown one of his old dress shirts, now festively besmirched with a rainbow of acrylic paint, over a pair of tights. Both wore expensive sneakers.

There were hugs and kisses all around. Ray started to introduce Steven, but it turned out they already knew him. He'd bought a big piece from the Dita von Teese series that now hung on the office wall. Promising Steven a preview of Eve's upcoming show, Alan headed off to get drinks while Eve took Jacqui into her big, bright studio to look at paintings in progress, including one of Jacqui.

In the meantime Ray, a regular guest out here, showed O around. It was lovely and serene, with ocean views out most windows. The walls were white and bare, the floors polished parquet. There was a big open studio with steel shelves for camera and lighting equipment and a darkroom to one side. A cozy den held deep couches and a giant television on which a satellite feed showed a sumo match from Tokyo. The kitchen would have been adequate to a medium-sized restaurant.

"You see," Ray told O, "it's possible to get rich off your art."

"Off Eve's art," O corrected. "My art you can't hang in most living rooms."

"That's why I keep telling you to shoot some different subjects," Ray said as they stood next to the long lap pool. "You really killed shooting fashion."

O made a look of distaste. "Shooting fashion nearly killed me and fine art doesn't pay. I like what I'm doing now. You know that no woman in history has ever shot that kind of material?"

Unlike O herself, Ray worried about her future, but whatever O ended up doing when she grew up, she'd secured a place for herself in the history of erotic photography that wouldn't be challenged soon. The combination of painstaking technique and authentic raunch she'd achieved was unlike anything that had come before and would doubtless inspire generations of imitators to come after. O was right, however. It wasn't going up in any museum any time soon.

Drinks – tea, water and lemonade – were distributed and Alan showed O to the dressing room off the photo studio. Steven helped him roll down a big seamless while Ray showed Eve the latest issue of *Forbidden* he'd brought as a gift. Alan and Eve collected porn of ever kind from every period, going back to 3-D slides on glass in a wooden viewing box from 1900. Eve found *Forbidden's* cheeky rankness endlessly amusing. After paging through it, she rolled it up and smacked Ray playfully on the head with it.

"These are filthy pictures!" she exclaimed in her Betty Boop voice. "You should be ashamed of yourself, you dirty, dirty man!"

"I am, deeply. I assure you," he laughed, fending off the onslaught.

Jacqui wandered into the small dressing room just as O was unbuttoning her dress.

"Let me help you with that, sweetie," Jacqui offered. O let her, but didn't respond to it as a sexual gesture. Eve wanted her hair up and she continued pinning it while Jacqui undid the long line of small buttons.

"A person could go crazy getting into this thing," she said.

"Depends on how you approach it," O replied, turning around and brazenly flipping up the loose skirt to reveal her defenselessness from the rear.

Jacqui agreed that could be practical for some things. O turned back around, smiling, and let Jacqui finish undressing her.

"Now that wasn't so difficult," O said.

Jacqui stared at O for a long moment. "No," she said, "but it was weird. Somehow me undressing you feels wrong, like you should be undressing me."

"We'll do it that way next time," O promised, kissing Jacqui lightly on the lips before slipping into a blue satin robe hanging from a hook on back of the door. She went out into the studio where the crowd had gathered to watch. Eve fussed about where to pose O first. She finally settled on a big pouf of black and gold velvet trimmed in black-silk tassels and cords.

O felt entirely clumsy working through easy positions she'd demonstrated while coaching a hundred models. Alan concentrated on his lighting checks, the way O usually did. Slipping off the robe, she felt oddly self-conscious. She'd been naked in front of rooms full of people many times, even recently. But she'd been fucked in those rooms and that was different. These people were just going to look.

Eve and Alan chatted about various options: kneeling on the pouf, lying on it with her legs up. Eve fetched a pair of exquisite vintage fetish heels with round toes from Alan's prop shelf and had O put them on, seating her at an angle. When Eve suggested she put her knees together, O looked over at Steven with alarm. He smiled and nodded, but O did it reluctantly. The only time in weeks she'd had her legs together was when they were crossed over Steven's shoulder.

Seeing that this was all making O uncomfortable, he steered Ray out onto the deck by the pool, leaving Jacqui behind, which Steven correctly figured O wouldn't mind.

"God, it's so beautiful," Ray said, looking out at the ocean. "I could move here tomorrow."

"I don't see you making a ninety-minute commute every day."

"We could wire up an FTP for the server and I could work from here."

"It's too quiet. You'd go nuts."

Ray thought about it.

"You're right. I'd go nuts. O and I are settled down, but we're not THAT settled down, if you know what I mean."

"Oh, I know what you mean."

Steven brought out a small leather slipcase from inside his jacket, extracted a joint and fired it with another DuPont, this one sheathed in black alligator. Finding the light breeze, Steven torched up with it at his back, taking a deep drag before handing the joint on to Ray.

"You like that Jacqui girl, don't you?" Steven asked.

"What's not to like?"

"Depends on your intentions. If they're casual, nothing's not to like. If they're otherwise, I'd say her complete lack of interest in anything serious at this time in her life, not to mention the fact that she's more into girls than guys, would be not to like."

"I'm thinking more of having her with O, not instead."

"I doubt that's going to be your choice to make."

Ray gazed at his brother through the cloud of smoke.

"What's that supposed to mean?"

"Our sharing arrangement works fine in theory. I think O may feel the same restlessness as you in spite of whatever we can give her together."

"How do you do that?"

"Do what?"

"Read my mind."

Steven took another hit.

"Somebody has to. It's not like you know what's going on in there. I always try to get you what you want. I'm thinking of having O stay up at Marie's for a couple of weeks. Given a little time, she'll have Jacqui on her knees in front of you."

"What am I supposed to do in the meanwhile?" Ray demanded, annoyed at where this was going.

"Marie doesn't hold them prisoner up there. O will be ten minutes away from you and twenty away from me."

"What aren't you telling me, Steven?"

Ray had picked up a few mind-reading tricks of his own.

"I'm thinking of having O pierced and marked."

"She's got a beautiful pussy," Ray protested. "You're not going to clutter it up with a bunch of fishing tackle, are you?"

"I wouldn't dream of messing with perfection. No, I'm thinking of someplace that would only be visible when there was a ring in it."

"And what kind of mark?"

Steven's gaze was steady.

"My mark."

"You do remember she and I live together, right?"

"Wrong. You each have a place to live and you alternate back and forth. O is your slave, not your girlfriend."

"And you want her to be your slave exclusively."

"I won't pursue that against your wishes. But If Jacqui were delivered up to you the way O was to me, would you turn her down?"

Ray looked at Steven for a long time, trying to read The Great Stone face. That he was already stoned himself didn't make it any easier.

"You don't run my life, Steven," he said at last.

"If I did, it wouldn't be so messy."

They went back into the kitchen for Ray to grab a beer. His throat was dry from the smoke and the conversation.

When they returned to the photo studio, O was draped backward over the pouf while Eve attempted to gently shoo a large, friendly marmalade cat out of the shot. Once the frame was clear, Alan snapped off a final half dozen and called a wrap. O folded herself in a perfect crunch, arms and legs straight, then sat up to take the shoes off and give them to Eve in return for the robe. Jacqui came over, clapping.

"Dude, you rocked that," she said, giving O a high-five. O slapped her hand in return, but she wasn't sure about any of it. O asked Alan if she'd be intruding by looking over what they'd shot.

"No problem," he said affably. "I'll put it on the computer in my office, and you and Eve can go through the frames after dinner. She's not going to do a painting from a pose you don't like."

Steven and Alan shared a bottle of Chimay ale while Ray seared steaks on a huge stainless steel grilling island not far from the pool.

"I hear you bought that John Willie from Vasta Images," Alan said, too casually.

"Got a pretty good price on it," Steven admitted.

"Interested in any others?"

"Always. Are you really selling?"

"I have six of them and I can't really show them here anyway. The buyers we have these days are pretty vanilla."

"At least you've got buyers."

"Not so many. If it weren't for T-shirts and greeting cards, we'd be out of business. I'm thinking of giving this place back to the bank."

Steven was genuinely shocked. "After you spent five years building it?"

"Things are different now. We don't sell a lot of seventy-thousand-dollar canvases these days. For the first time since when we lived in New York, Eve has to paint to keep a roof over our heads. Her hands give her a lot of grief and I don't like to see it."

"I wish I was in the market for a house. I might take a couple of those Willies off your hands if you'll agree to buy them back at the original price when things get better."

Alan looked at Steven somberly. "Do you really think things are going to get better?"

"They will for somebody. They always do."

"Whoever it is will probably need a lawyer but not necessarily a painter."

"Okay," Steven said. "I'll buy any Willies you'll let go of, but I'm also in for the first painting Eve does of O. Just don't let her cover up too much."

"Eve will like that. She's tired of doing prissy pin-ups. It will be a nice change to show some skin. I'll bring out the Willies after dinner."

Over steak and asparagus the talk was politics, photography, vintage smut and e-publishing, which Alan believed might be his and Eve's salvation, though Steven feared it could just as easily be their ruin. Steven had little difficulty picturing a copyright infringement beef in Vancouver.

After dinner when the girls retired to Alan's cluttered office on the upper level, Steven happily wrote out a check for four J.W. pen-and-ink drawings and two watercolors. Like most of Willie's surviving larger pieces, they were harsher and more explicit than the more demure, but still beautiful, sketches that had run in *Bizarre Magazine*. There were bare breasts, whip marks and steel shackles in most of them.

It was a pretty pricey dinner once the O portrait was figured in, but Steven never felt guilty spending money on art. The kind he bought was a lousy investment that could only be liquidated to some other pervy collector, but he didn't intend to sell it anyway. Steven had already made arrangements for his whole collection to go to The Center for Sex and Culture in San Francisco. It always surprised Steven how many lawyers died *in testate*. Clearly, they were no more able to consider their own mortality objectively than anyone who employed them.

Having been shot only a few years after his mother killed herself, Steven had no illusions about how quickly life could end. Much of the extravagance of the way he lived was attributable to a bone-deep understanding that he really couldn't take it with him.

What he took with him that night was a trunk full of the best fetish porn ever created, two sleeping girls in the back seat and a rather morose brother staring out the window at a full moon low over the sea.

Only the moon and the sea felt permanent. Everything else was up for grabs.

CHAPTER FIFTEEN

Back in the world the day after the trip to Malibu, O had a lot of catching up to do. As usual, the fading L.A. summer managed one final burst of blast furnace heat that made O want to hide indoors, but when things needed doing, O did them. There was a repaired power pack to be picked up at Samy's Camera, where she splurged on a new leather case for her Leica point-and-shoot. She expected to be using it more frequently in the coming days. Then there were the usual things that working people did on their days off: bank, cleaners and supermarket. O was careful about her diet, buying mostly fruits and vegetables and lean protein, but allowed herself the treat of a pint of *Dulche de Leche* premium ice cream.

In anticipation of her coming indulgence, O dropped off her groceries at home and jetted out to the nearby gym to work up a good sweat on the treadmill. She hit the machines for half an hour to work on her arms, back and abs, all of which were surprisingly sore from the previous day's posing. It had been so long since O modeled, she'd forgotten how strenuous it really was to assume and hold positions of unnatural beauty for substantial periods of time.

The gym was the only place O was ever seen in sweaty T-Shirts and tiny camel-toe shorts. The clientele was mainly gay and her nipple jewelry hardly merited a glance through the wet fabric over her chest. Many dramatic body modifications were more ostentatiously displayed by those whose pursuits there extended beyond mere physical fitness.

Eager to wash the drying salt trails off her skin, O had been headed for the locker room when the cell phone clipped to the waistband of her shorts vibrated to life. O had previously left her phone in her gym bag, but after the ordeal of having a previous cell phone stolen and needing to rebuild everything stored in it, she never let this one out of her sight.

It was a text from Ray, strangely blunt and cryptic: "Need 2 see U right now. My place. As you are."

The last three words made O swallow hard. She had always gotten out of bed before Ray to make herself presentable so his first vision of her in the morning wouldn't be much different from his last the night before. Looking down at her perspiration-saturated workout clothes, O whimpered quietly. She didn't want anyone, least of all Ray (or Steven for that matter) to see her in such disarray.

Still, an order was an order. Swinging her well-worn Ghurka carryall over her shoulder, she headed straight for the red-and-black Mini-Cooper Clubman she treasured for its ability to fit in a parking space no bigger than a washing machine and for the large, easily accessible cargo compartment in which she could stow her camera gear. She tried brushing her hair in the vanity mirror, concluded there was no point in worrying about any of it, considering her appearance as a whole, and headed into late afternoon gridlock between Los Feliz and the Hollywood Hills.

Ray's texts were usually flirty and fun. There was no mistaking the gravity of this one. Was it something about the magazine? Or worse, something about Steven? Whatever had necessitated such an imperative summons, she didn't have a good feeling about it.

Pulling into the driveway next to Ray's car at the top of the hill, she heard something that brought her up short when she got out. O realized that she hadn't heard Ray's acoustic guitar in months, but there was no mistaking it. Ray had talent to burn as a musician, but since his brief rocker phase hadn't done much with it beyond cranking out a few tunes at the occasional party. In their early days together, he'd played and sung for O almost every day. The music, like the regular marks she wore with such deliciously secret pride under her skirt, had faded away over time.

O walked up the curving steps to the deck quietly, not wanting to interrupt. Even before she could make out the words, she felt a surge of affection at the sheer sweetness of his voice, a lasting gift from his mother.

Ray, clad only in rumpled shorts, sprawled on the deck chair, his beloved Martin D-Twenty-Eight Dreadnaught guitar across his lap. He strummed each chord with easy precision. His eyes were closed and his face dreamy in that way O loved. She stopped, put down her bag and just listened.

The song had been written a decade or more before O was born. She had heard it a couple of times on classic rock stations but couldn't recall the title or the group that had recorded it.

But there was no mistaking the melancholy with which Ray infused the lyrics. She came over and sat down next to him on the double width deck chair. He looked over at her, silenced the guitar with his palm, and started to say hello. O put a finger over his lips, asking him to go on. Ray seemed pleased, went back to playing.

O put her hand on Ray's bare knee. For once she called him by his name. "Ray, what's wrong?"

He looked at her, still smiling. "You know, I kind of like you this way. Remember that rafting trip on The Russian River?"

"You didn't bring me up here to relive old times. Talk to me."

Ray gently set the guitar upright in its padded steel rest next to the chair, put his arms around O and held on as if to keep from drowning. "I must have gotten you coming out of the gym."

"That's me, sweaty and stinky."

"Never have minded you that way."

"I know. You and your brother both. Sorry you didn't get to deconstruct me yourself."

"Ah yes, my brother."

Ray let O relax in the chair, folded his hands over his chest. "You've made quite an impression on Steven."

"He's made a quite a few on me."

"I'm sure he works you good and hard."

O took off her Ray-Bans, rolled half over onto him so their eyes could meet. "Why am I here, Ray?"

"Steven wants to amend our contract. He intends to take sole possession of the property, that being you."

O just stared at Ray a beat, wide-eyed. "I don't understand. I thought you were sharing."

"I can still have you at his discretion, but you'll no longer answer to me as your Master. Only to him."

O felt the familiar flush of anger rise in her face. Though seldom seen, she had a fearsome temper she kept chained to the floor. "You agreed to this?" she demanded.

"Between the two of you, I didn't see any point in fighting it."

O's voice rose. "Between the two of us? I haven't consented to this. Steven hasn't even brought it up with me."

"Isn't that what you said you preferred, for us to just decide what we want and make you do it?"

"It doesn't sound to me like you decided anything."

"I think someone else got my proxy."

"What the fuck does that mean?" O's soft brown eyes had gone virtually black.

"He's more your type than I am and we all know it. Even if Steven hadn't come along, sooner or later you and I would have ended up friends and partners, not Master and slave."

"You are so wrong." O stood up, stripped off her T-shirt, peeled down her shorts and kicked the discarded pile away instead of stacking it up as usual. She stepped out of her red-soled espadrilles and knelt on the hard concrete next to the chair.

"You were the first man I ever called Master. You opened a whole world to me. You gave me the chance to make pictures like the ones in my head. You think I can just turn my back on you? I'll never stop being yours. I'll prove it right now."

O reached for Ray's fly, but he caught her wrist and pulled her up into his lap instead.

"I know what you feel for me. But I've always assumed there was someone out there who could give you what you really require. I kept you distracted with the job and the parties and the Very Important Pervert status. But I'm really a dom, not a Master. I like to play at it. When it's expected of me all the time it wears me down.

"Steven has an inexhaustible supply of Master mojo that I don't. And I wouldn't want it if he could give it to me by transfusion. I thought your time at The Mansion and being able to get your fix of the real thing from Steven now and then could fill in the gaps, but I see how serene you are with him and how restless you are with me, even when things are good."

By now, tears streamed over O's cheeks.

"And I'm restless too," Ray continued. "Honestly, I'm not ready to go where you and Steven can and I may never be. I knew it could come to this when I gave him a key to your collar. It was the lesser risk. I figured this way I'd still have you close, and I want that."

"I want it too," O said, choking back sobs.

"Me you want. Him you need. You can have both, but we all understand that need is stronger than want."

O pushed away from Ray's chest and glared at him. "Maybe I don't want either one of you, or all your crazy bullshit."

Ray managed a laugh of sorts. "I don't buy that any more than you do. We have nothing to lose by trying to move forward, because there is no going back. I've already gotten my things out of your house. I left the key on the mantle. Only Steven has access at will now."

Ray's words fell on O's heart like heavy, black stones. The truth of them was that solid. Her ragged breathing steadied as she brushed away the tears.

Again, O realized, someone had loved her and she had hurt him. Someone had tried to be the man she needed and couldn't be. This was O's fate. She could give everything, but only to someone who didn't require it. Just as her need for formality and consistency exhausted Ray, his need for affection and reassurance exhausted her. At times it was convenient, how easily she could get her way with him by pleasing him with so little effort.

But her ability to do so left her feeling empty, untried and untested, unappreciated for the very thing that made her who she was. Steven alone seemed not just to want it from her, but would take it by any means necessary. She knew Ray needed O's dark desires in her pictures, but in real life, they had turned more and more into a regular couple.

O hadn't told Ray much about her time at The Mansion, how she'd relished it – the anonymity, the cruelty of strangers, the strictness of the routine, the freedom from everyday life and its interruptions. No one could ever find fault with the way she served as their slave, however easy or grueling their requirements might be. O felt that confidence only one other place, at Steven's.

She looked down sadly, unable to meet his eyes. "I'm so sorry. I never meant you any harm." God, this again. How many times in O's life was she destined to say those words?

"You haven't done anything wrong. This is about what we are. It's not as if I'm dying or moving to Thailand or something. We've got a magazine to put out, friends we want to keep and, frankly, I still like fucking you and don't want to stop."

O couldn't help smiling, even while sniffling.

"I like fucking you too. Always have. Always will."

"Now those are words any man would be pleased to hear."

They both turned suddenly, caught and guilty, at the sound of Steven's booming voice as he climbed the steps from the driveway. Unusually casual, he wore a black ANJ-3 bomber jacket with a hot babe painted on the back, a silk T-shirt, and a red silk scarf embroidered with a black dragon. The cuffs of his cargo pants were stuffed into the tops of laced and buckled military boots.

O suddenly felt sickeningly aware of her appearance. It was one thing when he'd wrecked her as he did every time they were alone together. It was quite another to be discovered in such a condition. She started to scramble off Ray and get on her knees, but Steven told her to stay where she was.

O froze straddling Ray's lap while Steven lifted her face for a look that made her want to die. She knew her eyes were red from crying and her sweat-shiny face and breasts streaked with tears and grime.

"Really, Ray, what have you been doing to this poor woman?" Steven asked with mock outrage.

"Torturing her with words, I'm afraid."

"Better to use hot irons."

O felt another wave of tears cresting over her lower lids. "Please, Sir," she implored Steven, "I don't want to give Ray up."

"You're not giving him up. He's giving you up and we're going to help him with a suitable replacement. His privileges with you won't be affected."

"But we won't be together anymore," O said mournfully.

"It will be different," Steven said, stroking O's limp, greasy hair. "But it will also make better sense."

He looked down at Ray, whose expression was quizzical. "You know, I don't think reassuring words will do the job. Would you mind getting a couple of whips, some lube and O's collar?"

"BRB," Ray answered, motioning O to stand so he could get up. While he trotted off to the house, O and Steven stood still, looking at each other. O's eyes were still leaking.

"You're rather stunning like this," Steven said calmly. "Easy to picture all kinds of terrible things that might have left you so torn up."

"Sir, you are a real bastard sometimes.

"Only sometimes? I must be getting lazy. Come here."

O shuffled forward until her nipple rings touched Steven's leather-armored chest. She glowered up at him. Taking her by the throat with one hand, he slapped her wet face hard with the other.

"That's for calling me a bastard," he said cheerfully. Then he kissed her just as hard.

"And that's for being such a hot mess."

Steven wrapped her in his arms and let her cry into the smooth, cool leather of his jacket.

"Maybe if I'm lucky you'll keep doing that through the whole thing."

"What whole thing?"

Ray came back with O's collar over his wrist, a pair of heavy, red-leather floggers with mean, knotted ends over his arm, and a black plastic bottle in his hand. Putting down the bottle and the whips, he circled O's neck with the silver band while Steven held her firmly by the upper arms. Feeling Ray's kiss on her neck, hearing the click of the lock behind her, O wondered if Ray would ever do these things to her again.

And yet, feeling the heat of both men's bodies so close, she found herself responding helplessly. Steven could see it in her eyes. When he reached down to seize her between the legs, expertly rolling her clit back and forth between her labia, he could see it on his fingers after he took them away. He showed O her own wetness.

"You're such a slut, O," Steven said without a trace of reproach. He liked sluts. "Even when you're pissed off your cunt is still wet."

"Yes, Sir," O said, giving in again to the part of her over which she had no control. "I'm incapable of shame down there."

"How about it, Ray? Don't you think this scruffy little whore deserves a good whipping?"

"Oh, at the very least."

Ray's mood had improved considerably. O's was definitely on the upswing. She often used sex to numb her sorrows and this was a perfect occasion. It wasn't as if she'd never wondered what it would be like to have both brothers at the same time. How could she not have? It was a common fantasy, and one of fairly few O hadn't acted out. She wouldn't have chosen these circumstances, but in a way, that made it better.

Steven had O hold out her hands for some lube, opened his fly and made her masturbate him while Ray used the flogger on her back. It was one she'd never felt before, surprisingly stiff with a real bite to it. Normally she didn't like floggers much, but the extra weight of the impacts jarred her just right. Now she cried for real, but her hands never faltered. The harder Steven got, the harder she worked and the harder Ray whipped her.

Steven tugged her up *en pointe* by her rings, keeping her still so Ray could distribute the impacts evenly on her back and bottom. Ray wasn't a technical wizard like Steven when it came to such things, but he did have a knack for wielding heavy leather instruments, which had been part of O's initial attraction to him. He didn't take it easy on her either. She couldn't remember him ever whipping her this hard.

Ray wasn't angry, or even sad at that point. He just wanted to step up in Steven's presence as always. He knew he'd never raise his game to Steven's level, but at least he could deploy his particular skills to the best use. Each blow was stout enough to rock O forward, her breasts bouncing off the leather of Steven's jacket as she struggled to maintain her posture while her hands worked determinedly away. She wanted the hard shaft inside her, and what was undoubtedly an equally alert one behind.

After Ray had given her a solid fifty, leaving her pale back cross-hatched with the unique signature of the flogger's braided tails, Steven pushed her into Ray's grasp so he could work on the front with the other whip. Careful not to snag O's jewelry, Steven started slowly, familiarizing himself with a new implement. Ray's grasp was harsh. He bent her back so her feet almost left the deck. She could feel the heat of his body against hers and her supposition about how hard he would be proved correct. This, too, was a thing Steven and Ray had done before and Ray knew how Steven liked his targets presented.

Once he felt sure of the flogger's action, Steven set to work with a vengeance, though he wasn't angry either, but rather excited, as O could clearly see from the gleam in his eye. He lashed her everywhere, working his way up and down methodically from collarbones to thighs. O's breasts, belly, and legs were soon striped and throbbing. The unpredictable upswings between her legs, which Ray kicked wide for Steven's convenience, elicited pained yelps every time. The knots, Steven knew, would tenderize her down there perfectly for what was to come.

Leaving O to Ray's rough fondling, Steven quickly got out of his clothes. Ray had left his in the house. There were no neighbors in the line of sight to witness two naked men with whips tossing an equally naked woman back and forth between them.

As a finale, Steven ordered O to stand at attention with everything presented while the two men circumnavigated her, striking unexpectedly at random. O knew she had best stay still to minimize the inevitable wrapping, but took many strokes on her sides and around her hips regardless. The leather was heavy and it wasn't easy for her to keep her balance. The effect was deliriously intense. The two men she most desired both now exposed as her, doing their best to hurt her as she leaked from her eyes south. O was grateful not to have fallen over when they finally tossed the whips aside.

Panting, wild-eyed, hair sticking to her face, flesh crimson as if from a blotchy sunburn, O looked like she'd been dragged from a medieval dungeon to be burned at the stake for witchery, though that was hardly what Steven and Ray had in mind.

Instead, Ray tossed a large cushion down on the redwood slats and they made themselves comfortable, side-by-side, facing out from the deck chair. O immediately dropped to her knees on the cushion and set to purpose, sucking one while jerking the other, then trading off. Steven gripped her head while she sucked Ray, moving it up and down until she gagged and choked, Ray doing the same for Steven when it was his turn.

Ray was longer but Steven was thicker, requiring O to vary her technique slightly each time she was yanked from one cock to the other. Now saliva dripped onto her chest along with tears. O felt ever so used and it was ever so delicious, better even than she'd pictured it.

"Well?" Ray said at last.

"Now or never," Steven replied.

They dragged O to her feet, one holding her under each arm. To her surprise, Steven cupped her burning buttocks and hoisted her until she was horizontal in mid-air, her head on his shoulder, her arms wrapped around his massive back. Ray came in from underneath, draping O's legs on either side of his neck and applying his mouth to her recently flogged regions. He was just as avid and adept as his brother, sucking in as much flesh as possible, applying his tongue in slow circles. His style was almost identical to Steven's.

Held aloft between them, O felt her head begin to spin and she squirmed involuntarily, wailing for permission to orgasm at the last possible instant. Steven whispered it in her ear and O came, thrashing between them, howling so loud Ray wondered if someone might call the cops. He wasn't too worried. There had been plenty of noise up there before with no official intervention.

Lowering O carefully to her feet, Steven bent her forward, instructing her to hold onto Ray around the middle. Taking the black bottle and squeezing out plenty of gel, Steven methodically greased both O's holes, starting in front where she was, as usual, quite wet already. He lingered in the back, working his fingers into her ass, which was still clenched from the proceedings thus far. Her rosebud opened for him easily now, after so much practice, and his thorough application deep in her rectum made O grateful she hadn't found time to eat that day. Still, she hoped she was clean back there. Much as O preferred fastidious preliminaries to anal sex, she knew this time it wouldn't matter what she preferred.

Ray wondered aloud how they should do it. Steven suggested standing up would be practical, given that both men were approximately the same height and O was so small and light. That settled, Steven ordered O to bend low and put her hands flat on the seat of the chair. No one doubted who would enter first or where.

As ever, Steven was polite about it, opening O into a little gape with his fingers before sliding in the head. Her belly rose under her and she gasped, but held still until he was all the way in, rocking slowly back and forth.

"Amazing," Ray said. "You always make it look so easy."

"I like girl-butt and girl-butt knows that," Steven said off-handedly, as if the two were conversing with O no more than a piece of deck furniture in the middle.

"And it's aye, aye, up she rises," Steven said once he was settled comfortably to the root in O's ass. Ray scooped up her legs, and, holding them apart, stepped in from the front. There was a bit of awkwardness as Ray had to free up one hand to spread O and guide his way in, but she felt in no danger of being dropped. Surrounded and packed by so much man meat, she knew she wasn't going anywhere, nor would she have wanted to. No matter how many times she'd fantasized about this, nothing could have prepared her for the reality – the fullness, the alternating internal friction, the body heat all around her, the strength of the hands grasping her not a bit gently.

Geography now properly arranged, they held her in a seated position, impaled fore and aft, rocking her back and forth between them. O was usually a pretty quiet ride, but not this time. Her arms around Ray, she babbled and squealed, hammering forward at him, then back onto Steven. The feeling of their respective cocks inside her, separated only by a fraction of an inch of membrane, was overpowering.

They were aware of the close quarters too. If the implications of having so little girl between their rigid members might have raised disquieting questions, those questions had all been answered over the years for Steven and Ray. This was certainly far more intimate than most brothers would ever be, but it was also as intimate as they would ever get with one another. Delightedly bouncing their writhing toy up and down, they waited for the inevitable scream pleading release. Both shouted their assent, laughing while O let out an ear-splitting wail. She clenched so hard inside they both felt it simultaneously, and it sent both of them over as well, howling and pumping jets of hot liquid up into O's stuffed piping. It wasn't the first time Steven and Ray had felt each other's throbbing orgasms through a tiny wall of woman and it wouldn't be the last.

Minutes later, they all lay on a big towel, drained and dizzy, Steven and Ray laid out next to each other, O draped across the two of them.

"We have to do this more often," Steven said, finally regaining the power of speech.

"Good idea. What do you think, O?"

She murmured something that neither heard, then rolled onto her back, arms and legs splayed over both of them.

"I said I'm available at Steven's pleasure," she repeated.

With that simple statement, the new status quo was established. Once they'd all showered and smoked, O would go back to Ray's first, gather the few necessities she kept there and spend the night with her ankle chained to Steven's bed. No matter who he shared her with, including Ray, she now belonged to Steven and they all knew it beyond a doubt. Grief over Ray still haunted the back of O's mind, but the anticipatory pounding of her heart overpowered it.

Now, at last, she would be truly alone with Steven and no longer have to deny that she had wanted it that way since their first time together.

CHAPTER SIXTEEN

The transition proved smoother than expected. O felt a stab of sorrow at the sight of Ray's small, empty closet under the stairs at her house. It felt strange not to see his toothbrush in the rack in the bathroom. But for as much time as Ray had spent there, it had only ever been O's domain, bought with her money, decorated to her taste and kept in the tight order she imposed on everything in her world, most especially herself.

The gifts Ray had given her – the red leather Smythson jewelry box, the Cartier mantle clock, the Mark Ryden painting Ray found creepy but bought for her anyway – didn't seem to belong any less. Neither did O herself when at the office, working late on a photo edit or helping Ray pick out a cover. Ray still felt perfectly at ease slipping a hand under her skirt or having her service him there when they found themselves together after a long day. He didn't have to ask Steven's permission or hers. If anything troubled O about Ray's acceptance of the new status quo, it was the ease of it. She entertained the dark thought that he might be secretly relieved in some way.

The impact of their redefined arrangement was even less apparent at Steven's. The few things O had kept at Ray's – a small selection of cosmetics and toiletries and a couple of decent outfits to spare her the walk of shame when she stayed over after some event for which she'd dressed in a manner unsuitable for daylight – she moved to Steven's in one carload. Steven dedicated a guest bathroom to O's use and, miraculously, found an available section in his vast closet for her "getaway clothes."

Again, the fact that Steven adjusted to the change so readily was the only thing that weighed on O's mind. Had they intended this all along? Had things like this happened between them before? Did any of that really matter? O didn't mind being traded back and forth between them like a bicycle to be ridden at will. Reassuringly, neither of the men in her life threatened to smother her liberty beneath their affections.

What reservations O had were easily forgotten amid the pleasing distractions of Steven's ready access to her, and her freedom to explore the world he'd built himself. Having the entry codes to his quarters, O liked to wander around and marvel at the quantity and variety of things he'd accumulated. Steven had given O leave to poke around at her leisure when left on her own, though in deference to him she remained bare in her heels and collar, ready should he suddenly appear. However, one place she did not venture without him was the back room. She could have spent hours, days, there examining every instrument of pleasure and pain he kept at his disposal. She had been generously invited to borrow whatever she wished to prop out her photography. O feared spoiling some surprise Steven might be incubating and resolved never to do so.

Not that she didn't spend plenty of time back there. Clearly entranced by his versatile new plaything, Steven found many ways to amuse himself with O's person.

Once he locked her in the standing cage with her hands cuffed behind her, challenging O to use any means at her disposal to persuade him to let her out for an orgasmic reward. O loved this game, offering her ringed breasts between the bars, turning her back to masturbate him with her conjoined hands, kneeling to suck him with her face pressed against the locked door, bending her small frame double and bracing herself against the opposite wall of the cage so he could fuck her from behind. She was out in less than a quarter of an hour, to their mutual amusement.

Another time, Steven impulsively decided to give her some instruction at the pool table, making the game more challenging by inserting the big, ringed, steel plug in her tail first and making her keep her heels on. O had very little experience at this game and would have expected to fare poorly under the best of circumstances, much less handicapped by Steven fondling her breasts, rolling her clit between her swollen labia, tugging the ring and otherwise taking advantage every time she had to bend or stretch to make a shot.

O found this immensely arousing, but somehow it inspired a fierce determination to concentrate on the task at hand. Steven clapped with glee as she sunk one ball after another despite his best efforts to distract her. It was a bit comical, but O experienced a surge of pride when the eight ball dropped into the leather mesh. To demonstrate his admiration for her fine performance, he carried her to the bed and fucked her all afternoon, pausing occasionally to refresh the marks she now wore constantly with the beautiful riding crop from the hook in the living room. Unlike with Ray, O was quite certain she'd stay marked for as long as Steven owned her.

O's visits to Steven's office became so routine that Constance came and went, paying her no notice as she struggled to remain upright against his desk while he toyed idly with her most sensitive spots during phone conferences. If Constance found anything peculiar about O's nudity or her situation, she said nothing about it. Constance was the kind of milky-skinned, ginger-haired, curvaceous Celtic girl O found irresistible, but Steven had cautioned her against any advances. Constance was happily married, entirely heterosexual and, most importantly, an employee, one who had ample grounds to support a lawsuit on the basis of what she'd seen alone. It wouldn't do to have unruly slaves crawling up her skirts.

The only time Constance actually paused to watch their activities came about as a result of O's initiative. Knowing Steven kept a bottle of liquid silicone in his desk drawer, O asked permission to show him a trick she'd been working on at home with her favorite dildo. Warning that it could get a bit messy, she persuaded Steven to take off his trousers before she seated him on the couch.

Though feeling faintly ridiculous in his shirt, tie, socks and shoes, Steven was, as usual, hard by the time O laid down on her back in front of him. Propping herself on her elbows, she asked permission to take off her high heels. Thoroughly greasing her small, soft, freshly pedicured feet, O went to work on him with them, clasping his shaft between her high arches, working the head with her toes. Pumping away with her strong legs, giving him a naughty pink wink with every stroke, it didn't take her long to achieve the desired effect, a spurting eruption of ejaculate coating her soles, in the midst of which Constance strolled in to deliver the day's mail.

Constance glanced over at them, waiting for Steven to pump out the final spurts before delivering a rare opinion.

"Well, that certainly looks effective," she pronounced crisply. "I'll have to try it at home sometime."

Then she strolled back out.

Steven and O both burst out laughing.

"You're going to get me in serious trouble one of these days," he said when at last he could speak.

"It's a good thing I know an excellent lawyer, Sir," O replied. Demonstrating her flexibility, she took hold of each ankle in turn, bringing her feet up close to her face so she could lick them clean, showing off her intimate geography in the process.

"I trust Sir will never again accuse me of modesty," O snickered between licks.

"I'm going to get you back for this," he warned.

"I certainly hope so, Sir," O said tauntingly.

Dressed again and on her way out, O paused at Constance's desk and cleared her throat. Constance looked up from a long yellow pad.

"Is there something I can do for you?"

O looked uncharacteristically sheepish. "I hope I didn't make you uncomfortable earlier. When Steven takes the initiative I don't think about how things look to anyone else but it's different when I'm the one starting things."

Constance reached over the desk and patted O on the cheek.

"Darling," she said, "I'm English. When we're born they cane us instead of spanking us. Steven was very direct with me about the work environment here and I saw no problem with it."

Constance went back to studying her pad.

"Steven's not even the most perverted boss I've worked for," she said, "and at least he doesn't attempt to include me in his amusements, which is more than I can say for some."

That was the first and last conversation O and Constance ever had on the subject.

A week later Steven made good on his jovial threat. He took O to dinner at BLT Steak, one of the better restaurants on Sunset, with his friends Jake and Anna. Jake was an awesome civil liberties specialist with The First Amendment tattooed on his arm under his impeccably suited sleeve and Anna, chic in an Armani suit, was a rising star at the hot agency of the moment. She had the most perfect, delicate features O had ever seen on a woman who wasn't a model and the kind of slender but nicely rounded body that bespoke early mornings in the agency's private gym.

O wore a black silk dress with a daring plunge and a long skirt, slit up one side. What Jake and Anna didn't know but soon suspected was the presence of something underneath that dress – a slender, murderously tight rubber-lined locking chastity belt fitted with thick wedges front and rear and a small, strategically located vibrating pad on the crotch strap. A control box and battery pack taped in the small of O's back was fitted with wires leading down to sockets at the bottom of the spring-steel harness.

By pushing buttons on a tiny remote control in his trouser pocket, Steven could administer a delicious buzz from the vibrating pad or a nasty shock through the intruding probes. He did so randomly throughout dinner, most often when O was trying to make conversation, causing her to jump and moan while pretending to cough, squirm on the banquette and, for once, blush all the way from the roots of her hair down the open V of her neckline.

After exchanging knowing glances through the first two courses Jake, legendary for his blunt candor, demanded to know if Steven was doing something evil to his poor companion.

"Yes he is," O replied, giving Steven a look of mock indignation. "He's got this thing locked on me ..."

O's explanation ended in a yelp when Steven gave her a good, long shock.

"Well then," he said cheerfully, "let's see what's for dessert."

Steven left the vibrator on at full power while O struggled her way through a perfect *crème brulee*. The combined sensations were so overwhelming she finally had to put her spoon down, grab the table and climax with her eyes and mouth clamped shut.

When O finally regained some semblance of composure, Anna insisted they go off to the lady's room together.

"This I've got to see," she said. Still dizzy, O rose unsteadily to her feet and followed Anna, whose manner brooked no resistance despite her angelic face.

When the two men were alone, Jake's rough, angular face broke into a wide grin. Jake was an ex-band-roadie who went to Burning Man every year and had worked with Steven on some of the biggest obscenity trials of the past decade. If anyone could ever take Martin's place in Steven's life, it was probably Jake.

"Looks like you've found a keeper this time," he said, offering a knuckle-bump.

"I haven't had much luck when it comes to keeping anyone."

"You think that's a matter of luck?" Jake was an ace at cross.

Steven admitted he didn't really believe in luck. "Ruling out pure chance as an explanation for you remaining single as long as I've known you, what else comes to mind?"

"Ask yourself, Jake. Would you want to live with me?"

Jake grimaced. "It's bad enough having to share a hotel suite with you. I haven't been told to hang up my clothes so often since I moved out of my mother's place."

"The defense rests."

Mercifully, the girls returned, giggling and poking each other in the ribs.

"Hey, let's order some cappuccino," Anna suggested wickedly. Steven knew that Anna shared some of his tastes, a contributing factor in her five-year engagement to Jake with no wedding yet in sight.

O groaned. "What I really need is a stiff drink."

"I can't imagine you'd need a stiff anything at this point," Anna said.

They all laughed.

Back at Steven's, O lay sprawled across her Master's lap, watching the late news with him while he stroked her back and gave her rump an occasional swat.

"That was truly evil, what you did to me tonight," she said.

"Thank you. I'm sure you'd agree you had it coming, so to speak."

O rolled over and swatted him with a skull-embroidered velvet throw pillow. "Monster." She tossed the pillow aside and looked up at him.

"I never said I wasn't," Steven answered without a trace of shame. "And that's Sir Monster to you."

"You're the most fun of all the monsters I've been with ... Sir."

Steven sat her up, held her in his arms and kissed her affectionately. "Now there's a compliment I can appreciate."

"I never know what to expect with you, but one thing I'm sure of is that wherever we go I never have to feel afraid of anyone else."

It seemed a good moment to change the subject. "I was thinking of giving you a short vacation if you can take the time off."

"How short, Sir?"

"Just a few days."

O pushed away to look more clearly into Steven's face. "I'm not going back to The Mansion am I?" O didn't find the prospect displeasing, especially if Steven would come out to visit. She rather liked the idea of him using her like a common house girl. It was his motives, of which she was never entirely certain, that gave her pause.

"Marie has a smaller place here in the city where she keeps a few very select young women she trains for specific Masters."

"Do I seem to need further training, Sir?"

There was a resentful edge in O's voice.

"Hardly. I know someone who does and so do you. It will be sort of a working vacation, but you won't mind the work."

O had been having such a good time she realized she'd forgotten what she really was to Steven – his slave.

"You mean the work of seducing Jacqui for Ray? I won't pretend not to enjoy it."

"You never do," he said, playing with O's hair as he held her head against his chest. "We'll go shopping this weekend and then I'll take you up to Marie's. I promise this will all make sense eventually."

"That, Sir, is a statement of which I always prefer to remain dubious."

"Wisely."

They shared a long kiss before Steven switched off the TV and sent her off to get ready for bed.

Watching her walk away, enjoying the calculated sway of her departing back (which bore the traces of a recent encounter with his favorite single tail), Steven had a rare moment of doubt.

Would it all make sense? It was a statement of which he too preferred to remain at least somewhat dubious.

Steven liked the way O preserved her mystery by adhering to her unbending principles as a proper slave. Steven could expect no less of himself as her master. This pretty much ruled out overly personal questions regarding aspects of O's life and history unattached to that part of her that belonged to him. It felt strange to be curious about anyone anymore.

Marie was an outside source of information on which Steven would rely in any case. Not only would O be at Marie's to accomplish the particular task Steven had set for her, Marie would be observing the manner in which O did so.

CHAPTER SEVENTEEN

The Drive, as the locals called it, was one of the few West Side venues Steven haunted. He'd trimmed his conspicuous consumption a bit in observance of his mother's reliable wisdom when it came to shopping, a subject on which her expertise was not in doubt.

"Buy nothing," she had advised, "that you don't love absolutely."

Tragically, there was little left in that category that Steven didn't already own in several variations. He still shopped at least one weekend a month to stay in practice.

For the Saturday mission, from which he expected them to return heavy-laden with cargo, Steven had loaded O, Jacqui and Ray into the big Mercedes SUV. It was Steven's least favorite of his fleet. He regarded German cars overall as lacking in style, and the G563 AMG didn't even make the attempt. Basically a black-primered bank vault on all-terrain tires, it was impregnable to anything less than a stinger missile, reasonably well-behaved in traffic, quicker off the line than might be expected, but save for its inimitable three-spoke logo, completely undistinguished. Even its interior was Spartan and practical. Equipped for medium-duty in alpine terrain, it was all grey leather and carbon fiber.

The festive quartet within was more colorful. Fall, such as it existed in Los Angeles, had reached that awkward phase of concrete-baking heat during the day followed by desert chill at night and they'd all dressed accordingly.

O was a strictly practical consumer. She usually knew exactly what she wanted and where to find it, paid whatever it cost once there and went home with nothing else. Within the restrictions imposed since her return from The Mansion, she uniformed herself sensibly for today in a simple red dress with a pin-tucked bodice and wedge-heeled sandals. She allowed herself the luxury of a big, red hat to keep the sun off her fair skin.

Jacqui wore jeans with about three inches of zipper that only the tall, slender, and young should wear, with a hippie blouse and desert boots, a big, shapeless hobo bag slung over one shoulder. Ray saw it as a long-sleeved thermal T-Shirt and leather vest kind of day, though he jazzed things up a bit with silver-trimmed engineer boots and a wide Chrome Hearts belt to match his aviator glasses.

Again, Steven followed his mother's advice. If one is going to rob a bank, one should dress properly for banking. His black pique polo shirt was emblazoned with an embroidered purple and yellow crest, his crisp, pleated slacks belted in yellow suede to match his Gucci sneakers and a yellow and black silk bandana around his neck. It was still warm enough for his Montecristo Panama planter hat to shelter his eyes in addition to his vintage four-panel Persol shades.

It caused him a certain sardonic amusement as they climbed down from what Steven called his "Beverly Hills technical" to realize that they looked pretty much like everyone else from the neighborhood. At least they didn't stand out as tourists. In no world anyone would visit during this lifetime would they ever stand out as tourists.

He'd laid out the order of battle in the valet lot at Ralph Lauren, where he chatted up the captain in Spanish as usual, and as usual wasn't even handed a ticket. His tank would be parked right up front when they returned. Only the ex-governor's Humvee had priority placement.

The clubby interior was bustling. Steven was glad to see signs of economic life anywhere in what he feared might become a high-budget version of Manila. Jessica, a tall, slim, twice-divorced department manager who looked like she was born in high-end equestrian gear, greeted them all with hugs, though she really only knew Ray and Steven from their excursions with various companions. Jessica swept the girls away for a survey tour of the latest merchandise while Steven and Ray found their respective salesmen in the men's section.

Lowell, who had spent one season on HBO playing a werewolf, still sported fashionable stubble with his chalk-stripe linen suit. He immediately engaged Ray in some good-natured shadow boxing over at the Black Label section where everything was tight and narrow, leaving Steven to seek out James, which was like hunting a shark in the middle of a school of mullets.

Wiry, dapper and sharper than Steven's Damascus razor, James was the store's top earner, having done over a million in sales the previous year. He worked the floor like no one else, stashing high-roller clients in three dressing rooms at a time, darting among them, his arms piled high with Purple Label stock, which was his specialty.

Nevertheless, when Steven appeared, everyone else went on hold, not because Steven was such a whale (most of Steven's big-tickets suits and jackets were bespoke on a yearly binge in London), but rather because he was fun to talk to. No man may be a hero to his valet, but Steven's parade of stunning girlfriends, his collection of hot cars and his unchallenged status as chief defender of the city's carriage trade *demi-mondains* made him a hero to his haberdasher.

"Any good homicides cooking?" he asked brightly.

"None so far today, but Saturday nights are always promising. What's new that I should see?"

"Man, I've got something that's really you, but it's totally sick."

"You're already in my wallet. Let's have a look."

Jim opened one of the walnut panels in the wall of the PL room and produced a scarlet tailcoat with brass buttons and black velvet collar trim.

"Is that not sick, I ask you?" James asked him.

Steven had a quick look at the price tag.

"Now that's sick. For that kind of money I can fly to England and have Huntsman run me up one of these."

"Yeah, but you won't get it until next year. This is here now. Give it a try. I just want to see how it looks on you because I can't picture it on anyone else."

Steven stood in front of the fitting room mirror and slipped on the red coat. Unfortunately, if fit as if made for him. Sleeve buttons, a slight lowering of the collar in back and it would be ready to go. But go where? Steven hadn't attended a hunt breakfast in some time.

"Well, do you love it or not?"

James knew about Steven's mother's rule.

"I'm afraid I do, but I have to put this to a vote."

"Where have you got the ladies hidden?"

"In the lady's department, what did you think?"

James escorted him there to model it for them. Every head turned as the two men ambled through the store, talking about porn and drugs and the latest behind-the-scenes dramas on The Drive.

When they caught up with Jessica, O was already pinned into a liquid silk pleated skirt the color of buffed pewter. It swung on her beautifully, and the short, silver-embroidered tunic on top of it didn't even need pinning. Steven was a sucker for anything that closed with hooks at the top and remained open at the bottom.

"She'll take it," Steven told Jessica.

"She was hoping to get her credit card out before you got here," Jessica reported quietly.

Steven took out his black one and handed it to Jessica.

"I don't think she'll fight me too hard for it."

Wearing the crimson tailcoat, Steven appeared in the mirror behind O.

Would you go out with me in that if I wore this?" he asked.

O waited for the last pin to turn around for a good look.

"If you wear that, Sir, we might end up staying in."

That seemed a good enough review. Excusing himself while O went back to the dressing room, Steven pulled James away from an Iranian guy who was already checking out with a pile of rugby shirts.

"Done deal," Steven said. "Better get Alma."

"You bring any chocolate?

Steven drew a big, unopened bar of Valhrona chocolate from his bag, a bittersweet blend that was 70% cocoa. James elbowed Steven's ribs in admiration.

"Never drops a stitch."

"It's insurance to make certain Alma doesn't."

A slender Russian seamstress who had sewn for the Bolshoi, Alma was about Steven's age with big glasses and a regal bearing. She ruled the back shop like Ivan Grozny. One could never be too nice to Alma, who was under no obligation to return the sentiment.

"I see," she said in her lingering Muscovy accent, "you're buying a circus now. Aren't you lucky we had this in stock?"

"I'm lucky you were here today," Steven said, handing her the chocolate bar.

"Flattery is useless but bribery is always good."

Alma dropped the chocolate bar into the small basket she carried and went to work with her chalk and tape.

"Yes, this is good," she said, wagging her head from side to side. "Your arms almost match."

She marked up the sleeves, satisfying herself with the tape once the cuffs were set.

"Working button holes I assume?"

"For the price you could throw them in," Steven dared to suggest.

Alma laughed.

"For that I'm going to charge you a hundred dollars for each hole, not counting the buttons."

James wagged a warning finger at Steven.

"Don't mess with Alma. She's already sent three customers to the E.R. today."

Alma gave an exasperated shrug as she chalked a line across the tops of Steven's shoulders to remind her about lowering the back of the collar.

"What can I say? I'm slowing down. When do you need this?"

Steven looked at himself in the blazing tailcoat.

"Need it? The next time I work as a doorman at the The Plaza Hotel."

"Two weeks. Don't call on Monday and ask if it's done. Thanks for the chocolate."

She kissed him on both cheeks and marched out, passing Ray and Jacqui on their way in. Ray was zipping up a short leather jacket with a diagonal closing that reminded Steven of a *Panzer* wrapper.

"What do you think?"

Ray lacked the dandy's swagger with which Steven wore even a hospital gown.

"It works," Steven conceded, "as long as you stay off The Eastern Front."

His eyes were on Jacqui, who was made in some better world expressly for the short, tight silver-leather skirt and black silk off-the-shoulder top she wore. Sparkly silver-gray tights that made Jacqui's legs even longer and strappy sandals completed the look. Steven motioned her forward.

Jacqui gave him a model's spin.

"Everything fits her," Ray said. "They've got her picture on the wall at the factory."

"They should."

Ray settled up his half of the tab and left all their goods to be loaded into the car. They went out the front door into the heat and the crowd, both happily diminished as it grew later in the afternoon.

"Let's go here next," O said with uncharacteristic excitement.

Within the rarified confines of Hermés, most of the customers were Asian and all the help wore blue suits with one or another of the marque's signature scarves. Here, apparently, O ruled. The staff descended on her like a close relation back from overseas. A lot of air got kissed, and compliments exchanged before Julia, O's girl, swooped in to deliver a serious hug.

"It's great to see you," she said and meant it. Steven was a bit mystified by O's popularity here, where the staff tended to be friendly but formal.

"How's business?" O asked.

"Started slow, but got crazy right after lunch."

O introduced the rest of her party, explaining that Julia could find anything in the store in less than a minute. Julia amended that to half a minute. She was a pretty brunette about O's age with an air of unaffected enthusiasm about life.

"Well," Julia asked, scanning their faces, "what are we looking for today?"

She tugged lightly on the end of Steven's bandana.

"I have another one of these in gray and black."

He told her to break it out and ring it. In this store there were no wrong choices.

Jacqui, who hadn't been here before, headed straight for the orange leather iPad cover, Ray following.

O always went to the riding gear first, Julia and Steven in tow. They paused to admire a bright red jumping saddle.

"Isn't that beautiful?" Julia asked. "Makes me wish I wasn't scared of horses."

"That would go well with your new coat, Sir," O teased.

Julia wanted in on the joke.

"Okay, what did he buy?"

"A scarlet tailcoat at Ralphie's."

O tried not to laugh.

"Sounds dashing," Julia said, relieved to have found the right word.

"Yes, I'll be dashing for my life if I ever wear it outside," Steven said somewhat ruefully.

Suddenly O's eyes lit up at something she saw in a rack near the glass counter.

"Look at that!" she exclaimed, going directly to a row of riding whips stood like sentries in their wooden cradle. They were all beautiful and beautifully made. A couple of them had twisted wood shafts like the one Steven had used on O, but the one that had drawn her attention was a heavy, round-shafted crop with a ball head and short flaps at the end. It was wrapped in woven straps of the thinnest, finest leather ever seen in alternating bands of red and blue.

O and Steven stared at it as if it were The Lost Ark. Julia came up behind them, smiling.

"So which one of you rides?" she asked brightly.

O pointed at Steven.

"Thought so." Julia drew it out of the rack and handed it to him. "These are still made in our own workshops and they do just a few in each color combination every year. I think there are a hundred of these."

Steven hefted it from the hilt.

"Nice balance. Good weight. Looks like a worker."

With that, he put out his hand and gave himself a hard enough whack to startle them all. He didn't even flinch.

"It has a good action too. Stiff with a heavy bite."

O reached out to take it from Steven.

"With your permission, Sir?"

He handed it to O who gave it to Julia.

"There's something else I saw here too."

They all followed O to men's jewelry, where O pointed to a heavy key chain with a nautical shackle at one end.

Julia unlocked the case and brought out the chain on a grey velvet cushion. O fastened it to a belt loop on Steven's trousers. She reached into his pocket for his house key case, opening it and removing the empty jump ring for the car keys he kept on a big silver fleur-de-lis currently in the valet garage. She snapped the case onto the ring and put it back in his pocket.

"Voila," O said triumphantly.

Steven looked down at what O had assembled. It was sharp and he was inclined to buy it because O had sought it out for him, but this time she got the jump.

"Just put everything on my company card," O instructed Julia, reminding her that the information was in the computer.

"No problem," Julia said, removing the tag from Steven's new chain and hustling off to the register.

"Are you sure that's wise?" Steven asked, treading very lightly in what felt very much like a minefield.

"I would like to do this if Sir will allow," O said, looking at him steadily.

Steven nodded. "Thank you, that's very generous," he said, "but you may regret the whip."

"I trust you'll make sure I do, Sir."

O smiled and turned her back to Steven, sticking her rump out just enough to break the tension of the moment.

Steven gave it a discreet pat and all was quite back to normal when Julia returned with the charge slip for O to sign.

Steven had an intuition that there was something more to all this than he'd seen, but knew better than to pursue an explanation at the moment.

They stopped a couple of other places, passing the yellow and black Bugatti parked outside Bijan (surrounded by kids with cameras as always), the usual knots of European and Asian shoppers and the casually dressed ex-wives for which The Drive was just a big supermarket aisle.

Ray was able to keep Steven out of Mont Blanc, but not easily.

"Not one more fountain pen for a year," he scolded. "You made me promise to have you sedated if necessary."

Steven grumbled a bit, but he really had gone overboard on the Andrew Carnegie.

There was no keeping anyone out of Cartier, where each did a different kind of damage. O took Steven's rubber-armored Santos lighter upstairs to be filled. She couldn't have been gone more than fifteen minutes – long enough for unattended kids to get in trouble in a candy store.

Ray made the first wrong move. He'd always fancied those bracelets that screwed on with their own little gold driver, so he bought one for Jacqui, who was perfectly happy to take it, gave him a kiss and turn to show it to Steven. He alone knew what lay ahead for these two; it was too soon for this, and Jacqui was too quick to acquiesce in it.

She was no stranger to things that locked on and fully understood their meaning, but did not see this in that context. Why should she? They hardly knew each other and Jacqui was the kind of girl for whom men impulsively bought things. But things like this in their world were not to be accepted so lightly. Steven was grateful they didn't have a necklace in the same style.

Then Steven misbehaved himself. Kyle, the store's manager, came over to shake his hand. Kyle was short and stout, with heavy horn rims and a trimmed mustache. He could be quite formal and forbidding, but no one was like that with Steven. He didn't allow it.

"Would you like to see something beautiful?" he asked rhetorically. Who doesn't want to see something beautiful?

Steven nodded toward Jacqui, still busily checking out her new hardware at the counter.

"More beautiful than that?" Steven asked edgily.

"Depends on what you're looking for."

Kyle was gay, but beautiful was beautiful. Steven followed him back to the watch department where he brought out a limited edition Rotonde Day/Night. Its face was made of rotating silver guilloche dials inscribed with the sun and moon. Several blued hands pointed at different circles of numerals. This was an extremely rare twenty-nine-jewel auto-wind with a thirty-six-hour reserve. Kyle said there were only three left, one each in Los Angeles, New York, and Singapore. It cost no more than the down payment on a modest condo.

Steven knew a thing or two about watches. One thing he knew was that this kind held its value, might even appreciate, but only if kept in the box in a bank vault. Just like cars or pens or any other luxury item, it would depreciate forty percent the first time he ever put it on. It might or might not recover that forty percent in his lifetime, depending on all kinds of things that couldn't be predicted. Museum watches were great investments for museums, but for consumers, not so much.

Steven strapped it on. At forty-four millimeters and made of a split wafer of white gold, it felt like a quarter he'd flipped on his wrist, especially by comparison to the big, square black-anodized Bell and Ross NATO pilot watch he'd been wearing all day. It was absolutely piss-elegant and entirely unnecessary.

"I'll take it," he said, pulling out a green crocodile billfold.

They were just finishing up the paper work when O came down the steps from the service department. She didn't like what she saw one bit. Steven had the best game face, but even he looked caught and guilty. Ray, having suddenly realized that he'd blown a wad of cash so he could see a girl he'd just met smile while still in the company of his barely-released slave, felt more than a little self-conscious. And Jacqui made matters worse by holding up her wrist and grinning at O like she'd just found a new penny.

"Look what I got!" she said, sounding every minute of twelve years old.

O marched up to Steven just as he inscribed his florid signature on the warranty card with a little retractable fountain pen he carried in his shirt pocket. She got a good look at the bottom line. Just how rich and just how crazy was this man? For the first time, she seriously asked herself those questions.

"Your lighter, Sir," she said icily, extending it to him on her open palm.

Steven thanked her and dropped it in his pocket.

"May I see what you bought, Sir?" O asked in a tone that, irrespective of their roles, left only one possible answer.

"Of course," Kyle interjected, ever so delighted to distract her by opening the red leather box and giving her a peek. As a jeweler, he saw a lot of greed, and had much practice at keeping his smile in place while tensions mounted around him.

O took the box and studied the watch carefully.

"It is beautiful, Sir. I'm sure it keeps excellent time. What niche does it fill?"

For once in his life, Steven wasn't quite sure what to say. "Niche?"

That was a pretty fatuous comeback, even in his estimation.

"What does it do that all the others don't?"

"Well, it has these concentric dials, you see ..."

Ray and Jacqui gathered round as he pointed out its features. O looked supremely unimpressed. Thinking back on that first night when she'd marveled at his self-control while looking her over in all her naked splendor, she felt somewhat let down to know he was less resistant to the charms of an intricate cuckoo clock.

"I'm sure you'll get a lot of enjoyment out of it," she said finally, closing the watch box and the subject with it.

Ray, ironically choosing that moment to check out the old Rolex Daytona that had been the first item in Steven's collection, reminded everybody about the fitting. He volunteered to go get the car, as the upper lot would be closing, and bring it down to the garage at the end of The Drive. Steven insisted on doing it himself. Ray could escort Jacqui down to the end of the block. Heading back to toward Little Santa Monica, O challenged Steven for the first time. Once she submitted as she had to him, she did not judge, but her demanding principles were essential to all that made her desirable.

"Do you know the Russian word *'poshlost'*, Sir?" she asked, looking at the dark red bag hanging from his wrist.

"I spent my last deployment at NATO HQ as a liaison officer. I speak five languages fluently, including both Russian and Japanese, and a few others conversationally. I do believe I catch your drift."

Steven's voice was hard but not angry. He had been lectured about his vices many times.

"I grew up understanding the necessity of luxury," O explained. "I indulge myself plenty. But with the world the way it is, don't you feel like Marie Antoinette sometimes?"

"O, there's something about money that people who haven't had it just don't understand. You can't get rid of it. It keeps breeding on itself like some kind of virus. Once you reach a certain point, no matter how much you spend, you end up with more than you had at the beginning of the day. I came from nothing. I'm smart and I work hard, but I've also been lucky and I know it. If you've got that kind of luck the least you can do is spread it around. That's my story and I'm sticking to it."

They had come to the lot where the smiling valet waited with Steven's keys. He gave the man a large tip, opened the door and watched O climb in. When they were alone he looked over at her. Her expression had softened.

"I just need for you to understand one thing," she said in a tone of finality that, much to Steven's relief, suggested it really would be just one thing, at least in this regard.

"I don't fit under a bell jar."

Steven smiled his slightly crooked grin and made it all better.

"No, O, you most certainly don't. It would be a terrible waste to keep you that way. In my own defense, I know how to use the beautiful things I acquire."

O smiled back at him.

"That you do, Sir.

In a short journey, Steven drove the Mercedes exactly three blocks to the basement garage of the pseudo-Florentine Via Rodeo. On the lowest level of this *Ponta-Vecchio*-as-Strip-Mall, there was an expensive, exclusive lingerie store that, true to its London origins, marketed matter-of-factly to the well-heeled and stiletto-heeled swells of Albert's Perveratti.

Behind the black-draped doors of this cozy den of de-bauchery it was Ray who had juice as *Forbidden*'s editor. He got more than just a serious hug from Violet, the manager, who wore the same pink Fifties-style button-front smock as the other personnel, but did more for it.

All three of the girls on the floor were pretty East Side refugees in club makeup with hints of ink poking out from un-der sleeves and through low-buttoned bosoms. The uniforms were cut closer and shorter than their Ozzie-and-Harriet era inspirations; management preferred them held together with the fewest possible buttons. Fishnet stockings and medi-um-heeled maribou mules were also standard.

French Vietnamese, Violet was a blend of Western archi-tecture and Eastern detail. Sinuous, long-waisted and slen-der-stemmed, she wore her smock open in a neat triangle down to her wide belt, revealing lots of golden skin and presenting the finest bust money could buy in one of the firm's signature ornate black-and-pink push-up bras. All the uniforms stopped above the knee, but Violet had raised hers a few additional inches, making it unambiguously clear that her stockings were attached by garters. Her hair and eyes were lustrously black.

Violet's hug for Ray was more than professionally friend-ly. It went on long enough to suggest something that became indisputable when she casually flung an arm over his shoulder and kissed him as boldly as the store's requisite heavy red lip-stick would allow.

O had always come alone to this place to pull items for photo shoots and knew from the stroke-inducing invoices that Ray had a hook-up here, but hadn't known it was that kind of hook-up until now. It would hardly have mattered to her when she was still Ray's exclusive property and mattered even less now.

Still, O had never really thought about how Ray's priv-ileged position at *Forbidden* made him a worthwhile bed-post notch for every fetish *femme fatale* in Los Angeles. She wouldn't have cared much if she had known, having force-fed her feet to many an aspiring model, but the thought of Ray out in the world on his own roused a certain protectiveness. Ray's impulsive purchase of the bracelet for Jacqui had definitely brought it to Defcon Two.

O had a feeling Steven shared that protectiveness and that it might not be unrelated to the impending mission at Marie's for which they'd all come to this shop in preparation.

After peeling herself off Ray, Violet gave Steven a more correct cheek graze, hugged and rocked Jacqui like a younger sister and extended O a confident, friendly handshake.

"I've seen your photographs in the October issue," Violet said in her surprising West End accent. "They were fantastically dirty and we all loved them but I'm not sure the owner's would have liked seeing our credit at the end.

Ray laughed.

"And how was business the week after the magazine came out?"

Violet rolled her eyes. "Through the roof. I had to send to New York for an emergency shipment."

Ray affected his best Bay Ridge accent. "So hey, you no beech-a-to-me, capiche?" They all laughed.

"Let me lock the door and we'll get started," Violet said.

She literally closed it in the face of a tourist couple, brusquely inviting them back at ten the next morning before locking up and pulling the black curtains tight.

The whole place was done like the front parlor of a small Parisian brothel from *La Belle Epoque*, complete with red-flocked wallpaper, beaded lamps and deep velvet couches. There were mirrored cases along the back wall and a short hallway to the spacious dressing rooms. In between, there were racks and racks of scandalous split knickers and peek-a-boo bras and other bits of lace that got more expensive as they diminished in size and modesty.

It made O wince inwardly to think that they would now be buying lingerie for her here, when Ray had gone through her closet like a buzz-saw after her return from The Mansion, disposing of all her back-hooked bras, a pile of panties from La Perla and any of her Wolford body suits that didn't open in the right places.

But Steven had explained that Marie liked her girls girly and had strict preferences regarding what was worn at Franklin Street. Ironically, Jacqui's ostensible purpose on this excursion was to help O acquire the proper wardrobe, a truly stunning reversal of roles. O might have balked were it not done under Steven's authority.

Jacqui went right to work, sifting through the racks while Violet took O's measurements and Bridget, a small, round sales girl whose dialect was more East End than Violet's, took down O's specs in centimeters. Steven and Ray sank in the couches, Ray with a glass of champagne, Steven with some sparkling water from a plastic bottle imprinted with the store's logo on a pink label.

"With a waist like that, you'd corset beautifully," Violet observed, pulling the yellow tape tight around O's middle. O shot an alarmed look over her shoulder at Steven.

"Please, Sir. I have some custom-made ones from Mr. Pearl. I'm sure Marie won't mind. I'd hate to leave them."

"I'm envious," Violet admitted. "And O is right. We just do show corsets here. What she's got is the genuine article."

Marie liked the genuine article.

Jacqui came over with an armload of merchandise, handing it off to Bridget.

"You can put them in the same dressing room," she said. "O's seen me naked and now it's my turn."

O raised an eyebrow. Jacqui did not want for self-confidence. It was a good town and a good time to be young and hot.

In the satin-draped dressing room, which had its own gold-silk-upholstered bench and a giant gilt-framed mirror hanging from the ceiling, O and Jacqui got out of their street clothes. O started to unbutton her dress, but Jacqui stopped her.

"Oh, can I please? I've been so patient."

Jacqui got O's dress half undone and stopped to gawk at O's chest.

"They're so big," she said with awe.

"I'm only a thirty-four double-D," O insisted.

"No, I mean those rings. May I touch?"

"Of course."

O never minded being touched by pretty girls, especially when they asked nicely. Jacqui tugged lightly, rolling steel and flesh in her long fingers. She had a nice touch. O was certain Marie required that.

"They must have hurt like hell."

"Just during the stretching. When they got past eight-gauge they really were a misery for a while. Couldn't touch them, much less play with them, for almost six months."

Jacqui clutched her own chest and whimpered.

"You're a braver woman than I," she said.

"That's pretty funny coming from the one who insisted on batteries in the cattle prod."

"Oh it's not the pain that would bother me. But not having them touched for months? I'd go insane."

"If you ever have it done, believe me, you won't want anyone getting near them until they're completely healed. I had to grit my teeth every time I went into an air-conditioned room. Picture that in this town."

By then, O was down to her sandals, impressing Jacqui with how fast she could get naked.

"Well that was sure easy."

"I'm easy. I'm supposed to be."

"You go around bare-ass all the time?"

"I get a dispensation for work. I can wear plain cotton under my work clothes, but I can't be seen in them outside the studio."

Jacqui noted the fading marks everywhere from Steven's last whipping.

"How long have those been there?" she asked, reaching out to trace them gently.

"A few days. Steven's had a busy week. He tries to make sure I always have some, but they never last as long as I'd like."

"Have you noticed that they tend to fade faster when you get it more often?"

"I think your body gets used to it," she said. "Don't know why, but it certainly isn't because he hits any lighter."

"I wouldn't figure."

O didn't want to travel this road just yet.

"Let's see if we can peel those jeans off you."

It took some doing, but O got Jacqui down to her purple sweat socks pretty quickly. She had a lot of practice at high-speed stripping during her locker-room days. Jacqui shook out her hair and stood in front of the mirror next to O, the two of them an appealing contrast. Jacqui towered over O in all her smooth perfection, but O had the curves.

"Let's start with me. I already know what I want," Jacqui suggested.

It was easy enough. Jacqui's chosen black bra was mostly theoretical, just tiny lace demi-cups underneath that left her breasts entirely exposed, framed by slender satin straps rising to the halter. Proportional tits had their advantages. O's super-structure needed more support.

Neither liked the garter belt that went with.

"Too square across the top," Jackie said.

O agreed that it would be a crime to cover up a belly like hers, and Jacqui kissed her on the forehead. "You know what every model wants to hear."

"You all want to hear the same things."

The narrower style with the shorter straps showed more. The ensemble was all black, except for the socks, which O decreed had to go. Leaning out of the curtains, O asked for a pair of size C seamed stockings in black. Bridget pulled them from a drawer, asked O if she'd like to borrow a robe. Before O could answer, pink satin kimonos appeared for both.

Jacqui left hers on the bench after fastening the stockings and straightening the seams, critically appraising herself in the mirror.

"What do you think?"

"Makes you look like a whore."

Jacqui's face lit up.

"Excellent. Maybe she'll treat me like one."

O suggested they go show the boys.

This was why Steven had arranged the special after-hours fitting. Money couldn't buy everything but it could pay for the privilege of having girls model almost nothing in a commercial setting. Violet didn't even blink at Jacqui's lack of protection where it mattered most.

"Well," Jacqui asked, doing walks and turns in front of the couch, "do you like it?"

Steven looked over at Ray, who had the familiar glazed expression Steven knew so well.

"It works," he pronounced.

"This one's a keeper," Jacqui told Violet.

"Just make a pile in the dressing room for the things you want. We'll hang up the rest."

This was the first time Violet had seen Ray in here with a model. She'd always rather appreciated that. At least he'd picked a good one.

It was O's turn next. From the items Jacqui had brought in, O made a counter-intuitive choice: a half-bra – solid underneath with a transparent scrim of lace over the top of each cup through which O's rings were fully visible. The garter-belt was just a thin strap at the front, leaving O's abdomen completely unprotected, but with three tiers of short, lacy petticoat starting at the hips and resting atop O's upper cheeks. A quick lift, or even draft, would expose her back there too. Everything was white, including the fully-fashioned stockings she chose to go with it.

Satisfied all was in place, she walked purposefully out into the store, aware that the shadows of her last whipping and her bold rings would be fully visible. O was not a model and made no elaborate moves, simply going to Steven, giving him close front and back views.

"I know it's not your sort of thing, Sir," O said, a bit self-consciously. Steven preferred her as bare as possible, even taking off her shoes and corsets more frequently than she would have expected. Nevertheless, he knew Marie best.

"Good instincts," Steven said. "Marie should love it."

That was a relief. O hadn't bought this kind of thing for herself since she was in school. She passed Jacqui on the way back to the dressing room. O really liked what she saw this time: a strappy bra and matching suspender belt. This time it was Jacqui who had gone with all white, making the whole thing look like it was made from bandages.

"How about it, Ray? Would you do me in this?"

Ray looked up into her face. Jacqui's eyes narrowed and her lips pouted out like a sexy gremlin.

"If we were alone your virtue would be in serious danger," Ray managed.

"Good thing I have no virtue to endanger," she said, heading back to the dressing room.

There she found O admiring herself in the mirror in something Jacqui might have bought for herself. It was a bodysuit in heavy black lace, low in the front but otherwise covered, save for generous windows starting above the belly-button, cut equally high on the hips and completely revealing from O's lumbar vertebrae to just below her rear cheeks. Her rings glistened right through it.

Jacqui stopped cold at the sight, suddenly aware of O as she hadn't been before.

"Now that's wicked," she said admiringly.

"I hope it's not too concealing."

"Not where it counts, sweetie."

Jackie demonstrated by giving O's crotch a friendly pat.

When O emerged, heads turned, followed by stunned silence.

"Well, somebody say something please," O finally insisted.

"I say turn around," Steven ordered.

O showed them her completely unprotected hindquarters.

"You don't think it makes me look too dominant do you?"

"The bare-ass thing pretty much neutralizes that issue," Ray offered helpfully.

Steven reminded her sternly to be sure and bring it back with her from Marie's, which was just what O hoped to hear.

Not to be outdone, Jacqui's final ensemble consisted of a short mesh girdle with nothing but a medium width satin strap up the front attached to a matching collar. But bare as it left her breasts, the sweetest treats were elsewhere. The girdle's elastic stopped just above her thighs and the satin waistband knotted with a big bow. Jacqui's back and bottom were fully presented as target areas. A convenient cutout at the center seam of the girdle left Jacqui conveniently available from any direction.

O helped her fasten the hooks at the collar and fluff up the back bow. After a moment of cold calculation, she slipped a hand between Jackie's legs and ran it over the softness exposed by the window.

"I rarely even think about this when I'm shooting," O said, "but I couldn't help wondering how you'd feel when we were in the studio the other day.

Jacqui didn't resist O's light stroking, looking her mischievously in the eye.

"So how do I feel?'

"Even better than you look. Just waxed?"

"Yesterday. Marie's very strict about keeping us all nice and smooth."

"Then I should fit right in."

O took Jacqui's hand and put it to the front opening of the bodysuit. Jacqui drew a naughty finger between O's labia, then brought it to her lips and sucked with closed eyes, as if it were the most delicious confection she'd ever tasted. Then she looked boldly into O's face, touching the end of her nose with the wet fingertip.

"You and I are going to have some serious fun together."

Jacqui took a last look in the mirror and tripped out to the showroom, O following at a respectful distance so as not to distract attention.

Jacqui made a circuit around Ray and Steven.

"Do the gentlemen approve?" she asked playfully.

"I'm not sure there are any gentlemen present," Ray said, "but I think we can agree it's fantastic on you."

"Knowing Marie, I'm sure you'll get whipped plenty in it," Steven said.

"I certainly hope so."

It must have put the idea in her mind, because Jacqui stopped at one of the glass cases on her way back to the dressing room, eyes widening at a skinny, evil dressage whip. It had a a pink handle, from which dangled a jeweled heart on a charm.

"Could I see this please?" Jacqui asked, tapping on the glass. Violet brought her keys and opened the door, bringing the thing out and handing it to Jacqui, who seemed transfixed.

"You do know that those really sting, right?" Violet asked.

"Oh, yeah," Jacqui said, a smile creeping across her lips.

She brought it over to Ray.

"Try it on me, please."

Ray hesitated a beat but came to his senses quickly enough, standing to take the whip in his hand. He flexed it a couple of times to get the action right, then gave Jacqui a good one right across the open space in the cut-out girdle. Jacqui yelped and jumped forward a couple of feet. She turned to face him, smiling and rubbing her ass.

"Thank you, Sir. That was perfect. I'm going to give this to Marie as a present."

Taking the whip from Ray, she handed it to Violet.

"This is on me. Gift for a special friend."

It was all over but the reckoning. While Bridget packed everything into pink boxes, Violet swiped Steven's card once again. For the pink-handled whip, Jacqui fished a Hello Kitty vinyl wallet out of her shoulder bag and unsnapped it. Jaws dropped all over the room. It was packed with crisp hundred dollar bills. Jacqui peeled four of them off and slid them across the counter to Violet.

"I would like a receipt," she said.

After a bit of farewell macking between Violet and Ray, they were down in the garage where, like always, Steven's car waited up front. As expected, the cargo compartment was now filled with boxes and bags.

"I'd call that a successful day," Steven concluded, popping the big SUV into gear.

"At least as far as the local economy is concerned," Ray added. "Anybody interested in dinner?"

Jacqui's hand went up first, waving her new bangle in the air.

"Starving here," she said.

"I could eat," Ray said, as if it was news. Ray could always eat.

"And you O?" Steven asked.

Knowing this would be her last night at Steven's for a while, O would have preferred to go straight home.

"I'll vote with the majority," she said.

The majority ultimately voted for Chinese food at The Mandarette. It had been a long day and fighting their way into someplace trendy on a Saturday night was too much work. Besides, Steven had something to discuss with O in private and sooner would be better.

Over salt-and-pepper Shrimp, Steamed Fish with Ginger and Scallions and Mongolian Beef, they reviewed the day's events while Ray gazed at Jacqui ever more intently. This might be easier than expected, Steven hoped, but only with O's full participation. She seemed solemn, distracted, as she poured his Tsingtao for him. Her usual reverence for a good meal seemed to have deserted her. Jacqui's assurances that they'd all have a great time up at Marie's didn't lighten her mood any.

CHAPTER EIGHTEEN

In the morning, O had gone home briefly, with Steven's permission, to assemble a few things for her stay at Marie's in addition to the items they'd bought, which were clearly intended for special occasions. She took a quick shower and made herself up lightly, remembering to give her lips and nipples a little extra color in the likely event that Steven would see her naked.

O packed a small Halliburton roller with some lingerie of her own that had survived Ray's sorting process, along with her beloved under-bust corsets, one in black of course, the other a sensuous pale pink that matched O's nail color and most of her anatomy. She tossed in a pair of tall pumps the same shade, so that when corseted and shod in the most confining way, she'd still appear molded out of bare flesh. She had borrowed Steven's ballet boots as well, which she loaded up alongside a pair of extravagant white satin mules with heels so high, soles so thin, and a single strap across the front so narrow, her feet seemed to float in space when she wore them, which was seldom. Extra stockings were a must. O would have bet Marie had a supply of them, but O never depended on anyone else to have what she needed. She brought along nude, black and white, all seamed and with Cuban heels of course.

She was equally economical in her choice of cosmetics. Aware, from the thousands of photographs she'd shot, how significant seemingly minor differences could be, O knew exactly what lipstick, liner, rouge, mascara and shadow worked for her. She tossed in a few hygienic items and tucked her laptop into the compartment in the lid. Her carry-on was barely full. It was like getting ready for a vacation at a nudist colony.

But then, she recalled, she'd brought along nothing at all for her stay in Pasadena. She hadn't known she was going to The Mansion until Ray had picked her up. After he'd cut her out of her underwear she had literally arrived with the clothes on her back. And those had come off as soon as she was in the door.

O pictured reenacting that same scene with Jacqui. She couldn't deny the shudder of anticipation that went through her at the thought of taking a blade to Jacqui's bra straps and panties as Ray had to hers; delivering her up hand-cuffed, thinly wrapped and trembling as O had been. O involuntarily squeezed her thighs together, trying keep from dripping at the whole idea.

O would never have done the thing on her own; she was now determined to do it without fail. Steven's orders gave her permission not only to set aside her own convictions, but also to thoroughly enjoy doing so. There weren't a lot of sins left for O to commit in this life and the thrill of reveling in one of the few remaining was intoxicating. She would, at least briefly, go from slave to slave trader and had already been assured the consequences were not her concern. There was liberation in being made to do bad things that, O well knew, caused a lot of trouble in the world. She felt it this morning nonetheless. She had her misgivings about the whole venture, but most exciting ventures inspired misgivings.

And when she put on the austere white blouse and short black skirt she knew Steven liked with nothing beneath she felt a strange, new closeness to him. She'd learned in school that the word "conspire" came from the Latin for "breathing together." It captured the clammy intimacy of sharing a not necessarily harmless secret with only a few of those it would involve. Slipping into her gleaming black "uniform" pumps, she was ready for the road, wherever it led.

Returning to the living room with her case, she started at finding Steven waiting in a white silk jacket, black linen shirt, and black linen trousers. She knew he had the key to her house, but this was the first time he'd used it. He smiled broadly, embraced and kissed her in that demanding way she loved, then stepped back to take a look.

"Good choice," he said. "Marie appreciates a touch of formality, particularly if it's suggestive."

O almost blushed realizing how little protection she had given herself. The blouse was thin enough that the outlines of her nipple rings stood out clearly and if she bent over in the skirt, she'd reveal the lower halves of her rear cheeks. But there was nothing for it. She was quite sure the rule forbidding modesty would be ruthlessly enforced where she was going.

Steven enjoyed watching O delicately lower herself into the seat of the Bentley coupe.

"Still tender back there?" he asked with a laugh.

O laughed too.

"You mean after being beaten and buggered like a British sailor?" she asked good-naturedly. "It's hard to find an inch of me that isn't tender, inside or out."

Before sending her home the previous night, Steven had to try out the new whip they'd bought. That had led to predictably ferocious and perverse coupling that had left her striped and sore in all the right places.

"I'm sure Marie will appreciate that."

"Sir, am I permitted to know a little about you and Marie?" O asked as Steven nosed up the ramp.

Passing the *taquerías* and *iglesias*, all busy on one of the last bright Sundays of the year, Steven revealed more than he'd expected to.

"Marie originally started out as Martin's client. She'd come to us after we got in the paper over that Beverly Hills Madam thing. She was about your age then, had already been running her own escort agency for a couple of years until the vice bulls took her down in a sting. I remember how cool she was for someone up on felony pandering charges. The first thing you have to do in a criminal case is tell the client the worst that can happen, so if you manage to spare them execution they think you're a wizard. Otherwise, they all expect probation and a couple of weeks' community service. She didn't bat an eye when I read her the statutes she was charged with violating and the potential penalties they carried. Unfortunately, I was already working a multiple homicide, so Martin got Marie's case. I remember being a little jealous."

"Because you found her attractive?" O asked.

"The sight of her made my hands sweat, but sex with clients is a bad, bad career move. No, I was jealous of her intelligent questions and realistic expectations. Criminal defendants tend to be arrogant assholes with no idea of how much trouble they're really in. Marie was like a professional gambler looking at the downside of a bad bet. She wanted to cut her losses and get on with the game. That's a dream client in our business."

"How did it come out?"

Passing into Silver Lake, everything changed within a block. The wide boulevard was lined with fashionable cafés full of fashionable people having fashionable conversations over fashionable brunches. This was a younger, not-yet-made-it-crowd compared to their counterparts west of La Cienaga but they'd be over there soon enough.

"Martin was the most able negotiator I ever met," Steven said flatly. "He didn't try to charm or bully or humor the opposition into seeing things his way. He just summarized his trial strategy for them in a calm, unflinching tone that left other lawyers watery in the knees. He knew every exploitable clause in every article on the books and had the weaknesses in the prosecutors' cases all sorted out before he sat down with anybody. He was a lovely guy, but he could be very intimidating in his soft-spoken way. After one meeting with the lead counsel for the DA's office, he got Marie walked on a promise to destroy her client list and close up shop."

O blinked in disbelief.

"That was it?"

"That was it. And they really had her, too. They'd flipped one of her girls on a drug beef and sent her back wearing a wire. They had credit card slips and surveillance tapes. They could have crucified her."

"What did Martin say to them?"

"Just what I would have, although I'm sure he was more diplomatic about it. He threatened to take the case to jury and introduce Marie's black book as Defense Exhibit One."

"Ah yes," O said with a sigh. "The little black book."

Steven grinned.

"Except that there was no little black book. Marie was much too smart to keep one. The prosecutor had her figured as just a typical crook whose bragging could bring down a bunch of more important people; people who would then become his mortal foes."

"So Martin bluffed him."

"It's all about reading the opposition. Some ambitious deputy might have gone for the headlines without considering what it's like to live in this town with powerful enemies. The DA assigned an old-timer to Marie's case and Martin figured there was a mutual interest in settling things quietly. As usual, he was right."

O hesitated on the next question but they were turning onto Franklin Avenue and she had to know.

"How did it get from that to you and Marie walking down the aisle together ... Sir?"

"Once the fix was in, she was no longer the firm's client, so the quarantine was lifted. I asked her out to lunch. We ended up back at her place. She knew what I was all about from a few minutes of casual conversation. In her trade, it's also important to figure out what the client really needs you to know, but isn't quite sure how to tell."

"She must have known you liked it on top."

"And she was curious about that. She didn't generally attract dominant men because most dominant men are pussies. They can't deal with a woman who has plans of her own."

O had been let down by more than one ostensible dom who wanted her to fuck him in the ass with a strap-on as soon as they were alone. Her iron self-possession prevented most from even getting to ask.

"Anyway, as you'd expect, that wasn't an issue with us. I have no problems hurting any woman who wants it."

"And Marie found out she wanted it from you."

"But not everything that came with it. I've dialed things back a lot since then. If we met today, we'd just have some fun and leave it at that, but I was very insistent on getting married. I had to make it official."

O stared at the side of Steven's face, wondering what he must have been like less a dozen years' miles on him. The idea induced a brief shudder.

"The evolution was surprisingly natural. Martin was my best friend and we spent a lot of time together. A natural affection developed between them, just as Marie was beginning to realize that a slave's life wasn't for her. Eventually she admitted she was having more and more trouble 'going there' with me, as she put it. We'd been married a couple of years by then. I was already doing pretty well and she could have really soaked me, but she didn't ask for anything. We filled out the paperwork and filed it together at the county clerk's office."

"And Marie and Martin ..."

"She was already fucking him by then. It was the only dishonest thing he ever did in his life, I think. It bothered him much more than it bothered me. I half expected it would happen from the start. I was best man at their wedding."

O shook her head.

"You're hard to figure sometimes, Sir. You enjoy taking but you can also be very giving when it's not expected."

"I could see that two people I loved were miserable because they thought they were doing something bad to me, which they weren't. I ended up with two happy friends instead of an unhappy wife and a resentful partner. I'll never understand why people can't think these things though more logically."

"But Marie's no longer married to Martin."

"Martin's dead. He died of a heart attack on a racquetball court at thirty-nine. He and Marie only had a couple of years together. I'm glad they were good ones."

O was beginning to regret opening this box. Steven's habit of giving direct answers to direct questions could be disconcerting to say the least. Nevertheless, she had one more that needed a response, whatever it might be.

"Sir, are you absolutely sure we're doing the right thing here?"

"It's unwise to be absolutely sure about anything. I make this as good a wager as any."

That wasn't much help.

"I don't know if Jacqui's a good match for Ray. He's been very good to me and I feel like I've already hurt him once. Jacqui's very young and all about Jacqui and what Jacqui wants. I'd hate to see Ray fall for her and get kicked to the curb. He's a pretty sensitive guy."

Steven laughed.

"Gee, I hadn't noticed that."

He turned his eyes from the road for an instant to look O in the face, alert for any sign of weakening resolve. He didn't see it, but he did see a little furrow of concern between her plucked eyebrows before he want back to watching the traffic.

"You understand why I need you to give Jacqui to Ray as your slave the way he gave you to me. I don't know if she's capable of falling for any man, but I suspect she's already half-way there with you."

"Sooner or later they'll have to be alone with each other, Sir. What happens then?"

"Do I look like a gypsy to you? I don't know if they'll live happily ever after, or if she'll just be a transitional object for him while he recovers from his latest self-inflicted injury. It's a good thing he recovers quickly, especially when he's got some-one new and hot to distract him."

"Sir is going to a lot of trouble to clear his conscience."

"You sound surprised."

"I wasn't sure you had one."

"That makes two of us."

O was relieved when they pulled up in front of the neo-Aztec façade of Marie's place on Franklin.

The stairs from the street were steep, winding and en-closed by thick foliage. Steven carried O's case to the ornate wrought iron gate and rang the doorbell, which chimed a short melody.

In a clatter of high heels, Jacqui came down to let them in. She was in the pink today: pink leather collar and cuffs trimmed with white lace, a tiny pink satin bra and a six-strap garter-belt to match, holding up white stockings. Her pink patent fetish pumps were truly perverse, a suggestive match for her pink lips. The sheer, black peignoir thrown over her ensemble wouldn't have covered much even if she'd bothered to lace it shut. She threw her arms around O, who noticed that

Jacqui no longer wore the gold bangle Ray had just bought her.

"Hello, beautiful," she said, kissing O on the cheek. "I've told everybody all about you. They're dying to meet the girl I've been panting after. Have you had lunch yet?"

Before O could answer, Jacqui darted over to give Steven a quick hug and kiss.

"And how are you, Sir? Will you be needing any services performed today?" Jacqui asked, smiling up at him with a girlish eagerness of which he was skeptical.

"Do you do circumcisions?"

Jacqui scowled at him comically.

"I'd suggest four skin-divers for that," she shot back.

"That's good," Steven conceded. "Mind if I steal it?"

Jacqui shrugged.

"Why not? I did. Come on in. We're just setting the table."

Jacqui was a clever one. Steven hoped she wouldn't prove too clever for Ray.

"What happened to the bracelet Ray bought you?" O asked.

"It's in Marie's desk drawer. She thought it was premature so she took it off with one of those little screwdrivers. She's collected a few bracelets no one came back to claim."

They followed Jacqui into the big, dark front parlor, which was completely walled off from the street but opened onto a glassed-in courtyard with a long swimming pool down the middle. The parlor had a massive stone fireplace surrounded by deep couches and chairs in burgundy velvet. A vast Persian rug softened the tiled floor. The marbleized walls were decorated with Marie's collection of Parisian bordello art; two large vitrines flanking the fireplace held her collection of pre-war brothel artifacts, ranging from boudoir clocks with risqué faces to ivory dildos.

The parlor gave onto a big dining room where the other three girls currently in residence set out china and crystal on a long table draped in light-green damask and illuminated from above by a blood red Murano glass chandelier. All wore scraps of expensive lace in various pastel colors along with stockings, garters and heels. Only two beside O bore the identifying shackle ring.

A small blonde with hourglass curves accentuated by the perfect features of a Vargas pin-up arranged the silver with a taller blonde who might have been her less-perfect sister. The tall girl had big brown eyes and a thick lower lip lending her a pleasingly bovine placidity. Her full, rosy breasts were unbound beneath a transparent under-blouse that stopped above the navel. She was a bit narrow through the ass and hips, one of which was extravagantly illustrated with a big, brilliant floral tattoo, but her legs stretched all the way to China, or at least to her strappy sandals. An exquisite Japanese girl in a body harness of pale blue ribbons that accentuated her perfectly proportioned after-market chest concentrated intently on rearranging an extravagant bouquet in a black crystal vase.

As always, the whole atmosphere was so aggressively feminine Steven wanted to plunder it like a Hun. Marie had organized every detail to induce such desires, but unlike The Mansion, plundering was discouraged here. Only Marie, the other residents, and their masters were allowed to indulge under this roof.

Jacqui clapped her hands twice, getting the attention of the other girls.

"Everybody, this is O, our new sister."

They all stopped work and gathered around O and Steven. Jacqui made the introductions. The smaller blonde was called Laurel, the tall one Angelique. The Japanese girl was Noriko. Each curtsied in a deliberately quaint manner, said hello, and kissed O on the lips while Jacqui playfully undid a couple of buttons on O's top.

"Wait until you get a look at what's under here," she said in a husky voice.

"I think we'll have the unveiling in private."

The girls froze at the sound of Marie's voice as she descended the spiral stairs. She wore a long black-chiffon negligee trimmed in satin and high-buttoned Victorian-style boots. The girls all dropped to their knees, heads bowed, at Marie's approach. She and Steven embraced and kissed.

"How's my favorite ex-husband?" she asked.

"Still single," he replied.

"That's a relief."

She turned to O and extended a hand.

"And you must be O."

O took Marie's hand firmly.

"I have no choice in the matter, Ma'am, as with many things."

Marie smiled over at Steven.

"She is a quick one, isn't she?"

"That's the half of it," Steven replied, grinning broadly.

"Jacqui, take O's bag and put it in your room. She'll be sharing with you."

Jacqui's face lit up.

"Thank you, Ma'am!"

She seized O's case from Steven, groped him shamelessly, kissed O on the cheek and hurried off.

Marie asked Steven if he was staying for lunch.

"Not this time. I'm trying out a new fencing partner down at the club."

"I know how you hate being late to stab someone. Come on back where can talk."

Marie turned with a rustle of chiffon, and started toward the corridor that led to the other rooms around the courtyard. O and Steven followed. The house had been reconfigured so the hallway ran along the glass wall surrounding the pool. Glass doors opening into the girls' rooms were ranged every few feet down the opposite wall. Each was painted a rich blue that matched the water in the pool, giving the house the air of a well-tended aquarium stocked with exotic specimens. The carpet underfoot was so thick it felt like freshly-mown grass.

Marie's office was at the opposite end of the house where the hallway terminated in mirrored double doors Marie could see through from inside. The large room looked directly out onto the pool and the jalousied inner shutters were open, affording Marie a commanding view of her domain.

It was an elegant room, anchored by an Art Nouveau escritoire with a large, green velvet fan-back chair behind it and a deep sofa covered in striped silk brocade. The fabric on the walls matched the couch. A huge lacquered cabinet, in which Marie kept her computer safely locked away, dominated one side of the room. Opposite Marie's vast inlaid black antique desk an intimidating, meticulous stage-set reproduction of a small Harley Street surgery with a gleaming white-tiled floor made an ominous contrast. Its glassed-in cabinets holding steel instrument trays and an articulating black-and-white gynecological table complete with restraining straps implied every kind of invasive procedure. Pendant lamps with old-style Edison bulbs crackled overhead.

O shivered at the sight, which brought back unwanted memories of the humiliating and painful examination to which she'd been subjected her first night at The Mansion. A woman doctor in latex whites had opened, inspected and probed her, testing her for everything relevant, from gag reflex to pain threshold to orgasmic response. O hoped she wasn't in for more of that here.

Steven settled onto the couch. Marie sat up straight in the tall chair behind the desk. O started to sit down next to Steven, but Marie stopped her with an upraised palm.

"Come here and hold up the front of your skirt," Marie said firmly.

O did as instructed, feeling more rudely revealed by showing her most sensitive anatomy first before unveiling anything
else. Marie appraised the view at leisure, pronouncing it perfectly delectable before delivering a brief orientation.

"That's the one part of you that will never be covered
during your stay here. The girls will be encouraged to touch
you there at any time and required to on occasion. You'll do
the same with them. You may not touch yourself or prevent
yourself from being touched by the others. You will depend
on your slave sisters and on me for the relief you'll require
frequently. Steven tells me you have strong sexual appetites
and everything in this place is calculated to stimulate them.
Other than Steven, who can visit when he wants and put you to
whatever use he pleases, you'll serve no men here. But you will
serve me and you will be generous with the others. I'm sure
you won't find that too unpleasant."

"No, Ma'am," O said, stifling an unwise giggle. Standing
their with her skirt lifted was like being tutored by the dean of
girls at some school she could only wish she'd attended instead
of the stuffy, snobbish institutions among which her parents
had bounced her as she managed to get herself in trouble at
each.

"You can remain standing while you disrobe for us, O,"
Marie said in a firm but pleasant tone. "I'd like you completely
naked please."

O undressed by the numbers, starting at the top and folding each article of clothing onto the couch as it came off. There
wasn't much, just the blouse and skirt. O was barelegged and
had only to remove her shoes. She bent over to reveal herself
totally as she set them neatly next to the couch. O came to attention, legs spread and fingers laced behind her neck. Marie
brought out O's Mansion file from the desk drawer, comparing
the printed-out pictures of O exposed in various lewd postures
to O very much in the flesh. While O stood trembling on pointed feet, Marie scanned the reports in the file. It was impossible

to tell if she approved or disapproved of the evidence presented.

Marie signaled O to approach the desk.

"Steven's explained his whole scheme to me," Marie said sternly. "I have reservations about it, but I've agreed to go along. I'll do everything possible to make it work. I dislike manipulating my girls — other than physically that is — and I'm very fond of Jacqui. She's the only un-owned one I let stay here, because I enjoy her company and don't want her getting herself into trouble as she's fond of doing. Whatever Ray's shortcomings, at least he can advance her career and he'll certainly do her no harm. On the contrary, I suspect she'll eat poor Ray alive, but that's Steven's problem."

Marie looked over at Steven, who sprawled on the couch, enjoying the show.

"Hardly news," he said with a shrug. "I've been pulling Ray out from somebody's choppers since the day he was born."

"You'll be sharing a room, and also a bed, with Jacqui," Marie continued. "You'll dress and undress each other, bathe each other and feed each other. You'll also hurt each other when required. Bend over the desk."

O lowered her shoulders, putting her breasts within Marie's easy reach. Marie hooked an index finger through each of O's rings and pulled hard enough to make O flinch.

"Steven doesn't believe in punishing slaves, and I generally agree. It only produces the opposite of the desired end by feeding their masochistic desires. But don't be fooled by the languid atmosphere. Our discipline is strict and I have no hesitation about enforcing it in ways you won't like. That's why my word is respected. You seemed uneasy when you saw our medical facilities. If I'm inclined to be cruel to you, that's probably where I'll do it."

Marie released O's aching tits and let her stand up straight again.

"Before I found my way into this line of work, I trained as a nurse-practitioner. I know quite a bit about women's bodies and I've learned even more about their minds. A certain amount of shared suffering will contribute to the bond Steven hopes to create between you and Jacqui. You can count on me to make sure you both get more than enough. I can expect your full cooperation?"

"Yes, Ma'am," O said, almost in a whisper. Accustomed as she was to having her way with women both in the studio and in the bedroom, O wasn't used to being intimidated by anyone of her own sex.

Marie stood, came around the desk and motioned O back into the middle of the room. She circled O's waist with both hands.

"I understand you have a taste for corseting," Marie said.

O confirmed it.

"What's your maximum reduction?"

"Four inches, Ma'am, but only for short periods. Two inches I can wear all day."

"What do you think, Steven? Shall we sculpt her a bit for you?"

Steven thought it over.

"I do like seeing her curves exaggerated."

Marie concurred. "

We'll keep her compressed regularly. With proper diet and exercise, she should come back to you a little more constructed, in addition to the modifications you already have planned. Enough talk for now. Let's get her dressed for lunch."

O always found it titillating to be discussed in the third person in her presence, but couldn't quite shake the momentary discomfort of being found in need of further "construction." O had invested a lot of labor into molding herself as she was. She had some of the model's usual insecurities, even though she'd never modeled.

Marie pressed a button on the underside of her desk and a buzzer sounded faintly from the front parlor. In a moment, O's companions entered, did the required curtsy for Marie and formed a line in front of the desk to either side of O. Jacqui had a brightly-woven basket under one arm and a tape measure draped over her collared neck. Laurel carried one of the boxes from the lingerie store. They greeted Marie in unison, much to Steven's amusement. Just as Steven had taught Marie a lot about what turned dominant men on, Marie had shown him a lot about what excited submissive women. The "dollhouse" atmosphere of Marie's private retreat was carefully engineered around those insights.

"Laurel, let's see what O brought for her debut."

Laurel took the black ribbon off the pink box and opened it, bringing out the white ensemble one piece at a time and inspiring much delighted laughter from the girls. Angelique held up the open-front garter-belt.

"Very practical," she said coolly.

"Not for you," Laurel shot back. "Yours should be open from the rear."

"You're one to talk," Angelique replied, pinching Laurel's behind.

"These two compete for the A Squad around here," Jacqui explained.

"Angelique wouldn't care if her pussy were sewn shut," Noriko said.

Angelique warned her not to give Marie any ideas.

"This all seems well-chosen," Marie concluded after inspecting the contents of the box. "Let's see it on."

O took the bra and started to put her arms through the straps. Marie took it away from her and handed it to Jacqui.

"Here you're not allowed to put on or take off anything by yourself," she chided. "Hold your arms out straight."

She handed the bra to Jacqui, who took her time shaping the cups around O's breasts before hooking them together in front. More accustomed to dressing others than being dressed, O stood stiffly while Jacqui fastened the garter-belt, playfully lifting the ruffles in back.

"Oh dear, must have been a sudden breeze," Jacqui said innocently, provoking an outburst of laughter from the others. Jacqui pointed at the couch.

"On your back, Sister"

It was the first of many times O would be called that. It would take some getting used to. She had, after all, been brought up as a nominal Catholic.

O lay down, legs raised in a wide split so Laurel and Noriko could roll on the white stockings and clip them to the garters. O put her head in Steven's lap. Steven dropped a hand casually over O's conveniently disposed pussy, finding it quite moist as usual. O's face had taken on the heavy-lidded languor Steven knew so well.

"Enjoying yourself so far?" he asked.

"Yes, Sir. Very much. I'm afraid I might get spoiled here."

"No danger of that," Marie interjected drily.

"Okay, who's got her shoes?" Jacqui demanded. Angelique held up the white satin mules.

"You mean these?"

She and Laurel slipped them onto O's feet.

Steven took his hand away so O could stand.

"Collar and cuffs now, Jacqui," Marie instructed.

Jacqui set the colorful basket on the desk and wrapped the measuring tape snugly around O's neck. She called out the circumference. Noriko took down the statistics in a small red-leather-bound diary with a gold pen as Jacqui circumnavigated O's body, measuring each wrist and ankle separately. Once the statistics were inked, Angelique popped the lid off the basket. Searching through the various sizes of restraints within, she brought out a full set of collar and cuffs.

They differed subtly but significantly from those worn at The Mansion, and from the set Steven had commissioned for O. A gently faded brown leather instead of the usual black, their hasps and rings were brass rather than steel and they were an inch narrower than the more industrial gear to which O was accustomed. The leather was deliciously soft on O's skin, but closely fitted and thick enough to be sturdy in use. Each was secured with a small gold heart-shaped lock as the girls fluttered around O clicking them shut.

Once the operation was completed, everyone just looked at her in silent admiration for a beat.

"Quite the juicy little bon-bon, isn't she?" Angelique drawled.

O had imagined herself many things over the years, but a juicy little bon-bon had not been one of them. Steven had seen her dressed this way in the store and appreciated her for her beauty as always, but here, surrounded as by such heavily sensual musk, he felt the powerful urge to slam O against the nearest wall and nail her into it. Marie had been slammed against a few walls by Steven back in the day and momentarily missed it.

"Sure you can't stay for lunch?" she asked.

"I'll be back soon, I promise," he replied. "May I have a moment with O before leaving?"

"Of course," Marie said. "Come on, girls. I think Rosemary has something special in the kitchen to welcome your new sister."

Standing and sweeping the others out like a flock of schoolgirls, Marie looked back at Steven with a strange tenderness, shutting the door behind her and leaving them alone. Steven took O in his arms.

"You can't imagine how much I want to fuck you right now," he said.

O wrapped a leg around him, plastering her thinly-covered body against his linen shirt and trousers, where she felt the familiar bulge.

"Yes I can, Sir" she whispered.

With some difficulty, he peeled her off and put a little distance between them.

"We'll catch up on that when I visit. Meantime, you have work to do. There are many distractions here. Mustn't lose sight of the mission objective."

"That's not a thing either of us would do, is it, Sir?"

The question came edged with an unfamiliar anxiety, but he chalked it up to the new surroundings and the complex task ahead.

"That's my good girl."

The kissed hungrily, hands searching each other's bodies for a last tactile memory to hold close during their separation.

Steven walked O out to the table, around which the others stood. He kissed each good-bye, Marie last, and headed for the door.

CHAPTER NINETEEN

The business district had long been a ghost town on Sunday afternoons, but no longer. After many false starts, the downtown real estate explosion had finally detonated, much to Steven's good fortune. The coming of expensive residential spaces had brought restaurants and shops and, shocking as they were to Angeleno sensibilities, pedestrians. An odd mix of hipsters, suits, and street people, they were out in force on this bright Sunday afternoon, sucking down lattes, slurping up gelatos or chugging wine from paper sacks as they threaded their way among the spavined refrigerator boxes and piles of rags marking the dwellings of the city's less fortunate.

The Athletic Club bustled with families bringing the kids for a swim at the indoor pool and middle-aged men, drunk before five, shouting at referees on the bar's TV sets. Steven had someone new to kill and did his best to focus his energies as he changed in the locker room, emerging once again in his black tunic and mask.

With Morgan gone to the desert, he was left to pay the hourly for the club's new coach as a fencing partner. Though the multiple dials of the Breitling Old Navitimer on his wrist said he was right on time, the soft-spoken young black man with whom he'd booked the match on the phone was waiting for him when he got to the fencing hall.

They shook hands genially, Steven insisting that he must have been late, Mike (aka Mike the Spike), insisting that he must have been early. Mike was a serious competitor who spent most of his time teaching rich kids how to hold a foil. Aware of Steven's murderous reputation, Mike looked forward to some serious competition for a change.

It wasn't important for Mike to know that Steven had done some arm-twisting at the board meeting to get him hired. Though the club's legendary basketball coach had trained many young African-Americans who had gone on to glory at Staples Center, a certain crowd Steven called The Hancock Park Fossils had wanted a swordsman from some Eastern prep school. Reminding them that a black American had dethroned all the aging Italians and Hungarians to bring home Olympic gold in saber fencing not long ago, he invited anyone present to challenge Mike, the young up-and-comer whose name he had forwarded, for themselves. There were no takers and Mike got the job.

Now it was Steven taking up his own gauntlet. Chatting as they did their stretches about all Mike's competition experience, Steven realized he'd need to bring his A-game if he didn't care to be embarrassed. Though still in his mid-twenties, Mike had won so many collegiate and amateur tournaments he seemed likely to end up under the five circles himself someday. If Steven had to lose at least he'd be losing to a worthy opponent.

As expected, Mike took Steven out three times running.

"Well I'm dead as I'll ever be," Steven said with a laugh.

Mike laughed too.

Over a beer in the lounge they talked about how they came by their enthusiasm for such an archaic sport.

"All you need is one good teacher," Mike explained. "Mine was a retired Marine DI from Pendleton who volunteered at a community center in Compton just to keep in shape. He was even older than you, but he had all the moves."

"You could probably show him some new ones now," Steven said. "You know you've graduated when you kill your coach."

They clicked beer glasses.

"I wouldn't take it for granted. He brings something to it not many fencers do."

"Actual hand-to-hand combat experience," Steven said.

"No shit. I saw him in his dress blues at his daughter's wedding. She married a Marine like her old man. He had so many ribbons, he was practically wearing them on his back."

"I met guys like that when I was in the Navy. It always seemed wrong that they had to salute me. I did most of my hitch in front of trial boards."

"No kills at all?"

Steven hesitated an instant. "Not while in uniform."

Mike didn't press him on it. In fact, Steven had seen some action in The Balkans, but mostly after the fact. As a counselor for the CID detachment assigned to IFOR, he'd become entirely too familiar with the stench of recently opened mass graves and the equally vile scent of corruption that dirty wars enable.

"There are battlefields everywhere," Mike said. "I lost my nephew in a drive-by about a block from our house."

Steven shook his head.

"There's no safe refuge."

"Amen to that," Mike agreed, finishing his beer. "You want the same time next Sunday?"

"I'll try not to expire from old age in the meantime."

They laughed and shook hands and Steven took his leave. He had one other appointment prior to meeting Ray for dinner.

Jan Harkness had been the blazing nova of star tattoo artists back when celebs showed off their ink on the covers of supermarket magazines. Tats from Jan were as desired, and as hard to come by, as a Harley Silver Anniversary Fat-Boy. The pricing was comparable.

But at the very height of body-art's go-go years, Jan was gone-gone. She'd dumped her big, red-walled shop on Melrose Avenue and set up a small studio next door to her shabby apartment in a shabby building on a shabby block of a fairly shabby Hollywood street south of Sunset. She took new clients only by referral and used the money she'd piled up through hard work and thrifty living to travel the world, acquiring odd skills and odder companions along the way.

Jan and Steven had been friends since he'd sprung her long-since-rejected musician boyfriend from the slammer. Jan had touched up a couple of holidays in Steven's shoulder piece, which she'd instantly recognized as a Horiyoshi II, leading to the kind of story Jan loved. Hearing that Steven had been flown to Osaka by a *yakuza oyabun* whose passport Steven had pried out of the State Department and given the tattoo in gratitude, she'd decided he could hang.

Neither her appearance nor her attitude had changed much since. Her hair was still black-black. She still wore black librarian glasses (earned fair and square when she'd taught life-drawing at Carnegie-Mellon before The Tattoo God spoke to her). She still had an impossibly perfect comic-book shape, in no way hidden by the black tights, big belts and low-cut tops she favored. Jan still probably had some undecorated skin someplace, but of the substantial percentage on view, scarcely a millimeter lacked a souvenir from a fellow artist. Some of her work was lyrical, like the fruits-and-flowers left sleeve. Some of it was biker-badass, like the Viking skull on her right ankle.

Meeting Steven on the second-floor asphalt walkway of Jan's sun-bleached cinderblock hideout, she gave him a linebacker's hug, though with Jan's legendary rack it certainly didn't feel like one. Jan's strength had come from rolling bodies around and she stood about six feet, even without the high-heeled boots she habitually wore.

"Get your ass in out of the sun, stranger," she said in her friendliest bark.

The studio was tiny but bright, made more so by Haitian paintings and *Dìa de los Muertos* mementos she'd picked up in her wanderings. Steven pulled up a big, dark red kilim pillow from the pile against the wall and settled in under the window while Jan went off to make him some tea in the closet-sized kitchen.

"So where you been laying low?" she asked, as if it had been a couple of weeks instead of a couple of years.

"The Inns of Court, where else?"

"Still making the streets safe for thimble-riggers and jack-rollers?"

"Please. My clients are murderous gangsters," Steven said in a tone of mock indignation.

"Well that changes everything."

She knelt in front of him, bowed her head and presented a celadon teacup from a black lacquered tray.

"*Ippuku sashi agemasu,*" she said.

Steven bowed in response.

"*Otemae chodai itashimasu,*" he replied, taking the cup. "Thanks for seeing me on a Sunday."

She sat cross-legged on the floor facing him, drinking some tea of her own.

"I'm always glad to see you, so long as it isn't through chicken-wire."

"That reminds me."

Steven reached into his jacket for the leather joint case, slipped it open and torched up with the Dupont French Foreign Legion lighter. Jan spotted it instantly, asking for a closer look as she took a hit off the joint. She hefted it, fired it once just to hear the inimitable "ping" when she closed the lid.

"Nice. Didn't know you'd been a Legionnaire."

"Hardly. In the Legion, it's march or die. In the Navy JAG it's cocktails at five. I won it in a pool game from a snotty One-REC commandant when we were all with the blue-helmets."

Steven never lied, but he did leave things out. He had worked with the liaison team in Kosovo. But he had also prosecuted two bent Navy junior officers and a half-dozen NCOs who had thrown in with the Albanian mob, landing girls trafficked from Moldova on the Adriatic Coast in Zodiacs for transshipment to points west. They'd get out of Leavenworth sometime before the next ice age. Not a subject he cared to discuss.

He asked where she'd been recently. Jan did the inventory in her head.

"Let's see, this year I was in Japan for The Fire Festival. Then I spent a month in Bali. I came back through Europe so I could catch the Salzburg Festival. You know half the musicians are Chinese now?"

"That must make the Austrians nuts," Steven laughed.

"Hard to tell."

"I think that's why Austria makes me nervous."

"I'm sure it has nothing to do with the Anschluss or anything."

This time they both laughed. Then Jan got serious.

"I don't hear from you since Christmas before last, and all of a sudden you have to see me right away. What's so important that we have to meet on a Sunday?"

"I want you do to something for me in a couple of weeks, and I figured I'd should give you as much time as I could to work on the design."

"This just keeps getting better. First I'm doing business on my one day off, and now I'm taking a commission that's going to make my calendar an exercise in quantum physics."

Steven brought out a folded sheet of paper from inside his jacket and handed it to Jan. She opened it up and peered at it intently. The crude drawing on it was simple but bold: a bow with a long ribbon draping from each side and a circle above it containing Steven's initials.

"It's a good thing you don't have to make a living off your art," she concluded, handing it back to him. "Unless I'm mistaken, that looks very much like a slave tag."

"Exactly."

"You know what I think about putting names or initials on anyone."

"Unless it's your mother or a dead best friend, it's bad luck."

"Why are we going against both our principles this time?"

Steven brought out his cell phone, running his fingers over the touch screen. Steven passed the phone to Jan in exchange for the nearly finished joint. She flipped back and forth among O's look-book shots from The Mansion.

"Nice. How tall is she?"

"About five-three."

Jan held up Steven's attempt at drawing a flash.

"Is this roughly to scale?'

Steven gave an embarrassed shrug.

"As close as I could get to what I have in mind."

"That's a mighty big tattoo on a small woman. No lasering it off if anyone changes their mind."

"Ours aren't the kinds of minds that change."

Jan looked at him for a long moment.

"I'll need to talk to her first, without you in the room."

"No problem. She'll expect it."

"She'll have to sign the consent form too."

"I wrote the consent form, Jan. I expect you to make everyone sign it. I don't do civil litigation."

She grinned at him.

"Don't worry, counselor. I get all their John Hancocks. I just want to make absolutely sure you're both absolutely sure."

"When you meet O, you'll have no doubts."

"Okay, let's see what we can do here."

Jan gave Steven back his phone, fetched a big, orange Rodia pad and an Aurora black demonstrator sketch pencil. Spreading Steven's folded sheet on the floor, she looked back and forth between it and the paper in front of her as she drew, holding the pad upright so Steven couldn't see what she was doing.

"Don't even think of looking over my shoulder," she said, reading his mind.

"So what part of this girl's anatomy are we talking here?"

"Lower lumbar."

Jan looked up with visible distaste.

"Not a tramp-stamp, I hope. That would be putting graffiti on Vermeer."

"Something much ruder. I want the bow to loop about an inch above her tail bone so the ribbons drape over her ass cheeks."

"Sort of gift-wrapping her anus for yourself."

"Exactly."

Jan turned the pad around and held it up so Steven could see. The rendering was perfect, the bow just the right size, the ribbons the prefect length, the open circle big enough for two letters of modest scale. The quickly executed outlines of O's back view reflected Jan's long service teaching others how to draw the human body. Though just a few curved strokes, it was unmistakably O.

"Fantastic! Just what I'm looking for."

"You won't have any trouble finding what you're looking for with this over it. Any particular color in mind?"

"I was thinking of a dark pink."

"That's very sick of you."

"I figured you'd approve."

"Let me see that picture of her bending over again."

Steven gave her back the phone, and Jan studied it carefully.

"Not much pigment in her skin. The color should be pretty stable. What font for the letters?"

"Some kind of script, but nothing too frilly."

Jan got up, went to a small bookcase next to her household shrine and brought out a thin volume of type styles, handing it to Steven. He went through it carefully, checking out the letters "S" and "D" in each.

"How about German Blackletter?" Jan teased.

"Not sure I want to look at that every day," Steven replied. "Although Lucida Blackletter is kind of nice."

"If you're going there, I'd stick with Lucida Calligraphy. It holds up better over the long run. Check out Monotype Corsiva and see what you think."

Jan picked up her drawing pad, took the book back from Steven, carefully tracing his initials from the sample alphabet. She held up the results for inspection.

"I like that," Steven said. "It's rather elegant."

"Come back in a week. I'll have a color flash for you."

Steven reached for his wallet, but froze at Jan's notorious hairy eyeball.

"Don't you dare."

"It's a rush job on someone you don't know and you'll have to do it as an outcall up at Marie's."

"Don't care. I didn't charge you for the lock on the back of Marie's neck either. How is that fine woman these days?"

"Content. You can see for yourself when you do this."

"Does she have a flat, stable surface I can work on?"

"How about a vintage operating table?"

Jan laughed.

"Sounds like a party."

Both stood for a farewell hug.

"I'm really happy for you," Jan said. "I never thought the *El Veijo* would take a mate."

Steven stiffened in her arms.

"Careful not to draw conclusions," he said.

"That's the one thing I don't draw," she said, letting him go.

In an architecturally austere and pricey Mexican restaurant off Flower Street, Steven found Ray already seated, midway through a Mojito and perusing the bill of fare. He looked smart in his new Panzer coat, a flashy red scarf around his neck. They fell into deep green vinyl at the opposite end of the round booth.

Ray asked if O was all settled in up at Marie's.

"I imagine the settling-in process is well underway by now," Steven said, consulting the big Breitling watch. It was starting to get dark by seven now. Los Angeles did have distinct seasons, but they were measured in time rather than temperature.

"I already ordered us some guacamole," Ray said as the redheaded waitress put a Bohemia and a chilled glass down in front of Steven.

"Hello, Mr. Diamond," she said pleasantly. "Amy's cooking tonight and she says she'll do the *carnitas* on the lean side for you."

"Tell her I thank her and my cardiologist thanks her."

They all laughed. Steven returned the menu and the waitress drifted back toward the computer to key in their order.

Ray was impatient for details Steven didn't care to provide.

"O likes girls and girls like O. She'll fit right in. What are you having?

"Chicken Mole. Anyone else I know up there at the moment?"

"I assume you mean Jacqui."

"Isn't that called leading the witness?"

The guacamole arrived on a triangular black plate. The chips in the basket were hot and the *pico de gallo* was fresh. It wasn't as easy to find a good Mexican restaurant in L.A. as most tourists assumed, and once discovered, such places were quickly overrun, which was why Ray and Steven often ate here on Sunday nights.

"No, it's simply recognizing the obvious."

"Tell me you didn't think Jacqui looked hot in that half-bra thing."

"She'd look hot in a feed sack. I'm sure she wakes up looking like that, though if she doesn't cut back on the partying, things could change. You'll want to keep an eye on her when there are liquor and drugs around.

"There are always liquor and drugs around, especially where I go. Anyway, why is that my problem?"

"Everything about Jacqui's going to be your problem."

"Fuck you. I knew you were sandbagging me."

"If somebody put that girl at my feet, I don't think I'd consider myself sandbagged."

Steven took another scoop of guacamole. The texture was perfect, chunky rather than homogenized. "What, you're so sure you're the only smart guy in the room?"

Ray said it good-naturedly, but that was an aspect of Steven's character that got on his last nerve.

"If I'd wanted to conceal my objectives, I don't think I'd have paraded her in front of you in various states of naked. And what was up with the sudden urge to slap a screw-on bracelet around her arm?"

"Yeah, well, it was an impulse buy, kind of like that watch you picked up. What makes you think Jacqui's even interested in me?"

"She's not interested in you, yet. Right now she's interested in O, but you're next on the fun wheel. She'll be plenty interested in you by the time O serves her up. But if you want the arrangement to last, you'll have to keep her that way."

Ray stretched back in his chair, caught the waitress going by and ordered another Mojito.

"Not everyone is like you."

"Everyone is like everyone. That's what I've learned in life."

"Let me rephrase that. Not everyone is like The Terminator. I had feelings for O. I still have feelings for O. You've just snagged her like you did that Cartier watch and you're dangling some bright, shiny object in front of me so I won't notice how you snaked my slave."

Steven thought that one over and nodded.

"I'd say that about covers it. But in all fairness, it was your idea. I'd never have touched her if you'd told me not to."

Conversation stopped while the entrées were served. Amy had remembered Steven's déclassé preference for flour tortillas. They were nice and warm too.

"I wanted to share my most precious possession with the only person in this world I trust."

Steven slapped his hand over his heart.

"I'm wounded by your sense of betrayal."

He got serious about wrapping up some pork and peppers.

"You and O were done and you both knew it. That's why you outsourced her to The Mansion. You needed a break from the intensity."

It was Ray's turn to do the thinking-over as he sliced into the black-sauced chicken breast.

"O does run on a two-twenty line."

"And you're wired for one-ten. Jacqui's a sweet, funny, sexy party hamster that juices up behind a good whacking. Do you really need anything more right now?"

"I can find that on my own."

"I've never known you to have a problem getting laid," Steven conceded. "But I've seen the way you look at Jacqui. You felt you had to balance the scales by giving me something I really wanted and you did. Now I feel like they're tipped the other way. Jacqui is something you really want, but if you don't get her on your terms, you'll end up in the mole sauce like that chicken."

"Gee, thanks for the vote of confidence. I look to my big brother for that."

"You wisely look to me for straight answers, since everyone else kisses your ass, Mr. Smokin' Magazine Publisher. Only Jacqui won't do that unless she thinks it's her idea."

"And you believe O can put that idea in her head."

"Or somewhere further south."

Ray ate in silence for a moment or two.

"You know, Ray," Steven finally said, "I'm not the only one who's uncomfortable with how things have shaken out so far. O still has feelings for you too, just not the kind you'd prefer. Would you please let everybody off the hook by allowing us to do something nice for you?"

"You're so good at making me feel like an ungrateful fuck."

"You are an ungrateful fuck most of the time, although I have to say you got one up on me with O."

"So what's my part in the grand scheme?"

"Just play along. Once O has Jacqui in the right frame of mind, we'll all start going places together, hanging out, fooling around. Pretty soon you'll be out in Pasadena locking a collar around Jacqui's pretty neck. Your job is to have a good time. I'm confident you can handle it."

"Steven," Ray said, shaking his head, "you are, and will remain, a complete enigma."

"How's the flan here? I can't remember."

"Kind of like Jacqui, smooth and creamy."

"That's more like it," Steven said. "Hang onto that thought."

CHAPTER TWENTY

The Santa Ana winds had finally gone offshore, leaving the night air warm, velvety and heavy with the scent of jasmine. It felt almost indistinguishable from the deep blue water of Marie's pool, where O and Jacqui swam naked in slow, lazy strokes. Their leather collars and cuffs were stacked carefully next to the water, tiny padlocks in a gleaming pile. The house was dark but for the lights in and around the pool and a dim lamp somewhere in Marie's quarters at the back.

With her long, lean limbs, Jacqui covered a lot more distance with each stroke, but O's strength allowed her to keep up as they did their languid laps. She admired the uncontrived sleekness and grace with which Jacqui glided through the water.

"So what's the story with Angelique and Laurel?" O asked. "I can picture Laurel taking the collar for the right man. Angelique doesn't seem suited to that life."

Jacqui blew some water out from between her delectable lips.

"Because she's an ice-cold bitch?

"I wouldn't have put it quite that way, but ..."

"Angelique wasn't always like that. I met her when she first started modeling, which she only did to please the Master she was with back then. She was bubbly and enthusiastic about it all."

"Bubbly isn't the word that comes to mind when I think of Angelique."

"You probably wouldn't think of sweet and goofy either, but she was all that. She just fell in love with the wrong man."

This time O spat out some water.

"Love, the deadliest toxin outside the fangs of the Black Mamba."

"It was for her. I met the asshole once. You know how some people give off a mean vibe even when they're trying to seem nice?"

"I know the type."

"Angelique told me the only time he really got off on fucking her was when she was crying."

"Did he give a lot of pain?"

"Not the physical kind. He liked messing with her head. The more she tried to please him, the worse he treated her."

"I hate men like that."

O took a break, sitting on the shelf at the shallow end, her arms stretched along the concrete lip. Jacqui joined her.

"I grew up with a couple of those," Jacqui said. "They're no threat to me. I like nice guys."

O felt a stab of remorse over Ray. He was a nice guy, the kind any woman might love, except O. "Angelique never intended to do porn," Jacqui went on. "She was working for some tech company in San Jose when she met her so-called Master. He got her to move down here and make videos just so he could use them to humiliate her. It gave him a hold over her, knowing she couldn't go back to her old life after all the super-hard gonzo shit he talked her into doing."

"I believe this is what's known as a suitcase pimp," O suggested.

Remembering, Jacqui looked skeptical.

"I never saw him take any money from her. And I wouldn't call him lazy. He was a graphic artist who made a pretty good living on his own. He bought the house they lived in."

"And he just pushed her to do gang-bangs and *bukkakes* so he could accuse her of enjoying it?"

"Exactly. Except that she did, at least in the beginning." Jacqui said. "Enjoy it, I mean. He broke something in her, but he also set something free, and when it got loose ..."

"Bye-bye Master Wrong."

"Laurel took her in because they both needed roommates. Laurel was already working up at The Mansion part time. She got Marie to put Angelique on with her. Now they're inseparable. When Laurel landed herself a daddy, she told him she'd only let him collar her if he took both of them."

"Sounds like trouble to me," O said, wringing the water out of her hair.

"I give it six months," Jacqui replied with a shrug. "They're real subs, but they're not that into guys, or straight guys at least."

From what O had seen earlier in the evening, it wasn't hard to deduce Angelique and Laurel's common interests.

"Why would Marie enable something she knows will fail?" O wondered aloud. The question wasn't entirely about Marie.

"Because she's an enabler. She gives people what they think they want and if it works out, great. If it doesn't, she offers them things to make them feel better."

O was silent for a long time. If there was one thing O was not, it was an enabler, and yet here she was, helping Marie pack Jacqui for shipping. That she was starting to like Jacqui didn't make it any easier.

She looked at Jacqui, who stared up at the crescent moon. She seemed too young for Ray and, like O, too set on her own path. She was also accustomed to getting her way, as youth and beauty so often do.

O hoisted herself out of the pool onto a thick fleece towel she'd laid out for them before they went in. There was just enough of a breeze to give O a shiver. Jacqui pushed off from the wall and turned to stare at O's chest. She observed that O's rings stuck out even further when she was cold. O leaned forward into the blue light from below.

"Care to look?"

"Rather touch."

"I couldn't stop you, could I?"

In a house with many rules, O's favorite forbade any girl from refusing the advances of another. All curiosities and desires were eventually satisfied, as were grudges and resentments.

Earlier in the day ,O had sat in Jacqui's lap, having her hair brushed. Together, they had watched Angelique hold Laurel down so Noriko, a former professional dominant with impressive technical skills, demonstrated how smoothly a small girl could take an even smaller fist.

Laurel had yielded with predictable ease, eyes rolled back in her head, rosy complexion darkening to fuchsia, spine rigidly convex, while Noriko effortlessly turned her inside out. Angelique's face was completely expressionless throughout the performance, but O suspected she hadn't enjoyed it much.

The rules didn't require Angelique's direct complicity, even to the point of pouring the lube from a black crystal bottle over Noriko's balled knuckles, but to have done less would have been an admission of giving a shit. As Noriko well knew, Angelique would sooner have had her thighs whipped, something she made no secret of hating.

Going down on Jacqui's perfect pink parts as she lay stretched out on a towel next to the pool, O had realized that, lovely as Jacqui was, O wouldn't have enjoyed it half so much if she weren't doing it for Steven. There was something in O that only Steven had ever switched on. It transmitted itself through her to Jacqui, whose cries, even muffled by her own hand, rose into the perfumed night.

The regimen at Marie's was more complex and detailed than that at The Mansion. As the others had recited each article to O during lunch at Marie's direction, she quickly realized that they were calculated to maintain a high emotional pitch. The cultivated air of constant vulnerability would eventually deliver up slaves more defenseless and yielding than any amount of physical duress — not that duress was in short supply either.

After that lunch, O had been secured to a low, wide table in the living room with maroon silk sash cord. She'd been spread wide and each girl had been required to use fingers, tongues or whatever of the other instruments laid out easy to hand to get her off before being tapped out by the next one.

Only Jacqui had been excused from the exercise, designated by Marie to assist with whatever toys, penetrative or vibrating, might be needed. O had given herself up to pleasure without troubling herself over what would happen later. Three orgasms from three pretty girls in under an hour was hardly a challenge.

Marie had made her point. The carefully contrived atmosphere of strictness combined with lassitude would inevitably give rise to the spontaneous drama on which her charges thrived. Of all the girls' schools to which O had been consigned during her youth, none had been so well-suited. Too bad her family couldn't have packed her off to this place. Much conflict would have been avoided.

Marie presided with an amiable imperiousness, giving individual attention to each girl as needed without showing favor for any. She deliberately took a different one upstairs with her each night to her private retreat, where there could be little doubt about Marie's primary orientation.

It was a large, high-ceilinged room with black marbleized walls, sculptured black carpeting and heavy black velvet curtains over the windows. All the furniture – the tufted chaise; the long dresser; the oval wall mirror; the small, round table and two tall, narrow chairs; and most of all, Marie's enormous bed with its elaborately sculpted head and foot boards – was either lacquered or upholstered in high-gloss black and slathered in scrollwork. Lit by black glass chandeliers and ornamented with black vases and columns and swaths of black damask, it was a theatrical den of iniquity direct from precode Hollywood.

There were heavy iron rings at the corners of Marie's bed. Every girl brought before her, accompanied by her designated sister, was stripped completely before being cuffed to a pillar for a working over with a heavy flogger and a short, light single-tail, front and rear. Each girl's companion was dismissed after securing Marie's choice for the evening to the huge bed with black silk rope hitched to the iron rings. After tasting the bound girl's flesh at her leisure, Marie gave her a solid shagging with a big, red strap-on. Otherwise naked, Marie wielded her after-market equipment better than many men used that with which they were born. Marie's body was an architectural wonder of streamlined curves, smooth and unwrinkled despite her age, voluptuous and athletic in equal measure. Unlike so many professional dominas, her manner was gracious if stern. She affected no air of being a goddess. She just was one, and rather Teutonic at that, with her golden hair and pale-blue eyes.

Afterward, each girl was required to show her gratitude on her knees with her hands locked behind her while Marie stood above, guiding her partner's head movements. Sometimes she sent them back to their rooms when she was done. Sometimes she kept them over if she felt like company.

O hadn't been surprised to find herself in Marie's chambers that first night. Though a bit wrung out from her earlier initiation, she had taken and given her best as always. If Marie had any complaints, she kept them to herself.

In the soft halo of the silk-shaded beside lamp, they had lain together, O curled up under Marie's arm, O's face snuggled to Marie's breast, their legs entangled. They had passed a brilliant blue glass pipe between them, Marie periodically firing it with a gold lighter O was sure had been a gift from Steven. They had talked into the night and O had learned much. She had dared to ask if she was the first girl Steven had brought here, not sure what answer she'd have preferred. Marie had confirmed that O was the only one.

"I love him dearly," Marie had explained, "but he is a slut. He comes up to The Mansion to pluck the prettiest flowers. Sometimes he takes one home for a few days, but he always brings her back. Until now, he never seemed the least bit interested in keeping any of them, much less putting his mark on her."

Marie had sensed O's unease at the revelation.

"Steven is not Ray. If he does want you as a slave, that's what you'll be to him."

"It wasn't that way with the two of you, was it?"

"For one thing, I was in love with him," Marie had explained. "I think he was in love with me, but I wouldn't swear to it even now. He was always a perfect gentleman, except in bed, where he was a perfect brute. I never cared to fuck any man more than twice, three times at the most, but I wanted him all day every day. You know that place he goes when he's doing what he wants to you?"

O knew that place very well.

"I wanted to live in that place with him. I'd never so much as had a spanking before, but I was down for just about anything with him. He could have pushed me harder than he did and I'd still have wanted more."

"What happened?"

Marie had taken a deep drag and passed the pipe to O.

"That scar on his shoulder, did he tell you how he got it?"

"He said an ex-client shot him."

"That's not quite the whole story. Steven was taking some local gang leader to the federal courthouse for sentencing. I met the man once when he was out on bail. Very handsome in a cold way. He and Steven seemed to be great friends.

"But the day the judge was going to send the guy over for running a bunch of meth labs out in San Bernardino County, something happened on the courthouse steps. Steven caught a glimpse of one of the other gang members out of the corner of his eye as he brushed up against the client on the way in. Have you ever watched Steven fence?"

"I'm sure he's very good judging by that case full of trophies in his office."

"He's better than good. He was a champion in college and in the Navy. Even now, he's got the reflexes and moves of a man half his age. He saw the gun pass from hand to hand and didn't hesitate. He jumped his client and they fought for it right there in front of the statue of blind justice and about a hundred witnesses. The client managed to put a bullet through Steven's shoulder, but that was the only round he got off. Steven yanked the poor bastard's arm down so hard he shot himself in the gut."

"Jesus!"

O didn't know why this shocked her, but picturing it had given her the chills.

"There's more. Steven jumped up and stood over the gangster, pointing the gun down at him. It was some kind of large-caliber pistol and the stomach wound might already have been fatal, but Steven didn't wait to find out. He pumped two more rounds into him, one in the chest, one right through the third eye."

"It was self-defense."

From Marie's description, O wasn't entirely sure.

"The first bullet, certainly. But in this state once an assailant is incapacitated and no longer a threat, you're supposed to quit. Steven didn't quit. He killed that fellow when he didn't have to. It wasn't exactly murder, but it could easily have been voluntary manslaughter."

"How did he get away with it?"

Marie had shrugged with a cynical weariness that made O sad for her.

"The system protects its own. Most of the people on the steps that day were lawyers, cops or judges. None of them saw a thing. It was ruled a justifiable homicide in a fifteen-minute hearing."

"Were you afraid of Steven after that?"

"No more than before. He was no danger to me or anyone else who didn't threaten his safety. That wasn't why I left him. It was the way he took the whole thing in stride that did it. I was frantic when Martin came to drive me to the hospital, but by the time I got to Steven's room, he was sitting up in bed, all bandaged up and flying on morphine, joking around with a bunch of policemen and paramedics. I swear, everyone in the room was laughing like the crowd at a late show in Vegas."

Marie took another hit, casually wrapped a finger through one of O's rings.

"I wasn't afraid of Steven. I was afraid for him. He'd only let me see the parts of his life he thought I could handle. I never realized what kind of world he lived in and what could happen to him there. It had never occurred to me that one day he could go off to work with that big grin on his face and never come home. His complete fearlessness frightened me. That was what I couldn't live with."

"But why would you leave him for Martin? They were in the same business."

"No, darling. They were in the same practice. Martin was the cerebral type and quite possibly he was the sweetest man who ever lived. He specialized in white-collar cases. His clients were mostly embezzlers and con artists. He wisely avoided any situation where he might have had to do what Steven did. It just wasn't in him. Steven made me feel safe in one way, but Martin made me feel safe in quite another."

"And yet you lost them both anyway," O said.

"I didn't lose Steven. We just went our separate ways. He couldn't have been nicer about the divorce. He understood why I made the choice I did, and he was glad to see us happy. At Martin's funeral, Steven walked me up the aisle just like he did at our wedding. As the executor of Martin's estate he set me up in this business. Steven was all wrong for me as a husband but I've never had a better friend and I never will."

O had asked Marie if she wanted her to stay the night, and Marie kissed her on the forehead.

"You should wake up with Jacqui. She's the real reason you're here. Don't forget that."

O wouldn't forget that. Neither would she forget what Marie had told her.

Part of what O liked about Steven was his seeming indestructibility. O didn't want to worry about anybody, ever. That was part of what had gone wrong with Ray.

Sitting on the rim of the pool, dangling her legs in the water and watching Jacqui ease back into a position of neutral buoyancy, rivulets running off Jacqui's exquisite geometry, O felt a surge of enthusiasm that washed away all doubts for the moment. The wonderful thing about the world Marie and Steven had built was that, within it, everything not forbidden was mandatory.

"Do you really want to touch me?" O asked coyly. "What if I only let one part of you touch me?"

Jacqui gave a defiant laugh.

"I could get you off with an ear if I had to. You come when the wind blows up your skirt."

"That's because I'm not wearing anything underneath. It's against the rules."

"I like your rules," Jacqui said. "But I also enjoy wearing jeans and a big stain on the front isn't that attractive. I'm like a milk carton. I tend to leak from the bottom."

O laughed out loud. She spread her legs wide and opened herself.

"Is this the part you want to touch?" she asked.

"Oh yeah," Jacqui replied, a hungry look in her green eyes, which were a less alien hue than when she wore her contacts. She started paddling toward O but stopped when O raised a hand.

"Just a minute, young lady. I said you could only touch me with one part of you."

"Fuck! I hope it isn't my ear."

"I'll give you more to work with, but it will be a challenge. Go get some rope."

"You just stay right there, Sister."

Jacqui climbed out of the water, threw her big towel over her shoulders and scampered back in the house.

It wasn't going to be hard to stay in shape around here. Between the grueling workout which Marie put them through every morning and the non-stop sexual activity that took up most of the rest of the day and night, hormone levels and cardios were constantly elevated.

Jacqui returned in a blink with a healthy length of sash cord. She tossed it to O and dived gracefully back into the deep end, swimming over while shook out the coils.

"It was fucking freezing out there," Jacqui said. "Aren't you cold?"

"You're going to make me forget about it, but first ..."

O slid back in the water and waded over to where Jacqui stood, waiting and dripping.

"...We'll do the challenging part. Turn around."

Jacqui turned, automatically folding her arms in the small of her long back. She knew the drill.

"This is going to be interesting," she said calmly.

"You have no idea."

O had started out doing her own rigging for photo shoots and though she didn't consider herself an expert, a simple, secure box-tie was no problem. Two loops above Jacqui's small, round breasts and two above, a simple hitch in between to give them a bit of a squeeze, then a line over each shoulder, meeting in a mid-back square-knot into which she bundled Jacqui's arms. O finished it all off with a double hitch and asked Jacqui how it felt. Jacqui rolled her shoulders and lifted her arms, which was pleasant to watch, and pronounced O's work "downright cozy."

The bondage wasn't meant to be the difficult part. O took Jacqui by the strategically placed front loop and led her to where the bottom started to slope away so that when Jacqui stood she was submerged from the ribs down. O climbed out using the ladder. Bringing her towel back to sit on, O opened herself as before and motioned Jacqui to come forward.

Jacqui's lids dipped and her smile narrowed the way they did in the studio when things started to get fun.

"I like the way your mind works," she said with a low giggle.

"We'll see about that."

As soon as Jacqui was within reach, O grabbed the rope harness, bringing Jacqui's face right up against her. Jacqui tried to nuzzle her way in, but didn't get the chance. O used the harness to pull her down into the water, Jacqui's red hair floating up like a cloud above her. She kicked and struggled a little, but O held her firm until she stopped fighting. Only then did she bring her back up, coughing and spitting.

"You evil bitch!" she said with a laugh, once she could talk.

O cocked an eyebrow.

"Still like the way I think?"

"Even better."

"Then get busy."

O steered her back in by the harness, but this time, she let Jacqui show what she could do without her hands. O was suitably impressed, though not surprised. Girls who made it to Marie's didn't need a map to find their way around down there. Jacqui lapped and sucked in all the right places. She didn't need her hands either.

When O felt started up the curve she held back, ducking Jacqui under again. This time, Jacqui did her best to stay still while submerged, so O held her down longer, until the struggling was involuntary. Dragging Jacqui back out, gasping and choking this time, O slapped her hard across the face.

"Still want it?" O demanded.

"Yes, Sister! Please let me get you off."

"Since you put it so sweetly ..."

This time, O, having made her point, let Jacqui do her best, as O was certain she would now. O wrapped her legs around Jacqui's shoulders, heels pressing in against Jacqui's back. She even reached down to give her a little help.

Every wish was granted here, but there were always terms. At least, unlike in the world at large, the terms were clear.

CHAPTER TWENTY-ONE

O adapted to the routine at Marie's with surprising ease. Her workaholic nature made vacations a misery, but here, the labor and languor were compulsory, so it wasn't her fault that she slept in every day. The rooms were just large enough to accommodate a vanity with a round mirror and a low stool, a dresser adequate to what little they wore and a bed large enough to be comfortable for two but small enough to ensure physical contact throughout the night. Everything was done in white, and each chamber had a small, white-tiled bathroom attached, with no door in between. All bathrooms had tubs accommodating both girls at once.

The girls slept in their collars and cuffs, which could only be removed for bathing or swimming. Each girl held the key to the other's locks. Once O discovered that Jacqui preferred to be held from behind in her sleep, O rested soundly on the firm mattress, her arms around Jacqui, cupping the tall redhead's breasts.

At ten a.m. sharp, they were awakened by a light knock on the door from one of the staff, giving them the thirty-minute warning. The staff at Marie's was very different from the hard men in black who ruled over the girls at The Mansion.

They were quite pleasant and deferential, all Latinas from one family ruled over by Bianca, who had started a business cleaning houses in The Valley for porno girls that eventually brought over her entire clan. All were happily married mothers who wore plain, gray uniforms, kept things clean and ignored whatever didn't require their attention. As Bianca herself often reminded Marie, they weren't the ones going to hell.

The only household tasks performed by the residents were the setting of the table and the serving of whatever Rosemary, Bianca's mother, turned out in the kitchen. The meals were all light and healthy and delicious, and it was not unknown for one of Marie's little darlings to sneak in and get a snack from Rosemary under a veil of strict secrecy — as if anything could be a secret from Marie. Once a girl gained six ounces, the snack bar was closed.

Jacqui took O through the routine the first morning they woke up together, starting with cuffing O's hands behind her and brushing her teeth for her. It was one of the stranger and more intrusive sensations O had experienced, but Jacqui told her to just pretend she was at the dentist, which actually helped. She gave O's hair a quick comb-through, but that was all the preparation needed before the morning workout.

O found it more than a little problematic dealing with the lack of a closing bathroom door the first time, but Jacqui had no such inhibitions. Unlike O, Jacqui belonged to the worldwide tribe of models, to whom life was one giant dressing room where privacy had never been invented.

O readied Jacqui in the same way, taking some of the same liberties Jacqui had when O's hands were cuffed, in the process determining just how hard Jacqui liked her nipples.

From then on the routine never varied.

The entire company formed up naked, single-ranked in the long, narrow gym opposite their sleeping quarters across the courtyard. The room was mirrored without mercy.

Equipped with six exercise stations, each was fitted with its own weight machines, slant bench, and treadmill.

Marie, topless in tights and boots with a nasty driving whip in one hand, inspected them all as they stood at attention on their toes, keeping their legs apart and their hands behind their heads. Based on her observations, Marie gave each the specifics of her exercise routine for the day.

The lists proved surprisingly demanding, clearly more so for some than others. While O and Noriko trotted along on their treadmills, barely breaking a sweat, Laurel struggled, red-faced, through her crunches on the steeply tilted board. Jacqui's small breasts were an advantage with the fly machine, but Angelique clearly dogged it on the elliptical trainer, earning many a sharp rap across the back and belly from Marie's whip.

O felt that whip too. Marie had concluded that O's tread-mill had been set lower than necessary and twisting the dial to speed it up. O was sweating profusely a few minutes later while Noriko still trotted happily along at an even faster clip. In fact, she raised the incline unassisted, grinning as O watched in amazement each time she made the adjustment.

"Hey," Noriko explained, "I can't let you *gaijin* bitches show me up."

The routines concluded with all the sweating, panting girls on their backs, open legs to the mirror, working their internal muscles with short, ball-ended steel bars they were required to push in and out by squeezing their kegels.

Marie walked back and forth behind their heads with a spring-loaded probe attached to a digital pressure gauge. As each girl finished her set, Marie squatted down, put a disposable plastic cover on the probe and tested the strength of their contractions. It was a particularly trying moment, as they were already fatigued inside and out. But if the numbers on the box didn't spin up high and fast enough, Marie inflicted another set of squeezing and releasing. Sometimes, Jacqui deliberately tightened up to obstruct the insertion of the probe, earning herself a sharp crack of the lash across her lower abdomen. Giving O a quick wink, she would then take the probe in easily and squeeze it so hard Marie had to forcibly extract it, earning a cheeky expression of gratitude Marie chose to ignore.

Breakfast was served back in their quarters, wheeled in on a cart with steel domes to keep everything warm. The same rules applied. First Jacqui cuffed O and fed her sliced grapefruit, cereal and excellent Jamaican coffee with steamed milk. Then it was O's turn to do the same for Jacqui.

Bathing was a trial of self-control, since they had to take their leather cuffs off each other. They were, of course, to keep their hands off themselves and not interfere with their partners using big sea-sponges to scrub them down. But in the warm, scented water, some cheating always seemed to occur beneath the curtain of bubbles, starting with that first day. Washing Jacqui's hair, O had boldly pinched the girl's nostrils shut, forcing Jacqui to open her mouth so O could kiss her deeply.

Sitting low on the stool in front of the mirror, which Jacqui deliberately blocked so O couldn't see what was being done to her face, O was always surprised by how deftly Jacqui applied the simple makeup required. Jacqui, it turned out, had gone to cosmetology school, originally intending to work as a makeup artist because she didn't consider herself pretty enough to model. Part of the reason Jacqui found such satisfaction in front of the camera lay in her surprise at finding herself there at all.

In return, O usually wound Jacqui's hair in a lovely up-do, with a few loose, auburn tendrils to give her a pleasing, freshly fucked look. Jacqui loved it, always giving O a powerful hug and a good groping.

Each girl had three drawers in the dresser, more than enough room for the skimpy frills they wore, and space on a shelf above it for shoes, carefully lined up, heels out. On the first day, Jacqui picked out stay-up stockings with wide stripes and a sheer, black bed-jacket with ruffles. Black patent peep-toe heels decorated with big white-patent flowers completed the look. As O re-collared her, Jacqui appraised herself skeptically in the mirror. O reassured her that she looked like a proper harlot. Jacqui was relieved to hear it.

O went with all black that time, including the corset she'd brought, asking Jacqui to lace it extra tight. Thereafter Marie let O sleep in a simple muslin cincher as part of her training. By the time O left this place, Steven would be able to see her with her waist compressed the full four inches any time he wanted. Each day before lunch there was an instruction period. Sometimes Marie tutored them on fine points of protocol, such as how to greet a fellow Master-slave couple for the first time, or how to negotiate limits according to what she was permitted when loaned out for use. Other times, they got basic training in simple bondage in case their masters needed assistance restraining a visiting slave. There was always a posture walk in heels with two books balanced on their heads and one in each upturned palm of their outstretched arms, viciously weighted clover clamps jingling on their anguished aureoles.

Lunch was the big meal of the day, delivered from the kitchen for each girl to serve, dish by dish, to all the others. Marie joined them for this meal and the atmosphere was surprisingly relaxed. They told dirty jokes and bawdy stories, talked music and movies, teased each other good-naturedly. It took a bit of effort for O, to whom nothing was more comfortable than silence, but her boarding school experience was useful. She had learned the art of small talk where it was still treated as an art.

After lunch, the rest of the day was given over to deliberate indolence. Occasionally one or more of them would go out shopping or to do errands, as they were allowed, but most of the time they lay around the living room or the pool, reading from Marie's library of elegant pornography or playing video games on their tablets or listening to downloads through headphones. There was a large flat-screen monitor that dropped down from the ceiling on which Laurel and Angelique watched videos of gay men fucking while the two of them made out.

O usually took this time to edit pictures with the computer she'd brought along. She went a bit mad if she was out of the studio for more than a week, but at least laying out sets or Photoshopping qualified as work, which soothed her compulsions somewhat. She also began taking *shibari* lessons from Noriko, figuring she might have to do her own rigging on some hypothetical shoot in the future.

Noriko was quite the expert with boiled hemp, as she'd proved by hanging Laurel from one of the forged lifting eyes buried in the ceiling of the living room. She'd been feeling generous that time and left Laurel for Angelique to enjoy rather than taking advantage herself.

Noriko was quite cordial and welcoming to everyone except Angelique. One day she even requested Marie's permission to give O a massage, though the girls weren't usually allowed to get naked until after dinner.

On the massage table in the gym, Noriko showed herself to be as adept with her hands outside a woman's body as inside. O was a tightly wrapped bundle of tension most of the time when she wasn't being fucked, and Noriko found many productive spots for working deep into O's hard sinews. She'd located a spasm in O's arches that actually produced moans.

"Every girl in this place has knots there," Noriko observed. "It's from wearing heels all the time. I have them myself."

O offered to do her the next time.

"You can do me any time," Noriko replied. "You're the only one here I respect. The others are a bunch of lazy cows."

The compliment took O by surprise. She'd kept a certain distance from everyone but Jacqui and didn't realize she was being observed so closely.

"I used to work as a pro-domme," Noriko explained. "I have certain standards, although honestly I have trouble living up to them myself. It's funny. When I was a mistress I had male slaves who used to piss me off all the time with one thing and another. I couldn't imagine it happening, but I promised myself that if I ever ended up a slave somehow, I'd never do any of those things. Since I was collared, I've done every single one of them at least twice."

O agreed that being a perfect slave was pretty demanding.

"I'm never satisfied with my own submission. I obey as gracefully as I can, but then I think back on it and see ways I could have served better."

"Lucky for us, I don't think the guys notice the things we do. They punish us when they're in the mood, not when we deserve it."

O asked Noriko how she came to be on the other end of the whip in the first place.

"I'm still not sure," Noriko answered. "I used to do doubles with a pro-sub, a lovely Russian girl who was into it for real but could still keep her boundaries. She works up at The Mansion now. She was a gem who attracted the best clients. I'd say about a third of them were guys I'd have at least considered going out with for free."

"Except that they were dominant and wanted to watch you do things to your partner."

"Exactly. I wasn't tempted for that reason, until one day we got this man who was ... different. He was very handsome, tall with gray hair, and very confident. A lot of clients are nervous and unsure of themselves, but not this one. He knew exactly what he wanted. He watched quietly while I gave my partner a real going over — hard bondage, hard whipping, ass-fucking with a strap-on. Then he stepped in and for the first time ever, watching a client with another woman made me jealous. He was just so good, the way some men are. He didn't forget anything. He used every part of her just like he

wanted to and I swear she must have had about a dozen orgasms by the time he had his."

"Sounds like quite a show," O offered tentatively, aware
that she was hearing something very confidential.

"That's just it. It wasn't a show. He let himself be what
he needed to be with no guilt or anxiety at all. Most of them
are ashamed of what they like, so they cover for it with a lot of
bullshit bravado. Everything was completely natural to him.
That's appealing in any man."On top of all that, he turned out
to be a big studio exec running a whole division. He had a couple of ex-wives and he was still rich. Next time he called, I figured he wanted to book another double. Actually he wanted to
ask me to dinner. I'd normally be totally suspicious of something like that, but I just knew he wasn't bullshitting me. He
really did take me out to dinner. He turned out to be funny and
smart. We had a great time and he took me straight home, the
perfect gentleman in every way. Afterwards it dawned on me
that this had been the first real date I'd gone on in years. Then
I called him. When we got together I admitted that I'm really
submissive but hadn't found a man I could stand the thought
of seeing me like that. That was — until him."

"And now he owns you."

"He retired me from work, got me anything I wanted and
fucks me into next week every time I see him. I don't know
why, but rimming his ass is as natural as breathing."

Realizing how similar she and Noriko were, it wasn't hard
for O to understand why even a successful professional mistress might hand over the whip to the right man.

O had no use at all for gender essentialism or EvPsych
bullshit. It was not in the nature of every driven, ambitious
woman to find solace at the boots of some Type A powerhouse
like Steven or the man whose initials Noriko wore on a gold
tag attached to a ring through her right labium. But for some
women, no other kind of man would suffice.

CHAPTER TWENTY-TWO

The only reasonable way to get from Steven's place to Mount Washington was via the One-Ten Freeway, generally regarded as the worst stretch of bad road in the whole system. Originally built as The Arroyo Seco Parkway, it was meant for stately motorcades from the mansions of Pasadena to the white marble monuments of the financial district. All short, steep ramps, narrow shoulders and hair-raising turns, it was utterly unsuited to the relentless commuter traffic now risking their lives daily on what the guys in the Motor Division had dubbed The Ribbon of Death.

It was, however, perfect for a mid-afternoon shake out of the new model Morgan Plus Four. Steven hadn't put many hours on it yet. It was exquisitely impractical for much of anything with its tiny trunk and vestigial back seat. But despite the odd marriage of the old Morgan oblong grill and bug-eye headlamps to a streamlined Italianate body reminiscent of a Bugatti Type 35, its lineage under the sheet metal was unambiguous. Quick and sticky, it ate up the switchbacks through the avenues like a practice lap at Goodwood.

Steven figured Albert would appreciate it. Steven glanced down at his chronograph, which was black-faced and trimmed in burl wood to match the Morgan's dash. He was right on schedule. Albert also appreciated punctuality.

Albert's eye for quality goods had served him well as a consumer journalist, a celebrity journalist and now a pornographic journalist. He was, just possibly, the smartest man in town, and therefore of great value to Steven among many others. There was Ray's version of what was going on at the magazine, and then there were the cold facts, for which Steven relied on Albert.

The facts must be very cold indeed for Albert to grant Steven an audience. A lifetime of smoky clubs and noisy bistros had left him functionally agoraphobic. It was easier to get face-time with the Pope than to meet with Albert in person.

Steven found him on his big redwood deck, stretched out in an Adirondack chair with a copy of *The Economist* spread face-down over his ample midsection. His round sunglasses were tipped back and he appeared to be sleeping in his weathered Henley and sweat pants.

"Albert?" Steven called from the steps, "are you home?"

"No," Albert replied without moving, "I'm not home anywhere west of The Hudson."

Ditching the magazine, Albert climbed somewhat creakingly to his feet and came over for the ritual hug-and-handshake.

"Okay," Albert said, "let's see it."

They descended the stairs to the street together, Albert's flip-flops flapping with each step. Reaching the asphalt, Albert circled the Morgan, scratching his chin and furrowing his brows.

"It's a crazy idea," he said, "like going directly from a steam locomotive to a bullet train, but it kind of works in that English way. Leave to the Brits to invent a steampunk car. How's the ride?"

"Stiff and bumpy."

"Well, at least that hasn't changed. It gets my blessing, my son. Come up and have some lemonade."

Steven settled into a chair across the small redwood table from Albert. The deck was sheltered from the sun by a big, old-fashioned green canvas umbrella that opened with a hand crank. A cool breeze bore the news of impending autumn. Through the open French doors, he could hear Albert rattling around in the kitchen, emerging moments later with a red tray from some long-gone resort bearing a couple of juice glasses and a large, sweating pitcher. Albert sat and poured, waiting for his cue.

"Why am I here?" Steven asked.

"Because you want to talk about O. And I want to talk to you about *Forbidden*. I'd say you have reason to worry about both. I'm worried and I'm not a worrier."

Albert picked up his copy of *The Economist* and tossed it across the table to Steven. "Check out the masthead page."

Steven extracted his spectacles from inside his leather shooting-jacket with its padded shoulder and bellows pockets. Studying the page he saw nothing unusual.

"It's there, at the bottom – *TheEconomist.Com*. It even has its own smart-phone app. How long has *The Economist* been around?'

Steven gave it some thought.

"At least a hundred years, I'd guess."

"It was founded in 1843," Albert said triumphantly. "Fucking 1843 and they've got a fully interactive website, while *Forbidden*'s Internet footprint remains invisible. Everybody I know has a site or a blog or something. This big, flashy book we crank out once a month might as well not exist for an audience of millions that gets most of its media product from the web."

"Apples and oranges, Albert. *The Economist* is in the news business. Its readers are stock traders strung out on Red Bull. They go into seizures unless they know everything that's going to happen tomorrow by yesterday. *Forbidden* is a picture-driven stroke book for discerning perverts to jizz over at their leisure. So tell me what you've got in mind for this Internet scheme Ray and O and everybody else is arm-twisting me to sign off on. I know you're the instigator of the whole mad scheme and I want to hear the pitch directly from you."

Albert tapped a low-tar cigarette out of the box in the pocket of his sweat pants, lit it with a wooden match from a French café striker on the table. As part his cultural Cold War with Los Angeles, Albert remained an unregenerate smoker.

"We need to use the Net for what it does best," Albert said. "Promoting a something you can actually sell. Media products can't make a dime online. The bright spot is Internet retail. It's a giant, open-all-night Home Shopping Channel. I'm picturing a very slick site that offers bits and snips and extras from the magazine – behind-the-scenes footage from photo shoots, interviews with naked models, event feeds, interactive parties – but not the same content we put in the book. If they want to see the pictorials or read the full text of anything, they have to click on the "buy" button. We can offer monster subscription deals for the print version that way because we don't have any direct mail costs or other circulation bullshit. We outsource all that to a fulfillment operation and ship the paper copies straight from the warehouse as one option and offer downloadable PDFs at full price as the other option."

"This 'we' you're talking about, Albert, who the fuck is 'we?'"

"Not you or me or Ray, that's for sure."

"This would require hiring people. People cost money."

"Not a lot of people and not a lot of money. There's a surplus of talented web designers out here and I think we may have found the right one, or rather he found us. Once the thing is up and running, you put on one staff producer to oversee the content and do everything else with stringers and automated tech support."

Steven shook his head. "I'm picturing bags with dollar signs and wings on the sides fluttering out the window."

"I'm not a numbers guy, but I'll bet you can make this happen for a hundred grand. Your toy car cost that."

"My toy car, as you put it, is fun to drive. I hate the Internet. I wish Al Gore would come back and uninvent the fucking thing. It's as boring as Speakers' Corner in Hyde Park multiplied by a couple of billion."

"You think the management at *The Economist* embraces a similar platform because they're such avid techies?"

Albert topped off their lemonades while Steven pondered. "Okay, who are you selling me?" he asked at last.

"His name is Eric Barton. He worked in the digital division at RSA before he went solo. You should see the stuff he's built. It's got a compatible sensibility about it, very slick and very sexual. His client list reads like the ad bank for *The Robb Report*."

"We're not *The Robb Report*. We can't afford someone who's used to peddling super-yachts."

Albert smiled in that satisfied way Steven knew presaged the unveiling of an angle. "Ah, but that's where we have an advantage. See, Eric's one of us, if you know what I mean. He's nuts for *Forbidden*. He contacted me about working there. He's already got all the money in the world that you didn't get first. He wants to do this thing and if we offer him a face-saving flat rate with a small back-end on web-related revenues, he'll jump at it just for the imagined fringes."

"I'm automatically suspicious of anyone who wants to emulate my brother. How old is the kid?"

"I'm pretty sure he's 2257 legal."

"That's comforting. When do I meet our child prodigy?"

"Sooner would be better. He's kind of ADHD. He's all hot for us right now but something else could come along."

"It better not come along after I've hired him."

"That's what contracts are for."

"Put us together. It can't hurt to talk."

Albert flashed his seldom seen grin and high-fived Steven across the table. "I'll hook you up with Eric as soon as the stars align correctly. Bring O if you can."

"What's O got to do with this?" As he often did in court, Steven was pretty sure he already knew the answer.

"He's a huge fan. Crazy about her work. I think she's sort of a crush object with him."

"And that's meant to encourage this venture?"

"She could probably negotiate him down to bread and water."

"Is he cute?"

"Adorable, but not her type at all. If you sent her out on a date with him, she'd be completely unimpressed, and he'd be yours for life and beyond."

Steven didn't like where this was going at all. Recreational pimping was one thing. Entangling it with business was quite another, as Marie had found out the hard way. His partnership in The Mansion was proof of his confidence that she'd learned her lesson and Steven didn't need that kind of schooling.

"I'd need to discuss that with O."

"She belongs to you. Why not use her for something practical? I think she'd enjoy that kind of service."

Steven looked at Albert in wonder as always. "How do you know so much about O and me?"

"Everyone has to talk to somebody. You've got Marie. O's got Albert."

"Good thing I have you too."

"I'm aware who writes the checks, dad. I know as much as anyone can about O. I brought her over with me from Condé."

Albert stood up and strolled to the railing around the deck to peer through the metallic haze toward downtown. Steven followed. Once there, he produced the joint case and alligator upholstered Dupont. They fired up together.

"You're making it very hard for me to say no, which isn't usually a problem," Steven said.

"That's why I figured we'd better get business out of the way first. Once I heard you had her up at Marie's and that you wanted to talk to me, I knew I'd better use the window of opportunity before you were too preoccupied with other matters. I normally don't violate friends' confidences, which is why I hear them, but in this case, I'm making an exception."

"Why?"

"Because I think you're starting to need her and that could contribute to my worries, if not put to greater purposes. Ray and I need you on board with our plans. I don't want you caught off guard by something that might shake them up."

"Okay, I'll bite. What was she like before she got together with Ray?"

"Crazed. She hated shooting fashion. She loved dressing the girls and staging the scenarios, but good as she was in the studio, that's how bad she was in the office. Couldn't stand the whole corporate thing. The marketing side hated her. She wouldn't listen to anybody, wouldn't work on any team projects. She was the queen-hell-bitch-diva of all the shooters who worked for us. I had to go over my own editor's head a few times to keep her from getting axed. Thankfully, the art department loved her, so James let her stay on until we both decided to jump ship."

Steven took a deep drag, blowing the smoke out through his nostrils. "Hard to imagine her like that. She's been nothing but helpful to Ray."

"That's because she's happy. She likes what she's doing, even if it pays about a quarter of what she's used to."

"It's pretty unusual to see someone do something for reasons that don't involve money. I mean it happens, but it's not common."

"Money's been more a curse than a blessing in O's life. Have you ever Googled her under her real name?"

"Why would I do that?"

Steven was genuinely indignant at the idea. He didn't snoop on his lovers and wouldn't have been pleased to think of them doing so to him.

"Because you're a successful attorney who's getting serious about a girl you hardly know whether or not you admit it. I wouldn't go through her underwear drawers if I were you, but I would do a background check just to see if she has any exes listed under missing persons."

"Actually, I do go through her underwear drawers, but not because I'm looking for concealed weapons. I know from hustlers and crooks and she's definitely neither."

"It's worse than that. She's a very wealthy girl."

Steven thought about it for a minute. O's house, her wardrobe, her jewelry. Fashion photography paid well at her level, but she was casual about money in a way that only people who hadn't worked for it could be.

"How wealthy?" Steven asked, bracing for the worst.

"We don't even have that kind of wealth in this country. Her father is the head of North American operations for ILMG."

Steven winced. "As in 'International Luxury Marketing Group?'"

"Yep, the conglomerate that's bought up every overpriced brand name in most of the world. They almost snagged Rolls out from under the Germans' noses. That company is all about appearances. You don't get a job like O's dad's unless your middle name is 'of.'"

"This explains a few things."

"Here's the rest. When O was about ten, her old man dumped her mother and married some Swedish model. From then on, O was incarcerated in the most prestigious educational institutions money can buy. She got thrown out of most. They were hoping to bribe her into one of the Ivies, but she stuck it to them again, this time by getting a full scholarship to The Chicago Art Institute. That's where she assembled the portfolio she put on James's desk when she showed up in New York. She really wanted to shoot actualities for VF or something like that, but they pushed her right over into doing runway stuff."

"I guess she didn't fall as far away from the tree as expected."

"Oh yes she did, which is how we got to be friends. My parents thought journalism was a disreputable trade and I wasn't very popular at home either. Now we can't even tell our families what we do for a living. I suppose we really showed them. Ray said you took her into Hermés and they made a big fuss over her. Want to know why?"

"It did seem a little strange."

"They're the last hold-outs when it comes to family-owned designer labels. O's father wants to put that jewel in his crown but so far, they're pushing him back. O knows ILMG's got people working on the sales floors of all their bigger locations and that it gets back to daddy every time she goes in there and spends her trust fund helping them fight him off. It doesn't amount to much in real terms, but it definitely makes a statement."

Steven knew most people would envy O's problems, but he didn't. He'd dealt with the unhappy children of the unhappy rich enough to understand that unhappiness may be defined many ways, but always felt the same.

"Sounds like a hard life," he said with a sigh.

"Have you ever seen an easy life?"

It was a good question. Steven thought it over a minute. "Mine, maybe."

"It is now because you made it that way. Back when you were just the son of a blacklisted writer and an alcoholic nymphomaniac, it was probably pretty rugged."

"Guess so." Steven fixed his cross-examiner's gaze on Albert's round, bespectacled face. "Why are you telling me this?"

"Because you've been a good and helpful friend, and it's always advisable to balance the books, as I think you understand. O is perfect just as she is. You and she both built your lives by force of will and you're very attached to them. She may be your slave and all that stuff, but I wouldn't underestimate her determination to protect the things that matter to her. I've worked with her and I promise you, she can be as immovable as The Glendale Galleria."

"Duly noted. Thanks for the upload."

"Any time, bro. I like my life too. Speaking of which, want to go down to Chi's for dim sum?"

"It's a little early for me. Besides, I have one last appointment today."

"Something important?"

"Anything involving a jeweler is probably important."

Albert slapped his ever-expanding forehead. "Did you hear anything I said?"

Steven stuck out his hand and Albert took it. "Get your friend Eric teed up. We'll make it happen."

Taking the Two Freeway to its end, Steven puttered along in the thickening late afternoon traffic on Glendale Boulevard down to Sunset. There was hardly anything left of the old Silver Lake that had been a rough neighborhood when Steven was a kid. The red-tiled building tucked in the middle of an Upper Sunset curve had been a somewhat dilapidated bodega where Steven sometimes stopped for a Coke while riding his bike down to the Vista Theater, but now it was the freshly painted shop and studio of his longtime friend Lola, L.A.'s most sought after body piercer. She was to steel what Jan was to ink, but a more charismatic cultural presence as well.

In the early, activist days of the city's emerging BDSM scene, Lola had been a performance artist, an event organizer and a highly visible, highly vocal representative to the vanilla world through mainstream media, collegiate outreach programs and workshop presentations. She had also been the first close friend Steven made when he began his emergence from the closet.

In her early twenties Lola, fresh from the deeply suburban West Valley, already had rings and studs in all kinds of places, likely and unlikely. Over the years she gleefully abandoned all pretense of passing as a weekender. By now, she had as many holes in her anatomy as Heinz Sauce had ingredients. She was also entirely tattooed, with massive black wings covering her back all the way down over her ass and colorful mermaid scales adorning the rest of her to below the ankles. She'd assured Steven that the scales could be found everywhere south of her waist, and she did mean everywhere. He had taken her word for that, thinking it bad form to insist on visual proof.

And yet, rebelliously exotic as she appeared, she was entirely free of Jan's brooding volatility. She had a merry, high-pitched voice, was given to outbursts of hilarity at the slightest cause and generally wore a smile, as much or as little as she might otherwise have on.

Curbing the Morgan outside the red building, Steven rang for admission at the black painted front door, pausing to admire the array of rings, barbells, jeweled ear-lobe plugs and other decorations in the window.

CHAPTER TWENTY-THREE

Feeling a need to inform Ray of his change of heart concerning the website, Steven tapped the button on the round Bluetooth ear set and called Ray's office. It was nearly seven, but Ray was still at his desk. While Ray's judgment was questionable at times, his diligence was not.

Steven suggested they have dinner and then take a drive out to Pasadena. Both were temporary bachelors at the moment. Ray didn't need much persuading. He and Jasper had spent a long afternoon doing the next issue's pre-edits and Ray could use a drink.

Picking Ray up in front of the round-windowed building on Sunset, Steven cruised over to Musso and Frank's, parking the Morgan by the back door. They took charge of a round red leather booth on the bar side. Steven ordered his usual: a Stella, a cup of cream of tomato soup, broiled lamb kidneys with bacon and a side of creamed spinach. Ray chose the Caesar and a small fillet, watching his brother put away yet another meal he was sure would send Steven to an early grave. Steven caught the look.

"Quit fretting over me. This is my idea of health food."

"That's the part I fret about," Ray replied, shaking his head.

"Look on the bright side," Steven suggested, taking another gulp of Stella, "If I drop dead from eating lamb kidneys here, I'll die happy and you'll inherit all my money."

Ray rolled his eyes. "Isn't there something important you're supposed to be telling me?"

"I'm getting to that. I was up at Albert's today."

"He let someone in?"

"Desperate times call for desperate measures. He browbeat me into caving on the website."

Ray's face lit up. "I can't believe it! What did he use, hypnosis or drugs?

"He played the unfair advantage of making sense," Steven conceded somewhat ruefully.

"He didn't call you a Luddite did he? I warned him against that."

"No, he swatted me on the nose with a rolled-up copy of *The Economist*. Anyway, I'm ready to pull the trigger on this mad scheme."

"I'll get right on it," Ray said. "Eric's been waiting to hear from me for weeks."

"Just make sure I see a spreadsheet prior to our meeting with genius boy. I need some baseline numbers before he starts adding on the accessories."

Ray and Albert had lots of plans for the site. Before Steven could stop him, he unspooled a whole list of them, much of it in a language not among any of the six Steven spoke. Steven made him promise not to discuss business on the drive to The Mansion as he signed off the check with a torpedo-shaped Waterman Edson.

Shortly they were roaring out the Two-Ten in Steven's car, Tom Waits wailing on the stereo. The Morgan's fog lights cast yellow halos ahead of them through the low-lying marine layer that descended during dinner. Cozy weather for where they were headed.

The Mansion lay at the bottom of a deep hollow buried back in the Pasadena hills a few winding miles from the freeway. It was first identifiable as a patch of trees in the otherwise sere landscape where the desert encroached. Behind its electronically lifted iron gates, it looked much as it had a century earlier: the biggest, most extravagant palazzo erected by any of the earliest California oil barons.

The original owner had made it particularly extravagant in commemoration of the fortuitous event that paid for it: a delay on The Red Line had prevented his assistant from transferring a deed during business hours that would have handed over a tract of land under which lay a lake of crude oil.

His grandchildren had donated it to the county because no one could afford to maintain a twenty-eight-room mansion as residential property anymore. It had been a charter school for a few years but after the Northridge Quake, it no longer met earthquake standards and the county no longer had the necessary fifteen million dollars to bring it up to code.

It was in pretty shabby shape when Steven and Marie first looked at it but under some layers of institutional paint, it had lost little of its garish charm. Its great rooms were still lit by a couple of million worth of Tiffany glass and the secret library, where no students had ever been allowed, still had its naughty Joel Chandler Christy murals of Native Americans partying on the prairie in lush pastels. Steven had been particularly amused by the scene portraying a naked, blonde female settler tied on horseback being led toward a tepee where she undoubtedly faced a long night.

Using Marie's reconstructed client list and Steven's multi-layered corporate ownership plan, they'd raised enough money to buy the place and renovate it within a year. It had been duly chartered as a private club to which the original investors had been granted lifetime memberships with full privileges. All admissions since (there were over two hundred now, though only assembled in numbers for the occasional gala) had been sponsored by the founders and paid a staggering yearly fee to belong.

Marie oversaw the management, delegating most of the daily routine to bright, attractive young men and women as discreet as they were efficient. Attendants, male and female, in black turtlenecks and black jeans maintained order with the help of surveillance cameras in the ceilings, walkies on their belts and short stinging floggers that commanded attention without inflicting damage to the establishment's most valued assets.

Marie kept The Mansion stocked with no less than twenty-five girls, with more available part-time as needed, which they tended to be at certain seasons of year. Though half the membership lived in other cities, many in other countries, Marie's service corps consisted entirely of locals, never far out of sight or out of mind.

They were an oddly congenial mix of high-end escorts, porn performers, hunters of wealthy husbands, bored ex-wives of previous wealthy husbands, sensation seekers and an ardently sincere minority of deeply submissive beauties either at the pleasure of their masters or hoping to find a master at whose pleasure to be.

Ranging in age from eighteen to forty-five, they were of every race and nationality with two things in common: Each had her own unique physical attractiveness that translated to the kind of fuckability O had discussed with Jacqui; and at Marie's insistence, all were genuinely aroused by the pleasures of cruelty. Other than the owned slaves of specific members, the girls were paid handsomely for their labors, though none signed on solely for the money. Marie understood that sexual subjugation, unlike mere sexual enjoyment, could not be feigned convincingly for long. The men — and by now, a few women — who paid such exorbitant sums to visit wouldn't be satisfied with anything less than authentic submission.

To maintain the proper atmosphere, disobedience to any of Marie's long list of rules resulted in physical punishment (as opposed to the more painful economic sanctions employed in regular bordellos). By accepting the terms of the unwritten contract, all agreed to regular use by any member whose eye they caught, or by any attendant struck with an urge to indulge.

As Marie could not be everywhere at all times, she also wielded authority through a half-dozen bisexual pro-dommes dressed in belly-baring leather tops, tight leather jodhpurs like hers (but with strategically snapped panels through the crotch) and tall boots. They were a merry and good-looking lot who understood their presence was as much decorative as functional. The boys liked seeing them dispense a whipping or lead their charges along on leashes. They also lent assistance in private quarters when needed.

The great triumph of Marie's aesthetic sensibilities was the costume she designed for the house slaves. Marie had been a drama major in college; her specialty in production design was reflected in the mixture of classicism and modernity with which the girls were dressed. She'd struck a very good bargain at Syren, the latex couturier of choice for cinematic superheroines, for a steady supply of the basic pattern in different sizes and colors.

Each girl wore a two-piece latex outfit in one of several assorted jewel-tone colors. The skirts were pencil-tight, but easily accessed with the removal of strategic zipped panels front and rear, the zippers covered in contrasting rows of latex ruffles. The rear panels were cut out to expose the buttocks through a window just large enough to administer a casual spank. The gaps in the front panels plunged from the navel to where there could be no doubt that all the girls were shaved bare.

The bustiers were high in the back, but scooped below the breasts, which were framed by ruffles matching those on the skirts. During the orientation week for new talent the most challenging test often proved moving in silent grace atop the tall mules color-coordinated with the dresses, but in time they all learned how to display themselves most appealingly with every movement.

All were cuffed and collared in black-patent-leather. Their lips, eyes and nipples were shaded with battle-tested color, though none wore perfume. Most of the members were married and wives could smell infidelity with the olfactory capabilities of bloodhounds. Each girl had an engraved nameplate on her collar so members could summon her specifically.

Though they weren't supposed to speak unless spoken to and to keep their eyes averted, these regulations were often observed in the breach to no great consequence. Most still managed to earn a whipping for something, such as smoking on the terrace, at least once a day if only to attract the attention of the members.

The committed slaves-in-training got an informal education from the house girls that had been known to subvert the plans of more than one aspiring master. In all, they were a merry group of luscious, licentious, lash-loving ultra-femmes exactingly screened by Marie for their aptitude at having a good time themselves while showing a good time to others.

Steven and Ray were expected, having called ahead to see who was on duty. Josh, the chief attendant on the night shift, took the Morgan after some affable car talk and the huge Tiffany doors at the massive portico swung inward on their retrofitted hydraulic hinges as Steven and Ray approached.

Svetlana and Eugenia waited to greet them in the round marble foyer. They knelt as Steven and Ray entered, per protocol, but jumped up and hugged them both as soon the boys gave the signal. Svetlana, in sapphire blue, was tall and blonde, resembling a Russian model frequently seen on the magazine covers O had shot in her previous life. She had the same excellent Russian bones and a subtly exotic Siberian tilt to the eyes, but she was more a Victoria's Secret-type than a runway type. She wasn't quite tall enough and her fair, Slavic flesh spilled from the cut out top of her service uniform a little too generously. Her "imperfections" made her quite popular here.

Eugenia, Ray's chosen companion, was a light-skinned black girl who had worked as a dancer. She had big, round eyes, boldly sensual features and what was generally conceded to be the best ass in the house, which she'd balanced with some carefully calibrated augmentation in front. Her uniform was transparent to show off her caramel skin. She adored Ray and the feeling was nearly mutual, though her refusal to model for *Forbidden* exasperated him. Holding her hard against him, he got a good handful of Eugenia's fabled derrière.

The party paused in the foyer where a vaguely Eastern-European attendant in the customary black turtleneck and black jeans sat at the concierge desk where Steven and Ray signed in. The attendant had a quick, discreet look at their status in the database to verify their tests for every known STD were current before logging them.

"Enjoy yourselves, gentlemen," he said with a slight accent. Eugenia enthusiastically promised they would.

Ray made Eugenia walk ahead of him so he could enjoy the view on the way to the big, dark-paneled library. She gave her hips an extra roll to make sure he did. Steven wrapped an arm around Svetlana's middle and they ascended the vast, circular staircase together. Completely ignoring the rules he'd had more than a minor hand in writing, he asked her how she was doing.

"Okay, Sir," Svetlana replied in her husky, still slightly accented voice. "Just busy enough."

"The blue uniform really flatters you," he said.

"You mean it shows off my milk veins, Sir," she replied. Svetlana had an acute memory for what men liked about her.

Steven put an arm around her waist and they went upstairs so he could trace those veins.

The library, with its risqué murals, was empty so late on a weeknight, but a welcoming fire blazed in the huge black-iron hearth. Ray settled in on a deep, green leather sofa to one side of it and commanded Eugenia to bring him a brandy. She poured it from a decanter on the mantle, requiring her to stretch up with her back to him. She took her time about it, gliding over to him, glass in hand, then kneeling next to the couch and offering it with upraised hands.

Dipping a finger into the amber liquid, Ray painted a circle of it around each of Eugenia's nipples, which had been dusted a shade darker for emphasis. She trembled a little, still holding the glass overhead, when Ray bent down to savor the cognac from the tip of each breast. Their points hardened immediately on contact.

"Missed me?" Ray asked, taking the glass from her trembling hands. Eugenia nodded vigorously. Though she was here working off her student loans, Eugenia enjoyed her duties and allowed herself the luxury of liking some of the men she served. Ray was on her short list.

"I've missed you too."

He took a healthy swig from the glass and motioned Eugenia off her knees so he could pass it from his mouth to hers. He held her by her collared throat to feel her swallow it. The taste lingered in their kiss.

"I have a few things on my mind from which I'd like to be distracted at the moment," he said. "Any new smut here I'd enjoy?"

Eugenia raised her threaded eyebrows and gave him a mischievous smile. "Just your kind of thing, Sir."

She got up in a rustle of clinging rubber, went to the bookcase and brought back a big, marbleized folio, its lid tied shut with a red ribbon. When she started to kneel again and pass it to him, he patted the couch and bade her sit down instead. It was an order and she had to obey, even if slaves weren't generally permitted on the furniture.

Pulling Eugenia close, Ray put the folio across both their laps and undid the ribbon. "Show it to me," he said.

Inside was a tall stack of exquisitely tinted pastels by an English artist whose work Ray particularly enjoyed. In fact, he had probably financed this limited edition with illustrations he'd bought for the magazine. This batch was particularly lurid, set in some nineteenth-century penal colony where naked women with impossibly long waists and legs, breasts of every size and shape, complexions of various hues, and consistently outsized vulvas were subjected to a variety of diabolical sexual tortures. Their tormentors, both male and female, wore only boots and looked as lustful as their tearful captives appeared terrified and agonized. The beating and buggering and branding to which the prisoners were subjected seemed somehow to leave their beauty miraculously untarnished.

Turning the leaves with one hand, Eugenia unbuttoned Ray's jeans with the other, though she should technically have waited until ordered to do so, and slipped in a delicate, long-fingered hand. What she sought wasn't difficult to find, her leisurely stroking timed to the flipping of the pages. They made it almost halfway through before Ray set the artwork aside to lower Eugenia's head into his lap, working his hands through her shiny curls. It had been a long time, and she wanted to dive on him but started respectfully, as she'd been taught. Here, the men always set the pace. There was no rule governing how deep she could take him, however, and she put that omission to good use, swallowing his length fully at the conclusion of each circular head motion.

In one of the suites upstairs, lovingly restored in the fashion of a pre-war Parisian boudoir, Steven let Svetlana undress him and hold a robe open for him so they could get comfortable on the large, damasked draped bed. Steven lay on his back while Svetlana poured him a half-shot of scotch, as much as he ever had. She gave herself a little less than that at his insistence. This too was against the rules, but they knew each other well enough to adjust the terms a bit.

It hadn't always been that way. Steven was apprehensive about foreign girls, particularly those from east of the Danube, no matter what kind of paper they had. He didn't just fear a possible trafficking bust, though that was a real concern; he despised traffickers ever since his stay in The Balkans and wouldn't knowingly funnel one cent their way.

But Svetlana had checked out completely with his connections at State. She had a legitimate green card, a diploma certifying her as a veterinary assistant and documents going back to her arrival seven years earlier. She hung on to the accent strictly for theatrical reasons.

Still, because of his suspicions, Steven had made a point of getting to know her and found her to be intelligent, mordantly funny and clearly doing what she did by choice.

She handed Steven his drink and sat down on the bed next to him, putting her back up straight against the headboard so her breasts would be at eye level. He noticed a few fresh marks on Svetlana's breasts from something that looked like it must have hurt.

"How many times have you been used today?" he asked, watching Svetlana lower her extended eyelashes as she sipped her drink.

"Only three, Sir."

"Tell me about them."

Svetlana stretched out alongside Steven, rolling in against his sturdy frame. She dropped off one of her mules so she could stroke his leg with her bare foot. "The first was an overnight guest who just wanted a morning BJ with his breakfast. Easily pleased. Then I ran into Tomas, the attendant from Barcelona, on the stairs back from the kitchen. He's the one who gave me the marks. I make big sad eyes at him so he wants to beat me."

She lifted her face and made big sad eyes at Steven. He immediately wanted to beat her. "He put me up against the wall right there and flogged me with the whip from his belt. Then he took off the belt and hit me a few times with that. Of course, his pants slipped down. Then he turned me around to face the wall. What could I do?"

"Stick your ass out at him?"

"You think I am a woman of loose morals, Sir?"

Steven grinned at her.

"I think you know how to take advantage of a good opportunity."

"I was a little wet from the blowjob, and Tomas has such a nice cock. I had to kick off my shoes so he could fuck me because he's shorter than I am, you know? Don't tell him I said that, please, Sir."

"Rub your tits on me and I promise I'll forget."

Svetlana swallowed the last of her drink, put the glass down on the nightstand and dug a black bottle of expensive silicone lube out of the drawer. While Steven watched, she lubricated her cleavage thoroughly, rubbing her nipples so he could watch them get hard. Setting the lube aside, she undid his robe and slid down along his body until she could squeeze his hard-on comfortably between her breasts by pressing them together with her hands. Svetlana was in high demand for this particular use.

"The third guy was kind of fun," she continued, looking up at Steven and rubbing her torso in slow circles over his lap. "English, I think. He ordered me for one of the special rooms downstairs where he put me on the impaling stand and used this crazy little toy he brought back from Japan on me. It looked like a flashlight and I was afraid at first. You know how I hate anything electric, Sir."

"Except for vibrators," Steven reminded her.

"That's different. Anyway, it wasn't that bad. When he touched me with it the thing made a big, loud spark, but it just felt like being snapped with a rubber band. I started to laugh. Then he started to laugh. It was kind of a crazy situation, squirming around with this big dildo up against my cervix while he shocked me all over. The shaft was up me so far I couldn't do much to get out of the way."

"Poor darling."

"Eventually I had to beg him to fuck me before I pissed myself."

Steven slipped his hands into Svetlana's armpits and dragged her across his knees.

"Are you a wicked bitch, Svetlana?" he asked, affably.

"Only when I get the chance."

He began spanking her rump, nicely exposed by the cut-out skirt, firmly but affectionately. "You know I'm already sore from Tomas, Sir."

"I certainly hope so."

"You are an evil man."

"Just as you deserve."

He slapped Svetlana's tail just hard enough to raise her existing set of marks before flipping her over and zipping the front panel out of her skirt. He felt her hands on his head as his face sank between her long, slender legs, which crossed over his back in violation of how she'd been taught to wrap them around a man only once he was inside her. She accepted his attentions greedily, talking to herself in Russian, forgetting he could understand her. He lifted his face and shook his head.

"Such language, young lady. I would never call you those dirty names."

Svetlana hid her face in the pillow, truly embarrassed.

"Oh my god," she said. "I didn't know you were listening. Maybe you should call me dirty names yourself. I must have earned it."

Steven rolled on top of her, slipped inside and pinned her hands above her head. Fucking her in long strokes, he whispered every vile word of Russian he could remember in her ear. A few minutes of that and she was slamming her hips against him with all her might, her Russian babbling now too fast and disjointed for him to follow, although the general idea was clear enough. She came with a howl that could have attracted wolves all the way from Siberia.

"Okay my little *shelava*," Steven said, pulling out of her and planting a knee on either side of her head, "make big sad eyes for me."

She looked up at him defiantly.

"Nyet! Mudak!" She hissed.

"Easy for you to say."

He slapped her across the face twice, hard. She gave him the big sad eyes he requested and threw in a few tears. Still holding her wrists down with one hand, Steven jerked himself with the other, glazing Svetlana's perfect face with a thick coat of icing. She started to laugh again, trying to lick down the spurt that splattered closest to her mouth.

"You are a horrible, evil man. Now I have to do my whole make-up over... Sir. "

"No, you just have to go in the bathroom and wash up so you can come sleep with me."

His tug on her collar brought her back to reality. "I am at your service of course, Sir."

He let her out from under him so she could stumble off to the sink and then fell on his back, smiling happily.

Before going to sleep, they broke another house rule by smoking a joint out on the balcony. It was chilly and even with their fleecy Frette house robes belted shut, they still huddled together for warmth.

"I've gotten soft here," Svetlana said, exhaling a plume of white smoke. "Back home the train stations are colder than this inside."

Steven assured her that California reset everyone's thermostats the same way. After a moment of silence, she looked into his eyes and asked him about O.

"Why her?"

There was clearly both incomprehension and some pain in Svetlana's tone.

"Why not her?"

If Svetlana knew something in particular, Steven wanted to hear it.

"She's colder than a Russian train station. The whole time she was here, she never said a word to any of us. She obeyed all the rules, wouldn't go along with any fooling around like the rest of us. She thinks she's better than we are."

"O tries to do everything perfectly. Sometimes she tries too hard."

Svetlana pondered.

"I understand. Most people don't try at all."

That was the unfortunate truth of the world. Steven and Svetlana both knew it entirely too well. He suggested they go inside. It had been a long day.

Chapter Twenty-Four

At ten a.m., Eugenia woke Ray up with her mouth as ordered. He lay back, letting his mind come around last after other parts were already in full morning salute. Eugenia laughed and wriggled delightedly when he dragged her across his lap for a good spanking. His cock burrowed in the crease of her stomach while his hand came down repeatedly on buttocks so solid, Ray felt his palm giving out before her skin tone darkened appreciably. Bidding Eugenia to open her legs, he slipped his tingling hand in between, where the weather was as warm and humid as expected.

Rolling over on command, Eugenia climbed up Ray's frame and staked herself onto him in slow, swirling circles. He clipped her wrist cuffs together just to make it all a bit trickier, but she could still brace against his chest as she raised and lowered, rocked back and forth and swung in lazy swirls. Ray let her do most of the work, busying his hands with her tits, getting their dark tips nicely tumescent. Slipping a couple of fingers in between them, Ray found a productive spot, working it adroitly to get Eugenia pounding down on to him harder and harder.

As she'd explained to him one time, living in a beautiful place with a bunch of beautiful girls, wandering the halls all day in a costume that never let her forget why she was there and witnessing or participating in perverted sexual acts whenever the opportunity arose, she was pretty near the edge most of the time. It didn't take much to push her over. She barely had time to mutter a breathless request for permission before jamming down on Ray's marble-hard shaft and coming with a sudden outburst of friendly obscenities.

Ray unhooked her cuffs so Eugenia could fall comfortably onto his bare chest, her arms flung around the back of his neck. He let her lie there, rubbing her breasts against him and stirring her insides with his stick until he eventually gave the order to finish him where they started. Eugenia scrambled south, sucked him hard and fast, and swallowed her reward in three eager gulps. She lifted her damp, shiny face to smile up at him. In private they, too, tended to set the house rules aside.

"Man, I wish you'd come around more often," she panted. "You always make it nice for me. Some of these other pompous fucks could use a few lessons in how to show a girl a good time. So just where have you been keeping yourself?"

It was a daring question. The girls were under strict instructions never to ask the members about their personal lives.

"I've been pretty busy at work," he tried unconvincingly. Eugenia shook her head, curls bouncing.

"I know that's bullshit. When have you let business get in the way of fucking?"

"Busted again." Ray shrugged. "I have no gift for lying at all."

"That's another thing I wish was more common," Eugenia said. "Gets pretty old, hearing the same fairy tales over and over. Love those guys who got their training from some secret château in France. They hip-wrap me every time. What's happening with you and O? How did she end up here while you stayed away?"

Ray didn't know where to begin.

"For a while, I was a pretty big part of her life, but I think I'm being edited out."

"She didn't break your heart, did she?"

Eugenia looked ready to throw a punch at somebody.

"It's complicated. She didn't leave me. We sort of drifted apart and rather than let her get away completely, I passed her on to my brother."

"You boys every lived down south by any chance?"

"Hey, it's not like she's our cousin or something."

They both laughed. Eugenia suggested they look on the bright side. Now she and Ray would be seeing each other more often. Ray didn't counter that, instead ordering her to get her uniform on and bring him some breakfast. Eugenia saluted, jumped out of bed and wriggled on her latex skirt. Ray helped lace her into the top, eliciting a few giggles by elaborately "adjusting" her breasts in the ruffled window.

Opening the curtains, Ray looked out on the green lawns of The Mansion, and beyond them to the dusty hillsides. The sky was bright and dirty. In a couple of hours, he'd be working again, but for the moment he allowed himself the luxury of falling back into bed awaiting Eugenia's return.

The unaccustomed time-out from his hyper-scheduled routine tempted Ray to a thing he generally avoided: thinking about his life.

Not that it was a bad life. It felt like freedom, but was it? Ray suffered no false modesty regarding his own accomplishments. He'd beaten the odds, and Steven's skepticism, by turning a profit from a sharp X-rated magazine at a time when magazines had the life expectancy of mayflies. His actually brought in a few more dollars each month. The shadow of Albert's gloom-and-doom prognostications might lie over it, but however long it lasted, *Forbidden* would have earned its place next to *Bizarre* and *Exotique* and even *Playboy* in mapping a sexual frontier of its own time and place.

But without Steven, Ray knew he'd be like millions of other bright lads, dreaming the dream instead of living it. Steven, who had no dreams of his own, could only have underwritten Ray's out of love. He certainly hadn't acted on faith. Nothing Ray had done in his life to that point would have inspired any. He'd already proved he would never be an artist or a musician himself, but Steven had given him credit for the educational value of failure.

It was a bit early in the day for all of this, but it made him feel better about O. She really did have more in common with Steven than she had with him. She obviously thought she belonged to Steven. If Steven was prepared to throw over all his practical reasons for never taking a slave of his own to have her, maybe she was right.

Eugenia put a stop to his ruminations just in time, returning with a white wicker tray and setting it on the bed over his lap. She was back in service mode, saying nothing as she draped a napkin across his unveiled legs and took the steel dome off a plate of Eggs Benedict. Ray looked suitably delighted.

"You remembered!"

He pulled Eugenia's face down for a quick kiss, followed by a quick squeeze of a breast that came recklessly within range. Ray patted a spot on the mattress next to him.

"Sit here and keep me company."

Eugenia sat down on the bed and swung her legs up under her so she could get nice and close. These moves had to be learned just right. Linen tended to stick to latex. Eugenia rested against his shoulder while he ate. She even performed a useful duty or two, such as grinding the pepper on his eggs. In return, he gave her the orange slice, which she sucked clean with casual suggestiveness.

There was a rap on the door, but Ray had no time to ask who was outside before Steven entered. He was shaved, showered and dressed for the road.

"You look like you had a pleasant evening," Ray said, detecting a little extra swagger in Steven's stride.

Steven nodded toward Eugenia.

"And you look like you had a pleasant morning."

"Hey, I'm casting here. Don't you think Eugenia would make a terrific model for a girl-girl layout?

Eugenia had to laugh.

"Give it up Ray. I'm going to finish my MBA and make some real money. The last thing I need is a bunch of dirty pictures floating around on the web."

"Speaking of which," Steven said, "in the unlikely event you make it to the office, give your pal Eric a call and get the meeting happening. Shoot me an email with some dates. I'll be at my desk."

"What, no one to stab today?"

"I've already had a run this morning."

Ray was incredulous.

"In the Pasadena smog? Are you trying to kill yourself?"

Steven pointed an accusing finger at Ray's plate.

"If you keep eating like that, I'll outlive you."

"Said the great carnivore. I'm glad we don't share a room anymore. The sound of your arteries hardening would keep me awake all night."

"Hey, my LDL is lower than yours. And don't start counting my money either. I decided last night to leave everything to a cat shelter."

Eugenia giggled. Ray pinched her nearest nipple.

"Go ahead and laugh. You'll live to be older and richer than either of us."

Eugenia couldn't resist.

"You know what they say, fellas. Black don't crack. May I be excused so I can go fuck someone I'm sure needs it more than either of you?"

Ray let her go with a kiss on the cheek. She turned at the door and gave Ray a scolding glance before departing.

"Don't stay away so long, Raymond. My ass craves your particular kind of attention."

"I'll bear that in mind."

In the approved manner, Eugenia opened the door of the luxurious suite and backed out into the hallway, leaving them with a respectful view of her downcast eyes and lowered breasts.

"I wonder if she'd ever date me outside," Ray mused when Eugenia was gone. Steven sat down on a corner of the bed while Ray polished off his plate.

"I seriously doubt it. She's already married, and quite satisfied with that from what I hear."

"No shit. I didn't have a clue."

"That's why Marie doesn't let them talk. It's better to allow the members their fantasies. Anyhow, you've got something ultra-fine coming your way."

"If your conspiracy succeeds."

"Don't they all? There's a disposable razor in the bathroom. Your beard is starting to make you look like a back-up player for ZZ Top."

"I only wish I had their talent."

"I only wish you had their money. Then I could quit working."

Ray set the tray aside and climbed out of bed.

"You quit working years ago. Now you're just practicing."

"Eventually I'll get the hang of it. I'll be downstairs when you're presentable. Let me rephrase that. I'll be downstairs when you can find your clothes."

Sliding into his jeans, Ray felt something in his pocket. It was the gold screwdriver for the bracelet he'd impulsively bought Jacqui. He stared at it a long moment. Why had he been so extravagantly generous with someone he just met? Ray liked nice things, wasn't particularly tight with a buck and didn't mind putting a smile on a pretty face with an unexpected treat. But he wasn't impulsively extravagant like Steven and this spontaneous gesture had been far from cheap. Ray had acted from personal impulse and enjoyed it. Something about Jacqui's slightly imperfect grin made it worth seeing even at unjustifiable expense. That could be good or bad. Ray tucked the little gold screwdriver back in his pocket. Misgivings aside, it felt good having it in there.

CHAPTER TWENTY-FIVE

Half an hour later, the Morgan puttered down Sunset so Steven could drop Ray off at *Forbidden's* HQ. There was a welcoming party waiting inside.

The staff meeting was called for three. In the conference room, Lena checked out the PowerPoint system on the huge wall screen, tossing up random web pages, photos from gossip sites and YouTube clips. Jasper had his pad unfolded in front of him at one end of the deltoid conference table. Albert, who capriciously chose to clean up his act that day, sat near Jasper at the far end of the trapezoid from Ray and Lena. All had open laptops in front of them.

"I've scrambled the pagination for this issue a little," Jasper said. "Tell me if it works."

"I'm hopeless with covers," Albert admitted, "but that won't stop me from offering an opinion."

Ray pointed out that nothing could stop Albert from offering an opinion.

"Here we go," Lena said, popping the first slide up on the screen. It was a schematic map of the magazine, with each page labeled in print and color codes for different types of material – ads, editorial copy, photo sets, cartoons and standing features. They all took a long look at it before anyone said anything.

"I'm a little concerned about putting a column up against the lead feature," Ray said. "That's a lot of graywall."

"The feature has a ton of art in it. Take a look before you decide," Jasper insisted.

Fair enough. Ray nodded to Lena, who tapped on her laptop's keyboard. One by one, as if the screen were a game show scoreboard, the labeled rectangles flipped over to reveal Jasper's constructed pages.

"I like the masthead image," Albert offered. It was nice, a standing figure, naked and hooded in a spiderweb of chains from one of Darcy's layouts.

Ray was fine with it, but wasn't sure about one of the choices for the Table of Contents.

"That one seems a little tame. Don't we have something dirtier?"

Jasper explained that the set was a little thin and there weren't a lot of good horizontals he wasn't already using.

"Try pulling one from O's set," Ray suggested.

Jasper peered at his small screen, manipulated the touchpad for a couple of minutes. The revised TOC jumped up in a blink. Everyone stared in silence.

"It pops," Jasper said finally.

"I can't be wrong all the time.."

They all laughed. Ray wasn't wrong about the magazine most of the time.

"Okay, let's move on."

Each rectangle flipped over to reveal a photograph, drawing, or mixture of type and art.

"How many of these letters are fake?" Ray asked Albert, scanning the reader mail page.

"Three of six. We did get a lot of stuff I couldn't read on lined paper from various penal institutions.

"Okay everybody, here's your homework," Ray announced. "Get a friend to write in on this issue. Just a few lines. Ply them with drugs and alcohol and make them do it by email."

Everyone nodded and scribbled on stickies. Lena pressed on with the show.

"The hard isn't very visible in Feldman's set," Ray said, penciling something on a legal pad in a leather binder. He put a cursor up on the screen and moved it to where the insertion shots looked off-angle.

"I know this fucking machine is going somewhere, but I can't tell where," he said.

"That," Lena said, "is because he's a lazy old goat who won't take his camera off the sticks."

"Yeah, well, then let him move his sticks. And a little fill light wouldn't be a bad idea either. I need to see something go into something."

Jasper promised to diplomatically raise the issue with Feldman, who was an aging great of the pin-up genre fairly new to shooting hard kink. He had good ideas and his name drew gorgeous models, but he wasn't a dynamo like O. Who was?

When O's set of Jacqui popped up, there was an audible murmur of satisfaction in the room. This was more like it. Every image was riveting, suffused with Sade's voluptuousness of cruelty. The centerfold of Jacqui pinned open on the Y-frame was the embodiment of tempting vulnerability.

There were comments from everyone around the table, but Ray didn't hear them. He was looking at Jacqui's face. She looked scared and excited and pitiful, but mostly just plain lovely. Would she ever show him that face in private? He'd know the answer to that question soon, one way or another.

The advice columns were next up. Ray wanted a new headshot for Marie's *Slave Quarters Q&A*. The current one, featuring Marie in blue latex, was getting too familiar.

"Give me something a little more retro," Ray said. "You know, something kinda Bill Ward."

Jasper promised to make it happen.

Jasper was absolutely right about the feature. It was an interview with a legendary French illustrator whose images were so vivid and shocking they took the curse off the long stretches of print. Ray was sold, instructing Jasper to go ahead and run it in the designated well.

Jasper looked relieved. He wasn't eager to tear the pagination down and start over.

"Do you think we're light for pissing in this issue?" Ray asked them all.

"I think Josh's set covers that pretty well. I practically had to wear rubber boots to lay it out," Jasper said.

Ray seemed satisfied.

The cover, which Jasper and Ray had already chosen privately as usual, was the last card turned over. It displayed Jacqui in the hanging cage, the bars placed just right to keep the cover ID legal. Jasper had blown the image a little larger, bringing Jacqui closer to the front of the frame. The red lipstick on her frightened face suggested just what Albert's copy implied, that she was an unfortunate American tourist grabbed from a nightclub and plunged into some subterranean hell of a foreign prison. Ray liked the way the metallic font in the logo picked up the highlights from the cage bars.

He read Albert's screaming cover line out loud.

"Shock-Tortured Tart's Anal Agony – "I'm Still Sore Back There!"

They all thought it was pretty funny.

"I like it." Ray said. "Very subtle."

"Have you looked at this book recently, bro?" Albert asked wearily. "We don't do subtle."

Ray raised his hands in a gesture of surrender.

"It's perfect. The rest of the cover copy is great too. You I don't worry about."

"Thank you, oh wise and beneficent Sire."

"It's a picture-driven book, Albert," Ray reminded him consolingly. "You have to push the text over the top to get the readers' attention."

"Readers?" Albert said in a tone of mock amazement. "You mean people actually read this magazine?"

"I have only your word on that," Ray shot back. "Okay, this issue's approved. Let's get it moving."

Everyone stood to drift off, but Ray asked Albert to stay behind. Albert sank back into his Aeron chair.

"What have I done?" he asked when they were alone.

"You've talked my brother into meeting with Eric the Kid. It looks like we're going for the site after all."

Albert, who might never have looked surprised in his entire life, looked even less so than usual at this news. He knew that Steven was not one to resist the facts.

"Eric's in Berlin at the Venus show. Back in about ten days. The important thing is that we're moving on this deal."

"I bow before your wisdom," Ray said. "You and Eric set it up however you please, but I get final approval on site content."

"You're the one with the instincts," Albert conceded, throwing his hands in the air. "You just tell Eric what you want on there and that's what you'll see."

"I hope he'll prove as flexible as you think. That's not his reputation."

"No worries. Steven has the right bait."

"Steven always has the right bait. Want to hike over to Delphine?"

"If the magazine is buying."

"With what I pay you, I'm lucky not to be parking cars at Delphine."

"Monopoly prices, my friend. How many mainstream editors are going to give up their ambitions to work on this material? Meet you in half an hour?"

"Sounds good."

Albert shuffled out, leaving Ray gazing up at Jacqui's magnified image on the big screen. Was it really possible? Were they really going to tie a bow around her neck and give her to him? She gave good face to the camera, but what was she really like? She'd been flirtatious and charming for an afternoon in Beverly Hills, but how would she be on her knees in front of him every day? Looking at Jacqui's picture, he couldn't deny his eagerness to find out.

At least Ray had spent the afternoon looking at images of beautiful girls doing dirty things. Once in his office, Steven had been presented with much less interesting material to view, but with much more at stake. He'd just sat down after stopping to change into dark blue double-breasted gangster suit when Constance bustled in and dropped a bradded sheaf of papers on the desk in front of him. The print looked exceedingly fine. He asked her what it was, mildly distracted by the fit of her emerald green dress.

"The contract for the sale of the Santa Fe plat."

"I assume you've read it."

She shot him a look of indignation. "Of course I've read it. You think I sit around here all day filing my nails?"

"No, they're plenty sharp enough. How bad is this monstrosity?"

"I've seen worse. They really do want the property. The down-stroke isn't all that smashing. I've flagged it on Schedule A..."

Steven flipped the through the pages until he came to the little green tag Constance had attached. "Twenty million in front and another forty on execution? They must not want it that bad."

"The earnest money is non-refundable, so they better be serious. You'll like the ninety-nine-year ground lease terms better. They're on Schedule B with the blue flag."

Steven located it, put on his round spectacles and did some serious reading. "You're right," he conceded, "I do like these numbers better. Especially the five percent bump in each of the first three years."

"And there's an option to take it in equity once the complex opens," Constance announced triumphantly.

"Assuming they get it built and occupied. How many widows and orphans are we making homeless for this thing?"

"None. It's nothing but rail yards and warehouses. Everybody down there is homeless already. The idea is to develop it for mixed residential and commercial use. The zoning is already in place."

"So long as they don't build any offices. Downtown doesn't need another square foot of office space."

"They intend to finance with Urban Core money. The government won't subsidize it for anything but apartments, theaters, condos, shops and restaurants. It's meant to be a public space. They want to run a shuttle line between Union Station and Staples."

"At my age and the speed of transit construction around here, the only way I'll ever ride it is on a draped catafalque. Leave it with me. I'll hack my way through the underbrush and give them an answer tomorrow."

"Promise? I don't think I missed any land mines, but you shouldn't sign anything without reading it yourself."

"Constance, you're going to make an excellent lawyer as soon as you overcome your principled nature."

She wagged her red head at him, the wag traveling down the rest of her to her green pumps.

"See? I've already got you fooled into thinking I have a principled nature. By the time my principled nature and I get done, this will be my office."

"Fine. Just try to avoid heavily-armed clients."

"No worries. It's strictly civil practice for me. I've seen enough yobbos come in and out this place to last a lifetime.

Mind if I take off early? I have a hot date with my husband. And you've got some reading to do."

He watched Constance depart in a symphony of hydraulic movements. Lucky husband.

Steven sighed, trying to focus on the intricacies of the purchase offer. He'd hoped the previous night's adventures might cure him of his restlessness, but he couldn't help thinking about O. He didn't like not having her around even if he had been the one to send her off on the mission to Marie's. Steven rarely gave much thought to those not present, but he found himself wondering what O was doing right now, and what she was thinking. He could find out the answer to the former easily enough with a call to Marie. As for the latter, he seriously doubted he'd ever know.

Chapter Twenty-Six

Marie's house was quiet most of the afternoon. Laurel and Angelique were out at the movies. Noriko was at the weekly rope dojo working on her horizontal suspensions. Jacqui had gone off to read for a part in a soft-core cable series. As usual, Marie retired to her office after lunch to handle scheduling and other paperwork concerning The Mansion.

It was both a passion and a job for Marie. When she was out there, descending the spiral staircase in Marlene Dietrich drag to greet an eager crowd of stylish admirers, she was the elegant, clever, *maîtresse de salon* she lived to be. But the price of those moments was many hours of bookkeeping, housekeeping and girl-keeping. Somehow she always knew where everyone was supposed to be, where everybody really was and how to get them all from one location to the other. She knew which members were in town, which were expected and what or who each might have in mind. O occasionally passed the open door of Marie's office to see Marie firing off emails and giving instructions by phone through her headset at the same time. It looked like hard work.

O fully grasped the mathematics of effort invested and reward received. More importantly, she understood that work was the most reliable refuge from the woolly unpredictability of a life without an organizing principle.

That's why she spent her afternoon at the long table with her laptop open and rows of pictures displayed in front of her, back supported by her red corset, which she'd had Jacqui lace down to a three-inch reduction before leaving. O had added a red-embroidered shelf-bra, red seamed stockings and red satin heels, always conscious of Marie's expectations.

O had a girl-girl that needed a last edit and after that a bit of cleaning up on the final selections. O wasn't a doctrinaire realist, but she believed that Photoshop, like makeup, needed to be applied in the proper amount for the situation.

It helped that both girls were beautiful. One was Eastern European, but had been here a long time and had a rowdy, raunchy sense of humor that made her fun to work with. She was the domme in the set. The other girl, a petite Valley blonde, wasn't all that into girls, but hadn't done a lot of bondage and found it new and different. It had been a good shoot and as O trashed every image that was a little out of focus or awkwardly composed, a good set began to emerge.

It would have been the most tedious gig in the world for many people, but O liked post work almost as much as photography itself. It was all about that last inch. A project wasn't done until it was finished. In some sense, it wasn't even complete before the magazines rolled off the presses, but that was beyond O's responsibility. The creation of a certain reality was her part of the process. Delivering that reality to readers was up to Jasper and Albert and a bunch of people O never met who did different things in the production cycle to make it all happen.

O admired people like Ray and Steven and Marie who could keep many plates spinning simultaneously, but she was meant to spin plates one at a time to absolute perfection. Evening had started to come early. By the time the last reflected sunshine faded off the pool outside and the underwater lights came on, O had as close to what she wanted to see in print as she was going to get. She closed the monitor just when dinner, the wonderful aroma of which had begun to drift from the kitchen, was served.

By then, the rest of the girls had straggled back and wandered to their quarters to change, but Marie, already dressed for dinner in the long, sheer, satin-trimmed robe, had stood over O as the last few pictures were tucked into their folders, sitting down for a moment of shared solitude before the starving horde descended.

She praised the precision of O's work.

"I'm never satisfied with it," O said, "but I always feel like I'm getting closer."

"I could say the same," Marie agreed. "Tonight I'll need you to do something very precisely. The success of our little project depends on how well it goes."

O laughed. "Thanks for putting me so at ease."

"I do that with everyone all day long. Consider it a compliment that I trust you not to need it. Jacqui's tonight's whipping girl. You're the one whipping her."

O wasn't surprised. It would have come up anyway as a matter of arithmetic, but Marie would interfere in the order if she had a purpose, which she often did. In this instance, it was obvious. The girl who does the whipping enjoys the submission of the one she whips for the entire night. Jacqui would be laid open to O as dinner would be served – ritualistically.

"Jacqui is not a cream-puff," Marie cautioned. "You'll need to step up to it. You have to do more than just hurt her. You have to surprise her."

A slow smile crept across O's face. "The way you spend all day reassuring people, I spend all day surprising them," she said.

Marie put her hand to O's cheek. "Steven will be visiting tomorrow. He has some very special things for you. I'm looking forward to watching you earn them after we eat."

Anticipating this trial, O had laid plans of her own.

"With your permission, Ma'am, I'd like to go and change. I think I have something more appropriate for the task we have in mind."

"We?"

"I promised Steven my full collusion in his scheme. It was either that or refuse to participate in it at all."

"You've certainly made a believer out of him. We'll see how you do with me."

O excused herself and hurried back to her room, where Jacqui was already wriggling into the sheer, ribbon-fronted girdle she'd bought on their shopping spree. It was a perfect choice, leaving her entirely exposed in front and mostly naked to the crease of her buttocks below the bow in the rear.

"Let me help you with that," O offered, coming over to hook the satin choker in back and tuck it under Jacqui's collar.

"So, heard the latest?" O asked coolly.

"That it's us tonight? Why do you think I chose to wear this? I hope you'll really give it to me. I need it bad."

"You always need it bad."

"This is true."

Jacqui turned around and kissed O on the mouth. "Don't you dare be nice to me, at least not until later. I want to show these bitches something."

"I want to show you something," O said calmly. "Now it's your turn to help me. Let's find that other thing we bought." Moments later, they assembled at the table with the rest, all dressed in their finest frills and lace. Noriko wore her special white satin kimono. O had never known there was such a thing as a fetish kimono before her first trip to Japan, but it hadn't taken her long to discover that there was a Japanese equivalent to every perverse invention of the Western mind.

Noriko's, cinched with a narrow red and gold obi, was not only significantly shorter than anything a proper Japanese woman would wear outdoors, it had outrageously long and full sleeves that came down to her knees. When she turned, she revealed that it was split wide from armpit to waist on both sides. It was quite convenient for hands to slip inside the openings and roam freely over her small body while she modestly kept her arms folded in front of her, the huge sleeves concealing whatever was going on behind them. Her hair was secured with chopsticks and she'd done her face in a toned-down version of a geisha masque. Barelegged, she wore white *tabi* and a pair of customized *okobo*, lacquered white with red peonies painted on the sides. No respectable geisha would have served tea in such an outfit, but a *Shimibara tayu* would perform other services wearing it with pride.

She stood behind the chair to Marie's immediate right. Laurel and Angelique decided it would be fun to do twinsies tonight, as they sometimes did just to enhance their slightly creepy sisterly resemblance. Both dressed in silver-gray demi-bras trimmed in pink lace, matching garters with multiple straps attached to smoky gray stockings and gray suede pumps. Neither wore panties, per the house rules, but there were napkins already spread over all the chairs for them to sit on. As Jacqui had observed, girls tended to leak from the bottom — or at least she did.

At the last moment, O had quickly piled Jacqui's hair on top of her head, realizing it would otherwise be in the way later. She'd secured it with a big white satin bow matching the wide strap that came up the front from the mesh girdle's trimmed waistline and the perky white bow in back. Shiny white mules and white stay-ups with three rows of velvet trim over the elastic at the tops completed the look. It would be no problem getting Jacqui completely naked when the time came.

O, in her black lace bodysuit, was the most covered, except for the part of her that would be in public, which was totally exposed. She'd made Jacqui kneel and lace up her red-soled knee-high boots, which Jacqui kissed after the lacing was complete.

Dinner service was as orthodox as every other activity under Marie's roof. Marie sat down first. All the others followed, except for Jacqui and O, who stood at the far end of the table. They went immediately to the kitchen to bring out the first course, a cold lobster salad, which they served to each of the others in turn, starting with Marie. Then O and Jacqui sat down while Noriko circled the table, pouring wine for all, bowing to kiss Marie's hand before sitting down.

"Well, then," Marie said, looking pleased, "isn't this all just like we'd pictured it? This is how good life can be. Let's enjoy it."

They went at the lobster salad like a girl's volleyball team. The chatter was animated and the flirtation anything but subtle. Angelique had already kicked off a shoe and extended a long leg to Laurel's chair, working her stockinged foot in between Laurel's legs. Marie, drinking her wine, slipped a hand into the wide slit of Noriko's kimono, pinching her nipples until they poked quite shamefully through the thin silk. O fed bites of lobster to Jacqui, who spontaneously knelt next to O's chair to receive them with hands behind her back.

When Marie rang the small silver bell to signal for the entrée, Angelique had to get her shoe back on in a hurry to fetch it, as they were next in the order. Noriko made another round with the bottle. Angelique and Laurel returned with the salmon coulibiac and grilled baby vegetables, which they dished out in turn to a chorus of oohs and aahs. As the buzz of conversation rose in volume, Marie signaled Noriko to stop pouring. The girls were permitted to get slightly lit, but never drunk. She wanted their full attention for what was to follow.

In the meantime, she entertained them all with a story to which they listened attentively. Long ago, when Marie, then a young escort, had attended a film festival as the guest of an Italian film magnate. After a ceremony in honor of an elderly German woman who had directed many brilliant films over the years, only a few of them for the Nazis, they'd all gone drinking with some up-and-comers.

Following some schnapps and champagne, the aged director had answered an eager young film student a little too candidly when asked how she'd gotten her start. Though in no way political herself, the director had received an invitation to a private meeting with an admirer of her work named Adolf Hitler, upon whom she had, in her own words, "performed fellatio," earning herself a very *freundlichst* interview with Josef Goebbels. She had related all of this without a hint of shame, calling for a celebratory glass of schnapps at the conclusion, compelling them all to drink a toast with her to the good old days.

"So," Marie said. "When you girls are all married off to your respective robber barons and potentates and you find yourselves feeling a bit guilty about how you rose in the world, you can console yourselves with the knowledge that not one of you had to blow Hitler to do it."

There was an outburst of high-pitched laughter around the table, followed by a round of applause, which died quickly at the tinkle of Marie's bell. "I think we're ready for dessert now," she said.

O and Jacqui, nearest the kitchen, started to rise, but Marie motioned them to stay seated. "Angelique and Laurel can get it. Noriko, would you drop the ropes please?"

The room fell silent except for the clicking of Laurel and Angelique's heels on the way to the kitchen. O and Jacqui exchanged a look. "It's your call, O. What do you want to use?" Marie asked.

"I'd like the pink dressage whip Jacqui gave you, if you don't mind loaning it to me, Ma'am."

Marie's look made Jacqui shudder, exposed nipples hardening. "I can't think of a better way to initiate it," Marie replied. Her smile was even more chilling.

Meanwhile, Noriko brought down a pair of long, thick, red silk ropes swagged from the draped ceiling between the table and the glass doors to the illuminated swimming pool. Each had a snap-swivel at the end.

"Well," Marie said to Jacqui, "I suspect you'll be eating your dessert standing up."

Jacqui looked down at the table. "Yes, Ma'am," she said, more excited then afraid.

Jacqui sat very still while Marie sent Noriko to retrieve the pink whip from upstairs.

Laurel and Angelique appeared, each carrying a large silver tray. While Angelique set small, black dessert plates with skull motifs on the table, each brightened with small scoops of mixed gelatos and shortbread cookies, Laurel poured coffee into black cups. Noriko returned with the whip, went straight to O and knelt by her chair, offering the whip on upraised palms held above her bowed head in the proper manner. There were no accidents here; this was why O and Jacqui had been seated at the end of the table.

O took the whip, nodding to Noriko, who went back to sit next to Marie. Marie stirred some cream into her coffee while Angelique sugared Laurel's for her. All eyes fell on O and Jacqui.

O unsnapped the little charm dangling from the pommel of the dressage whip and set it on the table. Swishing the slender, evil instrument through the air, she brought the tip up under Jacqui's chin.

"On your feet, pretty bitch," O said evenly.

Jacqui whimpered, lips turning down. She wished she hadn't encouraged O quite so much. Both stood, pushing in their chairs. O watched Jacqui round the end of the table to take her position between the two ropes. This was always done in the same fashion. The whipping girl had to stand facing the table so the others could see her face and she could see theirs. A whipped back, after all, is pretty much a whipped back no

matter whose. The view from in front was often more dramatic.

O snapped the swivels at the ends of the ropes to the rings
on Jacqui's brown leather cuffs, turning them so Jacqui could
get a good grip on the soft, braided silk. She reached under
her to the center-split in the girdle's crotch and stroked Jacqui
open, working in a couple of fingers. Jacqui's knees trembled,
but she stayed in position. O's fingers came out shiny and wet.
She held them up in front of Jacqui's face.

"You can hardly wait, can you?" O said quietly.

"Not much longer, Sister. I've been waiting for this since
the day you got here."

O promised not to disappoint her as Jacqui eagerly sucked
her fingers clean.

There wasn't much to strip off the tall redhead. Tucking
the whip under her arm, O started by undoing the bow holding the back of the transparent girdle together, reaching down
into Jacqui's suddenly exposed rear cleavage and grabbing
her hard between the legs. Jacqui's head rolled in a circle and
her eyelids closed slowly. O lingered for a bit before undoing
the choker and slipping the filmy garment down Jacqui's legs.
Jacqui lifted her feet to step out and O folded the fabric carefully, placing it on Jacqui's chair.

Flexing the dressage whip, she returned to contemplate
Jacqui's smooth, perfect form, now clad only in stockings and
heels, the way O was so often at Steven's. It was still too much.

"I want the rest off too, please," O said.

At a gesture from Marie, Angelique and Laurel went to
work, taking off Jacqui's shoes and setting them beside her
chair, before rolling down the stockings and tugging them out
from under Jacqui's ankle cuffs. Completely exposed, Jacqui
observed the interdiction against modesty by setting her bare
heels far apart.

Marie nodded to Noriko, who got up and pulled a bell-
cord that retracted the ceiling ropes, silently raising Jacqui's

arms, pulling her whole body taut. Marie wondered how far O would take this. She would not allow Jacqui's entire weight to be suspended by the wrists, but just as the girl was stretched to the limit of her ability to stand on her own, O told Noriko to stop. The hoist locked off automatically, holding Jacqui immobile but not straining.

O had rehearsed this night repeatedly in her mind. She had spent much of her life dominating girls in one setting or another, but always in her own way, on her own terms. Here, her purpose was to advance Steven and Marie's scheme. If Jacqui were to give it all up to O so O could later surrender her to Ray, O would have to hurt and scare her. Nothing less would command Jacqui's respect. This would require an unexpected twist or two.

Jacqui's eyes followed as O paced back and forth in front of her, inspecting her from every angle. Jacqui tried to stay still as a statue, but her toes kept awkwardly scrabbling for better purchase, producing a ballet of unintentionally seductive movements. Remembering how much Steven enjoyed seeing O in a similar predicament, she let it go on a bit before steadying Jacqui up with a hand wrapped through the front of Jacqui's collar.

"I see you're already shiny," O said, noting the rising flush and glow of Jacqui's fair skin. "Are you afraid of me?"

"Yes, Sister, but not in a bad way," Jacqui said with an unexpected smile. O smiled back.

"I'm going to hurt you then, but not in a bad way."

Well, they'd agreed on that much. What followed was less anticipated.

"You know, I've always wondered," O said in a contemplative tone, "how far I could get one of these things down a girl's throat."

O deftly dropped the tip of the dressage whip toward the floor, bringing the slender handle's flared cap up next to Jacqui's face. Jacqui glanced over at it, eyes widening as she realized what O was about to do. She started to say something, which was either the right move or the wrong move, depending on its intentions.

O reached up with one hand, pinching off the air through Jacqui's nostrils, once again insuring that Jacqui's mouth would stay open. Tipping Jacqui's head back by the nose, O slowly threaded the whip handle down Jacqui's gullet. There was something so unexpectedly invasive and inventively cruel about the act, it provoked a appreciative whispers around the table. Laurel sat in Angelique's lap, being fed small spoonfuls of gelato and sips of coffee. Marie had turned her chair to watch and Noriko sat cross-legged at her feet, the toe of Marie's boot casually grazing the side of Noriko's breast through the now-gaping window of the kimono.

Jacqui was not going to give this up easily. She'd had much bigger things down her pipes before. But the whip handle was thin, ticklesome and completely rigid. Worse, it was nearly four feet long and Jacqui could imagine dire consequences if O pushed this too far.

Inevitably, Jacqui began to choke and cough, her stomach muscles rippling and breasts bouncing as she teared up and tried to twist away from O's grip on her nostrils. Satisfied, O slowly withdrew the handle, holding it up in the light. The whip glistened with spit a good nine inches down.

"No wonder the boys love you," O laughed. Jacqui sucked in air and righted herself.

Again holding the whip under her arm, O slapped Jacqui across the face twice, brightening the pink of her cheeks.

"Now that I've satisfied my curiosity, the remaining question is where to whip you first, Sister."

This, too, would need to be unexpected. With a sudden lunge, O brought the whip slicing in sidewise, striking Jacqui along her right breast from the nipple all the way back through the armpit. It wasn't a vicious stroke, but it raised an instant pink line and made Jacqui yelp, mostly out of surprise.

"Your breasts seem a little sensitive," O said. Again tucking the whip, she hefted one in each hand.

"And a bit swollen. Are you ovulating by any chance, Jacqui?"

"Feels like it, Sister," Jacqui admitted. "After a few months here we all begin to cycle together. It makes certain days kind of dangerous." Her eyes were already misty from the first endorphin rush.

"So your tits are not only tender but swollen as well. And I'm sure you're quite excitable," O continued.

"Yes, Sister! I've been horny as hell all day."

This time, Jacqui smiled. The conversation had drifted to more pleasant terrain, but it wouldn't stay there long.

"But being a little more hormonal than usual, you probably cry more easily."

This wasn't fair, but as Marie had pointed out, justice was never as important as pleasure.

"I guess you're going to find out, Sister."

This time Jacqui's tone was edged with stubborn defiance, just the emotion O had hoped to provoke.

"We just might," O agreed, stepping back to take her distance. The whip was long but Jacqui was tall and O wanted to make her work neat as well as effective. She started on Jacqui's slender belly, beginning at the breastbone and working her way down, laying the stripes exactly three inches apart and taking plenty of time in between. Jacqui dug her toes into the carpet and didn't budge a millimeter as the thin, thread-wrapped shaft fell across her navel. O had taken a wide-legged stance to Jacqui's right side so the length of the whip fell evenly across Jacqui's lower abdomen. But when she got to the tops of Jacqui's thighs, O stepped in front and delivered two searing cuts directly to Jacqui's bits. Jacqui's legs clamped together and she yelped, but it turned into a laugh as she got herself back in position.

"Good one, Sister," she said.

"Glad you liked it," O replied affably. "I'm sure you won't mind a couple more."

This time, O brought the whip back even further. It whistled through the air, landing with hard splat on something wet. Jacqui let out a howl that ended in a hissed "Yes!" O knew that Jacqui almost never got hit as hard as she wanted. O could relate to the frustration of looking more delicate than she was.

Honoring that awareness, O concentrated on Jacqui's breasts, working from underneath in tiny increments toward the bulging nipples. They both knew from experience how it would feel when the whip cut directly across them. Jacqui screamed the first time, and on the second, couldn't help trying to twist out of the way, giving her left breast a break at the expense of her right. O restored the balance by laying an extra slash over the one that had been spared.

Aesthetically, the stripes over the upper curves were the most appealing, especially viewed from above later when the girl was on her knees, as Jacqui was destined to be. O was extra careful to make those six perfectly straight.

The room was silent but for the whip's blows, Jacqui's cries and heavy breathing as the lashing continued and the audience lost its inhibitions. Having marked her territory on Jacqui's erogenous zones, she moved on to less predictable territory, striking the undersides of Jacqui's arms and her inner thighs. The latter produced some squirming as always, but O didn't linger down there. Even girls who were lashed frequently took lasting marks there, and Jacqui would surely be back in front of the camera soon.

Running a hand down Jacqui's front, now oozing perspiration from every pore, O felt the ropey welts rising. They were thin and shallow and wouldn't stay long, but they certainly added pleasing highlights to the pinkness of Jacqui's complexion. O paused to suck Jacqui's puffy, stinging nipples, rolling the tall redhead's big, hard clit back and forth between tenderized lower lips. Jacqui swayed in rhythm.

Jacqui dipped her head and kissed O's shoulder.

"Could I please have some on the back, Sister?" Jacqui asked sweetly.

"Since you put it so politely," O replied, "I'll make it even better."

Looking over at the table, O gauged the available talent as a photographer would. Angelique, though no one's favorite except Laurel's, was the tallest. And she had certainly studied advanced feminine anatomy. O asked Marie if Angelique could come and kneel in front of Jacqui while O worked from behind. Angelique shot O a hateful look, but rules were rules.

Marie had devised them, enforced them and would be the last to make exceptions. With the wave of a finger, she had Angelique on her knees in front of Jacqui, fingers opening the bound girl wide so Angelique could apply her tongue to the sweetest parts. Jacqui looked down, grinned, and thanked Angelique, knowing she was receiving an act of obedience rather than affection. That was fine. Jacqui and Angelique had each exchanged their share of blissful moments with girls for whom they felt no fondness. Angelique's fingers and tongue were able and practiced and that was all that mattered.

Surveying Jacqui's expanse of unmarked back, O had to decide once again where to start. Men always went straight for the ass, but O was not a man. Being careful to avoid Jacqui's collared neck, she started at the shoulders, moving back and forth, painting each side with scarlet chevrons. Jacqui's flanks were next, the skin there thin and delicate.

By now O shamelessly masturbated through the wide opening at the bottom of the body suit with one hand while whipping with the other. O had no interest in cruelty for its own sake. Unless it was directly connected to sex, it served no useful purpose. Like Steven, O became more aroused the more pain she inflicted.

For those watching from the front, it wasn't entirely clear what was being inflicted. Jacqui could come from whipping alone under the right circumstances. Having Angelique lapping away at her with technical expertise and no emotion added another element of mixed sensations. The rest watched the play of emotions across both Jacqui's face and O's as each stroke pushed them closer to a verge.

O still resisted the obvious target, stinging Jacqui's strong, stretched calves, even lifting her ankle cuffs to snap the mid-section of the whip through Jacqui's arches while Angelique held Jacqui in position around the waist and buried her face deeper in between Jacqui's freshly-whipped thighs.

Finally squaring off to target Jacqui's rump, O put all the force of her small, strong body into every stroke, balancing them carefully, alternating cheeks the way Steven did on her. Feeling herself nearing the point of no return, O willed herself to keep on masturbating while applying the strokes up and down from the under-curves of Jacqui's ass-cheeks to the upper surfaces where they converged. The marks were deep and almost black, the tightly-woven threads of the whip's wrapping showing up as darker lines at the edges of each point of impact. Impressive as they were, these traces wouldn't last on such frequently flogged flesh.

Jacqui's knees quaked and she shoved down against Angelique's face. Holding Jacqui steady with a hard grip around the knees, Angelique applied that last little bit of suction where it counted, to push Jacqui across the threshold. Jacqui threw her head back and woke up every coyote in the Hollywood hills. O lashed away, slapping at herself until Jacqui was done. O dropped the whip and kissed Jacqui passionately, having to stand on tiptoe to reach Jacqui's face, while Angelique and Noriko carefully unhooked Jacqui from the ropes, easing her to a proper kneeling position. Tears rolled down Jacqui's face, as much to her own surprise as anyone else's. She wasn't a crier, and no part of the pain O had inflicted was beyond her endurance. But the high drama of the moment, the surroundings, the onlookers and the fact that it was O at the other end of the whip had affected Jacqui in a way she hadn't felt before.

O took Jacqui by the collar, walking her over on all fours to present her back for Marie's close inspection. It was an impressive canvas of carefully applied abstract geometry, lines crisscrossing with increasing depth until they reached Jacqui's bottom, which was a uniformly brilliant hue of vermilion. Marie stroked Jacqui's back, feeling the burning ridges of O's measured strokes.

"Nicely done, O," Marie said. "You can claim your prize now."

"Oh, thank you, Ma'am," Jacqui cried out, seizing Marie's hand and kissing it for an instant before O grabbed Jacqui by her collar again, dragging her to her feet. Holding Jacqui next to her, O bowed to Marie.

"I'm glad you found that satisfactory, Ma'am."

O's words carried more than one meaning, and Marie's nod of approval applied to them all. O put the whip down on the table in front of Marie and headed off to the hallway, leading Jacqui by a collar ring. Applause followed them out. O had passed this test with flying colors, all of them different tints of red.

CHAPTER TWENTY-SEVEN

Following Jacqui down the hall, O could fully enjoy the vivid evidence of her labors. O caught up and put an arm around Jacqui's middle, pulling her close. She felt damp and shaky.

"Think you'll live?" O asked.

"Oh yeah. I'll live to do worse to you."

"Can I get that in writing?"

Back in their close quarters, Jacqui turned, catching O off-guard, and trapped her against the door. She kissed O so hard O thought she might black out for a moment. Jacqui finally relented, grinning in O's face.

"No woman has ever even come close to doing me that way," she announced, gripping O's thick rings through the body suit's lace top. "And, just so you know, we all agree you've got the best natural rack in the house. Even better than Angelique's."

"Thank you and thank you. You took the whipping very well."

Jacqui laughed again.

"Took it? I loved it. You could have gone on like that all night."

"My arm would have fallen off," O said. "Let me get out of this thing. I'm sure it's scratchy against all that raw skin."

Looking down at her zebra-striped torso, Jacqui shrugged.

"Medium-rare maybe, but I wouldn't call it raw."

The two of them had O stripped in seconds, falling on the bed in a tangle of limbs. After some playful wrestling, O got on top.

"So now that I'm yours, what are you going to do with me?" Jacqui asked, grabbing O between the legs.

"I'm going to sit on your face so you'll stop talking and eat me."

Jacqui rolled onto her back, spreading all her limbs wide as she'd been trained. Resting her hands on Jacqui's hipbones, O placed a knee on either side of Jacqui's head and lowered herself to Jacqui's eager mouth.

Jacqui, like O, was not merely bi-curious. Her lesbianism was entirely authentic in its own way. She had an insatiable appetite for cock, but her emotional life revolved mostly around women. The connection between them was different from that between Laurel and Angelique, but no less intense. Tonight had sealed it forever and the night was far from over.

As O rocked back and forth, moaning, eyes shut tight, hands gripping Jackie's sides, she remembered something very important about who she really was, and what she needed that could only be had from another woman.

She had hurt Jacqui as she would expect a real lover to hurt her under similar circumstances and Jacqui demonstrated her gratitude just as O would have. Only with Steven, and for very different reasons, would O experience such an ecstatic paroxysm. It went on and on in convulsive waves, after the last of which she fell, face forward, into the wet folds between Jacqui's legs.

Scrambling her small frame around to lie belly-down on the mattress, she set about slurping and lapping with similar hunger, but when Jacqui's rapid breathing and clutching of the sheets seemed to presage an approaching orgasm as well, O lifted her head, told Jacqui to hold off for just one more minute and hurried over to her small suitcase. Propped on one elbow, idly playing with herself, Jacqui watched and wondered. O came back with a truly scary implement: a stainless steel dildo at least a foot long with a massive round head and a curved shaft thick as a drainpipe.

"It looks dangerous," Jacqui said apprehensively.

"You'll be pleasantly surprised," O assured her, wrapping her lips around the huge knob to wet it down.

Lying again between Jacqui's legs, O very slowly slid it into her, carefully working it to just the right angle while Jacqui looked down at her with widening eyes.

"That thing is freezing," Jacqui said, glancing at her own stiffening nipples.

"You'll warm it up, just relax," O instructed. "I'm not going to fuck you with it."

"That's a relief."

"You're going to work that part yourself. Just squeeze your muscles around it. The weight does the rest."

It was true. Jacqui had never felt anything like it. It seemed to rest inside her in the perfect spot. Every contraction against its unyielding girth pushed it just a fraction of an inch deeper into that spot, making Jacqui grateful for her morning exercises. O held it by the knurled grip at the other end and went back to using her tongue between Jacqui's spread labia. Casually tossing a leg up Jacqui's body, O extended a small foot to Jacqui's lips. It was a quirk of O's, a small gesture that meant something only to her. Jacqui opened wide to get it in her mouth, sucking at it with rising enthusiasm as O nibbled away down below.

In just a few minutes, Jacqui was squirming like a hooked eel and reaching down to press the steel prod in deeper. Red hair flying, Jacqui's head thrashed back and forth on the pillow as she screamed loud enough for everyone downstairs to hear, not caring a bit whether they did or not.

Only when she was calm again did O ease the massive hunk of steel back out.

"It's fucking amazing," Jacqui announced.

"It was designed by a couple of guys from MIT. This was the prototype. They gave it to me to test out."

Jacqui giggled.

"I can't imagine why."

"Hey, it's not my fault I get more pussy then they do. I'm surrounded by it all day."

"Poor O. I feel so sorry for you."

They shared a good laugh while Jacqui hefted the steel bar.

"Also handy for home defense. I gotta get me one of these here things," she said.

"I'll call them tomorrow and have one sent out. They're doing their first production run now."

Jacqui opened her arms so O could lie on top of her. The salt in O's sweat stung Jacqui's streaked flesh.

"I'm going to wear some really tight jeans tomorrow to remind me of what a devil doll you are."

"Yeah," O said, meaning something else entirely. "That's me all right. Want to take a bath?"

"Sweet!"

In the adjoining bathroom Jacqui admired her battle scars in the mirror while O ran a steaming torrent into the large tub.

"Check this one out," Jacqui instructed, pointing at a particularly angry welt bisecting her left breast. "You really got me good."

O apologized, explaining that she was right-handed and in the moment tended to hit harder right to left.

"It's like a golf slice. I try to correct for it, but I can never get the stroke quite even."

Jacqui squatted down, putting her arms around O's shoulders.

"Did that sound like a complaint to you?" She asked.

"Not at all. I'm just a perfectionist."

"Then you should be happy, because that was the most perfect whipping I ever had."

Jacqui kissed O lingeringly on the mouth. When they finally came up for air, O offered to wash Jacqui first.

"Promise you won't do anything mean to me?" Jacqui asked warily.

"No way. You'll have your hands on me next."

O poured bath salts from a glass jar into the full tub, the water instantly turning a brilliant blue. Small clouds of vapor swirled over the surface. Using the small passkey hanging in the bathroom, they opened and peeled off each other's leather cuffs and collars. O nimbly swung her leg over the high marble rim and stepped in, offering Jacqui a hand. Both sunk slowly to their knees, letting the water embrace them.

"Does it sting?" O asked.

"Umm. Sure does," Jacqui purred. O shrugged. It was a little exasperating to meet another woman as unabashedly masochistic as her, but it was also kind of fun. Despite the lack of any physical resemblance, they really were sisters in a sense. O urged Jacqui to lie back so she could soap her.

"Careful with that sponge, Eugene," Jacqui warned.

Jacqui folded her arms behind her shoulders and visibly unwound. O used the sponge very gently, sopping up the warm, soapy water and squeezing it onto Jacqui's tenderized pelt so it foamed up nicely. She dabbed it lightly over every inch, starting with Jacqui's hands and arms. Much had gone into the making of this moment. O's growing awareness of her fondness for Jacqui didn't make it any easier.

"Do you think a woman can really be a slave to another woman?" She asked.

"It can happen," Jacqui said, "but I don't see it often."

O agreed.

"It's not a shortage of dyke slaves that's the problem. It's a shortage of good lesbian mistresses. Just casting a model that looks the part and can go through the motions is hard enough. I can find ten perfectly good submissive girls for every one who can domme convincingly."

"What about Marie?"

"She's the real deal," O said admiringly. "I wish we could clone her."

Jacqui lowered her lids. Her voice was tender with longing.

"I think you're the real deal."

"As a Mistress or a slave?"

"Both," Jacqui said. "You always bring it, whatever you do."

That was the essential thing in O's life and Jacqui had tapped it with a finger so lightly.

"What's your family like, Jacqui?"

"Bunch of lucky rednecks. Ever heard of tar sand?"

O thought about it a second.

"Sand with oil in it, right?"

"They're sitting on about ten thousand acres of it back home, but it hasn't made them any smarter. My mother still never makes it past noon without her first drink. She's the family terror and her problems are everybody's problems. My dad is remarried and outta Dodge. I see him and his trade-in wife about twice a year. He left when I was so young I hardly remember him. I've got one brother who's in the Army. He takes after his mom, so I hope they don't let him near anything that blows up."

"The Beverly Hillbillies."

"With a twist of frontier orneriness."

"At least you don't have to send them money."

"Ah, but I do," Jacqui said in a conspiratorial whisper. "Mom's clueless about it. She's always getting in some kind of scrape and needs bailing out. Each time, I take a little something in return. I'm going to end up owning that land and all the oil they can squeeze out of it."

"Good for you. It's important to have something of your own. No one else in my family understands that. They think I'm just a crazy bitch because I'd rather work than cash checks from Switzerland."

"Trust funder?"

"Big time, if I wanted to be. I just can't stand the company they attract."

O's sponge lingered beneath the waves over Jacqui's neat, pink slit.

"You got me nice and clean there already," Jacqui said with a sigh. O instructed her to roll over so she could do the back.

"Yes. I think I could belong to you," Jacqui said, answering the question before O could ask it.

"Careful. That's the kind of thing that leads to complications."

"Not with me. No time for that shit. There's a certain ratio of orgasms to hysterical two a.m. phone calls that must not be exceeded."

"True that," O concurred. "Girls are high maintenance if you let them be."

"I'll bet you wouldn't."

"I don't give them time. I'm actually a predatory butch in femme's clothing. I dine and dash."

Jacqui laughed, flipping back over and giving O a splash with her foot.

"Don't tell me I was only a snack. I saw that look in your eye. I'll bet I could keep you interested."

"I'd be worried about getting dependent on that," O said honestly.

"No more than I'd be dependent on what you give me."

So far, this was just too easy.

"When I think about being owned," O said with careful consideration, as she looked Jacqui in the eye, "I can only think of belonging to a man. It's funny. I don't have much other use for them. But that thing that goes everywhere with them, it makes a difference."

Jacqui shook some shiny beads of water out of her hair.

"I do love cock. There's something about kneeling in front of it that just seems natural."

"It's called a few thousand years of conditioning, and I've quit fighting it. Next week Steven's coming up here to tattoo my ass. Then he's going to stick another ring through some part of me."

Jacqui sat up, smiling brightly, offering her wet hand for a sloppy high-five.

"Congratulations, O. That lucky bastard."

"He is a lucky bastard and he knows it. That's what makes him tolerable. He's been unlucky before and he's grateful for what he's got. Most men like him are arrogant. He's confident. Big difference."

"He's a better fit for you than Ray," Jacqui admitted. "Too bad in a way. Ray's such a sweetheart."

"And I," said O, "am a black heart. My mother told me that. She said I had a little black heart. Don't underestimate Ray. He can really bring it where it counts. He's got a lot of his brother's warped imagination. But he lacks that little black heart."

Jacqui leaned forward and crossed O's chest with the tip of her index finger.

"I want into that little black heart. First time with any woman. I can give up a lot with Marie, but I want to give it all up with you."

"I'd have killed to hear that a few months ago. Now it's not even mine to give. If I'm going to be Steven's property, and I am, I'm going to be all about it. That's just me. If you want me, you have to take the world that goes with me."

"I wouldn't mind being sister slave for you with him. I think he's hot. But I'd need some alone time with you for sure."

"The alone time is no problem. But it wouldn't be Steven you'd serve with me. Ray felt the scales were out of balance when he had me and Steven had nobody. Now Steven has me and ..."

"He feels the scales are out of balance because Ray has nobody."

"Ray has any girl he wants, but none he can call his own." Jacqui looked pensive.

"Ray," she said. "I'd have to think about that."

"It's a serious thing. I'd expect you to be as much Ray's meat as I'm Steven's. That's the only way I could have you without feeling like I was cheating. I'm not a cheater."

"I am," Jacqui said with an evil smirk. "I can really get into it when I want something different from more than one person at the same time. This wouldn't be like that, though, would it?"

"No. It would all be out in the open. Tell you what. When they finish with me up here, we could all try spending some time together. See how it goes. It's not like we'd keep you locked in the tower."

"Damn! And I was so hoping for that."

O leveled her steadiest gaze, the one that peered through the viewfinder.

"I'm not kidding, Jacqui. I need Steven, but I need you too."

"I don't know about needing Ray. I like him. I'd do him for sure."

"That's not enough," O said firmly as Jacqui washed O's salty armpits. "We have to form a circle, like my name. Steven has me. I have you. You have Ray. Through you, Ray has me."

Jacqui started to say something but O silenced her with a finger over her lips.

"Like I said. Let's give it some time and see what develops. No obligations until we're sure."

O was already sure, but didn't want to spook the prey she'd stalked with such care. She stood them both up and they took turns rinsing each other with the hand-shower. Neither could resist the temptation to turn it over between the other's legs, but they were too wrung out to make anything serious of it.

Lying in bed, Jacqui's head on O's stomach, they passed the silver filigreed pipe Ray had given O what seemed an eternity ago.

"Man," Jacqui said, exhaling a plume of green smoke, "every part of me is sore except my asshole."

O promised to get that part next time. Stroking Jacqui's damp hair, O felt that paradoxical surge of power that only slaves feel. She would once again deliver a treasure to her master that only she could have secured. If she wasn't altogether guilt-free, it was hardly as if she was handing Jacqui over to a terrible fate.

O shared Steven's desire to see Ray properly partnered. Having gotten to know Jacqui better, O realized she'd been too quick to dismiss her as yet another of the parade of shallow, scheming doxies who passed through the studio. Jacqui might share some outward similarities with the others, but there was something more, and more interesting, going on inside.

Setting the pipe aside, O pulled the covers over the two of them and shut off the lace-shaded lamp next to the bed.

There was something yet to be done before she left this place with her winnings and that too would demand nothing less than all she had to give. O had no interest in anything that required less. She considered that about herself for a moment as Jacqui's breathing grew slow and regular in her arms.

There were things O could never anticipate that made life an interesting series of problems to be solved, but one thing of which she was certain was that she would never spend another moment of that life anywhere she didn't belong.

CHAPTER TWENTY-EIGHT

Secluded in Marie's office, O braced herself on the back of a chair and leaned forward for Jacqui to tighten the laces of the under-bust corset made so exactingly to match O's skin tone. O's slick-soled nude pumps didn't afford much traction, but she did her best to push forward against Jacqui's tugging. Steven had phoned to say he would be coming by in an hour with something important for O, which didn't give O much time, but that was O's problem, not Steven's.

"I know you can get another inch out of it," O insisted.

Jacqui, dressed in her "work clothes" – a black cotton garter-tank that covered all but her most private real estate (which still bore traces of O's recent dressage work) and opaque black stockings to match – dug her black stiletto pumps into the carpet and strained at pulling O's already compressed waist in a bit further.

"That's it if you're interested in breathing," Jacqui declared.

Jacqui posed her in front of Marie's tall rolling mirror, a big smile spreading across her face as O stared at the transformation.

"I think it's pretty spectacular myself," Jacqui said.

413

She wasn't wrong. The corset took O's narrow middle in a good three inches, exaggerating her breasts, hips and buttocks even further. With only the faint contrast of her brown leather collar and cuffs and her nude high heels, O appeared to be sculpted entirely of gleaming flesh, Jacqui having oiled her exposed areas lightly before wrestling with the cincher.

Her proportions were so extreme she resembled an unpainted mannequin. O was going for that effect. Though never fully satisfied with her appearance, she was at least grateful for her rigorous exercise, light diet and regular lacings. In profile, the impact was even more arresting.

"Well," O conceded, "at least it's comfortable."

Jacqui threw her hands in the air.

"You're insane! I'd be passing out about now."

"You just have to breathe from your diaphragm," O explained, "and it's good for you in reasonable doses. Helps take the weight off your spine."

Unconvinced of the practical benefits, Jacqui admitted that the look was, literally and figuratively, breathtaking. To underscore the point, she stole a kiss and copped a feel.

"Steven's going to want to fuck you the minute he walks through the door."

O smiled wickedly.

"That's just what I'm hoping."

They didn't have to wait long to find out. Both turned guiltily at the sound of voices in the hall as the door swung inward. That their hands were all over each other was only to be expected and neither Steven nor Marie had any objections, though they did stop chatting long enough to enjoy the girls' momentary shyness.

Having just come from a meeting with a new client looking to beat a money-laundering rap, Steven was still dressed for work in a black-and-white glen-plaid double-breasted cashmere jacket, matching tie and black shirt. The sharp seams of his gabardine trousers terminated in two-inch cuffs, breaking fully over the tops of a pair of wingtips with plaid inserts to go with the tie and jacket. Today Marie wore a long, sheer white-lace Victorian gown, buttoned up to the neck but with nothing under it. She didn't need a corset to achieve curves much like O's, having been gifted with them by nature.

"I hope we're not interrupting," Marie said, amiably.

O and Jacqui immediately dropped to their open knees and put their hands behind their necks.

Steven's face lit up at the realization of how much he'd missed seeing O daily and how glad he was to see her now. Marie signaled them to stand for inspection while Steven put Jan's rolled drawing, which he'd just picked up *en route*, on the desk. Jacqui took a half-step back, as O was the one being presented. O squared her shoulders to give her breasts maximum thrust. Her nipples so hardened at the sight of him, her thick rings had already begun to tilt outward. She felt momentarily dizzy as much from excitement as the constriction of her middle.

Steven gazed at her in obvious delight before taking her in his arms and kissing her hard enough to squeeze what little breath she had out of her, despite which she managed to kiss him back just as ferociously.

Feeling under her, Steven found her quite juicy in the front and obstructed behind by a steel disk similar to the base of the plug she wore for him at home. She expected to be thoroughly used on this visit and had prepared accordingly.

Finally separating their lips, Steven held O at arm's length so he could admire her in greater detail. His big hands almost met around her middle.

"Fantastic," he said, "I couldn't have asked for a more inspiring welcome."

O smiled up at him, rubbing the outside of her thigh against the bulge in his trousers.

"I can tell you approve, Sir."

"I'll demonstrate my approval after I show you what I've brought along."

He turned to Jacqui for a more sedate but still rudely familiar embrace.

"You're looking very fine as well, young Miss," he said, eyeing her up and down. "Quite slutty, in fact."

"Why thank you, Sir," Jacqui said brightly. "I'll be happy to wear this for you any time."

In a gesture so forward it should have earned her another whipping, she took Steven's hand and put it on the only part of her that wasn't covered. Marie made no move to interfere. Pretty things were meant to be touched. Jacqui was as wet as O, though Steven understood that it was O's proximity, and not his, that produced the effect.

"I'll hold you to that," he said.

"I'm sure you'll hold me to all kinds of things, Sir."

This was definitely pushing it.

"Come with me, Jacqui," Marie said firmly. "These two need some time alone. Besides, I want you to console Laurel. Angelique's out getting drunk with some boys, and she's feeling abandoned."

"Yes, Ma'am," Jacqui said, bowing her head as they exited. She turned back in the doorway to blow O a kiss.

As soon as the door closed, O was back in Steven's arms. She stayed there a long time while his hands traveled up and down her body, finally settling in a grip around her boned middle. All she knew for now was that he found her extremely pleasing, which was enough.

"It looks like your project with Jacqui is on schedule," Steven said.

"It's gone more smoothly than expected, Sir. I had some reservations, but the better I know Jacqui, the more right this seems. As long as I'm around to keep her in line, she'll serve Ray very well. Probably better than I did. They have more in common."

"I think I have him convinced of that too, at least in theory."

"I'm convinced and I've been with both of them. So what
did Sir bring me?" O asked at last.

He swept her over to Marie's desk, giving her rings a tug
on the way, and unrolled Jan's drawing, weighting the corners with small, square leather bags of copper shot Marie kept
stacked for the purpose. O turned on Marie's antique swing-
arm pharmacy lamp, positioning it over the drawing. Both
were silent a long time while O studied it. O spent a lot of her
time looking for imperfections. In Jan's work, there were none
to be found. The proportions of the ribbons and the execution
of the calligraphy were perfect. But the color was troubling.

"I don't usually wear pink, Sir."

Steven laughed out loud.

"That's a good one, considering how you're dressed today."

O had to give him that.

"And when I'm looking at this, I doubt you'll be wearing
much more."

She couldn't argue with that either. But it was so big and
bold and it would be on her for life. Any attempt to remove it
with a ruby laser would leave a nasty blotch. Many men and
women would see this tattoo in the coming years. Indeed, suddenly thinking for the first time of the difference in their ages
and all it implied, O realized they'd be looking at it after Steven
was dead.

Well, fuck them. This mark would then be a memorial to
the only real master O had ever had or ever would.

"Could you show me where it goes please?"

Steven backed O up to the rolling mirror, adjusted it to
one side and unfurled the drawing over the small of O's corseted back, letting the ribbons trail across her bare bottom. With
the initials just above her tail bone, they fell several inches
down either cheek. At the beach, O always stayed covered

against the sun. That was fortunate, because a bikini would certainly reveal more than just some additional skin once this thing was on her.

The question was starkly simple. Did she belong to him or not? If she was his property he was as entitled to ink her skin as to engrave a watch. The comparison made her smile.

"It's perfect," she declared resolutely, turning to put her arms around him. The drawing fluttered toward the floor but he snagged it in mid-air, bringing it around between them for another close look.

"You're the one who has to live with it. If you want any changes, you'll need to make them now," he warned.

"If it always has the effect on you I think it will, Sir, I wouldn't change a line."

"I'll leave it here. You have until next Monday to think it over."

O swallowed hard. Next Monday wasn't far off. But it was as good as any other Monday.

"There's something more," Steven said. He put the drawing on Marie's desk and took a small brown-paper envelope from his pocket.

"Hold out your hand."

Steven tapped the ring out into O's open palm. At first sight, this was less problematic. It was the color of her steel nipple jewelry but heavier for its size – ten gauge by one and a half inches in diameter.

"What's it made of?"

"White gold."

"It's beautiful, Sir. But isn't it a bit small compared to what I already have?"

O turned back toward the mirror and held the ring down over her clit hood.

"If I were going to put something there," Steven said, "it would be thicker. As it is, I'm sure this size will be quite conspicuous enough."

O felt a sudden chill deep in her compressed gut.

"Then where does it go, Sir?"

Steven turned O straight to the mirror and held the ring in front of her upper lip.

"It's a slave ring, O. It goes through your septum."

O stared into the mirror wide-eyed, then put her hand over her face. She turned to look up at Steven with a desperate expression.

"Sir, I make my living in public. I'm not a teenager with black nail polish."

Steven reassured her he would never interfere with her other life. He took her hand down and dropped the U-shaped black retainer into it from the envelope.

"With this in, the piercing is completely invisible. Once the piercing heals, which takes about a month, you'll be able to switch it in and out with the ring easily. There might be occasions on which I'd have you wear the ring in public, but only when and where it would be appropriate. It's mainly meant for just the two of us."

O held the ring up to her nose with shaking fingers, looked at herself in the mirror. Why was this so much more difficult to contemplate than the tattoo? It could be worn discreetly and even disposed of if ... something not to think about. Her alarm wasn't a matter of vanity. O imagined it would look rather pretty in an exotic sort of way. She was certainly no more vain about her face than about her breasts.

The tattoo merely declared possession of her ass, and what was that after all? But a ring in the middle of her face signified ownership of her, like a piece of livestock. Did she wish to be something more to Steven? Absolutely not. Once she realized how strictly her acceptance of this token would define that boundary, her doubts faded like smoke. With the ring there, Steven would never be able to look at her face without seeing that of a slave. It might unite them in one sense, but it would separate them in any other.

She turned and threw her arms around him happily.

"I love it!"

Steven held her tight.

"That's a relief," he said. "I wasn't sure if we'd hit a hard limit."

O reminded him that she didn't have many of those. Thankfully, he didn't choose this moment to question her about them.

"Marie's going to pierce you herself," he said, returning the ring and retainer to their envelope and tucking it back in his pocket.

"She's very good with these things, and I'm sure you'll recover quickly, but you'll be out of commission for a bit after all the work is done."

It was far too broad to even be considered a hint.

"Well then," O said, her heart suddenly lighter than air, "perhaps Sir should make use of this slave while the opportunity is at hand."

Steven laughed.

"I suppose it wasn't difficult to read my mind."

"It wasn't your mind that gave you away, Sir."

O stroked the front of his trousers; the bulge within was still prominent.

"May I?"

Steven nodded. O unbuttoned his fly while he carefully undid his necktie. As soon as O had his rigid cock exposed, she slid to the floor, folded her hands behind her head and went to work while he finished undressing at leisure. Steven shrugged off his embroidered braces, tossing them with his jacket and shirt to Marie's desk. He pushed O back by the shoulders just long enough to step out of his trousers.

O took one look and her face illuminated with surprise and delight.

"You wore your sock garters for me, Sir!" she exclaimed.

"It seemed the least I could do under the circumstances," he said with a slightly embarrassed shrug. He was more accustomed to girls dressing for him. He felt a bit like a player in an ancient blue movie standing there in his shoes and socks, but was soon too distracted to care.

Leaning in, O took him to the back of her throat over and over, holding him there until she choked quietly, repeating the motion over and over. The meds Steven swallowed on the way over had fully kicked in and he was hard as granite. Looking down at the exquisite living figurine into which O had molded herself, he got even harder. He told her he'd need to fuck her very soon.

O looked up from her labors.

"The corset somewhat limits my movements, Sir. I can be fucked standing or lying down, but I don't have much mobility on my hands and knees."

Steven promised to keep that in mind as he lifted her under her damp armpits to kiss her again, perching her on the edge of Marie's desk, where O settled her weight onto the plug inside her. She'd deliberately chosen an extra large one for their reunion as a self-imposed gesture of compliance with whatever he had in mind. O opened her legs wide, put her hands atop her head and sat up as rigidly as the corset required. She held the pose with increasing difficulty, shuddering and moaning while Steven kissed and caressed her in the most forceful and intrusive ways. She expected to be rocked back on Marie's desk and fucked at any moment, but Steven was never predictable in that way.

Leading her to Marie's leather-padded, white-enameled surgical chair, he made O sit while he worked the levers to lower the back and raise the steel knee crutches that hinged conveniently open for him to step up. And to think, O had shivered at the sight of this contraption when actually, considering what she was wearing, it was quite comfortable. She put her head back on the round leather pads while Steven lifted her legs into the steel cradles, which settled in nicely beneath her knees and under her girl-colored heels.

Climbing onto on the raised plate at the end of the table, Steven bent down to kiss her everywhere, sucking and biting her rings, working his way along the crease of her belly to suck her swollen, craving vulva into his mouth. O never thought it odd that her master would "service" her in this way. The more aroused she was, the more pliable she became, which made the act an assertion of power rather than a concession to her desires.

Though unrestrained, the stiffness of the corset made her virtually helpless on her back, hardly able to lift her head and look down to watch. After so long denied the skill with which he applied himself to her, she was soon babbling and pleading for permission as if she'd never come in her life. He nodded without stopping what he was doing and O did indeed come as if she'd never come in her life.

Her legs shook on either side of his shoulders, rattling the steel struts holding them high. Her whole frame, constrained by the corset as it was, went even stiffer and she threw back her head with a scream so loud she involuntarily lifted a hand and slapped it over her own mouth to avoid alarming the entire house, not that orgasmic screaming was there.

Steven stood, wiped his face with the back of his arm, and held O's shaking body against his, rubbing his cock on her freshly tenderized, sopping wet membranes. She reached down to stroke him.

"I really need that inside me, Sir," O panted.

On that they could agree. Steven gripped her corset hard enough to make O gasp and hooked her roughly with a slow forward thrust to the wall of her womb.

It was an interesting sensation. The big steel bullet in O's rectum and the downward pressure of her corset reshaped her internal anatomy, making it even tighter than it was naturally, and shallower as well. The friction was delicious for both of them. Steven reached down to grab her breasts, rocking her back and forth on what felt like a bar of iron.

Realizing how effectively she was immobilized in the situation, he took the opportunity to shower O's breasts with a salvo of hard slaps, making them bounce merrily, and turn a nice rosy shade of pink. O closed her eyes and absorbed the blows, letting the angle of the table work for her as she rocked her hips. The slight anoxia from the binding of her waist made it all very dreamlike. She imagined him looking down to see the ring through her nose, imagined him turning her over to admire his symbol of ownership. The heat trapped under the unyielding satin was fierce. Sweat beaded up on O's flushed chest and dripped under her arms. She was going to be the messy, smelly girl she wanted to be when this was over. In the meantime, she needed to come again, badly.

Before granting O's plea, Steven wrapped his right hand around her collar, squeezing her carotids tighter and tighter, her breath coming in ragged, rasping gasps. Lightheaded and dizzy O, lifted herself up as much as she could, slamming onto him with all her strength.

He looked down at her shiny face, now a darker hue than any other part of her, admiring her endurance. One of many things they had in common was the ability to keep themselves in check at all times, except when they chose to let themselves go. At that moment, O did exactly that with an even louder scream.

Once O was done, Steven let her lie back and breathe as best she could, enjoying the spectacle of her chest rising and falling and the unusual frictions to be found inside her.

"Think you can stand up?" he asked, smiling down at her. She raised her hands for him to assist her. Steven ordered her to turn around and brace herself on the table. The inflexible corset compelled her to bend from the waist and thrust her backside out to present her rear. Unable to look back over her shoulder, she felt the slow withdrawal of the plug, and heard the steel bullet land in a bowl on a nearby stand.

The insertion of skilled digits widened her back passage even further. Realizing how much she missed this, a long, low moan escaped her lips. Parting her cheeks, he slid into her easily, O's internal muscles tightening around only when she felt his full length inside her.

Using the end of the table to steady herself, O shifted her weight back and forth between her high heels, rolling her hips as much as her situation allowed, pressing her rump hard against his unyielding abs. Though not bound, she felt delightfully small and helpless, held in place by his grip around her middle. The enforced shallowness of her breathing made her dizzy. She needed permission again, though this time she was able to keep the noise level down a bit, concentrating on the intensity of the sensations within.

When O stopped shuddering and corrected her position, Steven abandoned all pretense of being a gentleman and pounded her ruthlessly, dragging her back to fill her insides with a hot gush of pent-up liquid lust. He growled like a beast, roughly slapping her backside until he was entirely spent. Through the binding satin, O felt his hand press affectionately down on her back, but he made no move to withdraw.

"Thank you for using me so well, Sir," O said.

"Thank you for being so fucking adorable," he replied, feeling a bit winded himself. If what they did at home was a complex ballet, this had been more like a torrid tango, violent and tender at the same time.

Handing her a wet wipe to staunch the leaking when he finally pulled out, Steven offered to unlace her corset.

O's back ran with rivers of sweat and her entire midsection, still narrower then normal from the compression, bore the long, parallel indentations of the boning, a look Steven and O both liked. They showered together in the black-and-green tiled bathroom adjoining Marie's office, O in her terrycloth turban, and both wandered down the hall to her room in luxurious, generic guest bathrobes for a little quiet time together.

Lying in the bed O usually shared with Jacqui, they fired up a joint Steven had brought with the rubber-armored lighter he carried most often in public. They talked about ordinary things – the magazine, an upcoming shoot O had planned when she returned from Marie's. They concurred that spending more time as a foursome with Ray and Jacqui should be the next phase of operations.

Fortunately, that conversation had just concluded when Jacqui came in, unaware that O had brought her master there. Jacqui knelt and excused herself for interrupting, but when she turned to go, Steven instructed her to remain. Jacqui was pleased.

"It does smell very good in here, Sir," she hinted.

Steven re-lit the joint and invited Jacqui to join them. O moved to one side of the bed so Jacqui could fit in between. Still quite exposed in her garter-tank when she crawled into bed, Jacqui felt O's arm drape over her, O's hand casually settling into the unprotected territory between shirt and stockings. She rolled happily back into O's embrace and took a hit from Steven. Jacqui wanted to see what Steven had brought for O, but was told that would have to wait for his next visit. Steven promised she'd be present at the unveiling.

"I'd make her tell me all about it anyway," Jacqui said in a blasé tone.

O grabbed her hard down below, making her jump.

"Like you could make me do anything, you little shit," O said in mock indignation.

"I can make you come."

"That's just because I'm easy."

They all laughed. Steven hadn't realized it before, but as much as Ray needed a new slave, O could use a friend. He suspected it was difficult for O to make female friends, or friends at all for that matter. The easy camaraderie and physical playfulness between O and Jacqui made him happy for her. It also got a rise out of him.

As Steven wore no belt, or anything else but an open robe, this did not pass unnoticed.

"You have a beautiful cock, Sir," Jacqui observed as if talking about the weather.

"I'm very attached to it myself," Steven said wryly.

"You ought to see it when he's excited," O chimed in.

Jacqui moved a little closer to Steven.

"That sounds like an invitation to me," she said.

O correctly pointed out that such would have to come from Steven. He promised not to put up a fight.

Jacqui rolled over half on top of him, rubbing her body against his and searching for the handhold she quickly found. It stiffened rapidly in her grasp.

"I see what you mean," Jacqui said as a second wave of vascular dilation washed through Steven. Jacqui slid down to take him in her mouth, where he rose to full strength immediately.

O took hold of the back of Jacqui's head, instructing her in a calmly commanding manner just how he liked this task performed. It was a casual thing done in a casual way, without much fanfare. While Steven kissed O and played with her rings, Jacqui demonstrated her skills with the ease of long and constant practice. She got him off in a matter of minutes, swallowing with a noisy gulp whatever O hadn't already extracted. O left Jacqui lying with Steven to fetch his clothes.

"She's so different in private," Jacqui said after O closed the door.

"I like that about her," Steven said. "Not many people know the difference between public and private anymore."

"I guess we'll all be seeing more of each other now."

Steven told her to count on it.

"Speaking of enigmatic personalities, what's your brother really like?" Jacqui asked. "I always see him at work or at some party. He seems nice, but that's all I know."

"He is nice," Steven confirmed. "He has a sweetness about him that he gets from our mother. I think that's why they were so close."

"You taste nice and sweet," Jacqui giggled.

"I drink a lot of apple juice."

Jacqui propped up on an elbow, suddenly interested.

"So that really works. I've heard about it but never noticed a difference before."

"Most of the guys you know probably smoke and drink."

Jacqui admitted she had been known to smoke, drink and do other things herself.

"God, I hope that doesn't make me taste bad."

"O certainly doesn't think so."

"O is a worse gash-hound than any guy I ever met."

Jacqui got serious.

"This thing you and O want me to do, I'd never go for it with anyone else. Ray's practically a stranger, and he's a publisher. Some girls jump-start their careers by fucking publishers, but that's never worked for me. I can't pretend to care when I don't."

"In this town, pretending to care when you don't is an art form. You'll like Ray. He's fun. He kept O interested for a surprisingly long time."

"Well, at least he's cute."

"And doesn't he know it. He got the cute genes."

"What genes did you get?"

It didn't sound like an idle question. Jacqui could go from frivolous to earnest without taking a breath.

"The hard-ass DNA of my old man I suppose. I inherited our mother's vices and my dad's stubborn streak. It's kind of a rough mix."

Jacqui studied Steven's face.

"Doesn't it wear you down, having to think for everybody?"

"I've been doing it so long it feels natural."

"Thinking for one person is enough work for me."

Steven brought her up for an affectionate kiss.

"From my brief experience, I'd say you do that pretty well."

O came back to find them both grinning.

"Did I miss something?"

"Yes. She told me all your secrets," Steven teased.

"That would have taken a lot longer."

This was a good place to leave things. He let the girls have their fun getting him dressed, O instructing Jacqui on every precise detail in case she had to stand in someday. He kissed them both goodbye – friendly with Jacqui, passionate with O – leaving them wrestling on the bed.

He stopped by Marie's office on his way out to retrieve the drawing for O's tattoo. He found Marie studying it with an unreadable expression.

"It's beautiful," she said, rolling it up and tying the string. "I just hope neither of you regrets it later. I see a lot of tattoo regret with my girls."

"Who are you worrying about?" Steven asked, "O or me?"

"Both of you. And what you've got O cooking up with Jacqui worries me too. You always seem so sure of what you want I can never tell how serious you really are."

Steven sat on the corner of Marie's desk.

"Maybe that's why we're not married anymore."

"It's hard to live with a man who's more difficult to read than The Dead Sea Scrolls."

Steven touched his lips to Marie's forehead.

"You miss Martin don't you?"

"Every day," Marie said matter-of-factly.

"Me too. He was the only person who ever understood us both."

"And we understood him. He was incapable of dissimulation."

"That helped him in court. Judges took him at his word. I have to work harder to convince them."

"If this world had more people like Martin in it," Marie said wistfully, "it would be a better world."

Steven shook his head. "He lived so carefully and I never passed up a risk. It should have been me instead of him."

"I know this will come as a shock to you Mr. Diamond, but things happen in life that not even you can control."

Marie handed Steven the drawing. He reminded her he'd be back promptly at two p.m. Monday. She assured him he was in her calendar.

It was dark when Steven drove away. The nights had definitely gotten chillier. The Bentley had heated seats, along with every other useful amenity and a few that weren't. He settled into the warm leather and switched on the CD player, skipping through a few choices before finding Elvis Costello. He sang along to "Every Day I Write the Book," enjoying the sound of his own voice. He generally showed others the consideration of restricting his vocalizing to the car.

Hungry and tired, he wanted only to go home, eat something and stare at the big screens for a few hours. The world would simply have to do without him until morning. He supposed it would probably hold up until then.

Chapter Twenty-Nine

The following Sunday found O and Jacqui out on the deck for the dressage drill Marie had ordered for noon when the sun would be warmest.

Even from a distance, Jacqui looked impossibly tall. She stood, otherwise bare, in boots laced to the knees that had rounded leather, steel-shod "hooves" instead of soles and curved, spring-steel plates covered in leather that rose under the arches to keep the wearer pitched as high as possible. Jacqui fairly towered over O, who wore a light, sheer robe over her strappy lingerie to prevent tan lines. Marie gave them plenty of time to get ready before coming down to review the results.

"Why do I always get the fucking pony thing?" Jacqui moped, ducking down so O could tighten the straps around Jacqui's face harness and straighten the puffy white plume rising jauntily behind the triangular leather forehead guard. She left the rubber bit, cut short for a girl's jaws, hanging free from the headgear for the moment.

"Because you've got the legs for it."

"Just one more inch and I could have been a real model." O laughed.

"One more inch and Ray could have been Rocco Siffredi."

"Wow," Jacqui said, crossing her legs involuntarily. "Is he really that big?"

"Just kidding. It's a nice, manageable size and he's very polite with it, which I can't always say is true for Rocco."

"You've done Rocco?"

"No, silly, I've shot him. Could you at least try to hold still?"

Jacqui straightened up to let O buckle the straps on the red-and-black leather body harness, making them good and tight, as expected. Jacqui hardly had a belly, but the belt sank in far enough to emphasize her waistline. The twin straps above and below her breasts squeezed them boldly outward. A spritely white horsehair tail mounted on the belt matched Jacqui's head plume. It was purely decorative. Tails attached to inserted plugs dangled dispiritedly between the wearer's legs.

"Please tell me I don't have to neigh."

"You better not," O warned. "Marie hates that. You're not a pony. You're a girl in a pony harness. That's the whole point."

"I never really did understand the point, except that when the reins are pulled back, the girl gets fucked."

"You seem to have grasped the essentials. And you do look adorable."

"I know. It's that little, red curl that sneaks out under the headpiece. Happens every time."

"I'll give you something to take your mind off it."

O reached into the red leather tack satchel and pulled out a martingale fitted with a pair of silicone phalli, one a little smaller than the other. Both turned in slightly at the top so the would rub together through Jacqui's thin wall of tissue whenever she moved. Looking at it, her eyebrows rose in despair.

"You're not really going to put that in me, are you?"

"No," O said. "You're going to do it yourself."

O handed Jacqui a pair of rubber gloves and a lube bottle.

"This is cruel and usual," Jacqui complained.

"Come on, you know what they like to think about when your haunches are moving up and down. At least that's what Ray thinks about."

"So Ray is into this?" Jacqui asked, snapping on the rubber gloves and anointing the plugs that would soon be in her with thick globs of lube.

"Used to take me to The Mansion for it twice a month. They've got a track out there."

Jacqui pinched O's cheek.

"Bet you made a cute little pony."

"Yes I did," O said with mock indignation. "I may be only three hands high, but I'm very spirited."

Jacqui burst out laughing, just as O expected, enabling O to buckle the bit in easily.

"That's not fair!" Jacqui protested in a somewhat distorted voice through the rubber bar between her teeth. She started making sucking noises behind it immediately.

"You're going to drool on your tits no matter what you do," O said. "That's part of it. They want you wet and sticky all over when you're done. If you're a smart pony, you'll give them a good show and get down to the fucking part that much sooner."

This was not news to Jacqui. She had been typecast in this manner before. There was even a cover of *Forbidden* on which Jacqui wore a small saddle. It amused her to think how easily she could have outrun her supposed riders, even in her hoof boots. Jacqui had grown up riding real horses and the other things young people do in mountainous regions. She wasn't an athlete, just athletic by default.

Jacqui squatted down and eased in the twin probes with a look of intense concentration on her bridled face.

O enjoyed watching. Ray had always made her do this part herself too. Seeing Jacqui struggle to stay on her hooves while, blinded by her blinkers, she worked the intrusive silicone towers into each hole made O wonder how she herself had looked in the same situation. O buckled the center strap to the tight waist belt. Jacqui slowly stood up straight.

She moaned, mumbling through her bridle about the unfairness of life. O peeled the gloves off Jacqui's hands and tossed them in steel trashcan nearby. She fastened Jacqui's wrists to the harness ring.

"Now for the finishing touch," she said with an evil grin. She brought six small brass bells, equipped with clips, out of the tack bag. Jacqui's eyebrows lifted to a pathetic, prayerful peak when she saw them; she hated the racket from harness bells. Complaining was always allowed, and hard limits always respected, but short of outright refusal, compliance was expected. Jacqui understood that when she moved in. O started with the collar rings and worked her way down, snapping a bell to each wrist and ankle cuff. When she was done, Jacqui lifted a leg and shook it, just to hear the surprisingly loud clang of the small clapper in the ankle bell, leather-caged features scrunching in annoyance.

"Who knew you had such hidden musical talents?" O said sarcastically. Jacqui looked daggers at her, but O knew she would not gain Jacqui's submission by giving in to every minor gripe.

Marie marched up, wearing only a white tailcoat, tight leggings and boots. She carried a long lunging whip. O curtsied while Marie conducted a through inspection, checking the straps and buckles for snugness. Giving Jacqui's long reins a tug to tilt her head back and pulling up on the belt at the same time, Marie extracted some inarticulate gurgling, accompanied by an involuntary hoof-stamp.

Marie complimented O on her thoroughness. "Thank you, Madame," O said. "I had to do all my own rigging for shoots before I could hire an assistant."

"Let's get started then. Walk with me, O. We'll take Jacqui around the pool."

Marie collected the reins and tapped Jacqui on the right rear cheek with the whip. "Forward, girl. Shoulders back. Tits out. Knees up."

Jacqui whined, but obeyed, pulling the reins taut and lifting her legs as high as possible with each step as they advanced toward the far end of the pool. Each time Jacqui raised either leg, things moved around inside her, as the jangling of the brass bells reminded the onlookers. The group quickly grew to include all the girls at the house, turned out for lunch in their lacy best. Just a few steps and Jacqui was panting and whimpering. It was hard for her to walk straight, but each time she deviated from the line or her posture wavered, Marie laid a hard lash over her shoulders or on either side of her "tail." Jacqui yelped with each stroke, but it was a happy yelp.

Jacqui never tired of leather on her flesh. Nevertheless, she wasn't one to deliberately misbehave and soon had a pretty good gait going, legs rising and falling rhythmically, hips rocking back and forth to agitate the harness's concealed elements. The bells clinked cheerfully in time, conveniently obscuring O's conversation with Marie from overhearing by the small but riveted audience watching them make their circuits of the pool.

"Tomorrow's the big day," Marie said. The reins were long enough for Jacqui to be out of earshot as well and she had more urgent concerns demanding her attention.

O admitted to being a little nervous.

"Who wouldn't be? Permanent modifications are no small matter."

"That's not what worries me," O said. Up ahead, Jacqui shook her head, trying to slurp up the long stringers of spit drizzling down her chest. Her skin began to shine from the heat and exertion.

"What then?'

"I like being Steven's slave. I never thought I'd say that about anyone. I don't even mind being marked as his property. We wouldn't have gotten this far if I had any doubts. I just hope he'll be satisfied with things as they are. Sometimes I get the feeling he wants more."

"More than to own you?"

"Sometimes," O said, "I look into Steven's eyes and see my Master. Other times, I see a lonely man. He can have me any way he wants physically, but that's all I can offer him. It has to be enough."

Marie thought about it, flicking Jacqui with the whip lightly here and there just for fun. Steven was less immune to the need for human contact than he let on. There were clear boundaries to O's slavery. Just as her body and any uses to which it could be put would be Steven's domain, the rest of O's life had to be entirely her own. She and O had something in common there as well.

The love of her life being conveniently dead, Marie never had to explain her emotional unavailability. But if she were to meet Martin today, however much she might like him or even physically desire him, he would never breach the walls around her heart as he had years ago. By now those walls were too high and too sturdy.

She tried to think of something comforting to say, though she knew O's misgivings weren't entirely unjustified.

"Steven's not the needy type. He takes wonderful care of himself and isn't looking for anyone to take over the job. Every now and then, some poor woman falls in love with him only to discover that he's already in love with Steven Diamond."

They made one more circuit of the pool in silence, except for the ringing of the brass bells, the clank of Jacqui's steel-bottomed boots, and her heavy breathing. At last, Marie tugged on the reins, bringing the small caravan to a halt in the cool shadows beneath the eaves of the house's rear deck. Jacqui dripped sweat. Her face was purple. Her legs shook from exertion and a river of saliva flowed down between her breasts and over her quivering belly. She was striped everywhere from

Marie's whip, but when Marie came around to look her over again, Jacqui stood up straight and kept her eyes forward. It wasn't so much Marie she sought to impress with her stalwart obedience as O.

When, at Marie's instructions, O released the bit, ,Jacqui shook her head and worked her jaw to regain her power of speech. The rings had left little circles at the corners of her mouth.

"Please, Ma'am," she begged, "could I have some water?"

Marie sent O into the house for a bottle and as soon as she was gone, Jacqui gave Marie that naughty grin.

"And after that, could Ma'am please put on her cock and ride me properly?"

"Jacqui," Marie said, "you have no shame whatsoever."

"None, Ma'am. Should I?"

"No, dear. You're perfect just as you are."

Jacqui looked down at her grime-streaked, whip-scored geography and laughed.

"If you say so, Ma'am."

She lifted her right leg and shook it again, to amuse Marie with a slightly impudent jingle.

O reappeared with bottled water, which she had to hold over Jacqui's face so the tall redhead could suck from it, as Jacqui's hands were still fastened in back. At Marie's instructions, O went to the familiar drawer in the upstairs bedroom where Marie's custom-molded after-market parts were kept.

By the time O returned, Jacqui was already down on her hands and knees on a long, high-density-foam pool pad and Marie knelt behind her, waiting. The center strap with its penetrating appliances had been tossed aside, gleaming with Jacqui's secretions, but Marie still held the reins, keeping Jacqui's back straight and her head up.

O didn't need to be instructed to fasten Marie's gear in place, or to grease the business end of it before Marie drew in the reins, slowly backing Jacqui toward the stake protruding from Marie's groin. O even knelt to hold Jacqui open and guide Marie in. Strap-ons had no agenda of their own and were unlikely to work their way to their destinations unassisted.

Jacqui settled back onto the newest intrusion with a happy exhalation of breath, responding to Marie's rein tugging by rocking back and forth. Always conscious of her mission, O went around to hold Jacqui's face, kissing her through the bit and looking into her eyes while the spasms rippled through Jacqui's lean frame. Jacqui was usually more a whimperer than a screamer, but she couldn't hold back a loud cry at the conclusion of her ecstatic moment.

Once O unstrapped the face harness and extracted the sticky bit, Jacqui asked Marie if there were any services she could perform in return. Marie suggested Jacqui husband her energies; she would be the one sharing Marie's bed that night. She instructed O to get Jacqui cleaned up for lunch and stepped out of her apparatus, leaving it for the girls to clean and put away.

"You looked really good out there," O said.

"I just hope Ray doesn't want that too often. I'm a lazy bitch. I'd rather take a good whipping, suck some cock and lie on my back."

"No problem," O assured her, "Ray's pretty lazy too."

Once in a while, Ray could get motivated for something elaborate, especially with a new or occasional partner, but over time tended to drift toward a more vanilla approach, which had been part of O's frustration with him.

It was a frustration she knew she'd never feel with Steven. If only she could keep things contained within the walls of the back room, all would be well.

After tomorrow, there would be no turning back from wherever she and Steven were headed.

CHAPTER THIRTY

While O and Jacqui did their equestrian practice, Steven occupied himself with equally anachronistic pursuits. He was as excited and conflicted as O regarding tomorrow's irreversible steps toward a life neither had ever known or expected to know. Like her, he channeled his jitters, if that was the word for what he felt, into physical activity.

Grateful Mike was available, Steven slashed away at him as they danced back and forth along the strip. The fencing hall was empty on a Sunday afternoon, and they took advantage of the solitude to act like real sword-fighters, as saber fencers considered themselves to be by comparison to those who played around with foils.

"You couldn't hit a wall with that sticker," Steven shouted through the mesh of his mask as he parried Mike's always startlingly quick advance. "You aren't fast or accurate."

Another thing that differentiated saber fencers from the more sedate brotherhood of the foil was their disdain for courtly etiquette. They enjoyed riling each other up.

"Says the dead man walking," Mike shot back, sweeping across Steven's chest with the upper edge of the blade. Steven had seen that one coming and leaned back so it whooshed past him. By now, he was hip to many of Michael's tricks. But then, Michael was hip to many of his.

Steven lunged at the arm that had just flown past him and missed by an annoying millimeter as Mike turned back to the offensive again.

"I'm sure to kill you this time," Mike declared as they got back to first positions. "That is, if you don't die of old age first."

"You don't get to be my age by letting smart-ass kids rattle you," Steven fired back, accompanied with a feint right and a thrust left. Mike was a little slow on that left leg and Steven caught him right in the gall bladder. Mike looked down and laughed.

"Well, I guess there's a first time for everything," Mike said between deep breaths as he lifted his mask.

After four matches Steven had finally scored. He offered to buy a celebratory drink in the lounge.

"Love to," Michael said, "but tonight's my anniversary and I'm taking Tony out to Café Giovanni."

"Nice. I like the draped booths. Very romantic. How long have you guys been together?"

Mike did some math in his head.

"Well, with the law and all, we were married and then unmarried and then married again. It's simpler to just say we've been partners for seven years.

Steven was impressed.

"My record is three. How do you do it?"

"Don't be stubborn."

"That's it?"

"If your partner really wants something enough to fight over it, why fight? Why not make them happy instead?'

Steven was inclined to be stubborn. So was O. Definitely a thing to consider.

"Thanks for the advice," Steven said, extending his hand for Michael to shake. "I'll try to remember it."

Mike smiled at him.

"That's the tricky part."

Steven ended up alone in the dining room with *The Times Book Review* and his thoughts. Spectacles perched on his nose, he tried to concentrate on the words. His mind wandered again and again to the coming day. It had been many years since he had done anything fraught with such symbolism.

Putting the wedding ring on Marie was the last such occasion. That hadn't come out too well. But this seemed a more sensible approach for the man he now knew himself to be. He was a man of property, and O would soon be the most valuable of that property. The show was on, and he would play his part, as he did so often.

By the time he got home, a dense fog had cloaked the whole neighborhood. Flickering neon signs on the tops of ancient terra cotta apartment towers around his high nest were about all that was visible through what looked like soaped windows. Lounging on the huge silver couch in his red-trimmed black robe, pipe in one hand and lighter in the other, he watched some good gangster TV on cable before bed. His last thoughts were of O, and of what he should wear to such an occasion, the exact nature of which had no code spelled out in any reference book. He would have to improvise. He was good at that.

The fog stayed the night and the morning dawned cold. The cloud banks over the San Gabriels were almost black, but Steven had lived here long enough to know it wouldn't actually rain. He went through his morning ritual a bit faster than usual. Always punctual, for this event he hoped to arrive a bit early.

It was going to be a long day and one not to be forgotten, which was why he dropped his own small Leica into the pocket of his mid-length lambskin double-breasted jacket with the broad shearling collar. Beneath, he'd tucked a black cable-knit cashmere crew neck, worn over a heavy twill shirt from his friends at Turnbull & Asser, into a pair of pleated, wide-legged black-and-grey tweed slacks. He deliberately wore the Barker-Black buckled boots he knew O liked, though sock-garters wouldn't be needed this time. A festive red woven-silk scarf, his black safari hat, a pair of Dunhill driving gloves, and he was ready to go.

He'd given Constance the day off and headed straight down to the garage. This was an occasion, and it called for the occasion car, the Auburn that was the pride of his collection. With its boat-tail, bank-vault construction, outdoor exhaust plumbing in gleaming chrome and spoked wheels, it was truly something grand from a grander time. It was also a challenge to drive, even with its restored running gear, but it kicked over with one punch of the big button on its engine-turned dash. The motor, which could have powered a locomotive, warmed up quickly. Louder than a modern car, Steven could hear the different components working under the mile-long hood, but the note from the tuned exhaust was smooth and low. Even at eighty years of age, the Auburn was a goer. It gave Steven hope.

It was not, however, a stopper. Its giant drum-brakes were singularly unsuited for the hillier terrain around Marie's house. Fortunately, in the light Monday traffic, the straight ride up Virgil to The Triangle was easy enough and Steven felt curiously comfortable today in the huge seat, which was up-holstered in tufted red leather. The errand he was on was both ancient and modern, not unlike Steven himself.

He knew with absolute confidence that he could have been plunked down in any historical age and would still have come out very much the man he was, positioned as firmly in whatever occupation was the era's equivalent to his own. He was no less mortal than any other man, but no small part of his success in life was owed to that about him he knew to be eternal. Every time and place had men like Steven. It required them and they were always to be found, though never in great numbers and invariably at great cost.

A trustworthy and fearless mercenary, whether John Hawkwood or Steven Diamond, rarely made history but often cleared the path for others to do so. Unlike Ray, who meant to leave a legacy of something to be admired in a future he'd never live to see, Steven was content to make his mark in private, just as he would today.

Amazingly, on Franklin Avenue, Steven found a parking space ample enough to berth the Auburn's mighty keel. Its steering wheel would have been right at home on the bridge of a motor yacht, which the whole car was engineered to resemble, and required much the same combination of brute strength and finesse to operate. The Auburn's door weighed as much as most modern cars, and shut with a clunk that must have announced Steven's arrival. The wrought-iron gate buzzed him in while he was still climbing the steps.

Marie had prepared the household for the occasion, with all the girls accept O and Jacqui lined up in ranks on either side of the entrance. All were dressed in their most alluring, least concealing patchworks of lace, satin and silk. Marie herself had chosen yet another of her collection of nouveau Victorian, high-necked gowns, this one in white with a long, matching pinafore, lending her a medical air. She and Steven hugged and kissed while the girls went to their knees and bowed their heads as the two of them walked toward the spectacularly set table. The red chandelier was illuminated against the gray light from the windows, reflecting off the red tablecloth, set entirely with black plates, glasses and utensils.

No one pulled these things off like Marie, and she had outdone herself this time. She and Steven had barely exchanged pleasantries when Jacqui, in the black demi-bra and suspender belt they'd acquired on their shopping expedition, led O on a leash attached to her collar to greet them. Other than a long, sheer, white veil, a white brocade under-bust corset laced to the maximum reduction and tall white-satin pumps, O was naked. Her collar and cuffs were cut from shiny white patent and her hands were fastened behind her. First Jacqui knelt off to one side so O could come forward and drop to her knees in front of Steven. She bestowed a single kiss from her perfectly polished lips on each of his boots. She didn't raise her eyes to him until he reached down and tilted back her head so he could bend to kiss her mouth. It was a long kiss, and Jacqui waited patiently for it to end before she handed O's leash to Steven.

Steven brought O to her feet and embraced her, kissing her in an unabashedly sexual manner, pulling her up on her heels by her nipple rings, the better to stimulate his appetite.

Angelique took Steven's hat, coat, and scarf and, at Marie's suggestion, all sat down to lunch. O was to be well fortified for the ordeals ahead. Rosemary had seen to that with a hearty meal of fresh greens and lobster pot pie. Steven was amazed, yet again, at how O could tuck into such a robust meal with her middle constricted so severely.

Conversation was animated as always, but there was a certain gravity to things, given what all knew lay ahead. Everyone drank wine except for Steven, who never had developed a taste for it, and O, who knew that alcohol made tattooing bloodier.

O was particularly quiet, moving her chair as close to Steven as possible. During the meal, he paused now and then to caress her here and there, O offering whatever parts seemed to engage his interest as conveniently as possible. Subdued as she was, he still found her quite wet. When his hand traveled across the swells of her chest, he felt the familiar thumping of her small heart. He couldn't imagine that she feared the relatively minor pains she would soon endure, but shared some inner anxiety about the irreversible nature of what they were about to do.

As the raspberry sorbet was cleared away, O leaned over to whisper something in Jacqui's ear. Jacqui excused herself and clicked off down the hall. A surprise of some sort was in the offing. As a black dish of dark chocolate truffles went around the table while coffee was poured, there was some light-hearted conjecture about what it might be. O smiled slyly, but deflected all questions until Jacqui returned carrying a big, thick photo album bound in shiny black leather with a silver *fleur-de-lis* riveted to the cover. She gave it to O, who in turn passed it to Marie.

"This is probably my last day here for a while. You've all been so good to me in so many ways, I wanted to leave something behind so you would remember me as I'll always remember you," O said, looking around the table. Marie studied the album's cover, waiting until O asked her to open it. Everyone, including Steven, jumped up to look over Marie's shoulder as she began to flip through the creamy, vellum pages.

On each was a glossy print from O's small camera, which Marie had allowed her to keep with her because of Steven's trust in O. Steven was wrong about things from time to time, but he wouldn't have lived this long as a poor judge of character.

The room soon echoed with gasps and giggles. O had made a documentary portfolio of daily life at Marie's that seemed to capture its feeling with an artlessness only an artist could have achieved.

In one image, the girls lay in a naked, sweaty heap after a particularly demanding exercise routine in the gym, Marie standing over them, whip in hand, grinning broadly. In another, Jacqui gazed up hungrily from O's POV just before lowering her face between O's black-stockinged legs. Laughter erupted at the selfie of O's startled ecstatic expression, taken with the camera at arm's length, as Jacqui went to work on her. There was a surprisingly tender image of Laurel curled up naked in Angelique's arms, slumbering contentedly with her face resting on Angelique's fabulous breasts, displayed proudly through her unbuttoned lace top. Angelique's affectionate smile was as unexpected as sunlight bursting through brooding clouds.

In another shot, all the girls sat around the table in their lingerie, concentrating fiercely on giant, gilt-edged playing cards during what was clearly a very serious poker game. The lack of chips on the table suggested stakes of an unusual nature. Jacqui, eyes crossed, coughing out a bong hit with her ear buds in and her hair in curlers, had everyone in stitches. Noriko, kneeling to dress her ropes while the others watched, could have come from the Meiji era. Marie, seated at her dressing table while Jacqui brushed her hair, was serenely Junoesque, looking in the mirror to make sure the job was done to perfection.

There was even an image of Marie in the kitchen, laughing uproariously as Rosemary pretended to carry on a conversation with a smoked duck. One particularly striking image showed the whole household naked in the pool at night. It was eerily lovely, timeless and from a mysterious world where no man had ever set foot.

No one present could even remember O taking these pictures, though all recalled the occasions and offered comments that brought more laughter.

Steven felt honored to be granted such intimate entre to Marie's private world. He took out the red Montegrappa fountain pen scrolled with the silver dragon from his shirt pocket and handed it to O. She uncapped it, thought for a moment, then carefully wrote an inscription inside the front cover of the album in her tall, elegant hand.

"For Marie and all my beautiful sisters," it read simply. "As you live in these pictures, each of you lives in my heart."

O blew the ink dry and handed the album to Marie, who brought O's face close by the front collar ring and kissed her on the mouth. One by one, the others lined up and did the same. It was a melancholy moment as all realized that O would be leaving later that day, and might be gone a long time. Only Jacqui, who came last, smiled down at O.

"How did I let you sneak up and get me in curlers?"

"I waited until your eyes were closed," O explained calmly. "I was going to use the one of you smoking and douching at the same time, but it seemed a bit rude."

"No shit," Jacqui said. "Then I guess you won't mind my taking a picture of you when Marie sticks the needle through your nose."

Jacqui crossed her eyes and opened her mouth, miming a scream. Everyone cracked up again.

"Which reminds me," Marie said, glancing down at the rose-gold Piaget watch Steven had given her for her fortieth birthday, "Jan's due here any minute. Jacqui, take O to my office and get her ready."

Marie stood, put her arms around O, and placed O's hand in Jacqui's. The two of them set off down the hall, whispering, while Marie and the others closed in around the book again for another run-through.

Unobserved, Steven slipped into the kitchen, sneaking up on Rosemary, who bossed her cousins through the washing up. When he was about two feet away, she spun on him suddenly, large butcher knife in hand.

"I don't know what you're thinking," she said ominously. "But if you come any closer it won't matter."

Steven laughed. He loved Rosemary's complete comfort with the exotic environment and the ease with which she kept herself and her family members apart from it.

"Actually," he said, "I was thinking I might get another cup of coffee."

"All you have to do is ask," Rosemary said, putting down the knife. "Estella," she barked in Spanish at her youngest cousin, who had the most promising culinary skills. "Make the man a cappuccino with an extra shake of chocolate."

She turned to Steven.

"Want a shot of brandy in that?"

Steven answered in his own impeccable Spanish.

"Thanks, but I'm not the one getting tattooed and pierced this afternoon, and if I were, it would be a bad idea."

"Every man in my family has a tattoo and not one of them was sober enough to remember when or where he got it," Rosemary said with a laugh.

"When I was in the Navy, that was pretty common too."

Rosemary eyed Steven suspiciously.

"How come your Spanish is so good?"

"I represented Pablo Escobar. I wanted to make sure we understood each other very clearly."

"Well, if I ever need a lawyer I know who I'm calling."

"I hope you never do, but I'm telling you right now I'll take my retainer in culinary services."

"Actually, I've been thinking of starting a catering business. Maybe you can help me with the license application."

Steven pulled out a red alligator card case from his back pocket and handed her one of his blue business cards.

"I don't usually do licensures, but I'm sure I can get the forms filled out for you. Call anytime."

Leaning against the counter, watching the staff wash up, he sipped his cappuccino and wondered why he always enjoyed being backstage or in the kitchen or up on the scaffolding or down in the garage. Steven was endlessly fascinated by the inner workings of things. He suspected that fascination somewhat explained why a middle-aged man took such satisfaction in playing with miniature steam engines. It never ceased to surprise and satisfy him when a few drops of oil, some water and a fuel tablet made the flywheels go around.

He loved knowing the tricks of every trade, however remote from his own, and had long ago discovered that the most important part of any operation was usually invisible from the public entrance. Not given to much introspection, he accepted the fact that he was a backdoor man in several senses of the word, and that this served him well.

Grabbing a cookie to finish off with his cappuccino, Steven went to Marie's office to see how the preparations were proceeding.

Jan had already arrived and gathered with O, Jacqui and Marie in the medical suite attached to Marie's office. The examination table was flattened out and O laid on it face down and naked, providing Steven one of his favorite views. It showed off the supple muscularity of her back and limbs, and provided a particularly pleasant presentation of her perfectly round rump. Jacqui sat on a low, three-legged stool and held O's hand. They were still whispering. Steven presumed the topic was Ray, but didn't want to limit O's options by joining in. Marie stood by a Mayo stand draped with a disposable sterile pad. Jan mixed bright pigments in tiny paper cups using a narrow steel spoon. A row of striped autoclave bags had been laid out neatly nearby, along with a stainless steel alcohol sprayer and a pile of folded gauze wipes. Her machine, a fabulous example of retro-tech with scrollwork side plates, was already strung to copper connections at the forked end of a long, old-fashioned cord which was wrapped in red thread. The cord led to a thoroughly modern power pack on the floor Jan could operate with a treadle switch. Marie's antique pharmacy lamp cast a pool of illumination over O's backside.

Jan wore ruthlessly tight black jeans, tall boots and a painted black leather vest, also cut tight as well as low. Like many heavily tattooed people Steven had known, Jan dressed like a rocker's dream, but was cautious in her private life. She'd had fewer than a dozen boyfriends, most of them musicians, and been utterly faithful to them before kicking them to the curb for their inability to return her faithfulness.

She'd been explaining the whole process to Marie and the others before looking over at Steven's entrance. She leaned toward him for an air kiss, but already had her black latex gloves on and had to limit further physical contact.

"Glad you could make it," she said dryly.

"Didn't want to get in the way."

"Now there's an idea I'd like to see catch on."

Steven knelt next to O's face and took her other hand.

"So far?" he asked.

"I'm pretty good at lying down, Sir."

"She's scared shitless," Jacqui translated.

O's hand was uncharacteristically cold and clammy. Steven gave it a good squeeze.

"So was I," Steven confessed, "and my hosts did everything possible to make sure I stayed that way."

"Let me guess," Jan said. "They had you go to some shady bar in Shinjuku, kept you waiting an hour, then showed up in shiny suits and sunglasses."

"I see you're familiar with the local customs," Steven said with a laugh.

"Been through the whole thing several times. Bet they took you someplace in a big black Caddy where a small bearded fellow about a thousand years old looked at you like a side of beef he'd already decided wasn't good enough."

"Yeah, I got the old guy. I did his boss a solid and the ink was a bonus."

"Did it hurt much?" O asked. She was scared, but not of pain. That part of it made her want to rub her thighs together. She was afraid she might not be as perfect a subject as she intended.

Steven pulled over Marie's desk chair to sit near O's face. Marie settled on the couch. She had never seen this done before and wanted to commit every minute of it memory.

Jan stroked O's lower back and upper buttocks with a gloved hand.

"Normally, I'd shave this area before starting," she said. "But there's not much here to shave."

O explained about the laser.

Jan was a little incredulous at how thorough O had been. "They even did your back?"

"They did everything, and I mean everything. Sometimes it was like sitting on medium-rare sunburn the next day."

"Well, this job should be easy," Jan said happily. Though masochistic clients squicked her as a rule, she liked O immediately. She always knew who belonged in the club with Steven and her. The club's motto was: "It's weird, but it's me."

Jacqui's face was lit with anticipation.

"I can't wait until this is done. It's going to be so hot."

O suggested Jacqui could use the finished work to guide her tongue. When it came to licking girl-ass, she was endlessly greedy.

"Why, does my tongue need guidance?" Jacqui asked, fluttering her thick lashes.

"You manage just fine and you know it."

Jan picked up the machine and pumped the foot switch. There was a loud crackle at the contacts that made everyone jump.

"Well, that's working," she said matter-of-factly, setting it down so she could unroll the drawing for the transfer. Spreading it out across O's upper rear cheeks, Jan sprayed the tracing paper down with the alcohol. O didn't move, but she did break out in goose bumps at the chilly blast.

Jan concentrated on getting the transfer in the perfect spots, smoothing and patting the paper, appraising it until she was satisfied before peeling it away.

On O's body, precisely centered over her tail bone, was the purple inked outline of Steven's initials and the ribbons. Everyone gathered round to look at it but O, who had to remain prone.

"What do you think?" Jan asked.

"It seems perfectly centered to me," Marie observed.

"Higher, lower, or just right?"

Jan wasn't going to fire up the machine for real until there was absolute unanimity.

"I know whose vote we really need," Jacqui said. She'd been entrusted with O's small camera to record critical moments in the ritual. She flashed it over O's back, brought the image into the monitor and held it down so O could have a look.

"It's pretty big, isn't it?"

O's tone conveyed more pride than apprehension.

. Jacqui said it would go well with the corset. She asked everyone else to look up so she could take their pictures too. They all smiled.

"You can shoot some more when I'm done, but I don't want the strobe while I'm working," Jan warned. Jacqui responded to her tone immediately.

"No, Ma'am."

She put the camera down on Marie's desk.

"Can you get music in here?" Jan asked Marie.

"No problem."

Marie opened a tall lacquer cabinet to one side of the desk and revealed a small control panel.

"What would you like to hear?"

"It's O's choice. She's the one getting the ink."

O suggested The Velvet Underground. Marie tapped a few buttons and the room filled with Lou Reed's quaky voice. She turned the volume down a bit and excused herself, not wanting to crowd Jan in any way. Exiting, she reminded Jacqui to make sure O got plenty of water.

"Should we restrain her?" Jacqui asked eagerly once Marie was out of the room.

"She won't need it," Jan assured.

"But it could be fun," O said.

"I wouldn't let anyone else do this," Jan cautioned. "And I better not see any pictures of me putting ink on someone who can't run away."

There wasn't much to it. The table was already fitted with restraining rings and all Jacqui had to do was scoop up a few small carabiners from a steel cabinet to hook down O's wrist and ankle cuffs.

O put her face to one side of the lowered headrest, making herself comfortable as possible. Steven stroked her hair.

"Need a pillow?"

She gave his hand an extra pump. "I'm fine, Sir. Jacqui's been instructed to care for my every need."

"Isn't she the lucky bitch?" Jacqui asked.

"I'll be keeping score for when it's your turn," O cautioned good-naturedly.

Jacqui couldn't imagine when that would be. Jan shrugged.

"You never know. Okay, let's get started. I use the outliner first. It's only got three needles, so it's pretty focused. This may be the hardest part."

The machine crackled to life again, but settled into a steady hum as Jan carved the first line into O's flesh. O tensed but didn't move a muscle.

"Think you can deal?" Jan asked. It wasn't a rhetorical question. She insisted every new client make a final decision after feeling the sensation before pressing on, lest anyone end up with half a tattoo.

"No problem," O said. She never thought of herself as having a high pain threshold and she certainly didn't consider it a boasting point, but it was a fact.

"It feels sort of like getting a haircut," she said. "A really deep haircut."

Everyone laughed.

"From this side," Jan said, "it's a little like trying to mow a portrait of Einstein into a rocky lawn with a rusty hand-mower."

Jan went on to inscribe the boundaries of Steven's mark in long sweeping strokes, pausing only to dip the outliner in the cup of black ink.

Steven felt O's hands get drier and warmer again, and the color returned to her face. He understood what happened when that first endorphin rush kicked in. He smiled down at her.

"Feeling a little high?"

"It's different than I expected," O admitted. "I thought it would be more like cutting."

Jan explained that the needles had to go in exactly the correct distance.

"Too shallow and the ink wears off. Too deep and your body fluids wash it away."

Soon Jan was working intently, hunched over O's back, while the others, including O, sang along to "Waiting For the Man." O's eyes looked as dreamy as if she'd just had her sweet taste.

Steven remembered how, after the first few strokes, his own tattoo had begun to feel good, or in any case he'd begun to feel high from it. Unfortunately, the tattooing had outlasted the high.

"They used the stick and ink on me," Steven volunteered. "It's kind of amazing, the way they sort of lift the skin up and punch the ink in from underneath."

"They've nearly all gone mechanical by now," Jan said a bit wistfully.

"It's not just a gangster thing anymore," O explained. "You see a lot of trendy girls hanging out in Roppongi with *manga* tattoos on their arms where they can hide them from their mothers when they get home."

Jan admitted that for Western-style *nukibori* the machine probably worked best.

Watching closely, Steven was amazed at the speed and precision of Jan's outlining as always. No matter how often he saw her work, it still seemed like magic. The flourishes at the ends of the ribbons made it all seem so effortless, but he knew, better than most, how difficult an art form this really was.

Jan told O when she switched from the outliner to the shader, with its wider array of needles, in order to put in the color. O actually sighed when it touched her skin.

"Now that feels more like a massage," she said. "A really deep massage."

Jacqui held the water bottle for O to take a drink while Steven went over to the stereo controls. The Velvets had rolled out and they needed another choice. They settled on Robert Johnson, but after Steven attempted the first chorus of "Kind-Hearted Woman," Jan suggested he restrict himself to listening. He was happy to do so; he was happy about everything at that moment, especially looking down at Jan's work and imagining the first time he would have O from behind after it was healed. Its permanent presence would remind him that he could do what he pleased with her, and that she was with him for exactly that reason.

There wasn't much blood, but the ink trails were raised and raw and by the time Jan got around to putting white highlights on the ribbons, which involved going back over freshly-applied pink pigment, O was shiny with sweat and gripping both Jacqui's and Steven's hands hard.

He remembered this part too. After the first couple of hours, the endorphins wore off and the shakes and chills of mild shock set in.

"I think I need to pee," O said in a voice seeming remote and distant.

Jan stood up and stretched her spine.

"Sounds like a good idea. Be careful walking. You might feel a little light-headed."

"Who said anything about walking?" Jacqui interjected, going to one of the medical cabinets, removing a gleaming, steel-lidded bedpan and grabbing a handful of wipes from a dispenser on the counter.

Jacqui and Steven unhooked O's cuffs and carefully helped her to a sitting position. Jan concentrated on opening a fresh pack of needles and installing them on the machine. She was often a witness to these small, ceremonial acts among her tribe of clients, but she never joined in.

O demonstrated the complete lack of embarrassment about bodily functions she'd developed while living in Marie's luxurious barracks. She pressed her palms into the white towels on the table and lifted up so Jacqui could slide in the bedpan. O and Steven kissed while the water Jacqui had fed O splashed against the metal. Steven was always impressed by how much a small woman's pipes could hold. When the last drops plinked, Jacqui gave O a quick swipe from underneath with the moistened wipe, slid out the pan and took it to the adjoining bathroom.

Steven helped O lie back down while Jan inked her needles once more.

"Almost done," Jan said reassuringly, bending to the final shading around Steven's mark.

"I won't deny I'm ready for it to be over," O said. Her face momentarily twisted out of its usual composure into a mask of real pain when the shader brushed against the outline of Steven's initials, but she composed herself, gritted her teeth and held onto Jacqui's arm. In a moment of inspired calculation, she looked Jacqui in the eye to show that she was, in fact, capable of tears. Jacqui's grip tightened in return, proving that it worked. Everything O did with Jacqui was meant to build an intimacy that would be O's gift to Ray, or more correctly, to Steven by way of Ray.

"All done," Jan pronounced. It had only taken two hours, but they were a very long two hours. At Steven's instruction, Jacqui brought over the rolling mirror while Steven helped O to her feet. O craned her neck over her shoulder to see as much as she could of the finished product.

Jan laughed.

"You can travel all over the world and see all kinds of things but the one thing you'll never see is your own back. You might catch a glimpse in a mirror at some twisted angle or look at it in a photograph, but there's a big part of yourself that's always visible to others and always hidden from you."

O noticed that Jan addressed the comment to Steven, not her. She didn't give him too long to think about the subject, turning her attention back to the angrily fresh tattoo.

"What you had in mind?"

"Better."

"It should be pretty well healed in ten days. I'm going to patch it for tonight, just to absorb any ink and fluid that might ooze out. After that, short showers, no baths for a week or so and no scratching or picking. Because once it starts to heal, it will itch like a motherfucker and until the ink sets completely, it can be knocked out."

O said she understood. Jan opened a package of large sterile gauze pads, unfolded a couple of them and started tearing lengths off a roll of surgical tape. Steven let her steady herself by placing her hands on his shoulders.

"Are you sure you're ready for the second act now?"

"I've been working up the nerve to do it for days," O replied. "If I crash out now, it will probably never happen."

Sometimes it was a matter of sticking with the plan or none of it was real at all.

Jacqui went to get the others. This was the ceremonial part of the affair, and if it was to be done, it had to be done properly.

Once all were assembled in the surgery they formed a line behind the table. Steven helped O get to it, scooping her up and lifting her the way she loved. O sat up straight, parted her lips and opened her legs. Steven came around to look her in the eyes. They were still a bit cloudy.

"You understand that this, even more than my mark on your back, makes you my slave," he said.

"Yes, Sir. I do. Many people wear other people's names or symbols. Only slaves have ringed noses," O said.

It was not quite true anymore, when kink affectations of all kinds had become commonplace, but in this context, with this person, it could have no other meaning. O wasn't a green-haired punker chick. This was a frontal assault on her emotional privacy, a thing she valued above all else, except for what she'd found with Steven. Whatever else she might be, O was certainly determined.

Marie entered, still in her white pinafore and boots by otherwise stripped for work. Steven still admired Marie's eternal curves, the template for so many men's fantasies, including his own at one time. She put a warm hand on O's thigh.

"I've done this many times," she said. "It's a simple procedure. I just need to know that your consent is completely solid. If you have any doubts, tell me now and we'll call it a day."

O's tone was firm, even though she was still shaky from the ink work. "I want Sir's ring and I'm glad you're the one making it possible, Ma'am."

Marie assented with a quick nod and a kiss on O's lips.

"I never doubt you when you've made up your mind to something."

She began giving orders to the other girls, who set to work gathering the needed items.

Noriko changed the towel on the Mayo stand and laid out the new batch of autoclave bags. This would be a less complex operation than the inking, but it was every bit as zero-critical. Jacqui gave O the authorization form from Marie's desk drawer and went over it with her in detail. Taking the dragon pen from Steven, O initialed each paragraph on the form, then signed off with her inimitable flourish and blew the purple ink dry. Jacqui slipped the form into an envelope that went straight back to the desk. Marie kept paper records of any procedure for which she could conceivably be sued.

Marie stepped up, looking at O's face critically.

"How are you feeling?"

"Ready," O said.

"That's what I needed to hear," Marie said. Looking at O's small, perfect cameo of a face, every muscle in it set with purpose, she had no doubts about O. She had always had some about Steven, but none he didn't share himself.

Angelique and Laurel rolled purple latex gloves over Marie's outstretched hands with audible snaps. O tilted her head back as instructed so Marie could measure the distance between O's nostrils with a tiny caliper. She seemed satisfied with the reading. Accustomed as she was having Marie's gloved fingers in her other orfices, O wasn't entirely comfortable with Marie's gloved fingers in her nostrils. Marie felt around for that sweet spot behind the cartilage where a needle would easily pass. O's small, round nose had more usable soft tissue than expected – a good thing.

"No problem here," she said. "Let's do it."

Noriko cranked the back of the table upright so O could lean back against it while sitting. Noriko, the house bondage queen, passed an armful of straps through the steel rings bolted into the frame around the edge of the table and tightened them down firmly from O's shoulders to her shins, making them tight enough to press into O's skin. Jacqui fastened down the wrist and ankle cuffs.

At Marie's direction, Jacqui cranked the leather pads on either side of O's head tight, forcing her to face front. Noriko added a strap across O's forehead, just in case she inadvertently jerked away from the needle, unlikely as that seemed. Marie wouldn't risk any unplanned perforations. All the other girls leaned forward, each putting a hand on O's shoulder. Steven kissed her and she gave back as much as her immobilized cranium would allow. He stood back to get out of Marie's way but his eyes never strayed from O's.

"This isn't as painful as you expect it to be," Marie explained, "But you will feel some pressure and you have to stay absolutely still."

O managed a smile.

"I don't see how I could do much else."

The ten-gauge needle looked as big as a shotgun barrel coming out of the bag, though it wasn't much larger than a thick toothpick in actuality. Lola dropped it into a small dish of alcohol Noriko had set out. Next came the retainer, the U-shaped black niobium staple that O could use to keep the piercing open while it healed, and thereafter when she had to go out in public. Angelique pulled the pharmacy lamp down a bit, and Marie fine-tuned the aim until the beam fell across O's nose but missed her eyes. Taking the receiving tube in her left hand, Marie smiled in a way unique to a perfectionist who is seeing something perfect.

"Looking good," she said, slipping the receiving tube into O's left nostril and the needle into her right.

"Now," she said calmly. "Just take a deep breath and relax."

In a single smooth movement, Marie brought the needle and the tube together. O didn't even flinch. As Marie had promised it really didn't hurt much, though O certainly felt the strange sensation of a foreign object where none had been before. She experienced an odd desire to cross her eyes so she could watch what was going on, which made Jacqui giggle.

"Now there's a look I haven't seen before."

"That's because your face is usually between my legs when it happens," O shot back.

"Okay, you two, no more talking until I get done."

"Yes, Ma'am," the two said in unison.

Marie deftly withdrew the needle from the tube, dropped it in a red sharps container on the stand and inserted one end of the retainer into the opening on the right side of the tube, which she then slipped out, leaving the retainer neatly in place. Its tiny black points stuck down out of O's nostrils like miniature tusks.

"May I see?"

Jacqui fetched a hand mirror from the bathroom. Returning to the silent room, she held it up to O's face. O took one look and burst out laughing.

"I can't believe I actually went through with it!" she exclaimed.

Everyone else started laughing too.

"If I had a dollar for every time I heard that, I could retire," Marie said.

O very carefully touched the tip of her nose.

"It feels twice its normal size."

"And yet it's completely unchanged from the outside."

Proving the point, Marie carefully flipped up the retainer so the points vanished in the darkness of O's nostrils.

"See? It's your little secret until you can put in the ring. You should heal up in about ten days, but I'd wait a couple of weeks before I put anything else in there. When you're ready, come by and I'll show you how to change out the jewelry."

Marie leaned down and kissed O through the leather headband strap. O thanked her for making it all so easy.

"Happy to do it," she said. "Congratulations to you both."

The whole household came around the table to kiss O on the cheek and hug her carefully, avoiding bumps as Noriko freed her from the restraints.

Steven hugged Marie and thanked her also, his trust in her validated once again.

"Just remember, no BJs until it settles down, and be careful in doggie position too," she said.

"I just wish I could wear the ring home now," O said.

"Judging from the hardware on your chest, I don't doubt you'll be wearing it all over town soon," Marie laughed. She knew full well, of course, how unlikely that was.Marie sent Jacqui off to pack O's small bag and her own. Tonight, both would sleep under Steven's roof. Jacqui suggested O accompany her so they could dress for departure. While Noriko took Marie's instruments to the antique but still functional autoclave, Steven brought out a joint he'd been waiting to smoke all day, firing it with a Dupont French Line lighter, lacquered with a sleek black finish . Marie took a deep hit and passed it back.

"Never thought I'd see the day," she said.

Steven knew just what she meant.

"It's not like I took a vow never to have another slave. I just stopped looking for someone and you know what happens then."

"When you're not looking for others," Marie observed, "they tend to look for you."

Steven suggested that she herself might be about due, but Marie shook her head.

"It's all about novelty for me. I won't mind if I never spend two consecutive nights in the same bed with anyone. Which reminds me, Steven. Thanks to you, I'm going to have two vacancies at once up here."

"Svetlana could benefit from some personal attention."

Not for the first time, Marie looked at him as if he'd lost his mind.

"Time to collect the knives."

"She likes girls and she'll appreciate the change of scenery. I never underestimate your ability to command loyalty, especially from a useful person. Svetlana's really quite observant."

Snapping off her gloves and tossing them into the lidded waste container, Marie circled Steven's temple with a fingertip.

"The wheels never stop turning."

Marie walked Steven out of the office, the rest falling in line behind her.

Steven would have O. Ray would have Jacqui. As only he could, he put doubt aside and set thought to purpose. He glanced at his watch as he waited; a Patek Phillipe with a midnight blue face and gold trim, it showed a rising moon in the phase indicator. Left to her own devices, Jacqui might have drifted off into an alternative reality on a cloud of cannabis. But Jacqui was unlikely to be left to her own devices hereafter. O led her back into the living room, both now dressed; O in the clothes she'd worn the day of her arrival, Jacqui in jeans, a massive sweater that hung off one shoulder, motorcycle boots and a multi-colored newsboy hat. O carried her small valise until Steven took it from her. Jacqui wheeled a well-worn roll-aboard behind her.

In the living room, farewells were exchanged. Marie cultivated a particularly physical intimacy among the girls of Franklin Street. Steven wasn't surprised to see tears in all eyes, even Angelique's, as they hugged and kissed O and Jacqui. The two of them playfully grabbed a breast here and smacked a bottom there while each impeccably whorish member of the sisterhood presented for a good-bye. Noriko promised to visit O's studio and rig a shoot as soon as O felt like going back to work. O assured her it wouldn't be a long wait.

Marie and Steven watched the pre-departure ritual shoulder to shoulder. She had seen all this before many times. More than once, she'd pulled one of her girls off another's throat, only to see them sobbing in each other's arms when one or the other headed back to The Mansion or off with a new man.

Chapter Thirty-One

O held onto Jacqui's arm going down the steep, uneven concrete steps from the front door to the sidewalk. It had rained the usual five drops, just enough to make cement and asphalt slick with a thin layer of dust and grease. When the three of them reached the bottom, Jacqui's jaw dropped in shock at the sight of the Auburn.

"You can't be serious," she blurted out.

"Not while driving it," Steven admitted.

"It was one of those things he just had to have," O explained.

Steven opened a bank vault door so Jacqui could clamber into the back, than helped O, who was a bit shaky, into the passenger seat next to him.

"This thing is bigger than my old apartment," Jacqui said, looking around the cavernous interior.

"Neater too," O added.

Steven fired up the massive engine and a mighty roar from the chromed pipes emerged through the hood.

"This isn't some kind of kit car is it?" Jacqui asked.

"No, it's a real one. I only take it out of the garage when I want it to rain."

Steven drove slowly going home. O sat even straighter than usual, keeping her lacerated back off the upholstery as much as possible. At least the massive weight of the car minimized bumps in the road.

O hadn't told Jacqui much about Steven or how he lived, and her amazement continued at the sight of his glass tower, the garage full of costly rolling stock and, most of all, his sybaritic hideout on the top floor. She gazed in utter astonishment across the vast central space with all its luxurious appointments to the glass wall behind which much of the night cityscape was displayed.

"Wow. It's like the bat-cave with windows," Jacqui said.

"Wait until you see the back room," O teased. "You'll never want to leave. I know this sounds weird but I'm starving for some reason."

Jacqui suggested that having her flesh shredded and punched all day could have something to do with it.

While they set down their things, Steven went to the kitchen and brought out the pile of menus. He fanned them out on the granite counter top like the giant poker deck from Marie's.

"Tell me what seems appealing."

Steven tapped the centralized remote control to turn on the lights. He picked up some combustible refreshments while Jacqui and O sorted through the menus. O almost never craved red meat, but at that moment, she needed a steak, on the rare side. Jacqui was easily suggestible where O was concerned. Before long, they were making choices from the bill of fare at The Pacific Dining Car, a revered steak house that was older than the Hollywood Sign. Never a favorite of Steven's, it was close and open all night, so he joined in, taking everyone's orders and phoning the delivery.

While they waited, Steven suggested if O was feeling up to it she could show Jacqui around and make her comfortable while he got out of his clothes. Leaving the kitchen, he cranked up the heat, knowing everyone would soon be less dressed. The radiant coils buried in the floor combined with the over-head registers to raise the temperature quickly.

Jacqui's head continued to swivel this way and that, eyes wide with astonishment, as O led her off down the hall. Steven went straight to his closet to methodically dismantle himself as usual, hanging his clothes on their dedicated hangers and stashing all the things he carried in their various cabinets and drawers. He could hear the girls' voices as they faded, but couldn't make out anything they said.

O, who had become an accomplished docent in Steven's private maze, explained to Jacqui how all the various auto-mated conveniences worked, pointed out some of the nastier art she thought Jacqui would particularly appreciate and di-rected her to the various bathrooms and closets.

"He really owns this whole place?" Jacqui asked, still not quite believing it even existed, much less that it belonged to someone she knew.

"He owns the whole building. He owns all those cars down in the garage. He owns a whole lot of things."

"Including you."

"Especially me. Even more so after today."

"And you own me?" Jacqui sounded skeptical about that.

"Let's just say I'd like to."

Jacqui looked out the windows down toward the shiny wet streets where the stoplights cast their festive colors in al-ternation.

"I think I could probably get used to this," Jacqui she said.

When they reached the back room, where the lights came up automatically as they entered, she threw her arms in the air and let out a shriek of delight.

"Now this I *know* I could get used to!"

O stood in the doorway and watched Jacqui tentatively explore the place – the heavy, shiny furnishings, the racks of whips and restraining gear, the sturdy suspension bar, the ring bolts and drain in the floor. She even stepped into the vertical cage and shut the door, looking through the bars at O with her most pitiful expression.

"On please don't tell me I'll have to sleep in here," she whined.

"Tonight you're going to sleep with us," O said. "But there's a lovely guest bedroom on the other side of the elevators so you can have some privacy when you want it. As for this room, you'll be here soon enough. We should get you ready. Slaves don't wear much around this place, so you might as well get used to it."

"Get used to being naked?" Jacqui laughed, tossing her cap on the bondage bed. She pulled her sweater off over her head to reveal a tiny black bra that barely contained her. "I don't know if I can handle that."

O helped her out of her jeans and boots, finding a suitable pair of uniform pumps for her from the collection ranked by size in one of the diamond-plate cabinets arranged along the wall. O also brought out a patent leather "guest collar" with no markings on it and a matching set of wrist and ankle cuffs. Starting at the bottom, she locked everything in place, pausing to kiss Jacqui's neck as Steven always did hers before snapping the tiny padlock on the collar.

It startled Jacqui just enough to produce a sudden head-shake, bumping O's newly punctured nose. O let out a yelp. Jacqui turned, embarrassed, hands covering her mouth.

"Oh god, did I just hit you in the nose?"

"Yes," O answered calmly. "That's why I'm holding it at the moment."

"I'm so sorry."

Jacqui very carefully put her arms around O, who brushed her cheek against Jacqui's breasts, now at the perfect attitude as she stood in her heels.

"Your turn."

Jacqui took extra caution undressing O, unbuttoning the white blouse and holding up the skirt so O could step out of it. Bright splotches of tattoo ink had already soaked through the pad on O's back. Jacqui pointed at it.

"Doesn't that hurt?"

"No worse than a skin peel. My nose feels kind of ... strange though."

Jacqui kissed the tip of it very lightly.

"It took a lot of guts, going through with this," she said admiringly.

"It was easier than I thought it would be."

"I don't mean the painful part. I know you're a tough bitch. I mean the other part."

O put her arms around Jacqui, rubbing their naked bellies together. "Don't worry. I'm not going to ask anything like this of you. Your body is your living. But I may ask something that's difficult in a different way, when the time comes."

Jacqui chose not to pursue that. Instead she brought O's collar, cuffs and shoes from the cabinet in the closet reserved for O's use. It had a mirror on the inside of the door so O could make sure she was perfect before presenting herself. There were several corsets rolled in their own cubicles but she wouldn't be wearing one tonight. Catching herself in the mirror, O saw a tired, pale stressed version she didn't like.

"Maybe I should fix my makeup or something," O said.

"Maybe we should get you away from the mirror for a minute."

Jacqui led O out of the closet by the hand.

O looked at her for a moment, wondering if she could really let this girl go when the time came. She supposed she'd find out then.

They rejoined Steven, now in his silk dressing gown and velvet skull slippers, which Jacqui found so charming she had to get down for a closer look, kissing each after inspecting the bullion embroidery. The view looking down was certainly pleasing.

"I do love it when women undress for dinner," he said, giving each a hug and a kiss. He was careful to put his arms around O's shoulders instead of her middle as usual. She bristled at feeling so fragile, but had to concede that she was, at least for now. Jacqui groped him good-naturedly, knowing O wouldn't mind.

The table was set for three: black tablecloth, black dishes decorated with the 17th/21st skull motto and black anodized flatware. Two of the aluminum chairs were covered with thick black bath sheets. Steven lit black tapers in black glass candelabras with a long wooden match from flat box decorated to match the humidor. The lights were dim and Gil Scott-Heron's jazzy spoken word came faintly from speakers in the ceiling and walls.

"The food should be here in about twenty minutes," he said, "leaving us just enough time for this."

Producing a fat joint from his robe pocket with a flourish, he fired it with the mother-of-pearl clad lighter O knew to be his favorite. It was reserved for special occasions, which this certainly was.

"Oh yeah," Jacqui said happily, taking a deep drag off the joint. O passed, still woozy from the various insults to her body that day, but Steven took a huge hit, exhaling what looked like a green thunderhead under the winged cable spots strung from the ceiling.

He pulled out a chair for each of them, watching O sit down with the utmost care before placing a small red velvet cushion behind her back. Jacqui and O got to sit side by side, facing the windows so they could enjoy the view of the city while Steven enjoyed the view of them. O wanted only water, but a lot of it. She felt dehydrated as well as drained. Jacqui had the same. Steven poured a Stella from the refrigerator into a chilled glass. Placing a big, heavy machine-age ashtray between the three of them, he sat down for the pass-around.

While they waited they talked about tattoos and piercings and photography and modeling. Jacqui had big plans for her own website. Steven was impressed with her technical virtuosity when describing the features she imagined for it, though he wasn't sure how much of this was just a daydream and how much she could or would actually do.

He'd had his doubts about Jacqui that day they all went shopping, but the more time he spent with her, the better he liked her. Her scheming was transparent enough to be harmless and there was something sweetly optimistic about her that her rough and raunchy history hadn't dimmed.

The phone on the kitchen counter buzzed. Dinner had arrived and a security guard would be bringing it up presently. Indeed, by the time Steven hung up, the young man was already at the door. He was new to the job and ill-at-ease finding his boss in a half-open robe, not to mention the two naked girls in plain view. Steven reassured him with a twenty-dollar tip and carried the bags to the kitchen. He started to unpack them, but both girls jumped up and shooed him out of the kitchen. They might not have prepared their Master's feast but they could at least serve it. Steven certainly didn't mind being fussed over by two lovely, fully exposed slaves, bending over at either side to dish up his salad and pour béarnaise on his filet.

Sitting across from him to eat their own meals, they gave him still more reason to be pleased. O, whose appetite was always hearty, ate like she'd been lost at sea for a week. She put away a giant porterhouse with such enthusiasm, he was surprised she didn't lick the plate. Jacqui, being young, athletic and active, did pretty much the same with her slightly smaller slab of meat. Hungry as she was, her manners bore the unnatural polish of Marie's strict training. Marie understood that men liked watching women eat and schooled those under her sway to do so in the awareness that they were being seen.

The meal disappeared with astonishing speed, concluding with a slice of chocolate cake they split three ways. The girls cleared the table, and O rinsed the dishes before putting them in the industrial sterilizer while Jacqui fetched her iPhone from her bag to check messages, responding with brief texts.

Steven kicked back from the table to watch all the activity, making it easy for O to come and straddle his lap, putting her head on his scarred shoulder, simultaneously reaching under herself to stroke him through the silk.

"That was wonderful, Sir. But I'm very tired all of a sudden. May we lie down so I can watch Jacqui service you?"

O didn't have to ask twice. Jacqui took off the geek glasses she needed to text when not wearing her contacts and put her phone away. Steven stood, took her in his arms and kissed her. He'd never kissed Jacqui before but found her surprisingly tender and relaxed, closing her eyes and opening her lips to invite his tongue. While Steven explored her with his hands, O sauntered somewhat wearily down the hall to the back room, returning with a slender, cutting dressage whip not unlike the one she'd used at Marie's, but all black with a flat disk pommel. She put it on the table next to Steven's hand. He broke off his kiss to look down at it, a bit surprised.

"Seems a little severe for a first time."

"It's what she needs. You'll have to hurt her for real if you want her at her best."

Jacqui pinched O's nipple hard enough to pry an "ouch" out of her.

"You just want to watch him do it, evil Sister."

O couldn't deny it any more than Jacqui could deny the accuracy of O's instructions.

They went off to the bedroom arm in arm, removing their shoes and placing them neatly side-by-side against the wall while Steven pulled back the thick duvet. O stretched out on one edge of the bed, yawned and patted the smooth, dark blue sheet. Jacqui laid down next to her, opening her legs to O's languid caresses.

Though spent from a grueling day, O was never too tired to enjoy Jacqui's taste. She made her way down to spend some time there. Jacqui raised her knees, put her hands on O's head, running her fingers through O's thick dark hair, and rotated her hips, pelvis rising and falling with each of O's circular head moves.

Steven watched, whip in hand, from the foot of the bed, until Jacqui's breathing grew rapid and her face turned red. Quite rigid from watching, Steven masturbated casually, flicking the whip back and forth with his other hand. Jacqui whimpered a few barely intelligible encouragements in her little girl voice and suddenly cried out for permission to come. Steven granted it as always, knowing from O that Jacqui had plenty more where that came from.

Jacqui clamped her thighs around O's face and grabbed her head, babbling out her thanks to both of them as she lifted her long back in total abandonment to pleasure. The spasms were short and sharp, finally diminishing to random twitches.

O rolled off her, stretching out on her side and propping her head with a hand once again to watch the rest of the show.

"Now would be a good time, Sir," she suggested to Steven.

He leaned across the bed, tapping Jacqui on her sweaty chest with the red cracker at the end of the whip.

"Come here and bend over, girl."

"Yes, Sir," Jacqui said, coming to her senses. O had told her how adeptly Steven handled a whip and she was eager to experience his stroke. A bit dizzy from coming so hard, she made her way along the bed, bending over the foot rail, placing her hands on the mattress and rising onto her toes to show Steven nice, straight legs and a properly offered bottom. He gave it a couple of playful slaps, for which she thanked him, then felt under her for the wetness and hardness he expected to find there. He wasn't disappointed.

"I've been wanting to do this since I first saw you," he said, squaring off to her right.

"Then you needn't wait any longer, Sir," Jacqui said brightly.

Steven's first stroke was crisp but not too deep, sweeping up from underneath to catch Jacqui across the crease of both buttocks. Letting the impact ripple through, she thanked him, suggesting he could go harder.

Steven took careful aim and laid on the first six strokes, neatly spaced as always, across the twin ovals of Jacqui's tail. They were sharp and she jumped slightly with each, but stayed in position, thanking him every time and asking for another. He switched sides and repeated the exercise. Jacqui's fair skin marked instantly, but Steven rightly suspected the stripes would fade quickly. Young bodies repair minor damage with an ease that he'd come to envy.

O watched, eyes gleaming, enjoying the view she never could when he did this to her. It wasn't the same in the mirror. In the room's muted light, Steven's movements were fluid and graceful and Jacqui's wide-eyed surprise at each impact, followed by a shudder and the pursing of her lips, made a charming spectacle.

He improved it further, ordering her to turn around, stand up straight and grab the rail. Knowing what was coming, Jacqui tilted her head back and braced, legs spread wide and breasts thrust forward. Steven worked his way down the front of her body, now broken out in a light sheen of sweat.

Starting on the upper curves of her breasts he spaced the lashes closely, getting a credible squeal out of her with two rapid blows right across the nipples. Her stomach was nice and springy, the thin whip ricocheting off each time, leaving behind a bright crimson streak. Jacqui knew where he was going with this and didn't shy away, tilting her pelvis up to provide a better target. With a quick snap, Steven caught her just across the clit, wringing out a cry of surprise, pain and exhilaration.

Panting and looking down at her new souvenirs, she begged to suck his cock in gratitude. O crawled down to watch as Jacqui sank to the floor and took Steven's entire length into her face while he shrugged off his robe.

This time, Jacqui needed no guidance applying herself to her work with every flourish O had taught her. She even dared to bat her eyes up at Steven, lacing her fingers behind her head so O could hold her hands while he throat-fucked her.

Jacqui's mouth was soft, wet and yielding. Thanks to O's precise instructions, he knew how to use it to the best advantage now, teasing Steven a moment or two between gulps to the back of her throat. Steven knew if he wanted to claim his prize in any other way, he'd need to do it soon.

Ordering her to climb onto the bed and lie down, he joined the two of them, holding himself off Jacqui's graceful, freshly striped body so O could open her up and guide him in. O rolled back on her side to watch Steven settle over Jacqui's lean frame, slowly pumping and grinding on top of her. Jacqui matched his movements expertly.

O had never watched Jacqui fuck a man outside the studio, but she wasn't at all surprised to find her as skilled and accommodating a mount for Steven as she had been for O after that first whipping up at Marie's. Jacqui's conscious desires might revolve around women, much as O's did, but like O when it came down to brutal carnality, she had a strong a taste for pure XY.

Wrapping her legs around Steven's back like a boa constrictor, she pulled him in as far as she could, gasping and pleading for harder, faster, deeper penetration. Steven was pleased to oblige, pinning Jacqui to the smooth sheets under the full weight of his massive frame. O rolled over to pinch Jacqui's nose and kiss her the way they both liked. It worked as expected. Soon as she could draw a breath, she was begging Steven for another climax.

Lifting off and gripping her collar so he could watch, Steven granted her wish. He was pleased by the way she kept her eyes open and her face still to let him see her have it. He felt her tense under him inside and out, heard her invoke various deities as she convulsed. Jacqui was, as O had observed in the studio, a most fuckable girl.

Like all of Marie's girls, Jacqui was on Norplant and immune to the risk of pregnancy. Rather than finishing in her mouth, which was where slaves most often received their masters' tributes, or even turning her over and using her ass in the manner for which he was known, he exploded inside her like a lover, the two of them clutching each other while he pumped her full of hot liquid in what seemed an endless series of gushing thrusts.

O stroked his back lightly, gazing affectionately at the two of them. She knew Jacqui was no threat to her situation, being already intended for another owner, but wouldn't have worried about Steven's obvious affection for her anyway. Long ago O had decided that she would never need anyone or anything badly enough to fear their loss.

When Steven finally fell onto his back, O scrambled over for a taste, sucking Steven clean and conveying their combined juices from Steven's cock to Jacqui's lips.

That night, with O's raw back turned to the wall, they slept in a tight knot, O's face to Jacqui's bosom, Jacqui's bottom in Steven's lap, his arms around them both. With the flip of a switch before losing consciousness, he lowered the shades on the twinkling lights of the city outside. All three of them would be back out in the thick of it tomorrow, but for now, there was silence and rest, accepted without hesitation.

CHAPTER THIRTY-TWO

O woke up alone to the sound of the shower blasting in Steven's bathroom. Though she wasn't as miserable as expected, her back still burned and her nose still felt as if she'd stolen it from a circus clown. Worse than either was the generalized muscle soreness from the sheer tension of staying still through her trials the day before.

And somewhere under that, not yet as obvious as the physical sensations through the haze of regaining consciousness, was the awareness of having been permanently changed. The word "permanent" about anything, even a hairstyle, made O shudder. The changes to her body were both more extensive and far closer to the original meaning of the word than anything that might befall a head of hair. Even if her scalp had been shaved, she'd still eventually go back to looking the way she had before. That could never happen again.

For the rest of her life, everyone who saw her naked would know she was owned, or at least had been. At that thought, she found her right hand sliding between her thighs. She might be in no condition to do anything about it but she was definitely wet.

O assumed Steven and Jacqui were fooling around in the shower, but he emerged from the dressing room alone and cleared for departure in the kind of suit he favored for court appearances: a charcoal-gray flannel so dark it was almost black, single-breasted with peaked lapels, and a double-breasted vest with a heavy silver watch chain disappearing into one pocket. He'd paired a rich purple tie with an equally royal shirt, made more so by a white spread collar. His purple wingtips were a bit daring for the halls of justice, but Steven never worried about attracting attention. His jacket was still draped over his arm as he joined O on the bed for a kiss good-bye.

No longer drowsy, she surrendered to it. An accessory to Steven's ensemble suddenly caught her attention like a bucket of cold water in the face as its cold metal surface touched her breast.

Steven was wearing a gun, a small automatic in a shoulder rig that crossed the back of his vest. He looked like a bad guy in a particularly lavish gangster movie. She half expected him to call her "doll-face" when he asked how she was feeling.

"No worse than if I'd been hit by the Blue Line, Sir," she said, sitting up with a theatrical yawn and stretch. The sheets fell away, inviting Steven to greet her breasts with an additional kiss for each.

Eyes clear, brows raised, she pointed at the automatic.

"What's that for?"

"Shooting people."

"Anyone in particular today?"

"Try though I did to avoid it, I have to go to court this morning."

"Don't they have metal detectors or something?"

"I hand it to the security guard before I go through. They know I've got a carry card."

"Hardly seems like you'd need it in a courthouse."

"Darling, courthouses are full of shady people. How do you think they end up there? I figured Marie would have told you by now about how I got the hole through my shoulder."

"She did."

The rushing water had stopped in the bathroom, replaced by the sound of a blow dryer.

O asked if she could have a look at Steven's weapon, a request he was unlikely to refuse in any context. He drew the automatic from its holster, checked the red safety-bar and popped out the magazine. He locked back the slide to make sure the chamber was empty before offering the gun to O.

It was a sleek little piece, art deco lines updated with rubber grips. Deeply blued, there was nothing flashy, or even particularly intimidating about it. O knew Steven wouldn't pull it to make a point. He might have a flashy fountain pen tucked away for that, but this thing was all business.

O hefted it, finding it lighter than expected. It hardly seemed capable of doing the job.

"It doesn't."

Steven held up the magazine.

"What's in here does the job. Three-eighty hollow-points. They spread on impact. Still doesn't have the stop of my Glock Forty but I hate the way that thing distorts the line of a good suit."

"I've seen one of these before," O said, releasing the slide and carefully holding it out at right angles from Steven so she could site down the barrel.

"It's German, isn't it?

"Sort of. It's a Walther PPK/S, an older model, fabricated in Virginia with German parts after Interarms bought out the original manufacturer. It shoots pretty flat for something with a four-inch barrel, though it does feel a little like a grenade going off in your hand. I didn't know you were such an enthusiast. We'll have to go out to the range some time and rip up paper."

"Sounds like fun, Sir. Maybe we can take Ray and Jacqui."
Steven smiled.

"That's my girl. Eyes on the prize all the time."

She looked up at him seriously, about to risk a question that might trespass on forbidden territory.

"What was it like?"

"When I shot that guy? Ever been in a car crash?"

"Once. I was driving an old VW on a gravel road outside Aspen with some silly boy. We hit a loose patch coming around a curve and I lost it. Did a couple of donuts and wound up in a ditch. Lucky we went off the low side."

"When the wheels broke away, did time seem to slow down?"

O nodded.

"It was very quiet. I tried to get the car back under control but everything seemed to be working backwards."

"In a truly mortal situation," Steven said, "your brain slows down to buy you a little extra time. It's a survival adaptation. That way if there's something you can do you've got a few heartbeats to make it happen. It felt like that when I saw the first shot coming. I had time to lunge sideways and make a grab for his hand. Unfortunately, real-time and processing-time are always slightly out of sync, which is how he managed to ding me before I put him down."

"Marie says you murdered him."

"Fortunately, the grand jury disagreed."

They were smiling when Jacqui shambled in with a towel draped around her hips. Seeing the gun in O's hand, she stopped short.

"Is this a bad time?" she asked cautiously.

"No worries. Just checking it out."

She gave the pistol back to Steven who carefully wiped all its metal surfaces with a corner of the sheet before reloading it and returning it to its holster.

"As your lawyer, I advise you never to leave your prints on someone else's gun."

O promised to bear it mind. Steven turned to Jacqui.

"I have to take Dr. Evil in front of the judge today," he explained. "Unless you have other plans, I'd appreciate it if you stayed here and tried to make O pretend she's lazy while I'm gone. Plenty of water and nothing strenuous, okay?"

Jacqui gave him a half-naked salute.

"Aye, aye captain. I'll lash her to the mast if she tries to do any work."

"Good girl. And thanks for last night."

Steven stood up, shrugged on his jacket, straightened the lapels and gave Jacqui a kiss. She slipped him some tongue, which he repaid with a bit of friendly fondling.

"Aren't you forward, young miss?" he scolded good-naturedly.

"Yes, Sir. I deserve a whipping for my impertinence."

The marks from the previous night's entertainment, intensified by the heat, of the shower, still showed clearly across Jacqui's breasts and bottom.

"The judge won't wait so your correction will have to. And don't try talking O into giving it to you instead. I'm sure you'd succeed."

Then he was gone. His broad back, jacket lying across his shoulders dead smooth, disappeared toward the front door. Jacqui flopped down on the bed with her head in O's lap. O casually traced the welts on Jacqui's breasts.

"What was that all about?" Jacqui asked.

"The thing with the gun? Just curiosity. Steven lives in a very different world from ours. I think he belongs there."

As usual, Marie had been absolutely right. Steven had described the whole episode in purely mechanical terms. He really did appear to have no emotional response whatsoever to having deliberately killed a man. If he'd ever lost an instant's sleep over it, no one would have known.

Where Marie had found that chilling, it reassured O. Clearly, Steven was extraordinarily adept at compartmentalizing things, another trait he and O shared. She did, however, have to accept the reality that Marie could not. It was just possible that the sight of his departing back would be the last O would ever have of him. That was the price. O had understood all her life that everything came with one.

"I wouldn't want to belong anyplace you had to go armed," Jacqui said.

O patted her on the head.

"Very sensible. Coffee?"

"Already made."

O felt achy and woozy getting out of bed, and Jacqui was extremely careful draping her in the light dressing gown of pale blue silk O kept for sleepovers at Steven's. Random blooms of color had seeped through the big gauze patch on O's lower back overnight.

It was sunny and warm in that unpredictable way so they took their coffee on the deck. While O peered through the giant binoculars, Jacqui put on her geek glasses and read the latest gossip blogs aloud from her tablet.

Afterward, they retired to the bathroom where Jacqui tentatively washed O down with the hand shower, a sponge, and some lovely blue gel that smelled like the ocean. Once soaked, the gauze patch fell away onto the wet floor of the shower, revealing O's new artwork. Jacqui let out a gasp, causing O to look over her shoulder in alarm.

"Everything okay back there?"

Jacqui stared at the tattoo, wide-eyed.

"It's incredible. You have to see it."

Taking O by the shoulders, she turned her so her back was reflected in the mirrored wall opposite the glass cube of the shower.

It was quite a sight. The freshly applied ink stood out in vivid color, highlighted by the angry redness of the surrounding flesh. It looked more like an engraving than a tattoo.

"I gotta get a picture of this," Jacqui said, darting for the doorway.

"Use the Leica in my bag," O called after her.

Gazing in the mirror as best she could, O was a little dizzy at the realization of how far she'd gone on this excursion. Steven's mark was big and bold, like him. O noticed that the very top of the banner where she bore his brand fell just below the hemline of the corsets O favored. She smiled, remembering a dress she had with a back plunge so low that his initials would be revealed. She made a mental note to be sure and wear it the next time they went out for an elegant dinner.

That would probably happen before her septum piercing was sufficiently healed to take a ring, but if she could wear that too, she would. O felt curiously liberated. She'd never have to explain herself again. Everything was right there on the label now. Warming her breasts under the falling water, she cautiously reached up and swiveled the retainer down as Lola had shown her. It was surprisingly painless.

Jacqui returned, camera in hand, to find O standing in front of the double sinks with a big smile on her face, admiring the tiny black spikes sticking out of her nostrils. Pulling O under the large skylight in the middle of the bathroom and making her pose naked with lank, wet hair, Jacqui snapped away, capturing the newly ornamented goddess just emerged from the water.

O had no blood sister, only a brother from whom she was estranged over his willingness to be whatever his father wanted him to be. But she did have Jacqui, and she was happier about it than she thought prudent. After all, she would soon have to give Jacqui away. At least she'd still be nearby, and O really couldn't imagine Ray keeping them apart. He wasn't possessive and had never been able to refuse O much of anything, which had been part of the problem.

It was a problem she knew she would never have with Steven. He was generous and flexible but after all arguments were heard, his rulings were final.

While Steven greased the wheels of justice, Jacqui and O spent the first of many days together. O sat at the kitchen counter, robe at half-mast, while Jacqui, indecent in one of Steven's T-shirts, whisked her up a bacon and cheese omelet with surprising dexterity.

"I had no idea you were so good in the kitchen," O said.

"Somebody had to be. My mother thought of the kitchen as the room where they kept the ice. She wasn't much better in any other room."

"At least she knew where the kitchen was. My mother always had her drinks brought to her on a silver tray. I suppose they taste better that way."

"Family life," Jacqui said with a shrug, grinding some pepper over O's plate before sitting down with half a grapefruit, some granola topped with Greek yogurt, and a big yellow mug full of coffee the color and consistency of motor oil.

"Money makes it look easy," O said. "People and things magically appear and disappear so smoothly you'd never know there was a problem. But there always is. It's just never discussed until it can't be avoided."

"At least I know my kids won't be sitting around talking this way about me. I've been trying to get my plumbing shut off since the day I turned twenty-one. Doctors keep telling me to come back when I'm thirty."

"My doctor didn't ask me one annoying question when I had mine done. I'll put her number in your phone."

"It'll be nice to ditch the Norplant. My body pumps out plenty of hormones by itself."

"If you really don't want kids, it's a lot more convenient this way."

Jacqui shook her head emphatically.

"Definitely do not want kids. I've done all the caretaking I need to for this life."

O raised her eyebrows pensively.

"I never thought about it that way. I just knew I shouldn't have children."

O was right. She shouldn't have children. Just as she'd learned to make an omelet, Jacqui had learned to keep things light and fun but she always saw more than she let on.

O suggested they drop by the magazine office to see how Jacqui's cover was coming along and show Ray O's new tattoo.

Jacqui asked if that was wise.

"Why shouldn't it be?"

"I'll bet it makes him want to fuck you."

"Ray and Steven aren't like that. They don't piss on each other's territory. If anyone's going to be fucking Ray, it's you."

Jacqui swirled her coffee and cocked an eyebrow.

"I know it's going to happen sooner or later. Will I like it?

"He's a terrific fuck."

"Like Steven?" Jacqui asked hopefully.

"Ray's a little more playful, but I wouldn't underestimate him."

"I'm afraid he might be too sensitive for me."

O admitted that had concerned her too at first.

"But the way you'll be with him it won't matter."

"And how will I be with him?"

O looked Jacqui in the eyes with a chilling certitude.

"On your knees as his slave, like I am with his brother. That's the arithmetic."

"Of having you."

"Exactly. As my sister slave you get privileges with me no one else does. And if you can keep Ray happy, which isn't all that difficult, I can be so very helpful to you in all kinds of ways."

No woman had ever spoken to Jacqui with such cold candor but if that threw her, she wasn't about to let it show. She got up, came around to stand behind O and casually dipped her hands into O's robe, finding the big rings to play with.

"You're very persuasive, aren't you?"

"I can be," O agreed. "When something's important to me."

"I'm flattered ... I think."

Jacqui didn't sound very flattered.

"Let me see if I have this right. I'm important to you because delivering me up to Ray will please your Master."

"More or less."

O finished her last bites, letting Jacqui's hands go where they wanted.

"And in return for that, I get you and all the wonderful things you and Steven can do for me."

"Do you have a better plan?"

O gently extracted Jacqui from her robe by the wrists, which she held in a surprisingly firm grip.

"You're a very bright girl, Jacqui. I've seen you at the computer. I'll bet you could have a real career in the real world. But you're a lazy stoner and not as different from your mother as you wish. Right now, the camera is your best friend but eventually you'll need some other friends if you want that nice little ranch back in Wyoming."

Jacqui's eyes narrowed.

"You'd be surprised how many offers like that come my way."

"No, I wouldn't. But I know you won't take them because whoever comes with them can't satisfy you. It may require all three of us, but we might just manage."

Jacqui contemplated her granola.

"In a funny kind of way, I've always thought of myself as property ... my own. What kind of upkeep do I need? How do I show myself off best? What's the most I can charge for renting myself out on a job? How much wear and tear will there be if I say yes? I guess I'd call myself a rental property. I kind of like being my own landlord."

"That won't be a problem. Strange as it seems, I wouldn't call either Steven or Ray controlling men in that fucked up way. Neither of them is possessive. They don't mind helping out with work if they see an opportunity for you, but they have exactly no interest in managing your outside life. They're content to take one part of you and let the rest of it be."

Jacqui patted herself between the legs and laughed.

"It's a pretty important part."

"Neither of them care what you do with it when they're not using it. They have much better boundaries than most boys."

Jacqui finished her coffee with a long gulp.

"Okay, I'm on board this far. Let's go say hello to my new lord and Master. I'm sure he wants a look at your ink while it's still fresh."

O, having planned a day off after what she'd presumed would be an ordeal, had no other obligations.

They both dressed casually for the visit, which in O's case meant a simple Anne Fontaine blouse, a short jacket with a peplum, a slim black skirt and medium heels. It took O longer to apply what she considered minimal makeup than it took Jacqui to get back into the clothes she'd worn the day before. Each in her own way dressed for herself, and not to the expectations of others.

Despite having been parked in Steven's garage for two weeks, O's Mini fired right up, its eager little engine hungry for some asphalt. Jacqui was glad O was a sensible driver. The small coupe was obviously a sleeper just from the way it rocketed up the ramp and out into the gray afternoon.

The slate sky seemed like good weather for Nina Simone. O clicked through the CDs until she found "I Put a Spell On You." They sang along to it. O had never heard Jacqui sing before. It was a pleasant surprise. She could growl on key more convincingly than O would have predicted.

Ray wasn't alone in his office when O and Jacqui arrived. O was always astonished to find Albert there or anywhere other than home, but always pleased. "Jacqui, this is Albert, the brains of the operation. He knows everything."

Albert's eyebrows shot up over his round horn-rims as stood to take Jacqui's hand and return O's embrace.

"Hello, Jacqui," he said in his most cheerful rumble. "Actually, Erasmus was the last man to know everything, back when there was less to know."

Jacqui laughed.

"I see what she means."

Ray rounded the desk to bring Eric into the circle. A boyish thirtysomething with shiny black hair and a thin mustache, he was small and solid in his lounge-lizard bowling shirt and black jeans. He had the characteristic pallor of those who lived in front of monitors. Ray announced him as *Forbidden*'s new website manager and resident tech genius (a bit prematurely, as Steven hadn't signed him onto the payroll yet), but Eric corrected that to "Consulting Geek" with a half-smile. He surveyed both women with an adolescent hunger they knew too well. Ray got on the intercom and instructed Lena to bring in the new cover proof.

"I think you're going to like this," Ray told Jacqui as Lena glided in with a slick, stiff sheet of heavy stock concealed by a routing sheet taped to the back and draped over the image. She set it down on Ray's desk and they all gathered round.

"You may recognize the model," Lena said in her customary tone of cultivated irony.

Flipping back the cover sheet, she revealed Jacqui hanging in the cage during the interrogation shoot. The caption next to Jacqui's worried face read: "Dear God, What Will They Do To Me Now?"

Albert liked the light kick at the back. O thought the color looked a little gray, but she was happy with the composition. Eric just stared, saying nothing.

Jacqui frowned.

"You promised to Photoshop the fat off my thighs," she said with exasperation.

O said she'd looked but couldn't find any. Jacqui pointed at the openings where her legs stuck out between the bars.

"See those bulges down there?" she demanded.

O sighed wearily.

"You're sitting on steel bars. We want to see them pressing into your flesh. If I'd rounded your legs completely you'd look like a Barbie doll."

"I really like the expression," Ray offered by way of distraction. Jacqui looked up at him anxiously.

"Are you sure? Do I look scared enough? I could have done it bigger, see?"

Jacqui's eyes grew huge and round, her jaw dropping open in a silent scream. Laughing, Ray jumped back theatrically.

"Whoa! That's too *Police Gazette* for our guys."

"This is fine," O said. "I wanted frightened and pathetic and aroused and you gave me that, as always."

O looked up at Ray.

"But I'm not thrilled with the color. I think it's a little muddy."

"I can have the prep house saturate the skin tone a bit more."

O hadn't yet taken a picture with which she was entirely pleased. If she had, she would probably have quit shooting by now.

Eric cleared his throat uncomfortably, looking up at Jacqui in her baggy bohemian disguise, trying to make the mental connection between the girl in the office and the luscious captive in the image.

O put the cover sheet back down and handed the proof to Lena.

"Promise me you'll remind him about the skin tone," O said. It was not a request. Lena promised, heading straight back to her office next door.

"Okay," Ray announced, "We've shown you ours. Now you show us yours."

O looked around the room. She had no problem displaying Steven's tag to Ray, and Jacqui had already seen it. Albert was an old friend with whom she'd shared many hotel rooms. No worries there. But the way this young stranger gawked at her had the unusual effect of making O self-conscious. No matter. As Steven's slave she still owed obedience to the brother who had surrendered her to him.

"Jacqui, help me out."

O bent over and put her hands on Ray's desk. Jacqui tugged O's blouse up out of the skirt, which she unzipped and pulled down past O's thighs. O held up the hems of the blouse and jacket so she was completely bare from mid-back to knee. The air went out of the room.

There was nothing quite like a fresh tattoo – the ink so dense, the flesh so obviously scribed, so swollen and angry. Eventually the body would accept what had been done to it and begin reclaiming its violated terrain like a slowly encroaching jungle. The swelling would subside and the colors would dim until the design appeared to have to have been there since O was born. In some sense, that would be true. But today it glowed like a neon sign.

"Nobody does those white highlights like Jan," Albert observed, as always, the connoisseur of everything.

Ray felt the cold hand of melancholia grip his heart for an instant but he kept it out of his voice.

"It makes a strong statement," he said after an uncomfortably long silence. O wiggled her ass at him a bit cruelly.

"But will it make your brother want to spread my cheeks?" she asked in a falsely ingenuous tone.

"I doubt he needs much encouragement to do that."

Ray had seen Steven spread the ass-cheeks of many other girls over the years. He wanted O to remember that.

Looking under her arm, O caught Eric's mesmerized gaze. She wasn't sure he'd fit in here or that she wanted him too. O enlisted Jacqui's help again, zipping her back up and tucking her back in. Turning to face the room, O bowed ironically for a short round of applause.

"You should show them the nose thing," Jacqui said.

Why not? Sliding a finger gently into each flared nostril, O flipped down the tiny black prongs of the retainer. Ray couldn't help smiling.

"You really did go through with it."

"When have you ever known me not to go through with something I said I'd do?"

Ray gave the matter some serious thought, stroking his chin whiskers and looking up at the ceiling. "Well, basically, never," he conceded.

Albert joked that there was something oddly diabolical about the tiny niobium tusks, as if they really belonged on top of her head. O accused him of knowing her too long.

Eric had had enough and more. Looking like he was fighting a panic attack, he grabbed his leather jacket, mumbled something about enjoying meeting the girls and departed with a promise to have a blueprint for the website in hand when they met with Steven.

"I think you blew his lights out," Ray said after the door shut behind Eric.

"I don't like the way he looks at me," O said flatly. "He's one of those guys who blames me for wanting what he wants."

"A problem you'll never have with my brother," Ray laughed.

Ray understood the appeal of Steven's guiltless embrace of his own vices. He didn't judge himself or anyone else for who or what they were, only for the things they did – a much more forgiving standard. He might want to pierce O and mark her but he had no desire to fix her whatsoever.

Still drained from the day before, O wanted to go back to her own place for a bit, see familiar things and perhaps take a nap. She suggested that Jacqui have dinner with Ray.

Jacqui realized that O's suggestion was actually an order. She wasn't unhappy with the prospect of an evening getting to know Steven's mysterious sibling and O conveniently left her no choice, patting her butt as she kissed her good-bye.

"Keep Ray entertained," O admonished. "I haven't been alone with Steven in a long time."

Jacqui promised to do her best, and O was sure that would be more than adequate. Delighting in showing Jacqui around his slick little empire, Ray introduced her to Jasper and they all looked at the final edit of Jacqui's layout. Aside from what Jacqui deemed some goofy expressions on her part, they all agreed it was incendiary. Jacqui asked a lot of smart questions about the software they used to design the pages.

Albert joined them for dinner at the Thai restaurant around the corner from the office where the waitresses put out their own pin-up calendar every year. The place was loud and packed, but Ray and Albert were such regulars the waitress took them past a line of scowling cineastes from the ArcLight Theater and straight to a table in the back. "When did this place get to be so popular?" Ray asked with some annoyance as they slid into a round, pink-vinyl booth with Jacqui in the middle.

"It's the whole neighborhood, pal," Albert said. "Creeping Disneyfication's turned it into a province of BH."

"I liked it better when it was seedy and dangerous. You could actually afford to live here. Remember when I had the place up on Las Palmas? We'd hit The Frolic and then head on over to Jumbo's Clown room."

Jacqui made a face.

"Jumbo's? Ewww."

"Ray only went there on week nights to watch the feature dancers from The Valley try out their new acts before going on the road. He did the back room at Sin-a-Matic on weekends," Albert explained.

Jacqui had heard about Sin-a-Matic, the last funky kink performance venue before slicker operations like Bar Sinister flooded the scene with tourists from over the hill – all gothed-out for the kind of S&M the Old Guard dismissed as "standing and modeling."

"I used to do live shows there back in the day," Ray said nostalgically. "It was amazing what they let us get away with."

"The place was always packed," Albert recalled with a shudder. "Ray dragged me there when I first moved to L.A. It smelled like a subway entrance and the music made your ears bleed, but Ray ruled the performance space. One night he split the whole room down the middle and had half the crowd lean against the wall. Then he made them drop trow while the other half worked out on them with floggers. Everyone did the flogger on the belt thing in those days. Thank god that's over. He got them all flourishing Florentines in unison. It sounded like the hull of a slave galley in there."

Jacqui found herself warming to Ray more every minute.

"I used to work at The Box in New York," she told them after Ray ordered a round of Singhas, some chicken sate and a plate of spring rolls.

"That place down in the old meat-packing district?"

Albert really did know everything.

"The one and only," Jacqui confirmed. "We did the dirtiest burlesque in town."

Ray shook his head.

"Damn! Sorry I missed your act."

Jacqui leaned in against his shoulder.

"I give an even better show in private."

"You're inspiring some very impure thoughts, young lady," Ray cautioned with a broad grin. Jacqui could put on a casual flirt with the best of them, and he appreciated it for what it was.

She turned to Albert.

"What's he good at?"

"Everything but fire play. That's a hard limit," Albert said with a smirk.

"Yeah, well, after I set my hair on fire that time the charm sort of went out of it," Ray admitted.

"That's on my no-list too," Jacqui said. "But I'm sure we could figure out something. I like the idea of being onstage with you."

Ray promised to give it some thought. If Jacqui became his she'd be onstage with him in one way or another for as long as they were together. That was part of what had distanced him from O.

After some tom ka kai, giant spotted prawns with lime and chili sauce, and a side of pad thai, all washed down with potent Thai beer that smelled faintly of formalin, the party split up. Walking back to the office together, Albert hunched against the evening breeze in the threadbare cashmere polo coat left over from his days at Condé Nast, they exchanged parting *abrazzos* and Jacqui climbed into the BMW with Ray. She watched Albert slump into his ancient Mercedes, which chugged reluctantly to life with a puff of diesel smoke out the tailpipe.

"Your friend Albert's an interesting guy," Jacqui observed as they rumbled out of the parking lot.

Albert would have been equally odd and equally at home in Weimar Berlin or Belle Epoque Paris. He existed on his own space-time continuum.

Ray suggested Jacqui come up to his place. She'd expected that and would have been disappointed if she hadn't heard it.

CHAPTER THIRTY-THREE

Winding up Outpost Drive, Jacqui feared she might find herself someplace as grandiose as Steven's. The relatively modest scale of Ray's mid-century-modern hillside redoubt was a relief, but she was duly impressed by the sweeping, basin-wide panorama it commanded. Metro L.A. lay below like a blanket of Christmas lights as far as the eye could see. Ray might not have Steven's proud tower in the town, but he had just as commanding a view. And when they got out of the car, the surroundings smelled as good as they looked – balsam and jasmine untainted by airborne grime.

"Nice up here," Jacqui said as Ray came around to walk her in. "Must have taken forever to find it."

Ray drank in a deep breath of night air.

"It was the first place I looked at. Pure luck. I didn't even have to arm-wrestle Steven for the down payment. He knows valuable property when he sees it."

"I guess that's why O has the tattoo on her back."

"I was pretty shocked by it. Steven doesn't even get his shirts monogrammed. He's starting to worry me."

Jacqui laughed.

"Yeah, well, don't get any ideas. I have to show my back for a living. And my front. And everything in between."

"So I've noticed."

Ray unlocked the door and Jacqui stepped into the spacious, glass-paneled living room ahead of him. Taking a quick inventory of Ray's modest comforts, Jacqui felt immediately at ease.

"Not much like Steven's roost is it?"

"Yes and no. You have your own idea of luxury."

Spotting an antique brass telescope near the window, she went straight to it, putting her eye to the viewfinder. "He's got something like this too."

"The older I get, the more I'm convinced that a lot more stuff is genetic than people like to think. He and I once showed up at our mother's house wearing identical shoes. She thought it was hilarious."

Jacqui turned to look at him directly, saying what she thought O would have said.

"I'm sure you're alike in a lot of ways."

"Only the important ones."

He came close.

"Time to retire the hippie princess for now."

Jacqui recognized the easy authority in Ray's voice. That too was something he and Steven shared.. Exactingly trained by Marie, Jacqui knew just how it all went from there.

"Yes, Sir," she said softly, raising the loose-fitting sweater over her slender belly and pink-tipped breasts. Ray watched her studied movements as she went to the ovoid couch, folded the sweater to drape over one arm and then sat down to remove her boots before shedding her tight jeans with minimal wriggling. She folded those and put them on top of the sweater, leaving her hat for last. When finished she slipped into a proper, open-legged kneeling position, put her hands behind her head and lowered her eyes.

Ray was free to look at her as long as he liked. After doing so without a trace of shyness, he came over to tilt her head back with a finger under the chin.

"I think you have the best face of any model we've ever shot."

"My ears are too big, Sir."

Ray flipped back Jacqui's auburn hair to reveal them.

"Bet they hear really well."

Jacqui knew better than to respond. She remained silently in place while Ray went to a blonde wood cabinet and opened its double doors. Daring a peek, Jacqui saw it was mirrored inside and hung with all the whips, cuffs, straps and other gear Ray might use on her. From O she knew in detail what Steven enjoyed, but O had been less forthcoming about Ray, other than to reassure her there would be no unpleasant.

"Do you like rope?" Ray asked as if it were a menu entrée.

"Smoking it or wearing it, Sir?"

"Both."

"I would say it depends on the quality in either case, Sir."

Oh dear, that came out snippier than intended, but Ray just laughed. He wasn't as strict about protocol as either Steven or Marie. He'd been laughing at rules all his life, including his own.

"I think we'll measure up, miss. Can you roll a decent joint?"

Ray directed Jacqui to the bright-yellow airtight plastic dive box in the kitchen cupboard where he kept his Indica. It was quite entertaining watching her get it on tiptoe with her hands folded behind her neck. Ray could enjoy the luxury of being lazy about matters of form was because others around him weren't. Jacqui deliberately put the box down on a low table so she could bend over and give Ray something nice to look at while she worked. Ray could not deny that Jacqui's lady parts were even prettier in person.

"Thump or sting?" he asked.

"Definitely sting, Sir, although thump can work if it's hard enough."

Ray had a tough time turning his attention from her, but his plans required concentration. There was a finely made faux fox-fur throw just a bit brighter in color than Jacqui's hair to be spread on the floor, a mile of boiled hemp in various lengths to be laid out and a pair of pro-grade paramedic scissors to get her free of it in a hurry if necessary. Jacqui eyed him surreptitiously through the V of her long legs, which she kept straight, remaining *en demi-pointe* as she'd been taught. The better she did her part of the act, the finer the performance she'd inspire in return.

Much of what Ray chose from the cabinet was familiar. There was the inevitable wand vibe, already plugged mated to a long yellow stinger Ray jacked into a wall socket. There was a handsome pair of well-worn floggers, heavy and black, finished with Turk's head knots at the handles. Ray's simple broad-head riding crop was nothing fancy but it looked well loved. Jacqui felt a little shiver and a surge of wetness when the rattan came out.

Jacqui liked things dirtier and more painful than her angelic face led some people to believe. The black clover clamps held together by a short chain and the ball-ended steel hook, not unlike the one that hung in Steven's back room, were reassuring. Whatever the differences between Ray and Steven, both understood that submissive women weren't fragile.

With everything laid out along the edge of the fur throw to Ray's satisfaction he turned his full attention to Jacqui, who dropped to her knees and offered up the finished joint, along with a souvenir lighter she'd found in the box from a strip club in Vegas. Steven liked ornamental things. Ray liked practical things. And he was nothing if not direct. Firing the joint, he slipped the lighter into the pocket of his jeans and directed Jacqui to unbutton his fly.

"With my hands or with my teeth, Sir?"

"Hands would be quicker," he said. Running her palm up his leg, Jacqui wasn't surprised to find something nice and hard, something she wanted to see. While Ray filled his lungs, Jacqui worked her way down, one brass button at a time, not hurrying or fumbling. She'd had a lot of practice at this.

Nevertheless, she was surprised by the aggressive rigidity of what popped out in her face. O had said she wouldn't be disappointed. It was a handsome unit and she couldn't think of anyplace it wouldn't fit nicely. It was always flattering for a naked girl on her knees to be greeted with such enthusiasm. That was, after all, what she meant to inspire by being down there in the first place.

"Nice," she said simply.

"Glad you approve. It's the only one I've got."

Ray skimmed off his black-silk gabardine T-shirt, revealing his smooth but not ostentatiously muscular gut, and tossed it aside. He told Jacqui to keep her hands behind her head and held the joint down in front of her face so she could take a hit. When she exhaled, Ray gave her permission to suck him. She went right to work with all the art and eagerness an inspired professional can deliver. Every few strokes, Ray pulled her head away by the hair and gave her another hit.

Whatever hesitations Ray had about the larger situation he certainly enjoyed this part. Fellatio from a pretty girl was never a bad thing, but it was even better from a girl he realized he'd begun to like. Had they met some other way they'd probably still have ended up right here. When Ray mumbled something about an ashtray, Jacqui playfully raised a hand to catch the warm debris from the burning weed. After each pass, she looked up at him with increasingly pleading eyes. He promised her she wouldn't go long un-fucked.

But first, she would be tied. No, Ray didn't do this with all the girls. He had put some time into learning how to do rope and saved his skills for those who could appreciate them.

When the joint was smoked down to a roach, he gave it to Jacqui to put into to the bright, ceramic, deltoid-shaped receptacle on the coffee table while he sat on one end of the couch and worked his way out of his boots and jeans. He was lean and muscular, like his brother, but without the theatrically over-developed shoulders that made Steven appear so massive. She generally liked her boys a bit more delicate anyway, but the delicacy had to be balanced with flexible strength.

Once naked, Ray had her stand in the middle of the room and fold her arms behind her back. Jacqui obeyed with her legs wide open. Much as she expected, he grabbed her by the crotch with a pleasing rudeness and pulled her close for a long, hard kiss. She'd been similarly greeted by on more than one occasion. It was sort of strange doing her lover's master's brother, and good nasty fun. Whatever similarities she observed, she would be smart enough to keep to herself. She wasn't surprised to find Ray a good kisser too.

Ray liked the teasing way Jacqui moved subtly out of position to rub her thigh up and down his leg. It was the kind of liberty he never discouraged. He didn't worry about being respected in the morning.

Following his hard-on across the room, he snatched up a long coil of rope, undid the hitch and spun it out toward Jacqui like a party streamer. He worked quickly and confidently, his touch just a bit rough when he moved her this way or that as he rigged a simple but elegant chest harness above and below her breasts. He cinched it in the middle to give her flesh a little squeeze before taking the loose ends over her shoulders to secure her crossed arms in the small of her back.

The clover clamps were a nice decorative touch, but Jacqui gritted her teeth even though he put them on expertly, slowly allowing the jaws to close where the pink of her aureoles met the whiteness of her breast-flesh. This type of clamp always bit hard and any tugging on the chain made each one even tighter. He proved that while kissing her some more.

Jacqui held perfectly still, noting the little things visible to someone who had spent a lot of time in bondage. His hands were warm and smooth. He didn't pinch or scratch her. The rope had been thoroughly treated and was much softer than it looked. She could feel the confidence in his touch.

Ray held her up to him by the clamp chain and rubbed his cock against her concave belly. His other hand found her quite wet, inspiring him to get her more so. Padding her shoulders with a leather cushion from the sofa, he laid her out on the fur throw and tasted, starting with the tender flesh extruded by the chest harness. Jacqui's moan turned into a cute squeak when he removed the clamps. The fuckers always hurt worse coming off than going on, but Jacqui was soon distracted in other ways.

From the minute his mouth made contact with Jacqui's lubricated machinery, his skill and dedication were evident. No licking or flicking for him. He tucked in between Jacqui's thighs as if to a banquet. Jacqui's arms were restrained but her legs soon wrapped around the back of Ray's neck as he lapped and sucked happily away. His hand crawled up her body, tweaking her tortured nipples through the clamps hard enough to hurt. He felt her shaking thighs grip his bearded face and heard a sweetly desperate plea for leave to come. He detached himself only long enough to grant permission.

Jacqui's orgasms were lovely from any angle. She made pretty, happy submissive girl noises, her whole body stiffening but staying still in the moment. No thrashing, howling histrionics of the type Ray instantly recognized as professional performance. Jacqui could certainly do all that for the camera, but in private she was pleasingly unaffected, a refreshing change from too many of the partners Ray tended to meet through the job.

She certainly didn't hold back, though. Squirming in her harness, Jacqui suddenly clamped Ray's head between her knees, jammed her bones to his face and let out a cry.

Far from done, Jacqui pleaded for cock and got some. After rather rudely applying a layer of silicone slick to Jacqui's pink tissues, internal and external, Ray raised her legs to rest against his shoulders and slipped in. As much as her trussed upper body would allow, Jacqui rose to meet him. He was pleased to find her a nice snug fit yet deep enough to accommodate him fully and comfortably, at least in this position. He just stayed there a moment, appreciating Jacqui's gamine charms and stroking her nicely tended feet. Then he initiated a slow, deep drilling that went on until Jacqui began swinging her hips and pushing up harder.

Ray had lots more to do, and this was just a prelude, meant to establish right away that Jacqui could and would be penetrated at his whim. Ray had met people who made a point of telling him that their BDSM "wasn't all about sex." He had no clue what else it could be about, ever. The two were as intertwined as the next set of ropes Ray intended to apply. But first, poor, desperate Jacqui would have to have another one.

Leaving her panting on the floor, Ray stood, his rod glistening with Jacqui's juices, and kicked her legs apart. She let them lie languidly in the fur, which felt so lifelike it briefly concerned her.

"This isn't a real fur, is it, Sir?" she asked in a tone that might have turned improbably scolding, given the circumstances. But Ray had long learned that animal cruelty was a deal-breaker with women under forty.

"No. It just costs as much."

That was only a slight exaggeration. The political resistance to natural pelts had created an upper-tier market in counterfeits.

Due diligence observed, Ray went back to his ropes, wrapping them in neat double bands around Jacqui's legs starting at the ankles. She watched with some amazement as he took his time and every opportunity to caress her exposed flesh between the bands, but his erection never wavered.

Performing complex procedures without losing concentration on their purpose was the BDSM equivalent of walking and chewing gum, yet few of those who had topped her possessed that ability. At some point, she became wrists and ankles to most of them, and they had to be reminded, after all the skilled labor was done, why they'd done it.

Once the leg bands were neatly wrapped, hitched off to one another by lines that would eventually help distribute her weight without tightening, he lifted her back and wrapped her belly in corset-tight loops he hitched to the webbing running from her collar bones to her toes. Ray finished a complete body harness as casually as lacing a pair of sneakers.

He asked her how it felt. Jacqui moved what muscles she could, which weren't many, but pronounced the finished product comfortable as a hammock, suspecting from experience that Ray would use it as one.

She wasn't wrong. Going to a heavy bronze marine cleat bolted into a wood-paneled wall Ray unfurled a tight figure eight of bright-red mountain-climbing line. Looking up, Jacqui saw a set of elegant, old-fashioned pulley blocks with a big hook dangling underneath slowly descend from the high-beamed, vaulted ceiling until it hung six feet above her, swaying gently in the breeze.

A short length of hemp, wound into a tight knot with two loose ends and a loop at the top, was all it took to secure the webbing on Jacqui's body to the hoisting gear over her head. A quick trip back to the boat cleat, and Jacqui could feel the hoist take up. The bands tightened around her just enough to be pleasantly constricting. An extra yank and she was back on her toes again, digging them into the softness of the fur throw, which provided no purchase at all. Jacqui was definitely going to swing.

Watching her little dance inspired Ray even further. He gave her another searching kiss before starting in with the floggers. He used both at once, circling her slowly, slapping her all over with the multiple tails in a leisurely fashion. He wanted her to feel the weight of the leather before applying it with conviction.

These were not ordinary play whips. Like Steven's, they were Marstons, still the standard against which others were measured. The balance between the weight of the handles and that of the leather blades was so perfect they could be used with effortless accuracy and delicacy despite their length and heft.

The sharp report when Ray shot the business ends across Jacqui's backside echoed, along with her surprised yelp, in the open space of the room. She made a pleasurable purring sound deep in her throat and thanked him. He promised to go harder, orbiting Jacqui in a cloud of surging leather. She stood firm as the impacts intensified and wide pink stripes began to appear between the outlines of the ropes. Like most floggers, these didn't hurt a bit, but their physics were impressive. Jacqui felt like she was being struck with a blunt instrument that left no lingering punch.

Ray hated showy technique, so there would be no Florentines, but he did shift the handles around, sometimes firing the combined strike of both whips from one hand, other times grasping them separately and slapping them against her from front and rear simultaneously.

Jacqui was starting to reconsider her ennui about flogging, but it didn't go on long enough to produce what would have been a probable orgasm. Satisfied by the even pink blush with which he'd painted her, Ray went for the cane, flexing it in front of her face. She gulped at his wicked smile.

"This is what you asked for," her reminded her, "and I do play requests."

"Yes, Sir. I was hoping you'd remember."

Jacqui had an odd, though not uncommon, relationship with the cane. It was the instrument they all loved to hate. It bit deep and the heat from it lingered.

Even used as lightly and accurately as Ray's short, sharp snaps at the fleshy parts, it was still rather like a bee-sting. He knew some interesting spots with it too, like the sides of her breasts and the backs of her calves. Only when Jacqui began to shift around and squeeze her legs together did he start laying straight lines across her rump, making her leap up after each stroke. He timed them just right too, with ten seconds in between for the second heat wave to course through. He stopped frequently to trace the marks, kiss her passionately or put invading fingers inside her, making her plead for cock.

Ray knew when the moment was right. Jacqui could certainly have taken more and he wasn't quite done hurting her but he had something very specific in mind.

Setting aside the cane, he took the rope off belay and scooped Jacqui up in his arms, lying her down on the throw and rolling her over just roughly enough to inspire a brief attack of the giggles.

It didn't last long, ending when she felt Ray pull her ankles together behind her, attaching them securely to her upper-body webbing. It was certainly the most relaxing open-legged hogtie she'd been in, but her helplessness was absolute. There was something chilling about the gentleness and speed with which he braided her hair from behind.

Ray told her she looked very pretty with braided hair, but that was not why he'd done it. He gave her a good look at the ball-ended hook that explained it all. With rubber gloves, thick lube and wipes from the cabinet he carefully anointed her smaller hole, working his way in against the rings of muscle. Jacqui found it surprisingly easy to relax them. Good hands never failed.

Ray wove more rope, this time spliced with the braid of Jacqui's hair. The loose end was firmly secured through the eye of the hook's shank, while the cold hardness of the ball at the other end invaded her most private entrance. A few more rope wraps and Jacqui could feel the traction on her head. If she didn't keep her skull back, the hook would be pulled in deeper than she might prefer. That was the essence of predicament bondage. Whatever she suffered from it would be largely self-inflicted, but inevitably she'd have no choice.

When she felt the pulleys take up from the back on the swivel snapped into the wide waistband, everything tightened everywhere all at once. She let out a gasp but it didn't stop him. He knelt down in front of her, stroking her upraised face.

"Anything feel numb?

"No, Sir, but it's challenging."

"Ready to go airborne?"

"Will you fuck me that way?"

"What do you think?" Ray asked with a laugh.

Back at the wall he took the rope up slowly. With the mechanical advantage of the blocks, he could lift her with one hand. Jacqui squealed involuntarily as she left the floor, twisting slowly in mid-air. Face pulled back, she could see her reflection in the big windows as she rose to hang, belly down, at waist height. A few little twitches and tugs proved she wasn't going anywhere on her own.

Having been strung up this way before, she'd never felt her weight so evenly distributed without a single hotspot. Ray was quite the wizard at this. She could have appreciated his expertise at her leisure, were it not for the intrusive hook. She decided he must have gotten that idea from his brother. Steven never hesitated to enable Ray's cruelty. Steven had plenty to spare and Ray could always use a bit extra.

Walking up in front of her, he put his hands on her face. "Well?"

"If it weren't for the hook I could probably take a nap in this, Sir."

"That's why it's there. Besides, it keeps your head up nicely."

He demonstrated the point by pressing his cock against her lips, which instantly gave way. Holding the line that kept her aloft, he swung her back and forth as she sucked, taking her onto him to the choking point, holding her there just enough to produce long strings of drool dripping to the floor, then pulling her back away. Unlike Steven, who'd had little vanilla sex in his whole life, Ray could appreciate far simpler pleasures. But once he'd acquired the skills he would never again prefer those pleasures to what could be had with a bit of ingenuity.

He kept at it until Jacqui's eyes began to tear, then gave her the reward he'd promised. Turning her around a hundred and eighty degrees he made her giggle again, but the giggling stopped when he stepped in between her stretched-open legs and grabbed her by the thighs. All he had to do was walk into her. The connection actually took some of her weight off the ropes, though his grasp on the hook-line prevented her from relaxing much. He used it to sway her back and forth, slowly at first but picking up the pace as he heard her breathing quicken.

Not all, or even most, women are so easily pushed over the edge by penetration alone, but that was still how Jacqui got off most of the time. Ray shafted her hard and fast enough to bring it on almost immediately. The tension of the position only made it better, simultaneously stimulating her in a variety of places. He let her have it with just a little begging as usual, but warned that there would be a cost.

When she was done, he stepped back, picked up the cane and gave her twenty good ones, five on each foot, five on each breast and the final ten up onto her stomach, as the rigging was in the way of her behind. Jacqui, sliding into a sort of trance, thanked him for every stroke. He gave her a couple of extra swats with the flap of the crop on her most sensitive spot, extracting a surprised howl of distress, before taking matters to their logical conclusion, staking her from behind and slamming her hips against his in a steadily increasing tempo.

Jacqui's tightly packaged body, now flushed and striated nearly everywhere, never looked so inviting and her sore buttocks in his iron grip felt firm and silken, though not so much as her insides which seemed entirely liquefied. He held her off for one last, long moment before plunging in and letting go with a sharp shout.

They were both amazed at how long it went on. He'd been saving something for her without knowing it, and now she got it all. She thanked him for her reward. Ray pulled out and walked around to let her suck out the last of it before going, somewhat unsteadily, to the wall to unwrap the cleat and lower Jacqui into the soft fake fur. She lay panting in her ropes, sweat beading on her skin and Ray laid down alongside her, dragging her into his arms. Jacqui was pretty much immobilized but she could still kiss. They did that for some time before Ray fell to one side.

"You rocked it, girl," he said.

"You did all the work, Sir."

"You let it happen and that's all that's required. Let's get this stuff off you."

Grabbing the shears, the first line Ray cut was the cinch from Jacqui's hair to the hook, producing a deep sigh of relief as she swiveled her head around, stretching out her neck.

"That was the most challenging part," she said. "But I totally dug it. You could have pulled the hook out and fucked my ass if you wanted."

"Unlike my brother, I don't usually bugger girls on a first date."

The both laughed while Ray eased the steel ball out of Jacqui's plumbing and set the shiny implement to one side. He snipped her arms loose next. Jacqui stretched them out to each side, rolling her wrists while he snipped through the cinches of the body harness.

"That's what I love about bondage," Jacqui said. "It feels equally good going on or coming off."

"Your hands are still warm so it must have been reasonably manageable."

"Give yourself some credit, Sir. After the way I've been tied up this, was like getting my hair done."

"Is that good? Should I have whipped you harder?"

"You could have, but I appreciate the way you took it easy the first time. I'm afraid to tell a lot of guys what I like because they try to prove something, if you know what I mean."

"I'm afraid I do."

Ray kept on cutting, massaging Jacqui's tingling flesh where the ropes had bitten deepest.

"Do you slice up your ropes every time?"

"I'm too lazy to unwrap them all. Besides, it's more hygienic this way."

"Must cost you a fortune."

Ray laughed.

"Costs me zip. It's one of the perks of running a kink magazine. People give me stuff for free. In return, I make sure to credit our vendors on all the layouts."

"Nice deal for everybody."

"The guys who make this merchandise are friends of mine. One of our biggest advertisers started out selling gear from the trunk of his car. The magazine gave him a real boost. He's got such a jumping Internet retail business, he's talked about buying me out."

Thinking of O, Jacqui gave him an alarmed look.

"You wouldn't go along with that, would you, Sir?"

"Selling the magazine? What would I do after that? Besides, we're finally starting to make some money and as much as he doubts it, I intend to pay Steven back for staking me."

"I don't think he worries about it much."

Jacqui was right. Steven had never expected to see a dime out of anything he invested in Ray's endeavors. At first he'd refused to accept the checks that Ray had started giving him, but respecting his brother's pride he took them now without hesitation.

Finally liberated, Jacqui stood and stretched, putting on a fine show for Ray. Her entire body was laced with rope marks, streaks, and red patches. Ray pointed her toward the bathroom so she could have a look. She scurried off to the mirror and let out a delighted whoop.

"All right! Will you take my picture?"

Ray called after her.

"Sure. I'll get my camera."

"Permission to pee in the meantime, Sir?"

"By all means."

Ray got up carefully. He was well aware of what he put himself through every time he did his best work. He found the point-and-shoot he kept in the bookshelf for this kind of occasion. Jacqui left the bathroom door open, having grown accustomed to living in places where bathrooms didn't have doors. The flash of Ray's camera caught her on the toilet seat in the lovingly restored green-and-black tiled guest bath.

"You fucker!" she shouted, throwing a spare roll of toilet paper at him that he easily ducked.

"If that shows up in the magazine I'll hate you forever," she said, blotting herself.

"Why? It's not like we haven't run pictures of you pissing before."

"Pissing in makeup is one thing. Pissing after you've been wrecked is another."

"You wreck very nicely."

He leaned down and showed her the image on the camera's small screen. She appraised it professionally.

"I do like the rope marks," she admitted. "What I can't figure out is why I never get my hair to look like this any other way."

"Freshly fucked is freshly fucked," Ray said with a shrug. "It's hard to stage in the studio even if you do get the real fucking. Porno hair is like a Roman helmet."

Jacqui agreed, getting up and washing her hands while he watched her in the mirror over the sink. They stepped out into the living room and Jacqui posed for a few shots, bending over to show off the cane strokes, squeezing her breasts together in front of the lens for a close-up to make sure he caught the indentations left by the clover clamps. Ray realized that as appealing as these images were he really didn't want them in the magazine.

After Jacqui fished her smart phone out of her big bag and downloaded the images from Ray's camera, he deleted them from the chip. For the first time in a long time, it occurred to him that with Jacqui as a partner, doing some live public performance again might be fun, but until they could stage something just right he preferred to keep their time together to himself.

While he went to fetch the robes he'd ended up buying at some ridiculously expensive resort to which Steven had dragged him, Jacqui looked around Ray's quarters. They were not unlike what she would have wanted for herself, if she could afford it. When her gaze lit on his guitars in their cradles – the big Martin next to an ancient, mint-condition Strat, her eyes lit up.

"I didn't know you played," she said as he held the white terry cloth wrap open for her to snuggle into.

"It's not entirely clear that I do."

She poked him in the ribs.

"Bullshit. I'll bet you're good. You're good at everything."

"I know a couple of people who would give you an argument there."

She asked him to play something for her. He sent her off to the kitchen for some water while he tuned the Fender and turned down the volume on an ancient Pignose portable amp he'd lovingly resurrected from a dusty box of loose wires. Jacqui came back with a blue tumbler she offered him kneeling properly. He took a gulp and cleared his throat, handing the glass back to Jacqui, who rolled off her knees to sit cross-legged, looking up at him expectantly.

"What do you want to hear?"

"I don't know," Jacqui said, rolling through the long and varied play list in her head. "Just play something soft and slow."

Ray plucked a couple of strings, did a bit of fine-tuning and strummed the opening chords of "No Expectations." When he closed his eyes and started into the first verse, Jacqui broke out in gooseflesh. Listening to his strong, clear tenor, she was suddenly aware of all the heartbreak and disappointment so adroitly concealed behind Ray's casual good cheer. She realized she could listen to that voice for a long time. At last she understood how O had come to be his before he'd given her up to Steven. Unlike O, who had eventually come to feel reproached by Ray's unforced tenderness, Jacqui felt free with him, warm and comfortable wrapped in the thick robe on the floor of his hillside hideout.

Though it was improper form, she decided she would ask to stay the night when they finished playing.

Chapter Thirty-Four

Home. O wasn't sure where that was anymore. She spent more nights in Steven's bed than in her own. Having Jacqui in the luxurious guest room next to Steven's office made it even easier to let the hours pass over there.

The glory hole shoot had been exhausting. The difficulty of keeping a unit on track rose exponentially with the number of live bodies in the studio. O's tattoo had reached the itching stage, and sweating made it worse, but O had refused to let it distract her or give in to the urge to scratch it. Fortunately, the talent had carried the action and she had been able to concentrate on the technical details of covering six simultaneous blow jobs given by one girl in a latex hood. Not since Fashion Week five years ago had O been so glad to put her camera down for the night.

Not long after, Steven heard the ding of the elevator outside his front door and the click of O's heels. She let herself in to find him sitting on the couch watching late night news on one of the big screens. The usual low-lying fog of gray-green smoke hung in the air. Jacqui, thinly covered by one of her not-quite-long-enough T-shirts, curled up asleep next to him, her head in the lap of his scarlet robe with the black piping. She wore no makeup and her hair was tied back.

Steven looked over his shoulder as O bent down to kiss him. She had stopped at home, taken a bath, put on some lips and eyes and a simple black dress trimmed in black lace to go with her black heels. She was tired and sore, hurting in some places and itching in others, but she intended that Steven never see her unprepared to serve.

Shutting off the news with the touch-screen remote, he reached up for her face, returning her kiss tenderly. He knew how hard she worked in the studio, knew she was tired and had no carnal intentions of his own at that moment. Still, intending to remain O's master, he had to make sure the one thing she never felt was unappreciated.

"You look lovely," he said.

"Thank you, Sir. I'm sorry the shoot ran so late."

"By definition, a shoot is something that runs late. That was one of the first things I learned when Ray hooked me into this business."

O looked down at Jacqui. She seemed so young and innocent, though her long bare legs were clearly those of a woman, not an adolescent girl.

"Did you wear her out while I was gone, Sir?" O asked playfully, her weariness fading in the rush of fear and excitement Steven never failed to inspire.

"No, she had a long day too, shooting a boring girl-girl web-cam show with a girl who wasn't into girls."

O shook her head. "Poor Jacqui. She hates that."

"At least you're happy with what you got."

O looked uncomfortable, as if Steven had accidentally uttered a curse.

"I never know how it went until I see the results. Even then I don't know sometimes. I'm sure every shoot will be my last one."

"That describes every jury trial I ever argued."

O came around the couch and knelt with her hands behind her head, her loose dress fanning out between open legs. When she bent to kiss the tops of Steven's velvet slippers, the dress fell open to reveal most of her unrestrained bosom. Steven reached down to stroke her hair as she lifted her head to kiss Jacqui lightly on the mouth. Jacqui stirred and moaned in her sleep. O kissed her again and she opened one eye.

"Hello, beautiful," she said in a hazy voice. "Going to a party?"

O suddenly felt self-conscious about being dressed.

"Not tonight."

She looked up at Steven. "Permission to undress, Sir?"

"By all means."

O stood, unbuttoning her bodice, while Jacqui sat up slowly, stretching and yawning.

She asked how things had gone in the studio. O didn't want to go over it again.

"It all looked good in the finder."

"She's not going to give you a straight answer," Steven said. "I asked her the same thing."

O put her folded dress on the arm of the big club chair at right angles to the long couch. Turning back and straightening her posture to show herself properly in her smoky stay-ups and heels, she requested permission to fetch her collar. Steven sent her off to the back room for it.

"You guys do this every time?" Jacqui asked.

"With some minor variations. We like a little bit of ritual. Keeps things powered up."

"I guess I was more tired than I thought. Mind if I go to bed?"

"Not at all."

Jacqui stood up slowly, bent down to kiss Steven good night and jammed her feet into a pair of flip-flops.

"Come back for coffee when you get up," Steven suggested.

Jacqui promised she would just as O returned, collar in hand.

"Not staying?"

"Nope. He's all yours."

O managed a laugh.

"I'm all his."

Jacqui patted Steven's freshly cropped head.

"Lucky man."

She ambled toward the door as O knelt to present her collar. Steven took it, kissing the nape of O's neck as always before locking it on. He bade her stand up so he could examine her healing tattoo. Reaching behind the couch, he swiveled the big chrome swing-arm lamp over to illuminate the ink.

"Seems to be healing very evenly."

"It certainly itches evenly. Not to mention constantly."

Switching off the TV, Steven ordered O to bring some lotion from the bathroom and lie down across his lap. While she retrieved the bottle, he let his robe fall open so they would be skin-to-skin. Handing him the plastic dispenser, she stretched herself across his iron-hard fencer's legs. O was bare but for her pretty shoes, settling in so his cock nestled pleasingly against her navel. Neither felt the least bit aroused at the moment, though that could easily have changed. Steven, despite his intimidating manner, was surprisingly affectionate in private. Likewise O, for all her ironclad reserve, was surprisingly susceptible to affection as long as it remained purely physical.

Squeezing a big dollop of lotion into his right palm, Steven rubbed his hands together to warm it before applying it over O's fresh ink in slow, firm circles. She sighed, resting her face on her crossed forearms. The unguent sapped the burning irritation from her carved flesh almost instantly and made the colors all bright and shiny again.

"If only you could cane it instead."

"Just another week or so," he assured her. "You'll be able to put your ring in by then too."

"Good. I'm sick of feeling breakable, Sir."

Steven laughed.

"That's not a word I'd ever associate with you."

"I know. But a lot of people do. You'd be surprised how many men just won't hurt you no matter how nicely you ask for it."

"Rotten bastards."

Steven gave O a smack on the butt.

"God, that felt good. May I have another, Sir?"

"Next week, I promise. It's not like you're the only one who's been missing it. Sit up. I want to show you something."

O rolled off Steven's lap and sat up slowly. She watched him go to long table to retrieve a large album bound in herringbone wool and black leather.

Holding hers spine even straighter than usual to keep her greasy back off the leather, O remembered to place her feet well apart on the floor so as to remain always open between them, just as she kept her lips slightly parted in case he preferred to use her in that way.

Returning with the heavy album, Steven settled in next to her, hips touching, and opened the thick, sturdy covers.

"This artist is a Spanish guy with a fanatical following but a rather specialized body of work. He's one of my favorites. He has some clever ideas that might inspire you in the studio."

O leaned into Steven's side, resting her head on his chest while he carefully flipped the pages. Each had its own clear-plastic sleeve with a black-and-white line-art drawing tucked inside. Steven slid the album across their laps, focusing the lamp so O could see every detail.

The themes were familiar: perfect girls of varying facial and body types, all naked in stonewalled dungeons. Most were restrained on ingeniously complex devices for the convenience of the powerful male and female figures, also mostly naked, in torturing or violating them by various means. The images were unsparingly explicit yet strangely lyrical, the figures gracefully elongated. The art reminded O a bit of Goya.

"Same home town," Steven said, "but a few centuries apart."

"If you go to Spain today you'll see people who look very similar to these drawings on the street every day, though generally clothed," O observed.

"There's one particular piece ... ah, here it is."

Steven handled the drawing carefully by the edges as he brought it out for O's inspection.

The image was powerful. A tall, spectacularly curvaceous woman of perhaps thirty-five lolled in the arms of a muscular, bearded man many years her senior. He stood, holding her barely upright, close against his broad chest. His penis, jutting up under the woman's back, was equally impressive. He looked down at her with a strange combination of severity and tenderness. The woman's eyes were closed. Her face was filled with an ecstatic transcendence familiar from the images of martyrs O had seen on the walls of many an Iberian church.

But the most arresting aspect of the drawing was the scrupulously rendered evidence of intense and prolonged flagellation. The woman was marked from her collarbones to the bottoms of her feet. A variety of different instruments had been used on her with great patience and skill. A layer of broad strap marks had been applied first, followed by a global lashing with some kind of slender, cutting whip that left long narrow welts, the deepest of which oozed tiny rivulets of blood. The whipping had obviously gone on for hours until every inch of her exposed flesh was covered in thin stripes, inflicted with sufficient restraint to fade within a couple of weeks.

The woman was collared but otherwise unrestrained and though clearly too exhausted to flee or resist, showed no evidence of wanting to do either. Something profound had clearly transpired between the two of them. The viewer was left to conjecture the specifics from the visible aftermath.

"Now that's my idea of a good whipping," Steven said.

"You could whip me like that if you wanted," O replied without an instant's hesitation, eager at the prospect.

Steven looked over at her gravely.

"Careful what you offer. You know I'll do it."

"Why would I offer, otherwise?"

They looked into each other's eyes for a long moment.

"That would take hours. It's a bit late to start tonight," Steven said at last, "But we'll know when the time comes."

"I'll look forward to it," she said. "And I think these drawings would be a fine addition to your collection."

Steven promised to send a wire transfer tomorrow. Though O was sufficiently stirred up by the pictures to offer herself for any service Steven might want, they'd both had long days, were very tired and in need of a good night's sleep.

Steven pushed the buttons that activated the shutdown sequence. Shades descended. Lights went out. The thermostat dropped to sleeping temperature.

Steven had actually slept with few women since his divorce from Marie. He never forgot how safe and comfortable he felt sharing a bed with her, how much he missed it at first after they separated, when he realized how rarely he felt safe anywhere.

Not just any warm body lying next close to his would produce the same effect. Many produced the exact opposite, leaving him stiff and tired from restless nights and eager to send them off as soon as routine politeness would permit.

O's response to the image in the album revealed more than she knew. She passionately embraced the part of him that craved the extreme. She had a corresponding part that fit to it as the contours of their bodies fit when they lay unconscious. Both were hard. Both were warm.

The temperature falling around him made that warmth all the more welcome when they finally crawled into bed and O immediately slid over to him. He took one long look at his mark, newly struck in her flesh, wrapped himself around her and pulled up the thick down-filled comforter over both of them. Both were asleep in seconds.

CHAPTER THIRTY-FIVE

O ver the ensuing weeks Steven and O and Jacqui and Ray settled into a sort of "new normal," punctuated by occasional surprises and spontaneous adventures. Steven walked a few felons. Ray sent the next issue of *Forbidden* to press. O edited her glory-hole set and scheduled new shoots, as always, a minimum of two weeks in advance. Jacqui divided her time among Ray, O and Marie when she wasn't under the lights somewhere.

It was impossible to ignore the tightening circle of intimacy that surrounded them. Buoyant and sociable by nature, Jacqui's company made Ray even more so. He often proposed dinners after work and with Ray came Jacqui just as O came with Steven. Sometimes they dined at home; the girls in their black-lace aprons, heels and collars busy in the kitchen while Ray persisted in his doomed attempt to beat Steven at Eight-Ball.

Friday nights were reserved for supper at Franklin Street, where Svetlana and a new girl named Carmen – a spectacular Spanish beauty with gleaming black hair to the waist and perfect face haunted by sin – seemed to have settled smoothly into Marie's intricately structured routine. O sometimes caught a look in Marie's eye she couldn't read when Steven was busy wowing the girls with colorful tales of his checkered past. O was curious about that look, but both women were too obstinately discreet to discuss Marie's thoughts.

Afterward they often went up to Ray's cantilevered roost where, despite the nighttime chill of what passed for winter in Los Angeles, Steven and O (now given Jan's permission to soak in hot water) sat in Ray's Jacuzzi out on the deck, getting high and savoring the night cityscape below. Jacqui and Ray usually stayed indoors where Ray patiently taught Jacqui the eternal three-chord progression on the big Martin. From what sound leaked through the partially open sliding glass doors she was a quick study.

Wednesday evenings, when the crowds were lightest, they often walked from Ray's office to the luxurious screening rooms of the ArcLight Cinema, where tickets had to be bought online and the concession stands sold trail mix as well as popcorn. At least the prints were always flawless, the audio always clean, and the audience dutifully silenced their smart phones at the ushers' command.

The negotiations over which film to see were complex. They all liked very different things but somehow they inevitably agreed on some new release. Jacqui got her share of big noisy sci-fi and fantasy shows. O and Steven were occasionally allowed something foreign with subtitles if there was nudity. Ray chose gangster pictures, if they offered hot babes in peril. While watching, he amused himself with his new dolly in the double-wide aisle seats.

He'd discovered that femmes in jeopardy, whether from witch finders or futuristic super villains, got Jacqui hot and squishy. He made her wear short, loose skirts to the cinema under a long, fur-trimmed cashmere sweater coat he bought her. O and Steven took to calling them "the kids" when they weren't in the room.

On their own, Steven and O frequently ate at the club downtown. O never tired of watching Steven lunging up and down the fencing strip with Mike, sabers flashing, even though Steven usually got killed. From the observation seats, his joyful physicality had the same effect on her that costume dramas about lusty barbarians had on Jacqui. She even persuaded Steven not to shower after a match once in a while so she could inhale the perfume of his sweat later in the evening. Those were nights when O deliberately cinched her corset extra-tight, did her eyes and lips like a whore, and presented herself with some large object already deep in her posterior plumbing, knowing that he'd be particularly rough and cruel after combat.

Sometimes they all went shopping together as they had before O and Jacqui did their time at Marie's. But if there were to be gifts of any kind, the boys and girls did their shopping separately.

On one such mission, O surprised Jacqui in a dressing room at Neimann's after lunching on tarragon egg salad with caviar. O tried on some opera gloves and Jacqui seriously considered a long Dolce & Gabbana dress, boned and hooked like a corset, in the three-way mirror. Finished doing up the millions of tiny hooks at the back of the dress, O suddenly reached into her handbag and brought out a small brown envelope with the septum ring inside. Jacqui's eyes, enhanced by her green lenses that day, brightened even more and she clapped her hands gleefully.

"Can you wear it yet?" she asked eagerly.

"Watch this."

O popped the nearly invisible link out of the ring, holding it in one gloved hand while neatly flipping down the black retainer and sliding it out with the other. The gleaming ring, all the more dramatic against the black kid of the long gloves, easily slipped in through one of O's nostrils and out the other. Leaning toward the mirror, O snapped the continuous link in place and rotated the ring so it appeared an unbroken circle of white metal.

Satisfied with what she saw in the mirror she turned to Jacqui.

"Well, what do you think?"

Jacqui got in close, peering intently at the strange new object centered in O's face.

"Are you sure it's completely healed?" she asked.

"No problem."

O flipped the ring up and down with a finger. It moved as smoothly as a polished door knocker.

"I can even pull on it."

O tugged at it just enough to make Jacqui feel slightly dizzy.

It was a more startling addition than Jacqui had expected. Quite large against O's delicate features, it transformed her into something exotic and defiantly perverse. In her long gloves and fitted day dress, O might have just come from a charity luncheon, but it was hard to imagine what kind of charity event called for what was unmistakably a slave ring.

O felt uneasy beneath Jacqui's riveted gaze.

"Well?"

"It's fan-fucking-tastic is what!" Jacqui exclaimed, throwing her arms around O and then pushing her away for another look.

"Can I touch it?"

O laughed.

"Of course you can touch it, silly. It's not just for show."

Jacqui carefully took the ring between her thumb and index finger, moving it up and down, turning it slightly from side to side through O's perforated nasal flesh.

"It sends a message. More than the shackle ring. More even than the tattoo," Jacqui concluded.

"How do you mean?"

"Well, the shackle ring could be a fashion statement. And a lot of girls have their guy's initials tattooed on them someplace. But this can only mean one thing."

"Is that bad?"

"I think you should wear it out in public," Jacqui pronounced.

"Perhaps I will," O replied, "but not today. This was just for you."

O took the ring out and dropped it back in its envelope. Jacqui put her arms around her.

"Thanks for that, Sister. It's nice to know you trust me."

"We wouldn't be sisters if I didn't trust you. I still care about Ray and I wouldn't put him in the wrong hands."

Jacqui smiled slyly.

"Ray seems happy in my hands."

"I'm happier with your hands in me, but then, I'm a girl," O said.

They emerged from the bathroom laughing to total up their purchases.

That night, O met Steven at his place after calling first, as always, to secure permission to enter on her own. She never used her keys and codes without asking.

He came in to find her kneeling on a brocade pad on the table. She'd chosen a red and black corset for the occasion, short and tight so it compressed her waist mercilessly, while concealing nothing else. She also wore the gloves she'd bought, her best red-soled pumps and the patent-leather collar and cuffs reserved for formal occasions. She'd even lowered the lights and centered herself under them so they'd reflect off the ring in the middle of her theatrically-painted face just so. This would be the first time Steven saw it in there and O played the moment for maximum drama.

Steven put down his briefcase and approached wordlessly, examining O's face from every angle. Her eyes followed him helplessly. He looked particularly elegant that day in a black worsted suit with peaked lapels pick-stitched in red, a red double-breasted vest and red-and-black spectators he'd had to talk the traditionalists at Lobb into making for him.

Steven seemed utterly hypnotized. He found the ring flattering in a jarringly unsubtle way. O had created herself with such care, had maintained her look with such rigor, it was truly astonishing that she'd allowed so major an intrusion in a place where it could not be ignored or misinterpreted.

And she had done it for him.

O remained perfectly still, gloved hands folded behind her neck. She centered her gaze, but a tiny trickle of sweat down one armpit betraying her anxiety. What if he didn't like how it looked?

That concern dissipated like a smoke ring as soon as Steven grabbed and kissed her. Never before had he crushed her mouth against hers with such ferocity. To their mutual surprise, they could feel the circle of cool gold against both their upper lips.

Freed at last from Steven's fierce embrace, O slipped to the floor, deftly unbuttoning his trousers despite the gloves, and pulled him free so she could put her red-lacquered lips around what seemed the steeliest hard-on she'd ever encountered. Sure enough, the ring dragged up and down its length with each stroke, tickling her nose and adding a subtle new note to the sensations she so expertly produced with her sensitive, highly trained mouth. She dared a look up at him and a deliberately provocative question.

"Does Sir approve of the modification to his property?"

He smiled down at her.

"A definite upgrade, adding all the more to your value."

"Jacqui thinks I should wear it out in public."

"We'll have to selective about which public."

After a bit of further demonstration, O found herself lifted to the edge of the table and shoved rudely onto her back, just as she had that first time. He fucked her so hard she had to grip the opposite edge to keep from slipping over. Every time O's new ring danced in the subdued light from the pin-spots above, he seemed to go in deeper. She wailed for permission to climax and he roared an order for her to do it and do it now.

O thrashed her hips, pounded her gloved fists on the steel surface and screamed, the ring glinting as she flipped her head back and forth. For once, O's hair flew wild. Her heart was still pounding when she begged to suck him off like a proper slave.

Steven stepped free of her, watching her slide to her knees again, this time trembling from the aftershocks of her internal upheaval. She gobbled him ravenously. Steven leaned against the table to steady himself.

O didn't take long to produce the desired effect. She felt his hands grip the sides of her head, a sudden choking lunge followed shortly by a geyser of hot liquid spewing down her throat. She gulped and sucked until there was nothing more to be extracted. Not a drop escaped her gleaming lips.

"Sir seems pleased," she said when finally regaining the ability to speak. Her face was flushed, her eyes still glazed.

"I think that's safe to say," Steven gasped.

It was pretty much the same conversation they'd had the first time he penetrated her anally after the tattoo healed. Crossing a line past which there was no retreat had liberated something in both of them, even though neither had felt there was much left in need of liberation. Neither would ever look at the other again without thinking of the irreversible proof O would always wear of surrendering completely to his desires.

O stayed the night and, as had become her habit when doing so, got up before Steven to spread out his newspaper and pour his coffee. Everything else in the place was so automated there weren't many services for her to render. This troubled her for a reason she couldn't pin down. After all, he'd lived alone for many years and had the means to provide himself with the ultimate in conveniences.

Dressed in her naughty-girl uniform of sheer white skirt and short, loose-fitting black skirt, her patent collar and cuffs still locked on, she went over to his office to see if she could be of some use there. She'd been sleeping with her septum ring in at home for a week or so and didn't think to take it out there.

Constance entered to find her honing a box of red Smythson pencils with a huge chromed Spanish sharpener on Steven's desk. Bent over, O's tiny skirt, recently taken in at the waist, exposed the under curves of her behind. Constance whistled, surprisingly loudly, in admiration. O whirled around, pencil in hand. Constance stared at her in shock.

"My god, what is that on your nose?" she asked incredulously.

O dropped the pencil, reaching up to confirm that she had indeed forgotten to remove the big ring from her nose.

"Well," O managed, trying to regain her composure, "what does it look like?"

"A very large ring that appears to have been installed in a very permanent way."

"Sorry. Didn't mean to offend you."

Constance shrugged, agitating her creamy bosom atop her blouse sufficiently to momentarily distract O from her own embarrassment.

"Surely you can't imagine any of Steven's depraved whims still have the power to offend me."

Her tone was cool but friendly. She'd seen a number of women come and go through Steven's life and found O by far the most suitable, not that she'd presume to offer an opinion.

"I'll make sure not to wear it over here in the future."

"You needn't do so on my account," Constance assured her. "Steven's been in an exceptionally good mood lately, which makes things better for me. Whatever you're doing, by all means continue."

Constance nodded toward the dropped pencil, causing O to display herself even more when she bent down. She felt almost as if she might blush, a thing she hadn't done in years. Instead, she turned hastily to the sharpener and went back to work, furiously turning the big, wooden-knobbed crank.

Constance smiled, shook her head and repaired to the relative safety of the outer office.

Steven came in, as usual, right on time, wearing a black double-breasted blazer and gray and black striped trousers. He greeted Constance cheerfully, his good spirits from the night before still evident. She'd seen him pretty grim on more than one occasion. This was definitely better.

"Anything blow up yet?" he asked.

"Nothing this morning, but I'm optimistic about the Barker case. He should be calling any day now."

"Never count your crooks before they're arrested. What about the extradition hearing?"

Constance handed him an envelope with an official seal in the upper left-hand corner.

"If I had to guess without opening it, I'd say your client is going to be doing some traveling."

"We'll see about that."

He started toward the inner door.

Constance alerted him to the fact that O was already waiting.

"Good," he said. "I was afraid she'd gone home."

As he strolled by, a distinct spring in his step, Constance wondered where this was all going. She was accustomed to Steven's relief at finding himself unencumbered by the previous night's company so he could concentrate on his work. Hopefully, O wouldn't turn out to be bad for business.

O was kneeling by Steven's chair when he came in. She had stripped to black stockings and heels in the usual way. After bending to kiss the floor in front of him, she assumed her usual stance at the edge of the desk – legs wide, hands behind her head. He used the nose ring to tilt her head back for a kiss, asked her how she'd slept, and gave her an affectionate, if rude, caress from face to crotch before sitting down.

Lifting the earpiece out of its charger, he plugged it into his head, pushed a hidden button somewhere on top of it and barked a name into the microphone. His touch was already making O squirm by the time he got the federal DA in Western Pennsylvania on the line. He extracted two orgasms out of O and a continuance from the prosecutor before he dismissed his slave to go edit pictures.

CHAPTER THIRTY-SIX

The day was off to a less interesting start at Ray's office, though that would soon change. The mail Lena stacked on his own desk was a predictable assortment of bills from prep houses and printers, sample work from photographers he would never hire, solicitations for contributions to various worthy causes and letters to the editor penned by a bowling alley's worth of oddballs.

Toward the bottom of the pile he found something worth opening. It looked like an invitation, enclosed in thick expensive black stock, from David Phelps. Phelps owned the biggest, richest, highest profile nexus of kink-porn websites in the world, and would certainly be *Forbidden*'s most formidable online competition unless Ray could figure out a way to turn their prickly cordiality into something more useful. Though lacking his brother's appetite for Byzantine intrigue Ray was not without reserves of cunning. Their invisibility served them all the better.

Ray and David, as the two most influential players in the world of BDSM commerce, treated each other with unfailing, if wary, respect. Ray made sure that David's latest site launch always got a favorable write-up from the magazine and David bought the inside back cover of every issue to funnel traffic toward his billing service.

In some ways, even this modest exchange of courtesies was a conflict of interest. Ray lost a few subscribers a month to David's expensive live-feeds. David, who aspired to monopoly, didn't control everything worth owning in their market niche while Ray had *Forbidden*, which had resisted the electronic tsunami longer than David thought it should have.

As neither appeared looked likely to go away soon, guarded cooperation seemed the most prudent course. Though they were always diplomatic in public they didn't usually socialize.

David must have shared some of Ray's concerns about the prospect of going head-to-head in cyberspace. For the first time ever Ray and an unspecified number of guests were warmly invited to attend David's annual Halloween Ball, the most lavish event on the West Coast perveratti party calendar. Held at the vast former hotel in San Francisco where David's constellation of enterprises now headquartered, it sold out weeks in advance, and David was not one to drop the velvet rope without a good reason.

Ray would soon need real-time credit card processing, and David, who had a tendency to attempt eating things bigger than his head, could always use another revenue stream.

The flashy foiled and embossed red-on-black card in the envelope requested an early RSVP for VIP admissions. Like his brother, Ray instinctively understood the value of the personal touch. Punching the intercom button, he instructed Lena to call David on his private line.

Ray made a point of thanking David for the gracious invitation and upped the ante by proposing a contribution to the live entertainment. It had been years since Ray had an ideal partner for the kind of performance he used to do when the L.A. club scene was still happening. That Jacqui had modeled for a couple of David's sites before hooking up with Marie and that David had been trying to lure her and her magic hit-rate to return ever since surely wouldn't hurt. David sounded perfectly delighted in his polished Oxbridge accent.

Jacqui would be Ray's next call but he'd have to wait a bit. He knew she'd be having lunch at Marie's. Jacqui was diligent about making it up there regularly, unable to foresee a future in which she could be certain not to need shelter under Marie's roof.

At that moment, as the girls in residence performed the ritual of setting up for the midday meal, Jacqui lay on her stomach in Marie's black-sheeted bed, chin propped on hands, discussing that unknowable future with the one person in whom she confided. Marie stretched out in all her sleek nudity after having her carnal appetites satisfied by Jacqui's unequaled oral skills and listened more closely than her languid posture would suggest.

Jacqui felt a little odd gotten up in pink and gray lace as if she still lived there but she had no objections to satisfying Marie's agenda while pursuing her own. She just wasn't quite sure where to start.

"Ray isn't what I thought he was," she began.

"What did you think he was?" Marie asked.

"The usual shallow spoiled rich kid in love with the mirror. I only did him because O wanted me to. I figured he'd get tired of me almost as fast as I'd get tired of him and then O and I would be back together."

"Didn't happen that way?"

"He's fun and sweet. And he has a beautiful cock he actually knows how to use."

"Really Jacqui, there's got to be more to it."

"He's a good listener the way you are. He's actually interested in my opinions. He doesn't treat me like a toy. We're even attracted to the same girls. You know he's teaching me to play the guitar?"

Marie frowned.

"That's worrisome."

"It gets worse. We make each other laugh. We text each other in the middle of the day for no reason. I make myself go back to Steven's a few nights a week just to maintain minimum safe distance but then I can't sleep. I end up calling Ray so he can read to me on the phone until I drift off. If that doesn't work I get dressed and go over to his place to watch *Dr. Who* marathons on BBC America."

Marie shook her head.

"I'm afraid the symptoms are there."

"Symptoms of what?"

"A smart girl falling in love. That's dangerous for our kind. Boys are easily distracted. What if someone else comes along and he decides to trade you in?"

"He could have any of us by just snapping his fingers, but that doesn't seem like a priority. I haven't met one model he's fucked so far. The magazine is my only real competition."

"But he couldn't say the same about you."

"He's cool with my being bi. And he's not afraid to hurt me either."

"I can see that," Marie said, tracing a fresh red streak along the side of Jacqui's right breast.

"I haven't been serious about a guy since I was in high school but Ray isn't just a guy. He's kind of a soulful person."

"He must have gotten that from his mother."

Jacqui rolled onto her back, resting her head on Marie's chest. Marie twirled Jacqui's loose strand of auburn hair around a finger.

"It's not like I want to settle down and start popping out babies or anything."

"That's a relief."

"But I'd be a lying if I said I didn't have feelings for him."

"Stick to lying. You're supposed to be his sex slave and that's all. Feelings could get in the way."

"Like they did with you and Steven?"

"We had a different problem. Sit up. I have to dress for lunch."

Jacqui hugged her knees to her chest while Marie floated through the room in search of her sheer black-satin-trimmed dressing gown and some tap pants to go with.

Marie stopped, turning to face Jacqui.

"When I told Steven I was leaving him for Martin I had no idea how he'd take it. That was one part of our problem, actually, but by then it no longer mattered. He just shook his head and said 'Nature always bats last.'"

"Don't you hate it when men talk about love like it was a contact sport?"

"Famously, but sometimes they've got a point. No matter what I tell you to do, no matter what you try to do, you'll end up doing whatever nature demands."

Shrugging on the long robe, Marie sat down at the edge of the bed, putting her hand on Jacqui's leg. There were only so many sins even she could conceal.

"Steven and I saw your pictures after you shot for O the first time. I told him a little about you. Since Ray had sort of upset the order of things by giving O to Steven, we thought we'd steady things up by giving you to Ray. Steven ordered O to seduce you and deliver you up to his brother at The Mansion as a collared slave. But events seem to have surpassed our ability to manage them. That happens sometimes."

"Don't even try to tell me O's been faking it. I don't care how good a slave she is she'd never get over on me that way. I've been seduced by experts and none of them fooled me for a minute. What O and I feel for each other is real."

"We counted on that development. What we didn't count on was what's happened between you and Ray. We'd pictured something more like what O and Steven have but obviously it didn't shake out that way."

Jacqui's voice grew hard and tight.

"Ray's not Steven and I'm not O. We're human."

"So are they. So am I. We tried to do a *mitzvah* for both of you. It seemed safe enough. Ray's always had a romantic streak and I worried he'd get emotionally attached to you but I figured you'd keep your distance the way you always do."

Jacqui stood up angrily, eyes narrowed on Marie's face.

"I guess you don't know me that well, do you? What right do you have to pull the strings on other people's lives anyway?"

Marie had plenty of practice at talking down angry girls.

"None. We have no right. But we do have responsibilities. Once you all start letting us make decisions for you, we're accountable for the results. When Ray gave Steven the key to O's collar he set all kinds of things in motion. We tried to stage manage those things but they went off-book."

"Why didn't you tell me any of this? I'd probably have been cool with it anyway but it would have been nice to have a choice. See, there's this thing called consent ..."

Marie wearily silenced her with an upraised hand.

"I'm familiar with the concept."

Jacqui started to leak tears.

"But you just ignored it and manipulated all of us to get your way. How fucking vanilla is that?"

Marie stood up, took Jacqui's face in her hands.

"I don't buy the whole ends-justify-means approach darling. However, we do have to look at the outcomes realistically. Would you have been happier if we'd given you to a man you couldn't love? And how long would your relationship with O have held up if she hadn't invited you into the most intimate part of her life? There's nothing wrong with loving the man you call Master. Most of the girls here would be thrilled to trade places with you."

Jacqui turned away.

"Do you mind if I don't stay for lunch, Ma'am?"

"Of course not. Now that I've outed our little scheme what happens next is up to you and Ray. From here on you'll have to make your own choices. Just remember what Steven said.

Doesn't matter how you came to feel what you do. Nature is at the plate now."

Marie got up and put her arms around Jacqui, who stood stiff as a wax dummy.

"Ray's a good man. If this works out for you two we'll be nothing but happy for both of you. Why don't you try letting yourself have what you want?"

"Right now I don't know what I want but I'll keep you in the loop."

Jacqui pulled away and went off to find her street clothes, not bothering with a kiss, a curtsy or a good-bye.

Fifteen minutes later Jacqui stormed past Lena into Ray's office where he sat behind his desk, typing away on the publisher's page editorial for the upcoming issue. Looking up at Jacqui – her red face, her set jaw, her eyes blazing – Ray made the easy observation.

"You're pissed off, aren't you?"

Jacqui grabbed the arms of Ray's chair and spun him around to face her so she could spit out her accusation.

"You knew!"

He didn't pretend not to understand what she meant.

"In on it pretty much from the start. And so were you if you'll be honest enough with yourself to admit it. Don't tell me you didn't know O was launching you at me like a Tomahawk missile. You were just in denial about it because you're so hot for O like everyone else."

"Fuck you, you fucking fuck."

Tears welled in Jacqui's eyes.

"Fuck me for what? It started out to be all about the Master-slave thing and everybody was fine. Now it's turning out to be a love thing and everybody's got their knickers in a knot."

Ray stood and put his arms around Jacqui, who fell in against him, wetting his western-yoked, rose- embroidered shirt with tears.

"When were you going to tell me how this got started?"

"Can you think of a good time? Steven and I have been trading partners back and forth for years. Ask around if you want the gory details. There are plenty of witnesses. Nothing serious ever came of it until now. Sorry I don't have a slick alibi in my back pocket, but it's not like you haven't played similar games with both men and women."

It was true. Jacqui had largely gotten through life telling men what they wanted to hear, true or false. She'd fixed up other girls too and not always with good intentions.

"My grand parents on the Italian side were very old school,'" Ray said. "They were from neighboring towns and hardly knew each other. Their families put them together in an arranged marriage because it seemed like a smart play. Short version: they fell madly in love. My dad said he used to come home from school and find them waltzing to the Victrola."

He squeezed her tighter.

"I love you, Jacqui. Does it matter how that happened?"

"I love you too," she said, looking up from his wet shirt. It was a good thing this wasn't a mascara day. "I'm just not sure it's in the right way. I don't know if I can love you and still be the kind of slave to you that O is to Steven."

"They need to do it by the numbers. We can make it up as we go along."

Still sniffling slightly, Jacqui composed herself. Steely determination replaced the hurt and anger in her eyes.

"I think we should go through with the original plan anyway. I want my time at The Mansion like O promised. I want you to own me. I'm not monogamous and I never will be. And I'm way gone past bi-curious. I'll always need things I can't get from you or any man. But I want to be as important to you as O is to Steven. If that's going to happen it will have to be the way it was with your grandparents. Arranged or not, my slavery to you has to come from love. We won't make it two weeks otherwise."

"O was more right about you than she knew," Ray said pensively. "She told me not to formally collar you until you'd spent some time in Pasadena."

"I'll never be perfect the way she is but I deserve a chance to try. I'm going to prove to that little bitch that I can submit to a man I love even if she can't."

"Done deal. As soon as we get back from San Francisco."

Jacqui suddenly remembered the world beyond her immediate situation.

"San Francisco?"

"David Phelps is having his big party next week. I'm taking you and O and Steven along. I'd hoped to do a live feed with you from there."

Of all the reactions Jacqui might have anticipated, this would have been the last.

"You mean performing live, the two of us?"

"I haven't tried anything like that in a long time but with you I'm pretty sure I can still bring it."

Jacqui's moods changed as fast as the weather in the mountains of Wyoming.

"Well then," she said, "we better get in some rehearsal time."

She wrapped herself around him, kissing him fiercely. Wherever he was going was where she wanted to be.

Chapter Thirty-Seven

Steven and O didn't find out about their travel plans until the weekend. They'd gone out to Eve and Alan's for O to choose the image among Eve's studies that would become her state portrait. While O inspected Eve's small roughed-out color studies in minute detail, Ray pitched the upcoming trip.

"You've got to check out David's operation. It's the biggest thing on the map. Getting on board with his billing system would save us a ton of money. Most processors charge ten percent or more on transactions for adult content but with the rate David gets for all that volume, he can do it for us at half that and still make a profit himself."

"As long we can audit his books, you'll get no arguments from me," Steven said. "I don't know anything about Internet billing and I'm too old to learn. Besides, I might as well meet the guy just in case I end up suing him later. Constance can book us a charter. If we pretend to do business up there, I'll write it off."

"This one," O finally declared.

Steven wasn't surprised she'd picked the most explicit image. Shot near the end of the session, it showed O stretched backwards over the ottoman, one stockinged leg crowned with a sky-scraper stiletto pump straight up in the air, the other leg down and folded slightly back to reveal all. O's face was turned to camera, her expression coolly inviting. Her neck was already collared but O asked if Eve could add the new septum ring to her face. Eve swallowed hard.

"Septum ring?"

"A gift from my owner," O said without irony. She took the ring from her small purse and changed the retainer out for it. Eve looked at her face, had her turn her head this way and that.

"Okay, no problem as long as I don't have to think about how much it must have hurt."

"It was more pressure than pain," O started to explain before Eve covered her ears.

"You'll really like the tattoo," Ray insisted. Alan, who collected volumes of tattoo art among other things, got interested. He asked for a look very politely.

Ever accessible, O wore a white cotton blouse with a high self-tie neck and many buttons down the front. It was tucked into a short pleated-leather skirt that could be flipped up easily fore and aft. She had only to drop the skirt while Steven held up the back hem of O's top to fully reveal her now healed ink-work.

"Jan Harkness," Eve pronounced without hesitation.

"Often imitated, never duplicated," Alan added.

Eve tilted up the lamp from her drawing table to focus on Jan's work, craning her neck to catalog every detail.

Eve asked how O explained it at the gym.

"I work out at home," O said. "I don't show it to anyone who needs an explanation.

Eve marveled at the way the pink ribbon curled over from the bow framing Steven's mark.

"She gets such depth in the shading. And on skin yet. I have trouble making that work on paper."

Alan asked Steven why he didn't have any ink. Steven and Ray both laughed out loud.

While O put her clothes back together Steven slipped out of his thick black double-breasted sweater and pulled up his cashmere turtleneck with a little help from Ray, revealing the big bright imperial dragon covering much of his un-punctured shoulder and the upper part of his adjacent arm.

Alan wanted to know how Steven had managed to get traditional *Yakuza irezumi*.

"I helped a Japanese client with a tricky problem," Steven said in a tone that discouraged further inquiry.

"Makes me think of sushi," Eve said.

"Did I here someone mention sushi?" Jacqui asked eagerly, entering through the glass doors from the pool. Eve looked up at her as she came over to drape an arm around O's tiny waist. O had slept in her muslin training corset since the tattoo calmed down and working out extra hard to regain her extreme contours.

"Next time I want Alan to shoot some new pictures of you for me," Eve warned, pointing at Jacqui with the handle of a Winsor and Newton brush. Jacqui, who could never stay in a bad mood for long, couldn't have been more pleased at the announcement of a new Harry Potter book.

"Seriously? You want to paint me again?"

"I'm thinking something kind of Art Deco this time. Maybe we can borrow a couple of Borzois to pose you with."

"I'd fuck a couple of Borzoi's for a study."

Eve recoiled.

"Don't tell Alan that. He'll want to shoot it and then I won't be able to do the painting. Alan will give you a call when I get done with O's portrait.

Over expensive bites of endangered sea creatures at Nobu Steven and Alan talked about politics while Ray entertained the women with tales of the Hustler anniversary party to which he'd taken Jacqui the previous Saturday. He rolled them with his spot-on impersonation of Larry Flynt deliberately lowering his voice so women in low-cut dresses would have to bend down to hear him, allowing him shameless reconnaissance of their cleavages. Eve could not be tempted to try Alan's *uni* despite rave reviews but Jacqui slurped one down without hesitation.

"Yum! It tastes like the ocean but cleaner."

"Yeah," Ray pointed out, "because it filters all the pollution into the part you don't eat."

In the green-tiled privacy of the ladies' room Jacqui let O touch up her lips for her.

"You're not still mad at me, are you?" O asked.

"For pimping me off to your ex? I've got mixed feelings about it."

Jacqui had been tense and distant with O for days and O, having heard Ray's account of Jacqui's surprise visit to the office, understood why. Even now, though they were all having a good time and Jacqui was much lubricated with sake, the remoteness lingered.

"I mean the other part," O said.

"For working me like a chump at your Master's orders? You're lucky I didn't rip out your ovaries."

O cringed.

"I never meant to hurt you."

"If you try to apologize," Jacqui warned, "I really will rip out your ovaries. You've brought a lot of great things into my life so why don't we just let it drop?"

O put away Jacqui's lipstick, impulsively cradling Jacqui's breasts through her clingy celadon silk dress. Jacqui only wore bras for show and her nipples popped right out at O's touch.

"Do you still want me?"

"Of course, though I do intend to ass-fuck you with a giant strap-on first chance I get."

O smiled cheerily.

"I'd like that."

Jacqui looked exasperated in the mirror.

"How do you punish a masochist?"

O reminded her about a very old joke that started that way. Jacqui took her under the arm and steered her toward the swinging door.

"Come on, you sneaky little bitch. If we're gone too long they'll think I've killed you and stuffed your body down the toilet."

They were both laughing when they emerged and they napped in each other's arms in the cozy backseat of the Bentley coupe on the way home.

Ray and Steven sat up front talking like brothers.

"Come on, Steven. You can tell me. How much is Alan hitting you for O's portrait?"

"Forget it. You can't afford one of Jacqui and I'm not giving you the money. Eve's done a bunch of limited edition lithos of her. Buy one of those."

"I don't need anything as grand as what Eve's doing of O. Maybe just a study."

"When Jacqui models for them next time they'll give her one anyway. They have to sell the bigger pieces at full price. If they can get a show together it will cover their mortgage for a year."

"Are things that tight for them? I mean, she's a really famous artist."

"These days the art market is very conservative. Pin-ups are too campy for an investment. I got offered an original Vargas last month for five K. That's a fucking steal."

"Did you buy it?"

"Of course. It's being shipped out from New York as we speak."

Ray swallowed this news with some difficulty.

"The guy was a fucking genius. Why can't something sexual be taken seriously as art?"

"It can if it's older than Jesus. After that art was either sacred or profane. Profane sells better on the streets but sacred is blue-chip."

"What's the matter with people? Are they worried about their immortal souls or something?"

Steven sometimes forgot that Ray had been raised a Catholic though it didn't seem to have done him permanent damage.

"No, Ray. They're worried about the photographers from *Architectural Digest*."

Ray got a laugh out of that.

"I don't suppose you're expecting them to show up at your place."

"Actually, they sent someone to scout it. She never made it past the living room."

"That's the price we pay for being out."

"Only the least of it," Steven said. "Try making a campaign contribution and see what happens. You know you've achieved infamy when politicians won't take your money."

Deep in the garage under Steven's tower, kisses were exchanged and ways parted. It had been a long drive and all Steven and O wanted was to burn one and go to sleep.

As usual, she stripped and knelt for collaring at the door, then followed him into the dressing room to attend him as he'd taught her. Watching her move gracefully amid the racks, cabinets and drawers in only her stockings and heels, his ring and his mark very much on display, Steven felt lucky in a way he never had before. He was well aware of his material good fortune, but O was a prize he would never have expected to win.

O presented herself on the bed for her ankle chain, asking if Steven desired any further services. She could happily have spent her whole life with his cock inside her but she got a lot of satisfaction from a simple hand-job or some quick fellatio.

Tonight he simply lifted the covers so she could slip in and snuggle up to him. That was fine too. He was so solid. For the first time in her life O felt entirely safe with a man. What she thought he wanted she was confident she could provide indefinitely.

Something from which neither was safe, unfortunately, was the phone on the steel chest at Steven's side of the bed. It was an old-fashioned land line connected to an even more old-fashioned answering service so that whoever called it would be greeted by a human voice regardless of the hour. The service had standing instructions to accept all collect calls.

Steven referred to the service as Bad News Central. He knew from years of lawyering that good news rarely arrived after ten p.m. The service didn't call often but when they did someone was in trouble serious enough to convince the service operator to put them through to Steven. If he was home he always answered. If he wasn't the service tracked him down relentlessly. Only a few people even knew the line existed. They understood they were pulling the fire alarm when they dialed the number.

In the darkest hour of the night, that phone ripped Steven and O from their dreams and each other's arms. He lunged for it, pausing just long enough to clear his head.

"Anybody dead?" he asked the service operator.

From the way he groaned at the reply, O guessed he'd have preferred an affirmative answer. Apparently nobody was dead at the moment but someone probably wished to be.

Though O was a heavy sleeper like Steven she came around fast just as he did. Steven was sitting up now, a grim expression on his face. He didn't like what he was hearing.

"Can't this wait until morning?" he asked, already knowing the answer.

"Okay, put her through," he said wearily, draping his arm around O's shoulders as she sat up next to him.

He confirmed to the calling party that he was indeed Steven Diamond and yes, the female voice on the other end of the line had followed instructions correctly in calling him. He cut off what sounded like an apology.

"So what did she do this time?"

Steven listened to the anxious, staccato outburst through the receiver and slapped his forehead.

"Ah, Jesus. You really need to put a leash on her. If you can't do it ,the agency better find someone who can. Call Mark when we get off the phone and remind him I bill triple my hourly for this bullshit. Where is she being held?"

There was a brief pause during which Steven's expression got even grimmer.

"I don't have to write it down. I know where it is. I'll be there in half an hour. Nobody talks to anybody before that. Are there any photographers outside yet? So far so good, I guess. If any media people show up, you have no comment and you will have no comment. Just stay put."

Steven clicked off the phone and put it down. O looked up at him, clearly worried.

"What's going on?"

"Absolutely nothing interesting. Go back to sleep and I'll be next to you before you wake up."

O wasn't satisfied.

"Sir, please, I ..."

"A somewhat talented young actress with bad habits has gotten herself arrested again. I represent her agency on criminal matters for an exorbitant retainer so when she gets slammed I have to pry her loose. She's at the West Hollywood sub-station now and if I leave her there until morning every paparazzo in town will be waiting outside for her walk of shame."

"Would you like me to come with you, Sir?"

"No need for both of us to be out all night."

"Won't you have to take her home once she's released?"

"Her new assistant sounds like a scared teenager. I'm not sending an intoxicated client anywhere with one of those."

"Don't you think it might be wise to have a witness with you ... Sir?"

Steven looked at O quizzically. He wasn't sure how much of his other life he really wanted her to see. He had always been careful to keep the sordid details of springing fuck-ups hidden from those he knew personally. But O did have a point and why, if she were really his slave in all the things, would he deny her the chance to make herself useful? It occurred to him that she just might turn out to be useful in ways he hadn't considered.

"Okay, but you won't enjoy it. Put on something modest while I make bail for the silly bitch."

O looked at the illuminated display on the short-wave radio next to the phone.

"At this time of night?"

Steven picked up the handset again.

"Judges are always available to set bail for the right defendant."

Steven hit a two-digit speed-dial code and put the phone up to his head. It rang a long time. O could hear Steven's voice clearly from the dressing room where she sought out her little corner of rack space in search of a simple gray button-front dress and her long cashmere wrap-coat to put over it.

"Hey Barney. It's Steven," she heard him say into the phone. "Yes, I'm all too aware of the time but I need the usual favor and I need it right away. Suspect's legal name is Allison Kemp. The sheriffs have her down in WeHo. Fuck, I don't know Barney... DUI, resisting arrest, assault on a police officer, overtime parking. I'm sure there's more. She's get plenty of money so set it as high as you want. No, she's not a flight risk. Where the fuck would she go? Thanks, Barney. Lunch at The Palm is on me."

O, dress half-buttoned, stood at the mirror running a tortoise-shell brush through her hair when Steven made his next call. Some of the well-buffed charm had begun to creep back into his voice.

"Good morning, Ms. Romano. What are you doing at work so late? Yes, I suppose we share that occupational hazard. Listen, I need you to bond out one Allison Kemp down at West Hollywood. The judge is calling in the order right now. I'm sure it will be stratospheric but believe me, her agency's good for it."

O heard Steven laugh drily.

"No, she's absolutely not worth it as far as I'm concerned, but if you or I had to choose our clients on that basis we'd both be out of business. Thanks pal. I'll have the security note on your desk by nine-thirty."

Getting out of bed, Steven felt curiously old. Every ancient injury from his colorful past ached as he hoisted himself to his feet. O emerged from the dressing room, coattails swirling around her bare legs, to find him stretching, naked, with his back to her. The round white shoulder scar of the exit wound left by a dead man's last shot was clearly visible in the overhead lights Steven had switched on.

O felt a wave of sympathy for him, realizing that he was doomed to solving other people's problems for life. Such a life would break her in two. With all his money, why didn't he just retire? She could ask the same question of herself. It wasn't like she needed to earn a living from her photography. But what would either one of them do without the organizing principles around which their days were strung together?

O offered to get Steven's clothes for him but he found it easier to do it himself than to tell her what he needed. The shearling collared jacket and some black jeans would do. This wouldn't be a formal occasion.

O had never been in the town car before. It had its own dashboard computer terminal, banks of radio scanners, a satellite phone and a huge hand-held spotlight mounted on a curly cord next to the steering wheel.

"Wow, your very own cop car, Sir."

"It was built for the Federal Executive Protection Service. It's even got mounts for a barrier cage in the back. If you'd like I can have you stand out on a street corner in something trashy, pick you up, cuff you and make you suck my cock in the back seat."

O squirmed and hugged herself. "You're making me very wet, Sir."

"Yeah, well, fun's over for tonight. Buckle up. We're taking the short-cut to hell."

Wilshire Boulevard was a blur outside the smoked windows as Steven raced the stoplights. Evidently he wasn't concerned with getting a ticket. Imagining how the blacked-out car must look she doubted any stray patrol unit would choose to pull it over.

Less than twenty minutes later they pulled into the parking lot behind the low, nearly windowless hexagon of the Sheriff's Department West Hollywood Branch HQ. The lot was mostly full with cruisers, unmarked command cars bristling with antennas, a couple of armored vehicles and rows of civilian rides that brought the deputies to and from work. Steven unhesitatingly parked in a spot clearly designated for official vehicles only. What were they going to do, write him up?

In his mannerly way he came around to open the massive armored passenger door for her and they went inside through the fortified entrance in back.

The fluorescent lights cast a sickly blue-green tint over everyone and everything. The gray tiled floor looked dingy, the institutional green walls faded and weary. The smell of Lysol hung heavy in the air, with an undercurrent of whatever the Lysol was intended to scrub away. The rows of incongruously bright-hued plastic chairs were largely empty but for a single slumped-over figure of indeterminate age and sex swathed in dirty rags and apparently out cold from drink, exhaustion or death.

The only other occupant was a very nervous young woman in a pricey designer motocross jacket. She was thin and gaunt with short brown hair falling in a messy fringe on her forehead. She had the dazed look of someone in a place where she deeply believed she didn't belong. As soon as Steven and O appeared she jumped up and ran to him, hand extended.

"You must be Mr. Diamond," she said in a high, thin voice.

He took her hand, which was cold and clammy.

"I guess I must be since I'm here."

"Becky Chandler, Charlotte's executive assistant. Boy, am I glad to see you."

"I get that a lot in places like this."

Allison, aka Charlotte Vale, had gone through a platoon of assistants already. Steven gave this one about a week.

Becky began rattling off a breathless account of the evening's misadventures, beginning with drinks at The Marmont and deteriorating rapidly thereafter. Steven calmly assured her that everything would be fine and suggested she have a seat next to O, who led her away with an arm around the shoulders. O looked back at Steven. He mouthed his silent thanks. He was glad he'd brought her along. She truly did have a way of making herself useful that he didn't associate with women of her particular tastes.

At the front of the waiting room next to a cork board plastered with rumpled notices of warning, wanted posters, calendars of community events and volunteer sign-up sheets, a tall, lean African-American sheriff's sergeant with graying temples and a trimmed gray mustache sat at a desk behind a thick, bullet-resistant plexiglass screen. His khaki shirt was adorned with many sleeve stripes and a row of ribbons below his shiny badge attested to his service on the street, now long past. The sergeant was reading an early copy of The New York Times and took no notice when they came in.

Motioning O and Becky to a front row seat, Steven strolled to the window and cleared his throat. The sergeant looked up. Recognizing Steven, his face broke into a surprisingly welcoming grin.

"Good evening, counselor," he said in a resonant basso through the mesh in the center of the shielding. "To what do we owe the honor?"

"Hello Sergeant Wilkerson," Steven replied, getting as close to the wire as possible. "I've come to take an unwelcome guest off your hands. I believe Judge Robling's already called about her."

"Ah, yes. That would be Miss Kemp. I can't say she'll be missed."

Wilkerson picked up a telephone receiver, punched a couple of buttons and said something Steven couldn't make out through the heavy polymer layer between them. He did hear Wilkerson laugh before putting the receiver back in its cradle.

"It will be a few minutes, Mr. Diamond. They have her downstairs in AdSeg."

"To protect her from the other tenants?" Steven suggested caustically.

"To protect them from her I suspect."

"Might I have a glance at the squawk?"

Stroking his chin, Wilkerson looked at Steven sternly.

"You know I'm not supposed to let you see that."

"I'll never tell."

Wilkerson rocked his head back and forth, thinking it over. Having decided, he shuffled through some papers in a wire-mesh basket on the desk and passed a legal-size sheet through a slot to the tiny ledge of counter where Steven stood. Steven picked it up, pulled out his glasses and started reading.

"It was a nice quiet night until she got here," Wilkerson said.

Steven didn't look pleased at what he saw and when he lifted the top stapled sheet to go on to the second page he winced visibly.

"Did she really do that?" Steven asked with a pained look on his face.

"It's all downhill from there. I will never understand why a young person with everything a young person could want in this world would fuck up her life like that. I see it happen all the time here and I still don't get it."

"I'm a lawyer, not a shrink. I just get them cut loose. Luckily, I don't have to fix them."

Even before the heavy door with the small chicken-wire-reinforced window opened with a loud buzz, Steven could hear the commotion coming down the hallway. This was going to be fun.

The door swung wide and a striking young woman fell through, kept from hitting the floor only by a muscular female deputy, also black, holding her up by one arm. Allison was handcuffed securely but struggled in the deputy's grip anyway.

"Let go of me, you fucking bitch!" the prisoner howled.

"Whatever you say, lady," the deputy replied, releasing her grasp and letting Allison lurch, stumbling, into the middle of the room. Allison whirled around in a tangle of blonde hair and heavy necklaces. Her face – startlingly beautiful even when puffy, dirty and red-eyed – twisted into a sneer of contempt. She opened her luxuriant lips as if to say something but stopped when the deputy's hand went to the stun gun on her garrison belt.

"One more word and you'll be doing the dry-fish ballet," the deputy said in a tone that could not be misinterpreted.

Steven stepped in between them.

"Thank you, Deputy ..."

He glanced hastily at the uniformed woman's nameplate.

"Deputy MacMillan. I'll deal with things from here."

The Deputy tilted her head toward Allison.

"Does that belong to you?"

"No, but I'll take it off your hands."

"Best of luck. You'll need it."

Snapping a long black jailor's key off its ring, Deputy Mac-Millan advised Allison to hold very still if she didn't want to go home with a cast on her wrist, then popped off the handcuffs, holstering them on the garrison belt. Allison jumped away.

Before going back through the heavy door, Deputy Mac-Millan shot a parting scowl at her.

"I'd strongly suggest you pull your head out of your ass before it gets permanently stuck in there."

Allison's world-famous lips started to curl into an obscenity and the deputy's hand went back to the stun gun. Steven wagged a warning finger in Allison's face. His granite features somehow hardened a bit more. He spoke in a tone O had never heard before and hoped not to hear again.

"That will be quite enough out of you."

Allison's words were slurry but the sarcasm dripped through.

"Whatever you say, dad."

"I'm bored with this game. Next time, you can rot down-stairs until you're arraigned as far as I'm concerned."

Allison glowered at him, her legendary chest, half out of a ripped, stained silk top, heaved rapidly. Her huge blue eyes were pinned tight. Her low-rise jeans seemed to hang on her hips by hidden strips of Velcro glued to her skin. A big diamond captive-bead ring sparkled from her navel at the center of the exposed expanse of flat belly between the hem of her blouse and the wide gaudy concho belt cinched around her waist just above the legal limit. She smelled of alcohol and speed sweat.

O recognized her, of course, but was truly shocked at her wrecked condition. No wonder Steven had so little use for movie stars if this was how he customarily saw them.

"I'm going to tell the agency to fire your ass for talking to me like that, MISTER Diamond."

Steven looked levelly into Allison's bloodshot eyes.

"Walk out with me or stay here," he said in that icy voice. "It's your call."

Allison tried to focus her gaze, looking briefly like she might end up on the floor after all, steadied up and followed Steven shakily to the window in front of the booking desk where Sergeant Wilkerson shook his head, a look of grim amusement on his weathered face.

"Hard to believe she's somebody's daughter," he said through the wire.

Steven picked up the offense report from the shelf where he'd set it down, flipped it open to the second page and held it up in front of Allison's face.

"Can you read that okay?"

"Yeah. I can read just fine," she hissed.

But then, reading it, her angry face collapsed into a childish pout.

"Right then," Steven scolded. "That's why the agency has to post a hundred thousand bucks for you to sleep it off at home tonight. If we don't get you out of here in a hot minute there'll be about a thousand photographers waiting in the parking lot to capture you in all your glory for the tabs."

Steven passed the report back through the slot to Wilkerson in return for a clipboard with a form on it. Pulling out a sterling Breguet ballpoint from his inside jacket pocket he signed off on the form. Wilkerson took it back, looked it over and tossed it into a slotted wall rack.

"She's all yours, Diamond. Hope we don't see her back here any time soon."

"That," Steven said, "is not up to me, thankfully."

He turned to Becky and O, both of whom stood up and came forward, Becky rushing to grab her boss before she could run into anything sharp.

"Charlotte, are you okay?" she asked anxiously.

"Yeah, I'm just great. Can't you tell?"

Allison shook off Becky's hands. "

Don't fucking touch me!" she hollered. "Don't you ever fucking touch me again or you'll be back waitressing like that."

Baring her perfect teeth, which were stained with lipstick, she snapped her fingers in front of Becky's face. Becky's lip trembled. She looked ready to burst into tears.

O had had about enough.

"You don't need to talk to her like that," O said calmly. Before Steven could warn O not to get involved, Allison rounded on her, fists balled and arms out as if to strike.

"And who the fuck are you to tell me what to do?"

Steven quietly went to *en garde,* ready to fling Allison across the waiting room, but O coolly stood her ground.

"Whatever you're thinking," O said quietly, "I wouldn't advise it."

Allison lunged at O who took a half step back so Steven could grab Allison's arm. Then O whipped the small Leica out of the shoulder bag she'd thrown on when they left the house and fired off a half dozen frames directly into Allison's soiled, bleary mug. Allison thrashed madly in Steven's iron grip.

"Hey lady," Wilkerson yelled through the barrier, "no pictures allowed in here!"

"Sorry, Sergeant." O replied politely. "My mistake."

She slipped the camera back in her bag as Allison screamed and cursed and threatened to kill her.

"Now then," O said, stepping up to look Allison, who was fully a head taller, directly in the eye, "you just settle down and do what the nice man tells you if you don't want those pictures up on TMZ by eight o'clock."

Allison started to say something, saw the look in O's eye and shut her jaw with an audible click.

Steven nodded at O.

"Thank you. That was very helpful."

A thin smile played across O's lips.

"It was my pleasure, Sir."

Still holding Allison by one arm to keep her from knee-walking away, Steven turned to Becky.

"We'll follow you to her place. She rides with us."

Becky looked desperately confused.

"I don't know. I'm supposed to be responsible for her."

"And how's that working for you?"

"Okay. She lives on Upper Sunset. I'll be waiting outside in a black Fiat."

"Smart girl," Steven said. "When I call your boss I'll try to think of something constructive to say after I finish ripping him a new one. Go on. We'll catch up."

Becky sprouted wings and flew through the door while Steven more or less dragged Allison out after her, O at his side every step of the way. Steven had no doubt that if Allison misbehaved once more, O would mop the pavement with her. He too had seen the look in her eye, and it was chillingly familiar. Steven and O apparently had yet another thing in common. Oddly, he found himself wondering what other surprises O might have in store.

At Steven's suggestion O rode in the back in case Allison, who Steven more or less dumped in the passenger seat of the huge sedan, needed strangling. Allison fussed at him a bit as he buckled her seatbelt but was quickly succumbing to the combination of exhaustion, intoxication and defeat. She slumped against the door and managed a final bark at Steven.

"Don't you dare start lecturing me, you fucking jerk," she spat.

Before Steven could return the thrust with some sharp rebuke Allison's face suddenly went gray. Beads of sweat popped out on her forehead. She spun toward the window, frantically fumbling with the button to roll it down, and vomited violently out into the cool night air, choking and heaving a few more times prior to collapsing back into the seat in a stupor. O reached forward to feel for a pulse in Allison's neck.

"Still alive I'm afraid, Sir."

Steven rolled up the window from his side.

"If you think of it, please remind me to add having the car detailed onto my bill when I send it over."

The tension broken, they both burst out laughing.

"There is a certain rough justice in the world, isn't there?" Steven observed.

"That there is, Sir," O replied as they pulled out of the lot behind Becky's tiny Fiat (the special red-and-black trimmed Gucci edition needing only a vanity plate that said "Assistant") for the ride up into the Hollywood Hills.

"One thing, though," Steven said. "You will have to delete those pictures."

Steven glanced in the rear view to see that O already had the camera out and was busily cleaning the images off the chip.

"Already done, Sir. I don't sell ugly."

Allison muttered something, shifted in her seat and began to snore.

"Charming," Steven said sarcastically.

"It's sad, really," O said. "I've seen her in a couple of things. She's got a lot of talent."

"Maybe she'll last long enough for the rest of her to catch up with it. The survivors write books after a few trips through rehab."

"I begin to see why you have such a grudge against show business, Sir."

"I just don't understand why the process of entertaining people has to be so brutal," he said sadly. "Roman gladiators got better odds than these lost souls. They come out here loaded down with insecurities and a bottomless hunger for validation. What they find is a vast freak show offering unlimited opportunities to be humiliated and rejected in different ways on a daily basis. They go to open calls where casting directors walk down endless rows of people who all look pretty much alike, stare at each of them for fifteen seconds and then thank them for coming in. They never even explain why they pick one over another. It's guesswork on one side and luck on the other. And it doesn't hurt to have relatives in the industry."

O asked if that wasn't true of every industry.

"Maybe so, but in show the line sucks worse than anywhere, except maybe for pro sports. And in the same way there's not much in the middle. You go to the Super Bowl or you end up coaching at some high school in Minnesota. Here, you get paid ten million bucks to make a dumb comic book movie or you end up hostessing at The Cheesecake Factory."

He glanced over at the semi-conscious Allison, shifting uncomfortably with her face against the back of the seat.

"I grew up around big names and lots of money, Sir," O said. "I saw plenty of human wreckage. But certain people just deal with the situation naturally. They're grateful for the breaks they get along the way and they don't take themselves too seriously."

"Personally, I prefer to have some control over my own destiny."

O laughed.

"And everyone else's too, Sir."

"Yeah, well, somebody's got to be responsible."

He nodded toward the snoring celebrity next to him.

"If I don't clean up messes like that, who will?"

O conceded she couldn't do it, wouldn't do it, no matter how much they paid her. Steven mulled that over. It seemed to him that she'd be pretty good at it.

Winding up through the switchbacks above The Strip, they stopped behind the Fiat in front of an enormous Italianate villa with lights burning in every window. Becky leapt from her car and ran to the passenger side of the huge Lincoln. Steven rolled down the window.

"Careful there. Your boss left her dinner on the door."

Becky looked down, jumping back with a repelled exclamation. Steven got out and came around to help her lift Allison out of the car and half-carry-half-drag her to the front door of the house.

"This is where my services stop," he said.

"Thank you. I'll take her from here."

Steven handed Allison off rather gently into Becky's arms.

"I'm grateful for what you did back there," she said.

"Every minute of it was on the clock. Accounting's going to have a collective coronary when I invoice."

"You know," Becky said sadly, "she can be very nice. I mean, really charming and funny and generous. I'm sorry you had to meet her this way."

"I'm sure she's a saint and her mother loves her. Keep an eye on her. If she starts twitching or stops breathing, call nine-one-one. Just don't call me, okay?"

O was already sitting up front when Steven got behind the wheel.

"Welcome to my glamorous life," he said.

"Sir, you don't know glamour until you've snipped off a model's tampon string while she's tied up."

Despite their fatigue they were inexplicably ravenous and stopped at The Pacific Dining Car for breakfast among the late shift of doctors from the hospital across the street and the early shift of senior officials headed for City Hall. As always, Steven got the best booth in the center room, where he put away a small filet, two eggs over medium and a pile of hash browns. O was satisfied with a mushroom omelet and some orange juice.

"You were good back there," Steven said, pouring some more decaf.

"I have a little experience dealing with difficult people, Sir."

She smeared some marmalade from a tiny jar on a piece of brioche, an indulgence O figured she'd earned after such a long night.

"I assumed that when I took you along, but I didn't anticipate the thing with the camera. Very effective improvisation."

"It was much like you said, Sir. Time slowed down when she lunged at me. I had just enough to come up with something."

"I'm glad you invited yourself along."

For the first time since Marie, Steven realized he'd met a woman who might mean more to his life than a temporary respite from it. Something not previously imagined now seemed possible.

"If you ever get tired of taking pictures and want into law school I can make it happen and you'll have a partnership waiting when you get out. We've been a little short staffed since Martin died."

O did her best to conceal the horror with which such a notion filled her. She wanted to be anything in the world to Steven but his law partner.

"From what I've seen of your client list so far, I might as well stay where I am," she said, hoping to slide through with a dismissive quip. From the look on Steven's tired face, which for once failed to defy gravity, O could tell the idea still lingered.

Fortunately, the full force of a PSD power breakfast was hitting him and Steven called for the check.

Half an hour later, they were back in bed as if the whole experience had been a dream. Once again Steven had made something un-happen. That was his peculiar magic in life. The more O saw of it, the more it mystified her. It wasn't something she hoped ever to need. Weary as she was, it took a few moments for her to curl up against his big back and fall down deep into a dreamless slumber.

Sleep didn't come so easily to Steven though he was just as tired. Something had changed that night. O would always be his slave but now he'd let her inside the wire where she'd proved herself capable of being something much more. For the first time in a decade he found himself wondering that might look like. It might look like love. He hadn't seen it in so long he was surprised by how easily he still recognized it. Even more surprisingly, he realized how much he'd missed seeing it.

CHAPTER THIRTY-EIGHT

O, dressed in her at-home "uniform" – black stay-ups, shiny red-soled heels a mile high, her septum ring and leather bands at the neck, wrists and ankles – sat on Steven's desk doing her cigar service. She went about it with her usual precision, neatly clipping off one end of the mighty Cohiba *robusto* with the special round-tipped scissors, placing the newly exposed tip between her red-stained lips (O had abandoned smearable gloss of any kind by now) and ignited it with a long cedar match from a lacquered box decorated with gold medallions to match his humidor. Taking exactly two puffs to satisfy herself that she'd gotten an even light she looked up and opened her mouth, letting the smoke escape in a languid imitation of her signature.

Satisfied, she passed it to Steven who took it, kissed O's wrist and went on talking into his headset as he drew in the first savory cloud.

"There will be four of us," Steven said into the tiny boom mic. "I don't think we need a Gulfstream. But I wouldn't mind something a little special in the way of a cabin crew."

Something Marie said on the other end of the line made him smile.

"Good choices as always. The usual suite at The Clift will be fine and if you don't mind calling Francis I'd like a nice table at Michael Mina for the first night. We'll need something roomy for the airport pick-up. I'm sure we'll bring twice as much luggage as we need. Sure you don't care to join us?"

Marie said something else that made Steven smile through the green nimbus forming around his head.

"Don't blame you a bit. If anything interesting happens I'll give you a full report."

Steven clicked off the headset with an invisible switch on the top of the earpiece.

O thought it all sounded like a grand occasion.

"Only because we're going."

Steven set the smoldering cigar in the crystal ashtray, pulled O forward by the front ring on her collar and kissed her.

"I'll have to wear more than this, I suppose," she said when he gave her back her lips.

"At least when we first get there. I'm sure you have something that will make an impression."

"Do we need to make an impression, Sir?"

"That can't be avoided so it we might as well be a good one. Perhaps you should give Jacqui a little wardrobe assistance."

O raised an eyebrow.

"I have just the thing in mind for her, Sir."

"No one gets her but Ray."

"I can make sure of that too," O said. "Will I be similarly restricted, Sir?"

"I haven't decided. We'll see if there's anyone there I'd like to watch fuck you."

O traced the inside of Steven's tropical worsted thigh with the toe of her shoe, opening herself for viewing in the process.

"If you do I'll try my best to give you a good show, Sir."

"If you can tear yourself away from scoping out models."

"It is a business trip."

"Business is pretty much what David's all about. He knows we're going forward with the web edition. I doubt the invitation was coincidental. We'll see how he intends to cut himself a piece of our new franchise."

"Each of you has something the other might want."

"Be a good girl and text Jacqui to tear herself away from Ray and get packing so we can be there by dinnertime."

O slipped off the desk, knelt to kiss the tops of Steven's brogued boots and backed out of the room, giving Constance a nice look at Steven's mark from the rear. Constance slipped by her, steno pad in hand, and sat down in front of Steven's desk.

"I never thought I'd say this," she began, "but I'm starting to like having O around. I rather miss her when she doesn't drop by."

"But does she miss us, or anyone else for that matter? I have my doubts."

"Good point, Mr. Diamond. I got a call from Mark at the agency while she was in here. Didn't think it was worth interrupting you."

"It wasn't."

Constance consulted the notes on her pad.

"Let's see. Profuse thanks, sending over a bottle of your favorite scotch, owes you beyond repayment and so on. I told him he could start by checking his email. I've already billed him."

"That should ruin his day."

"He said that actress girl – what's her name? – Allison something, wanted to apologize if she said anything rude last night."

"She was going to but she threw up on my car instead."

Constance raised her ginger eyebrows.

"I suppose that makes a strong statement in its own way."

"Not the one intended. I'll be gone for about seventy-two hours. Other than Marie I don't want to hear from anyone about anything."

"I'll tell them all you're looking at offices in Tierra Del Fuego. Should put the frighteners on them."

"Exactly."

Constance moved to the couch and crossed her legs, two things she rarely did.

"Mind if I ask you a question?"

"You already have."

"Fair point. Something specific."

Steven put his headset back in its charger.

"Why are you still taking these missions yourself? Any other practice this successful would delegate everything but trial work to junior associates. There you are bailing out drunk movie stars in person."

"When someone pays me the give-a-shit rate the least I can do is give a shit. If you leave things to people who don't have a direct stake in the outcome they rarely make that kind of investment. Besides, I like what I do. Martin and I really had more fun at the Public Defender's office than anyplace else."

"Just the thing for that old PTSD, eh?"

"You better not be writing a book, Constance," Steven warned good-naturedly.

"I have thought of pitching your life as a reality series."

Steven got up, brushed down the wrinkles of his cashmere jacket and started toward the door.

"Seventy-two hours, Constance. Put up the out-of-office auto-reply on the email."

"Sure you won't go into withdrawals or something?"

"I'll be too busy."

Back across the hall O called Jacqui, who was frantically tearing Ray's place apart in search last-minute necessities pre-staged there that had since gone missing. O calmed her down and had her put Ray on the phone. He was laughing at the spectacle of Jacqui running around the house in her underwear. O suggested he get her high immediately so she could remember where she'd stored all her things when she was stoned previously. She also reminded him to feed her some lunch, as she was even more scattered when her blood sugar dropped.

Moving on to Steven's personal haberdashery, O systematically packed his black Vuitton trunk. He'd need something dressy in which to go out tonight, of course. The black wool crepe double-breasted suit from Anderson and Sheppard traveled well. O felt a special affection for it, and the red shirt and black pleated tie to go along. He'd worn these clothes when they met. By now she had the inventory of all his shoes, socks, underwear, braces and jewelry catalogued in her mind. Then there were lighters and pens and wallets and other accessories to be stashed in the trunk's various drawers.

A couple of sweaters were always wise for a city that didn't seem to understand the principle of central heating in the same way Steven did. There would have to be extra shirts, scarves, gloves, boots, his silver travel shaving brush and collapsible silver cup, a watch or two and, of course, a few special items he might want during more private moments.

For the ball itself Steven had given her a specialized list of items for the particular ensemble he'd had run up by Gieves and Hawkes Military at Number One on The Row. He'd had to use all his lawyerly skills convincing them to make it for him. The stiff-necked sentinels at Firmin had been even less willing to supply the furnishings that went with, but Steven had a way of getting what he wanted.

O, who had been traveling since childhood, had wisely packed her Goyard valise and train case at home the night before. She would bring only garments she was certain to wear and the minimum practical requisites needed to assemble each of the looks she'd cataloged on a written manifest by long habit. Her bags were already waiting by the front door when she rang downstairs for Sumners, the afternoon security guard, to bring the Mercedes LE around.

With minimal assistance from the tall shaven-headed guard, Steven loaded in the trunk and a matching London bag for the items he preferred to keep close at hand. Service personnel were specialized by occupation. Security guards were not porters and didn't appreciate being treated as such.

Steven had ditched his suit in favor of the leather A-2 jacket with the historically accurate CBI patches on the front and a risqué nose-art pin-up painted on the back. He put on his aviator glasses and a leather ball cap, kicked the big machine into gear and headed for the ramp.

Ray and Jacqui were still scrambling around at Ray's place when Steven and O got there. Jacqui had her nylon roller bags lined up like soldiers on the front stoop but Ray hadn't finished dismantling his vaporizer and Jacqui still needed to roll one for the road. Like most serious potheads they didn't pack their stashes until the last minute lest they space out their most critical travel supplies. It wasn't like there was any weed to be had in San Francisco or anything.

Jacqui was uncharacteristically chic in slim, white embroidered jeans, a short white-suede jacket with fur trim and matching boots. No sweatpants, newsboy hats or Uggs for her today. It wasn't often she hitched a ride on a chartered jet and if she was mistaken for a movie star so much the better. O wore the kind of seemingly prim blue suit – cut impossibly high and tight to show off her corseted curves – intended to inspire impure thoughts. Just in case that didn't do it, the low-cut, ruffled silver-satin blouse under the unbuttoned jacket and the heels not made for walking would surely produce the desired effect.

Throwing on his battered black motorcycle jacket, Ray heaved the remaining baggage into the back of Steven's miniature tank and they all piled in for the short trip over Laurel Canyon up to the Van Nuys airport. Jacqui and Ray made out and sang a somewhat out of synch *a capella* rendition of "Girl On Fire." O and Steven exchanged a look.

"This is what I get for double-dating with my kid brother," Steven sighed.

Ray pretended to take umbrage, reminding everyone that he'd gotten the invitation, a fact of which Steven was very much aware. Ray was the one who got the invitations but Steven was the one everybody wanted to see. Ray might have the tickets but it was Steven who bought the drinks.

The chartered Learjet 75, silver with blue stripes, waited on the apron, ramp down and door open, as Steven swung around the hangar onto the broad expanse of baked concrete in the flattest depths of The San Fernando Valley.

A couple of beefy ground crewman in green shirts unloaded the Mercedes onto a long dolly while the traveling party climbed aboard, O going first to give Steven a glimpse of the smoky stocking-tops under her fitted skirt. Like Steven, O was never completely off-duty. And, like Jacqui, she now wore a narrow silver choker with a single ring in front around her neck.

The plane's interior was done entirely in stitched anthracite leather and shiny carbon fiber. Jacqui looked around and declared she would never fly coach again. Jacqui had, in fact, flown coach to India and was more accustomed to traveling with a backpack than designer suitcases but she could get used to most things that looked good, tasted good or felt good.

Marie had even provided a pair of "flight attendants" from The Mansion, Eugenia and Svetlana. Both wore utterly indecent travesties of classic stewardess uniforms cut from an electric blue shade of translucent latex. The tight sleeveless blouses opened with snaps and only came down as far as the belly button, exposing pleasing expanses of flesh above skirts so short it was impossible to serve drinks in them without revealing the lack of anything worn beneath. Matching tiny caps were pinned into their tightly coiffed hair and slender blue-patent-leather slave collars circled their necks. The fin-

ishing touch was shiny blue heels high enough to be dangerous in any kind of turbulence.

The door to the flight deck was, of course, closed. The
charter service Marie used was known for its discretion.

Ray greeted Eugenia with a hug that lifted her off the
floor, introducing her to Jacqui as his favorite playmate from
The Mansion. They kissed and greeted each other as "Sister."

Steven was pleased to see Svetlana, all the more god-
dess-like with her hair piled atop her head. The uniform was
extremely flattering to her and she worked it, adding a little
extra thickness to her Natasha Fatale accent as she took O's
order for a Campari and soda.

The seat-belt light came on with a chime and the engines
spooled up outside. Steven and O strapped themselves into a
row of large loungers along one bulkhead. Ray and Jacqui took
the circular banquet around the table opposite. Their hostess-
es provided pleasant viewing strapping themselves into the
jump seats behind the cabin door.

The plane swung smoothly out onto the taxiway, pausing to bring the engines to full power. Outside the windows
the sky was gray under a low cloud cover. Steven figured it
would be a bit choppy going up but nothing compared to the
bouncing of the helicopters he'd flown off the decks of aircraft
carriers during his Navy hitch.

Jacqui, however, couldn't resist a squeal, hugging Ray as
tightly as their seat belts would allow when the plane throttled up and roared down the tarmac. Like all Learjets the seventy-five was configured as an STOL for landings on skimpy
strips in places like Mustique and Gstaad. It blazed into the
air at such a steep angle the G-force pinned them all to the
upholstery.

"Holy shit! It's like being shot out of a cannon," Jacqui
yelled over the engine noise.

Steven checked the big square Bell&Ross chronometer on
his wrist and clicked one of the pushers to activate the timer.

As Van Nuys fell away beneath the marine layer the jet made a wide swing and climbed out, headed north. Steven and O shared a knowing smile. The aircraft could easily have reached cruising altitude in half the time but corporate pilots were trained for smooth ascents and terror-free landings. Both O and Steven had rattled their way through much rougher air in far less reliable equipment all over the world. Some had lacked doors, much less pressurized cabins.

Rising through the bumpy air to level out at thirty-five thousand feet the jet's engines throttled back and the sensation of movement faded. Svetlana and Eugenia rose from the jump seats and went to work in the galley. Svetlana poured O's aperitif and the sparkling water Steven requested. Eugenia popped open a bottle of sparkling cider for Ray and Jacqui.

Jacqui unbuckled herself and straddled Ray's lap so she could look out the porthole as the plane swung out over the white-capped Pacific far below. Eugenia dipped extra-low, showing off to both sets of passengers when she set the glasses on the table.

"We brought some refreshments of our own," Ray said, holding up a fat reefer from a pocket inside the leather jacket. Eugenia smiled broadly at Ray and Jacqui.

"We've really missed you out The Mansion since my little sister here's been keeping you at home, Sir. You always bring the best smoke."

"We'll have to come and visit together," he said, firing up with a titanium torch lighter.

Jacqui was all naughty, girlish excited when she took the joint from Ray.

"I've always wanted to do this," she said. "I had to use my electronic one-hitter in the head on the way back from London last time."

"You can pretty much do what you want on these flights," Eugenia said, taking the joint from Jacqui.

Svetlana was more reserved, doing a credible imitation of a real flight attendant as she dipped to serve drinks off a silver tray. Her blue-gray eyes met Steven's only briefly, making him wonder what it was she didn't want him to see. With the upper three buttons of her top open there was plenty else for him to look at.

"I never knew you were pierced," he observed, noting the gold stud through Svetlana's right nipple.

" I don't always wear it, Sir. Some men like jewelry and some don't. Better to give them a choice."

O complimented Svetlana's practicality. Each in her way made a living from knowing what men wanted to see.

"Svetlana has beautiful breasts," Steven said.

"Thank you, Sir," Svetlana replied rather formally.

"May I see them?" O asked. Svetlana looked at Steven for approval. She didn't take instructions from other collared girls. Steven nodded. Svetlana started to put her tray down on the table next to O's seat but O stopped her.

"If you don't mind, I'd like you to hold that for me please."

Still looking at Steven, Svetlana held perfectly still while O undid the remaining snaps. Svetlana's top burst apart, spilling out a cascade of smooth flesh every bit as appealing as Steven promised. O reached up and hefted Svetlana's breasts in her hands.

"They really are fabulous, Sister."

"Thank you, Sister," Svetlana replied, unfazed by O's gentle manipulations, though her nipples did harden and swell noticeably, the more so for the standard dark red tint applied to all The Mansion's house girls.

"Would you mind if I took a picture of them?"

"Of course not."

O brought the small Leica out of her handbag, directing Svetlana to lean down further and hold the tray up under her as if she were performing a real flight attendant's duties.

"Perfect!"

O snapped off four frames. Turning the camera around, she showed Svetlana the image. Svetlana couldn't keep from smiling.

"Very Helmut Newton," she said.

"Exactly. He'd have loved it. Or at least he wouldn't have griped about how much he hated digital photography."

Svetlana was impressed.

"You knew him?"

"I modeled for him when I was eighteen. He'd turned into a bitchy old queen by then. Fortunately I was more patient in those days."

Svetlana let the tray drop to her side, but made no attempt to cover up, expecting further instructions. She didn't have to wait long.

"Would it be all right if she sat down next to me so you could get a picture of both of us?" O asked.

Steven stood up obligingly so Svetlana could take his place. Sitting on the edge of the table swinging her legs, Eugenia watched, hearing Ray and Jacqui giggling about something behind her; her ass, most likely. The skirt was low enough in the back to reveal some butt cleavage, of which Eugenia had no shortage.

O slipped off her jacket, folded it on the seat next to her and opened her blouse so she and Svetlana were equally bare from the waist up. O put a light hand around the back of Svetlana's neck, gently easing the Russian girl's head onto O's shoulder. Steven could see where this was going.

"It's only a one-hour flight," he reminded them.

O reached over to tweak Svetlana's pierced nipple.

"I'm sure we can make good use of the time, Sir."

Kneeling in the aisle, Steven told them to hold still and fired off a few shots. He reviewed them, showed them to Ray, Jacqui and Eugenia who all agreed O and Svetlana made a lovely couple. Steven finally presented the small screen to his two subjects. Svetlana reached up to tug on one of O's rings.

"You have very nice breasts too," she said, turning to take the nearest in her mouth.

Moments later the cabin was full of discarded clothing. Eugenia lay on her back on the table with her legs in the air while Jacqui guided Ray's cock into her and played with her clit. Steven sat down to receive the shared oral attentions of O and Svetlana, who alternated working on him together with passing him back and forth between them. At the critical moment both lifted their chests to him so he could splatter their geography equally while Jacqui pulled Ray out of Eugenia just in time to swallow.

Eugenia slid off the table to fetch warm damp cloths while everyone enjoyed a good laugh. High-fives were exchanged in honor of Eugenia's and Svetlana's induction into The Mile High Club of which Steven, Ray, O and Jacqui were already long-time members in good standing.

By the time the seat-belt lights came on above San Francisco Bay, into which the sun was setting bright orange, everyone was buttoned up and strapped in as if nothing unusual had happened. Swooping down over SFO the jet touched down lightly, taxiing toward a waiting blue Chevy Suburban parked outside the charter service's hangar.

Before deplaning, Steven rapped lightly on the cockpit door. An athletic young co-pilot greeted him with a smile.

"May I help you, Sir?"

"Just wanted to thank you for the smooth ride. Next time I come up on my own maybe we can hot-rod a little."

The co-pilot, who Steven instantly made as a recent Air Force discharge, shook his hand.

"I'm sure we'd enjoy that."

An older, grayer head turned from the pilot's seat to give Steven a grumpy thumbs-up.

"Damn Skippy I'd be up for that. I can barrel roll this thing without spilling a drink and they make me fly it like an airborne bus driver."

He appraised Steven with a weather-beaten squint.

"What branch were you in, if you don't mind my asking?"

"Four years in the Navy, two more in the active reserve."

"Not some Miramar Miracle I hope."

"No, Captain. Just an old sea lawyer who got a taste for landing on steel plate."

They all shook hands, exchanged business cards and made vague plans, little knowing that Steven would ultimately see them through for the same reasons he liked to hang out in the kitchen at Marie's. These gentlemen might have some interesting and useful stories to tell.

The breeze from the bay was cool and wet, scented with the ocean and Jet Forty. Clacking down the steel steps in her stilettos O asked Steven if there was anything that failed to engage his curiosity.

"Only the things I know too much about already."

O weighed that.

"I'll try to make sure I don't wind up in that category."

Steven promised she'd always be an open case to him.

"You make it sound so dirty, Sir!"

Ramp rats in orange vests wrestled their bags into the back of the Suburban. Steven sat in the passenger seat. Ray happily climbed in between O and Jacqui, getting a hand around the thigh of each. Eugenia and Svetlana got the third row. They looked quite cozy in the long cashmere wrap-coats Marie considerately provided for occasions when it was necessary to be warm or decent or both while out on the town in latex.

Ethan, the driver from the hotel, was a clone of the entire staff – tall, good-looking and respectfully casual in his gray sweater and black slacks. Swinging around the long curve toward the city lights, which had begun to come on in the gathering dusk, he asked the usual questions about where they'd come in from and how long they'd be in town. O had something else on her mind. She leaned forward onto the back of Steven's seat.

"If I may, what was that business with the pilots, Sir?"

"The LJ Seventy-Five is about as close to a tactical fighter as you'll find in executive charter. It's favored by celebs and drug dealers."

"The type of person who might need your services."

O didn't miss much.

"Ordinary tourists get advice from cab drivers. My clients get their referrals from pilots and concierges."

"One reason to write off the trip," O suggested.

Steven suspected David would give them a better one soon.

CHAPTER THIRTY-NINE

The Clift's typically informal Ian Schrager-style lobby was full of those same fashionable people having a fashionable good time Steven saw everywhere. What they all did for a living he had no idea but they must have been pretty good at it from the way the dressed and the confidence with which they carried themselves in a time of widespread insecurity.

The Mansion girls, who'd been assigned a smaller room on a lower floor, were understandably eager to change. Jacqui and Ray headed straight for the noisy bustling Redwood Room, which the renovators had thankfully left intact. O and Steven rode up to the top floor alongside the bellman and a cart piled high with extravagant luggage, every piece of which the bellman could price in his head. This party clearly belonged in the big suites.

Known for its tiny jewel-box spaces, the hotel had wisely been designed with four luxury units at the top affording spectacular views of the city and the bay. It came equipped with separate sleeping quarters and a spacious bathroom. There was a recessed seating area with two big armchairs across a low blond-wood table from a wide bench tufted in red leather, several wide-screen TVs and a mirrored black-marble bar.

O and Steven settled into adjoining chairs while the bell-man went through his spiel about available hotel services and room features. Steven made sure he got his first name and cell phone number before he slipped him a hundred and sent him on his way.

O looked out the window toward the festively strung lights of The Bay Bridge.

"It's always so beautiful up here. I forget."

"I'd move my practice if this town had more crooks."

O laughed, getting up to unpack Steven's things and put them in the closets and dresser drawers.

"Maybe they've just got better crooks," she suggested over her shoulder while hanging up Steven's black suit.

"No shit. These kids figure out new ways to steal faster than politicians can write laws against them. L.A. used to draw all the best scammers, but I think a lot of them have moved north."

Steven changed the subject.

"Your project with Jacqui and Ray seems to be going smoothly."

O admitted she couldn't take much credit.

"I underestimated how well they'd hit it off. They're like a couple of high school kids on a permanent date."

"Jealous? Maybe just a little?" Steven teased.

"I think it's sweet," O pronounced. "If Sir would like to have a shower, I could lay out your things for dinner."

Steven took the green leather shaving kit from his satchel and headed for the bathroom, pausing to let O hang up his travel clothes in a closet bigger than many of the hotel's entire rooms.

Naked before the mirror, Steven assembled his portable shaving brush, daubed it in a plastic tub of Trufitt and Hill lime shaving cream and slapped the lather on his face. Opening his Damascus razor, he was reminded of another reason why he liked flying charter. Try getting something like that past Security.

Steven could have O come in and scrub his back with a quick summons but he needed them both dressed and feared that would be a step in the wrong direction. Instead, he showered alone, hammering himself with the fierce blast from the huge overhead sprayer.

Emerging in nothing but a splash of Orange et Verte and a towel the size of a Bedouin robe he'd wound around his middle, he was once more impressed with O's industry.

On the vast bed she'd laid out the black suit, a black shirt with mitered double-cuffs, some scandalous braces, the pleated tie, a pair of black boxer briefs and tall socks with a single gray stripe up the sides. His favorite gray and black high-button boots stood at attention at the foot of the bed and his square white gold cuff links sat in the open jewelry case on the bedside table next to the Patek Philippe.

But what O had done with herself was even more impressive. Having given her makeup what little patching it needed, she'd twisted her hair into a chignon anchored with a vintage diamond comb and stuffed her breasts into the top of a black-lace long-line corset that held them up for the world to admire. She'd exchanged her stay-ups for fully fashioned stockings attached to the lower hem of the corset by six wide elastic straps, her seams as straight as the edge of Steven's razor, and climbed into black patent pumps with heels so high they raised her whole frame several inches. She wore simple jet earrings and a matching choker with a black ring instead of her customary silver collar.

As usual, her working parts were completely exposed and when O bent down to attach the braces to Steven's trousers she gave him a good look at them.

"You're being a bad girl, flirting with me when you know I don't have time to fuck you."

"I didn't know I was flirting, Sir. Perhaps I should be spanked as a reminder."

"Then we'd be late for sure."

Steven slipped into shorts and sat down on the bed, watching her while he rolled on his socks. She went about each task like a little fetish automaton, but consciously so, ever aware of his gaze without looking over at him once.

When he'd finished buttoning his shirt she knew to turn and put in his cuff links for him. Her pearlescent-nailed fingers were as adept at buttoning his trousers as at opening them and she tightened the braces just enough to drape the pleats properly. Kneeling, she kissed the top of each shoe as she fastened its gore, straightening his two-inch cuffs to a perfect break.

She raised her eyes to him, fluttering her impossibly thick lashes.

"Sir seems less disapproving now," she half-whispered.

"You do everything just right," he said admiringly.

"There is no other way to do them, is there, Sir?" Not for the two of them.

Steven knotted his own tie with a casual precision that only a man who had done it every day for four decades could, the ends matching up neatly on the first try. O fussed with his pocket square – plain silver with black rolled edges – until it stood up like the sails of a three-masted schooner. She fetched his silver-cornered wallet, the Carnegie pen, a barley-patterned silver card case and his round black glasses, slipping them into their various pockets one at a time. Then she stood back and appraised him just as he had appraised her.

"Very handsome, Sir," she concluded.

He told her she was the prettiest valet he'd ever had. O sniffed at that notion, reminding him that he'd never had a valet. What she didn't say was that in the world in which she'd grown up men usually did. It was from watching her father's valet at work that she'd picked up such a deft touch at dressing men.

For O the rest of the ritual was much simpler. She slipped on a dark-blue-velvet dress rising precisely to the line of the corset, to which it conformed dramatically once Steven did the hooks up the side. The dress was long but slit daringly high on the right, leaving her readily accessible when seated. Opera gloves with wrist buttons and a beaded clutch were all she needed. Steven draped her bare shoulders in a ruffled stole, also velvet, but a darker blue burned out in a floral pattern. He offered her his arm and she took it.

Down in the lobby Steven checked his watch a third time and mumbled something about lazy stoners.

"It's only two minutes after, Sir," O reminded him. She understood that life was hell for the punctual but it was their burden to bear. Ray didn't make them bear it long. He and Jacqui emerged from the green-lit depths of the mirrored elevator and started toward them, laughing.

Hugging each other by the numbers, they passed around the compliments. Yes, Jacqui was breathtaking in the black satin D&G dress, boned to mid-thigh and held together by a million little fasteners down the back. Her silver collar was very much in view on her slender neck, which was impossibly long in the way O's waist had gotten to be impossibly narrow. The velvet-laced gladiator sandals made her decisively taller than Ray. Ray had actually gone to some trouble, looking quite trim in a narrow-lapelled slate-blue suit with a skinny knit tie and petrol derby shoes.

"Where's our entourage?" Steven asked, wondering about Eugenia and Svetlana.

Ray told him Marie gave them the night off to go clubbing. They know a lot of people up there.

Steven had no doubt about that and he didn't mind their absence. The evening would be relatively protocol-free, at least at the beginning. Steven was certain it would get more so as the strange double date unfolded.

The blue Suburban waited outside, young men dashing to assist the ladies into the back seat. Ray got in with them, as usual, and the old guy rode up front, as usual. The heat was blasting, there was music playing and Steven was glad he hadn't bothered with an overcoat, though as a native Angeleno, he considered anything north of Santa Barbara to be the Arctic.

Mina's new space was airy and bright. They all agreed the old location had been a bit funereal. Here the friendly but correct staff of young people who didn't want to be actors seemed more at home. Brandt welcomed them at the door and showed them to their usual table where they settled into the mid-century modern seats with enough implements on the table in front of them to perform orthopedic surgery. Thoughtfully, the napkins were black, as lint was a constant menace to all the darkly attired men and women in the spacious room.

Big windows gave out onto the street where people walked by under the lights in pairs and groups, a mix of tourists and locals taking in the gentrified zone around Front and Battery. Steven was struck once again by how heterosexual the center of town had become since his time at The Presidio. This was a whiter, straighter, cleaner city than he remembered, but at least it was a city.

Looking over at O he caught a glimpse of some similar nostalgia. For O, Manhattan was Paradise Lost. As her father bought up more and more of the places where fashion, which had once been O's trade, set rules for everywhere else, she felt ever more uncomfortably visible there.

When she showed up in the Style section of *The Times* at fashion week twice in the same season it was definitely time to move on. Albert, who had spent most of his life in Manhattan, had been delighted to join her.

A round of chilled Absolut shots and a platter of Osetra appeared unbidden to an enthusiastic welcome. Steven remembered some kind of toast in Russian from the Kosovo detail while O piled blini high with tiny grey eggs topped by dollops of sour cream.

"The commander over here's gotten wasted with the finest officers of many lands," Ray proclaimed proudly.

"It's true," Steven admitted, "and I'm a lightweight by comparison. Everyone thinks the Russkies are bad, but the French are more consistently drunk, the English are more loudly drunk and the Japanese put them all to shame in every category." O pointed out that Steven forgot the Germans.

"They take it through a rubber tube at each end."

Everyone laughed.

Ray and Jacqui would have to finish off the fifth of Charles Krug with only a little help from O. Steven and everyone else would be happier if he stuck to a nice Belgian beer.

Jacqui had a great story from her stint as a latex model in Stuttgart but the waiter appeared, pad in hand, and attention turned to the menu. No decisional paralysis in this crowd. There would be the seasonal seafood presentation for O, venison for Jacqui (who had shot and dressed many a deer back in Wyoming), a rare rib eye for Ray and the lobster pot pie the patrons wouldn't let the proprietor take off the menu for Steven.

All talk of business was forbidden tonight. Ray and Steven knew there would be no escaping it once within the walls of David's fortress twenty-four hours from now. At the moment Ray and Jacqui were very much preoccupied with one another and Steven and O with the two of them.

Something was happening before their eyes that neither had anticipated. Ray, the unavailable chick magnet and Jacqui, the unobtainable fetish goddess, were doing a pretty good impression of two high school seniors in love. O's labors had been almost too successful and she felt a slight twinge of regret over it. She enjoyed being able to pull Jacqui's strings with the skills she'd polished during those boarding school seductions.

It wouldn't be as easy as she'd thought to hand them over to Ray, but that was coming.

Steven was simply amazed at seeing his brother happy. Ray's neon grin was famous but behind it was the sorrow Steven had seen in Ray's long, brooding silences as they watched their mother's decline. Steven did what he could for Ray but the two of them had been wounded in such different ways neither could fix the other.

There was nothing like a copper vat of lobster and cream to float away bad memories on a sea of cholesterol. But the best distraction had been saved for after dinner. When the entrées were cleared O and Jacqui excused themselves to the ladies' room, leaving Ray and Steven to conjecture what would go on in there while waiting for the white chocolate *lozenge* and the tiramisu that O and Jacqui would be required to feed each other to the last bite.

Steven might have had consent concerns about any kind of public acting out potentially observable by some hapless couple trying to convince the woman's parents, just in from Salt Lake, that they shouldn't worry themselves with the things they'd heard about this town. However, as those things were largely true, Steven didn't feel it was his responsibility to uphold someone else's idea of what passed for civic virtue in this town.

Returning, both O and Jacqui walked much more carefully, taking smaller steps and holding hands as they descended the short ramp into the dining room. Like the gentlemen their mother had brought them up to be, Steven and Ray stood to pull out the girl's chairs for them, the better to watch them settle their backsides ever so gingerly. The seating was rearranged with O and Jacqui now separated only by the corner of the table.

Jacqui looked on ruefully as O passed the small black control box over to Ray. O's impressive posture would be even more rigid for the hard, thick, bulbous plug Jacqui had helped her insert where it would be the most challenging.

Each girl was required to explain precisely what the other had done when they were alone. Jacqui now wore the device Steven had used on O when they'd gone to dinner with his friends. O was already being stretched in anticipation of how she would be made to serve when the got back to the hotel.

Ray slowly ramped up the vibrations under Jacqui's dress while she swallowed each bite of date cake. O struggled to keep from rubbing her thighs together as Jacqui made her lick the spoon clean after every scoop of jasmine cremeux. Their flushed faces nearly touched in the soft candlelight.

"You're evil with that thing," Jacqui said through gritted teeth, turning her glittering green eyes (fully enhanced with the tinted contacts) toward Ray. "You know I will scream if you make me come," she warned.

"No she won't," O said. "She'll just make a pathetic face and whimper."

"Some sister you are," Jacqui started to say, the last syllable suddenly jumping up a few octaves when Ray maxed out the remote. Steven looked idly around the room. Not a single head had turned. Yes, it would be nice to live where scandalous behavior wasn't so marketable a franchise.

On the ride back to the hotel Steven again sat up front with the driver, occupying him with tourist bullshit while Ray held Jacqui's arms behind her so O could extract another orgasm with the remote control.

Up in Steven's suite, clothes came off rapidly, or as rapidly as Ray could undo all the tiny hooks on Jacqui's dress. O stripped to her heels, corset and stockings, revealing the ruby-red crystal on the base of the ovoid steel plug buried in her bottom when she bent over to retrieve her septum ring from the red kidskin jewelry roll in her valise. Satisfied that it was properly centered with the removable segment hidden, she devoted her attention entirely to undressing her master.

O carefully put away each item, lingering over his boots to remind him of his regard for the view she provided from above, all the more enhanced by the glittering jewel between her cheeks and the inked ribbons trailing off toward the sides of her haunches.

Ray capriciously left the stimulation belt locked around Jacqui's hips once he got the dress off her and played idly with the remote control while tossing his clothes here and there around the room. Jacqui squealed and doubled over, shaking from the shoulders down as she sank to her knees.

Ray had learned to accept Jacqui's need for pain. He held in the shock button longer than he would have on his own before switching to the vibe and bending down to kiss her. Jacqui begged him to pinch her nipples really hard before letting her suck his cock. He practically lifted her off the floor, smothering her yelp with his hard-on. After that, the humming of the vibrating belt and Jacqui's slurps and sighs were the only noises from that side of the room.

O draped Ray's red shirt over the top of a lamp to soften the light on her way to fetch the purple silk robe with which Steven traveled and an outrageous pair of Tom Ford brothel slippers embroidered with naked odalisques. She held the robe for him while he slipped into it, knelt to keep the slippers in place so he could step in.

"May I bring us something to smoke, Sir?" she asked as he settled into one of the round deco chairs in the seating area. Steven watched the red crystal flash from between O's rear cheeks while she went to the desk to fetch a joint from Steven's engine-turned silver cigarette case and a matching vintage Dunhill Rolagas.

Returning to the chair, O lit the joint and took a deep drag before passing it to Steven. He slipped the lighter into the breast pocket of the robe and pulled O carefully onto his lap so she could sit without being jabbed by the jeweled stopper plugging her piping. He tenderly hooked a finger through her nose ring and pulled her close for a lingering kiss.

Together they enjoyed the show Jacqui and Ray staged for them. O knew that Ray had stopped paying attention to them but she caught Jacqui's eye long enough to exchange a wink, cut short on Jacqui's side by Ray's sudden tap on the shock button. Jacqui squeaked and twitched but kept on sliding Ray's shaft in and out of her face in a steady rhythm. Jacqui loved an audience and Ray wasn't exactly shy himself.

"They make a very handsome couple, Sir," O observed.

Steven agreed. Noticing a fresh set of slender pink marks neatly laddered over Jacqui's torso, Steven noted that Ray had upped his game for his new partner. Why not? Steven considered himself a product of all the women who had ever given themselves to him. He had learned from each, at least as much as they had learned from him. O was the most enlightening yet.

Pulling out of Jacqui's mouth and lifting her off the floor, Ray scooped her up, her arms, legs and head dangling, and carried her to the wide tufted-leather bench opposite Steven's chair. He dropped her on her back none too lightly. Jacqui bounced nicely, giggling and squirming when Ray turned the vibrating prods back on.

He left her to it while he searched out the tiny key to Jacqui's steel belt from the pocket of his discarded trousers, tossing it over to O who neatly plucked it out of the air. Jacqui moaned in frustration when Ray suddenly switched off the vibes.

"Would you mind getting that thing off her, please?"

"My pleasure, Sir," O replied, cautiously lifting off Steven's lap. Key in hand, she crawled onto the bench with Jacqui who looked over at her suspiciously.

"You've got that twinkle in your eye," Jacqui said warily. "You're going to do something mean to me, aren't you?"

"Who, me?" O asked innocently. She slapped Jacqui hard across the face, first to the right, then to the left. Jacqui laughed, reached up and grabbed O by the collar.

"Kiss me, bitch," she said in the most commanding tone she could muster.

"Gladly."

O stretched out on top of Jacqui, O's small body easily enfolded by Jacqui's long arms and legs. They kissed deeply, rubbing against each other's flesh in the red-filtered light. Ray came over for a hit from the joint and the two men watched their slaves wrestle playfully while the smoke formed a cloud overhead.

"Aren't we a couple of lucky bastards?" Ray asked rhetorically.

"You know I don't believe in luck."

Eventually, O squirmed from Jacqui's grasp, reclaimed the key she'd lost in the tangle of limbs and pushed the taller girl down.

"Hold still if you want to get fucked," O instructed.

"Oh, yes, Ma'am!" Jacqui answered quickly, spreading herself out so O could get in between her legs and unlock the belt from around Jacqui's middle. The light-gauge spring-steel popped open, revealing the grooves it had temporarily inscribed up Jacqui's smooth abdomen.

"Be nice," Jacqui warned, grabbing a handful of O's hair.

"Don't you trust me?" O asked, deliberately wiggling the twin probes as she slid them out of Jacqui's insides. Jacqui clamped her legs around O's hips and lifted up so O could slide the belt from under her and toss it on the floor.

"Poor thing," O said, staring at Jacqui's swollen wetness. "You've had such a demanding evening already and we're just getting started."

Jacqui stuck out her lower lip.

"You're all a bunch of cruel perverts taking advantage of a defenseless slave."

"Let me make it up to you," O said with a wicked grin. She lowered her face between Jacqui's legs and went right to work. Jacqui rolled her eyes, grabbed O's head and ground her crotch against O's mouth.

"Damn, girl, you don't play fair at all!" She exclaimed. Ray and Steven enjoyed the spectacle of Jacqui squirming and thrashing and beating the padded bench with clenched fists, waiting for the desperate cry for permission to come yet again. Jacqui had an endless supply of real orgasms stored up from all those she'd had to fake for the camera. Jacqui lay gasping her entire body flushed bright pink, while O tormented her with the occasional lick to her most hyper-sensitized spots.

Ray sat down next to Jacqui on the floor so he could shot-gun her a hit. Jacqui inhaled deeply, stroking Ray's big granite-hard cock as she looked up at him.

"Glazed like a jelly donut," he observed, smiling down at her glittering green eyes.

"Oh yeah. Give me a minute and I'll show you some serious payback."

Jacqui sat up with some assistance from Ray, O rocking back onto her heels to get out of the way. Jacqui pointed at her.

"Now it's your turn to scream."

O wasn't given to screaming but was perfectly pleased to let Jacqui try and make her do it. Clearly the girls had planned something in advance.

O rose from the bench and offered Jacqui a hand. Jacqui took it, standing up woozily as if she might topple off her heels. Ray and Steven shrugged at each other while O led Jacqui over to O's open epi leather suitcase. O's intentions became clear when she brought out a small zippered leather bag from which she removed a black bulb syringe, a couple of pairs of short black-latex gloves and a clear-plastic bottle of viscous liquid. But that wasn't all she'd brought along. Next she took out and carefully unrolled an exquisitely stitched single-glove made of soft red kidskin. It seemed impossibly small for any girl to actually wear but O was more limber than most of the bondage models she shot and could easily touch her elbows together in back. She turned to Steven.

"May we be excused for a moment please?"

O led Jacqui off through the suite's bedroom leaving Steven and Ray alone to smoke for a moment.

"Well, I can see where this is leading," Ray said.

Handing Steven the reefer he went to the open steamer trunk where he poked around a bit and brought out a nasty-looking coiled snake-whip.

"You seem to have found what works for Jacqui," Steven observed as Ray took a couple of practice flicks in the air, furled the whip and parked it on his shoulder.

"I can be just as mean as you are with the right encouragement."

Steven glanced over at Ray's still-stiff spear.

"Jacqui gives good encouragement."

Ray looked down at himself and laughed.

"It points to her like a compass needle whenever she's within half a mile."

"I assumed you were just that way all the time," Steven said, exhaling a gust of green smoke.

"I think it runs in the family."

Steven looked down at his own lap where the flag stood at full-mast also.

"Mine's chemically assisted," he explained.

"Yeah, right. Tell me you don't pop a chubby every time O walks by."

"I never lie," Steven declared righteously.

"Good thing for us the girls appreciate it."

"I think we're about to be shown some appreciation right now."

O and Jacqui emerged side by side. O's arms were ruthlessly welded behind her from the shoulders down inside the tightly laced leather sleeve, which was held in place by suspender straps looped through O's armpits and snapped to the top of the single-glove.

The compression thrust O's breasts outward even more spectacularly than usual. With her waist cinched by the corset and her hands thrust down into bottom of the sleeve, O looked like one of John Willie's watercolors come to life. She stood up very straight for maximum effect while Jacqui walked her over to where Steven sat, Jacqui's gloved fingers in the opening previously occupied by the jeweled plug. They managed to cross the room quite gracefully, stopping in front of Steven and Ray.

"Turn around, Sister," Jacqui said firmly.

O turned and nuzzled in between Jacqui's breasts so Steven could see how O was held open from behind by Jacqui's invading digits.

"I got her all nice and clean back there, Sir. She's hoping you'll use her primarily in that way."

Steven reached forward to trace his mark inscribed in O's flesh.

"She's lucky to have such a helpful friend."

"Sister, Sir," Jacqui corrected.

"I'm happy to oblige," Steven said, "but I think we'd like you both on your knees for a bit first."

O turned around and the two girls knelt smoothly with Jacqui's fingers still in place. Despite the immobilization of her arms and Jacqui's distracting penetration, O got to her knees without a wobble. At Marie's they had learned to work together with the smoothness of oiled ball bearings. While O lowered her face to Steven's lap, Jacqui lifted her head so Ray could loop the whip around the back of her neck and pull her mouth onto him.

The room was silent but for the sounds of heavy breathing and distant traffic out on Geary Street. O's head bobbed up and down over Steven, her nose ring flashing in the reflected lamplight and her constricted limbs completely straight down her back. Jacqui's head swung back and forth in front of Ray, who remained standing, using the looped whip to guide Jacqui's movements. Steven reached under O to roll her thick rings between his fingers through the stippled flesh of her nipples.

Jacqui switched out her ungloved hand for her mouth, continuing her attentions to Ray as she lifted her eyes to meet his.

"I think this would be a good time, Sir. Would you assist me please?"

"No problem."

Ray put the whip down on the back of the chair. Jacqui finally withdrew her fingers from O's bottom, peeled off the greased glove and tossed it aside.

"Up you go, princess," Ray said, gathering O off the floor and swinging her over Steven's chair. Compared to Jacqui, O was practically weightless. He lowered her carefully, holding her by her corset-compressed waist, while Jacqui guided Steven in from below. O threw a stockinged leg over each arm of the chair and slowly impaled herself while Jacqui supported her back.

"You're all much too good to me," Steven said huskily.

"I'll remind you of that the next time I need a check," Ray shot back.

Steven would have laughed but he was preoccupied with the sensation of O's sphincters opening to admit him. He reached around her and gripped her breasts, holding her upright in his lap while she acclimated to his substantial girth in her tightest passage.

Using only her strong legs to raise and lower her body O swung her pelvis around in slow circles, drilling herself as deeply as possible. Steven held her leather-bound arms against his chest, grinding up into her from below. Jacqui continued to stroke Ray while putting her mouth to O's unoccupied and unobstructed anatomy from the front. O gasped, squirming helplessly in her restraints.

A sheen of sweat rose over O's body. She couldn't inhale very deeply due to the constriction of the corset. O's bosom rose and fell with her short rapid breathing. Her head lolled against Steven's neck, the white-gold circlet in the middle of her face bouncing as she writhed under Jacqui's practiced attentions. She feared Jacqui would take her over the edge too soon, making it more difficult for her to surrender to Steven's upward thrusts, which grew harder and more urgent with every stroke.

Finding himself idle, Ray took up the whip and applied it to Jacqui's stretched back, teasingly at first, then with increasing force until the stripes rose. Jacqui wriggled her spine sinuously and made a happy gurgling noise, but would not be distracted. She intended to get that scream out of O but first there was something she just had to try.

Seemingly undisturbed by Ray's increasingly hard lashes, Jacqui lifted her head and gave Steven her pained, come-drunk smile. Her face was wet with O's juices and her own perspiration.

"Want to feel something nice and dirty, Sir?" she asked Steven.

"Always."

Jacqui slipped two fingers inside O's unused socket to stroke Steven's cock through the taut flesh between O's holes. She was quite skilled at finding just the right spot deep inside where she could simultaneously make O toss her hair and cry out while inspiring Steven to pump even more ferociously from below. By then Jacqui's back was crosshatched with red streaks from the Ray's single-tail and her available hand had wandered down to locate her hard, swollen button.

Putting her mouth back to work with one pair of fingers buried deep in O's most humid terrain and another equally busy with her own, it didn't take much longer for the inevitable chain reaction to occur. First O went stiff, her insides pumping around Steven's invading hardness as the long-awaited wail was torn from her lips. Her response triggered his, unleashing a torrent of hot lava up past her tightening internal muscles, his hot breath against her cheek as he let out a low, guttural growl. Jacqui lurched forward flicking madly away at herself, her high whining cry muffled in O's cleavage.

Ray stopped whipping, folded his arms and stood over them all with a wide grin on his face. He'd often wondered if he'd ever really seen Steven happy, though Steven made sure Ray never saw him unhappy. At that moment, Ray had no doubts about anything. His brother to whom he owed everything was entirely satisfied with the gift Ray had given him.

And Ray was by no means displeased with the devious, sweet, funny and unpredictable girl Steven had used to return the favor. Reaching down, he took a handful of Jacqui's auburn curls – carefully set for the evening out – and dragged her to her feet so she could scamper off to the bathroom.

Running in heels with her typical lightness afoot, Jacqui was only gone a few seconds, returning as Ray helped O out of the chair. A few dabs at O's behind, a couple of strokes up and down Steven's still-stiff ramrod and everything was nice and tidy again. Jacqui unsnapped the shoulder straps of the single-glove and yanked it down off O's aching arms, undamming a river of sweat down O's spine. O stretched and shook out her arms. She had been much too involved to notice how intensely they'd begun to tingle in their confinement. Jacqui pointed at her laughing.

"You look like you've just been fucked in the ass!" Jacqui proclaimed.

There was no denying it. O's hair had completely come apart. Her make-up was wrecked, as she'd decided earlier to wear mascara that would run, and her septum ring had shifted to one side.

"And you look like you should be fucked in the ass." O replied without thinking. Suddenly the room got quiet. Steven shot Ray a puzzled look. Ray shrugged.

"Um, we haven't done that yet," Jacqui said, shy and a bit embarrassed. O had been waiting for this moment and now it had arrived. Jacqui was no anal virgin, but neither was she as experienced as O in such things. She hadn't deliberately withheld that part of herself from Ray but he hadn't demanded it and she hadn't thought to offer it for more than a finger or a toy of some kind.

The look in O's eye sapped Jacqui of all will and resistance whenever she saw it. She had no doubts what would happen next.

"Well Ray," Steven said, "I think you're about to take full possession."

Looking down at himself, Ray seemed a bit worried.

"I don't know. She's awfully small back there. I don't want to hurt her in a bad way, if you know what I mean."

"O once told me that no woman's a slave until she's given up her ass. I suspect that was O's whole purpose in organizing things as she did, not that she didn't get something for herself out of it."

O gave Jacqui a challenging look.

"I fear my anal virtue — such as it is — is in danger here," Jacqui said.

O took her in hand.

"If you don't mind, I'd like a few moments with Jacqui."

"I'm sure we'll all benefit as a result," Ray said agreeably. Jacqui gave him a rueful look.

"I hope all of us includes me, Sir."

"You most of all," Steven insisted as O led Jacqui off to the bathroom.

"I assume this was your idea," Ray said, sinking into the unused chair.

Steven shook his head.

"Not guilty this time," he replied as he got up to find his discarded robe.

"Nice for you, the way O drops girls at your feet."

"Unlike the way they just fall at yours."

Neither had ever suffered from a shortage of feminine attention, but Steven had to work a bit harder for it. He'd seen girls in twos and threes physically drag Ray home from some of L.A.'s trendier watering holes.

O came out of the bedroom with a big plug-in vibrator wrapped in coils of extension cord. She found a socket near Ray, stung the vibe and handed it to him.

"If you don't mind, Sir. Won't be much longer."

Ray cheerfully told her to take her time, but she scampered back through the suite anyway.

"I think she's more excited than I am," Ray observed.

"Your motives are different."

It was the kind of cryptic remark from Steven that Ray had learned not to question. Any explanations Steven had to make would be heard soon enough or never.

True to her word, O returned shortly leading Jacqui on a leash of smooth, black leather attached to Jacqui's collar ring. Jacqui crawled alongside her, swaying her hips like a very large and potentially dangerous panther already in heat. Jacqui even rubbed her face against O's leg when they reached the appointed spot in front the chairs.

O's hands were now sheathed in the short black latex gloves again and she held the bottle of thick grease in one of them. The marks had blossomed into red vines all over Jacqui's back and buttocks. O had pulled the pins from Jacqui's hair, which now hung in tendrils around the sides of her face. Jacqui was barefoot, giving her a more feral look. The visual effect was as striking as O intended.

O offered up the leash to Ray in return for the vibrator, suggesting they start with something familiar. Ray understood the hint. Giving Jacqui's leash a sharp tug, he signaled for her to crawl up into his lap facing him. Pausing only to offer a slavish kiss where it mattered most, Jacqui climbed into Ray's arms while O slipped him into her from below. Settling her knees onto either side of his lap, Jacqui put her arms around Ray's neck and showed what she could do. She could bounce up and down fast or slow, roll her hips side to side, sit up straight and spear herself to the hilt while rubbing her breasts into his face for easy sucking and licking and lean back so far she could lay her palms on the floor. That proved dangerous, as O seized the opportunity to slash Jacqui back and forth across her torso with the coiled whip Ray abandoned. O's aim was true and Jacqui made no attempt to protect herself from. When Jacqui finally got dizzy and had to right herself, she presented Ray with new scarlet decorations at eye level.

Steven quietly got up and found himself a *figurado* from his cylindrical alligator-bound travel humidor, clipped the end with a round guillotine cutter he sometimes used as a watch fob and fired up. Normally, he would make O do these things for him but her labors were better invested elsewhere at the moment. While Jacqui and Ray kissed and nuzzled, O knelt under them on the floor, applying her mouth to their point of connection.

Steven watched from the other chair, puffing his cigar and admiring O's ingenuity. There was no lazy passivity in O's slavery. She colluded fully in everything Steven did to her and everything he wanted done to others.

Whatever she was doing down there must have felt pretty good, judging from the way Ray threw his head back and stared blankly at the ceiling.

Grabbing Jacqui's hipbones, Ray hammered fiercely away pounding another climax out of her so quickly she barely had time to stammer a request for it. Neither Ray nor Steven was doctrinaire about such things, but both appreciated a good-faith attempt to obey the rules.

O crawled up Jacqui's back, hooking an arm around Jacqui's collar. The moment had arrived for her to show Steven what she'd accomplished.

"If I may suggest, Sir, I think it's time to get this girl down on her hands and knees."

Ray lifted Jacqui, who was nicely limp and floppy, out of his lap. She slid to the floor where O positioned her with great precision – face to a pillow Steven tossed them to put over the carpet, hands folded behind her collar, tail raised to what O calculated would be the correct height, given Jacqui's long legs.

"Now you just keep your head down and your ass up and let him use you as he pleases," she whispered sternly.

"Yes, Sister," Jacqui panted. She was a bit afraid in addition to being awash in hormonal bliss, which made it all the better.

Kneeling next to Ray, O parted Jacqui's rear cheeks to show off the puckered rosebud between.

"Isn't it darling?" she asked. "It's like nothing's ever been in there."

"You know that's not true, Sister," Jacqui insisted, resting her chin on her hands.

They ignored her and she forgot what she was going to say next when she felt the delicate point of O's tongue teasing a most sensitive spot. A shudder traveled up and down Jacqui's long spine. O raised her head to kiss Ray's cock affectionately, found the lube bottle and squeezed a big clear drop onto her gloved fingertips.

"Shall I open her little flower for you, Sir?"

"By all means."

Ray watched as O gently rubbed in the thick shiny liquid, first one with one finger, then with two. Jacqui sighed and arched up her rump to make it more accessible. She relaxed easily under O's practiced touch until she'd dilated just enough for O, after applying another squirt of lube to Ray, to ease him into her with excruciating slowness. Ray looked on, fascinated, as if the part O was slipping into Jacqui's backside belonged to someone else. Ray had never been in hands as skilled as O's and never expected to again.

Nevertheless, he was quite happy to find himself inside the warm dark tunnel where O fitted him so deftly despite its tightness. Ray was a gentleman about these things, holding still until his belly lay against Jacqui's buttocks, allowing her to make tiny movements while she adjusted to the sensation. Only then did Ray begin slowly pistoning in and out of her.

O looked over at Steven, meeting his eyes, the blue of which reminded her of The Mediterranean at Cap Ferrat. Her expression was solemn with expectation. There was something she needed him to understand.

He nodded to her respectfully. Steven knew exactly what O was doing. She was fulfilling her promise to deliver Jacqui to Ray as his slave, approximating what O was to Steven as closely as possible. O favored Steven with one of those rare, brilliant smiles that always lifted his spirits.

"You're a wicked, little whore," Steven said affectionately.

"Thank you, Sir. I do my best."

At O's request Steven tossed them another pillow from the bed for O to put under Ray's knees. O found the vibrator and switched it on. Jacqui jumped at the sound of the powerful electric motor but Ray was holding on much too tightly for her to go anywhere. She was quite defenseless against O's application of the round humming head of the device right where it would be most effective.

Jacqui's noises changed tone, sinking an octave to some more animal sound arising from deep in her belly. Now Jacqui pounded back against Ray oblivious to what hole he was in. O reminded her by snapping off a glove with her teeth, spitting it to the floor and doing to Jacqui with her clean fingers what Jacqui had done to her when O was staked onto Steven. O was more or less ambidextrous from years of handling camera gear and didn't miss a useful spot with the vibrator while stirring Jacqui's internals with a bare hand.

Suddenly inspired, Steven got up, went to the open steamer trunk and came out with the slender rattan cane he and O prized most. Walking around behind Ray, Steven ordered Jacqui to put her bare feet in the air. Jacqui complied, rocking her weight on her knees as she offered up her soles. Steven gave her six good ones on each foot making Jacqui cry out nearly to the point of sobbing.

As expected, the cruel lashing put Jacqui right over the top once more. Not bothering to ask, or caring about the consequences of failing to do so, Jacqui climaxed again with a high-pitched whine and fell forward right off of Ray and onto her face. O turned off the vibrator, set it aside and ruthlessly yanked Jacqui back into position with the leash Ray had dropped when Jacqui lunged forward.

"Get back up here like a good fuck-doll," O barked. Jacqui responded with the appropriate gasped apologies and promises to hold still. After plugging her backside once more with Ray's throbbing, purple-headed shaft, O peeled off the other glove, stood up, took the cane from Steven and mercilessly thrashed Jacqui's tail until Ray was finished pumping it full of every drop he'd held back all evening.

A look passed between Steven and Ray that no one else would have understood.

Jacqui, face still down, didn't see that look. She wasn't unaware of Ray's history with Steven but she didn't care much about it. What had developed between Jacqui and Ray was a thing of its own. Steven didn't know much about what people call "falling in love," but he had seen it before and liked the idea, mystifying though he'd always found it.

Leaving everyone else to get untangled and cleaned up while O circled the room naked, camera in hand, recording more "crime scene" images for that eventual book, Steven went to the glass door of the small, round balcony and took his cigar outside. The night air was cold, but the draft up Steven's robe was pleasant after the heat of the previous hours. The taste of the cigar made him think of chocolate. The lights of San Francisco's hills were scrimmed with the fog moving in off the bay.

Not only had O succeeded in making Jacqui Ray's slave as Ray had used the facilities of The Mansion for O's training to serve Steven, she had gone further. She had provided Ray with the suitable life partner she herself could never be for him. The formal collaring at The Mansion would proceed in due course, but the union between Jacqui and Ray was already a fact on the ground.

For the first time in their lives as brothers, Steven envied Ray.

Through the crack he'd left open in the sliding door Steven heard the three of them laughing inside. It was getting cold. Time to go in. Steven took a last puff. When he turned to the door, O stood waiting, disheveled and sweaty, the portable silver ashtray held in both hands with the lid already opened. She flashed Steven that smile again as he entered. Twice in one night. Things were going very well indeed.

CHAPTER FORTY

Saturday, the skies were clear and the sun was out, but the air was chilly and gusty. Early starters already wandered around the streets in costume, though in San Francisco the distinction wasn't always immediately obvious. That the holiday fell on a weekend this year was good news for the tourist bars from the open doors of which a celebratory roar had risen steadily since noon.

Steven's entire party gathered across from Union Square in the rotunda of Neiman-Marcus to fortify themselves with lunch before some serious shopping. Jacqui was back in jeans, a long sweater and sensible flats, O elegant as usual in a short, black, belted cashmere coat, a gray leather pencil skirt, a tight black turtleneck through which her rings showed quite shamelessly and knee boots.

Eugenia and Svetlana seemed a bit torn back from what had turned into a long night of indulgence involving a couple of Silicon Valley boys and some illicit powders. Nevertheless, they'd cleaned up well, Eugenia in a snug lambskin jacket and stretch pants well chosen to show off her striking curves and Svetlana in a long embroidered shearling coat and round fur hat that emphasized everything Russian about her. Her eyes were hidden behind huge sunglasses and gold chains dangled around her long neck.

They all congratulated Jacqui on her formal initiation into the sorority of dedicated butt-girls while Steven ordered mimosas for the ladies and a Diet Coke for himself to go with his – what else? – lobster club sandwich. Ray scolded him once again about de-populating the lobster beds single-handedly while tying into a cheeseburger. O, thinking of a corseted night ahead, chose the salad Niçoise. The other two girls went for smoked salmon and Bloody Marys.

Like generals over a map, they laid out their shopping plans for the afternoon, with the girls splitting off in a pack to drift through the levels of luxurious indulgence below while the boys braved the out of doors.

Steven had already decided to drag Ray down to the Ghurka store and replace his battered carry-on with something respectable.

"If you're going to be chartering jets you need something that doesn't look like it was stolen by gypsies," Steven explained as they hoofed their way alongside the park. Steven had dressed practically for shopping – a double-breasted, shawl-collared black sweater under his black Burberry trench, one of the last made before the line went all khaki.

Ray blanched when he saw the price tag on the sturdy Garrison bag Steven dragged to the counter for him but there was no point in arguing with Steven about how he spent his money. Fifteen minutes later they'd be at Mont Blanc so Steven could buy himself a limited edition fountain pen in varnished wood that looked rather like a medium Corona cigar.

"How many of those things do you really need?" Ray asked while Steven loaded his new writing instrument with violet ink.

"Signing shit is the most important thing I do. Think how you'd all feel if I stopped."

Ray couldn't argue that point.

"You're a one-man stimulus package."

"Listen," Steven said, "the only reason for tolerating the existence of overpaid hacks like myself is because we spread it around. All the working stiffs out there would be entirely justified in turning to cannibalism if we stopped spending money."

Steven had a point. The stinginess of rich people both puzzled and annoyed Ray. He'd seen it in action with their mother's family, who could easily have made all their lives more comfortable had they not withheld their resources to demonstrate their limitless disapproval of every choice the woman had made in her entire sad life. Ray suspected Steven took some vengeful pleasure in making more money than their mother's dour kin would ever see and spending it on things that would outrage them.

Strolling Maiden Lane, where Ray stopped to pick up a cannoli from a sidewalk café, they speculated about David's motives for inviting them up. Ray figured David just wanted them to anchor his guest list. David was certainly attuned to their world's notions of celebrity. Steven shook his head.

"I suspect darker motives."

"You always suspect darker motives."

"How often am I wrong?" Steven had him there. "I guarantee you some kind of offer will be put on the table tonight. We've got a sophisticated audience he'd like a piece of."

Ray looked alarmed. "You wouldn't really partner in with him, would you?"

"Don't worry. I never give more than I take back."

"True, that."

Knowing O's tastes well by now, Steven ducked into Hermés to pick out a huge dazzling scarf in a black and gold harness pattern, scooping up a pair of hammer and anvil cuff links for himself on the way out.

After a final stop at Cartier so Ray could secure a pair of earrings for Jacqui to match her screw-on bracelet (which she'd started wearing again), they returned to the hotel to re-charge for what would surely be a long night.

A couple of hours later the girls showed up at their door in a noisy pack. Heavy-laden with designer shopping bags they gathered in the living room where Steven and Ray watched them tally their loot. Eugenia had made the biggest score, a pair of crotch-high Christian Louboutin boots. Svetlana, who was careful with money as a rule, had treated herself to a Vuitton make-up case stamped with her initials. Jacqui's raid on Wolford had netted an assortment of elegantly provocative stockings and a two-piece lace body suit with a removable bra. O's purchases were small and select. From David Webb, she'd acquired an elegant jeweled serpent cuff and at an antique store she'd spotted an amethyst stickpin for Steven.

Steven insisted O take off her blouse before he knotted the new scarf around her neck. It would be perfect to cover a collar should a collar need covering. She kissed him affectionately for it.

It was decided to order appetizers and drinks from room service so the girls could all help each other dress for the ball more efficiently. Steven was dubious about the efficiency part, but happy enough to oblige.

While Svetlana and Eugenia went back to their room to retrieve the outfits Marie had chosen for them, O and Jacqui stretched out between Steven and Ray in the bedroom to catch the news and pass around a joint. O and Steven watched Ray tenderly put the new earrings through Jacqui's lobes. Jacqui held up the bracelet so O could take a smiling picture of the matching set.

Jacqui had already started undressing Ray when the buzzer sounded from the door so Steven went to meet the bellman. By now the entire hotel staff knew who rented this room. Service was quick and friendly.

The bellman made polite chatter while wheeling in and setting up trays full of carpaccio, shrimp, chicken skewers, stuffed quail and other small savories before breaking out the two bottles of champagne Steven ordered. Their server commented on how good the room smelled. Steven excused himself long enough to fetch another joint that O had just finished rolling, and handed it off to their server along with an ample cash gratuity. Steven found the best way to get people out of a room in a hurry was to give them money.

Half an hour later, the suite was filled with half-naked girls eating, drinking, smoking, teasing each other and their male hosts and helping each other into their costumes.

Some needed more help than others. O, whose own war paint, including nipple stain to match her lips, went on in a couple of minutes assisted Jacqui with some eyelash glue before slicking the tall girl's whole body with silicone polish for what Jacqui had brought.

There wasn't much of it, just a white-bordered bright-blue-latex G-string that barely covered, a matching blue-latex top cut below the breasts and a long blue latex skirt, full but equipped with interior straps so it could be buckled up to expose a leg or even higher to expose everything.

O poured a pool of polish into the palm of her hand and smeared it all over Jacqui's vulcanized geography until the rubber gleamed. Jacqui had brought high slides with clear straps to enhance the impression of a full-size doll. She used an electric curling iron to create a great pile of red ringlets on top of her head.

What Marie had packed up for her charges made them both moan with distress when the zippered hanging bag was opened. Both had worn full-body chastity harnesses before and their faces fell at the sight.

Lock-on bras with shiny rubber-lined steel cups pushed their breasts together and upwards most invitingly, but made them completely inaccessible without keys to round locks that closed them in the back.

Short lengths of chain connected the bras to high-cut steel belts, also padded with rubber. Matching locks front and back connected the padded steel plates covering the Vs between their legs and the mean steel straps that pushed their buttocks out wide while denying access front and rear. A narrow rubber-trimmed slit in each front-plate displayed a flash of pink but was mainly there for practical purposes and too small to admit anything larger than a finger, as Jacqui mischievously demonstrated while Ray and Steven snapped the locks shut.

"At least we can piss through them instead of having to hold it all night," Svetlana said with little enthusiasm.

Even the steel-trimmed strappy sandals with their brutally high heels locked on at the ankles.

"No action for us tonight" Eugenia said disconsolately.

"I don't know about that," Steven said consolingly. "Marie knows that putting you on display and making you hard to get will drive demand."

Steven held up two small keys, each on a silver chain.

"These will enable you to pop off your armor in a flash. However, each of you will be wearing the other's key so nobody can get to you without your partner's help."

He draped Eugenia's key around Svetlana's neck while Ray awarded Eugenia's to Svetlana.

"Marie doesn't trust some of the people who show up at David's parties so she's made sure neither of you can be had unless you both think it's a good idea. You'll have an excuse to turn down anyone you don't want or who can't be verified in the data base by blaming your friend."

"But they can still do things to us in other ways," Svetlana observed apprehensively.

Eugenia hugged her.

"Not while I'm around, Sister. All I see is a few BJs and hand-jobs in our future."

Svetlana shrugged. She'd endured far worse much of her life. At least the belts had no internal working parts. The two girls assisted each other with the shiny matching cuffs while Ray and Steven locked steel-banded collars around their necks as a final touch.

Turning to the mirrored wall they admired the striking effect.

"No helmets with horns?" Svetlana said drily.

"Promise me you won't try to sing Wagner," Eugenia said. "I'd have to mercy that."

Svetlana stiffened indignantly.

"I have a good voice," she insisted.

"Girl, you couldn't hit a high note with a hammer," Eugenia teased. "But you do have a sexy growl."

Svetlana growled and bit Eugenia on the bare shoulder.

O and Steven retired to their bedroom so she could assist him into his costume: G&H's perfect recreation of an Imperial German Uhlan cavalry general's uniform. The plastron tunic was a rich green trimmed in red and decorated with gold shoulder boards, gold aiguillettes and bullion garter stars. The gray breeches had wide, red stripes up the sides. The tall riding boots were topped with old-fashioned brown collars. With Steven's short hair and square shoulders he looked like he'd just stepped out of a daguerreotype from 1917.

"All you need is a monocle and you could pass for Eric Von Stroheim in *Grande Illusion*," O said admiringly.

"The steel neck brace might be a deal-breaker."

O stood up into his arms, enjoying the sensation of her nakedness against Steven's uniformed body. Parade-dress on a man who could carry it always got her wet.

"I wish we could just stay in tonight," she said plaintively. She had a dark presentment about the evening ahead but it was formless and irrelevant. This was the mission for which they'd come.

"If you don't get some clothes on it could happen," Steven warned, "and then I'll never know what David was up to."

O handed Steven a black satin corset from her suitcase. He laced her expertly, working his way down to pullers he tied in a big bow once O's mid-section had been reduced to a cruel minimum.

O's dress was a long whisper of utterly transparent black lace, open in front to the top of the under-bust corset. Steven's mark was clearly visible through the delicate fabric clinging down her spine and the long skirt was slit up the front to the legal limit. Stepping up into her steep round-toed stilettos, she did a turn for Steven.

"Do you approve, Sir?"

"If I approved any more you'd be on your back now."

O knelt and presented Steven with her collar. She wore no restraints tonight. Jacqui and Ray would perform at some point but Steven and O preferred to remain dress extras.

They entered, Ray giving the door jamb a perfunctory knock. He had shrugged on a Chrome Hearts leather blazer decorated with silver accents, matching jeans with nicely tarnished silver studs up the sides and down the fly and a silk jersey T-shirt. The cuffs of his jeans were stuffed into similarly ornamented biker boots. Ray could easily have been mistaken for a rock star, but then, that happened however he dressed.

O, still on her knees, looked over at them as if she'd just been caught doing something improper.

"Hope I'm not interrupting anything, general," Ray said cheerfully, giving his brother a crisp salute, "but they just called from downstairs. The car is outside."

Steven gave O a hand up.

Jacqui asked if anyone had a camera. O shot her a scornful look. Someone always had a camera. The small Leica was in O's beaded deco clutch on the bed. Jacqui got it out and summoned the other girls for a photo op.

"My, don't you all look fine?" she said, framing the two couples in a nice shot. The camera flashed. Eugenia reviewed the image on the small screen, wagged her head, not quite sure.

"One more, just to be sure. Everybody think of something really dirty."

They all smiled and the camera flashed again. This time Eugenia liked what she saw on the small screen.

"Better," she said, handing the camera to O who passed it back to Jacqui for an official portrait of Steven and her against a gray-fabric upholstered wall. Jacqui framed the shot expertly. Looking at it, O decided she'd adjust the image to sepia-tone when they got back and vignette it so it resembled something shot in a pre-WWI whorehouse on Berlin's old Ku-Dam.

The Mansion's standardized cashmere cover-ups concealed the house girls' armor completely, buttoning all the way up to cover their collars.

"At least we won't freeze," Eugenia said as she did up Svetlana's last button.

"Where I come from we go swimming in this weather," Svetlana joked. Eugenia asked to be reminded not to visit Svetlana at home. It wasn't likely anyway. Svetlana wasn't going home, ever.

O had brought along her ankle-length Napoleonic pelisse – black barathea with frog closures and white fur trim at the throat, wrists and hem. Its broad skirt swirled when she turned. She'd packed her opera gloves and a veiled round hat of the same fur as the trim of her coat. She slipped the septum ring into her nose last. This would be the first time she'd worn it in public. The wisp of lace over her eyes made it stand out even more.

Jacqui had only her gypsy coat to wear over her latex patches. She worried about it shedding on her polished surfaces. Ray reminded her that it would be pretty dark most of the time where they were headed and who knew how long she'd keep any of it on anyway?

Steven tossed a velvet-collared green cape over his shoulders. Ray buttoned up his jacket. Out into the hall they want looking like some kind of traveling dance troupe – a not entirely inaccurate comparison.

The heat was pumped up in the Suburban in anticipation of drafty costumes and Ethan had already dialed up Annie Lennox singing "Love is a Stranger" on the CD player. He complimented them all on their striking appearances in a carefully worded sound bite and assisted the girls into the dim interior of the huge vehicle. Steven couldn't imagine what it must be like navigating the hills of San Francisco in such a behemoth and didn't care to try.

Ethan not only knew where they were going but just enough about the place to make conversation without intruding into private matters.

CHAPTER FORTY-ONE

Over in the Tenderloin, The Royale Hotel had been a swank hostelry for most of the previous century. It eventually closed down as the neighborhood deteriorated. The city attached it for back taxes but by the time gentrification hit, it was in such disrepair while squatting on such a valuable piece of dirt no one knew quite what to do with it. There it sat abandoned until financial conditions forced the city to sell it off. David was waiting with cash in hand from the half-dozen booming websites he already operated back when the money was really good.

There had been some griping in the neighborhood and from some professional East Bay scolds about "pornifying the neighborhood." David had worked the local press expertly while solidifying relations with the city government by fronting up a couple of year's worth of property taxes in advance – things an MBA from The London School of Economics would know to do.

Saddled with a crushing mortgage just before the economic time bomb detonated, David suddenly found thirty-dollar-monthly website memberships not so easily sold anymore. Fortunately, his background in finance prepared him for market fluctuations. He created new sites with slightly different content, hired new people to run them, expanded the studio spaces and installed cam stations to run 24/7 for the new talent he recruited.

On weekends the company picked up extra change and banked good will by sponsoring community events. It was an exhausting business and for all the cash flow not much liquidity was left over at the end of each month. Still, it enabled David to live grandly and supplied him with whatever company he wanted whenever he wanted it.

Steven knew all this in some detail, mainly from Albert, and Ray understood the broad outlines. Ray helped with David's mortgage payments by renting out the hotel's elaborate fantasy environments as backgrounds for *Forbidden*'s more ambitious photo features. O did some of her best work there and Ray was open to the idea of further joint ventures, though he and David eyed each other with prudent skepticism.

Steven's role in the current mission was to secure whatever assistance David could lend in getting *Forbidden*'s site successfully launched without giving up the farm in return. David was the market leader on that side of the fence and the only person Steven would consider taking in as a partner, rather than just a hired service provider, precisely because he commanded the largest percentage of gross eyeballs riveted to performance perversion on any given night.

Leaving behind another hundred for Ethan, Steven asked him to stay close by as they had no clue when they might be leaving. Ethan was quite happy to sit in the truck and do his homework from hospitality school.

The wide flight of concrete steps leading up to The Royale's doors were lit up with a couple of spotlight trailers and a red carpet had been laid out but there were no photographers in sight, thanks to the big men in dark suits standing guard at the foot of the stairs. Couples and small groups, mostly in black, made the climb. The inevitable velvet rope was attended by a couple of large men in black jackets and a slender young girl with a bleached-white bob who checked off the guest list on a clipboard at a small table under a kerosene heater. The heater was turned all the way up in deference to the list girl's transparent latex dress. Her nipples were still hard enough to put up a fight with the snug rubber blouse.

O had shot this girl, who went by Anguissette, a couple of times and they exchanged a friendly kiss before all the names were checked off on the list and they were waved inside.

The lobby – cavernous and dark with ancient floral-print carpeting – was boisterous, packed with young people fetishisted-out in rubber and leather. They drank from plastic cups and shouted at each other to be heard over the brutal industrial noise coming from the nearer ballroom. There were many corsets on women and kilts on men, cruel shoes of every design, whips slung on waist belts, Steampunk Victorian dresses, black nails and lipstick on various genders, masks and hats and acres of bare flesh, tattooed, pierced or factory-issue. No one seemed to be much over thirty-five and most would be considered attractive by conventional standards in the conventional attire they undoubtedly wore by day.

The crowd might be bigger than usual for the occasion and the costuming more elaborate, but in this world every day was Halloween.

As usual, Ray was recognized by almost everyone. Those he didn't know, Jacqui did. The two of them were soon swallowed up in a maelstrom of knuckle bumping and air-kissing. Steven and O hung back together, taking the lay of the terrain.

"I think that's where we want to go first," Steven shouted, pointing at an old-fashioned open-cage elevator on a far wall.

She nodded, seizing Ray by the arm. With Ray came Jacqui, Eugenia and Svetlana close behind. They formed a rank, snaking through the crowd with O in front and Steven at the rear. Squeezing into the overloaded elevator, Steven closed the cage behind them. The elevator was operated by a tall, leggy, dark-haired girl with nicely augmented breasts. She wore a red-latex Spencer jacket, matching pillbox hat, black-fishnet pantyhose and high heels. The rest of her wares were fully on display.

On the alert for them, the girl told Steven's crew they were expected in the VIP suite and pushed the lever over. The elevator clanked to life. They watched the floors go by as it rose, stopping on Twelve where they found themselves in a much quieter space, though still large, decorated in red with imitation Edwardian furniture.

This room was also crowded but the people were a bit older, better dressed and better behaved. Clustered in small knots, chatting amiably, many seemed to know each other. Here and there a girl was bent over a couch for caning with her skirt flipped up or on the floor sucking her master's cock while he casually conversed with a few relaxed comrades. At the far end of the parlor in front of a big marble fireplace that was clearly a stage prop a pale redhead was strung naked and spread-eagled on a heavy whipping frame of polished wood where two women in black leather worked her over with floggers front and rear. The whipped girl by turns giggled and yelped while her owner – a big, ruddy, bearded guy in a long frock coat – leaned against the frame watching. He occasionally leaned over through the flying leather to offer his girl a sip from a glass of amber liquid.

Steven and Ray barely made it into the crush before David himself appeared. A pleasant sort with dark wavy hair, a perpetual twinkle in his dark eyes and a trim physique in a vested black suit correct for any bank, he hugged Ray first and O next before offering his hand to Steven and Jacqui. They introduced him to Svetlana and Eugenia. He took their hands politely, calling out a woman's name over his shoulder.

Another house slave, this one rounder with short pink hair, a short blouse and a shorter skirt, appeared from the crowd to take all their wraps. The room got quieter with the unveiling, particularly when Sventlana and Eugenia revealed their metalwork. David looked them over, amused.

"Well, I can see these two won't be getting in any trouble," he said cheerfully.

Eugenia warned him not to count on that.

He led them all over to a long bar where a pony-tailed man in a red velvet vest poured drinks. Eugenia requested a glass of red wine, Svetlana vodka and tonic, Jacqui a dirty martini and Ray a beer. It was sparkling water only for Steven and O. David went behind the bar and poured a scotch.

"So what do you think of the place?" he asked, quite sure of a positive answer. All agreed it was impressive so far but wanted to see more.

"I promise you the full tour, starting with my office."

All drinks collected, Steven suggested Eugenia and Svetlana enjoy theirs while the rest followed David back through a swinging round-windowed door behind the bar.

They entered an office with rows of desks and computer stations, whiteboards posted with schedules, banks of multiple servers and other things more associated with the nearby world of Silicone Valley. The old brick walls and arched windows were still there but lines of overhead track lights, turned down low, suggested a thoroughly modern corporation that could have been engaged in nearly anything.

Unlike Ray's office, where it was nearly impossible to find a wall not pinned with some shocking image, all evidence of pornographic activity was conspicuously absent.

"It's like a machine shop in here during the day," David said leading them through. "The ringing phones and the clicking keys are enough to drive a person crazy."

"Not the worst problem I can imagine," Ray said. He needed no reminding that his own operation would fit comfortably in half a floor of this fortress.

Passing through another set of saloon doors they found themselves in David's sanctum, a spacious, dark-paneled room full of buffed leather furniture surrounding a vast, old and somewhat cluttered partners' desk with a big computer monitor on it and an incongruously futuristic chair behind it.

As they entered, a familiar figure stood up from a high wingback in front of the desk. Everyone stopped cold. It was Eric, dressed in a black T-shirt and jeans. He had a drink in his hand and Steven guessed it wasn't his first.

Steven and Ray looked at one another. Something they weren't going to like was about to be revealed.

"I know you've all met before," David said brightly as Eric came forward with his hand outstretched. "He's my guest this weekend as well."

"What a coincidence," Ray said. Ray had a temper much like his mother's with which Steven was only too familiar. He feared the rest of the room might soon become acquainted with it.

Nevertheless, hands were shaken and greetings exchanged, if stiffly.

"I was just showing Eric how we track our live feeds when you got here," David explained as the others found seats. Steven and Ray made a point of sitting on either side of Eric. They'd done enough deals together not to need hand signals.

"Is this merely technical curiosity, or is there something more to it?" Steven asked, hoping to kick whatever was planned into operation as quickly as possible. He always preferred to be on the advance and made his easiest kills early in the match.

"I've been chatting with Eric about doing some work for us," David said, dropping into his chair and spinning it around full circle. He'd had a couple of drinks as well.

"David's thinking of starting a round-the-clock live streaming channel," Eric said, parking on the edge of the desk and taking another swallow. "Not just cam girls either. He wants scheduled programming like a real network, but interactive."

"That's going to take up a lot of bandwidth," Ray countered. "And it's going to need a lot of personnel to manage the traffic."

"That depends on how efficiently it's automated," Eric replied. "If the system's architecture is designed to funnel the traffic efficiently and the interactive elements use synthesized voices I think it can work at a reasonable overhead."

Steven suggested such a project might take up a good bit of Eric's time. Eric's attention had wandered to O, at whom he stared glassy-eyed. If he made her uncomfortable, she wasn't about to let him know it.

"But aren't you coming to work for Ray?" Jacqui asked. She knew how to make a question sound innocent but she was already onto this game.

"I'm prepared to offer him substantial incentives," David said.

"Well, I see it's time to collect the knives," Steven replied.

For once, Ray designated himself the naysayer.

Turning to David with a murderous look, he pointed out that having them up here to watch him steal Eric out from under their noses wasn't really necessary. An email would have been fine. Ray got up and turned toward the door.

"Oh really," David called after him, "that isn't what I have in mind at all. I don't care to have your brother suing me for soliciting breach of contract. Do come sit back down."

Ray did it, but the look he gave Eric brought on a gulp.

"I think there's an opportunity for all of us here and I'm hoping we can all take advantage, in the mutual sense."

Steven strongly suspected David's intentions involved taking advantage in the individual sense but he was interested in hearing out the case. One of the things Steven collected was a list of scams and how to obstruct them.

"It would seem to me that your biggest problem will be meeting the demand for fresh content around the clock," Steven observed calmly. "I know you're set up for it pretty well here in terms of physical facilities but it's people who cost money. You pay for a machine and it stays bought. If you want people to come around and do interesting things for the camera you have to keep paying them."

"Well someone does, don't they?" David agreed.

"So what does the mortgage on this place run you, David?" Steven asked. "Half a million a month?"

David smiled but it didn't make it as far as his eyes.

"I forget you're also a real estate mogul. I'm sure you've already done the math in your head."

"And that's before you even turn on the lights," Steven continued. What kind of staff are you running?"

David swirled his drink, stared at the ceiling.

"Full-time? About twenty-five. That doesn't count day-rate players and I put the cam girls on straight rev-share a few months ago."

"I heard about that," Jacqui said. "I was in a dressing room the other day where they were talking about putting a bounty on your balls."

David laughed convincingly.

"Darling, it's not like they have to pay for those, or even for the time I give them on my sites. I just can't afford to subsidize their bad habits. With memberships down and our increasing dependence on pay-per-view some additional revenue streams would make everybody happier. I'm hoping to solve that problem with Ray's help."

"And I'm to perform this miracle how?" Ray asked, shaking his head in disbelief at what he heard.

"If you were to wire the magazine's studios for shoots, set it up so the models could maybe do short Q&As with the viewers during breaks between set-ups," Eric said, "it would provide us with hours of fresh material every week. Maybe we could even wire the office to do feeds from meetings and auditions and so on, kind of like a cable series. Think of these segments as webisodes in a reality show based on your magazine."

"Let me see if I understand this correctly," O said in an icy voice. "My models and crew and I are to perform like trained seals while anonymous voices from the ether bark inane requests at us. Is that about it?"

"You can regulate outside participation as much as you want," David offered genially. "I wouldn't expect you to deal with interference while you're actually shooting."

"I run a closed set because I want a certain intimacy with my talent. This may be hard to understand for someone who operates a puppy mill but it's part of the reason your stuff looks like Amateur Hour and ours meets professional standards," O said dismissively. The smile faded from David's face.

"That hasn't stopped you from shooting stills here," David replied, his good nature fraying. "It's not as if we bring nothing to the table. You're staging to invade my market about which, without Eric's input, you know little. Many other print operations have come online and died in months."

Ray shot a poison glance at Eric.

"We thought we'd retained his expertise to get us over the bumps."

David stood up, came around the desk and put his arm over Eric's shoulders.

"When it comes to site design and setting up physical systems, our friend here has no competition. Unfortunately, he knows ... I believe the proper term is jack-shit ... when it comes to marketing. You're not going to pay the rent off of advertising on the web, I can promise you that. I've given up selling placements. Businesses aren't convinced web advertising works and they won't pay for it. It's going to come down to numbers of views, my friends. How many people are willing to pay to see what you've got? I have hundreds of thousands of sign-ups who don't even know you exist."

"Just out of curiosity," Steven asked, "what is the Alexa rating for all your sites combined?"

Steven never walked into a negotiation with unfinished homework.

"It varies by site, but as a group, well under ten thousand. I'll show you."

Steven pulled his round glasses out of his tunic as David turned the big monitor around. A few key taps and the screen lit up with graphs and columns of figures.

"We've had some ups and downs, but the overall trend is clear enough," David said, trying to keep the triumphant edge out of his voice.

Jacqui whistled.

"You're in the top percentile for unique visits."

Jacqui had done some homework of her own for her potential fan site.

"More people hit us in an hour than see your magazine in a month," David said, looking straight at Steven, who crunched the onscreen numbers and came to the same conclusion.

"There's no way I'm going along with this unless we can compensate our talent for content we provide you," Ray declared flatly. "That would bump our shooting costs through the roof."

"If you're making enough every month I'm sure you can work something out with them," David said. "It's not like they're particularly camera-shy."

"And who's going to keep all this running if you have Eric up here?" Ray demanded, seeing that the game was going against him. He could tell by the look on his brother's face, lit by the glow of the display, that Steven was weighing all this as he weighed everything, pragmatically.

The squeeze was on. Everyone in this room wanted something someone else had and the walls were closing in. Ray hated that sensation. He knocked back the rest of his beer and smacked the bottled down hard on David's desk.

"Let's suppose, purely theoretically, that we went for this deal," Steven said calmly. "Just hypothetically, how many hours a week of content would you expect us to provide?"

David's smile reminded O of the one Steven deployed for public situations.

"We could start off modestly as an experiment.

"How about twenty hours a week?"

"And in return?"

"We handle all the online purchasing for *Forbidden*, push it on every site and offer it through all our affiliates. We can sell entire issues as PDF downloads at your full newsstand price and a fucking hell of a lot more of them than you can by chucking them onto the racks."

Ray wasn't sure whom to be maddest at now.

"Steven, you can't be serious."

"In return for this you would expect what share of our revenues?" Steven pressed.

"Why none, of course. Perhaps a trade-out advert or two, but the PDFs would be all yours."

"And the income from the streaming," O said quietly, "would be all yours."

"Not necessarily," David insisted. "We'd expect to cover our expenses, but anything above that we can split evenly. That should help defray your additional production costs."

Steven stood up slowly, leaning across the desk into David's face.

"In other words, your numbers are descending after years of growth and you need to broaden your demographic. It's not our money you want, it's our readers."

Eric took another swig of his drink and sneered.

"All fifty thousand of them."

Now it was Steven's turn to show his cards.

"I realize that's not a big number by electronic standards, but our readers have more disposable income than your members. I know you'd like to upscale some of your operation.

You already have those viewers who want rough and raunchy. Slick, however, is what we market and you still don't do that very well. You're coasting along but new memberships are flat and I don't know where you're going to find them if you can't reach out to a better class of pervert. What you really crave is respectability and our brand has it."

"I don't hear anything very good from the models these days," O said, seeing a chance to strengthen Steven's hand. "They tell me you're dropping your rates and cutting back on bringing in out-of-town talent."

"Last time I was up here, I had to stay in the fucking slave dorm with all the live-in girls," Jacqui interjected, "just in case you've been wondering why I haven't returned any calls from your talent department."

"I wasn't aware that you weren't," David said soothingly. "We'll get you a nice hotel room next time."

"Already got one, thanks," Jacqui said with an affectionate nod toward Ray.

O could hear the gears turning in Steven's head. That uniform looked all too appropriate on him. He was reading the map like a latter-day von Clausewitz.

"It's worth some thought as a loose proposition," Steven said at last. "But what about him?"

Steven cocked a thumb toward Eric.

"Everyone wants him like grass on a golf-course. Once this game's in play, we'll be dependent on him to keep us up and running. If he's working for you ..."

"Precisely!" David exclaimed, throwing his arms in the air. "Without him, as your friend Albert knows, you'll be doing your whole start-up by trial and error. Errors can be lethal at the beginning. I'd actually prefer him to stay down in Los Angeles with you. I have plenty of technical support up here. I need a first-rate systems designer and engineer to get our joint venture going and so do you. You also need servers, credit card processing and if you're going live with anything you'll need on-site hosting."

"Too bad I hate Los Angeles and love it up here," Eric said blandly.

David's manner grew as chill as a London winter.

"I have no interest in using anyone as leverage where you're concerned, Mr. Diamond. Your reputation precedes you."

"My reputation as what?"

"Someone we'd rather have inside the tent pissing out than outside the tent pissing in."

Slowly, both men began to smile, easing the tension. Ray looked back and forth between them incredulously.

"I'd like to think I have a say in this," he snapped.

"The person who has the most say in this is him."

David motioned toward Eric with his glass. "And all I have to offer him is money."

"I'm sure he makes plenty of that doing what he's doing."

Eric raised his glass.

"No hard times at my door, gentlemen."

Steven turned to Eric.

"So what do you want in return for your guaranteed participation in this project until it's stable?"

Eric turned his slightly blurred gaze toward O.

"Her."

Steven couldn't suppress a laugh.

"She's not on the table."

"She'd be on the table with her legs in the air if you told her to, do it," Eric shot back.

Now Steven turned from David to freeze Eric with a deadly look.

"O is my property. If and when I choose to loan her out it's occasionally, briefly and entirely at my own discretion. I have no intention of sharing her with you."

"No worries. You and I have different approaches," Eric said disdainfully. "I just want a chance to show her something new."

Steven looked over at O, who cocked an ironic eyebrow. There was unlikely to be anything new that Eric could show her. A faint smile crossed her lips, not lost on Ray or Jacqui, both hardly believing what seemed to be happening before their eyes.

"Many a bargain has been struck between men over the body of a woman," David pointed out helpfully.

"Just one time," Eric said, a pleading note sneaking in. "If she doesn't want anything more with me after that I'll still deliver on my end of the bargain."

Steven wondered how this would work. O would surely scorn Eric's best efforts unless ordered to do otherwise, an order Steven wasn't prepared to give on a regular basis. Eric would be angry then and their new operation would be in his hands. Steven didn't like that idea at all. David, Steven and Ray all wanted this presumptuous little fuck and the presumptuous little fuck wanted O.

Steven had a hunch O could fix this problem better than he could. For once, someone else would have to pull his brother out of the well. He wasn't sure why he trusted O to do that but it felt right. Steven made many of his better decisions on instinct.

"I'm prepared to let Eric have some time with O but I'll need assurances in writing regarding our arrangements with both your company and Eric going forward."

David laughed.

"The assurances I need from you can't legally be put in writing. I believe that's a felony in this state."

"I assume there's a comfortable room someplace private in here."

"Got nice enough digs for myself up on the top floor. They can use my place to get acquainted while you and I handle the paperwork. I've already got Eric signed on an exclusive fee-for-service binder. We'll need to work out an amendment."

Ray started forward.

"You little prick! You had that all along and you ran this shit on us? I ought to ..."

Steven cut him off with a wearily raised hand.

"You ought to take Jacqui out there and enjoy the party for a while."

Ray's eyes hardened in that casually lethal Sicilian way.

"Yeah. Okay. Fine. You all work it out among yourselves. But if any of this interferes with the way I run the magazine, you'll need a new publisher. Good luck with that."

Ray grabbed Jacqui by the arm.

"Let's go. I'm over this."

"Yes, Sir! Me too, Sir."

Jacqui looked back at O, distressed, as Ray led her out of the room.

Once they were gone, David opened his desk drawer and brought out a small key ring with a red tassel on it. He tossed the key to Steven who gave it to Eric.

"O, I'd like you to go with him. Try not to damage him too much. It appears he's indispensible for the moment."

O knelt, kissed Steven's gleaming boot, stood to follow Eric from the room without so much as a backward look at her master.

"Pretty well-trained, that one," David observed, reaching back into the drawer for a small round mirror piled high with white powder, a handful of plastic straws cut to three-inch lengths and a gold single-edged razor blade.

"She pretty much came that way," Steven said, looking uncomfortably at the pile of evidence David set between them. Steven grew even more uncomfortable when David offered him a straw.

"No thanks. I had mine about thirty years ago."

David shrugged, expertly sliding out a couple of, thick rails from the pile with the blade.

"Please yourself."

He pleased himself by inhaling the two rails so quickly and thoroughly the mirror wouldn't have need polishing afterward. David's face flushed and he choked back a dry cough. Steven expected this behavior from clients, not partners.

At that thought, he drew out his silver card case, popped it open and slid one of his Nile-Blue calling cards across the desk to David.

"You might want to hang onto that," Steven advised.

David picked it up, flexing the heavy stock.

"Smythson and Company I presume," he said, tossing the card into the drawer. "Nice touch but unnecessary. I've got your contact information stored in my phone."

"Probably best to keep that in your wallet. They take the phone away first."

David laughed merrily.

"I'm touched by your concern, Mr. Diamond. I do have a lawyer of my own, as it happens. In fact, I even have some excellent paperwork from him for already prepared you to sign."

From a different drawer David produced three multi-page documents bound in red covers, setting two of them down in front of Steven.

"There's a copy for Ray but I don't imagine he'll read it."

"He leaves that part to me."

Steven flipped through sheets dense with performance guarantees, assignments and copyright boilerplate. There were no signatures on the last page as yet.

"Presumably this is open to amendment," Steven said in a warning tone.

"As long as the substance doesn't change. I think you'll find it fair enough. Given our visibility throughout the digital environment I doubt anyone can offer you better."

Steven pushed the papers back to David.

"I'd prefer you FedEx this down to my office. I'd like for my associate to have a look at it. She's more familiar with digital rights agreements than I am. My practice is pretty much limited to criminal cases."

"It will go out first thing Monday. And I hope we never have need of your particular services."

With that, David sliced off two more lines and vacuumed them up.

"I think we're done here for now," Steven said, standing up. David stood also.

"Absolutely. I hate taking time away from a good party just to make a deal for a shit-ton of new revenue."

"I hope your optimism is justified," Steven said. He didn't sound convinced.

"We're pretty good at making things happen," David replied, giving Steven a hard, glassy look and sticking out his hand.

Steven took David's hand in an especially tight grip, as this, he knew, was the real guarantee of everything David promised. It generally was in Steven's experience.

"Right then," David said, regaining his ebullience behind a bump of Peruvian marching powder. "Go explore my kingdom a bit while Eric gets his education. If you fancy any of the girls who work here just let me know. I highly recommend the little blonde we have on the door. Very dirty."

"I'll keep that in mind."

"No hurry. We're going to get to know each other's assets quite well I'm sure."

David undoubtedly had assets about which Steven preferred to know as little as possible but intended to discover them regardless before any ink was applied to paper.

Leaving David to his mirror Steven wandered out of the office wing into the main lobby, which was packed by now. He had a quick look at the blonde girl putting on the wristbands (red for guests, green for potential players already tested and in the database). She was a cute thing and dirty was good but Steven wasn't about to indulge until O was back at his side. He figured Eric would prove harmless enough but he didn't care to have his dick stuck in some luscious little treat if his appraisal turned out to be overoptimistic.

Instead, Steven wandered into the hotel's main ballroom by following the noise and the crush of late arrivals. The industrial thump from the DJ's booth in the corner was loud enough to have Steven packing in his compressible foam earplugs immediately.

In the great dim cavern that had once been the hotel's grand space for gala events the dark paneled walls and floors had been left as they were, along with a large bar at one end where a thirsty throng elbowed their way toward refreshment. On a stage opposite the most exhibitionistic players demonstrated their skills with *shibari* suspensions and single-tail whippings.

The room was lit from below and the paintings on the vaulted ceilings had faded to a uniform parchment color. Weary red vinyl banquets lined the walls and there was a mezzanine with partitioned booths one level up.

The tables had been removed from the area around the dance floor, replaced by play stations, each with its own piece of standing equipment. There were Saint Andrews' crosses, whipping posts, low benches, narrow tables edged with steel shackle rings, upright cages, steel-chain spider webs in sturdy frames, a medical table and an old-fashioned dentist's chair. Most of the gear was already in use, the sound of slapping floggers and the exclamations they produced occasionally rising above the din from the big speaker stacks. The smells of sweat, sex and alcohol hung heavy over the big room.

Steven knew that even more interesting and unique apparatuses were to be found in the shooting studios but these were generally closed to the public except by specific invitation. However, off to one side of the ballroom, there was an open double-doorway to a smaller bar where a line of men and women, each with a green plastic bracelet, lined up to one side for some particular purpose. Others, lacking the green bands, wandered in and out. Steven would have to have a look.

The long, narrow bar was more brightly illuminated for the benefit of a small video crew orbiting the center of the space where a padded horse had been bolted to the floor. A lushly padded, completely naked blonde girl with a Botticelli face and hair to match was strapped on the horse with her legs lifted by suspension hoists, spreading her open wide. Her arms were severely bound down behind her to the upper struts of the bench, emphasizing a spectacular set of natural breasts with pale nipples, one pierced with a small gold ring. Her spectacular mane hung almost to the floor below her. A leather-suited domina with a riding whip stood next to the panting, sweating, red-striped bound girl to supervise the line-up.

The men with the green bands had mostly unzipped their pants and were masturbating in anticipation, sometimes with the help of eager female partners, as they waited their turn for five minutes of throat-fucking and banging the well-used porn girl before the domina sent them to the back of the line. A few just stood around jerking over the girl's smooth flesh while others leaned against the bar, drinking and watching. A couple of ringers Steven recognized from videos he'd seen were allowed in close every so often to penetrate the gang-bang babe's ass, but they were the only ones approved to do so.

Scoring a club soda with lime at the bar Steven thought of O's description of the place as a puppy mill. The girl on the bench, who did her best to keep smiling and making happy noises even when her protector gave her a couple of hard strokes on the breasts and belly during tap-outs among the men, was clearly working hard to cope with all the traffic. Steven hoped she was being paid well.

Steven wondered what was happening to O. He wasn't worried. O could eat Eric's head in one bite. He merely hoped she wasn't utterly bored through what he was sure would be a fairly mundane encounter.

In fact, it turned out to be quite different and a bit more interesting, in a somewhat troubling way, than O expected. David's upstairs suite was chic and swank, with red leather furniture, a huge abstract contemporary rug and a round bed with ringbolts spaced around the frame on a platform. There were commanding views of the city through big arched windows. This must once have been the hotel's best room but it had been modernized with wall screens, dimmable overhead spots and a green marble counter with a steel sink and a small refrigerator. Hoisting bars raised and lowered by remote control dangled in front of the red couch and above the fur throw on the bed. There were framed mirrors everywhere. David clearly denied himself nothing.

O and Eric had been silent in the elevator on the way up, though she did look down to make sure he wore a green wristband. Once in the room, O immediately undressed in her systematic fashion, folding each garment and setting it atop a long Chinoiserie dresser, while Eric watched in frozen fascination.

Down to her shoes, corset, stockings and collar, O knelt in the middle of the room, knees apart and hands behind her head. She had hopes of sending this lad off happy with a nice noisy blowjob, rinsing her mouth, dressing and rejoining the party, but the way he looked at her without making a move left O with the initiative.

"How may this slave serve you, Sir?" she asked softly, not wanting to scare him.

Eric reassured her he had no intention of hurting her. O reassured him he was welcome to do so. She helpfully pointed out a leather umbrella stand full of crops and canes (a thing she'd expected to see in the vice den of any self-respecting Englishman).

"I've been told I'm at my best after a bit of a beating, Sir," O volunteered. She was actually playing with him. He was clearly the frightened one in the room.

"I'm not sure I could ..." Eric stammered, but she cut him off with the suggestion that she undress him first. He didn't refuse so she went right to it, unbuttoning his shirt and sitting him down on the couch so she could remove his boots and socks. Unzipping his fly, she boldly slipped her delicate hand inside, quickly finding it wrapped around something rather large and quite hard. It popped up to say hello. She greeted it with her mouth, all the while undoing his belt and slipping his trousers down over his knees without missing a beat. It dawned on her that this could actually be fun.

Once O had stacked Eric's clothes with equal precision she took the liberty of fetching one of the medium-thick canes and kneeling to offer it up to him. She was well aware that the last marks Steven had put on her were still visible across her chest and backside. She could imagine what a spectacle she made, the rings through her nose and nipples picking up the subdued light. Eric seemed paralyzed by the vision, but not for long.

Suddenly snatching the cane from her upturned palms, he instructed her to bend over the arm of the couch. O obeyed instantly, bracing her hands on the cushions and placing her feet far apart as possible. Anticipating a blow, she was surprised to feel a soft and knowing touch at the juncture of her thighs instead.

"You're wet already, you little whore," Eric said in a voice edged with anger.

"I can't help my nature, Sir," she answered smartly. O was not one to be shamed by some conflicted, inexperienced young man vainly attempting to put her in her place. "It's up to you to make use of it as you wish. Short of permanent damage you can do anything you want to me or have me do anything you want to you."

That was the magic incantation. O felt the rattan strike home in a bright flash. There was nothing timid in the blow. Eric slashed at her backside a half-dozen times, quite hard, then crossed behind her and repeated the action from the other side. This much he had obviously done before.

Grabbing her by the shoulders, Eric lifted O onto her heels. He planted her blazing tail on the arm of the couch and kissed her ravenously. He tasted of cigarettes and alcohol but she didn't care. This was obviously real to him and O always liked anything real. She kissed him back just as hard.

Taking her by the collar he led her to the bed and threw her down on it, where she naturally splayed herself out so he could dive in where he chose. Again to her surprise, he began with his face between her legs. He was good at this too. O had no patience for either men or women who didn't know what to do down there and his expertise came as a pleasant shock. Eric wasn't just good with machinery. And he was patient too, burrowing in to lap and suck until O amazed herself by gasping out a request for permission to come. Reaching up to pull her thick nipple rings, he raised his face and sneered at her.

"I didn't think you'd be so easy," he said.

And she didn't think he'd be so good. He granted his approval and she lifted her pelvis to grind against his face, her thighs squeezing shut around his skull. He actually made her scream, not an easy thing to do.

O's mouth was still open when Eric quickly swung around to shove that big hard rod down her throat. O choked and gasped, realizing she had very little control with his weight on her face. She still did her best to entertain him with her lips and tongue.

Eric was all over her after a few minutes of, yanking her legs apart to spear her to the mattress. He pulled her hair, smacked her back and forth across the cheeks, kissed her like a starving man bites into a juicy piece of meat. She found his roughness entertaining and encouraged him in her soft boudoir voice to pull her rings and crush her breasts with his hands while he hammered into her with what felt like a battering ram.

O went quickly from wanting him to come and get it over with as soon as possible to worrying that it would happen sooner than she'd like. Wrapping her legs around his back, she slowed him down a bit, suggesting that there were other pleasures to be explored if he had the patience.

He rolled off her, kicking back on the big pillows while O worked magic with her soft hot mouth. Coating an index finger with thick spit from the back of her throat, O worked it into a tight, tiny hole she had no doubt was previously virginal. Eric stiffened and clenched at O's insinuating touch but she sucked him harder and faster as she pushed in slowly until she found that secret spot that caused straight men such confusing and guilty pleasure.

Sure enough, she felt the blood throbbing in his veins, felt him rise off the bed to simultaneously fuck her throat harder and allow her to probe him more deeply. Knowing she could end this game in a matter of moments, O lifted her face to look up at him, suppressing an urge to laugh at how wide-eyed and intoxicated he seemed, and offered a suggestion that made his eyes light up.

Excusing herself for a moment, O left Eric on the bed to slip into the bathroom, which was all white tile and chrome and reminded her of a room in which she'd stayed at The Dorchester. The lube was in the medicine cabinet as expected.

Returning to bed, O let Eric watch, fascinated, while she greased herself in the hole they had in common, then roll up onto her hands and knees to offer it. This, too, would be a first, and she was glad he let her guide him in. Big as he was he could have hurt her there in a way she wouldn't have liked, but by that point he was much more under her command than the reverse.

As she "suggested," he took it nice and slow, gripping the bones of her cincher while stroking in and out. The feeling was quite pleasant and O found her own hands working their way down to fine-tune the experience. What was it about demolishing innocence of any kind that so stirred her within? She might have judged herself harshly for it but she'd been this way since she'd first discovered sex and could be no other.

O's ability to lure or drive her partners into all they wouldn't have done otherwise was the nucleus of her power and she relished it just as she relished the sensation of Eric's pulsing cock buried to the hilt in her bowels. She couldn't have given it up if she'd been minded to try.

Sensing him getting close, she had another trick with which to dazzle him that would make for a fitting conclusion. Sliding off him, she rolled over and greased herself with lube between her breasts, carefully avoiding any smears on her costly corset. Offering them to him, she positioned him on top with his achingly hard cock in between, slipped a finger back into him and encouraged him to hold her breasts together around him and finish there. As predicted, the ferocity of his grasp prevented him from making a mess of her face. She would soon have to rejoin the party downstairs and didn't care to patch her makeup first. As soon as he rolled off her, she darted to the bathroom to make sure the river he'd spilled on her chest didn't flow down under the satin compressing her middle. She'd experienced that sensation and didn't find it at all to her liking.

After a quick whore's bath at the sink, she returned to find Eric lying on his back, gazing at the ceiling in a daze. Suppressing an urge to laugh, O cleaned him up with a warm, damp washcloth and delivered the message.

"For as long as you keep my Master satisfied, I'll do this and more for you. Lose him and you lose me," she said in a voice gentle yet firm. When she turned to discard the washcloth back in the bathroom, he stopped her, made her sit while he traced Steven's inked symbol of ownership at the base of her spine.

"Do you love him that much?" Eric asked incredulously.

O had never thought of it that way. She didn't think of love the way most people did, or nearly as often.

"It doesn't matter whether I love him or not," she said, unable to keep the annoyance from her voice entirely. "He owns me and that's all there is to it."

Eric started to say something, but O was already up and dressing. She cut him off with a request to help tighten her laces. Hands still shaking, he fumbled with the long loops but O's guidance helped him straighten everything out back there.

He jumped up and tried to kiss her again at the door but she stopped him with a finger to her lips. She had to go and present herself and didn't care to do so looking as if she'd just done what she'd just done.

Out in the hallway, headed for the elevator, O smiled. She had just changed someone's life while he'd had no lasting effect on her own whatsoever. All she wanted now was to find Steven and update him on the successful completion of her mission.

No stranger to noisy crowds, O was perplexed by his invisibility in the throng until she found her way into one of the large, unisex bathrooms off the main lobby.

Shouldering her way through sweaty bodies, she located him in a circle of voyeurs gathered around the square Turkish-style toilet David had installed in the middle of the white octagonal floor for shooting purposes. Svetlana, still in her full chastity armor (which she had decided was actually the perfect attire for the occasion, sparing her the need to fight off rough hands), squatted over the drain, her high heels planted firmly on the foot rests, shooting an amber stream through the rubber-edged slot in the front plate of her leather belt. Eugenia, who had persuaded Svetlana to liberate her from the lower half of her costume, stood astride the toilet receiving

Svetlana's oral attentions while hushed onlookers enjoyed the show.

O appeared silently at Steven's side, slipping her arm under his. He looked over at her, smiled and kissed her.

"Can't take those two anywhere," O said, shaking her head in mock disapproval.

"I don't know," Steven mused, "seems to me they've made a few friends for us tonight. How did it go with you and Eric?"

O laughed. "He'll recover."

"You must have outdone yourself," Steven said admiringly.

"I don't think he'd ever been with a woman he could do anything he wanted to, or who would do it back to him."

Steven grinned. "I see. Like that was it?"

"Let's just hope he doesn't require frequent recharging. He's so not my type."

Eugenia grabbed Svetlana's shoulders, got off with a loud yelp that echoed through the bathroom and provoked a round of applause from the onlookers. Svetlana shook a few yellow drops off the bottom of the steel belt, stood and allowed Eugenia to help her onto the floor.

"Looks like the show's over for now," O said.

"I think the next act is on the main stage. Ray and Jacqui have something planned."

"I'd like to see that, Sir."

O had convinced Ray that it would undermine her authority as a photographer to be shown off among potential models. In fact, O simply didn't care to offer herself for anonymous viewing, preferring to preserve her personal pleasures for personal situations.

From what O and Steven saw as they butted their way toward the front of the ballroom, Jacqui had no such reservations.

The volume in there had risen even further – the sounds of leather splatting on flesh, of loud cries and low moans, of cracking single-tails and buzzing gadgets merging with the crunching industrial noise from the huge speakers to create a sort of electronic and biological fugue.

When they made it to the edge of the large well-worn stage with its slightly tatty curtains, a wiry, shirtless, bearded man of sixty was twirling around a tall, short-haired blonde woman with Junoesque proportions in mid-air, an elaborate rope harness holding her perfectly, nakedly upright, as if standing *en pointe* above the stage. They smiled radiantly in a single spot fired through the darkness.

It was a lovely moment and there was much applause when the bearded man jumped up, lowered the woman with the release of a hitch and unwrapped her as she descended, boiled hemp falling all around her. He quickly stripped away her body harness once she was steady on her feet. They kissed to more applause and he led her a bit unsteadily down the steps Stage Right where the woman's male friend waited with her clothing.

The applause didn't stop when Ray and Jacqui came on-stage next. Both were familiar to this crowd and the way the clapping, whistling and shouting escalated as they bowed to the room reminded Steven of the beginning of a popular magic act.

It was magical in its own fashion. Ray had arranged to have a small table set up for the black box he'd brought. Long wires trailed away from it into the blackout behind them. Jacqui still wore her blue rubber-doll costume, now supplemented with shiny chrome cuffs and short chains at wrist and ankle. The long skirt was gathered and buckled at her waist, framing her delectable treasures.

Ray led her out to stage center, took her in his arms and kissed her. She threw the chain over his shoulders, held him tight and ground against him. Another wave of cheering inspired Ray to turn Jacqui around, where the skirt was also hitched up in back, and make her place her fettered hands on her knees so he could spank her.

He gave her good, hard open-handed swats that left neat prints on her milky flesh, but were mere love taps to a girl more accustomed to the dressage whip. Jacqui pursed her lips in a perfect circle and jumped forward just a couple of inches with each blow.

After ten solid impacts, Ray spun Jacqui around and kissed her again, mauling her exposed breasts. He yelled an order into her ear over the noise and she made a pouty face, but obeyed. The blue latex popped open with a few snaps, practically flying off her until she was down to her silver collar, shackles and fuck-me shoes. There was an audible gasp at Jacqui's sheer perfection in the halo from the spotlight. The crowd would have been perfectly satisfied to see as much as they had so far.

Ray stood Jacqui at attention in the center of the pool of light, leaving her to be admired. At the small table he took off his shirt and laid it next to the black box. He pulled out a small metal plate, tucking it into the waistband of his jeans. Colored LEDs glittered within the box when Ray hit the switches. Jacqui shuddered at a menacing crackle from behind her.

Ray approached slowly until he was just inches from Jacqui's back. She didn't move a muscle, eyes front while he brought his fingertips close on either side of her body. He almost touched her before the purple sparks shot from his hands, arcing to Jacqui's erect ribcage. She jumped and let out a squeak.

Trying to regain her composure, she squared her shoulders, but when Ray moved his hands up and down her flanks, lightning bolts flying between them, Jacqui began to writhe and moan, eyes rolling back in her head.

Ray circled her slowly, lingering over her most vulnerable spots without actually touching her, while the static charges made her dance like a marionette, her shiny chains rattling.

Ray knew exactly where to apply each jolt to inspire Jacqui's best performance.

Prodding her to the table with his sparking touch, he made her bend over and stick out her rump so he could send trails of blue bolts up and down her spine, making her wriggle in time to his moves. Passing his hands underneath he illuminated Jacqui's tender giblets to another round of shouting and clapping.

"He's gotten really good," Steven shouted over the din.

"He was always good," O shouted back.

O liked watching Ray in action, loved seeing the sweat rise on his chest from the labor of concentration. Having no desire to serve as his foil onstage, she could at least be a good audience.

Ray jolted Jacqui back out on the proscenium to assume her upright stance. He waved his hands over her head, making her curls rise like smoke as the static charge crackled by. O could see Jacqui's skin gleaming, her long legs trembling. She knew exactly where this was leading.

At an order from behind, Jacqui shut her eyes. When Ray reached around her this time he was no longer attached to the generator. He held a glowing wand vibe in his right hand. Wrapping an arm around Jacqui's collared neck he pulled her to him and applied the new device.

Jacqui let out a cry of surprise. She'd expected him to shock her again but this was far more startling. And there was no escape from it. Jacqui kept her legs open and stood like a statue, the hum of the device rising. Her nipples hardened and her whole body shook but Ray was relentless. Eventually, as expected, Jacqui sang for the crowd, every muscle on her lean frame rigid, until her orgasmic aria was done and she turned to sink into his arms.

The spot went out and the applause rolled forward in a tidal wave, shouts and squeals riding on top of it like foam. When the lights came up, the stage was empty but for the table and the box, which were removed by a couple of David's minions.

O and Steven went backstage where Jacqui stood quivering with a big pink towel around her, still in Ray's arms. She and O exchanged kisses. Steven thumped Ray on the back as Ray buttoned his shirt.

"You looked good out there."

Ray gave Jacqui a squeeze.

"Anybody looks good standing next to this one."

Ray pulled Steven and O into his embrace, forming a protective ring around his sweating, trembling companion while she put her rubber scraps back on over her lubricated skin. Jacqui was seriously in need of a drink.

Steven asked if Ray had seen Svetlana and Eugenia.

Following Ray's directions, O and Steven took the elevator down a level to look in on Steven's charges. Marie's girls were his responsibility and he had to make sure they were in good hands, or in any case, the hands they preferred.

Anguisette, the petite blonde they'd met at the front desk, pointed them down the hall to the right as she slithered past them into the elevator. O caught Steven looking up as her legs disappeared in the elevator shaft.

"Like that one, do you, Sir?"

"David says she's fun," Steven replied, dropping an arm around O's middle and steering her in the direction the blonde girl had sent them.

"Would you like me to get her for you, Sir?"

"I'd like you to get her in the studio and then bring her home."

"Consider it done, Sir."

Steven knew he could.

At the end of the corridor a former wine cellar had been converted into a medieval dungeon rather more convincing than most right down to the dank walls of stone blocks. There were a number of interesting devices, including a body cage and a flogging frame, conveniently provided for the use of the guests.

Svetlana had managed to get her tall bare chassis strapped backward over a big wooden wheel that rotated through a water trough. Her hair hung in limp wet ruins around her head and her makeup was equally undone. Her whole body glistened from previous immersions and rivulets still ran down between her breasts from her most recent dunking. Somewhat to Steven's surprise, she was laughing even as she shook her head and spat, cursing in Russian between coughing fits.

A tall body-builder in a leather kilt, also laughing, slowly turned the wheel while Svetlana screamed and yanked uselessly at the chains holding her leather cuffs. He stopped the wheel just before her face touched the water again, walked in front of her and flipped up the kilt, leaning forward so Svetlana could stretch her neck off the wheel to get her wet face underneath. His eyes widened immediately.

In the maze of different shooting environments David had created an alternate universe was only one door down the hall, where O and Steven found Eugenia in her favorite sort of predicament. This studio had been done up like the inside of a laboratory, complete with stark stainless-steel furnishings and corrugated metal walls. A look at all the apparatuses in shelves and glass-front cabinets along one wall confirmed the time jump to The Machine age.

Under an elliptical OR lighting array, Eugenia was pulled taut on a vertical slant rack, discarded steel belt and cups piled on the floor nearby. A fat, smooth, red phallus mounted on the end of a reciprocating shaft driven by the flywheel of an electric motor between her ankles slid in and out of her just a little too lazily. A slender dominatrix with black curly hair and a leather dress boned all the way down to her ankles alternately adjusted the speed of the shaft and teased Eugenia with a pistol-grip vibrator. The domina's companion, a man with a black beard trimmed to a point, sharp features and a bright gleam in his eye, had unlaced his leather trousers and stood at the head of the rack just close enough for Eugenia's leather-cuffed right hand to get a good grip where it counted.

Eugenia stroked diligently away in time to the adjustments of the machine.

"What I like about fucking machines, Sir," O whispered to Steven, "is their complete indifference to the pleasure of whoever they're fucking."

Eugenia shut her eyes and moaned. Steven asked O if she thought the girls would be all right on their own.

O listened to the pitch of the grunts, yelps and laughter and shrugged.

"They're all consenting adults with green wrist bands," she pronounced. "Marie teaches her little darlings how to take care of themselves and each other."

Steven proposed they leave the car for the others and take a cab back to the hotel. O was just as ready to be out of there. She felt like she'd been to the same party on at least three continents. Actually, counting the time in Sydney, she'd make that four. Whether in a deconsecrated Belgian monastery or a Caribbean beach resort, they all had much in common.

The streets were crowded now with the denizens and visitors who made San Francisco America's number one party town. There was lots of yelling and loud laughter among the throngs who had dressed up for a night of indulgence and those who just dressed that way daily and blended in a little better on this particular occasion. Taxis were scarce but Steven had lived in New York. Snagging wheels on Halloween night was rugby with no rules.

In the cab, rattling up and down the hills back toward Geary, Steven asked O what she thought of David's operation.

"He's put in some new things since I was here last but the mood is the same. Work all day and party all night. I'm not surprised there's a lot of burnout. I've shot too many of David's models that just sort of fax it in. After a hundred live feeds they forget what it was that attracted them to this life. He sucks people dry."

Eventually Steven expected to be looking at David through bullet-resistant glass. David would be wearing jail orange instead of a vested suit then, but whatever problem Steven had to solve for him would not involve Ray. Steven would see to that.

There were many things about this arrangement he didn't like, but he knew enough to know what he didn't know and if Ray and Albert insisted that Eric was indispensible Steven would accept the terms that came with him, to a point.

He was glad when they got back to their suite. While O finished washing off Eric under the shower, Steven stood on the terrace, smoking black Afghani hash from Ray's ornately engraved silver pipe. The fog had begun rolling in off the bay once again, lights blinking under the translucent blanket.

It had been a successful trip, if not entirely as imagined. O had closed the deal with Ray and Jacqui beyond a doubt. That they enjoyed performing together and would begin their relationship with a shared enthusiasm sweetened the deal for the two of them.

And Steven had closed his deal with Eric and David. He was less optimistic about the prospects for that arrangement. David was not as firmly in control of the great engine he'd constructed as he seemed and could derail it unexpectedly at any moment. The confidence he needed at the throttle could not be found in the pile on the mirror.

Eric presented a different kind of problem. Steven wasn't sure what kind of problem that would turn out to be, but he was certain he'd find out soon enough.

CHAPTER FORTY-TWO

The flight home was a less festive affair. Svetlana and Eugenia had somehow managed to get into their sexy stewardess costumes but were both wrung out from the previous night's adventures and were allowed a merciful nap strapped into their seats.

Jacqui and Ray snuggled up under a blanket, plugged in their ear-buds and watched the clouds glide by outside. Only Steven and O seemed fully alert and disposed to conduct an informal inquest into the evidence revealed on the trip. O was confident of her ability to handle Eric and Steven certainly had plenty of experience extricating young financiers from the quicksand into which they were prone to stepping. Neither much enjoyed the prospect of these labors but it was clear enough that *Forbidden*'s odds over time were still long and only the assets recently secured were likely to shorten them.

Meanwhile, there were photo edits to be done and contracts to be studied under an electron microscope.

Steven was at his desk doing just that with the sheaf of papers David had given him when Constance buzzed him from the outer office. She had already examined the paperwork herself and found no ticking bombs in it but Steven never signed anything until he'd read every word on it even after a good pre-screening. He had brought out an enormous old Mont Blanc Diplomat 149 and was about to scrawl his signature on the dotted line in sapphire ink when the sleek Danish phone chimed.

Constance told him Eric was on the phone. Already dressed in his Belstaff Panther jacket for a sunset ride along Mulholland at the wheel of the Morgan with O at his side, he really wasn't eager to take the call, but Eric was part of this week's new business.

What Eric had to say was nothing if not new business but of a kind Steven wouldn't have anticipated for any week he'd ever lived through or ever hoped to. He was sufficiently unsure he'd heard the young man's high shaky voice correctly to make him repeat what he said. The words were committed to memory in advance. Steven didn't doubt their sincerity for an instant. One thing he'd never met in his travels was a disingenuous love-crazed fool.

In the tone he used to calm clients off the ledge he assured Eric he'd take up the matter immediately and get right back to him. He capped the pen and put it back in his pocket. Yet another new wrinkle had appeared in the already-treacherous surface of this unfamiliar terrain. There would be no further advancement until it was smoothed out.

O appeared exactly on time as always, dressed for motoring in a cropped red-twill jacket and a long pleated skirt reaching the tops of her laced boots. The scarf Steven bought her in San Francisco was knotted jauntily at the shoulder to complete the look. Of course, the red-trimmed black blouse under the jacket was completely transparent, as she opened her buttons to show him. She bent to demonstrate she wore only stockings under the skirt by flipping her pleats up over her head.

Having just snapped the wrists of his yellow and black driving gloves Steven gave her a couple of good smacks before turning her around for a kiss.

The days had gotten short and darkness came early so they had to putter through rush hour traffic all the way to Laurel Canyon. O was in good spirits – happy with what she'd done in the studio earlier that day and looking forward to a spectacular view, a good dinner and some sweet suffering at the hands of the man who owned her.

Steven was unusually quiet on the way up the canyon. O wondered what was on his mind. He knew, as she didn't, that there would definitely be suffering, but it might not be all that sweet.

At the crest of the hills, Steven pulled over so they could watch the city light up at their feet. He had brought along a nice fat joint, ignited with a lacquered Dupont, a red dragon emblazoned on its black field.

After each had taken a hit Steven turned to O with a weary expression she'd never seen.

"What is it?"

Steven never pulled a stroke with O.

"Eric thinks he's in love with you."

O slammed her hand down on the dashboard, hard.

"Oh for fuck's sake! I didn't mean to blow his lights out."

"Whatever you did worked a little too well I'm afraid."

O shook her head.

"That's what I get for sticking my finger up a guy's ass. I'm sure he thinks it's some profound experience he could never have with another woman."

"There's no shortage of women eager to stick something up a guy's ass but apparently he only wants you. He thinks I'm a monster for marking you. He wants to deliver you from slavery to a monster."

"I'm perfectly happy with my monster, thank you very much."

O turned and threw her arms around Steven's shoulders, something a taller girl would have found difficult in the coupe's tight cockpit.

"I'm so sorry, Sir. I only meant to give him a little extra motivation."

"I'd say you succeeded."

Steven stroked O's hair. This wasn't her fault. She'd just obeyed like the proud slave she was and outdone herself in his service as usual. Eric was too new and inexperienced to recognize it for what it was.

O sat back, face set in hard determination.

"We've got to do something about this right away. If it goes on it'll wreck everything. Eric will go away angry and rejected, straight to David's arms."

"And that will be the doom of *Forbidden*'s best shot online."

There was a long uncomfortable silence as they watched the sun sink. O let the joint go out, its red ash cooling to black while she pondered her next move.

"Well all right then," she finally pronounced.

"Sounds like a plan," Steven said with all the enthusiasm he could manufacture. "Care to let me in on it?"

"Eric thinks he wants me for himself. Fine. Let him see me as I really am and we'll find out if he means it."

It was an interesting approach. Steven didn't press for details. The set of O's jaw made him feel even sorrier for a young man who was about to be taught an unforgettable lesson. Steven had been administered plenty of those by the women who had submitted to him over the years. The bullet in his shoulder had hurt less.

Their dinner at the Bel Air was uncharacteristically quiet. Steven tried to make conversation but O seemed preoccupied. Steven realized how much he enjoyed their funny and flirtatious public outings, of which this was not to be one. Either the joint in the car or whatever was on her mind had given O an even heartier appetite than usual. She rarely ate red meat but Steven watched in some amazement as she determinedly consumed an order of steak tartare followed by a thick chunk of wild turbot in lemon butter. It was all protein, clearly intended to fortify O for something.

She also, quite deliberately, let the jacket fall open so he could see the steel flashing on her chest through the mesh blouse. Though she hardly spoke, she definitely didn't ignore him. Seated side by side in a round booth it was easy for her hand to find its way under the napkin in his lap. The act was surprisingly forward, done without asking permission. Steven neither encouraged nor obstructed it, concentrating on an excellent Wiener Schnitzel and a bottle of Pilsner Urquell. O took no alcohol, knocking back two double espressos instead at the end of the meal.

Steven started to ask for the dessert menu but stopped when O's grip under the table suddenly tightened. She looked at him.

"Please, Sir. I need you to take me back to your place right away."

It was as close to an actual demand as she'd ever made. Steven called for the check immediately.

The traffic had subsided by then. Steven wound out the Morgan through the curves of Mulholland Drive, lights going by in a blur. He could feel the urgency of O's need to be in private with him though he had no clue why.

The mystery was soon solved when they got back to Steven's. Instead of undressing and fetching her collar as usual, O asked Steven to follow her to the back room. It seemed strange to see her there with clothes on, stranger yet to watch her study the art on the wall so intensely. Finding the image she wanted, she led Steven over to look. It was the one of the naked whipped woman with the ecstatic expression, which Steven had framed and hung on the wall by now. O pointed at it.

"Do your remember that I said I'd let you whip me like that, Sir?"

"Not the sort of thing one forgets."

"Would you please do it now?"

"Why now?"

"I want you to whip me like that and use me however you like. I want you to be as brutal as you've ever felt like being toward any woman. When you're done, I need you to send for Eric."

Steven was rarely shocked by anything but O had managed it.

"Why in the world would you want me to do that?"

O sank to her knees sobbing, wrapped her arms around his legs.

"Please, Sir. I beg you for this. And when he gets here please put me on display in the most humiliating way possible."

Steven understood at last.

"That's rather drastic," he said calmly, reaching down to lift her tear-streaked face so he could look her in the eye. "Are you sure it will work?"

"It has to. There's no other way. You and Ray need him. For as long as he still believes he could mean something to me you'll never be able to trust him."

Steven had no trouble imagining the many ways in which O's plan could go horribly wrong. For once in his life he would let someone else assume the risk. He could ask himself why later.

"Go prepare yourself. I'll be back in a few minutes."

O was on her feet and gone in a whirl of fabric, her heels clicking across the rubber floor toward the bathroom.

Steven had been doing what he did so long he'd forgotten the thrill of conflicting desires. The prospect of unleashing his most violent urges on someone he found so compellingly desirable was dizzying. But when he allowed himself to consider the purpose of what he was about to do the ugly words "service top" wandered across the black screen behind his forehead. Had anyone but O proposed such a thing for such a reason he would have refused instantly.

Steven could hardly wait to get his pills down and his clothes off. Instead of neatly hanging everything up and putting it all away in the dressing room he tossed everything on the bed and went looking for his boots. He was already. How would he proceed? What things would he use and in what order?

As always instinct would rule. His ability to let it was what made him attractive to O as it had others before her. He couldn't disappoint either of them if he simply set the beast free in the arena.

He found O waiting for him on her knees. She'd already locked on her leather ankle and wrist cuffs but was otherwise completely naked – no corset or high heels for this occasion. Instead of her usual locking choker a high stiff posture collar sat between her open knees. Her septum ring shined from the middle of her face. Her eyes were cast down, her arms folded in the small of her back, her posture perfectly vertical. She'd tied her hair back in a short practical ponytail so it wouldn't get in the way. The big loop at the back of the biggest steel plug already protruded below the meeting of her ass-cheeks.

Steven was also naked but for his riding boots, his steely cock swinging past O's face as he bent down to grab the punishing neck restraint, locking it tightly around her vulnerable throat. The leather-covered flange in front forced her chin back so she couldn't avoid his eyes.

"Up, bitch," he said simply.

O rose slowly and gracefully until she stood so high on her toes she barely touched the floor. She laced her fingers behind her head and waited without so much as a shudder despite the delicacy of her balance.

Taking the tall collar by the big single ring in front, he yanked her head back by the hair, pulled her face up and kissed her. She returned the kiss in kind but without moving a muscle anywhere other than her mouth. Even when he took hold of the lower ring and tugged at it, she held absolutely still. They stood that way for a long moment in the half-lit chamber, their bare bodies hardly touching.

Eventually Steven broke it off and stepped back to luxuriate in the anticipatory thrill of O's skin as a blank canvas. He made her turn a full circle in place very slowly. Her armpits had already begun to trickle and her breathing was visibly more rapid. She maintained her form unwaveringly. He made her stop when she again faced him.

Grabbing her between the legs, he squeezed roughly. O was juicier than he'd ever felt her, no minor thing given her more or less constant state of lubricity. Whatever its purpose might be the ensuing ritual had taken on a life of its own.

Steven started slowly, almost casually, with a couple of hard slaps to O's face, leaving a print on each cheek. His hands would be the first instruments used. Circling around her he smacked her breasts and buttocks with open palms. O steadied herself on her toes after each impact. Steven imagined that her feet would soon begin to cramp but she would resist begging for mercy until it was impossible to do otherwise.

His slaps alternated with firm caresses. He pulled her up hard by the nipple rings only to suck the points of her breasts in a way he knew she liked. He worked the plug ring slowly up and down making her internal muscles tense even harder.

Then he surprised her with a light balled-fist punch to her hard little gut. It didn't hurt much but the sudden violence of it bent her over and made her stumble back half a step. O quickly reassumed her stance. Steven had struck her this way before and she always found it pleasant. This time would be different.

"Harder please, Sir," she asked, a smile flickering across her lips at the realization that she'd been wanting a bit more of that violence than she knew.

Steven orbited her like a boxer around a punching bag, thumping her ribs, her buttocks and the underside of her breasts. O struggled for equilibrium, coming back to attention after each thump. Red knuckle-prints began to appear in the spots Steven favored.

Ordering her to thrust out her pelvis he struck her just once at her most critical juncture. It wasn't nearly as painful a blow as it would have been to a man but its sheer rudeness caught her off-guard. O gasped and stumbled, only to be caught in Steven's tight embrace.

Lifting her off the floor, he sat her down on the edge of the bed, placed a hand in the middle of her sternum and pushed her back hard, laying her out flat. O spread out wide, pointing her hands and feet to the corners of the padded platform so he could easily attach the short chains and clips always ready in the rings at the farthest corners. She was glad there was enough slack in her wrist chains to give her something to hold onto. She'd need that soon.

Steven lay down next to her, stroking her firmly from the neck down.

"Just think of all the things that could happen to a girl in your situation," Steven teased.

"I expect I'll be made to come first, Sir."

"And why would I do that?"

"Because it drains me and weakens me and makes me more sensitive to pain ... Sir."

Taking the steel water bottle from the cart next to the bondage bed Steven strolled to the cooler and filled it full. Bringing it back, he leaned down over O's face, took a mouthful of cold water and applied his lips to hers so she could suck it out. Like a swimmer coming up from a dive she gasped for another drink. Steven gave her an even bigger gulp this time. Keeping O hydrated would be very important.

His lips, cold from the water, made O's nipples tighten around her rings until they stood up. His kisses on the red blossoms left by his fist were more frightening than comforting.

O jerked in her chains when she heard the electric vacuum pump come on. Steven applied himself between her legs just long enough to get her wet so the acrylic tube would fasten onto her girl-flesh as tightly as possible. Once again he passed the tube with the control valve up to O's right hand knowing she'd abuse herself with it far more severely than he would have.

Peeling back O's full firm lower lips Steven gently centered the tube over O's clit and gave the command. He pressed in as O thumbed down the valve. There was no intermittent tapping this time. O applied maximum vacuum and kept it on until her tender tissues were stretched up into the clear cylinder in a most unladylike fashion. She tossed her head as much as possible in the stiff collar and moaned at the torture she inflicted on herself. Watching her intently, Steven masturbated with one hand and tugged at the anal plug with the other.

Satisfied O was sufficiently tenderized Steven, shut off the pump and took the place of the clear plastic tube, applying a more intimate kind of suction. O was already nearing the begging stage, but Steven didn't want her to have her first one that way.

Sensing she was close he climbed on top of her, took hold of her captive wrists and pulled himself in, taking his time but not stopping until he felt the back wall of her interior. The large steel ball deep in her guts pressed upward against the back wall of her womb, making her even tighter. O daringly looked up at him and thanked him for raping her so nicely first.

Steven's movement on top of her was slow, driving, relentless. By now there was no part of O, inside or out, of which he hadn't calculated the exact responsiveness. This was how he wanted O coming – pinned under him like prey.

"You know I'm going to hurt you as soon as you orgasm."

"Yes, Sir. I've earned it."

"Justice doesn't concern me at the moment."

His unhurried grinding drove O insane. She pounded up at him as hard as her restraints would allow. She whimpered in frustration, unable even to lift her head, and finally let out a string of incoherent breathless pleas. Steven picked up the rhythm and felt O go stiff under him almost immediately, biting his shoulder to keep from screaming. There would be plenty of that later.

Giving her absolutely no time to rest, Steven unsnapped her chains, pulling O onto her feet when she was still twitching. Holding her high by two fingers hooked through her big collar ring and two more holding the other ring between her buttocks, he made her tiptoe over to the hoisting bar where red and black padded suspension cuffs dangled, waiting. They were large enough to slide over O's more delicate locking restraints. Steven buckled O into them above the fragile wrist bones, warning O to get a good hold on the. O wrapped her fingers around the leather.

The hoist took up more gradually than O would have preferred, letting her feel the tightening of every muscle in her arms and shoulders until she was taut as a violin string. Steven snagged a pair of long chains off the walls, using them to pull O's legs apart toward the inset bolts in the floor. It wasn't an uncomfortable position, though it didn't help much with the light-headedness, but it was vulnerable enough.

As if to underscore the point Steven came over and gave her a thorough groping, lingering over his favorite spots, casually rubbing his hard-on against her leg.

"You like being used as a masturbatory object, don't you?"

Despite her discomfort O couldn't help smiling.

"I love it, Sir."

"Adequately greased, there isn't an inch on a woman's body that can't be made into an erogenous zone."

Steven had proved this theory many times, demonstrating it in O's armpits, at the backs of her knees and in the crooks of her elbows. Much as she enjoyed being used unconventionally it only made her more eager for penetration.

But first there would be a proper warm-up, front and rear, with the big heavy black Jay Marston floggers. Among the last Marston made before retiring, they were created expressly for Steven, with long tails and weighted handles secured with elaborate Turk's head knots.

Neither Steven nor O preferred the flogger to sharper, stiffer instruments but it was the proper thing with which to begin. Steven stood just far enough away for the final third of the leather blades to make full contact. He moved around O's tense architecture firing the thongs just hard enough to deliver a solid thump.

There was little danger of doing any serious damage with a whip that displaced most of its energy against air-resistance before reaching the target but Steven made sure the target list was challenging. O's steel-stuffed bottom came in for the worst of it but no part was spared. There were soon wide pink stripes across her breasts and belly right down to the waterline.

The flogger was particularly sensual in its solid splat across O's shoulder blades, producing the fluttering eyelids and quiet sighs Steven liked hearing. He almost regretted needing to move on to less pleasant thing but that was the nature of the occasion. It was Steven's ability to make a plan and stick with it even when his dick was hard that O admired about him in these moments.

The short, heavy red-and-black woven single-tail with the feathered ends was next. Steven swung it in long arcs meant to lay dramatic stripes from O's collarbone across the top of her bosom down to her hip. He went back over the flogged terrain of O's shoulders and rump to put bright highlights on top of the uniform pink undercoating he'd applied.

Every so often he stopped and came over to toy with O, rolling her clit between her puffy labia, inserting a couple of fingers to press against the verdant pad of internal flesh behind her pubic bone or back against the unyielding steel sphere just a membrane away. He tilted her head down as much as the high collar permitted so she could see where she'd dripped on the black rubber flooring.

"Sir doesn't expect me to be embarrassed, I hope," she said breathlessly.

"I know you better than that. I just wanted to remind you of what you are."

"I am a pain slut, Sir."

"Well, that's settled."

He knew her arms would start to tingle soon. It was time to wind things up here. What better finale for the first movement than the cutting swish and whistle of the dressage whip?

It was the only whip about which O had mixed feelings. Nothing stung quite so deliciously but she still feared it, depending on where it landed. Gripping above its disked pommel, Steven landed it everywhere from O's aching calves to her inner thighs to the sides of her breasts to the backs of her upraised arms. He slashed it down across her navel repeatedly, only to bring it up with a snap between her legs.

O yelped and thrashed and twisted, but the severity of her bondage allowed no escape. She was teary-eyed when he stood in front of her, sheltering her nipple rings with a cupped hand as he lashed the upper curvatures of her chest, leaving a vivid map of pain over her sweating, panting bosom.

And then that movement was over. He lowered the hoist just enough so he could undo her hands and feet and let her sink into his arms. Again, there would be no rest. He made her sit on the floor so he could switch out her ankle cuffs for specialized inversion restraints that came half-way up O's calves and opened out over her insteps. The leather was soft and filled with high-density foam but the buckles were extra tight so she wouldn't slip in them.

O's minimal weight was an advantage when she swung upside down, her hands free so she could support herself on the floor until she was completely head-down over the floor. Steven brought her up to the proper altitude, hooked her cuffs together in back with a couple of carabiners and stepped in front of her. He took her by the collar ring and skull fucked her. In the merciless collar O couldn't move her head at all but she didn't need to. Her mouth was there to be used and Steven took advantage until O choked and spit ran down the sides of her neck.

Swinging like this, O made an excellent punching bag, a thought that occurred to her just before Steven's fist found her belly. Again, he didn't do it hard, but the surprise made her gasp for air. He let her dangle while he fetched the cane, going back to work on her whole body as she twisted in mid-air. The burning strokes fell everywhere from the backs of O's thighs to the undersides of her swaying breasts. When he paused occasionally, it was to stuff her flushed face with stiff meat.

O had started feeling dizzy from twisting and swinging but every nerve ending suddenly snapped awake when she heard the cane swish down from above to land right between her aching legs. O's screech was muffled by another mouthful of Steven. It would take all her concentration but she wouldn't bite him even as he gave her six more right down the center of her open groove. The pain reverberated all through her and she feared she might be unable to keep from gagging if he kept jabbing at the back of her throat.

Then she saw his boots briefly disappear from her limited field of vision and heard a vibrator hum to life. He was back and it was on her before she could brace for the new sensation. Now she urgently wanted Steven back in her mouth. He let her suck happily while the blazing strokes of the cane turned into pleasurable tingling from the wand. There was no way O could ask for a climax but she had one anyway, her lips sealed around the only object in the world that mattered to her at the moment.

As the spasms subsided, O felt her hands being freed from behind her. She opened her palms to touch the floor while the electric motor of the hoist slowly let her down. Steven unstrapped her stinging ankles and sat on the floor for a few moments so O could stretch out with her head in his lap. She nuzzled him as much as the collar would allow. His hands explored her body freely, reading the braille he'd inscribed on her.

"Does girl need to be fucked now?" he asked genially.

"Girl begs to be fucked, Sir, please, but also for more whipping."

O's voice was husky but her resolve was unshaken.

This time Steven strapped her face down on the spanking bench, settling her knees firmly into the V-shaped leg supports and cantilevering her hips over the far end for easy access. A few tight straps over her striated upper back, hands to the rings at the front of the horse and she was presented from the rear defenselessly. As a final flourish, he unscrewed the ring from the steel stopper and tossed it aside, leaving her still filled from within but her small hole open and exposed through the hollow shaft.

Steven stepped up behind her and slid in without warning, leaning his weight against her while he thumped away. O rested her head to one side and let herself be used in a different way. Again, there was nothing she could do to resist or assist. When he reached underneath to work some of his clever magic, she knew she'd give it up again soon, triggering another round of scourging. She made no attempt to prevent the inevitable, asking for permission in a soft, dreamy voice.

Of course, as soon as she had it, he applied his thickest cane to her bottom, which was perfectly placed for it, hitting her with loud thumps that left wide, deep stripes. She'd feel these every time she sat down for the next week. O could never stop herself from crying out when it hit, and she didn't try. After he'd gotten his first ten in, he stepped up to fuck her again from the rear, swatting her raw bottom open handed between strokes. Pulling out abruptly he came around to her face, running now with black tears, and put her mouth to work for a minute. The position was awkward for that, especially with her neck immobilized, but she did her best and it inspired him.

Releasing her from the horse, Steven made O crawl to him on the floor between the mirror and the bed. Sitting on the edge, he kicked her lightly in the side, a signal to roll on her back and masturbate while licking the bottoms of his boots. Every so often, he reached down to slap her using the black crop with the twisted wood handle. She provided many targets of opportunity, not even attempting to move out of the way. There was something she craved and she would try to win it by demonstrating the urgency of her need.

Allowed back onto her knees, there was no subtlety to O's approach. Sweeping some stray, sweat-soaked hair out of her face, she dived on him furiously, taking him in deep enough to stop her breath, staying there coughing for a few beats then pulling back out. Red-faced from gagging and choking, O granted herself a little mercy by concentrating on the head with an educated tongue, letting her mouth go slack when he grabbed her hair and forced his rigid meat back down her gullet.

O suspected he might come this way but just when that seemed inevitable he grabbed her under her sopping armpits and lifted her onto the bed, ordering her up onto her knees with her small, soft, supple feet in the air.

The bastard caned them at a steady tempo, allowing enough time between strokes for the sensation to build. Each impact burned furiously. O struggled to keep still after he'd striped her arches with five solid snaps each. When she began helplessly rubbing her bare feet together he knew it was time again. Tossing the stick aside, he climbed up and into her once more.

O couldn't believe she was coming again but for reasons she never understood having her feet whipped, much as she hated it, almost always brought on a climax. Steven could feel her clench around him.

When she was done he flipped her over and climbed on, holding her down with a brutal grip on the leather confining her neck and slamming into her. That was how he wanted his first one, flooding her insides with surges of heat as he threw back his head and let out a howl.

While Steven lay on his back regaining his strength O stood in front of the mirror examining her trophies. She was quite an amazing sight, striped everywhere she looked from her shoulders down. There were marks of every size, shape and color. Most would fade quickly enough, but the deeper imprints of the dressage whip and the heavy cane would be there a while.

"It's all lovely, Sir. Thank you," she said. "But I need more."

Steven had expected that. He would be a while getting hard again but he still had his practical applications.

Instructing O to lie down in the middle of the floor he fastened her hands down to the rings and lifted her legs with the suspension cuffs on the bar until they were straight and fully open. The open steel base of the plug still protruded from O's bottom and her pussy was the shade of a medium-rare steak. That was where he started with the crop, slapping it down repeatedly while O jerked and twitched.

There was worse to come. From the steel cylinder holding the harshest implements Steven brought out a short buggy whip, rigid for half its length, the rest an evil braided tail four feet long. It was tricky to use but Steven had much practice, as he demonstrated by laying it out over O's upper body with a side-hand stroke that bit viciously. No longer able to yell, O was reduced to mouthing the word "Ow" soundlessly each time the snake bit her. She'd stopped crying. Her eyes had taken on a dreamy, glassy remoteness. Her whole body gleamed with sweat.

Steven found her beyond beautiful this way, a martyred saint to some religion they had invented together. The expression on her face was unlike any he'd seen outside of a European cathedral. Nevertheless, he concentrated on placing one slash after another precisely two inches apart over her whole frame from shoulder to ankle. He even whirled the whip in the air a few times to bring the knot at the end down on her burning soles.

Releasing her ankles from the bar he slowly rolled O over so she was face down on the hard floor, unable to lift her head off the surface. Fastening her to the rings again he gave her another twenty on the back and bottom with the buggy whip.

When he was done O had gotten what she wanted. She looked very much like the woman in the picture, right down to a couple of tiny streaks of blood leaking from the harshest cuts of the whip. He freed her and helped her up onto her agonized feet so she could see the effect in the mirror. Turning around to confirm that her back was even more thoroughly crisscrossed than her front, she knelt before Steven and thanked him.

"But if Sir will oblige, there is one more thing I would ask."

Steven was hard again and quite sure he could do what was needed. Taking her by the hand and putting her back up on the bed on all-fours, he slowly extracted the steel plug and tossed it into a wheeled kick bucket, leaving her gaped open for easy entry. Her inner bands tightened around him as he pushed in slowly and for a long moment, they just looked over at themselves in the mirror, admiring the spectacle of O's violation.

Steven tried to ramp up his movements politely but O would have none of it. She slammed back, spearing herself onto him, working her fingers inside her front passage, slapping furiously at her clit until she came once more, screaming with a hoarse, broken voice.

Steven wasn't far from his own climax but in keeping with the intent of this all he didn't let her have it internally. Popping out, he gave O a brief break to squat over the floor drain and empty her bladder, a sight that still gave him a dirty thrill.

Barely allowing her time to finish, he put her up against a padded section of the wall fitted with hinged leg boards folded against it and a tiny padded ledge of a seat sticking out just below the boards when extended. The seat was cut out to take a shaft through the center and in a few movements, remarkably smooth given Steven's state of arousal, he had the boards down with O's legs strapped to them.

More straps held her torso against the padding. Her wrist cuffs were hooked onto ringbolts sunk next to the seat through which Steven pushed a steel bar with a short, fat, intrusive pink dildo on the end. Holding her bottom cheeks apart with one hand, he guided the dildo into O's freshly fucked ass and locked it into the socket provided for it in the floor.

"Comfortable?" he asked, tapping her lightly on the cheek.

"Not at all, Sir."

"Excellent."

Steven hinged the leg-boards apart so far O was stretched into a virtual split. She squeaked as she felt her joints strained to the breaking point, but Steven locked off the boards at the practical limit and stepped up to O.

They both knew what he was going to do. Gazing at her in all her gloriously scourged helplessness, he stood in front of her, jerking against her greasy belly until he suddenly rose on his feet, let out a yell and splattered her from her chest to her belly button.

O could not recall ever being so completely savaged and defiled and she thanked Steven for it in a soft whisper. He was the first man she'd met who never backed down from what he wanted to do. O had searched for such a man in high places and low, given many unlikely candidates the opportunity. Only Steven had never once failed to deliver.

You're a very dirty girl," Steven said when he remembered how to talk. She was, in fact, totally wrecked, covered in lines and spots of every color from crimson to greenish-yellow. Her hair was a tangled nest. Her makeup had melted like cake frosting. She stank of fear and sex and she was still dripping on the floor.

"Like I said, I'm not a girl who minds getting messy."

"Can you stay like that a while?"

"If you bring my legs in a little. You can always spread them again later."

Steven adjusted the struts and, keeping his eye on O the whole time, made his way to a red telephone mounted next to a fire extinguisher and first-aid kit in the corner of the room.

It was very, very late but that would make the effect all the more dramatic. Picking up the phone, he called Eric's number, which was already in the system's speed-dial.

After several rings, Eric picked up, his voice coming blearily through the receiver.

"Wake up, my friend. There's something you need to see," Steven said, smiling at O sardonically.

"What the fuck? It's four in the fucking morning."

"Trust me, you won't care once you get here. Where do you live?"

Fortunately, Echo Park wasn't far away.

"Are you awake enough to find a pencil? I'll give you directions."

Steven gave very fine directions. O saw the grin when Eric promised to get some clothes on and come right over. Steven called down to the guard's desk, giving instructions to escort Eric directly upstairs when he arrived, let him into the apartment and point him down the hallway.

After hanging up Steven went to O, leaned against the wall to which she was still strapped and kissed her affectionately.

"I've never whipped anyone quite that way," Steven said. "It was very liberating."

"It was, wasn't it?

"You'll be marked for weeks."

O laughed.

"I hope so."

He got the water bottle and passed another couple of gulps from his mouth to hers.

"Are you sure you want to stay like this until he gets here? I could always take you down and put you back while they keep him in the lobby."

O shook her head. Her eyes were still dilated from the endorphin rush.

"I wish I could stay like this for the rest of my life."

"Wouldn't that be nice?"

To keep O warm, Steven slid in between the leg boards and put his body against hers.

"Does it hurt when I touch you?" he asked.

"Yes, but not in a bad way."

They kissed and nuzzled for about fifteen minutes until the phone chimed.

"That was quick," Steven said on his way to answer it.

"I'm sure he's figured out it's got something to do with me by now."

Steven told the guard they were ready to receive company.

"Could you please spread my legs out more again, Sir?"

O winced when Steven cranked the leg boards apart. Their combined secretions had begun to dry on O in shiny patches. Steven briefly considered fetching a robe for himself, but dismissed the thought of leaving anyone bound alone, however briefly. Besides, he wanted Eric to be able to read the whole narrative at a glance and that called for Steven to stay just as he was.

They heard the door open and low voices somewhere out front. Steven turned the overhead lights all the way up, both of them blinking at the sudden brightness. It gave everything a clinical clarity that Steven knew would imprint itself on Eric's consciousness for a long time to come.

Dressed in a long leather overcoat, sweats and sneakers, Eric entered, looking around in amazement at the strange world to which he'd been transported at such a strange hour. His hair was unkempt and he needed a shave. He barely had time to give the room a looking over before his eyes landed on Steven and O, Steven idly playing with O's greasy, matted locks while he leaned against the wall. He looked up at Eric as though surprised.

"Hope you didn't get a ticket on the way over," he said cheerfully, giving O a kiss on the cheek.

"What the fuck? What's going on here?" Eric shouted, jarred into consciousness by the sight of them. The whole room was littered with whips, discarded lube bottles and other objects from O's forensic photographs, but Eric couldn't take his eyes off the naked, brutally lashed woman pinned to the wall like a butterfly.

"We were just having some fun and thought you might like to join in," O said brightly, smiling at him as if they were discussing a picnic. "I'm a little sticky and I'm probably still leaking semen out of every hole. Hope you don't mind."

His jaw dropped open as he looked back and forth between them.

"You wanted her," Steven said with a shrug. "Here she is."

Eric's face darkened. He started toward Steven.

"Motherfucker! I'll kill you!"

Steven raised his eyebrows, fixing Eric with a look O hadn't seen before. "I doubt that," Steven said quietly.

Eric squared off in front of them, breathing heavily, his face that of an angry wounded child.

"Now, now, gentlemen. No need to fight over me. There's plenty to go around. If you want to fuck me I'm obviously not going anywhere. Or you could take me down and make me suck your cock. I can rim you too if you want."

Eric looked at O angrily. "You let him do this to you?" he demanded.

"I begged him to do this to me. It's what I need."

Eric stared at them, anger turning to sheer astonishment. "Man, you two are really sick."

"And here I thought you wanted to save O from my clutches."

"Fuck that. You can have the bitch if this is what she likes."

Steven and O smiled at one another. "I'm so disappointed. I expected him to snatch me up in his arms and swing through the windows like Spiderman."

"They just don't make heroic rescuers like they used to," Steven said with mocking regret.

"You're evil! This isn't BDSM. This is just abuse."

Steven yawned and stretched. "You're entitled to your opinion." He turned to O. "How about it? Do you want to go home with the nice boy so he can be nice to you?"

O furrowed her brows theatrically, as if actually considering it. "I don't think so. I don't like nice boys."

Steven looked at Eric with a resigned shrug. "It's her call, Eric. I'm afraid you're just too good for her."

Eric stood his ground a few seconds longer before wrapping his coat around him. He stared straight at O when he spoke, his voice dripping with contempt. "Okay. I get it. You've made your point. You're too far gone for anybody human. You need this? Well, I don't. You can just stay where you belong until you get yourself killed or something. I'm out of here." Eric flipped Steven off, spun around and stormed out, his footsteps picking up speed in the hallway. They heard the heavy front door slam shut.

Steven put his forehead against O's and started to laugh. She quickly joined. "Did you see the look on that kid's face?" Steven asked, stepping back to crank in the leg boards and begin setting O free.

O was still laughing so hard tears ran out of the corners of her red-rimmed eyes. "Not since I told my little brother there was no Santa Claus," she gasped out, regaining her composure.

"Another brilliant coup, Holmes," Steven said, helping her onto unsteady feet. O went back up on her toes as soon as she felt the floor.

"Ouch! You really whipped me hard down there, Sir."

Steven unlocked the posture collar with one of the many keys spotted around the room and tossed it aside. Its impression was still clear around her neck. He slipped his arms under her knees and shoulders, lifting her up against his sweaty bare chest.

"How about I take you in and give you a bath before we go to bed? We can sleep all day if we want."

"Sounds lovely, Sir." She lifted her face, kissing him with all the passion she had left. "Thank you for hurting me so well. It was the best ever."

"I rather enjoyed it myself."

A few minutes later O lay in a huge tub of scented bubbles, Steven tenderly washing her back with a huge sea sponge. It must have stung, but O didn't even cringe as she took a hit off the joint he'd stopped to roll on the way to the bathroom. "Well," he said, "That's one problem solved."

"What if he won't work for you after this?"

Steven dunked the sponge and squeezed up some more water to send cascading over O's lashed breasts. "I picture a more professional relationship from here on," he replied in a business-like tone. "David will be happy to fix him up with some more appropriate companionship I'm sure."

O glanced over the mirrored wall. "Jesus. My eyes are redder than my butt."

"Got just the thing," Steven said, getting up off the low stool and going to the double-door steel medicine cabinet. He brought out a small white-plastic bottle and returned to the tub, showing it to O.

"Stein Solution!," she exclaimed. "I haven't seen that since I was in Paris. It's a model's best friend."

"Methylene blue and belladonna. Makes everything all bright and shiny. Tip your head."

O held perfectly still while Steven gently rolled back her eyelids and drizzled a few blue droplets into each. Blue tears trickled from the corners. "You're just full of surprises, aren't you, Sir?"

"I think the same could be said for you."

After administering a dose to his eyes Steven capped the bottle and set it on the marble rim of the tub. "Stand up and I'll rinse you off."

He extended a hand to help O out of the steaming water. Adjusting the thermostat on the marble wall, he dialed on the hand sprayer and held it while O turned slowly under the gushing stream, extending an arm to keep the reefer out of the rain. The hot water had made her marks even more vivid if that was possible.

"You're very beautiful like this," Steven observed, taking the joint from her with his free hand.

"Only you would think so, Sir."

O was already asleep under the covers of the big bed by the time Steven had finished turning off the lights and leaving a message for Constance to hold all his calls. It would be light soon and Steven never had liked approaching a day from this end. He looked forward to the warmth of O's small body in his embrace. He supposed it would probably be a bit warmer than usual.

CHAPTER FORTY-THREE

No longer capable of sleeping past mid-day, regardless of sins committed the night before, Steven sat up in bed slowly, aware of the double-glass-muted traffic noise, the winter light leaking in around the shades and his own mortality. He looked over at the spot where he expected to find O asleep after her grueling ordeal but she was gone.

There was a rose and an envelope on the pillow. He rubbed his eyes for a moment as if erasing the final frames of a lingering dream. But no, the rose and the envelope were actually there. With a remote control box by the bed, he activated the whirring motors of the shade risers to let in the city.

Holding the sealed envelope in one hand he twirled the rose in the other. It was the most perfect single rose he'd ever seen, at the most beautiful stage of its journey toward death and desiccation. The flower seller outside Langer's was the probable source, but how had O managed to slip out and return without waking Steven up? Steven may have been a sound sleeper but he had some kind of on-board radar that never went down. Any noise out of the ordinary always brought him to instant vigilance, thinking about guns.

O had probably left around eight when the flower seller opened for business, beautifying the desks of outer downtown. She'd managed to dress, take a half-hour stroll, slip back in to leave her tribute and vanish without stirring him from his slumbers. Was she that good or was he just used to her by now?

The envelope was one of his own, another interesting clue. She must have stuck around long enough for Constance to show up so O could talk her into handing over the stationery.

His first initial was written on the front of the envelope with the single bold stroke of one of his broad-nib fountain pens filled from the deep pool of sapphire ink in the black Lalique well on his desk. The color was blended to stand out legibly against the saturated background of the stiff stock.

The envelope was lightly tacked at the corners. He liked picturing O's clever tongue taking a precise lick at each.

Inside Steven found O's short message on a single sheet. "My Dear Sir," it read, "The color of this rose seemed right to remind you of the most memorable whipping of my life. Thank you for seeing it through to the very end. You are the only man I've ever known who could have done so. It is an honor to serve you. I look forward to doing so again while I still bloom as bright."

The note was signed with her single letter and a period. Steven had seen her legal signature often enough by now to know what it stood for but O was never one to waste a syllable.

Not only was it a perfect gesture but in so many ways typical – economical, effective and direct. That was how they communicated and he liked it. Getting slowly out of bed, his arms heavy and his calves aching, he took the rose to the kitchen to put in an empty absinthe decanter from the bar cabinet. He looked at it as the mighty caffeine factory chugged and puffed to life after he poured out the stale brew deposited in the steel carafe by the automated cycle at his usual wake-up time.

Not since he'd left home had Steven ever thought of himself as an unhappy man. Sometimes he was less than pleased with how things were, like everyone, but unlike everyone, he didn't take that personally or hold onto it long. He'd made himself the life he wanted and it was bad form to complain when things were going well, as they had been for a long time in that life.

But for all his success, his indulgences and his extravagances, was he really happy in the way he felt looking at O's perfect rose? He wouldn't have sworn to it under oath. He'd had many lovely moments with many lovely women. He'd even had a fine quality marriage until it hit the wall, and emerged from it with two friendships intact. Other than Martin's company (Martin having been unavoidably detained by an unexpected date with the Angel of Death), there wasn't much missing from his world, or so he thought.

He'd call O after he did the one important bit of business on the docket for that day. Using the phone on the granite counter he punched in Ray's number. Steven needed to know if Ray and Eric were in touch and how it was going if so. Last night had been a gamble. Steven had trusted O's instincts and hoped she'd been right.

Ray's voice on the phone was bright and cheerful. "No problems, Bro," he said. "Don't know what O did to Eric but he texted me first thing this morning about getting to work on the launch platform. Have you signed your pact with the devil yet?"

Steven knew which devil Ray meant. "No, but if Eric's still down for this arrangement I'll do it. No weirdness with him whatsoever?"

"Nope. He was all business. He even had a long list of expensive hardware you need to buy."

"That sounds normal enough. Go charge it all and send the receipts to the accountant's office. I'll have the partnership reimburse you."

"On my way. Thanks for making this happen."

"It was O who made it happen."

Ray suggested Steven give her a kiss for him and rung off. An expert blue-water sailor, Steven knew he was setting to sea with a weird crew and O lashed to the bowsprit but there was no turning back to safe harbor now. So far she'd brought him fair winds.

O wasn't home when he tried her and her cell went to voice mail immediately. He hoped she was finally getting some rest. He'd call her again later.

After the usual scraping and showering Steven still felt every minute of his age but his spirits were as young as in his dreams, where he remained twenty-eight forever. Physically creaky but in jaunty spirits, he whistled down the hall in a black blazer with white grosgrain trim and a skull patch on the pocket, a cream-colored ascot with O's amethyst pin jabbed through it, one of the black "work shirts" (double oversized pockets with a big pen slot on the left, button-down collar, turn-back cuffs) T&A made up according to his design specs, generously draped winter-white pleated trousers and saddle shoes. He'd mounted O's rose on his lapel in a tiny silver vase that went through the buttonhole.

Constance looked up as he entered, amused and appalled by Steven's Anglophile drag. "Misplace your boater did you?"

"It's out of season and I'm not going boating. What did you think of David's contract?"

"No obvious IEDs buried in it. Are you feeling all right today?"

"I was up pretty late. Why, do I look like shit despite my attempts to dazzle you with my style?"

"No, but you are smiling."

Steven stiffened indignantly. "I am not."

"Grinning, actually. And I heard you whistling in the hall. Would this have something to do with O's sudden need for stationery this morning?"

"Did she tell you anything?"

"She never tells me anything."

"Then I shouldn't either."

"The contract is on your desk. I flagged a couple of questionable items but I doubt they'll concern you."

"Thanks. You're the best."

Steven unexpectedly leaned down and kissed Constance on the cheek as he went by. She looked up, stunned, while he disappeared into his private quarters.

Planting his round glasses on his nose he went first to the items Constance had red-flagged. Steven simply struck out the clause giving David use of *Forbidden*'s content for a year after a termination event to defray front-end expenses. If anyone lost money on this deal they all would.

As for the sub-section dealing with Eric's obligations to both companies, Steven ignored Constance's question mark. He foresaw no further problems from that quarter.

On the final page, Steven affixed his inimitable scrawl, drying it with a weighty chrome rocker blotter. He hoped for O's sake that Eric had abandoned any notions of spiriting her off from her brutal captivity but had no doubt she'd set him even straighter if he tried it again.

Knowing he wouldn't be much good for the rest of the afternoon Steven seriously considered an early drink with O, Ray and Jacqui up in Hollywood, dinner to follow, if they could be wrangled for it. Constance rang to remind him he had fencing practice at the club at six.

Steven groaned. Taking on Mike in his present condition was symbolic suicide. Still, he'd booked the man's time and it was bad form to cancel at the last minute.

Back in the apartment, Steven grabbed his green-leather London bag and his saber. On the way to the club he called O again, barking her name into the headset's tiny boom. This time he got her on the line. She sounded happy if a bit weary also. She begged off on dinner but promised to wait for him at home. He offered to bring her something to eat but she assured him she'd be fine on her own.

Seeing Mike doing some deep stretches on the strip Steven was less certain of his own prospects. His hamstrings hurt just standing still. He apologized for being late, as he'd never been before, but Mike told him not to worry about it, promising to put him out of his misery quickly in any case.

It was no lie. Steven had given up his share of touches to Mike but tonight he found himself slashed to confetti three points straight. Back in the lounge for the customary beers and burgers Steven apologized for his desultory attempts at combat.

"Sounds like you had too much fun last night," Mike said, pouring them each another short glass from a tall Kirin.

"They would be an educated guess, I suppose."

Mike shook his head. "Man, some of these guys show up in such rough shape they have to be helped onto the floor, much less off it. I don't know why they waste their money. At least you always try to put up a fight."

"That's what I tell my clients. Must get to be a real bore putting down wheezy old hackers all day."

"Beats flipping these," Mike said, biting into his bacon-cheeseburger.

Steven said he couldn't imagine working with the public on equal terms. By the time clients met him they were already so scared they'd do just about anything he told them unquestioningly.

Other than on the strip, Mike had largely dropped his guard around Steven, as people usually did after realizing he meant them no harm. "Some of these guys don't give a damn to begin with and then they get drunk," he observed ruefully.

They both laughed.

Mike went on over the noise of some those guys cheering a basketball game on the TV above the bar. "I don't know how

I'd stand it if I didn't have Tony to go home to. Mind if I ask you a personal question about that?

Mike had never asked Steven a personal question about anything. "If I don't like it I'll just lie."

"How come you're not married?"

"I tried it once. I don't think I'm wired for it."

"You don't strike me as the type to quit after one attempt."

"After the next Olympics, you may discover that marriage can be an expensive hobby."

Mike laughed. "No way. Tony is never leaving me. Homicide, maybe. Divorce, not a chance. Seriously, a man your age with all you've got going, I'll bet there's some nice girl out there who'd devote her life to making you happy."

"In way, I already have that. I'm afraid changing the terms might fuck it up."

"You know that single people die seven years younger on average?"

Steven had heard that somewhere.

"Man was not meant to live alone," Mike concluded.

"I'll keep that advice firmly in mind," Steven replied, raising a schooner of ale.

In fact, Steen had a hard time getting the conversation out of his mind on the way home. He realized that he was excited at the prospect of seeing O. Usually after this much exposure to any one partner, he was more excited by the prospect of not seeing her. So why was he jamming in the Jag down Seventh Street to get back in such a hurry?

O was waiting as promised – something Steven could count on. She'd been watching some lavish period film on one of the big screens but shut it off as soon as he entered and sank to her knees. She'd already collared and cuffed herself but she wasn't completely naked as usual. Instead, she wore a short lightweight red-silk kimono, loosely belted at the waist that fell open when she knelt. Steven also noticed that the overhead cable spots had been turned all the way up and O had stopped him where the light was strongest.

"Welcome home, Sir," she said, looking down at his saddle shoes with a hastily suppressed smile.

O stood and undid the belt, letting the kimono flutter to the floor. Beneath it she was a Technicolor wonder. Her entire body was covered in lurid swatches of red, green, black, blue and yellow, accented with stripes wide and narrow, long and short. Little red welts covered her breasts and buttocks where whips had broken capillaries under the skin and thin scabs marked the places the whip had cut her. Steven could even see his fist prints on her lower belly as she rotated in the spotlight, hands behind her head.

"You're even more beautiful today than last night," Steven said. He meant it too. O's body may have been battered as if by rampaging Vandals but her face was radiant.

"The best part is down here," O said, rolling onto her back and raising her spread legs to show him the red lacework on her inner thighs and all points in between. Her intimate regions were swollen, purple and shiny wet. Instead of pumps, she'd worn the standard uniform mules from The Mansion so she could kick them off to show Steven the slender streaks on the bottoms of her feet.

Steven asked is she was as sore as she looked.

"No, Sir. Most of it really isn't bad, but I'm sure you could make it hurt if you wanted to."

It was an unambiguous invitation and he had no intention of refusing it. After using O's cherry-red bottom as a footrest while they shared the homecoming joint they quickly moved on to the bedroom. She undressed him in her systematic fashion, this time putting his clothes away neatly as usual, and helped him into the riding boots for which she never lost her taste.

In the back room he spread her out on the bondage bed and chained her cuffs down so he could make a through inspection, working his way along her body, pressing into each wound to interrogate O about how it had been made and what it felt like now. He lingered cruelly on her breasts, which had gotten the worst of it after her ass, though she sighed with pleasure when he sucked her rings between his teeth.

O couldn't keep from squealing when Steven went down on her. She was simultaneously hypersensitive and drippingly aroused. Steven reached up to squeeze her aching breasts while sucking her bruised clit into his mouth. The result was instantaneous. O barely had time to scream out a request before going stiff and twitchy, having her orgasm regardless of the consequences.

The consequences weren't too dire. Steven had, for once, gotten his fill of cruelty and was content to free O, put her on her knees and let her demonstrate her gratitude for a time. She was somehow even more devoted and attentive to the task than usual. Her striped back and blazing rump practically radiating in the big mirror as her face bobbed up and down over his lap where he sat on the edge of the bed.

Once more on her back, O felt the weight of Steven's body pressing on every wounded inch of her own. Instead of holding still to lessen the pain of contact she thrashed and writhed under him, thrusting her hips to meet his, rubbing her ravaged upper body against his chest. Wet as she was every, stroke still hurt when he fucked her, but she rose to take him in as deeply as possible.

Grabbing her by the collar Steven looked down into O's feverish eyes and staked her with all his might, injecting her deeply with one scalding shot after another. O remained tightly plastered against him feeling every thrust inside and out. For the first time ever they came simultaneously, her high-pitched cries harmonizing with his basso roar. Though a relative quickie by their standards, what their coupling lacked in duration was compensated in intensity. O sobbed against Steven's scarred shoulder while the moment of tender violence subsided.

Regaining his breath, Steven lifted his heavy frame off her far enough to look down into her watering eyes. She gazed back at him in a kind of wonder. All composure fled from her delicate features. Her face lay completely open to him for the first time the way her legs had from the beginning.

Wiping his forehead to keep from dripping sweat on her, Steven looked down on her with a consuming affection he'd never felt before. There was something he wanted to say to her that he'd scrupulously avoided saying to any woman since Marie, something he knew was dangerous to even think, much less speak out loud. But the urge was powerful and only hardened instinctive resistance prevented him from letting the single syllable spill out.

Instead, he freed O and rolled onto his side, taking her with him. He held her close for a long. She stared up at him, her eyes wide, lips trembling, as if injured in some entirely unexpected way. Whatever the sensation was, she couldn't endure it for long, burrowing in against his neck while he gripped her hair.

Minutes passed. In yet another unprecedented development they drifted off to sleep on the bondage bed, breathing slow, regular and synchronous. The exertions of the preceding twenty-four hours had drained them dry.

Steven had no idea how long they lay like that but when he awoke the lights were turned down low and one of his robes, long and black with triple rows of white trim, was draped over him. O, fully dressed, sat on the edge of the bondage bed watching him with a curious expression – tender, remote and sad.

Steven had never been able to read O as easily as he did nearly everyone else. In this moment she was entirely inscrutable. He had no idea what she was thinking or for that matter why she had her clothes on.

"Not staying?" he asked.

"Not tonight, if you don't mind, Sir. I think I should go home tonight."

A momentary feeling of alarm stirred in Steven's gut, but he smashed it down fast, managing an affable, sleepy smile as he sat up to let her drape the robe over his shoulders.

"Let me get dressed and I'll walk you down to the garage."

O sprung up and stepped back.

"That's okay. I'll be fine."

Steven stood, knotting the belt of his robe casually around his middle. He took O in his arms and kissed her once more. She kissed him back with reassuring fervor, letting him break it off.

"Are you sure you're okay?" he asked.

"I'll be fine."

O sounded edgy. For once she was stiff in his embrace. Steven knew better than to intrude on whatever was happening inside her. They'd been through a lot in a short time and it didn't seem unreasonable for O to want some respite by herself.

Kissing her on the forehead, he draped his arm around her middle and escorted her down the hall to the front door. They kissed again there. It felt more relaxed this time but O already had her hand on the doorknob.

"I'll call first thing tomorrow, Sir," she promised, stepping out into the hallway. Steven wished her a good night's rest he had no doubt she'd find and closed the door behind her, careful to avoid any parting eye-contact. He wasn't sure what just happened but it left him uneasy.

Steven liked living alone. He luxuriated in having so much space to himself, all composed to his most exacting specifications. Nowhere in a world with whose dangers he was far more familiar than most did he feel as safe as he felt here.

But for once the place felt empty, as if something vital was missing. His head was still clearing and it took him a beat or two to realize what that something was, that she'd just walked out and was riding the elevator down at that very minute.

Steven couldn't deny missing O already. It was a strange sensation. He'd trained himself never to miss anyone. Like a shameful secret, the need of another's company gave that person a power over him that he never cared to relinquish.

This was a moment Steven didn't want to relive. He decided then and there to make sure he wouldn't have to. For all the things he'd accumulated there might still exist in the world something – someone – he actually needed. O was his property. She wore his ink and steel in her flesh. She belonged to him in the only way he ever wanted any woman to belong to him. Surely that should be enough.

The realization that it wasn't troubled him but it was also unexpectedly exhilarating. That he was still capable of surprise was a revelation in itself.

It had been a long time since he'd wanted more than he had. As always, the only solution he could imagine was to get it and keep it.

CHAPTER FORTY-FOUR

Steven had planned to take the next day off but he awoke restless and needing to get something done. There was already a voice mail waiting from O that sounded perfectly cheerful and normal, though he couldn't quite shake the uneasiness he'd felt the night before when she left.

Fortunately, a little work had come in while he was away. One of his frequent flyers had crash-landed in front of yet another grand jury, this time regarding a rather substantial quantity of Oxycontin, now in the hands of the DEA but formerly believed to have been in Steven's client's possession. That was rich. Let them try and prove it.

There was also an invitation to teach a summer course at UCLA on *voir dire* examination in cases with high Q-factors. That sounded like fun. Steven liked spending time with young lawyers before the lights went out in their eyes and he found campuses comforting. Sitting at his desk he scratched down a note on a grid-patterned memo pad to have Constance confirm the dates.

Leaning back, Steven let his heavy shawl-collared dark-green cardigan fall open across the double pocket "work shirt" in black pincord.

Perhaps this might be a good day to drop by the Hollywood office.

Steven put on the kind of double-breasted suit he wore for trial, a black-and-purple striped shirt with double cuffs and a solid purple silk-satin Stefano Ricci tie. The dark purple wingtips would do just fine. It was cold and gray enough outside (was it really November already?) for the black crepe Charvet opera scarf Marie picked up at Bergdorf's on her last visit to New York, the long, black double-breasted cashmere Chesterfield and a broad-brimmed Borsalino fedora. After powering down a protein shake he tugged on a pair of snug purple-lined deerskin gloves on the way to the garage to fire up the Bentley coupe.

Ray greeted him warmly, wondering how Steven knew to show up at such an auspicious moment. Steven had no clue what Ray meant, which was far from unusual. With a great show of enthusiasm he led Steven down the hall to what had been a vacant office from the open door of which miles of blue cable now spilled amid a litter of empty cartons.

"Check out our new server room," Ray said, eagerly ushering Steven into a small space crammed with stacked hard drives, hubs and ports. Eric, in a T-shirt and jeans, lay on his back on the floor, his head and shoulders invisible underneath a tower he was wiring. Ray kicked him lightly on the bottom of a sneaker and Eric bumped his head on a frame rolling out to see who interrupted him.

"How are we doing?" Ray asked.

Eric stood up, brushing dust off his knees, an annoyed expression on his face.

"If you want to go Fox-Two on the launch date you need to let me do what I do without hovering like a fucking drone."

Ray laughed. "He's all charm when he's working, isn't he?"

The look that passed between Steven and Eric was entirely devoid of charm on either man's part.

"I see you've gotten right down to it," Steven said.

"Between your brother and David, I don't have much choice."

"Yeah," Ray said, "we've threatened to bonus him ruthlessly if he makes the deadline."

"I'm sure he'll be worth every penny," Steven said. "In fact, I've brought along something to sweeten the deal a bit more."

Reaching into his unbuttoned overcoat, Steven brought out a slender purple-alligator wallet and flipped it open, revealing a row of plastic cards adequate to leverage a small continent. One of those cards was entirely black on the front and white on the back, featureless except for the magnetic strip. Ray let out a low whistle.

"I was going to leave this for you, but since you're here..."

Steven handed the black card to Eric, who noticed an identical card in one of the other wallet slots.

"When you check your email you'll find directions to a location in Pasadena. It's a very exclusive club that you couldn't afford to join even with what we're paying you. I think you'll find everything you might want there, fully at your disposal for as long as you remain in our employ and don't abuse your membership privileges. There's a phone number in the email. Call and ask for Marie. She'll go over the details."

A smile that wasn't pretty curled Eric's lips.

"Will O be there?"

Steven took a step closer to Eric, covering just enough distance in the small cluttered room to make things uncomfortable.

"O belongs to me," Steven declared icily. "Her use by anyone else is entirely at my discretion. You may yet have another opportunity with her."

"If I'm a good boy and do as I'm told?"

Eric did sarcasm pretty well.

"You're being compensated for that part, and very well," came the even reply.

Steven handed the card to Eric who stuffed it into a battered trucker's wallet chained to his belt and stuck the wallet in the back pocket of his jeans.

"Thanks, dad. Can I use the car on Friday night?"

Steven turned to Ray, signaling the end of the previous conversation.

"Isn't Albert supposed to be here today?"

"He's in his office with the door shut. Enter at your own risk."

Steven left the room with a curt nod to Eric, Ray trailing after.

"You're not making this any easier, are you?"

Steven shrugged.

"You play the nice cop. Eric doesn't need to like me. In fact, I'd prefer he not be."

If Albert was glad to see Steven he gave no sign. His round shoulders, swaddled in a dark-gray tweed jacket haphazardly decorated with white cat hair, were hunched over his keyboard. Acrid smoke from a Turkish cigarette (a dispensation from law and custom in the office only Albert was granted) hung in a low cloud over what was probably a desk carefully hidden beneath piles of magazines, newspaper clippings, file folders, orange Rhodia notepads and tear sheets.

"Just let me finish this sentence before I forget the end," Albert said without looking up. Evidently he had noticed Steven's entrance.

Steven said nothing until Albert stopped tapping keys and turned slowly around in a brown leather swivel chair that had probably been there since the place was built. Albert hadn't bothered to shave today and his round face, made even rounder by his big metal-frame spectacles, looked puffier than usual. He gulped from a tall paper coffee cup with the imprint of some overpriced Hollywood joint on it.

"You're starting to show up here with alarming regularity," he said. "I hope this deal with David doesn't motivate you to oversee your investment more closely."

"This isn't an investment. I've regarded it as a K-1 loss since I wrote the first check."

Steven cleared a corner off Albert's desk and made himself at home there.

"I'm just passing through in search of advice."

"No shortage of that here. It's all equally bad too."

"Have you and O ever discussed the possibility of marriage?"

"To me? God no."

"I mean in general."

"Not in detail. We agree it's unnecessary unless you intend to have kids. O can't do that and wouldn't if she could."

"Has she been married before?"

"Not that I know of, but you have. How did that work out?"

Albert was entirely too quick sometimes. Steven shifted his weight uncomfortably. Albert took his glasses off and rubbed his eyes.

"I had a terrible premonition we might someday get into this conversation. I'm not an expert on the mating habits of high-functioning lizards but I believe sometimes one of them gets eaten in the process."

"Nobody knows O better than you."

"Precisely, chum. And that should give you pause. We've worked together since she was an intern at Condé and I know exactly as much about her as she wants me to. She's never lived with anyone, not even a roommate. She hardly speaks to her family. Sex is her hobby but I've never heard her associate it with anything domestic. One Christmas someone gave her a succulent and she re-gifted it to me because it was too high maintenance."

Steven shook his head.

"You paint a pretty bleak picture."

"I'm sure one of the reasons she came out here with me was to escape all the human wreckage she'd left in New York. You know what a small town it is. One time we were out to lunch at Raoul's and she saw some poor ex-lover who had attempted suicide when she made him dry. She put her money on the table, got up and walked right past him out the front door. Didn't say a word. Why do you think she likes L.A.?"

"Why would anyone like L.A.?"

Albert stretched, folded his hands over his unfashionable gut and laughed.

"You like it because it's your home town. She likes it because it's the most unromantic city on earth. And O's done a lot of traveling. When we'd been here about a year she told me she felt safe in a place where nobody seems attached to anybody. Ray was fun and he was helpful but the best thing about him was how little he demanded beyond the obvious. A man who puts his initials on a woman's ass probably wants something more."

Steven stood up, scowled at Albert.

"And that's the last time I ask you for personal advice."

Albert laughed.

"Can I get that in writing?"

He stood up too, draping his arm around Steven's shoulders.

"I love O myself and nothing would make me happier than to see her settle down with the right man. I just don't think he exists. You have something truly wonderful for which many would kill, probably have for all I know. Be satisfied with that. Realistic expectations are the key to happiness."

"If I'd gone by other peoples' ideas of what's realistic you and I wouldn't be having this conversation. As they say in probate court, where there's a will there's a way."

"If you're thinking what I think you're thinking you should have another look at your will. It might be needed sooner than expected."

Steven slipped away to head for the door. He turned back at the threshold.

"You're wrong about one thing," he said. "Not all the advice here is equally bad.

After Steven left Albert picked up the phone and called Marie who he knew would be meeting Ray for lunch any minute. From years of keeping secrets Albert had learned which to reveal and to whom.

The restaurant where Ray and Marie met was small and white with exposed bricks and pipes that paid tribute to its origins as a studio catering operation. Located on a dull and dusty stretch of Highland Avenue below Sunset Boulevard, it was starkly anonymous and easily overlooked, which it could afford to be. Much of its clientele had been enlisted on studio back lots and appreciated being able to catch a good lunch someplace unobserved.

Marie had already identified a couple of big-name actresses with their young kids and a producer or two by the time Ray showed up. In his tech jacket and fancy sneakers he fit right in. Marie had come from Franklin Street in a red equestrienne blouse, tight jeans and high boots, looking more like she belonged on a sound stage than anyone else in the room. Her slightly butch glamour played everywhere.

After placing their orders for a lentil salad with roasted beets and a prosciutto and Emmental sandwich respectively they huddled over their Virgin Marys and drew up the plans. Ray wanted something special for Jacqui's formal presentation as his slave at The Mansion's upcoming Founders' Dinner and Marie had a few ideas he liked.

He was psyched by the whole prospect in that boyish way Marie always found charming, though it was lost on Steven.

When Steven and Marie divorced Ray made sure Marie knew that his affection for her was uncompromised.

"No one knows better what a pain in the butt it can be to live with my brother," he had said. "I've wished I could divorce him myself more than once."

And yet the thing Ray and Marie shared and treasured most was their affection for him. It wasn't just the way he protected and cared for them. They both understood him as no one else did and held fast to the faith that somewhere inside Steven hid a nice guy struggling to get out.

"We'll have Jacqui ready when you arrive," Marie promised. "She'll be served up with dessert."

That seemed appropriate to Ray.

"She's a luscious little tart. I'm sure they'll all want to have a taste," Marie said. "Are you sure you're okay with that?"

"As long as I get the last bite. We like putting on a show together."

"What a loss you are to porn," Marie said with a laugh.

"Funny you should say that. O wants to shoot Jacqui and me together for a magazine set."

"I don't suppose you have to worry about it damaging your image."

"It's the way our readers like to imagine me. I'm living their fantasies for them."

"How generous of you."

Marie knew that Ray had, without trying, created a persona younger kinksters found appealing and that was part of *Forbidden*'s success. The male readers wanted to be him and the female readers wanted do him. When he'd been with O they'd popped up frequently on paparazzi websites and occasionally even made the pages of tabloids sold in supermarkets. Jacqui lacked O's dark charisma but she was pretty and charming and didn't miss much. She'd make Ray an excellent mate. Concerning Steven's situation Marie entertained fresh doubts.

"Do you think your brother's finally gone off his rails?" she asked bluntly over cappuccino and a split order of bread pudding with rum sauce.

"Maybe he's been off them all along and we're just noticing."

"I'm afraid he's developing an inappropriate attachment to O. You've lived with both of them. What odds would you give that?"

Ray looked up at the pipes in the ceiling and weighed the prospects.

"Let's see ... snowball in hell? Winning the Powerball lotto ..."

"When you put them together did it ever occur to you that Steven might fall in love?

"Not in the slightest. He'd be more likely to fall off The Matterhorn."

Ray was philosophical about his brother's mysterious obsessions and abrupt changes of direction.

"If it all falls apart they learn a lesson and neither of them tries it again. It's not like they have track records to uphold in the romance department."

None of them did. Ray and O hadn't worked. Marie and Steven hadn't either. What advice could they offer O or Steven? Marie was still troubled but didn't press it. Ray's attention was fixed on his own immediate future and might as well stay there.

"If you don't mind," Ray suggested, "I'd like to send Jacqui out to the mansion a couple of days earlier just to get her in the right head-space."

"Do you want her put on duty? There'd be plenty of demand."

"They can wait until the dinner. Let her play with the girls all she likes to keep her nice and juicy."

"I'll make sure she's well rehearsed for the event."

Marie looked at Ray for a long moment. For once, the sorrow concealed by his intractable affability was invisible even to her. He looked genuinely happy.

"You're completely sure about this, aren't you?"

"I wouldn't go ahead if I had any doubts. Why would I fuck up a couple of perfectly good lives?"

The question hung in the air like a dark cloud. Perhaps it was Steven who should be asking it. Perhaps Marie would have to ask it for him.

Back in the Rover after kissing Ray goodbye, Marie ordered the voice-dialer on her cell phone to track Steven down. He sounded entirely too cheerful on the phone.

The sun was already descending into the orange grit hanging over the L.A. skyline when Steven appeared in Marie's office at Franklin Street. She cut straight to the point.

"I figured it was only a matter of time before you went utterly mad," Marie announced, rising from behind her desk to go pour a scotch. "O is just the person to bring it on too. I warned Ray about that but if there's one thing you two have in common it's your immunity to advice."

Steven stretched out on the long black chaise.

"I get the feeling you're ahead of me on this," he said.

She drifted over, trailing a long black-satin dressing gown with her initials embroidered on it in silver bullion. She swirled the drink in her hand as she looked down on him. "How long have you known O?"

"Long enough if you're paying attention."

"You always pay attention, but not always to the right things, Steven. Unlike anyone else, I've actually been married to you and I've never wondered why lightning hasn't struck since. You already have O as a slave. Why in the world would you want her for anything else?"

"What makes you think I do?

"Albert ratted you out. He actually gives a shit what happens to you. If O even has a heart it's not included with the package she offers."

Marie motioned him to sit up so she could settle in next to him. She handed him her drink.

"Why don't you finish this and go fuck Angelique in the ass? She's back here this week and it might help both of you recalibrate your priorities."

"Not really interested in that at the moment," Steven said, swirling the amber liquid in the black crystal. Marie shook her head.

"Now you've really got me worried."

Steven put his arm around her shoulders.

"O and I wouldn't have to live a conventional life together. Neither of us wants a family. We're not jealous and we're both busy. I don't see how we'd get in each other's way."

"I didn't say the idea was impractical. I said it was insane. The longer you've lived by yourself the better you've gotten to be at it. You like your life the way it is. O feels the same way about hers. Why risk it all?"

Steven tossed down his drink in one swallow.

"Okay, that's definitely going down as a no vote."

Marie put her hand over Steven's and sighed. Steven stood and gave Marie back the glass.

"Thanks for attempting to protect me from myself. I can't think of anyone else who'd even try."

"When are you going to tell Ray?"

"After O says yes."

"And if she says no?"

"That would be a first."

Steven passed Angelique on his way out. She wore a curtained bra with cups open at the bottom and knickers consisting of a couple of straps and a bow in the back. Angelique was an artist with blue eye shadow when it came to making

herself look slutty. Steven had always admired her surly mag-
nificence. He greeted her politely and went straight to his car.

At home Steven did an extra mile on the treadmill, ordered out for sushi and sauntered across the hall to the office
in his sweats.

Steven had a low opinion of those who vetted their significant others on the Internet. What did that say about a person's confidence in his own judgment? What did he expect to
find out about O that he didn't know already? He drummed
his fingers on the cool shiny surface of the desk for a moment
before he pulled up the computer and started searching.

There was much to find. O had breathed a greater air than
the sooty soup of Hollywood from the day she was born. Her
family showed up in the kinds of magazines O had shot for at
the beginning. There she was with her family as a teenager in
Town and Country, all of them looking like the Von Trapps
in their Faire Isle sweaters on a skiing vacation at Vail. Her
father, a lean, hard, handsome robber baron, was no stranger
to the pages of the WSJ. Her stepmother rode dressage. The
way she looked in her breeches made her horse seem lucky.
O's older brother had an MBA from Wharton and had gone
directly into the family business. He was already married and
had couple of kids of his own. They all looked happy enough
with their slightly anorectic mom in the *Dwell* spread on their
tragically hip London townhouse.

Then there were the electronic relics of O's previous career – covers from *Vogue* and *V.F.*, a cheeky night-on-the-
town piece from The *NYT* Style section and a couple of can-
dids of her chatting with Tom Ford under a big tent during the
Milan show when O was still in her early twenties.

These were a little creepy. The O Steven knew seemed not
to have aged a day in ten years. Only really crazy people were
immune to the effects of time, mainly because they spent so
little of it on this particular planet.

Those glossy magazine covers were hundred-thousand-dollar commissions. Steven was no expert on the publishing business. In self-defense he'd acquired a working knowledge of its economics. O had been on course to a future of museum shows and coffee table books. She'd walked away – run away – from that future and all the money and prestige and access that went with it to shoot pictures of girls like Jacqui through the bars of cages.

Why would anyone do such a thing? Why would Steven continue to represent murderers when he could have a floor full of junior partners in Century City drawing up talent contracts all day?

Why did anyone do anything? Motive was the heart of any mystery, the missing piece that made the evidence fit together. It ran against Steven's steely pragmatism to contemplate making a life with someone of whose motives he was unsure. O's service was so passionate as to be indistinguishable from loving devotion but an aptitude for the former didn't ensure the capacity for the latter.

After all, the quality of her service to Ray had been equally impeccable. Yet she'd allowed herself to be handed off to a total stranger, surrendering herself to Steven with the heedless zeal of a novice nun. She'd accepted him as he was, in all that he was, no questions asked.

In his vanity, of which he was woefully aware, Steven hadn't even thought to question O's reasons. Perhaps that was mistaken. Or perhaps instincts forged in hotter, darker, louder places than the privileged realm from which O had descended were nagging at him out of habit.

Not wanting to know any more just now, Steven shut down the computer and left the office, the lights going out automatically behind him, shadowing his squared-away frame against the lights of the city where motives were eternally suspect.

CHAPTER FORTY-FIVE

Steven had told Marie that nothing was yet set in stone but he awoke the next morning convinced that something should be. Trusted friends had cautioned him against proceeding in haste. He'd wrestled with his own doubts. But Steven had made his own decisions for many years and once they were made he acted on them. That singular determination had brought him much of what he valued in life. It had also cost him plenty. On balance, the gains had been worth the risks.

Not for the first time, Steven had to make a point of telling Ray something Ray already knew. At least this time, it wasn't something Ray didn't want to hear. In fact, it brought out his legendary grin. A born actor, he did a fine job of feigning surprise.

"Holy shit!" he exclaimed. "The ice-cap is melting overnight. This is bigger than global warming. Alert the media."

They stood at the edge of Ray's deck watching while Jacqui lazed in the hot tub just out of earshot. She wasn't to be party to the happy news just yet. Steven passed Ray the joint he'd brought along.

"I figured you'd give me some shit about it," Steven said, sounding annoyed, "But you have lived with O and you do know her better than anyone but Albert. So speak now or forever hold your peace, and I mean that."

Ray hadn't ever known Steven to say anything he didn't mean.

"First of all, we didn't exactly live together. She refused to give up her own place and always slept there at least twice a week. I'd say I know her intimately but not well. We never talked about making anything permanent and I have absolutely no clue how she would have responded if I'd brought up the subject. Good luck with that."

Jacqui hoisted herself out of the water and showing off her sleek geometry in its full glory, steam from the cool afternoon breeze rising in wisps off her heated skin. She wrapped herself in a thick purple and padded over for a hit.

"Has Ray told you the good news?" she asked brightly.

"I haven't had a chance to get word in edgewise."

"He's going to collar me formally out at The Mansion after the Founders' Dinner. You better be there."

Momentarily forgetting his own domestic concerns, Steven smiled and dropped an arm over each of them, bringing them together with him in a powerful embrace.

"I wouldn't miss it," Steven said. "Congratulations and don't spoil him any worse than you already have."

He let them go.

Jacqui turned her attentions directly to Ray, fondling him through his jeans.

"I'm just getting started."

"Steven's thinking of asking O to marry him," Ray announced, having decided to include Jacqui in their discussion. Steven was reminded that no one could annoy him quite so adroitly as his brother.

Jacqui's eyes got huge. She let out a shriek and threw herself on Steven.

"That's fantastic! I'm so happy for both of you. You're perfect for each other."

Ray suggested maybe Jacqui should have stopped at "perfect."

Steven put his finger to Jacqui's lips.

"Not a word. No hints. Nothing, okay?"

Jacqui looked wounded.

"O's my friend and fuck-buddy. I wouldn't spoil the moment for her. I just wish I could be there to see the look on her face."

Steven rather wished for a preview of that himself. His research hadn't turned up anything conclusive. Albert and Marie were against the whole idea. Ray had effectively abstained from voting. Jacqui was all for it but that wasn't necessarily reassuring. Ray shrugged, looking at Jacqui with eyes full of happy anticipation, and observed, half-jokingly, that love was a beautiful thing.

Jacqui wanted to go out with Ray and Steven to celebrate but Steven had entertained enough of others' hopes and fears for the moment. He promised to report in when he saw the white smoke, which most definitely wouldn't be tonight.

Tonight dinner would be at O's. On the phone, she'd come as close to insisting as her status allowed. She must have a good reason.

Steven let himself into O's cottage with the keys and codes. The décor was so aggressively feminine and fetishistic he jokingly named it The Doll House. When he met with her there O usually dolled herself up to match in the choicest confections from her wardrobe department upstairs.

She hadn't done so for tonight. Steven walked into her *Belle Epoque* front parlor to find her kneeling in the middle of it, stripped to her heels, stockings, collar and the kind of simple black-muslin corset, laced brutally tight, she wore for fucking. Her septum ring was in place. All she'd added was a tiny ruffled lace version of the apron she'd worn to entertain his friends during the card game so long ago and slightly heavier than usual war paint. The lights were halfway up and something smelled very appetizing in the kitchen.

She bent down to kiss the tops of his buckled, rising on command for a passionate kiss and an abashed explanation. Her eyes were averted as she spoke.

"I hope you don't mind accepting your slave's hospitality, Sir," she said in her most formal manner, "but I felt less than satisfied with the way I left last time and I wanted to make amends."

Steven's assurance that none were necessary was pro forma. She would do what she must to regain her confidence in her status, as if the still vivid evidence of the whipping he'd given her left that in any doubt. He promised to exact whatever retribution was required.

She'd taken the liberty of borrowing a purple robe and velvet slippers from his closet (a privilege only O had ever been allowed), helping him into them and leading him to the table. Only one place had been set. O had eaten earlier and didn't want to be distracted while serving him.

And serve him she did – a beautifully presented salmon mousse accompanied by a foaming schooner of Stella and followed by fresh muscles on a bed of black pasta. At no point during dinner did O presume to sit down with him. Between courses she knelt at his side, silently stroking him under his robe. He had never seen her more humble and so obviously repentant. It made him wonder all the more what had been going through her mind during her hasty departure from their last encounter. With what he had in mind for them in the future such things would now have to concern him.

As soon as O cleared the dishes, rinsing them carefully while Steven watched from the table. Her purple latex work gloves were sweetly incongruous with what little else she wore. He was grateful for the lack of conversation, fearing he might let something slip at what would obviously be an inappropriate time.

Clearing the small table and abandoning her apron in the kitchen, O offered herself atop the pale blue jacquard cloth, arms above her head and legs raised. Steven indulged his taste for her sweets until he got her to melting temperature. Gently pushing herself away before it was too late to prevent an unscheduled orgasm, she slid down before straight-backed, slip covered chair and refreshed his enthusiasms as only she could, her face bobbing up and down in his lap.

True to his promise, Steven took her across his knees and gave her firm rump a good smacking until it matched the pink highlights of her tattoo. Though a punishment by no means equal to O's sins, it did the job. Her enhanced lashes were dewy as her pink slit, which she spread for him as she sat back on the edge of the table so he could wrap his arms around her constricted torso. He hadn't had her this way in some time. It was fun to watch her work her hips despite the rigid confinement of the cincher while he stood in front and pounded into her. She quickly broke a sweat from the labor and constriction.

Feeling O's strong legs clamp around him Steven knew she'd found a way to come despite all obstacles as she always did. He crushed her lips under his, feeling the hot breath from her nostrils and the smooth hardness of her nose ring on his upper lip. How she could so abandon herself to pleasure without disturbing her presentation – feet always pointed, shoulders always squared – was one of her many fascinations.

O hardly allowed herself enough time to catch what breath she could before slithering back to the floor to finish him off with her mouth, which was soon flooded with the creamy treat she craved. In buoyant spirits and thoroughly inspired by her teasing performance during dinner he gave generously, watching O's throat undulate under her collar with each gulp.

She was very neat about catching every drop and licking her red-stained lips clean before standing into his waiting arms, her rings rubbing against his perspiring chest. He instructed her to lower her lids so he could kiss her carefully decorated eyes. She made a purring noise.

"I'm not certain, but I do believe you're being tender, Sir."

Steven gave O's right breast a smack, making her giggle.

"Like that's such a rare thing."

"No, Sir. You're frequently tender to me. I just don't take if for granted."

"But you do like it."

"When it's earned ... Sir."

Steven thought that one over. It seemed to suggest more than it said.

"Does it have to be earned every time?"

"Affection by itself makes me uncomfortable. I'm afraid if you want it you'll have to beat it out of me, Sir."

Steven tried to imagine a lifetime of that. He knew that people changed over the years but attempts to influence the process rarely worked and frequently backfired. Albert was, as usual, correct. Realistic expectations were the key to happiness. Steven's most realistic expectations of O were that she remain who she was – always somewhat mysterious and never entirely within reach.

For once, Steven really didn't feel like going home but there was barely room for the two of them on O's O-sized mattress. They always slept entangled, but there was so little extra room Steven, an even less likely fit than Ray, feared if he turned over he might find himself on the floor.

As she reached up to switch off the stained-glass lamp on the nightstand and settled in with her back to him and her still-warm bottom nestled in his lap, it dawned on him that she, too, had created an environment entirely suited to her own needs and no one else's. She'd no sooner part with her *Petit Trianon* than he would with his massive bat cave.

Steven had pictured them ultimately living together but it might take a U.N.-brokered compromise to resettle them in a mutually acceptable location. Wherever they ended up, it would definitely need a bigger bed than this one.

Now it rained for real outside, wind-driven streaks rolling diagonally across O's swagged and curtained windows, black clouds piled up atop the hills in the distance. It was hard to believe that another Christmas would soon roll by.

When Steven was young, a year seemed an eternity. Now it went by in a month. Listening to O's steady breathing. Two decades from now O would still be a beauty and he would be an old man.

As usual when she not chained to a rail, O was up, dressed and out the next morning without disrupting Steven's sleep. He didn't mind waking up alone, but not in unfamiliar circumstances. It took him longer to assemble the ingredients in O's glass coffee press than he liked and his knees barely fit underneath the tiny table in the kitchen where he smeared some marmalade on a fresh brioche she'd left in a glass-domed plate for him.

Still, the view from the kitchen window to O's professionally tended garden was pleasing enough, misty and lush from the recent rain. The floral *Provencal* fabric on the kitchen walls was a cheery bright yellow and the glass-fronted cabinets were filled with rainbow-hued Fiesta Wear plates and glasses.

Though O had lived most of her life in the states there was something implacably European about her. If O was an enchanted princess from the place where fairy tales were invented, Steven was a grizzled king ruling over a dry, dusty realm where things were as real as a bag of diamonds and a suitcase with a head in it.

After rinsing his dish and cup Steven was about to take a shower in O's black-and-white tiled bathroom when he heard his cell phone chiming from the pocket of the jacket he'd draped over the back the chair out front.

It was Ray, very excited and a little annoyed. Didn't Steven know what day this was? He ventured a guess it was Tuesday, but wasn't sure of the date without looking at his watch. Ray reminded him that *Forbidden's* online launch was scheduled for that afternoon. O hadn't thought to mention it and Steven had been preoccupied with other things. He promised to stop by his place for a quick change and get right over to the office.

Everything had seemed fine the night before but Steven was still troubled by doubts about what could easily have been a polished performance from start to finish. Perhaps O had some intuition of his intentions and wished either to encourage them or distract him from them. Neither was possible. Steven was first, last and always a closer and while there was an important proposition on the table he could not be swayed.

CHAPTER FORTY-SIX

By the time Steven showed up in a long black-lambskin duster with diagonal pockets and buttons like a World War One aviator's coat, the rest of the gang was already assembled around the deltoid table in the conference room. Cables spilled from the doorway toward the servers and two monitors had been set up in the middle of the table – one to show the feed, the other to keep David on Skype from San Francisco.

Albert, Lena and Jasper had planted their Aeron chairs directly in front of the feed monitor while Eric and Ray engaged in some kind of low, urgent conversation with David. Jacqui, in camel-toe jeans, a sleeveless T-shirt and her beloved shearling coat, rubbed Ray's shoulders.

Steven quite deliberately stuck his head in between theirs and said hello to David, who was his usual amiable self. David explained that they had scheduled the launch right after their own most popular live feed, *The Trial*, a kind of reality show in which several of the newer girls in David's pen were put through the wringer according to instructions from the chat room participants. There evil suggestions were relayed in a spooky, feminine synthesized voice.

David, dressed for banking as always, was about to go online himself with the announcement. He'd been seeding all his sites with ads about this event for days. If he had to share Eric and so much else to secure a piece of *Forbidden Online* that chat room needed to stay full.

According to the counter there were seven hundred viewers in there now. Steven wasn't impressed with that number but David reminded him that on the east coast people were just getting home from work.

David's office suddenly lit up and so did his smile as he turned to face the camera as it bobbled subjectively into the room. He welcomed all members of his live action sites, eagerly assuring them that they were about to see something new in the world that they wouldn't want to miss.

David billed his feeds pretty much on the arcade model. Viewers bought blocks of time with tokens purchased through a credit card processor who bled David like a leach and threatened to cut off his billing every other week over some infraction of the terms of use. Steven, no friend to bankers, was glad he didn't make his living on that high wire.

Then the new cover of *Forbidden*, featuring Jacqui dangling in her cage, popped up to the cheers and applause of everyone in the room. Some very good studio instrumental with a pounding beat came up behind the image and the cover fell away directly into a gallery of hot shots from the session.

Periodic interview segments featured Jacqui, naked and collared, describing her experiences to an off-screen Ray. As a bonus Jacqui wound up the first block with a handcuffed masturbation to orgasm. Next up: a poised, bantering interview with O, shot in O's editing room as she sorted through the images that would make up the set. O looked alluring in a tight black cotton sweater with a few buttons open down the front and a short pleated skirt of black wool, but she made no attempt to seduce the viewers.

The feed cut to Blaine's studio. Blaine, who had shot video as well as stills, had no problem dealing with a behind-the-scenes unit on his set. The actualities crew started right out with him meeting Anguisette. She slipped in a plug for her work on *Bondage Machines*, one of David's other sites as she slipped an even larger plug into her *derrière* to relax her muscles while getting finishing touches in the makeup chair. Blaine described the variety of nasty things Anguisette would be put through in his calm affable manner, reminding her that she was free to decline anything she didn't want to do.

"I just hope they'll be something degrading involved," Anguisette drawled with affected ennui. "I haven't eaten in twenty-four hours. I've flushed myself out four times and taken enough Immodium to shut off Niagara Falls so I better get that milk enema you promised."

Blaine promised she wouldn't be disappointed. For the next block, the video crew followed Blaine around as Fiona, who rigged for most of *Forbidden*'s shooters, tied Anguisette in various demanding positions, starting in a kneel with elbows cinched together in the back. Nathan, a large black man with an even larger cock, throat-fucked her until her face turned purple. There was some rimming next, followed by clothespins and caning.

The sex went straight to anal in all variations, followed by a relight during which everyone smoked and had a few laughs. Anguisette casually masturbated Nathan all through the intermission before the promised milk enema was delivered.

Steven drifted over to the Skype connection to ask David how the numbers were trending. They were headed skyward. The count in the chat room had already doubled. Ray was thrilled. Steven asked if this happened with most launches and David conceded it did. Next week would be more typical. Still, the arrow was pointing in the right direction.

Steven still wasn't so certain *Forbidden* was pointed in the right direction. It had done well in a toxic atmosphere for publications because it sold dirty fantasies in deluxe packaging. How much illusion were they trading away for the unpredictable benefits of shooting in real-time?

No expert on these things, Steven counted on Albert and Ray to make the proposition work over time. Though he'd never thought he cared much about it one way or the other, the vision of this sideshow eventually replacing the physical elegance of *Forbidden*'s frozen moments of sublime excess altogether depressed him. Guys like Eric were constructing a new world around him and he wasn't sure he liked the looks of it.

Whatever they did, they'd still get in trouble and they'd still need him much worse than he needed them. At the moment it was Eric who needed to talk to him privately and urgently about something unrelated to either of their professions.

Taking Steven out into the back courtyard during an interview Albert had done in the studio with one of the magazine's illustrators, he eventually stammered out a request to meet with O once more up at The Mansion "to set things right." Steven patiently explained that things had already been set right but Eric made his best case. He respected O for who she was and wanted to make it clear that he understood how he'd misjudged her. It was important to him.

Steven promised to take up Eric's request with O, who would ultimately make the decision in this instance. There was something Steven wanted to make very clear as well. O was not part of Eric's contract. She would not be fed to him in addictive doses just to keep him around. Steven didn't like Eric's smarmy grin and didn't believe for a minute Eric's assurances that he was no less in it for the money than anyone else and would concentrate on business exclusively once this lingering bit of unfinished business was resolved.

At the end of *Forbidden*'s first-ever online presentation everyone in the conference room stood up clapping and whistling. By the sign-off the chat room was so full the servers were locking up, which drove Steven nuts every time the images on the screen froze but was nevertheless a good omen. David did some math in his head and gleefully announced they'd made more in the previous hour than *Forbidden* did in the first week after a new street date.

Steven hadn't seen Ray this excited since he'd gotten his first bicycle. He danced around the room, hugging everyone, slapping backs, grabbing mitts, high-fiving, knuckle-bumping, groping both Jacqui, who groped him right back, and Lena, who spiked him in the shin with a high heel. They all went out to get drunk after that. Steven watched them do it, his mind on other things. The Hollywood imitation of a London pub was so loud conversation was impossible and that was fine with him. He was destined for some conversation soon enough, though he'd as soon have avoided that too.

Back home and relieved to be there, Steven rolled over on his own big bed (which he had been glad to see again), his barely-belted black Pratesi robe lying mostly open across his body, and listened for some hint of unease through the Bluetooth disk planted in his left ear. The hint wasn't forthcoming.

"I really don't see the problem, Sir," O insisted on the phone. "His pride was hurt and needs a little patching up."

"Are you sure it's safe to be alone with him after the way we put him through the shredder?"

"I won't be alone. If there's a problem the attendants will put him in his car and send him on his way."

"So long as you understand that this isn't an order. I may require you to give yourself to men and women I like now and then but I have no intention of handing you over to an asshole who gets on my last nerve every time he needs patching up."

He heard O's rare and musical laughter through the tiny speaker in his head.

"You're the one he annoys, Sir. I don't find him difficult to manage."

O enjoyed certain strategic advantages in dealing with this troublesome techno prima donna. O was shooting tomorrow but could go out to The Mansion on Friday. She thanked Steven for his concern and promised to come to him immediately afterward, following a shower of course.

Marie was taking a short nap after dinner when Steven called but she was awake enough to promise a comfortable room for Friday's assignation and an attendant to quietly patrol the hallway outside throughout. She seemed relieved that Steven was still willing to loan O out at least occasionally.

Only Steven, who never hesitated to assume the worst, had foreseen the depth of Eric's rage at having been humiliated by O. He'd fled from the power of her submission like a frightened child and the child inside him was still furious.

Eric didn't even bother to request any particular type of room at The Mansion or give instructions regarding what O was to wear or how she was to be presented when Marie met him at the door. He showed up clean-shaven and in a crisply ironed shirt worn under a sport coat and over his jeans. He seemed unimpressed with the surroundings and uninterested in what they had to offer.

All he wanted was O. The particulars weren't important. This stirred some uneasiness in Marie but this wasn't her bargain to negotiate. Sending Eric with an attendant to one of the suites upstairs, she summoned O from the office where O had been working on her laptop. O was already dressed in the red version of the house livery, having stained her lips and nipples more garishly than usual. O assumed Eric wanted the slut who had shamed him and she intended to deliver on his fantasy just as she would Steven's or Ray's.

O felt a little guilty that the slight twinge of fear she felt in her gut at the thought of meeting this confused young man was exhilarating. Steven understood O's pleasure in fear and he could be pretty scary when he came at her with that look in his eye. But she knew Steven and there was something about putting herself in the hands of a stranger, one she'd deliberately antagonized, that made her unseemly wet.

Eric, already naked, sat in a tall chair next to the window when O entered. She knelt and waited per The Mansion's protocol of silence. Eric stood up, walked directly over to her, backhanded her across the face and ordered her to suck his cock, which was harder than it had ever been. Over the next hour he savagely abused and mistreated her, though she did manage to keep herself from getting fucked up the ass with no lube so that it would be in working order for Steven later if he wanted it.

Beyond that, O did her best to act bewildered and ashamed while he slapped her around and cursed her, but once on her back on the bed she whispered to him to go ahead and fuck her like he hated her. After that the whole thing was over in minutes, but not before O managed to wring a couple of orgasms out of it for herself.

Without a word, Eric dressed and left. O hobbled into the adjoining bathroom to see if Eric had left any evidence. She noted a couple of impact points that might bruise but nothing worth worrying about. As promised, she took a shower before driving to Steven's, pausing only to give a quick hallway BJ to the attendant who had stood watch in the hallway. The girls, forbidden to keep cash on the premises, tipped the staff with services in kind.

Steven was waiting at the elevator when O arrived. He had on his bomber jacket, black trousers and black boots. O had no doubt he wore his gun under that jacket and none whatsoever that he would go kneecap Eric with it at the slightest excuse. Before he could ask any questions she volunteered that she was fine and kissed him eagerly.

Eric's violence had merely whetted her appetite for more. Hoping to avoid Steven's detailed interrogation, she engaged his attention elsewhere. Steven rose to the occasion, stringing O up in the back room for a good lashing with his favorite single-tail for being such a slut (her favorite thing for which to be punished, as whipping was hardly a deterrent and she could do nothing about her unruly libido in any case). Afterward she found herself freed from the overhead bar and tossed face down on the bondage bed.

Steven couldn't be bothered to restrain her in any way, but he did pause to grease O's rear entrance before sliding his thick member slowly and inexorably into it. Beyond a few well-placed slaps and pinches he'd hardly bothered with foreplay but O supplied it with her own fingers while he pumped relentlessly away. That hadn't taken long either. O felt him spilling down her entrails in great heaving spurts. Boys were fun when properly pissed off.

O's hopes of avoiding questions were in vain, however. Lying on top of Steven back to front, she shared a joint with him and as few details as possible. Yes, Eric had been rude. He had used O to prove something to himself and she was confident he had done so. No she was not injured in any way and there was no reason why Steven should go put him in the L.A. River bed, however much he might want to.

"Besides," she pointed out logically, "if you do that, my sacrifice will have been for nothing."

Steven couldn't help laughing.

"Some sacrifice."

"It was rather stimulating being grudge-fucked with such sincerity."

"Let's hope you got it out of his system. Ray has to trust this jerk and he'll never put his hands on you again unless he fancies learning to write code with a bite-stick."

"I think he's done with me, Sir. And I'm certainly done with him."

Henceforward when they passed in the halls at the office she and Eric greeted each other with cold cordiality, neither having anything the other wanted anymore.

CHAPTER FORTY-SEVEN

Back behind his desk, Ray tried his best not to think about his disquieting lunch with Marie or his own unaccustomed nervousness in anticipation of the upcoming ceremony. Much as he and Jacqui loved performing together, this time it wouldn't just be their bodies laid bare. For once he felt a twinge of stage fright, though he was sure that would pass once the band struck up.

The more troubling consideration, to which he hadn't given voice even with Marie, was the change in his life that would come after. This was what real commitment felt like: exciting, scary and permanent.

Though he wasn't getting married in the traditional sense the way Steven planned to, he would no longer be single either. The whole image of the dashing young heart-beaker-about-town would dissolve once his feelings for Jacqui became common knowledge.

What about work? Would those he employed view him differently as half of a couple? Would they be on the lookout for evidence of inattention or loss of commitment to the enterprise? There was always drama among creative people. It was Ray's responsibility to keep that to a minimum.

And what of Steven? If he really did marry O would he lose interest in Ray's troubles? That had never happened before but the future was murky. Ray had hoped to bring them even closer together with the gift of his most valued treasure. Could he have accidentally done the exact opposite?

Steady creative employment was the obsessive goal of tens of thousands of Angelenos, only a tiny percentage of who would ever secure it. Working at *Forbidden* was a cush gig no one wanted to lose. Ray had always played the nice cop with his brother, the mean-ass rich lawyer, well cast as the bad cop upon whom all reprimands and/or firings could easily be blamed. He still depended on his big brother to finish the fights Ray started.

It was better to focus his thoughts on the upcoming festivities even if doing so produced abdominal butterflies. Jittery or not, Ray knew his and Jacqui's ceremonial bonding would be a joyous occasion, presenting themselves to the elite of their circle as master and slave, and as lovers, for they had become that as well. If Steven's prospects were less certain, Steven had made them that way. He'd be the one to live with the consequences for a change.

He got Jasper on the intercom and asked him to bring in the roughs for the redesigned landing page of the online edition. He knew that events outside this building were largely beyond his control and in the meantime there were plenty of things that needed his attention.

Marie felt much the same. She, too, was grateful for the myriad matters distracting her from personal anxiety. The Founders' Dinner wasn't the largest event on The Mansion's yearly calendar. The summer and winter galas drew bigger crowds and required more complex arrangements. But the strictly private affair now only days away brought together those who had been offered the first memberships in the inner circle and paid dearly for accepting.

They had no actual power over The Mansion's operations but their wishes could not be disregarded lightly. Not only did they continue to finance the operation with their money, they protected it with their privileged connections. In shielding their own involvement with Marie's establishment they also shielded her and for that they were to be kept contented – no easy task with those so accustomed to having their way.

A week in advance, Marie took up full-time residence at The Mansion to oversee every aspect of the preparations. She met with the kitchen crew to construct the menu, making sure that special meals would be prepared for the two vegetarians on the list. She'd entertained suggestions by the promising young woman she'd hired away from a legendary restaurant up in Napa as head chef. It was challenging task for the wholesome, freckled, frizzy-haired Jana to create a dinner appropriately indulgent and luxurious without being too rich and heavy, as the evening would eventually pivot to more strenuous pleasures.

Marie helped Aaron, a tall, somber African-American former police captain who had been her long-time chief of staff, brief the attendants. Most had been there long enough to know the drill, but could always stand to be refreshed on a few essentials. They were to be just visible enough to make the guests feel safe – parking their cars, leading them to the front door and then fading back into the woodwork. If a guest cared to see his or her companion used or punished the attendants were to make themselves available on request, but were otherwise barred from the dining room and the main salons.

The attendants were reminded to be especially vigilant about cameras or camera phones, collecting all electronic devices as politely as possible from each arrival.

Many of the house girls lived in other cities and only came out to The Mansion to work a few weeks at a time. For this one night the entire complement was expected to be in service. Marie herself made the arrangements to fly them all in a day or two before so they could readjust to The Mansion's routine. The girls from the Franklin Street house were added to the roster for the occasion. There could never be too many appealing and obedient slaves for this particular night.

Those already in residence hardly needed reminding of the importance of correct protocol in all things. The Founders' Dinner was a CMNF affair – clothed males and naked females. Each guest would have an escort for the evening, entirely exposed except for whatever shoes, jewelry or restraints her host would choose for her. The escorts would arrive early so the house girls could help them prepare. Most were now personal slaves though many had once been house girls themselves. The few members who still hadn't settled on a particular favorite would be assigned company from the staff based on feedback from previous visits.

Those girls not seated at the table would wear the standard uniform and attend to serving food, drink or anything else the guests might require. If ordered to render assistance in other activities as the evening wore on they would gather up whatever implements were needed and participate however commanded. The escorts would be allowed to speak at will, or at least at the will of their owners, but the house girls would observe the vow of silence as if they took it seriously.

Marie cautioned that in a room full of naked women those still partially concealed would be all the more conspicuous and should not expect to get through the event without being put to some kind of carnal purpose. They were reminded to wear no scent of any kind that might linger to incriminate attendees with suspicious spouses at home.

The maids and technicians would see to it that each guest's room was furnished with whatever items had been requested on the lists accompanying RSVPs attached to the Nile Blue formal invitations Steven ordered from London. There would be music from a naked all-female string quartet, chosen for their beauty as well as their virtuosity, during the reception in the front parlor but none at dinner. Volumes were to be kept low so as not to interfere with conversation.

Between briefings, Marie took calls from those flying in for the occasion, cheerfully promising their special wants or needs would be attended to diligently. She arranged for airport pick-ups, hair and nail appointments and massages. She booked in-town accommodations for those ostensibly traveling on business (even though after checking into various luxury hotels the occupants rarely returned to their deluxe suites).

Marie enjoyed this part of the job. She had that cardinal virtue of all great madams, an extraordinary memory. She happily reminisced with each caller about prior stays and hinted at amusements she knew would be to their liking. She remembered the preferences of each visitor more precisely than the girls who had actually had sex with them.

Then there was the inspection of the physical plant, which couldn't have been more thorough if conducted by a platoon of Marine drill sergeants from Twenty-Nine Palms. Floors were to be waxed and windows washed. Silver needed polishing and The Mansion's unparalleled selection of instruments of restraint and torture had to be checked out and properly adjusted. The dinner was always scheduled just ahead of the major holidays that most of the men spent with their official families and the big place would tend to be chilly. The climate control system required programming for naked-friendly warmth in every room.

A couple of days before the gathering Marie felt confident to go back into the city and buy herself something spectacular from Les Habitudes, the exclusive and stratospherically expensive boutique on Robertson Boulevard that specialized in lacy updated Victoriana. The girls who worked there all knew and adored her, the more so because she made no secret of her occupation or the nature of the festivities for which she shopped.

This year Marie's choice was a long black-lace gown – cut high and low and largely transparent in between – that emphasized every curve with darts and gathers and a row of close-set buttons from hem to neck in the back. The knee-length boots with black-lace panels were a perfect match.

Marie doubted it would all stay on through the night. She would have plenty of help getting out of it should the need arise. She dropped by Wolford while in the neighborhood to pick up a couple of extra pairs of stockings, just in case. She'd already chosen her jewelry: an art deco necklace from Van Cleef that would have made Catherine the Great envious and a couple of wrist bangles from David Webb that no man would ever buy for his wife. Marie was nobody's wife and this was hardly an occasion for subtlety.

CHAPTER FORTY-EIGHT

On the afternoon of the great occasion gainful labor was out of the question. Steven had already given Constance the day off. After a short and surprisingly blustery walk along the edge of the park for lox and eggs at Langer's he came back to a waiting queue of voice mails from newly arrived friends he rarely saw at any other time. He returned the calls, welcoming everyone back to Los Angeles, catching up on recent developments and promising an especially memorable evening to come.

While Steven pumped up the bonhomie among the boys he knew the girls would be frantically phoning Marie for last minute advice on manicurists and quick refresher courses in house protocol. This was the only day of the year when Marie's counsel was in the greater demand, and rightly so. She was the final authority on the details her devils desired.

Steven was knocking down billiard balls with his earset screwed into his head when O arrived at precisely four, just as the light from the windows began to fade. Fresh from the shower, his thick hunter green terry-cloth robe nearly swept the floor and he had to push the roomy sleeves back to shoot.

O had dressed in a simple red cashmere cardigan over a white high-collared silk blouse with a ruffled placket, a wide black-leather belt that emphasized the corset beneath and a close-fitting black knee-length skirt. Steven was surprised to see a spectacular vintage Chinchilla coat draped over O's arm. She disapproved of furs, especially in Los Angeles, but this one had belonged to her grandmother, she explained, and the statute of limitations on O's animal-rights-charter violations applied to pelts older than the wearer. It would be cold later and she didn't want to show up shuddering with her shoulders hunched. The bad posture of underdressed girls who insistently pretended that Los Angeles had no winter was one of O's favorite annoyances.

O's hair and make-up were already done. Freshly washed, styled and blown, her dark bob glittered with another family heirloom – a diamond and onyx clip from the Twenties that matched the clasp on her black silk-satin clutch. Putting the coat and bag on the table, she stretched up for a long kiss from Steven to test the durability of her lip-stain. It held up nicely. She'd had Renata come by the house to do her eyes, which were glamorized to just this side of whorish in a very calculated way.

Steven would bet that her nipple rouge was heavier than usual as well, which O confirmed by unbuttoning her blouse and popping the front of her minimal bra. Steven never tired of watching O's systematic striptease. As always, she neatly folded each article of clothing and set it on the end of the couch as it came off her, providing many viewing angles of her body in motion. Taking her septum ring from her clutch she slipped it into her nose and clicked it shut. Bare to the red-soled pumps and sheer black stockings, she clicked off to the bedroom for a moment during which Steven took and missed an easy shot on the Three Ball and brought him her collar. Kneeling, eyes averted, she held it on open hands above her head. He made her stand so he could kiss her neck before locking it on. This was the least varying of all their rituals. Whatever followed was pretty much improvisational.

"Seeing you so perfect inspires me to mess you up," Steven said jovially.

"That is the point, Sir, though I'm sure you'll enjoy it more after looking at me like this for a few hours."

He accused her of being clever and gave her a slap on the tail hard enough to make her laugh and yelp at the same time. She asked him saucily to do the other side so she'd be even. He obliged her with a second swat to the opposite butt-cheek. Pulling her back against him he reached around to massage her nipple rings, feeling the flesh harden and contract around them immediately.

O's voice was throaty.

"Please, Sir. I promised Marie I'd get you out there early."

"Absolutely right. Remind me to thrash you later for distracting me."

O reached back to grab a handful of him.

"I won't forget, Sir. I'll make sure I have it coming."

Steven sent O to the closet to collect the elements of his habit for the evening. It was a long list and Steven had plenty of time roll a big joint before O returned to lead him toward the dressing room.

Tonight, the scarlet tailcoat would make its public debut. Short of taking up fox hunting, a thing Steven had no intention of doing, this might be the one occasion for which it was appropriate. It had taken him a few late night phone calls to Snaith and Company in London securing "Death or Glory" brass buttons to replace the originals.

O did up the silver-and-black skull and bones studs on the bib front of Steven's black Marcella-bibbed wing-collared shirt and popped matching 17th/21st Sterling links through his thick cuffs.

"Hard to believe the Brits conquered the world wearing these things around their necks," Steven said as O went on her tiptoes to straighten the collar's wings.

"They regard discomfort as a test of character, Sir."

He couldn't argue with that. Attaching silver silk braces with alligator tips to his high-waisted trousers with braid stripes down the side, O helped him into them, tucking his shirt down and feeling him up once more before buttoning in his increasingly unruly anatomy.

"I can see what kind of mood you're in," he said with a laugh.

Steven held his cuffs up so O could roll on his high, red socks and shoehorn him into his high-button boots, planting a ceremonial lick on each. He even granted her the privilege of adjusting his sock-garters, in return for which she hugged his shanks into her cleavage.

Standing in front of one of the long mirrors Steven effortlessly knotted his black silk moiré cravat in one attempt, a skill possessed by no man in Los Angeles unaffiliated with the symphony. O loved watching him do his sartorial tricks. A younger, less weathered guy might have seemed affected and theatrical fussing with a regimental stickpin, but Steven was just a man out of time. It was easy for O to imagine him a daring comprador from The British East India Company as she pinned his bar of miniature Navy medals to his wide lapel.

"You've never told me what these were for, Sir," she said, smoothing their striped ribbons.

Steven looked down with knitted brows, as if struggling to remember.

"Let's see. I think the one on the left is for conspicuous consumption of Belgian beer. Next over is distinguished service in the whorehouses around Subic Bay. And then there's crossed golf clubs with oak leaf clusters for the most time spent hanging around the officer's club at The Presidio."

The truth was far less amusing. Besides the standard decorations any Navy officer received for avoiding courts martial, most of them came from his actions in Kosovo, which had made him much more popular with the U.N. commanders than his own.

O fussed with Steven's pocket square while he finished securing the double-breasted silk moiré waistcoat to match his cravat. O wound the Breguet repeater and slipped it in his vest pocket, sliding the fob on its heavy chain through the top buttonhole of the vest.

She collected his wallet with the Art Nouveau silver trim and the Mont Blanc Carnegie fountain pen at his direction while he palmed a small blue-velvet box from one of the burl wood drawers and slipped it into the other pocket on his vest. It took some persuading to get O's ring size out of the highly detailed computer profile Marie kept on all The Mansion girls but he had no doubts about its accuracy. When a new girl was inducted, they measured parts of her she didn't know she had.

Back in the living room Steven found the black opera scarf, white kid gloves and low-crown silk town shell laid out on the table across which O had draped the cashmere Chesterfield. She sat in his lap while they smoked the joint Steven rolled earlier. He'd bring another for the road in hi small leather slipcase and the pearl-finished Dupont lighter to fire it up at the end of what promised to be a very long evening.

In most previous years, Steven would have been thinking about which guests needed what kind of attention or wondering what new darlings the founders might be introducing to the establishment. This year, he would certainly have given some thought to Ray's big announcement, which was bound to raise some eyebrows considering that Steven would be with the girl Ray had brought last time.

Steven's mind was on something else entirely. He was an expert at keeping secrets but holding out for the right moment to produce the blue velvet box proved difficult. He wanted to put that ring on O's finger, throw her down and fuck her to the floorboards much more than he wanted to go to dinner. But a great trial lawyer is an actor of sorts and Steven understood the importance of setting. He'd already chosen the most dramatic available.

Steven slipped the fur over O's bare flesh. Most of the women came to the dinner wearing something they shed once inside, but O liked riding through the night naked under soft hides. If they got pulled over she had her lawyer conveniently by her side. She did miss the pitiless embrace of a corset, but felt sure her compressed waistline would still be obvious even unconfined.

Only the Roller would do for tonight. O deliberately flashed Steven climbing into it as he held the door open for her, closing it behind her with its unmistakably solid thump. The heaters in the red piped seats kicked on immediately once the huge engine turned over. O could feel the warmth rising beneath her before they were out of the garage.

It was still cloudy and the lambent incandescence of the city reflected back from the low cover. Los Angeles could be a magical place on a November night when viewed through the windows of a shiny Rolls while naked under a Chinchilla coat. O looked over at Steven. Could any man be so right for her?

Disdainful of flash and glitz, she was a sucker for style and elegance liberally applied atop a core of cruel, shameless lust. Steven was the beast who had haunted her dreams since she was a young girl. Now she belonged to him. She was his plaything, prisoner and tender piece of fuck-meat. O's fairy tales were a bit different than those of the other girls at school.

The Rolls made its stately cruise up the Pasadena Freeway, mercifully uncongested in this short interval between the home commute and the mad rush to Friday night's revels in Hollywood. They sang along to an old Kid Creole album. As the car warmed up O let the coat slip daringly off her shoulders to reveal an acre of creamy flesh. If he would have allowed it she'd have stretched out over the console and sucked his cock right there but Steven had outgrown that kind of risky entertainment, the results of which he'd seen in hospitals and courtrooms.

Every window in The Mansion was illuminated and attendants were already shagging the expensive cars of early arrivals when Steven came to the top of the driveway. Other vehicles were moved to park Steven's directly in front of the big double doors. He greeted the attendants by name. At least O was spared idle chatter with these men who had flogged and fucked her at will when she was just another collared girl in latex. O would rather have cloaked herself in the imposed silence she had so enjoyed during her previous stay but tonight she was required to make conversation.

Svetlana and Catherine, a deliciously mature redhead who lived at The Mansion full time in the diminishing hope of finding her own master, took their coats in the massive marble foyer. Marie had chosen them as greeters because they knew most of the regulars. All exchanged hugs and kisses, along with a little gossip.

"You know that Russian guy, Martinoff?" Svetlana whispered in Steven's ear.

Steven told her he'd gotten him taken off the watch list so he could travel in the states.

"I never expected to see him here," she hissed. "That man is a killer."

Steven smiled at her. Who wasn't?

"He's a billionaire oligarch with perfectly good manners who put up a lot of cash in return for the favor I did him. Who did he bring?"

"Some dancer from The Bolshoi."

"Better not flirt with Martinoff too much. The Bolshoi girls are a lot more dangerous than he is."

They all turned at the sound of Marie's voice. She came down the stairs looking quite elegant in her new dress and flashing jewels. She'd put her hair up and her bearing was nothing short of regal. There were more hugs and kisses. Marie pushed Steven back by the shoulders to admire his scarlet-jacketed splendor.

"It makes you look like a ringmaster," she concluded. Ringmaster indeed. Conscious of the small bulge in his vest pocket, Steven hoped Marie's appraisal was accurate.

"How are we doing so far?" he asked.

"Suspiciously well. The plumbing is working. The kitchen staff started on time. The musicians are tuning up in the main parlor. It worries me."

"Everything worries you. That's why you're so good at this."

"In my next life I hope I get some other mojo."

Steven asked about Ray.

"Pacing in the library like a nervous race horse. I haven't let him see Jacqui all day."

"It's a shame you don't do weddings, Ma'am," O said with a laugh. Steven and Marie exchanged a look both hoped O missed.

Marie herself led them into the sumptuous main parlor where the naked string players had just commenced with something light from Debussy. More guests arrived by the minute and the effect was quite striking – powerful men in black making conversation with beautifully revealed women resembling statues of the kind collectors kept hidden. House girls in bright latex circulated with trays of champagne flutes and canapés. O spotted a silver-haired publisher she knew from New York. She was confident he wouldn't recognize her under the circumstances and wouldn't acknowledge her if he did.

Of greater concern was the bald black fashion designer, piss-elegant in a green velvet smoking jacket cut from the original pattern of the garment with which P. Lorillard had caused such uproar at The Tuxedo Park Country Club, ending the tyranny of white tie and giving birth to the modern tuxedo. In a gesture to the old scoundrel, the designer wore pince-nez perched on his nose, the better to ogle the spectacular runway model he'd brought with him, whose eyelids and nipples sparkled with gold theatrical glitter to match her collar and shoes.

O had shot both of them for *Interview* back in the day, but they strolled right by her, oblivious. O realized how her nakedness and her septum ring made her an anonymous generic slave, nearly invisible to those who hadn't seen her this way before. She took some comfort in the notion.

Steven gave her a quick, quiet rundown on the more notable attendees. The heavy-set guy with the Teutonic blonde was the head of a sovereign wealth fund. He had recently been the object of some scandal for his own parties. The sleek lesbian dressed like Marlena Dietrich, her petite goth-girl slave clinging to her arm, bred polo ponies up in Santa Barbara. The tall good-looking man wearing a turban was a big Bollywood investor, his companion a mesmerizingly lovely Indian movie star. O had seen her picture many times but never before wearing only gilt high-heeled sandals and a gold collar. Her aureoles and lower abdomen were bordered in scalloped henna to make her sweet spots even more visible.

The jolly bearded fellow surrounded by laughing house girls was a prince from a small country with a lot of oil. O knew the ruddy gentleman in the kilt and Bonnie Prince Charlie tunic. He was a tabloid mogul from London and if she'd had a camera she'd have been tempted to use it as he ass-grabbed a passing server, nearly causing her to spill the drinks on her tray.

O's attention snapped back quickly when a fit, smiling middle-aged Japanese man in a white-tie ensemble that could only have come from Kiton brought his girl over to meet Steven. They exchanged friendly bows followed by a Godfather hug. O noticed the man was missing part of a finger. The girl, Yumi, was truly the most striking woman there in one important respect. She was almost entirely tattooed in the Yakuza style, her trim body a living mural of koi and dragons and exotic birds and flowers, her augmented breasts illustrated with peony petals. She had enlarged multiple piercings above and below and wore her hair short and platinum in the style favored by Japanese mob molls. Her face was made-up like a geisha, which strangely complimented her Western hairstyle.

Steven introduced the man as Nagasawa-san, the longtime Japanese client who had helped him master the challenging language in which they exchanged a few hushed words about business, which was evidently pretty good from the way they both laughed. Switching to perfect English he told O that the two of them must be his guests in Osaka where he would show them a truly good time. Steven could vouch for that promise having ridden around Nagasawa-san's hometown with a couple of carloads of dangerous boys through long nights of drinking and whoring.

His collared date seemed permanently bored until she noticed O's tattoo, at which she pointed with obvious admiration. There was some conversation in Japanese explaining that O was a photographer who belonged to Steven. Yumi extended her hand with a surprisingly warm smile and a request for a closer look. O obligingly turned so Yumi could trace Steven's initials with a fingertip.

"I think she approves," Steven said. "The ink over her pussy is Nagasawa-san's chop. I guess that makes you sisters too."

From the way Yumi eyeballed her O surmised they had other things in common. O couldn't decide whether she wanted to go down on her or photograph her. O's professional ethics required that it be one or the other. Except for Jacqui she'd never been physically intimate with any of her models and that had only been done under orders, conveniently absolving O of all guilt.

Nagasawa-san made the internationally recognized two-fingers-to-lips sign for smoking four-twenty. Steven promised they'd get to that after dinner.

O's attention was briefly drawn away by something that really did surprise her. It wasn't the slender, gaunt, white-haired producer with the hip narrow glasses perched on his nose. She'd seen him all over town. It was the Oscar-nominated actress he held on a leash, a dark-haired, golden-skinned stunner with the most luscious lips and fantastic curves in Hollywood. She'd been rumored to have her share of kinks. The rumors were confirmed not only by the leash and collar and the ranks of fresh whip marks up and down her body, but also by the strategic ink and metal in her most intimate regions. She couldn't be tattooed all over like Yumi for professional reasons but looked as if she'd have preferred it that way.

From a quick census of the room O concluded that half the founders were Marie's old clients and the other half were Steven's. It made sense. Both enjoyed confidential relationships with wealthy men to whom the astronomical cost of founding memberships was a trifling expense in return for limitless access to exactly the kind of sex they wanted with exactly the partners they preferred.

O felt a sudden rush of familiar anger toward her own class and all the privileges and entitlements she had rejected when she rejected her kin. It wasn't the luxurious world in which they lived that repelled her. It was the way those in other worlds were forced to live so these people could have everything they wanted she couldn't abide. As a young girl O had spent long periods at heavily guarded five-star hotels in Third World countries while her father negotiated licensing arrangements for luxury goods with corrupt and brutal overseers.

Once in India when she was about ten their driver in Mumbai had run over and killed a beggar in the street. Instead of being horrified, as O had been, the driver had jumped angrily out of the car, cursed the corpse, gotten back in and driven on. O's parents had turned up the air conditioning.

And to these people, Steven was what? Hired help. No matter how rich he got or what kind of influence he wielded, he was no different from the gardener who manicured their high hedges or the long-haired kid who brought them their drugs.

Marie understood that she was and always would be a madam regardless of how important the services she provided were to her customers. If she stopped doing so they'd just take their business elsewhere.

Did Steven know or care that he was equally expendable? He could save them from their own foolishness and cruelty over and over but if he didn't or couldn't they'd replace him with someone who would and could. It was that simple to them. The thought made her hate them all the more.

Thankfully, Ray appeared to divert O from these bitter reflections. If Steven looked like a circus performer in his red coat, Ray resembled a Las Vegas magician in his black tails. He came out of nowhere, through his arms around O and lifted her off the floor.

"Hello beautiful," he exclaimed, "is this sailor bothering you?"

Steven laughed.

"You get a lot of action with that line?"

"Hell, it was worth a try."

He set O lightly back on her heels. His face glowed with happiness.

"Okay," O demanded, "what have you done with Jacqui?"

Ray raised his hands.

"Haven't put a glove on her all day. Marie's keeping Jacqui locked up until show time and it's driving me nuts."

"More of a short walk than a drive in your case," Steven interjected.

"You're a fine one to talk."

O waggled her head from side to side, weighing the proposition.

"It should be a hell of a show," she concluded with a shrug
that made her nipple rings sparkle in the subdued lighting.

Ray agreed it would be, if he could control himself long
enough. Just then Marie went to the microphone in front of
the musicians, who fell silent at her approach, and announced
that dinner would be served.

"I'm so nervous I hope I can eat," Ray said.

Steven grinned.

"Based on experience I doubt that will be a problem."

The crowd filed out after Marie in a leisurely manner,
bare breasts and buttocks swaying amid a sea of elegant black
suits. The house girls followed.

The huge dining room where oil barons had once feasted
was done up to Marie's highest gothic standard, the long table
set with special black china trimmed in a silver chain motif.
Each place had its own menu, printed in silver on black stock.
The black glass chandeliers cast a flattering glow from above
enhanced by black candles set in clusters down the center of
the table. A variety of chairs, sofas and lounges slip-covered in
washable black fabric had been arrayed along the green-silk
upholstered walls.

Steven was seated at one end of the table, O to his right
and Ray to his left. To O's dismay David and Anguisette, new-
comers to this event, had been given the black velvet chairs
(in deference to their nudity the girls' seats were draped with
black Frette towels) on her other side. She needn't have worried. David was English and of the class accustomed to such
evenings. He looked perfectly at ease in an exact copy of the
tuxedo Brioni ran up for the latest cinematic James Bond.

David was already engaged in animated bi-lingual conversation with an Argentine telecommunications magnate
only slightly less handsome than Rudolf Valentino. His olive-skinned, black-eyed "date" was about six feet tall with-

out the heels, elegantly sculpted in every way, pearls strung through the gleaming black hair piled up on her head. David put their talking on pause only long enough to shake Steven's hand and give O an air-kiss.

Fortunately the seating chart placed O directly across from a middle-aged New Orleans plastic surgeon shellacked in Southern charm and accompanied by the most impossibly perfect woman O had ever seen. She was age-appropriate, more or less, but her large wide-set blue eyes, her smooth cheeks, lush pillowy lips and perfectly rounded chin made her look much younger. Her body was as flawless as those O shot, most of them twenty years this woman's junior. Looking at the surgeon's wife she realized that this sculptured vision was his finest work of art. He'd constructed her exactly to his specifications from her high spherical breasts right down to her trimmed-back lower lips that left her impressively enlarged clit rudely exposed. Being Doctor Pygmalion's prize had its benefits.

Marie took her station at the far end of the table, her chair pulled out for her by two of the house girls. Once everyone was settled and the girls began pouring wine as they circled the table, Marie rose again and clinked a silver spoon against her black crystal champagne flute.

She waited for the chatter to die down and the chairs to stop rasping over the deep-pile carpet before speaking.

"Good evening and welcome to our founding members and their beautiful possessions. Tonight we celebrate our good fortune and extend our hospitality those who make all this possible with their continuing support. Everything here is for your use and enjoyment and though I know some of you are rather shy ..."

Laughter rippled along the table.

"... I'm quite certain we'll be able to entice you all into wickedness in the course of the evening."

She raised her glass of Krug.

"To all our friends old and new (a quick nod to David who returned it with a dazzling smile), those who have come before (a tasteful reference to the half dozen founders who had met with some kind of fatal misadventure since the first such dinner) and those we have yet to know. May all your desires be fulfilled."

Marie sat down to ringing applause and turned her attention to the producer and his movie star. Celebrity gossip was a guilty pleasure she'd picked up as a more conventional sort of madam and she could never get enough of it.

As the small caviar *amuse bouches* appeared in front of them, served by bare-bosomed girls leaning extra-low to facilitate lustful gazes and brief caresses, Steven asked Ray how he was holding up so far.

"I was okay for the first couple of hours after I dropped her off here," he said. "Since then, it's been a pretty rugged seventy-six hours, three minutes and forty-seven seconds, not that I've been keeping track or anything."

O and Steven both laughed. When Ray was happy, everyone was happy. Unfortunately, as O and Steven both knew, the reverse was also true.

Protocol strictly forbade any serious discussion of business, the plague at so many Los Angeles social functions. This crowd was drawn together by very different shared enthusiasms.

The surgeon from New Orleans had just come back from Venice with his wife, who was smart and funny in addition to her visual splendor, where they'd put in after a private cruise on The Adriatic.

"Every year," he explained, "a bunch of us charter a small liner for what we call the Icarus Conference. During the day we do presentations on procedures where we reached just a little too high and got a little too close to the sun. Naturally, we like to hold this as far away from potential patients as possible."

O shuddered at the grimly amusing symbolism of molten wax to represent the consequences of surgical hubris.

While David and the Argentine mogul talked polo ponies with the lesbian horse breeder, enjoying a few laughs at the expense of the younger British royals with their half-goal handicaps, the olive-skinned goddess with the pearls in her hair complimented O on the beauty of her rings.

"I wish I had the courage to show my submission so boldly," she said in the kind of boarding school English O knew so well. She'd have had this one the first day of the term back then.

"Have you ever been fucked on horseback?" the woman asked.

O admitted that she hadn't but it sounded like fun.

"We have a special saddle you can strap a girl on with her legs spread. You should come down to our *estancia* and try it for yourself."

The lobster martinis were next – mixed in long-stemmed glasses with chunks of ripe avocado and a light dill-scented dressing. When Angelique dipped to deliver Steven's plate she made a point of swinging her legendary mammaries in front of his face, earning a nipple-hardening caress followed by a sharp pinch to each. She favored him with a teasing tail wag (reminding him of their shared appreciation for that part of her too) but performed her task smoothly if lingeringly.

As O savored each bite Nagasawa-san's *irezumi* covered geisha, accompanied by Noriko should any translation services be needed, came over to kneel next to O's chair. Noriko, who had been assigned to attend Mr. Nagasawa personally, knelt next to her.

"Pardon the interruption, Miss O," Yumi said in a voice seemingly too soft for her bold appearance, "but Mr. Nagasawa wants you to know that he greatly admires your work and would be pleased if you would take my picture for him sometime."

O reached down to gently tilt the girl's painted face this way and that.

"Please tell Nagasawa-san that I would be honored to photograph someone so spectacular."

The girl lowered her eyes.

"You are very kind, Miss O, but I am only what my owner has made me. If you will come to visit us he will hire the finest *kinbaku* artist in Japan to display me as shamefully as possible for your camera."

"I'd like to get my hands on some of those pictures," Ray interjected.

"You know the rules," Steven reminded him. "No shop."

O said she'd be delighted to fly over at Mr. Nagasawa's convenience, with Steven's permission of course.

"I might have to come along," Steven said. "It's been too long since my last kendo practice."

He leaned over to address the girl on her knees.

"Please tell Nagasawa-san we accept his invitation and will be very grateful if he makes the arrangements."

The girl dipped her head smartly.

"Yes, Steven-san. I will convey your acceptance. Please excuse me."

She and Noriko stood, bowed and glided back up the table to Yumi's smiling *sensei*, the huge serpent on Yumi's back undulating with each well-oiled movement. Both girls bowed and Noriko delivered her report in Japanese before Yumi sat back down. Noriko refilled Mr. Nagasawa's glass. He raised it to Steven, who lifted his in reply. If Steven ever needed to hide out somewhere he'd call Nagasawa-san first.

Marie had picked up three giant domed silver carts at a restaurant sale that were rolled in to serve the Chateaubriand. At each stop diners were invited to decide for themselves how large a slice they wanted off the savory, fragrant roasts. Predictably the men had much larger appetites for red meat than the women. Each plate also received a helping of grilled vegetables. It was a simple but elegant meal allowing everyone to choose portions that wouldn't weigh any of them down too much for the evening's later activities.

The house girls' service, which Marie had urged them to perform as seductively as possible, was meant to remind the diners of sweeter delicacies to follow. When guests, male or female, laid hands on their bodies as they bent down over the table the girls deliberately tarried. One or two of them, along with a couple of the founders' dates, ended up under the table before the main course had been removed. As expected, Laurel was among the first on her knees. For a girl who primarily preferred girls, her taste for cock was legendary and her diminutive proportions fit comfortably under the furniture.

Dessert, brought with coffee, was a light raspberry sorbet. Marie assured all that come midnight a buffet of snacks and more substantial pastries would be set out.

Steven consulted the chiming repeater from his vest pocket and looked up to Marie, who nodded. She kept time in her head from long practice monitoring sessions back in the day.

Now Steven stood and clinked his glass.

"Reluctant as I am to interrupt the colorful discussions in progress the time has come for me first to acknowledge the skill, grace and beauty of our hostess this evening ..."

He tilted the glass toward Marie to another round of applause and cheers, somewhat louder for the consumption of just the right amount of alcohol. Marie had instructed the girls not to pour too heavily as snoring would be unwelcome later.

"... and to congratulate my brother Ray, for whom tonight's festivities have a very special meaning."

Steven turned to Ray wearing his biggest, brightest smile.

"If I haven't told you before how glad I am to see you so happy, I'll say it now. You've worked hard to build something reflecting all that's good about the unusual life-paths we've chosen. I'm proud of your accomplishments and I'm truly gratified by the rewards your labors have brought you. I think it's time everyone got a good look at those rewards."

Ray grinned up at Steven when their glasses met. Marie clapped her hands and the house girls retired to the front of the room where they formed a line as they did for inspections prior to shift changes.

All heads turned toward the doorway to watch Eugenia and Svetlana usher Jacqui into the room. Jacqui wore only a long veil and long transparent skirt, both of the same white tulle. The skirt was split into four panels affording glimpses of gold beneath with the sway of her walk. She'd been locked into white cuffs behind her back and white boots with heels so extreme they resembled the dreaded bondage pointe shoes but with slightly flattened toes so she could at least stay vertical with her long legs straight.

Jacqui's hair, face and body were styled with meticulous attention. They'd given her extra-long eyelashes, bordello shadow and mascara and generous rouge on her lips and nipples. Long ringlets of auburn hair hung below the veil down each side of her face. A short hobble chain between her ankles forced her to take short mincing steps, balancing precariously but with surprising grace atop the towering stilettos. Jacqui had, after all, been a stage dancer before meeting Marie.

The dissonant elements of blushing bride and brazen harlot made Jacqui even more fuckable if that was possible.

Catherine followed behind holding a purple velvet cushion bearing a white collar with gold hardware Marie had commissioned for the occasion and a tiny gold key.

Familiar with this drill, Steven stood up and pushed his chair back from the table, his place setting quickly cleared from the damask cloth while the other diners gave Jacqui a standing ovation. Setting his chair off to one side so everyone could get a good view of what was to follow, he motioned Ray to trade places with him.

Ray sat down and watched, grinning merrily at the gravity of Jacqui's expression, clearly visible through the fine material, as she concentrated on being pretty for him.

Stopping just in front of Ray, Eugenia and Svetlana helped Jacqui to her knees, spreading the veil and skirt in circles on the floor around her. Catherine took position next to Ray, collar and key at the ready.

Marie and Steven both found elaborately detailed slave "contracts" hilarious (though for different reasons). With Jacqui's assistance, Marie had drafted brief believable vows. When Marie tapped her glass the guests fell silent but remained standing to get the best view. Jacqui's words, echoing slightly off the vaulted ceiling, resonated clear and strong in the large room.

"Sir," she began, "this girl kneels before you to humbly offer her obedience and loyalty and to pledge her service to your pleasure in whatever form you may demand. Girl begs with all her heart and desire for the honor of being your slave and surrenders herself to you without reservation."

No one caught the quick wink and smile that passed between Ray and Jacqui except Steven.

But Ray's voice was tender and strong in a way Steven had never heard before.

"Girl presents me with a jewel of rare price. I find her beautiful and pleasing in all respects. I accept her offer with a glad heart and promise to love, protect and cherish her as my most prized possession, to encourage her pursuit of excellence in all thing and to whip and fuck her regularly as she so richly deserves."

Everyone laughed, including Ray and Jacqui, though she tried to stifle it. He addressed her directly.

"Do you accept my ownership of you without hesitation and agree to abide by whatever rules I impose?"

"I do, Sir, with a joyous heart and a wet cunt," she answered, still stifling that giggle. For all the visual pomp Marie knew it was best to leaven these ceremonials with a bit of bawdy humor lest they become solemnly ridiculous.

"And I take you as my slave and so much more from this day forward."

Ray leaned down, pushed Jacqui's veil aside and kissed her at length, one hand wrapped firmly around her throat.

There was another eruption of applause. Steven stood by smiling proudly not only for his brother's happiness but also for the success of O's labors to bring it about. He motioned to O, who came to kneel next to him. Steven put his hand down to the side of her face and O leaned in against his leg.

"Right then," Ray declared, standing up, "Let's do it!"

Eugenia and Svetlana helped Jacqui to her feet, turning her to face the room. Ray took the gold-trimmed white collar from the cushion resting in Catherine's hands. Jacqui's "sisters" held the veil up out of the way. Ray circled Jacqui's long slender neck with the collar and kissed her up and down from her hairline to the tops of her shoulders. This produced a shudder from Jacqui and a ripple of amusement around the table. The gold padlock already dangled from the collar's hasp. All he had to do was put the ends together and snap it shut to another outburst of clapping.

The girls turned Jacqui to face the room while Ray fetched the key off the cushion and came around in front of her. When the skirt was parted everyone strained to see the new jewelry between Jacqui's thighs. Ray and Jacqui had kept it a secret from everyone but upon their return from San Francisco he'd had her labia pierced with gold rings, now locked together, effectively obstructing penetration in at least one orifice.

"Shall we open you for business, slave?" Ray asked.

"Please, Sir. I'm starting to trickle down my thighs," she answered, inflecting the script with a touch of sass.

Ray popped the lock, slipped it out of the rings with a magician's wrist-flourish and put it in his pocket. While he was down there, he drew a finger over her slit and held it up, gleaming wet in the candlelight.

"I do believe she means it," he said, getting a laugh from everyone.

"Of course, there's something to be done first, isn't their, girl?"

Jacqui's eyes lit up even brighter and she smiled her stoned gremlin smile.

"Yes, Sir!"

Eugenia and Svetlana bent Jacqui face down on the table where Steven had sat, her hips against the edge and her breasts spilling nicely to the sides of her narrow ribcage. The girls quickly freed her in back, allowing her to stretch her arms over the cloth and place her hands palms-down. Her "bridesmaids" undid the skirt, Svetlana taking it over one arm while Eugenia fetched the vicious pink dressage whip from Marie who had quietly sent Noriko to fetch it at the start of the ceremony.

Everyone formed a semi-circle around Ray and Jacqui, not wanting to miss a stroke.

"This will be your first whipping as my owned property," Ray said. "But it won't be your last."

"I hope not, Sir," Jacqui said, being cheeky in more ways than one. Stretching her legs and raising her rump as high as possible, she braced herself. He had promised not to be gentle.

"This time you will count them and thank me," Ray said. Usually they didn't bother with that kind of thing but this was not a usual occasion.

"Yes, Sir, please."

Ray had finally come to accept the passion of Jacqui's masochism and her insatiable appetite for indulging it. No longer hesitant, he slashed the air with the slender whip, planting it hard and straight across Jacqui's lower cheeks.

"One. Thank you, Sir," she shouted, more in surprise than distress.

While everyone observed, admiring Ray's technique and Jacqui's endurance, he gave her a full twenty – ten from the right and ten more from the left –so the stripes would align properly. He struck deep and the welts rose immediately to murmurs of approval from the audience, whose growing excitement was evident from all the fondling and grabbing going on. The actress was already sucking on the producer (hardly a rare event in this town, Steven noted to himself) while Yumi and Noriko helped Nagasawa-san out of his jacket and shirt to reveal his own vividly inked bodysuit.

Steven bent down and whispered in O's ear. She nodded and slipped quietly under the table to tease Jacqui with a hand from beneath. O and Ray nodded to each other knowing what would happen now. Feeling O's fingers that knew her so well, Jacqui looked down with slightly teary eyes to meet O's diabolic smile.

"Thanks, you little bitch."

Overhearing her, Ray landed an extra-hard stroke that made Jacqui jump and squeal.

"Sorry! I meant thank-you Sister!"

O just cocked an eyebrow and slid in a couple of fingers.

On the final stroke, Jacqui pleaded for permission to come as much from Ray's lashing as O's manipulations.

"How about it, everybody?" Ray said without looking over his shoulder. "She would let her have one?"

The round of whistling, clapping and cheering was just what Ray expected. He gave Jacqui an extra cut while O gripped Jacqui's crotch. Jacqui announced her gratitude with a deafening scream.

Striped and sweating, Jacqui stayed put while Eugenia unbuttoned Ray's fly and pulled out his cock. It was already as hard and straight as a lamppost but Eugenia sucked on it for a bit of added encouragement while Svetlana used the new gold rings to open Jacqui up for him. Ray took a step forward, grabbed Jacqui by the hips and let Eugenia and Svetlana guide him in. Jacqui took everyone a bit by surprise when she not only thanked him for fucking her in front of all these witnesses but declared her love for him as well. Ray surprised them even more by proclaiming his for her.

This was the signal for generalized amusements to commence. As Ray hammered on groups and couples formed around the room.

The dapper fashion designer sat in a huge chair at the wall absent his trousers (the better to show off his clocked socks and pony-skin high-button boots) while his towering blonde date rode up and down his shaft, lifting and lowering herself by bracing her hands on the chair's giant arms. Her back was to her master so both could enjoy the spectacle around them, to which her presence was no small contribution.

Nagasawa-san sent for some hemp rope and candles for his rites with Yumi. Noriko tied Yumi face-up on the table, back bowed, wrists to ankles. He ignited the candles with a gold torch lighter.

As soon as the rest of the table was cleared, the Argentine couple climbed up on it and began dancing a torrid tango to music only they could hear. The Belgian banker made his Amazonian blonde kneel and open her mouth for a large ball-gag before attaching her patent cuffs to a ring set high in the wall. He had one of the house girls lick her while he ornamented his date high and low with harsh miniature steel clothespins he slipped out of his jacket pocket. His companion's muffled moans turned to guttural growls when he threaded the clamps with coils of red string before ripping them off down the front of her body. Nostrils flaring over the gag, she came with a stifled cry when the last ones popped from her lower lips.

The room soon reverberated with sighs and moans and screams as the scent of sex permeated the air. O had returned to kneel at Steven's side. She wondered why they weren't joining in. Usually Steven was the first to kick off any kind of orgiastic activity.

Sensing her mystification, he extended a hand to help her up.

"This will go on all night," he said. "I'd like a few minutes to ourselves."

Puzzlingly, it sounded more like a request than a command.

"Of course, Sir."

O looked back from the threshold as they departed. No doubt this night would add to the legends of life at The Mansion. By then the party had begun dissolving into groups of twos, threes and fours, dispersing through the house in search of its various specialized quarters.

Steven led O from the dining room to the small library, passing a couple in an alcove along the way that couldn't be distracted. The man's rough caresses and slaps provoked yelping and laughter from his handcuffed, blindfolded date.

Once inside, Steven closed the door behind them. It was quiet and still by contrast and O had a strange feeling of cold dread deep in her gut. Why would he remove them from his brother's celebration? He didn't seem to intend anything physical, or at least he hadn't brought any props for the purpose. What was he thinking? For a sickening moment O wondered if Steven would be so cruel as to dismiss her on such an occasion, but whatever for? He seemed entirely content with her company and her service.

O racked her memory, wondering what she could possibly have done to set him on a course away from the celebration with an expression of such somber determination on his face.

Steven, who had stood before panels of stern military officers, international tribunals and The Supreme Court itself, still wasn't entirely sure how to phrase what he had to say. He had rehearsed several alternative approaches in his head. By the time they were safely sequestered in the library, with its titillating murals of Native Americans and captive settler girls hanging out at the big lodge house under cheerful Rocky Mountain skies, he had rejected all of them.

O immediately knelt when they were alone, lifting her spine and casting down her eyes. She was breathing hard and getting wet at the prospect of whatever Steven could only do with her in private. Persuaded this must be something so perverse he didn't want others to see him inflict it on her, the specifics almost didn't matter.

Almost.

Steven looked down on her in silence for an uncomfortably long moment.

In his experience nothing worked better than the truth – straight up, no chaser.

"You're especially beautiful tonight," he led out.

"I'm glad my appearance pleases you, Sir. Any girl would feel lucky to have a man find such enjoyment in the sight of her."

But even as she said this, O's eyes flicked up to meet Steven's. He looked at her with a calm determination that would not be flirted or amused away.

"I make no secret of it. I tell everyone you're even better than they imagine because you are. Most slaves just obey. You serve and please me in ways I never knew I needed. Now it's hard to picture life without those services and pleasures."

He began walking around her in a slow circle.

"It's not common to be surprised when you've lived a life like mine but somehow you never fail to give me more than expected. Ever wondered why I've been single since Marie?"

O had absolutely no desire to pursue this line of conjecture.

"I don't think about you that way, Sir."

"How is that?

"I respect the privacy of anything about your life you don't choose to share with me."

Steven knew a pat answer when he heard one. He'd heard a lot of them.

"Can you imagine how difficult it would be to lie to me successfully?"

O lowered her head.

"I'm sure people try all the time, Sir. But I wouldn't."

"No more than I would to you. It's funny where the turning points are. You and me and Ray on the deck. The sound of you singing with the tattoo machine crackling away over your back. The way you cold-cocked that bitch in the police station with a camera. Your defiant rejection of Eric's condescending sympathy. You know I'm incapable of slowing down and you're the first woman I've met in a very long time that can keep up."

O shuddered. "Permission to speak freely, Sir."

"I expect no less."

"I don't know where this is going and it frightens me. If things are about to change between us in some important way I need to know now. I beg you not to torture me by making me guess."

O's eyes brimmed with tears something Steven had only seen when O was in extreme pain and highly aroused.

"I have something for you."

Steven brought the blue velvet box out his pocket, hinged it open and held it down in front of O's face. O gasped.

The shackle ring inside shared the basic design of the one she wore every day, but the shackle was mounted through a tube set with an emerald that might not have been as big as The Ritz but was certainly competition for The Ritz-Carlton.

"Really, Sir, even for you this is extravagant. It's gorgeous but it doesn't seem right for a slave."

"It might be for a slave who is also engaged to become a wife."

O's head shot up. Her eyes were huge. This wasn't happening. This couldn't be happening. "Sir, I will ask you only once," she said in a tone of angry resignation, "is this a proposal to marry me?"

Steven smiled down at her. "That would have been next."

O stood, snapped the box shut and handed it to Steven who looked utterly bewildered. O's face was contorted with fury. "There is nothing wrong with the way things are! I don't want them to change."

"They already have. I fought it too, but the fact is that I love you."

O's jaw shut with a click. She put up her hands and turned away. Marching over to a large reading table she paused a moment, slapped her palms on the wood and choked back sobs.

"This isn't exactly how I pictured it," Steven said. It hadn't even occurred to him that he might lose this case and that was an error to which he wasn't prone. He had done that thing he knew better than to do: he had asked a question to which he didn't already know the answer.

O strangled her weeping. She turned to him jaw set, eyes cold, even as tears still ran down from their corners. Naked as she was, absent her cultivated vulnerability she looked like a lot of other dangerous women Steven had known.

"You have everything I can give you and it's not enough. It's not enough to own every inch of me, to put your mark on me and make me wear your ownership on my face. None of that is enough for you. It's my whole life you want. I can't give you that any more than you can give me yours."

She went to him, standing uncomfortably close.

"Where would I fit in your world, Mr. Diamond? Would I get more closet space maybe? I've already told you I can't live under a bell jar."

Steven remembered the impact of the bullet hitting his shoulder. This was worse, much worse. He knew nothing he could say would make it better but that didn't stop him from trying.

"Who gives a fuck about that stuff? We'll move someplace else and make a different life together. There's nothing I value more than I do you."

Now she really was angry.

"So glib, counselor. I'm sure you'll promise not to interfere in my career in any way and to let me have any diversions I want. And you'll mean it, which is the worst part."

Steven went over to the small round cart full of alcohol and glasses at one end of the room and poured himself a substantial shot of something brown, not caring what it was. "I have definitely lost the thread here, O. Help me out, will you? What, exactly, did I do so wrong?" He came back to stand face-to-face with her.

"You said you loved me."

No doubt about the accusatory delivery whatsoever. That was the thing about the truth. Once founding a case on it, you were stuck with it. "I said it because I meant it. I do love you."

O turned away in disgust. "Fucking Christ. Isn't there one man in this whole town who can draw between the lines?"

Now Steven was getting annoyed. It wasn't the cold wrath of which he was capable as much as a kind of frustrated disbelief.

"It's not like I planned it, O. I started out trying to give Ray the chance to put down his guilt and figured I'd enjoy myself in the process. My intentions were purely dishonorable. It just got bigger than that."

"Maybe it's that simple in your mind. I wanted a Master, not a boyfriend or a lover or a husband or anyone else whose feelings I'd have to worry about. I don't do love. I've seen how love changes people and I don't want any. I'm no good with feelings. I don't have the patience for us getting old and sick and tired of each other. You don't know me at all. I thought you were smarter than the others. Just like everyone else you make up some someone in your head who doesn't exist and fall in love with her."

She turned her back on him again. "This is the worst disappointment yet. Do you know how hard it's been for me to get what I need? I thought I'd finally found my very own Minotaur and he turns out to be fucking Ferdinand the Bull."

And that was as far as Steven would let anybody go, love them or not. He circled her and planted himself in her path.

"It would appear the petition is rejected. I hereby withdraw it," he said coldly, putting the velvet box back in his pocket.

If all she wanted from him was to be treated with sophisticated cruelty he felt eminently capable of it at the moment but it was already too late. She'd heard more than enough and was more than ready to draw a line under it.

"I will not be marrying you or anyone else. I have far too much to do in my life and no desire to ruin yours."

O tossed her hair back angrily and started yanking on her collar. "Will you please get this thing off me?"

Steven took the key ring with the monkey's fist knot out of his trouser pocket and placed it carefully on the reading table within her reach. When he spoke his voice was grim and hard.

"You want it off, you take it off."

O snatched the key, rotated the collar so she could fumble it into the lock and bared her neck, throwing the collar and the key at Steven's feet. Watching her carefully just in case she decided to emphasize her point by kicking him in the teeth, Steven squatted down and grabbed the discarded items, rolling up the leather collar and stuffing it into one of the jacket's interior pockets where it made an unseemly bulge. He didn't care about that at the moment. O popped the ring out of her nose and extended it to him.

"You can give this to the next one. And this too."

She pulled the shackle ring off her finger, folding his hand around it. Even as he put all the hardware back in his vest he didn't think he'd be able to stay mad at her for long, or at least not as long as she'd stay mad at him.

"I'm sorry to have hurt you in a bad way," he said, now calm if not collected, "but I'm not sorry for feeling what I feel and letting you know about it. You may remember what I said about secrets at the very beginning. There's a price for lying and a price for refusing to do so. I'll pay the latter. And for that I'll take the liberty of telling you I don't think you're doing either of us a favor. I believe we're good for each other and that we always would be. It's unfortunate that you can't see that. I'll ask Marie to find you some clothes and I'll take you home.

"I don't want to ride home with you."

This was actual pouting but Steven had already begun to cut the cord.

"Fine then," he said. "We'll have one of the attendants drive you back. Tomorrow we'll get on with our respective futures."

O began to cry again. Not the kind of crying she did when physical sensations overwhelmed her. She cried like every angry, injured woman Steven had disappointed in some way had cried.

"How do you expect me to do that? I work for your fucking brother. Everyone's going to know and everyone's going to ask questions."

"As I tell my clients, just because someone asks you a question doesn't mean you have to answer it. Neither of us has ever cared much about what others think. You're a tremendous asset to Ray's company and neither he nor I will jeopardize that in any way. On rare occasions when I run into you at Ray's office, which I don't frequent that often, I'll be perfectly correct, as will you. That's what we're both made of. I think we're done here, or at least I am."

With that, Steven marched straight through the door and closed it behind him, leaving O more naked than she'd ever been. She continued to cry, but not for the loss of a man, only of a master.

Steven caught up with Marie in the kitchen, which was blessedly noisy, bright and without visible sexual activity, other than the house girls scurrying through with various instruments of pleasure and pain.

"They're just setting out the late buffet," Marie said, not yet reading his expression, though it didn't take her long to catch up.

"Something tells me you've lost your appetite," she said, putting her hands on his shoulders. "Promise me you didn't ask O to marry you."

Steven shrugged.

"It seemed like the right thing to do at the time."

Marie was incredulous.

"Here? Tonight? Couldn't you have picked a quieter moment to go off the deep end?"

"Let's just say things didn't work out quite as I'd planned."

Marie shook her head.

"Everyone who knows either of you told you not to do this thing but no; you knew better than all of us."

"You can gloat later. O's in the library crying. She needs someone to dress her and take her back to her place."

Marie's face softened when she realized how much hurt Steven concealed.

"What will you do?"

Steven pulled a smile, but it wasn't up to his usual standards.

"There's a party in progress and I'm going to go have myself a good time. I guess I'm just a good time kind of a guy."

He kissed Marie on the lips in a friendly way and left the kitchen, though she tried to call him back. A tray full of dangerous-looking baked goods got in between them. Marie snagged a cookie off it as it went by.

She didn't feel generous toward O. In fact, she wanted to go tell O exactly what she thought of her. But to keep the peace she got on the intercom and called for an attendant.

Marie wasn't sure how the coming weeks would play out but she knew from long experience that O would be back, just not with Steven.

That tattoo was going to be a damned nuisance.

EPILOGUE

The next couple of weeks were like a bad flu. Steven lurked around in his empty tower with little enthusiasm for anything. He put in enough time at the office to prevent anyone from going off to jail owing to his neglect.

There were the expected condolence visits of course.

Ray, who could count on one hand the number of times he'd beaten Steven at pool, hammered him in two games of Eight Ball in a row, opening the way for a discussion neither wanted but couldn't avoid forever. Though Steven did his best to hide it, Ray knew him too well not to notice his uncharacteristic silences and his grim demeanor when he thought himself unobserved.

"Come on, Steven, you're not even trying," Ray said, dropping the second Eight Ball neatly into its called pocket.

"Could be because I don't give a shit."

Ray knew how much Steven hated being bested at anything. Not giving a shit was definitely a serious symptom of an illness with which Ray was too familiar.

"I suppose after you lose something that really matters the rest of it seems pretty trivial."

"Yeah, well, I have no one but myself to blame for the way things turned out," Steven set as he set up another rack and took a hit off a mid-afternoon joint. It was sunny and cool outside, the skies unusually clear. Everything seemed cheerful except Steven.

"I was trying to do something good," Ray said. He knew he wasn't responsible for what had happened between Steven and O but felt that way regardless.

"And you succeeded. You and O and Marie played your parts exactly according to the script. I'm the one who blew his lines."

Ray cringed. "I should have warned you about O's reaction to the L-word. I let it slip myself once and she dismissed it as a joke but she wasn't laughing. That's one reason I figured the two were such a good fit. I'd like to think I know my own brother. I never would have pinned you for a closet romantic. I wouldn't have given you O if I thought you were going to fall in love with her. She's not built for that."

Steven managed a reasonably strong break, putting down a solid and starting a run.

"So I discovered. Believe me, the whole deal was as much a surprise to me as to everyone else. I don't know what I was thinking with, but I'm pretty sure it was the wrong organ."

Ray put down his cue and came around the table to rest his hands on Steven's shoulders.

"Personally, I'm glad to know you're no more immune than the rest of us. Love is a good thing with the right person. Maybe this opens the door to something better in the future."

Steven shook his head and went back to lining up his next shot.

"Don't bet the rent on it. Love's great for people like you and Jacqui and I'm truly happy for you both. That turned out much better than I expected. But O and I aren't like you two. She knew it. You knew it. Marie knew it. I just didn't want to believe it. I'm convinced now."

Steven's game picked up rapidly. Ray could see Steven's steely resilience coming back.

"I think O made a mistake. She was too scared to let herself have what she'd always wanted. Maybe that could change."

"If you'd been in the room when she threw her collar at me I doubt you'd think so. Anyway, she and I are done now. When do you and Jacqui take off?"

"On the way to Templehof first thing in the morning, if I can get her out of bed. It's always easier getting her in. We're going to start in Berlin and drive south to Paris."

Steven put down his cue and wrapped Ray in a surprise hug.

"You set out to make two people you care for happy and they fucked it up all by themselves. Accept the rewards for your intentions and for once, please, as a favor to me, don't look for ways to beat yourself up over how things turned out. If anyone in this world deserves to be happy, it's you. You're a good man and I meant it when I said I'm proud of what you've done with your life. I should have said that more often. Now, if you'll let me concentrate I'll go back to thumping your ass in this game."

Ray stepped aside so Steven could finish his run and went away happy with the words he'd waited years to hear. He may not have proved himself much of a matchmaker but he definitely felt less like a disappointing brother. He was just sorry Steven had to take such a hard hit to bring them closer.

Marie stopped by to pick up O's belongings and return some things with which she'd been entrusted to give back to

Steven. Marie, who had maintained her friendship with Steven for many years by respecting his emotional privacy, didn't talk much. She put her arms around him, held him tight and said "Ouch" in a soft voice. That summed up the whole thing pretty well.

She explained that O had decided to take Nagasawa-san up on his offer and would be in Japan for several weeks. Steven promised he'd email appropriate expressions of gratitude for his client's hospitality to his ... what was O now? She was his former slave and a photographer who worked for his brother's magazine.

Most of the time, he was okay with that, but every so often something he saw or heard would remind him of O and it would be like a short, hard right to the gut. He'd wind up asking himself the kinds of questions he knew were irrelevant now.

Who had sinned? Certainly not O. She wanted a master and he had accepted her on those terms. Steven was the one who had changed the rules without bothering to negotiate revisions. Pretty presumptuous of him to assume she'd simply accede to the new stipulations. Had their situations been reversed, he'd have severed the relationship in much the same way, if a bit more diplomatically. He'd done that many times in the past when women wanted commitments from him other than those he'd willingly made.

And yet it was hard to put certain remembered moments out of his mind. He could still picture O covered in stripes, her face transported with religious ecstasy, after the fearsome lashing she'd begged from him to shatter Eric's heroic delusions. He doubted he'd see that expression on a woman's face again. He remembered her unpredictable laughter, her disciplined style, her meticulous service, her keen insight and her absolute fearlessness.

Then the memory would drift away like a smoke ring.

Steven stared at the big screens, smoked a lot of pot, slept on the living room couch, walked down to Langer's, played pool alone, always winning and losing at the same time. He'd even fenced a bit, though the symbolism of being eviscerated by Mike more often than not lessened his zeal for combat.

At least he picked up an intriguing new case. In an ironic demonstration of his ability to foretell everyone's future but his own, he was finally approached by the rabbi from the congregation of which the young diamond merchant currently sitting in a cell at Men's Central on charges of first-degree homicide was a member.

Much as Steven had suspected, the accused was guilty of nothing beyond obeying his boss's instructions to go to a hotel room at The Bonaventure and wait, not knowing that he'd find a bag of diamonds and a severed head there with the police already on the way. The rabbi had sworn an oath and put down a cash retainer raised in *shul*. It was possible that Steven would end up defending an innocent client after all.

Nights were the worst. They were long this time of year and the huge place seemed especially empty. But it was not Steven's way to dwell on past errors and misfortunes. Instead, he'd take a shower, get dressed and blaze out to Pasadena in the Mercedes coupe. Everyone out there knew, or at least had a vague idea, what had happened and the girls were glad to have him back.

Catherine was particularly eager to bestow comforting words and tender compliance, but Svetlana, who understood him better, usually suggested the downstairs dungeons, offering to let him visit his wrath on her. Steven made it a rule never to play when angry but he wasn't angry. He simply enjoyed hurting her as always.

She suffered very dramatically, whether from a stressful suspension, the invasive penetration of a small hole or a hard lashing with a snake whip. These things always made her very wet though she still wept when he fucked her, which never failed to inspire him.

One night they found themselves on the black-and-white marble terrace behind The Mansion. They shared a smoke, as was their way, Steven in a borrowed robe and Svetlana wrapped up in his cashmere Chesterfield.

"You know I hate it when you fuck me up the ass," she said, exhaling a cloud of carbonized Cannabis.

"And yet it always makes you come."

Svetlana shrugged. "I can't help that."

She thought long and hard before speaking. The men who visited her rarely shared confidences. Something about Steven made it safe to be honest, a feeling she seldom experienced.

"O was a very foolish girl," Svetlana said. "It's not a common thing to be loved as you loved her. The women here would give anything for that kind of love."

She looked at him squarely, her slightly tilted eyes rising at the corners.

"I know I would."

"Easy to say when you only see me at my charming worst. She knew I couldn't guarantee that every time."

"There are more important things in life."

"Not to O."

"Lives can be long or short. Don't waste the time wanting what you can't have."

Steven thanked her for the advice, kissed her and flicked the roach over the railing.

As they went inside he promised to return soon but Svetlana knew there was no predicting when that would be. Steven acted more impulsively than usual these days.

He had always been so certain of what he wanted and so adept at getting it. Seldom had he so completely failed to take an objective. Seldom had he chosen an objective so imprudently.

He'd been taught his lesson after he'd learned his lesson once again. He shouldn't have been surprised at O's reaction to his proposal. As he admitted to Ray, he would have done the same if he'd had the same expectations. Steven had nourished those expectations in good faith never imagining what unpredictable things might happen inside his carefully constructed emotional life.

He wasn't accustomed to missing anyone or being unhappy about anything for long. The day he'd come home to discover that his mother had checked out with no farewell he recognized with blinding clarity that those who wanted to be happy in life would have to see to it on their own. He might forget that for a moment, but it would come back to him.

And then one day he woke up feeling like living again. There was nothing unique about the particular day. In fact, the weather was cold and wet and most locals stayed home if they could.

But Steven needed what passed for fresh air in Los Angeles. He got himself cleaned up and put on his hound's tooth hacking jacket with the pleated back, a comfortable black cotton flannel shirt and some decent slacks. Buttoning up his black Burberry, he went off to have a drink in the bar where he and O had first met.

It might have been an exercise in morbid nostalgia for some, but for Steven it was more like the exorcism of a curse. He couldn't avoid all the places he'd been with people who had disappointed him or he'd soon run out of places worth going.

His best surprise in a long time waited at the bar. Morgan was back from Las Vegas. Somehow she'd gotten the management to give her back her old job.

"I hated Vegas," she told him. "Even more than I thought I would. It's the bone yard of rotted-out minor talents. Besides, I was sick of the cheesy costume and the goddamned skirt-lifting brats grabbing at me when their parents weren't looking. Did I miss anything while I was gone?"

Steven looked out at the downtown grid, where the lights of his city were on again.

"Not really. Care to come by the club tomorrow afternoon before your shift and kill me?"

She smiled, leaned across the bar and kissed him on the cheek.

"I'll look forward to it."

Steven realized he would, too.

Back home he found himself unable to sleep, restlessly wandering into his office in search of work to distract him.

Steven had considered returning O's jewelry. He just couldn't do it. Instead, he kept the box in his desk drawer along with her collar, even looked at it once in a while, though he harbored no illusions of ever seeing either the rings or the collar on O again.

For a moment it had seemed as if she might be the last one, but Steven knew in his heart there would always be the next one. He had merely needed reminding.

Dropping into the chair behind his desk, he took out the small box and opened it. For a long moment, he studied the things inside, thinking of what had been and what might have been. Then he put them back away and booted up his computer in search of situations that needed fixing. Sometimes, usually when he worked late and alone, he opened iTunes to something he knew he liked. Roxy Music's "More Than This" seemed right. Bryan Ferry's bravery in the face of inevitable heartbreak was always validating. A person could have hope and find life disappointing or abandon hope and find it merely grim.

In Steven's world, there was only room for what was and whatever had yet to be. Once again, he felt ready for both.

Ernest Greene has served as Executive Editor of the best-selling adult magazine *Hustler's Taboo* since 1999 and most recently as Chief Associate Editor for *Hustler's* All-Sex issues.

Greene, who is particularly well known for his groundbreaking approach to the presentation of unconventional sexuality related to consensual domination and submission, has participated in the production of adult video for three decades as a performer, writer, director and producer.

His body of work comprises over five hundred titles, including AVN award winners *Strictly for Pleasure, Mask of Innocence, Tristan Taormino's Ultimate Guide to Anal Sex for Women* and *Jenna Loves Pain*. With his wife, Nina Hartley, he has served as producer and director of the *Nina Hartley's Guide* series of adult sex education programs for video market leader *Adam&Eve Pictures*. The series has sold over three quarters of a million videos to date and now comprises forty titles. His own XXX features for *Adam&Eve, O: The Power of Submission, Surrender of O, The Truth About O* and *The Perfect Secretary: Training Day* have won multiple awards and are among the best-selling X-rated story-driven titles in recent years.